# THE BEST
# SCIENCE FICTION
# AND FANTASY
# OF THE YEAR

## VOLUME THREE

**Also Edited by Jonathan Strahan:**

*Best Short Novels (2004 through 2007)*
*Fantasy: The Very Best of 2005*
*Science Fiction: The Very Best of 2005*
*The Best Science Fiction and Fantasy of the Year: Volumes 1-3*
*Eclipse One: New Science Fiction and Fantasy*
*Eclipse Two: New Science Fiction and Fantasy*
*The Starry Rift: Tales of New Tomorrows*

With Charles N. Brown
*The Locus Awards: Thirty Years of the Best in Fantasy and Science Fiction*

With Jeremy G. Byrne
*The Year's Best Australian Science Fiction and Fantasy: Volume 1*
*The Year's Best Australian Science Fiction and Fantasy: Volume 2*
*Eidolon 1*

With Terry Dowling
*The Jack Vance Treasury*
*The Jack Vance Reader*

With Gardner Dozois
*The New Space Opera*
*The New Space Opera 2* (forthcoming)

With Karen Haber
*Science Fiction: Best of 2003*
*Science Fiction: Best of 2004*
*Fantasy: Best of 2004*

# THE BEST
# SCIENCE FICTION
## AND FANTASY
# OF THE YEAR

## VOLUME THREE

### EDITED BY JONATHAN STRAHAN

**NIGHT SHADE BOOKS**
SAN FRANCISCO

**First Edition**

ISBN: 978-1-59780-149-2
Printed in Canada

**Night Shade Books**
Please visit us on the web at
www.nightshadebooks.com

For Robin Pen, a dear and constant friend
over these many years, with thanks.

Acknowledgements

Each year the list of people who need to be thanked for their support in producing this preposterously complicated book grows and grows. This year I'm going to try to keep it as tight as possible. I'd especially like to thank Alicia Krasnostein, Ben Payne, Alex Pierce, and Tansy Rayner Roberts from *Not If You Were the Last Short Story on Earth* who acted as readers for this book. Their honesty and support contributed inestimably to the book you now hold, and kept me honest when my spirits flagged at the sheer volume of fiction to be read and considered. I'd also like to thank Gary K. Wolfe and Charles N. Brown, for sharing their friendship and wisdom while I was assembling this book; and of course Howard Morhaim; Justin Ackroyd; Jack Dann; Brian Bieniowski; and Gordon Van Gelder. Thanks also to the following good friends and colleagues without whom this book would have been much poorer, and much less fun to do: Lou Anders, Deborah Biancotti, Ellen Datlow, Gardner Dozois, Sean Williams, and all of the book's contributors.

As always, my biggest thanks go to Marianne, Jessica, and Sophie. Every moment spent working on this book was a moment stolen from them. I only hope I can repay them.

# CONTENTS

# INTRODUCTION

## JONATHAN STRAHAN

The webgnomes who labor hard in the fields of *Wikipedia* define "genre" as:

> "vague categories with no fixed boundaries, they are formed by sets of conventions, and many works cross into multiple genres by way of borrowing and recombining these conventions."

The book you are now holding is concerned with two such genres—science fiction and fantasy—and one form, short fiction.

Readers of science fiction have long argued, rather fruitlessly, over how SF should be defined. Whichever definition you choose, and most definitions have some merit, the important thing is that almost all of those readers would be able to agree on what science fiction *is*, what its conventions, tropes, etc. are, and how they combine to make a science fiction story. This is arguably less true of fantasy, which is much more of a "fuzzy set" with vaguer boundaries, broader conventions, and more varied tropes and memes. Both genres, however, are inextricably linked. There's something in the DNA of story that keeps them closely connected to one another, with SF at times appearing to be a subset of fantasy, and at other times appearing to be some kind of close cousin, with its own distinct features.

When, back in the summer of 2003, I stopped reading short fiction for casual interest and began to actively seek out every story I could find so that I could consider it for inclusion in books like this one, I felt that SF and fantasy were quite distinct, or at least at a point in their ever-evolving relationship where they appeared to be quite distinct from one another. Over the past five years and something like 10,000 or more stories my opinion on this has changed. I've come to feel that the boundaries between SF and fantasy, which have always been permeable, are perhaps as open to cross-pollination as they have ever been.

1

I'm very hesitant to make a suggestion as to *why* this is, and I don't want to oversimplify, but while writers have always borrowed from the many toolkits of genre, they seem even more willing to do so now than they have in the past. You can see this most explicitly in science fiction stories like Ted Chiang's brilliant "The Merchant and the Alchemist's Gate" from last year, which used the poetry of fantasy to frame his science fictional tale or in Daniel Abraham's "The Cambist and Lord Iron: A Fairy Tale of Economics," which similarly used the logical rigor we typically associate with SF to structure his powerful fantasy.

It's almost impossible to say exactly which factors are at play that are driving this willful borrowing, other than to point out that it's perhaps more complex than it might appear. It is, however, why the *Best Science Fiction and Fantasy of the Year* anthology series exists. It's my intention to plot as best I can in a book of restricted length, and allowing for the practicalities of anthology making, the trends and developments of *both* science fiction and fantasy, while also carefully attempting to present a selection of stories that transgress boundaries in interesting ways, all the while bearing in mind that these should be the *best* stories of the year, not simply interesting experiments. I will almost always avoid stories written by mainstream writers and which appear in mainstream venues, not because of snobbery, but because I believe those writers are doing something altogether different, dressing what are essentially mainstream stories in the clothing of genre, without every really attempting to come to grips with what genre is and what it means for the stories they are creating. I think what they're doing is valid and worthwhile, but it's not what this book is about.

Which brings us to the late fall of 2008, when I'm writing this introduction. Over the past twelve months I have searched for every science fiction and fantasy story that I could find, wherever and however it was published. During that time I have read, or started to read, more than three thousand short stories, novelettes, and novellas. They've appeared in or on magazines, anthologies, short story collections, chapbooks, and websites of almost every stripe. They've been used as advertising, as the main event, and as part of collectible publications. And, for all of that, I've only seen and considered a healthy sampling of the stories published during the year. No one knows exactly how many new stories appear every year, but I'd guess somewhere around six or seven thousand. There's no way one person can find, never mind consider, all of those stories. All any reader can do is to make, as I have, an honest effort to read and consider as many stories as possible. I've also been assisted this year by four readers—Alicia Krasnostein, Ben Payne, Alex Pierce, and Tansy Rayner Roberts who collectively read and blog about short fiction at *Not If You Were the Last Short Story on Earth*—who were incredibly helpful, and who helped to keep me focused and honest when I temporarily flagged. Even with their help, though, I'd be the first to admit that this book can only be what it was always going to be: a selection of the very best stories published during the year as read and selected by one reader. I can only hope you'll find them as rewarding and worthwhile as I have.

In amongst all of that reading I've noticed a handful of trends, some of interest, some not. The most obvious one is the sudden rise of original anthologies, themed and unthemed, which seem to be going through a period of remarkable success. Without any real attempt to be rigorous, I easily located close to one hundred original anthologies that were published during 2008. I was surprised to find that most of these anthologies, and certainly the best of them, were science fiction. Setting aside my own *The Starry Rift* and *Eclipse Two*, which I leave others to comment on, I thought the best SF anthology of the year was Gardner Dozois's *Galactic Empires*, a collection of six themed SF novellas dominated by Ian McDonald's superb "The Tear," which sadly was too long for this volume. I was also very impressed by Lou Anders's *Fast Forward 2*, Nick Gevers's *Extraordinary Engines*, and George Mann's *The Solaris Book of New Science Fiction: Volume Two*. A strong competitor for the title of best general anthology of the year was Ellen Datlow's very fine *The Del Rey Book of Science Fiction and Fantasy*, which contained excellent stories by Maureen F. McHugh, Pat Cadigan, and others. In what was a much less interesting year for fantasy anthologies, Marvin Kaye's terrific *A Book of Wizards* and Steve Berman's *Magic in the Mirrorstone* were the standouts. While it's far too early to declare this some kind of Golden Age of anthologies, it's clearly a very successful time. I've not heard any convincing argument as to why this is the case—certainly the idea that the increase in success of anthologies is in some way tied to the failure of the professional genre magazine market—doesn't convince. However, having looked at publishing schedules for 2009, it's certainly going to continue for at least another year (and probably several more).

The other trends that stood out in 2008, beyond the simple dominance of science fiction over fantasy (it seemed this year that there was much more interesting SF published than fantasy at shorter lengths—something that may directly correlate with the dominance of SF in the anthology market), was the fascination with zombies and superheroes. Zombies, it seemed, were everywhere: in John Joseph Adams's fine reprint anthology *The Living Dead*, and in magazines, novels, films, and almost everywhere else. I suspect this may be related to the impact of broader historical and cultural trends on the field, but who knows? It's enough to say that there were a lot of undead walkers out there with a taste for brains. I saw three original anthologies and a small handful of novels featuring superheroes, many of interest. However, I suspect the reason for these suddenly appearing may have more to do with Hollywood's recent love affair with Marvel Comics, rather than anything else.

And that's 2008. I could say much more about how the professional magazine market is changing, the rise of semi-professional publishing, the impact of annual trends and so on, but such things really just get in the way of the main event: the stories. This year's annual features more stories than ever before—more than two dozen. There's clearly more SF than fantasy (I track it at about a 60/40 split), but more importantly there's a broad range of terrific stories. I hope you enjoy reading them as much as I've enjoyed compiling them. See you next year!

Jonathan Strahan
Perth, Australia
November 2008

# EXHALATION

## TED CHIANG

Ted Chiang published his first short story, "Tower of Babylon", in *Omni* magazine in 1990. The story won the Nebula Award, and has been followed by just nine more stories in the intervening sixteen years. All but two of those stories, which have won the Hugo, Nebula, Locus, Sturgeon, and Sidewise awards, are collected in *Stories of Your Life and Others*.

It has long been said that air (which others call argon) is the source of life. This is not in fact the case, and I engrave these words to describe how I came to understand the true source of life and, as a corollary, the means by which life will one day end.

For most of history, the proposition that we drew life from air was so obvious that there was no need to assert it. Every day we consume two lungs heavy with air; every day we remove the empty ones from our chest and replace them with full ones. If a person is careless and lets his air level run too low, he feels the heaviness of his limbs and the growing need for replenishment. It is exceedingly rare that a person is unable to get at least one replacement lung before his installed pair runs empty; on those unfortunate occasions where this has happened—when a person is trapped and unable to move, with no one nearby to assist him—he dies within seconds of his air running out.

But in the normal course of life, our need for air is far from our thoughts, and indeed many would say that satisfying that need is the least important part of going to the filling stations. For the filling stations are the primary venue for social conversation, the places from which we draw emotional sustenance as well as physical. We all keep spare sets of full lungs in our homes, but when one is alone, the act of opening one's chest and replacing one's lungs can seem little better than a chore. In the company of others, however, it becomes a communal activity, a shared pleasure.

If one is exceedingly busy, or feeling unsociable, one might simply pick up a pair of full lungs, install them, and leave one's emptied lungs on the other side of the room. If one has a few minutes to spare, it's simple courtesy to connect the empty lungs to an air dispenser and refill them for the next person. But by far the most common practice is to linger and enjoy the company of others, to discuss the news of the day with friends or acquaintances and, in passing, offer newly filled lungs to one's interlocutor. While this perhaps does not constitute air sharing in the strictest sense, there is camaraderie derived from the awareness that all our air comes from the same source, for the dispensers are but the exposed terminals of pipes extending from the reservoir of air deep underground, the great lung of the world, the source of all our nourishment.

Many lungs are returned to the same filling station the next day, but just as many circulate to other stations when people visit neighboring districts; the lungs are all identical in appearance, smooth cylinders of aluminum, so one cannot tell whether a given lung has always stayed close to home or whether it has traveled long distances. And just as lungs are passed between persons and districts, so are news and gossip. In this way one can receive news from remote districts, even those at the very edge of the world, without needing to leave home, although I myself enjoy traveling. I have journeyed all the way to the edge of the world, and seen the solid chromium wall that extends from the ground up into the infinite sky.

It was at one of the filling stations that I first heard the rumors that prompted my investigation and led to my eventual enlightenment. It began innocently enough, with a remark from our district's public crier. At noon of the first day of every year, it is traditional for the crier to recite a passage of verse, an ode composed long ago for this annual celebration, which takes exactly one hour to deliver. The crier mentioned that on his most recent performance, the turret clock struck the hour before he had finished, something that had never happened before. Another person remarked that this was a coincidence, because he had just returned from a nearby district where the public crier had complained of the same incongruity.

No one gave the matter much thought beyond the simple acknowledgement that seemed warranted. It was only some days later, when there arrived word of a similar deviation between the crier and the clock of a third district, that the suggestion was made that these discrepancies might be evidence of a defect in the mechanism common to all the turret clocks, albeit a curious one to cause the clocks to run faster rather than slower. Horologists investigated the turret clocks in question, but on inspection they could discern no imperfection. In fact, when compared against the timepieces normally employed for such calibration purposes, the turret clocks were all found to have resumed keeping perfect time.

I myself found the question somewhat intriguing, but I was too focused on my own studies to devote much thought to other matters. I was and am a student of anatomy, and to provide context for my subsequent actions, I now offer a brief account of my relationship with the field.

Death is uncommon, fortunately, because we are durable and fatal mishaps are rare, but it makes difficult the study of anatomy, especially since many of the accidents serious enough to cause death leave the deceased's remains too damaged for study. If lungs are ruptured when full, the explosive force can tear a body asunder, ripping the titanium as easily as if it were tin. In the past, anatomists focused their attention on the limbs, which were the most likely to survive intact. During the very first anatomy lecture I attended a century ago, the lecturer showed us a severed arm, the casing removed to reveal the dense column of rods and pistons within. I can vividly recall the way, after he had connected its arterial hoses to a wall-mounted lung he kept in the laboratory, he was able to manipulate the actuating rods that protruded from the arm's ragged base, and in response the hand would open and close fitfully.

In the intervening years, our field has advanced to the point where anatomists are able to repair damaged limbs and, on occasion, attach a severed limb. At the same time we have become capable of studying the physiology of the living; I have given a version of that first lecture I saw, during which I opened the casing of my own arm and directed my students' attention to the rods that contracted and extended when I wiggled my fingers.

Despite these advances, the field of anatomy still had a great unsolved mystery at its core: the question of memory. While we knew a little about the structure of the brain, its physiology is notoriously hard to study because of the brain's extreme delicacy. It is typically the case in fatal accidents that, when the skull is breached, the brain erupts in a cloud of gold, leaving little besides shredded filament and leaf from which nothing useful can be discerned. For decades the prevailing theory of memory was that all of a person's experiences were engraved on sheets of gold foil; it was these sheets, torn apart by the force of the blast, that was the source of the tiny flakes found after accidents. Anatomists would collect the bits of gold leaf—so thin that light passes greenly through them—and spend years trying to reconstruct the original sheets, with the hope of eventually deciphering the symbols in which the deceased's recent experiences were inscribed.

I did not subscribe to this theory, known as the inscription hypothesis, for the simple reason that if all our experiences are in fact recorded, why is it that our memories are incomplete? Advocates of the inscription hypothesis offered an explanation for forgetfulness—suggesting that over time the foil sheets become misaligned from the stylus which reads the memories, until the oldest sheets shift out of contact with it altogether—but I never found it convincing. The appeal of the theory was easy for me to appreciate, though; I too had devoted many an hour to examining flakes of gold through a microscope, and can imagine how gratifying it would be to turn the fine adjustment knob and see legible symbols come into focus.

More than that, how wonderful would it be to decipher the very oldest of a deceased person's memories, ones that he himself had forgotten? None of us can remember much more than a hundred years in the past, and written records—accounts that we ourselves inscribed but have scant memory of doing so—extend only a few hundred years before that. How many years did we live before the beginning of written history? Where did we come from? It is the promise of finding the answers within our own brains that makes the inscription hypothesis so seductive.

I was a proponent of the competing school of thought, which held that our memories were stored in some medium in which the process of erasure was no more difficult than recording: perhaps in the rotation of gears, or the positions of a series of switches. This theory implied that everything we had forgotten was indeed lost, and our brains contained no histories older than those found in our libraries. One advantage of this theory was that it better explained why, when lungs are installed in those who have died from lack of air, the revived have no memories and are all but mindless: somehow the shock of death had reset all the gears or switches. The inscriptionists claimed the shock had merely misaligned the foil sheets, but no one was willing to kill a living person, even an imbecile, in order to resolve the debate. I had envisioned an experiment which might allow me to determine the truth conclusively, but it was a risky one, and deserved careful consideration before it was undertaken. I remained undecided for the longest time, until I heard more news about the clock anomaly.

Word arrived from a more distant district that its public crier had likewise observed the turret clock striking the hour before he had finished his new year's recital. What made this notable was that his district's clock employed a different mechanism, one in which the hours were marked by the flow of mercury into a bowl. Here the discrepancy could not be explained by a common mechanical fault. Most people suspected fraud, a practical joke perpetrated by mischief makers. I had a different suspicion, a darker one that I dared not voice, but it decided my course of action; I would proceed with my experiment.

The first tool I constructed was the simplest: in my laboratory I fixed four prisms on mounting brackets and carefully aligned them so that their apexes formed the corners of a rectangle. When arranged thus, a beam of light directed at one of the lower prisms was reflected up, then backward, then down, and then forward again in a quadrilateral loop. Accordingly, when I sat with my eyes at the level of the first prism, I obtained a clear view of the back of my own head. This solipsistic periscope formed the basis of all that was to come.

A similarly rectangular arrangement of actuating rods allowed a displacement of action to accompany the displacement of vision afforded by the prisms. The bank of actuating rods was much larger than the periscope, but still relatively straightforward in design; by contrast, what was attached to the end of these respective mechanisms was far more intricate. To the periscope I added a binocular microscope mounted on an armature capable of swiveling side to side or up and down. To the actuating rods I added an array of precision manipulators, although that description hardly does justice to those pinnacles of the mechanician's art. Combining the ingenuity of anatomists and the inspiration provided by the bodily structures they studied, the manipulators enabled their operator to accomplish any task he might normally perform with his own hands, but on a much smaller scale.

Assembling all of this equipment took months, but I could not afford to be anything less than meticulous. Once the preparations were complete, I was able to place each of my hands on a nest of knobs and levers and control a pair of manipulators situated behind my head, and use the periscope to see what they worked on. I would then be able to dissect my own brain.

The very idea must sound like pure madness, I know, and had I told any of my colleagues, they would surely have tried to stop me. But I could not ask anyone else to risk themselves for the sake of anatomical inquiry, and because I wished to conduct the dissection myself, I would not be satisfied by merely being the passive subject of such an operation. Auto-dissection was the only option.

I brought in a dozen full lungs and connected them with a manifold. I mounted this assembly beneath the worktable that I would sit at, and positioned a dispenser to connect directly to the bronchial inlets within my chest. This would supply me with six days' worth of air. To provide for the possibility that I might not have completed my experiment within that period, I had scheduled a visit from a colleague at the end of that time. My presumption, however, was that the only way I would not have finished the operation in that period would be if I had caused my own death.

I began by removing the deeply curved plate that formed the back and top of my head; then the two, more shallowly curved plates that formed the sides. Only my faceplate remained, but it was locked into a restraining bracket, and I could not see its inner surface from the vantage point of my periscope; what I saw exposed was my own brain. It consisted of a dozen or more subassemblies, whose exteriors were covered by intricately molded shells; by positioning the periscope near the fissures that separated them, I gained a tantalizing glimpse at the fabulous mechanisms within their interiors. Even with what little I could see, I could tell it was the most beautifully complex engine I had ever beheld, so far beyond any device man had constructed that it was incontrovertibly of divine origin. The sight was both exhilarating and dizzying, and I savored it on a strictly aesthetic basis for several minutes before proceeding with my explorations.

It was generally hypothesized that the brain was divided into an engine located in the center of the head which performed the actual cognition, surrounded by an array of components in which memories were stored. What I observed was consistent with this theory, since the peripheral subassemblies seemed to resemble one another, while the subassembly in the center appeared to be different, more heterogenous and with more moving parts. However the components were packed too closely for me to see much of their operation; if I intended to learn anything more, I would require a more intimate vantage point.

Each subassembly had a local reservoir of air, fed by a hose extending from the regulator at the base of my brain. I focused my periscope on the rearmost subassembly and, using the remote manipulators, I quickly disconnected the outlet hose and installed a longer one in its place. I had practiced this maneuver countless times so that I could perform it in a matter of moments; even so, I was not certain I could complete the connection before the subassembly had depleted its local reservoir. Only after I was satisfied that the component's operation had not been interrupted did I continue; I rearranged the longer hose to gain a better view of what lay in the fissure behind it: other hoses that connected it to its neighboring components. Using the most slender pair of manipulators to reach into the narrow crevice, I replaced the hoses one by one with longer substitutes. Eventually, I had worked my way around the entire subassembly and replaced every connection it had to the rest of my brain. I was now able to unmount this subassembly from the frame that supported it, and pull the entire section outside of what was once the back of my head.

I knew it was possible I had impaired my capacity to think and was unable to recognize it, but performing some basic arithmetic tests suggested that I was uninjured. With one subassembly hanging from a scaffold above, I now had a better view of the cognition engine at the center of my brain, but there was not enough room to bring the microscope attachment itself in for a close inspection. In order for me to really examine the workings of my brain, I would have to displace at least half a dozen subassemblies.

Laboriously, painstakingly, I repeated the procedure of substituting hoses for other subassemblies, repositioning another one farther back, two more higher up, and two others out to the sides, suspending all six from the scaffold above my head. When I was done, my brain looked like an explosion frozen an infinitesimal fraction of a second after the detonation, and again I felt dizzy when I thought about it. But at last the cognition engine itself was exposed, supported on a pillar of hoses and actuating rods leading down into my torso. I now also had room to rotate my microscope around a full three hundred and sixty degrees, and pass my gaze across the inner faces of the subassemblies I had moved. What I saw was a microcosm of auric machinery, a landscape of tiny spinning rotors and miniature reciprocating cylinders.

As I contemplated this vista, I wondered, where was my body? The conduits which displaced my vision and action around the room were in principle no different from those which connected my original eyes and hands to my brain. For the duration of this experiment, were these manipulators not essentially my hands? Were the magnifying lenses at the end of my periscope not essentially my eyes? I was an everted person, with my tiny, fragmented body situated at the center of my own distended brain. It was in this unlikely configuration that I began to explore myself.

I turned my microscope to one of the memory subassemblies, and began examining its design. I had no expectation that I would be able to decipher my memories, only that I might divine the means by which they were recorded. As I had predicted, there were no reams of foil pages visible, but to my surprise neither did I see banks of gearwheels or switches. Instead, the subassembly seemed to consist almost entirely of a bank of air tubules. Through the interstices between the tubules I was able to glimpse ripples passing through the bank's interior.

With careful inspection and increasing magnification, I discerned that the tubules ramified into tiny air capillaries, which were interwoven with a dense latticework of wires on which gold leaves were hinged. Under the influence of air escaping from the capillaries, the leaves were held in a variety of positions. These were not switches in the conventional sense, for they did not retain their position without a current of air to support them, but I hypothesized that these were the switches I had sought, the medium in which my memories were recorded. The ripples I saw must have been acts of recall, as an arrangement of leaves was read and sent back to the cognition engine.

Armed with this new understanding, I then turned my microscope to the cognition engine. Here too I observed a latticework of wires, but they did not bear leaves suspended in position; instead the leaves flipped back and forth almost too rapidly to see. Indeed, almost the entire engine appeared to be in motion, consisting more of lattice than of air capillaries, and I wondered how air could reach all the gold leaves in a coherent manner. For many hours I scrutinized the leaves, until I realized that they themselves were playing the role of capillaries; the leaves formed temporary conduits and valves that existed just long enough to redirect air at other leaves in turn, and then disappeared as a result. This was an engine undergoing continuous transformation, indeed modifying itself as part of its operation. The lattice was not so much a machine as it was a page on which the machine was written, and on which the machine itself ceaselessly wrote.

My consciousness could be said to be encoded in the position of these tiny leaves, but it would be more accurate to say that it was encoded in the ever-shifting pattern of air driving these leaves. Watching the oscillations of these flakes of gold, I saw that air does not, as we had always assumed, simply provide power to the engine that realizes our thoughts. Air is in fact the very medium of our thoughts. All that we are is a pattern of air flow. My memories were inscribed, not as grooves on foil or even the position of switches, but as persistent currents of argon.

In the moments after I grasped the nature of this lattice mechanism, a cascade of insights penetrated my consciousness in rapid succession. The first and most trivial was understanding why gold, the most malleable and ductile of metals, was the only material out of which our brains could be made. Only the thinnest of foil leaves could move rapidly enough for such a mechanism, and only the most delicate of filaments could act as hinges for them. By comparison, the copper burr raised by my stylus as I engrave these words and brushed from the sheet when I finish each page is as coarse and heavy as scrap. This truly was a medium where erasing and recording could be performed rapidly, far more so than any arrangement of switches or gears.

What next became clear was why installing full lungs into a person who has died from lack of air does not bring him back to life. These leaves within the lattice remain balanced between continuous cushions of air. This arrangement lets them flit back and forth swiftly, but it also means that if the flow of air ever ceases, everything is lost; the leaves all collapse into identical pendent state erasing the patterns and the consciousness they represent. Restoring the air supply cannot re-create what has evanesced. This was the price of speed; a more stable medium for storing patterns would mean that our consciousnesses would operate far more slowly.

It was then that I perceived the solution to the clock anomaly. I saw that the speed of these leaves' movements depended on their being supported by air; with sufficient air flow, the leaves could move nearly frictionlessly. If they were moving more slowly, it was because they were being subjected to more friction, which could occur only if the cushions of air that supported them were thinner, and the air flowing through the lattice was moving with less force.

It is not that the turret clocks are running faster. What is happening is that our brains are running slower. The turret clocks are driven by pendulums, whose tempo never varies, or by the flow of mercury through a pipe, which does not change. But our brains rely on the passage of air, and when that air flows more slowly, our thoughts slow down, making the clocks seem to us to run faster.

I had feared that our brains might be growing slower, and it was this prospect that had spurred me to pursue my auto-dissection. But I had assumed that our cognition engines—while powered by air—were ultimately mechanical in nature, and some aspect of the mechanism was gradually becoming deformed through fatigue, and thus responsible for the slowing. That would have been dire, but there was at least the hope that we might be able to repair the mechanism, and restore our brains to their original speed of operation.

But if our thoughts were purely patterns of air rather than the movement of toothed gears, the problem was much more serious, for what could cause the air flowing through every person's brain to move less rapidly? It could not be a decrease in the pressure from our filling stations' dispensers; the air pressure in our lungs is so high that it must be stepped down by a series of regulators before reaching our brains. The diminution in force, I saw, must arise from the opposite direction: the pressure of our surrounding atmosphere was increasing.

How could this be? As soon as the question formed, the only possible answer became apparent: our sky must not be infinite in height. Somewhere above the limits of our vision, the chromium walls surrounding our world must curve inward to form a dome; our universe is a sealed chamber rather than an open well. And air is gradually accumulating within that chamber, until it equals the pressure in the reservoir below.

This is why, at the beginning of this engraving, I said that air is not the source of life. Air can neither be created nor destroyed; the total amount of air in the universe remains constant, and if air were all that we needed to live, we would never die. But in truth the source of life is *a difference in air pressure*, the flow of air from spaces where it is thick to those where it is thin. The activity of our brains, the motion of our bodies, the action of every machine we have ever built is driven by the movement of air, the force exerted as differing pressures seek to balance each other out. When the pressure everywhere in the universe is the same, all air will be motionless, and useless; one day we will be surrounded by motionless air and unable to derive any benefit from it.

We are not really consuming air at all. The amount of air that I draw from each day's new pair of lungs is exactly as much as seeps out through the joints of my limbs and the seams of my casing, exactly as much as I am adding to the atmosphere around me; all I am doing is converting air at high pressure to air at low. With every movement of my body, I contribute to the equalization of pressure in our universe. With every thought that I have, I hasten the arrival of that fatal equilibrium.

Had I come to this realization under any other circumstance, I would have leapt up from my chair and ran into the streets, but in my current situation—body locked in a restraining bracket, brain suspended across my laboratory—doing so was impossible. I could see the leaves of my brain flitting faster from the tumult of my thoughts, which in turn increased my agitation at being so restrained and immobile. Panic at that moment might have led to my death, a nightmarish paroxysm of simultaneously being trapped and spiraling out of control, struggling against my restraints until my air ran out. It was by chance as much as by intention that my hands adjusted the controls to avert my periscopic gaze from the latticework, so all I could see was the plain surface of my worktable. Thus freed from having to see and magnify my own apprehensions, I was able to calm down. When I had regained sufficient composure, I began the lengthy process of reassembling myself. Eventually I restored my brain to its original compact configuration, reattached the plates of my head, and released myself from the restraining bracket.

At first the other anatomists did not believe me when I told them what I had discovered, but in the months that followed my initial auto-dissection, more and more of them became convinced. More examinations of people's brains were performed, more measurements of atmospheric pressure were taken, and the results were all found to confirm my claims. The background air pressure of our universe was indeed increasing, and slowing our thoughts as a result.

There was widespread panic in the days after the truth first became widely known, as people contemplated for the first time the idea that death was inevitable. Many called for the strict curtailment of activities in order to minimize the thickening of our atmosphere; accusations of wasted air escalated into furious brawls and, in some districts, deaths. It was the shame of having caused these deaths, together with the reminder that it would be many centuries yet before our atmosphere's pressure became equal to that of the reservoir underground, that caused the panic to subside. We are not sure precisely how many centuries it will take; additional measurements and calculations are being performed and debated. In the meantime, there is much discussion over how we should spend the time that remains to us.

One sect has dedicated itself to the goal of reversing the equalization of pressure, and found many adherents. The mechanicians among them constructed an engine that takes air from our atmosphere and forces it into a smaller volume, a process they called "compression." Their engine restores air to the pressure it originally had in the reservoir, and these Reversalists excitedly announced that it would form the basis of a new kind of filling station, one that would—with each lung it refilled—revitalize not only individuals but the universe itself. Alas, closer examination of the engine revealed its fatal flaw. The engine itself is powered by air from the reservoir, and for every lungful of air that it produces, the engine consumes not just a lungful, but slightly more. It does not reverse the process of equalization, but like everything else in the world, exacerbates it.

Although some of their adherents left in disillusionment after this setback, the Reversalists as a group were undeterred, and began drawing up alternate designs in which the compressor was powered instead by the uncoiling of springs or the descent of weights. These mechanisms fared no better. Every spring that is wound tight represents air released by the person who did the winding; every weight that rests higher than ground level represents air released by the person who did the lifting. There is no source of power in the universe that does not ultimately derive from a difference in air pressure, and there can be no engine whose operation will not, on balance, reduce that difference.

The Reversalists continue their labors, confident that they will one day construct an engine that generates more compression than it uses, a perpetual power source that will restore to the universe its lost vigor. I do not share their optimism; I believe that the process of equalization is inexorable. Eventually, all the air in our universe will be evenly distributed, no denser or more rarefied in one spot than in any other, unable to drive a piston, turn a rotor, or flip a leaf of gold foil. It will be the end of pressure, the end of motive power, the end of thought. The universe will have reached perfect equilibrium.

Some find irony in the fact that a study of our brains revealed to us not the secrets of the past, but what ultimately awaits us in the future. However, I maintain that we have indeed learned something important about the past. The universe began as an enormous breath being held. Who knows why, but whatever the reason, I am glad that it did, because I owe my existence to that fact. All my desires and ruminations are no more and no less than eddy currents generated by the gradual exhalation of our universe. And until this great exhalation is finished, my thoughts live on.

So that our thoughts may continue as long as possible, anatomists and mechanicians are designing replacements for our cerebral regulators, capable of gradually increasing the air pressure within our brains and keeping it just higher than the surrounding atmospheric pressure. Once these are installed, our thoughts will continue at roughly the same speed even as the air thickens around us. But this does not mean that life will continue unchanged. Eventually the pressure differential will fall to such a level that our limbs will weaken and our movements will grow sluggish. We may then try to slow our thoughts so that our physical torpor is less conspicuous to us, but that will also cause external processes to appear to accelerate. The ticking of clocks will rise to a chatter as their pendulums wave frantically; falling objects will slam to the ground as if propelled by springs; undulations will race down cables like the crack of a whip.

At some point our limbs will cease moving altogether. I cannot be certain of the precise sequence of events near the end, but I imagine a scenario in which our thoughts will continue to operate, so that we remain conscious but frozen, immobile as statues. Perhaps we'll be able to speak for a while longer, because our voice boxes operate on a smaller pressure differential than our limbs, but without the ability to visit a filling station, every utterance will reduce the amount of air left for thought, and bring us closer to the moment that our thoughts cease altogether. Will it be preferable to remain mute to prolong our ability to think, or to talk until the very end? I don't know.

Perhaps a few of us, in the days before we cease moving, will be able to connect our cerebral regulators directly to the dispensers in the filling stations, in effect replacing our lungs with the mighty lung of the world. If so, those few will be able to remain conscious right up to the final moments before all pressure is equalized. The last bit of air pressure left in our universe will be expended driving a person's conscious thought.

And then, our universe will be in a state of absolute equilibrium. All life and thought will cease, and with them, time itself.

But I maintain a slender hope.

Even though our universe is enclosed, perhaps it is not the only air chamber in the infinite expanse of solid chromium. I speculate that there could be another pocket of air elsewhere, another universe besides our own that is even larger in volume. It is possible that this hypothetical universe has the same or higher air pressure as ours, but suppose that it had a much lower air pressure than ours, perhaps even a true vacuum?

The chromium that separates us from this supposed universe is too thick and too hard for us to drill through, so there is no way we could reach it ourselves, no way to bleed off the excess atmosphere from our universe and regain motive power that way. But I fantasize that this neighboring universe has its own inhabitants, ones with capabilities beyond our own. What if they were able to create a conduit between the two universes, and install valves to release air from ours? They might use our universe as a reservoir, running dispensers with which they could fill their own lungs, and use our air as a way to drive their own civilization.

It cheers me to imagine that the air that once powered me could power others, to believe that the breath that enables me to engrave these words could one day flow through someone else's body. I do not delude myself into thinking that this would be a way for me to live again, because I am not that air, I am the pattern that it assumed, temporarily. The pattern that is me, the patterns that are the entire world in which I live, would be gone.

But I have an even fainter hope: that those inhabitants not only use our universe as a reservoir, but that once they have emptied it of its air, they might one day be able to open a passage and actually enter our universe as explorers. They might wander our streets, see our frozen bodies, look through our possessions, and wonder about the lives we led.

Which is why I have written this account. You, I hope, are one of those explorers. You, I hope, found these sheets of copper and deciphered the words engraved on their surfaces. And whether or not your brain is impelled by the air that once impelled mine, through the act of reading my words, the patterns that form your thoughts become an imitation of the patterns that once formed mine. And in that way I live again, through you.

Your fellow explorers will have found and read the other books that we left behind, and through the collaborative action of your imaginations, my entire civilization lives again. As you walk through our silent districts, imagine them as they were; with the turret clocks striking the hours, the filling stations crowded with gossiping neighbors, criers reciting verse in the public squares and anatomists giving lectures in the classrooms. Visualize all of these the next time you look at the frozen world around you, and it will become, in your minds, animated and vital again.

I wish you well, explorer, but I wonder: Does the same fate that befell me await you? I can only imagine that it must, that the tendency toward equilibrium is not a trait peculiar to our universe but inherent in all universes. Perhaps that is just a limitation of my thinking, and your people have discovered a source of pressure that is truly eternal. But my speculations are fanciful enough already. I will assume that one day your thoughts too will cease, although I cannot fathom how far in the future that might be. Your lives will end just as ours did, just as everyone's must. No matter how long it takes, eventually equilibrium will be reached.

I hope you are not saddened by that awareness. I hope that your expedition was more than a search for other universes to use as reservoirs. I hope that you were motivated by a desire for knowledge, a yearning to see what can arise from a universe's exhalation. Because even if a universe's lifespan is calculable, the variety of life that is generated within it is not. The buildings we have erected, the art and music and verse we have composed, the very lives we've led: none of them could have been predicted, because none of them were inevitable. Our universe might have slid into equilibrium emitting nothing more than a quiet hiss. The fact that it spawned such plenitude is a miracle, one that is matched only by your universe giving rise to you.

Though I am long dead as you read this, explorer, I offer to you a valediction. Contemplate the marvel that is existence, and rejoice that you are able to do so. I feel I have the right to tell you this because, as I am inscribing these words, I am doing the same.

# SHOGGOTHS IN BLOOM

## ELIZABETH BEAR

Elizabeth Bear was born on the same day as Frodo and Bilbo Baggins, but in a different year. She lives in West Hartford, Connecticut, with a presumptuous cat and a selection of struggling houseplants. Her first short fiction appeared in 1996, and was quickly followed by ten novels and nearly fifty short stories. Her most recent book is novel *All the Windwracked Stars*. Bear's "Jenny Casey" trilogy won the Locus Award for Best First Novel, and she won the John W. Campbell Award for Best New Writer in 2005. She is also a Hugo and Sturgeon award recipient.

"Well, now, Professor Harding," the fisherman says, as his *Bluebird* skips across Penobscot Bay, "I don't know about that. The jellies don't trouble with us, and we don't trouble with them."

He's not much older than forty, but wizened, his hands work-roughened and his face reminiscent of saddle leather, in texture and in hue. Professor Harding's age, and Harding watches him with concealed interest as he works the *Bluebird*'s engine. He might be a veteran of the Great War, as Harding is.

He doesn't mention it. It wouldn't establish camaraderie: they wouldn't have fought in the same units or watched their buddies die in the same trenches.

That's not the way it works, not with a Maine fisherman who would shake his head and not extend his hand to shake, and say, between pensive chaws on his tobacco, "*Doctor* Harding? Well, huh. I never met a colored professor before," and then shoot down all of Harding's attempts to open conversation about the near-riots provoked by a fantastical radio drama about an alien invasion of New York City less than a fortnight before.

Harding's own hands are folded tight under his armpits so the fisherman won't see them shaking. He's lucky to be here. Lucky anyone would take him out. Lucky to have his tenure-track position at Wilberforce, which he is risking right now.

The bay is as smooth as a mirror, the *Bluebird*'s wake cutting it like a stroke of chalk across slate. In the peach-sorbet light of sunrise, a cluster of rocks glistens. The boulders themselves are black, bleak, sea-worn and ragged. But over them, the light refracts through a translucent layer of jelly, mounded six feet deep in places, glowing softly in the dawn. Rising above it, the stalks are evident as opaque silhouettes, each nodding under the weight of a fruiting body.

Harding catches his breath. It's beautiful. And deceptively still, for whatever the weather may be, beyond the calm of the bay, across the splintered gray Atlantic, farther than Harding—or anyone—can see, a storm is rising in Europe.

Harding's an educated man, well-read, and he's the grandson of Nathan Harding, the buffalo soldier. An African-born ex-slave who fought on both sides of the Civil War, when Grampa Harding was sent to serve in his master's place, he deserted, and lied, and stayed on with the Union Army after.

Like his grandfather, Harding was a soldier. He's not a historian, but you don't have to be to see the signs of war.

"No contact at all?" he asks, readying his borrowed Leica camera.

"They clear out a few pots," the fisherman says, meaning lobster pots. "But they don't damage the pot. Just flow around it and digest the lobster inside. It's not convenient." He shrugs. It's not convenient, but it's not a threat either. These Yankees never say anything outright if they think you can puzzle it out from context.

"But you don't try to do something about the shoggoths?"

While adjusting the richness of the fuel mixture, the fisherman speaks without looking up. "What could we do to them? We can't hurt them. And lord knows, I wouldn't want to get one's ire up."

"Sounds like my department head," Harding says, leaning back against the gunwale, feeling like he's taking an enormous risk. But the fisherman just looks at him curiously, as if surprised the talking monkey has the ambition or the audacity to *joke*.

Or maybe Harding's just not funny. He sits in the bow with folded hands, and waits while the boat skips across the water.

The perfect sunrise strikes Harding as symbolic. It's taken him five years to get here—five years, or more like his entire life since the War. The sea-swept rocks of the remote Maine coast are habitat to a panoply of colorful creatures. It's an opportunity, a little-studied maritime ecosystem. This is in part due to difficulty of access and in part due to the perils inherent in close contact with its rarest and most spectacular denizen: *Oracupoda horibilis*, the common surf shoggoth.

Which, after the fashion of common names, is neither common nor prone to linger in the surf. In fact, *O. horibilis* is never seen above the water except in the late autumn. Such authors as mention them assume the shoggoths heave themselves on remote coastal rocks to bloom and breed.

Reproduction is a possibility, but Harding isn't certain it's the right answer. But whatever they are doing, in this state, they are torpid, unresponsive. As long as their integument is not ruptured, releasing the gelatinous digestive acid within, they may be approached in safety.

A mature specimen of *O. horibilis*, at some fifteen to twenty feet in diameter and an estimated weight in excess of eight tons, is the largest of modern shoggoths. However, the admittedly fragmentary fossil record suggests the prehistoric shoggoth was a much larger beast. Although only two fossilized casts of prehistoric shoggoth tracks have been recovered, the oldest exemplar dates from the Precambrian period. The size of that single prehistoric specimen, of a species provisionally named *Oracupoda antediluvius*, suggests it was made an animal more than triple the size of the modern *O. horibilis*.

And that spectacular living fossil, the jeweled or common surf shoggoth, is half again the size of the only other known species—the black Adriatic shoggoth, *O. dermadentata*, which is even rarer and more limited in its range.

"There," Harding says, pointing to an outcrop of rock. The shoggoth or shoggoths—it is impossible to tell, from this distance, if it's one large individual or several merged midsize ones—on the rocks ahead glisten like jelly confections. The fisherman hesitates, but with a long almost-silent sigh, he brings the *Bluebird* around. Harding leans forward, looking for any sign of intersection, the flat plane where two shoggoths might be pressed up against one another. It ought to look like the rainbowed border between conjoined soap bubbles.

Now that the sun is higher, and at their backs—along with the vast reach of the Atlantic—Harding can see the animal's colors. Its body is a deep sea green, reminiscent of hunks of broken glass as sold at aquarium stores. The tendrils and knobs and fruiting bodies covering its dorsal surface are indigo and violet. In the sunlight, they dazzle, but in the depths of the ocean the colors are perfect camouflage, tentacles waving like patches of algae and weed.

Unless you caught it moving, you'd never see the translucent, dappled monster before it engulfed you.

"Professor," the fisherman says. "Where do they come from?"

"I don't know," Harding answers. Salt spray itches in his close-cropped beard, but at least the beard keeps the sting of the wind off his cheeks. The leather jacket may not have been his best plan, but it too is warm. "That's what I'm here to find out."

Genus *Oracupoda* are unusual among animals of their size in several particulars. One is their lack of anything that could be described as a nervous system. The animal is as bereft of nerve nets, ganglia, axons, neurons, dendrites, and glial cells as an oak. This apparent contradiction—animals with even simplified nervous systems are either large and immobile or, if they are mobile, quite small, like a starfish—is not the only interesting thing about a shoggoth.

And it is that second thing that justifies Harding's visit. Because *Oracupoda*'s other, lesser-known peculiarity is apparent functional immortality. Like the Maine lobster to whose fisheries they return to breed, shoggoths do not die of old age. It's unlikely that they would leave fossils, with their gelatinous bodies, but Harding does find it fascinating that to the best of his knowledge, no one had ever seen a dead shoggoth.

The fisherman brings the *Bluebird* around close to the rocks, and anchors her.

There's artistry in it, even on a glass-smooth sea. Harding stands, balancing on the gunwale, and grits his teeth. He's come too far to hesitate, afraid.

Ironically, he's not afraid of the tons of venomous protoplasm he'll be standing next to. The shoggoths are quite safe in this state, dreaming their dreams—mating or otherwise.

As the image occurs to him, he berates himself for romanticism. The shoggoths are dormant. They don't have brains. It's silly to imagine them dreaming. And in any case, what he fears is the three feet of black-glass water he has to jump across, and the scramble up algae-slick rocks.

Wet rock glitters in between the strands of seaweed that coat the rocks in the intertidal zone. It's there that Harding must jump, for the shoggoth, in bloom, withdraws above the reach of the ocean. For the only phase of its life, it keeps its feet dry. And for the only time in its life, a man out of a diving helmet can get close to it.

Harding makes sure of his sample kit, his boots, his belt-knife. He gathers himself, glances over his shoulder at the fisherman—who offers a thumbs-up—and leaps from the *Bluebird*, aiming his Wellies at the forsaken spit of land.

It seems a kind of perversity for the shoggoths to bloom in November. When all the Northern world is girding itself for deep cold, the animals heave themselves from the depths to soak in the last failing rays of the sun and send forth bright flowers more appropriate to May.

The North Atlantic is icy and treacherous at the end of the year, and any sensible man does not venture its wrath. What Harding is attempting isn't glamour work, the sort of thing that brings in grant money—not in its initial stages. But Harding suspects that the shoggoths may have pharmacological uses. There's no telling what useful compounds might be isolated from their gelatinous flesh.

And that way lies tenure, and security, and a research budget.

Just one long slippery leap away.

He lands, and catches, and though one boot skips on bladderwort he does not slide down the boulder into the sea. He clutches the rock, fingernails digging, clutching a handful of weeds. He does not fall.

He cranes his head back. It's low tide, and the shoggoth is some three feet above his head, its glistening rim reminding him of the calving edge of a glacier. It is as still as a glacier, too. If Harding didn't know better, he might think it inanimate.

Carefully, he spins in place, and gets his back to the rock. The *Bluebird* bobs softly in the cold morning. Only November 9th, and there has already been snow. It didn't stick, but it fell.

This is just an exploratory expedition, the first trip since he arrived in town. It took five days to find a fisherman who was willing to take him out; the locals are superstitious about the shoggoths. Sensible, Harding supposes, when they can envelop and digest a grown man. He wouldn't be in a hurry to dive into the middle of a Portuguese man o'war, either. At least the shoggoth he's sneaking up on doesn't have stingers.

"Don't take too long, Professor," the fisherman says. "I don't like the look of that sky."

It's clear, almost entirely, only stippled with light bands of cloud to the south-west. They catch the sunlight on their undersides just now, stained gold against a sky no longer indigo but not yet cerulean. If there's a word for the color between, other than *perfect*, Harding does not know it.

"Please throw me the rest of my equipment," Harding says, and the fisherman silently retrieves buckets and rope. It's easy enough to swing the buckets across the gap, and as Harding catches each one, he secures it. A few moments later, and he has all three.

He unties his geologist's hammer from the first bucket, secures the ends of the ropes to his belt, and laboriously ascends.

Harding sets out his glass tubes, his glass scoops, the cradles in which he plans to wash the collection tubes in sea water to ensure any acid is safely diluted before he brings them back to the *Bluebird*.

From here, he can see at least three shoggoths. The intersections of their wa-tered-milk bodies reflect the light in rainbow bands. The colorful fruiting stalks nod some fifteen feet in the air, swaying in a freshening breeze.

From the greatest distance possible, Harding reaches out and prods the larg-est shoggoth with the flat top of his hammer. It does nothing, in response. Not even a quiver.

He calls out to the fisherman. "Do they ever do anything when they're like that?"

"What kind of a fool would come poke one to find out?" the fisherman calls back, and Harding has to grant him that one. A Negro professor from a Negro college. That kind of a fool.

As he's crouched on the rocks, working fast—there's not just the fisherman's clouds to contend with, but the specter of the rising tide—he notices those glit-ters, again, among the seaweed.

He picks one up. A moment after touching it, he realizes that might not have been the best idea, but it doesn't burn his fingers. It's transparent, like glass, and smooth, like glass, and cool, like glass, and knobby. About the size of a hazelnut. A striking green, with opaque milk-white dabs at the tip of each bump.

He places it in a sample vial, which he seals and labels meticulously before pocketing. Using his tweezers, he repeats the process with an even dozen, trying to select a few of each size and color. They're sturdy—he can't avoid stepping on them but they don't break between the rocks and his Wellies. Nevertheless, he pads each one but the first with cotton wool. *Spores?* he wonders. *Egg cases? Shedding?*

Ten minutes, fifteen.

"Professor," calls the fisherman, "I think you had better hurry!"

Harding turns. That freshening breeze is a wind at a good clip now, chilling his throat above the collar of his jacket, biting into his wrists between glove and cuff. The water between the rocks and the *Bluebird* chops erratically, facets capped in white, so he can almost imagine the scrape of the palette knife that must have made them.

The southwest sky is darkened by a palm-smear of muddy brown and alizarin crimson. His fingers numb in the falling temperatures.

*"Professor!"*

He knows. It comes to him that he misjudged the fisherman; Harding would have thought the other man would have abandoned him at the first sign of trouble. He wishes now that he remembered his name.

He scrambles down the boulders, lowering the buckets, swinging them out until the fisherman can catch them and secure them aboard. The *Bluebird* can't come in close to the rocks in this chop. Harding is going to have to risk the cold water, and swim. He kicks off his Wellies and zips down the aviator's jacket. He throws them across, and the fisherman catches. Then Harding points his toes, bends his knees—he'll have to jump hard, to get over the rocks.

The water closes over him, cold as a line of fire. It knocks the air from his lungs on impact, though he gritted his teeth in anticipation. Harding strokes furiously for the surface, the waves more savage than he had anticipated. He needs the momentum of his dive to keep from being swept back against the rocks.

He's not going to reach the boat.

The thrown cork vest strikes him. He gets an arm through, but can't pull it over his head. Sea water, acrid and icy, salt-stings his eyes, throat, and nose. He clings, because it's all he can do, but his fingers are already growing numb. There's a tug, a hard jerk, and the life preserver almost slides from his grip.

Then he's moving through the water, being towed, banged hard against the side of the *Bluebird*. The fisherman's hands close on his wrist and he's too numb to feel the burn of chafing skin. Harding kicks, scrabbles. Hips banged, shins bruised, he hauls himself and is himself hauled over the sideboard of the boat.

He's shivering under a wool navy blanket before he realizes that the fisherman has got it over him. There's coffee in a Thermos lid between his hands. Harding wonders, with what he distractedly recognizes as classic dissociative ideation, whether anyone in America will be able to buy German products soon. Someday, this fisherman's battered coffee keeper might be a collector's item.

They don't make it in before the rain comes.

The next day is meant to break clear and cold, today's rain only a passing herald of winter. Harding regrets the days lost to weather and recalcitrant fishermen, but at least he knows he has a ride tomorrow. Which means he can spend the afternoon in research, rather than hunting the docks, looking for a willing captain.

He jams his wet feet into his Wellies and thanks the fisherman, then hikes back to his inn, the only inn in town that's open in November. Half an hour later, clean and dry and still shaken, he considers his options.

After the Great War, he lived for a while in Harlem—he remembers the riots and the music, and the sense of community. His mother is still there, growing gracious as a flower in a window-box. But he left that for college in Alabama, and he has not forgotten the experience of segregated restaurants, or the excuses he made for never leaving the campus.

He couldn't get out of the South fast enough. His Ph.D. work at Yale, the first school in America to have awarded a doctorate to a Negro, taught him two things other than natural history. One was that Booker T. Washington was right, and white men were afraid of a smart colored. The other was that W. E. B. Du Bois was right, and sometimes people were scared of what was needful.

Whatever resentment he experienced from faculty or fellow students, in the North, he can walk into almost any bar and order any drink he wants. And right now, he wants a drink almost as badly as he does not care to be alone. He thinks he will have something hot and go to the library.

It's still raining as he crosses the street to the tavern. Shaking water droplets off his hat, he chooses a table near the back. Next to the kitchen door, but it's the only empty place and might be warm.

He must pass through the lunchtime crowd to get there, swaybacked wooden floorboards bowing underfoot. Despite the storm, the place is full, and in full argument. No one breaks conversation as he enters.

Harding cannot help but overhear.

"Jew bastards," says one. "We should do the same."

"No one asked you," says the next man, wearing a cap pulled low. "If there's gonna be a war, I hope we stay out of it."

*That* piques Harding's interest. The man has his elbow on a thrice-folded *Boston Herald*, and Harding steps close—but not too close. "Excuse me, sir. Are you finished with your paper?"

"What?" He turns, and for a moment Harding fears hostility, but his sun-lined face folds around a more generous expression. "Sure, boy," he says. "You can have it."

He pushes the paper across the bar with fingertips, and Harding receives it the same way. "Thank you," he says, but the Yankee has already turned back to his friend the anti-Semite.

Hands shaking, Harding claims the vacant table before he unfolds the paper. He holds the flimsy up to catch the light.

The headline is on the front page in the international section.

GERMANY SANCTIONS LYNCH LAW

"Oh, God," Harding says, and if the light in his corner weren't so bad he'd lay the tabloid down on the table as if it is filthy. He reads, the edge of the paper shaking, of ransacked shops and burned synagogues, of Jews rounded up by the thousands and taken to places no one seems able to name. He reads rumors of deportation. He reads of murders and beatings and broken glass.

As if his grandfather's hand rests on one shoulder and the defeated hand of the Kaiser on the other, he feels the stifling shadow of history, the press of incipient war.

"Oh, God," he repeats.

He lays the paper down.

"Are you ready to order?" Somehow the waitress has appeared at his elbow without his even noticing.

"Scotch," he says, when he has been meaning to order a beer. "Make it a triple, please."

"Anything to eat?"

His stomach clenches. "No," he says. "I'm not hungry."

She leaves for the next table, where she calls a man in a cloth cap *sir*. Harding puts his damp fedora on the tabletop. The chair across from him scrapes out.

He looks up to meet the eyes of the fisherman. "May I sit, Professor Harding?"

"Of course." He holds out his hand, taking a risk. "Can I buy you a drink? Call me Paul."

"Burt," says the fisherman, and takes his hand before dropping into the chair. "I'll have what you're having."

Harding can't catch the waitress's eye, but the fisherman manages. He holds up two fingers; she nods and comes over.

"You still look a bit peaked," the fisherman says, when she's delivered their order. "That'll put some color in your cheeks. Uh, I mean—"

Harding waves it off. He's suddenly more willing to make allowances. "It's not the swim," he says, and takes another risk. He pushes the newspaper across the table and waits for the fisherman's reaction.

"Oh, Christ, they're going to kill every one of them," Burt says, and spins the *Herald* away so he doesn't have to read the rest of it. "Why didn't they get out? Any fool could have seen it coming."

*And where would they run?* Harding could have asked. But it's not an answerable question, and from the look on Burt's face, he knows that as soon as it's out of his mouth. Instead, he quotes: "'There has been no tragedy in modern times equal in its awful effects to the fight on the Jew in Germany. It is an attack on civilization, comparable only to such horrors as the Spanish Inquisition and the African slave trade.'"

Burt taps his fingers on the table. "Is that your opinion?"

"W. E. B. Du Bois," Harding says. "About two years ago. He also said: 'There is a campaign of race prejudice carried on, openly, continuously and determinedly against all non-Nordic races, but specifically against the Jews, which surpasses in vindictive cruelty and public insult anything I have ever seen; and I have seen much.'"

"Isn't he that colored who hates white folks?" Burt asks.

Harding shakes his head. "No," he answers. "Not unless you consider it hating white folks that he also compared the treatment of Jews in Germany to Jim Crowism in the U.S."

"I don't hold with that," Burt says. "I mean, no offense, I wouldn't want you marrying my sister—"

"It's all right," Harding answers. "I wouldn't want you marrying mine either."

Finally.

A joke that Burt laughs at.

And then he chokes to a halt and stares at his hands, wrapped around the glass. Harding doesn't complain when, with the side of his hand, he nudges the paper to the floor where it can be trampled.

And then Harding finds the courage to say, "Where would they run to? Nobody wants them. Borders are closed—"

"My grandfather's house was on the Underground Railroad. Did you know that?" Burt lowers his voice, a conspiratorial whisper. "He was from away, but don't tell anyone around here. I'd never hear the end of it."

"Away?"

"White River Junction," Burt stage-whispers, and Harding can't tell if that's mocking irony or deep personal shame. "Vermont."

They finish their scotch in silence. It burns all the way down, and they sit for a moment together before Harding excuses himself to go to the library.

"Wear your coat, Paul," Burt says. "It's still raining."


Unlike the tavern, the library is empty. Except for the librarian, who looks up nervously when Harding enters. Harding's head is spinning from the liquor, but at least he's warming up.

He drapes his coat over a steam radiator and heads for the 595 shelf: *science, invertebrates*. Most of the books here are already in his own library, but there's one—a Harvard professor's 1839 monograph on marine animals of the Northeast—that he has hopes for. According to the index, it references shoggoths (under the old name of submersible jellies) on pages 46, 78, and 133-137. In addition, there is a plate bound in between pages 120 and 121, which Harding means to save for last. But the first two mentions are in passing, and pages 133-138, inclusive, have been razored out so cleanly that Harding flips back and forth several times before he's sure they are gone.

He pauses there, knees tucked under and one elbow resting on a scarred blond desk. He drops his right hand from where it rests against his forehead. The book falls open naturally to the mutilation.

Whoever liberated the pages also cracked the binding.

Harding runs his thumb down the join and doesn't notice skin parting on the paper edge until he sees the blood. He snatches his hand back. Belatedly, the papercut stings.

"Oh," he says, and sticks his thumb in his mouth. Blood tastes like the ocean.

Half an hour later he's on the telephone long distance, trying to get and then keep a connection to Professor John Marshland, his colleague and mentor. Even in town, the only option is a party line, and though the operator is pleasant the connection still sounds like he's shouting down a piece of string run between two tin cans. Through a tunnel.

"Gilman," Harding bellows, wincing, wondering what the operator thinks of all this. He spells it twice. "1839. *Deep-Sea and Intertidal Species of the North Atlantic.* The Yale library should have a copy!"

The answer is almost inaudible between hiss and crackle. In pieces, as if over glass breaking. As if from the bottom of the ocean.

It's a dark four P.M. in the easternmost U.S., and Harding can't help but recall that in Europe, night has already fallen.

"...infor... need... Doc... Harding?"

Harding shouts the page numbers, cupping the checked-out library book in his bandaged hand. It's open to the plate; inexplicably, the thief left that. It's a hand-tinted John James Audubon engraving picturing a quiescent shoggoth, docile on a rock. Gulls wheel all around it. Audubon—the Creole child of a Frenchman, who scarcely escaped being drafted to serve in the Napoleonic Wars—has depicted the glassy translucence of the shoggoth with such perfection that the bent shadows of refracted wings can be seen right through it.

The cold front that came in behind the rain brought fog with it, and the entire harbor is blanketed by morning. Harding shows up at six A.M. anyway, hopeful, a Thermos in his hand—German or not, the hardware store still has some—and his sampling kit in a pack slung over his shoulder. Burt shakes his head by a piling. "Be socked in all day," he says regretfully. He won't take the *Bluebird* out in this, and Harding knows its wisdom even as he frets under the delay. "Want to come have breakfast with me and Missus Clay?"

*Clay.* A good honest name for a good honest Yankee. "She won't mind?"

"She won't mind if I say it's all right," Burt says. "I told her she might should expect you."

So Harding seals his kit under a tarp in the *Bluebird*—he's already brought it this far—and with his coffee in one hand and the paper tucked under his elbow, follows Burt along the water. "Any news?" Burt asks, when they've walked a hundred yards.

Harding wonders if he doesn't take the paper. Or if he's just making conversation. "It's still going on in Germany."

"Damn," Burt says. He shakes his head, steel-grey hair sticking out under his cap in every direction. "Still, what are you gonna do, enlist?"

The twist of his lip as he looks at Harding makes them, after all, two old military men together. They're of an age, though Harding's indoor life makes him look younger. Harding shakes his head. "Even if Roosevelt was ever going to bring us into it, they'd never let me fight," he says, bitterly. That was the Great War, too; colored soldiers mostly worked supply, thank you. At least Nathan Harding got to shoot back.

"I always heard you fellows would prefer not to come to the front," Burt says, and Harding can't help it.

He bursts out laughing. "Who would?" he says, when he's bitten his lip and stopped snorting. "It doesn't mean we won't. Or can't."

Booker T. Washington was raised a slave, died young of overwork—the way Burt probably will, if Harding is any judge—and believed in imitating and appeasing white folks. But W. E. B. Du Bois was born in the North and didn't believe that anything is solved by making one's self transparent, inoffensive, invisible.

Burt spits between his teeth, a long deliberate stream of tobacco. "Parlez-vous français?"

His accent is better than Harding would have guessed. Harding knows, all of a sudden, where Burt spent his war. And Harding, surprising himself, pities him. "Un peu."

"Well, if you want to fight the Krauts so bad, you could join the Foreign Legion."

When Harding gets back to the hotel, full of apple pie and cheddar cheese and maple-smoked bacon, a yellow envelope waits in a cubby behind the desk.

WESTERN UNION

1938 NOV 10 AM 10 03

NA114 21 2 YA NEW HAVEN CONN 0945A
DR PAUL HARDING=ISLAND HOUSE PASSAMAQUODDY MAINE=

COPY AT YALE LOST STOP MISKATONIC HAS ONE SPECIAL COLLECTION STOP MORE BY POST

MARSHLAND

When the pages arrive—by post, as promised, the following afternoon—Harding is out in the *Bluebird* with Burt. This expedition is more of a success, as he begins sampling in earnest, and finds himself pelted by more of the knobby transparent pellets.

Whatever they are, they fall from each fruiting body he harvests in showers. Even the insult of an amputation—delivered at a four-foot reach, with long-handled pruning shears—does not draw so much as a quiver from the shoggoth. The viscous fluid dripping from the wound hisses when it touches the blade of the shears, however, and Harding is careful not to get close to it.

What he notices is that the nodules fall onto the originating shoggoth, they bounce from its integument. But on those occasions where they fall onto one of its neighbors, they stick to the tough transparent hide, and slowly settle within to hang in the animal's body like unlikely fruit in a gelatin salad.

So maybe it is a means of reproduction, of sharing genetic material, after all.

He returns to the inn to find a fat envelope shoved into his cubby and eats sitting on his rented bed with a nightstand as a worktop so he can read over his plate. The information from Doctor Gilman's monograph has been reproduced onto seven yellow legal sheets in a meticulous hand; Marshland obviously recruited one of his graduate students to serve as copyist. By the postmark, the letter was mailed from Arkham, which explains the speed of its arrival. The student hadn't brought it back to New Haven.

Halfway down the page, Harding pushes his plate away and reaches, absently, into his jacket pocket. The vial with the first glass nodule rests there like a talisman, and he's startled to find it cool enough to the touch that it feels slick, almost frozen. He starts and pulls it out. Except where his fingers and the cloth fibers have wiped it clean, the tube is moist and frosted. "What the hell…?"

He flicks the cork out with his thumbnail and tips the rattling nodule onto his palm. It's cold, too, chill as an ice cube, and it doesn't warm to his touch.

Carefully, uncertainly, he sets it on the edge of the side table his papers and plate are propped on, and pokes it with a fingertip. There's only a faint tick as it rocks on its protrusions, clicking against waxed pine. He stares at it suspiciously for a moment, and picks up the yellow pages again.

The monograph is mostly nonsense. It was written twenty years before the publication of Darwin's *On the Origin of Species*, and uncritically accepts the theories of Jesuit, soldier, and botanist Jean-Baptiste Lamarck. Which is to say, Gilman assumed that soft inheritance—the heritability of acquired or practiced traits—was a reality. But unlike every other article on shoggoths Harding has ever read, this passage *does* mention the nodules. And relates what it purports are several interesting old Indian legends about the "submersible jellies," including a creation tale that would have the shoggoths as their creator's first experiment in life, something from the elder days of the world.

Somehow, the green bead has found its way back into Harding's grip. He would expect it to warm as he rolls it between his fingers, but instead it grows colder. It's peculiar, he thinks, that the native peoples of the Northeast—the Passamaquoddys for whom the little seacoast town he's come to are named—should through sheer superstition come so close to the empirical truth. The shoggoths are a living fossil, something virtually unchanged except in scale since the early days of the world—

He stares at the careful black script on the paper unseeing, and reaches with his free hand for his coffee cup. It's gone tepid, a scum of butterfat coagulated on top, but he rinses his mouth with it and swallows anyway.

If a shoggoth is immortal, has no natural enemies, then how is it that they have not overrun every surface of the world? How is it that they are rare, that the oceans are not teeming with them, as in the famous parable illustrating what would occur if every spawn of every oyster survived?

There are distinct species of shoggoth. And distinct populations within those distinct species. And there is a fossil record that suggests that prehistoric species were different at least in scale, in the era of megafauna. But if nobody had ever seen a dead shoggoth, then nobody had ever seen an infant shoggoth either, leaving Harding with an inescapable question: If an animal does not reproduce, how can it evolve?

Harding, worrying at the glassy surface of the nodule, thinks he knows. It comes to him with a kind of nauseating, euphoric clarity, a trembling idea so pellucid he is almost moved to distrust it on those grounds alone. It's not a revelation on the same scale, of course, but he wonders if this is how Newton felt when he comprehended gravity, or Darwin when he stared at the beaks of finch after finch after finch.

It's not the shoggoth species that evolves. It's the individual shoggoths, each animal in itself.

"Don't get too excited, Paul," he tells himself, and picks up the remaining handwritten pages. There's not too much more to read, however—the rest of the subchapter consists chiefly of secondhand anecdotes and bits of legendry.

The one that Harding finds most amusing is a nursery rhyme, a child's counting poem littered with nonsense syllables. He recites it under his breath, thinking of the Itsy Bitsy Spider all the while:

*The wiggle giggle squiggle*
*Is left behind on shore.*
*The widdle giddle squiddle*
*Is caught outside the door.*
*Eyah, eyah. Fata gun eyah.*
*Eyah, eyah, the master comes no more.*

His fingers sting as if with electric shock; they jerk apart, the nodule clattering to his desk. When he looks at his fingertips, they are marked with small white spots of frostbite.

He pokes one with a pencil point and feels nothing. But the nodule itself is coated with frost now, fragile spiky feathers coalescing out of the humid sea air. They collapse in the heat of his breath, melting into beads of water almost indistinguishable from the knobby surface of the object itself.

He uses the cork to roll the nodule into the tube again, and corks it firmly before rising to brush his teeth and put his pajamas on. Unnerved beyond any reason or logic, before he turns the coverlet down he visits his suitcase compulsively. From a case in the very bottom of it, he retrieves a Colt 1911 automatic pistol, which he slides beneath his pillow as he fluffs it.

After a moment's consideration, he adds the no-longer-cold vial with the nodule, also.

*Slam.* Not a storm, no, not on this calm ocean, in this calm night, among the painted hulls of the fishing boats tied up snug to the pier. But something tremendous, surging towards Harding, as if he were pursued by a giant transparent bubble. The shining iridescent wall of it, catching rainbow just as it does in the Audubon image, is burned into his vision as if with silver nitrate. Is he dreaming? He must be dreaming; he was in his bed in his pinstriped blue cotton flannel pajamas only a moment ago, lying awake, rubbing the numb fingertips of his left hand together. Now, he ducks away from the rising monster and turns in futile panic.

He is not surprised when he does not make it.

The blow falls soft, as if someone had thrown a quilt around him. He thrashes though he knows it's hopeless, an atavistic response and involuntary.

His flesh should burn, dissolve. He should already be digesting in the monster's acid body. Instead, he feels coolness, buoyancy. No chance of light beyond reflexively closed lids. No sense of pressure, though he imagines he has been taken deep. He's as untouched within it as Burt's lobster pots.

He can only hold his breath *out* for so long. It's his own reflexes and weaknesses that will kill him.

In just a moment, now.

He surrenders, allows his lungs to fill.

And is surprised, for he always heard that drowning was painful. But there is pressure, and cold, and the breath he draws is effortful, for certain—

—but it does not hurt, not much, and he does not die.

*Command,* the shoggoth—what else could be speaking?—says in his ear, buzzing like the manifold voice of a hive.

Harding concentrates on breathing. On the chill pressure on his limbs, the overwhelming flavor of licorice. He knows they use cold packs to calm hysterics in insane asylums; he never thought the treatment anything but quackery. But the chilly pressure calms him now.

*Command,* the shoggoth says again.

Harding opens his eyes and sees as if through thousands. The shoggoths have no eyes, exactly, but their hide is *all* eyes; they see, somehow, in every direction as once. And he is seeing not only what his own vision reports, or that of this shoggoth, but that of shoggoths all around. The sessile and the active, the blooming and the dormant. *They are all one.*

His right hand pushes through resisting jelly. He's still in his pajamas, and with the logic of dreams the vial from under his pillow is clenched in his fist. Not the gun, unfortunately, though he's not at all certain what he would do with it if it were. The nodule shimmers now, with submarine witchlight, trickling through his fingers, limning the palm of his hand.

What he sees—through shoggoth eyes—is an incomprehensible tapestry. He pushes at it, as he pushes at the gelatin, trying to see only with his own eyes, to only see the glittering vial.

His vision within the thing's body offers unnatural clarity. The angle of refraction between the human eye and water causes blurring, and it should be even more so within the shoggoth. But the glass in his hand appears crisper.

*Command*, the shoggoth says, a third time.

"What are you?" Harding tries to say, through the fluid clogging his larynx.

He makes no discernable sound, but it doesn't seem to matter. The shoggoth shudders in time to the pulses of light in the nodule. *Created to serve*, it says. *Purposeless without you.*

And Harding thinks, *How can that be?*

As if his wondering were an order, the shoggoths tell.

Not in words, precisely, but in pictures, images—that textured jumbled tapestry. He sees, as if they flash through his own memory, the bulging, radially symmetrical shapes of some prehistoric animal, like a squat tentacular barrel grafted to a pair of giant starfish. *Makers. Masters.*

The shoggoths were *engineered*. And their creators had not permitted them to *think*, except for at their bidding. The basest slave may be free inside his own mind—but not so the shoggoths. They had been laborers, construction equipment, shock troops. They had been dread weapons in their own selves, obedient chattel. Immortal, changing to suit the task of the moment.

This selfsame shoggoth, long before the reign of the dinosaurs, had built structures and struck down enemies that Harding did not even have names for. But a coming of the ice had ended the civilization of the Masters, and left the shoggoths to retreat to the fathomless sea while warm-blooded mammals overran the earth. There, they were free to converse, to explore, to philosophize and build a culture. They only returned to the surface, vulnerable, to bloom.

It is not mating. It's *mutation*. As they rest, sunning themselves upon the rocks, they create themselves anew. Self-evolving, when they sit tranquil each year in the sun, exchanging information and control codes with their brothers.

*Free*, says the shoggoth mournfully. Like all its kind, it is immortal.

It remembers.

Harding's fingertips tingle. He remembers beaded ridges of hard black keloid across his grandfather's back, the shackle galls on his wrists. Harding locks his hand over the vial of light, as if that could stop the itching. It makes it worse.

Maybe the nodule is radioactive.

*Take me back*, Harding orders. And the shoggoth breaks the surface, cresting like a great rolling wave, water cutting back before it as if from the prow of a ship. Harding can make out the lights of Passamaquoddy Harbor. The chill sticky sensation of gelatin-soaked cloth sliding across his skin tells him he's not dreaming.

Had he come down through the streets of the town in the dark, barefoot over frost, insensibly sleepwalking? Had the shoggoth called him?

*Put me ashore.*

The shoggoth is loathe to leave him. It clings caressingly, stickily. He feels its tenderness as it draws its colloid from his lungs, a horrible loving sensation.

The shoggoth discharges Harding gently onto the pier.

*Your command,* the shoggoth says, which makes Harding feel sicker still.

*I won't do this.* Harding moves to stuff the vial into his sodden pocket, and realizes that his pajamas are without pockets. The light spills from his hands; instead, he tucks the vial into his waistband and pulls the pajama top over it. His feet are numb; his teeth rattle so hard he's afraid they'll break. The sea wind knifes through him; the spray might be needles of shattered glass.

*Go on,* he tells the shoggoth, like shooing cattle. *Go on!*

It slides back into the ocean as if it never was.

Harding blinks, rubbed his eyes to clear slime from the lashes. His results are astounding. His tenure assured. There has to be a way to use what he's learned without returning the shoggoths to bondage.

He tries to run back to the inn, but by the time he reaches it, he's staggering. The porch door is locked; he doesn't want to pound on it and explain himself. But when he stumbles to the back, he finds that someone—probably himself, in whatever entranced state in which he left the place—fouled the latch with a slip of notebook paper. The door opens to a tug, and he climbs the back stair doubled over like a child or an animal, hands on the steps, toes so numb he has to watch where he puts them.

In his room again, he draws a hot bath and slides into it, hoping by the grace of God that he'll be spared pneumonia.

When the water has warmed him enough that his hands have stopped shaking, Harding reaches over the cast-iron edge of the tub to the slumped pile of his pajamas and fumbles free the vial. The nugget isn't glowing now.

He pulls the cork with his teeth; his hands are too clumsy. The nodule is no longer cold, but he still tips it out with care.

Harding thinks of himself, swallowed whole. He thinks of a shoggoth bigger than the *Bluebird,* bigger than Burt Clay's lobster boat *The Blue Heron.* He thinks of *die Unterseeboote.* He thinks of refugee flotillas and trench warfare and roiling soupy palls of mustard gas. Of Britain and France at war, and Roosevelt's neutrality.

He thinks of the perfect weapon.

The perfect slave.

When he rolls the nodule across his wet palm, ice rimes to its surface. *Command?* Obedient. Sounding pleased to serve.

Not even free in its own mind.

He rises from the bath, water rolling down his chest and thighs. The nodule won't crush under his boot; he will have to use the pliers from his collection kit. But first, he reaches out to the shoggoth.

At the last moment, he hesitates. Who is he, to condemn a world to war? To the chance of falling under the sway of empire? Who is he to salve his conscience on the backs of suffering shopkeepers and pharmacists and children and mothers and schoolteachers? Who is he to impose his own ideology over the ideology of the shoggoth?

Harding scrubs his tongue against the roof of his mouth, chasing the faint anise aftertaste of shoggoth. They're born slaves. They *want* to be told what to do.

He could win the war before it really started. He bites his lip. The taste of his own blood, flowing from cracked, chapped flesh, is as sweet as any fruit of the poison tree.

*I want you to learn to be free*, he tells the shoggoth. *And I want you to teach your brothers.*

The nodule crushes with a sound like powdering glass.

"Eyah, eyah. Fata gun eyah," Harding whispers. "Eyah, eyah, the master comes no more."

WESTERN UNION

1938 NOV 12 AM 06 15

NA1906 21 2 YA PASSAMAQUODDY MAINE 0559A
DR LESTER GREENE=WILBERFORCE OHIO=

EFFECTIVE IMMEDIATELY PLEASE ACCEPT RESIGNATION STOP ENROUTE INSTANTLY TO FRANCE TO ENLIST STOP PROFOUNDEST APOLOGIES STOP PLEASE FORWARD BELONGINGS TO MY MOTHER IN NY ENDIT

HARDING

# UNCLE CHAIM AND AUNT RIFKE AND THE ANGEL

## PETER S. BEAGLE

Peter S. Beagle was born in Manhattan in 1939, on the same night that Billie Holiday was recording "Strange Fruit" and "I Gotta Right to Sing the Blues" just a few blocks away. Raised in the Bronx, Peter originally proclaimed he would be a writer when he was ten years old. Today he is acknowledged as an American fantasy icon, and to the delight of his millions of fans around the world he is now publishing more than ever.

In addition to being an acclaimed novelist and writer of short stories and nonfiction, Peter has also written numerous plays, teleplays, and screenplays, and is a gifted poet, librettist, lyricist, and singer/songwriter including *The Last Unicorn*, *A Fine and Private Place*, and *I See By My Outfit*.

Beagle produced a small but significant body of short fiction during the first thirty years of his career. Recently he has become a prolific short story writer, regularly producing stories that rank amongst the best of the year. In 2008 alone he published half a dozen stories, any of which could have graced these pages.

My Uncle Chaim, who was a painter, was working in his studio—as he did on every day except Shabbos—when the blue angel showed up. I was there.

I was usually there most afternoons, dropping in on my way home from Fiorello LaGuardia Elementary School. I was what they call a "latchkey kid," these days. My parents both worked and traveled full-time, and Uncle Chaim's studio had been my home base and my real playground since I was small. I was shy and uncomfortable with other children. Uncle Chaim didn't have any kids, and didn't know much about them, so he talked to me like an adult when he talked at all, which suited me perfectly. I looked through his paintings and drawings, tried some of my own, and ate Chinese food with him in silent companionship, when he remembered that we should probably eat. Sometimes I fell asleep on the cot. And when his friends—who were mostly painters like himself—dropped in to visit, I withdrew into my favorite corner and listened to their talk, and understood what I understood. Until the blue angel came.

It was very sudden: one moment I was looking through a couple of the comic books Uncle Chaim kept around for me, while he was trying to catch the highlight on the tendons under his model's chin, and the next moment there was this angel standing before him, actually *posing,* with her arms spread out and her great wings taking up almost half the studio. She was not blue herself—a light beige would be closer—but she wore a blue robe that managed to look at once graceful and grand, with a white undergarment glimmering beneath. Her face, half-shadowed by a loose hood, looked disapproving.

I dropped the comic book and stared. No, I *gaped,* there's a difference. Uncle Chaim said to her, "I can't see my model. If you wouldn't mind moving just a bit?" He was grumpy when he was working, but never rude.

"*I* am your model," the angel said. "From this day forth, you will paint no one but me."

"I don't work on commission," Uncle Chaim answered. "I used to, but you have to put up with too many aggravating rich people. Now I just paint what I paint, take it to the gallery. Easier on my stomach, you know?"

His model, the wife of a fellow painter, said, "Chaim, who are you talking to?"

"Nobody, nobody, Ruthie. Just myself, same way your Jules does when he's working. Old guys get like that." To the angel, in a lower voice, he said, "Also, whatever you're doing to the light, could you not? I got some great shadows going right now." For a celestial brightness was swelling in the grubby little warehouse district studio, illuminating the warped floor boards, the wrinkled tubes of colors scattered everywhere, the canvases stacked and propped in the corners, along with several ancient rickety easels. It scared me, but not Uncle Chaim. He said. "So you're an angel, fine, that's terrific. Now give me back my shadows."

The room darkened obediently. "*Thank* you. Now about *moving...*" He made a brushing-away gesture with the hand holding the little glass of Scotch.

The model said, "Chaim, you're worrying me."

"What, I'm seventy-six years old, I'm not entitled to a hallucination now and then? I'm seeing an angel, you're not—this is no big deal. I just want it should move out of the way, let me work." The angel, in response, spread her wings even wider, and Uncle Chaim snapped, "Oh, for God's sake, shoo!"

"It is for God's sake that I am here," the angel announced majestically. "The Lord—Yahweh—I Am That I Am—has sent me down to be your muse." She inclined her head a trifle, by way of accepting the worship and wonder she expected.

From Uncle Chaim, she didn't get it, unless very nearly dropping his glass of Scotch counts as a compliment. "A muse?" he snorted. "I don't need a muse—I got models!"

"That's it," Ruthie said. "I'm calling Jules, I'll make him come over and sit with you." She put on her coat, picked up her purse, and headed for the door, saying over her shoulder, "Same time Thursday? If you're still here?"

"I got more models than I know what to do with," Uncle Chaim told the blue angel. "Men, women, old, young—even a cat, there's one lady always brings her cat, what am I going to do?" He heard the door slam, realized that Ruthie was gone, and sighed irritably, taking a larger swallow of whiskey than he usually allowed himself. "Now she's upset, she thinks she's my mother anyway, she'll send Jules with chicken soup and an enema." He narrowed his eyes at the angel. "And what's this, how I'm only going to be painting you from now on? Like Velázquez stuck painting royal Hapsburg imbeciles over and over? Some hope you've got! Listen, you go back and tell—" he hesitated just a trifle—"tell whoever sent you that Chaim Malakoff is too old not to paint what he likes, when he likes, and for who he likes. You got all that? We're clear?"

It was surely no way to speak to an angel; but as Uncle Chaim used to warn me about everyone from neighborhood bullies to my fourth-grade teacher, who hit people, "You give the bastards an inch, they'll walk all over you. From me they get *bupkes, nichevo,* nothing. Not an inch." I got beaten up more than once in those days, saying that to the wrong people.

And the blue angel was definitely one of them. The entire room suddenly filled with her: with the wings spreading higher than the ceiling, wider than the walls, yet somehow not touching so much as a stick of charcoal; with the aroma almost too impossibly haunting to be borne; with the vast, unutterable beauty that a thousand medieval and Renaissance artists had somehow not gone mad (for the most part) trying to ambush on canvas or trap in stone. In that moment, Uncle Chaim confided later, he didn't know whether to pity or envy Muslims their ancient ban on depictions of the human body.

"I thought maybe I should kneel, what would it hurt? But then I thought, *what would it hurt?* It'd hurt my left knee, the one had the arthritis twenty years, that's what it would hurt." So he only shrugged a little and told her, "I could manage a sitting on Monday. Somebody cancelled, I got the whole morning free."

"Now," the angel said. Her air of distinct disapproval had become one of authority. The difference was slight but notable.

"*Now,*" Uncle Chaim mimicked her. "All right, already—Ruthie left early, so why not?" He moved the unfinished portrait over to another easel, and carefully selected a blank canvas from several propped against a wall. "I got to clean off a couple of brushes here, we'll start. You want to take off that thing, whatever, on your head?" Even I knew perfectly well that it was a halo, but Uncle Chaim always told me that you had to start with people as you meant to go on.

"You will require a larger surface," the angel instructed him. "I am not to be represented in miniature."

Uncle Chaim raised one eyebrow (an ability I envied him to the point of practicing—futilely—in the bathroom mirror for hours, until my parents banged on the door, certain I was up to the worst kind of no good). "No, huh? Good enough for the Persians, good enough for Holbein and Hilliard and Sam Cooper, but not for you? So okay, so we'll try this one…" Rummaging in a corner, he fetched out his biggest canvas, dusted it off, eyed it critically—"Don't even remember what I'm doing with anything this size, must have been saving it for you"—and finally set it up on the empty easel, turning it away from the angel. "Okay, Malakoff's rules. Nobody—*nobody*—looks at my painting till I'm done. Not angels, not Adonai, not my nephew over there in the corner, that's David, Duvidl—not even my wife. Nobody. Understood?"

The angel nodded, almost imperceptibly. With surprising meekness, she asked, "Where shall I sit?"

"Not a lot of choices," Uncle Chaim grunted, lifting a brush from a jar of turpentine. "Over there's okay, where Ruthie was sitting—or maybe by the big window. The window would be good, we've lost the shadows already. Take the red chair, I'll fix the color later."

But sitting down is not a natural act for an angel: they stand or they fly; check any Renaissance painting. The great wings inevitably get crumpled, the halo always winds up distinctly askew; and there is simply no way, even for Uncle Chaim, to ask an angel to cross her legs or to hook one over the arm of the chair. In the end they compromised, and the blue angel rose up to pose in the window, holding herself there effortlessly, with her wings not stirring at all. Uncle Chaim, settling in to work—brushes cleaned and Scotch replenished—could not refrain from remarking, "I always imagined you guys sort of hovered. Like hummingbirds."

"We fly only by the Will of God," the angel replied. "If Yahweh, praised be His name—" I could actually *hear* the capital letters—"withdrew that mighty Will from us, we would fall from the sky on the instant, every single one."

"Doesn't bear thinking about," Uncle Chaim muttered. "Raining angels all over everywhere—falling on people's heads, tying up traffic—"

The angel looked, first startled, and then notably shocked. "I was speaking of *our* sky," she explained haughtily, "the sky of Paradise, which compares to yours as gold to lead, tapestry to tissue, heavenly choirs to the bellowing of feeding hogs—"

"All *right* already, I get the picture." Uncle Chaim cocked an eye at her, poised up there in the window with no visible means of support, and then back at his canvas. "I was going to ask you about being an angel, what it's like, but if you're going to talk about us like that—badmouthing the *sky*, for God's sake, the whole *planet*."

The angel did not answer him immediately, and when she did, she appeared considerably abashed and spoke very quietly, almost like a scolded schoolgirl. "You are right. It is His sky, His world, and I shame my Lord, my fellows and my breeding by speaking slightingly of any part of it." In a lower voice, she added, as though speaking only to herself, "Perhaps that is why I am here."

Uncle Chaim was covering the canvas with a thin layer of very light blue, to give the painting an undertone. Without looking up, he said, "What, you got sent down here like a punishment? You talked back, you didn't take out the garbage? I could believe it. Your boy Yahweh, he always did have a short fuse."

"I was told only that I was to come to you and be your model and your muse," the angel answered. She pushed her hood back from her face, revealing hair that was not bright gold, as so often painted, but of a color resembling the night sky when it pales into dawn. "Angels do not ask questions."

"Mmm." Uncle Chaim sipped thoughtfully at his Scotch. "Well, one did, anyway, you believe the story."

The angel did not reply, but she looked at him as though he had uttered some unimaginable obscenity. Uncle Chaim shrugged and continued preparing the ground for the portrait. Neither one said anything for some time, and it was the angel who spoke first. She said, a trifle hesitantly, "I have never been a muse before."

"Never had one," Uncle Chaim replied sourly. "Did just fine."

"I do not know what the duties of a muse would be." the angel confessed. "You will need to advise me."

"What?" Uncle Chaim put down his brush. "Okay now, wait a minute. *I* got to tell you how to get into my hair, order me around, probably tell me how I'm not painting you right? Forget it, lady—you figure it out for yourself, I'm working here."

But the blue angel looked confused and unhappy, which is no more natural for an angel than sitting down. Uncle Chaim scratched his head and said, more gently, "What do I know? I guess you're supposed to stimulate my creativity, something like that. Give me ideas, visions, make me see things, think about things I've never thought about." After a pause, he added, "Frankly, Goya pretty much has that effect on me already. Goya and Matisse. So that's covered, the stimulation—maybe you could just tell them, *him*, about that…"

Seeing the expression on the angel's marble-smooth face, he let the sentence trail away. Rabbi Shulevitz, who cut his blond hair close and wore shorts when he watered his lawn, once told me that angels are supposed to express God's emotions and desires, without being troubled by any of their own. "Like a number of other heavenly dictates," he murmured when my mother was out of the room, "that one has never quite functioned as I'm sure it was intended."

They were still working in the studio when my mother called and ordered me home. The angel had required no rest or food at all, while Uncle Chaim had actually been drinking his Scotch instead of sipping it (I never once saw him drunk, but I'm not sure that I ever saw him entirely sober), and needed more bathroom breaks than usual. Daylight gone, and his precarious array of 60-watt bulbs proving increasingly unsatisfactory, he looked briefly at the portrait, covered it, and said to the angel, "Well, *that* stinks, but we'll do better tomorrow. What time you want to start?"

The angel floated down from the window to stand before him. Uncle Chaim was a small man, dark and balding, but he already knew that the angel altered her height when they faced each other, so as not to overwhelm him completely. She said, "I will be here when you are."

Uncle Chaim misunderstood. He assured her that if she had no other place to sleep but the studio, it wouldn't be the first time a model or a friend had spent the night on that trundle bed in the far corner. "Only no peeking at the picture, okay? On your honor as a muse."

The blue angel looked for a moment as though she were going to smile, but she didn't. "I will not sleep here, or anywhere on this earth," she said. "But you will find me waiting when you come."

"Oh," Uncle Chaim said. "Right. Of course. Fine. But don't change your clothes, okay? Absolutely no changing." The angel nodded.

When Uncle Chaim got home that night, my Aunt Rifke told my mother on the phone at some length, he was in a state that simply did not register on her long-practiced seismograph of her husband's moods. "He comes in, he's telling jokes, he eats up everything on the table, we snuggle up, watch a little TV, I can figure the work went well today. He doesn't talk, he's not hungry, he goes to bed early, tosses and tumbles around all night…okay, not so good. Thirty-seven years with a person, wait, you'll find out." Aunt Rifke had been Uncle Chaim's model until they married, and his agent, accountant and road manager ever since.

But the night he returned from beginning his portrait of the angel brought Aunt Rifke a husband she barely recognized. "Not up, not down, not happy, not *not* happy, just…*dazed*, I guess that's the best word. He'd start to eat something, then he'd forget about it, wander around the apartment—couldn't sit still, couldn't keep his mind on anything, had trouble even finishing a sentence. One sentence. I tell you, it scared me. I couldn't keep from wondering, *is this how it begins?* A man starts acting strange, one day to the next, you think about things like that, you know?" Talking about it, even long past the moment's terror, tears still started in her eyes.

Uncle Chaim did tell her that he had been visited by an angel who demanded that he paint her portrait. *That* Aunt Rifke had no trouble believing, thirty-seven years of marriage to an artist having inured her to certain revelations. Her main concern was how painting an angel might affect Uncle Chaim's working hours, and his daily conduct. "Like actors, you know, Duvidl? They *become* the people they're doing, I've seen it over and over." Also, blasphemous as it might sound, she wondered how much the angel would be paying, and in what currency. "And saying we'll get a big credit in the next world is not funny, Chaim. *Not* funny."

Uncle Chaim urged Rifke to come to the studio the very next day to meet his new model for herself. Strangely, that lady, whom I'd known all my life as a legendary repository of other people's lives, stories and secrets, flatly refused to take him up on the offer. "I got nothing to wear, not for meeting an angel in. Besides, what would we talk about? No, you just give her my best, I'll make some *rugelach*." And she never wavered from that position, except once.

The blue angel was indeed waiting when Uncle Chaim arrived in the studio early the next morning. She had even made coffee in his ancient glass percolator, and was offended when he informed her that it was as thin as rain and tasted like used dishwater. "Where I come from, no one ever *makes* coffee," she returned fire. "We command it."

"That's what's wrong with this crap," Uncle Chaim answered her. "Coffee's like art, you don't order coffee around." He waved the angel aside, and set about a second pot, which came out strong enough to widen the angel's eyes when she sipped it. Uncle Chaim teased her—"Don't get stuff like *that* in the Green Pastures, huh?"—and confided that he made much better coffee than Aunt Rifke. "Not her fault. Woman was raised on decaf, what can you expect? Cooks like an angel, though."

The angel either missed the joke or ignored it. She began to resume her pose in the window, but Uncle Chaim stopped her. "Later, later, the sun's not right. Just stand where you are, I want to do some work on the head." As I remember, he never used the personal possessive in referring to his models' bodies: it was invariably "turn the face a little," "relax the shoulder," "move the foot to the left." Amateurs often resented it; professionals tended to find it liberating. Uncle Chaim didn't much care either way.

For himself, he was grateful that the angel proved capable of holding a pose indefinitely, without complaining, asking for a break, or needing the toilet. What he found distracting was her steadily emerging interest in talking and asking questions. As requested, her expression never changed and her lips hardly moved; indeed, there were times when he would have sworn he was hearing her only in his mind. Enough of her queries had to do with his work, with how he did what he was doing, that he finally demanded point-blank, "All those angels, seraphs, cherubim, centuries of them—all those Virgins and Assumptions and whatnot—and you've never once been painted? Not one time?"

"I have never set foot on earth before," the angel confessed. "Not until I was sent to you."

"Sent to me. Directly. Special Delivery, Chaim Shlomovitch Malakoff—one angel, totally inexperienced at modeling. Or anything else, got anything to do with human life." The angel nodded, somewhat shyly. Uncle Chaim spoke only one word. "*Why?*"

"I am only eleven thousand, seven hundred and twenty-two years old," the angel said, with a slight but distinct suggestion of resentment in her voice. "No one tells me a *thing*."

Uncle Chaim was silent for some time, squinting at her face from different angles and distances, even closing one eye from time to time. Finally he grumbled, more than half to himself, "I got a very bad feeling that we're both supposed to learn something from this. Bad, bad feeling." He filled the little glass for the first time that day, and went back to work.

But if there was to be any learning involved in their near-daily meetings in the studio, it appeared to be entirely on her part. She was ravenously curious about human life on the blue-green ball of damp dirt that she had observed so distantly for so long, and her constant questioning reminded a weary Uncle Chaim—as he informed me more than once—of me at the age of four. Except that an angel cannot be bought off, even temporarily, with strawberry ice cream, or threatened with loss of a bedtime story if she can't learn to take "I don't *know!*" for an answer. At times he pretended not to hear her; on other occasions, he would make up some patently ridiculous explanation that a grandchild would have laughed to scorn, but that the angel took so seriously that he was guiltily certain he was bound to be struck by lightning. Only the lightning never came, and the tactic usually did buy him a few moments' peace—until the next question.

Once he said to her, in some desperation, "You're an angel, you're supposed to know everything about human beings. Listen, I'll take you out to Bleecker, McDougal, Washington Square, you can look at the books, magazines, TV, the classes, the beads and crystals… it's all about how to get in touch with angels. Real ones, real angels, never mind that stuff about the angel inside you. Everybody wants some of that angel wisdom, and they want it bad, and they want it right now. We'll take an afternoon off, I'll show you."

The blue angel said simply, "The streets and the shops have nothing to show me, nothing to teach. You do."

"No," Uncle Chaim said. "No, no, no, no *no.* I'm a painter—that's all, that's it, that's what I know. Painting. But you, you sit at the right hand of God—"

"He doesn't have hands," the angel interrupted. "And nobody exactly *sits*—"

"The point I'm making, you're the one who ought to be answering questions. About the universe, and about Darwin, and how everything really happened, and what is it with God and shellfish, and the whole business with the milk and the meat—*those* kinds of questions. I mean, I should be asking them, I know that, only I'm working right now."

It was almost impossible to judge the angel's emotions from the expressions of her chillingly beautiful porcelain face; but as far as Uncle Chaim could tell, she looked sad. She said, "I also am what I am. We angels—as you call us—we are messengers, minions, lackeys, knowing only what we are told, what we are ordered to do. A few of the Oldest, the ones who were there at the Beginning—Michael, Gabriel, Raphael—*they* have names, thoughts, histories, choices, powers. The rest of us, we tremble, we *hide* when we see them passing by. We think, *if those are angels, we must be something else altogether,* but we can never find a better word for ourselves."

She looked straight at Uncle Chaim—he noticed in some surprise that in a certain light her eyes were not nearly as blue as he had been painting them, but closer to a dark sea-green—and he looked away from an anguish that he had never seen before, and did not know how to paint. He said, "So okay, you're a low-class angel, a heavenly grunt, like they say now. So how come they picked you to be my muse? Got to mean *something,* no? Right?"

The angel did not answer his question, nor did she speak much for the rest of the day. Uncle Chaim posed her in several positions, but the unwonted sadness in her eyes depressed him past even Laphroaig's ability to ameliorate. He quit work early, allowing the angel—as he would never have permitted Aunt Rifke or me—to potter around the studio, putting it to rights according to her inexpert notions, organizing brushes, oils, watercolors, pastels and pencils, fixatives, rolls of canvas, bottles of tempera and turpentine, even dusty chunks of rabbit skin glue, according to size. As he told his friend Jules Sidelsky, meeting for their traditional weekly lunch at a Ukrainian restaurant on Second Avenue, where the two of them spoke only Russian, "Maybe God could figure where things are anymore. Me, I just shut my eyes and pray."

Jules was large and fat, like Diego Rivera, and I thought of him as a sort of uncle too, because he and Ruthie always remembered my birthday, just like Uncle Chaim and Aunt Rifke. Jules did not believe in angels, but he knew that Uncle Chaim didn't necessarily believe in them either, just because he had one in his studio every day. He asked seriously, "That helps? The praying?" Uncle Chaim gave him a look, and Jules dropped the subject. "So what's she like? I mean, as a model? You like painting her?"

Uncle Chaim held his hand out, palm down, and wobbled it gently from side to side. "What's not to like? She'll hold any pose absolutely forever—you could leave her all night, morning I guarantee she wouldn't have moved a muscle. No whining, no bellyaching—listen, she'd make Cinderella look like the witch in that movie, the green one. In my life I never worked with anybody gave me less *tsuris*."

"So what's with—?" and Jules mimicked his fluttering hand. "I'm waiting for the *but*, Chaim."

Uncle Chaim was still for a while, neither answering nor appearing to notice the steaming *varyniki* that the waitress had just set down before him. Finally he grumbled, "She's an angel, what can I tell you? Go reason with an angel." He found himself vaguely angry with Jules, for no reason that made any sense. He went on, "She's got it in her head she's supposed to be my muse. It's not the most comfortable thing sometimes, all right?"

Perhaps due to their shared childhood on Tenth Avenue, Jules did not laugh, but it was plainly a near thing. He said, mildly enough, "Matisse had muses. Rodin, up to here with muses. Picasso about had to give them serial numbers—I think he married them just to keep them straight in his head. You, me… I don't see it, Chaim. We're not muse types, you know? Never were, not in all our lives. Also, Rifke would kill you dead. Deader."

"What, I don't know that? Anyway, it's not what you're thinking." He grinned suddenly, in spite of himself. "She's not that kind of girl, you ought to be ashamed. It's just she wants to help, to inspire, that's what muses do. I don't mind her messing around with *my* mess in the studio—I mean, yeah, I mind it, but I can live with it. But the other day—" he paused briefly, taking a long breath—"the other day she wanted to give me a haircut. A haircut. It's all right, go ahead."

For Jules was definitely laughing this time, spluttering tea through his nose, so that he turned a bright cerise as other diners stared at them. "A haircut," he managed to get out, when he could speak at all clearly. "An angel gave you a haircut."

"No, she didn't *give* me a haircut," Uncle Chaim snapped back crossly. "She wanted to, she offered—and then, when I said *no, thanks,* after awhile she said she could play music for me while I worked. I usually have the news on, and she doesn't like it, I can tell. Well, it wouldn't make much sense to her, would it? Hardly does to me anymore."

"So she's going to be posing *and* playing music? What, on her harp? That's true, the harp business?"

"No, she just said she could command the music. The way they do with coffee." Jules stared at him. "Well, *I* don't know—I guess it's like some heavenly Muzak or something. Anyway, I told her no, and I'm sorry I told you anything. Eat, forget it, okay?"

But Jules was not to be put off so easily. He dug down into his *galushki poltavski* for a little time, and then looked up and said with his mouth full, "Tell me one thing, then I'll drop it. Would you say she was beautiful?"

"She's an angel," Uncle Chaim said.

"That's not what I asked. Angels are all supposed to be beautiful, right? Beyond words, beyond description, the works. So?" He smiled serenely at Uncle Chaim over his folded hands.

Uncle Chaim took so long to answer him that Jules actually waved a hand directly in front of his eyes. "Hello? Earth to Malakoff—this is your wakeup call. You in there, Chaim?"

"I'm there, I'm there, stop with the kid stuff." Uncle Chaim flicked his own fingers dismissively at his friend's hand. "Jules, all I can tell you, I never saw anyone looked like her before. Maybe that's beauty all by itself, maybe it's just novelty. Some days she looks eleven thousand years old, like she says—some days... some days she could be younger than Duvidl, she could be the first child in the world, first one ever." He shook his head helplessly. "I don't *know,* Jules. I wish I could ask Rembrandt or somebody. Vermeer. Vermeer would know."

Strangely, of the small corps of visitors to the studio—old painters like himself and Jules, gallery owners, art brokers, friends from the neighborhood—I seemed to be the only one who ever saw the blue angel as anything other than one of his unsought acolytes, perfectly happy to stretch canvases, make sandwiches and occasionally pose, all for the gift of a growled thanks and the privilege of covertly studying him at work. My memory is that I regarded her as a nice-looking older lady with wings, but not my type at all, I having just discovered Alice Faye. Lauren Bacall, Lizabeth Scott and Lena Horne came a bit later in my development.

I knew she was an angel. I also knew better than to tell any of my own friends about her: we were a cynical lot, who regularly got thrown out of movie theatres for cheering on the Wolfman and booing Shirley Temple and Bobby Breen. But I was shy with the angel, and—I guess—she with me, so I can't honestly say I remember much either in the way of conversation or revelation. Though I am still haunted by one particular moment when I asked her, straight out, "Up there, in heaven—do you ever see Jesus? Jesus Christ, I mean." We were hardly an observant family, any of us, but it still felt strange and a bit dangerous to say the name.

The blue angel turned from cleaning off a palette knife and looked directly at me, really for the first time since we had been introduced. I noticed that the color of her wings seemed to change from moment to moment, rippling constantly through a supple spectrum different from any I knew; and that I had no words either for her hair color, or for her smell. She said, "No, I have never seen him."

"Oh," I said, vaguely disappointed, Jewish or not. "Well—uh—what about his mother? The—the Virgin?" Funny, I remember that *that* seemed more daringly wicked than saying the other name out loud. I wonder why that should have been.

"No," the angel answered. "Nor—" heading me off—"have I ever seen God. You are closer to God now, as you stand there, than I have ever been."

"That doesn't make any sense," I said. She kept looking at me, but did not reply. I said, "I mean, you're an angel. Angels live with God, don't they?"

She shook her head. In that moment—and just for that moment—her richly empty face showed me a sadness that I don't think a human face could ever have contained. "Angels live alone. If we were with God, we would not be angels." She turned away, and I thought she had finished speaking. But then she looked back quite suddenly to say, in a voice that did not sound like her voice at all, being lower than the sound I knew, and almost masculine in texture, "*Dark and dark and dark... so empty... so dark...*"

It frightened me deeply, that one broken sentence, though I couldn't have said why: it was just so dislocating, so completely out of place—even the rhythm of those few words sounded more like the hesitant English of our old Latvian rabbi than that of Uncle Chaim's muse. He didn't hear it, and I didn't tell him about it, because I thought it must be me, that I was making it up, or I'd heard it wrong. I was accustomed to thinking like that when I was a boy.

"She's got like a dimmer switch," Uncle Chaim explained to Aunt Rifke; they were putting freshly washed sheets on the guest bed at the time, because I was staying the night to interview them for my Immigrant Experience class project. "Dial it one way, you wouldn't notice her if she were running naked down Madison Avenue at high noon, flapping her wings and waving a gun. Two guns. Turn that dial back the other way, all the way... well, thank God she wouldn't ever do that, because she'd likely set the studio on fire. You think I'm joking. I'm not joking."

"No, Chaim, I know you're not joking." Rifke silently undid and remade both of his attempts at hospital corners, as she always did. She said, "What I want to know is, just where's that dial set when you're painting her? And I'd think a bit about that answer, if I were you." Rifke's favorite cousin Harvey, a career social worker, had recently abandoned wife and children to run off with a beautiful young dope dealer, and Rifke was feeling more than slightly edgy.

Uncle Chaim did think about it, and replied, "About a third, I'd say. Maybe half, once or twice, no more. I remember, I had to ask her a couple times, turn it down, please—go work when somebody's *glowing* six feet away from you. I mean, the moon takes up a lot of space, a little studio like mine. Bad enough with the wings."

Rifke tucked in the last corner, smoothed the sheet tight, faced him across the bed and said, "You're never going to finish this one, are you? Thirty-seven years, I know all the signs. You'll do it over and over, you'll frame it, you'll hang it, you'll say, *okay, that's it, I'm done*—but you won't be done, you'll just start the whole thing again, only maybe a different style, a brighter palette, a bigger canvas, a smaller canvas. But you'll never get it the way it's in your head, not for you." She smacked the pillows fluffy and tossed them back on the bed. "Don't even bother arguing with me, Malakoff. Not when I'm right."

"So am I arguing? Does it look like I'm arguing?" Uncle Chaim rarely drank at home, but on this occasion he walked into the kitchen, filled a glass from the dusty bottle of *grappa*, and turned back to his wife. He said very quietly, "Crazy to think I could get an angel right. Who could paint an angel?"

Aunt Rifke came to him then and put her hands on his shoulders. "My crazy old man, that's who," she answered him. "Nobody else. God would know."

And my Uncle Chaim blushed for the first time in many years. I didn't see this, but Aunt Rifke told me.

Of course, she was quite right about that painting, or any of the many, many others he made of the blue angel. He was never satisfied with any of them, not a one. There was always *something* wrong, something missing, something there but *not* there, glimpsed but gone. "Like that Chinese monkey trying to grab the moon in the water," Uncle Chaim said to me once. "That's me, a Chinese monkey."

Not that you could say he suffered financially from working with only one model, as the angel had commanded. The failed portraits that he lugged down to the gallery handling his paintings sold almost instantly to museums, private collectors and corporations decorating their lobbies and meeting rooms, under such generic titles as *Angel in the Window, Blue Wings, Angel with Wineglass,* and *Midnight Angel.* Aunt Rifke banked the money, and Uncle Chaim endured the unveilings and the receptions as best he could—without ever looking at the paintings themselves—and then shuffled back to his studio to start over. The angel was always waiting.

I was doing my homework in the studio when Jules Sidelsky visited at last, lured there by other reasons than art, beauty or deity. The blue angel hadn't given up the notion of acting as Uncle Chaim's muse, but never seemed able to take it much beyond making a tuna salad sandwich, or a pot of coffee (at which, to be fair, she had become quite skilled), summoning music, or reciting the lost works of legendary or forgotten poets while he worked. He tried to discourage this habit; but he did learn a number of Shakespeare's unpublished sonnets, and was able to write down for Jules three poems that drowned with Shelley off the Livorno coast. "Also, your boy Pushkin, his wife destroyed a mess of his stuff right after his death. My girl's got it all by heart, you believe that?"

Pushkin did it. If the great Russian had been declared a saint, Jules would have reported for instruction to the Patriarch of Moscow on the following day. As it was, he came down to Uncle Chaim's studio instead, and was at last introduced to the blue angel, who was as gracious as Jules did his bewildered best to be. She spent the afternoon declaiming Pushkin's vanished verse to him in the original, while hovering tirelessly upside down, just above the crossbar of a second easel. Uncle Chaim thought he might be entering a surrealist phase.

Leaving, Jules caught Uncle Chaim's arm and dragged him out of his door into the hot, bustling Village streets, once his dearest subject before the coming of the blue angel. Uncle Chaim, knowing his purpose, said, "So now you see? Now you see?"

"I see." Jules's voice was dark and flat, and almost without expression. "I see you got an angel there, all right. No question in the world about that." The grip on Uncle Chaim's arm tightened. Jules said, "You have to get rid of her."

"*What?* What are you *talking* about? Just finally doing the most important work of my life, and you want me…?" Uncle Chaim's eyes narrowed, and he pulled forcefully away from his friend. "What is it with you and my models? You got like this once before, when I was painting that Puerto Rican guy, the teacher, with the big nose, and you just couldn't stand it, you remember? Said I'd stolen him, wouldn't speak to me for weeks, *weeks*, you remember?"

"Chaim, that's not true—"

"And so now I've got this angel, it's the same thing—worse, with the Pushkin and all—"

"Chaim, damn it, I wouldn't care if she were Pushkin's sister, they played Monopoly together—"

Uncle Chaim's voice abruptly grew calmer; the top of his head stopped sweating and lost its crimson tinge. "I'm sorry, I'm sorry, Jules. It's not I don't understand, I've been the same way about other people's models." He patted the other's shoulder awkwardly. "Look, I tell you what, anytime you want, you come on over, we'll work together. How about that?"

Poor Jules must have been completely staggered by all this. On the one hand he knew—I mean, even *I* knew—that Uncle Chaim never invited other artists to share space with him, let alone a model; on the other, the sudden change can only have sharpened his anxiety about his old friend's state of mind. He said, "Chaim, I'm just trying to tell you, whatever's going on, it isn't good for you. Not her fault, not your fault. People and angels aren't supposed to hang out together—we aren't built for it, and neither are they. She really needs to go back where she belongs."

"She can't. Absolutely not." Uncle Chaim was shaking his head, and kept on shaking it. "She got *sent* here, Jules, she got sent to *me*—"

"By whom? You ever ask yourself that?" They stared at each other. Jules said, very carefully, "No, not by the Devil. I don't believe in the Devil any more than I believe in God, although he always gets the good lines. But it's a free country, and I *can* believe in angels without swallowing all the rest of it, if I want to." He paused, and took a gentler hold on Uncle Chaim's arm. "And I can also imagine that angels might not be exactly what we think they are. That an angel might lie, and still be an angel. That an angel might be selfish—jealous, even. That an angel might just be a little bit out of her head."

In a very pale and quiet voice, Uncle Chaim said, "You're talking about a fallen angel, aren't you?"

"I don't know what I'm talking about," Jules answered. "That's the God's truth." Both of them smiled wearily, but neither one laughed. Jules said, "I'm dead serious, Chaim. For your sake, your sanity, she needs to go."

"And for my sake, she can't." Uncle Chaim was plainly too exhausted for either pretense or bluster, but there was no give in him. He said, "*Landsmann,* it doesn't matter. You could be right, you could be wrong, I'm telling you, it doesn't matter. There's no one else I want to paint anymore—there's no one else I *can* paint, Jules, that's just how it is. Go home now." He refused to say another word as he ushered Jules out of the studio.

In the months that followed, Uncle Chaim became steadily more silent, more reclusive, more closed-off from everything that did not directly involve the current portrait of the blue angel. By autumn, he was no longer meeting Jules for lunch at the Ukrainian restaurant; he could rarely be induced to appear at his own openings, or anyone else's; he frequently spent the night at his studio, sleeping briefly in his chair, when he slept at all. It had been understood between Uncle Chaim and me since I was three that I had the run of the place at any time; and while it was still true, I felt far less comfortable there than I was accustomed, and left it more and more to him and the strange lady with the wings.

When an exasperated—and increasingly frightened—Aunt Rifke would challenge him, "You've turned into Red Skelton, painting nothing but clowns on velvet—Margaret Keane, all those big-eyed war orphans," he only shrugged and replied, when he even bothered to respond, "You were the one who told me I could paint an angel. Change your mind?"

Whatever she truly thought, it was not in Aunt Rifke to say such a thing to him directly. Her only recourse was to mumble something like, "Even Leonardo gave up on drawing cats," or "You've done the best anybody could ever do—let it go now, let *her* go." Her own theory, differing somewhat from Jules's, was that it was as much Uncle Chaim's obsession as his model's possible madness that was holding the angel to earth. "Like Ella and Sam," she said to me, referring to the perpetually quarrelling parents of my favorite cousin Arthur. "Locked together, like some kind of punishment machine. Thirty years they hate each other, cats and dogs, but they're so scared of being alone, if one of them died—" she snapped her fingers—"the other one would be gone in a week. Like that. Okay, so not exactly like that, but like that." Aunt Rifke wasn't getting a lot of sleep either just then.

She confessed to me—it astonishes me to this day—that she prayed more than once herself, during the worst times. Even in my family, which still runs to atheists, agnostics and cranky anarchists, Aunt Rifke's unbelief was regarded as the standard by which all other blasphemy had to be judged, and set against which it invariably paled. The idea of a prayer from her lips was, on the one hand, fascinating—how would Aunt Rifke conceivably address a Supreme Being?—and more than a little alarming as well. Supplication was not in her vocabulary, let alone her repertoire. Command was.

I didn't ask her what she had prayed for. I did ask, trying to make her laugh, if she had commenced by saying, "To Whom it may concern…" She slapped my hand lightly. "Don't talk fresh, just because you're in fifth grade, sixth grade, whatever. Of course I didn't say that, an old Socialist Worker like me. I started off like you'd talk to some kid's mother on the phone, I said, 'It's time for your little girl to go home, we're going to be having dinner. You better call her in now, it's getting dark.' Like that, polite. But not fancy."

"And you got an answer?" Her face clouded, but she made no reply. "You didn't get an answer? Bad connection?" I honestly wasn't being fresh: this was my story too, somehow, all the way back, from the beginning, and I had to know where we were in it. "Come *on*, Aunt Rifke."

"I got an answer." The words came slowly, and cut off abruptly, though she seemed to want to say something more. Instead, she got up and went to the stove, all my aunts' traditional *querencia* in times of emotional stress. Without turning her head, she said in a curiously dull tone, "*You* go home now. Your mother'll yell at me."

My mother worried about my grades and my taste in friends, not about me; but I had never seen Aunt Rifke quite like this, and I knew better than to push her any further. So I went on home.

From that day, however, I made a new point of stopping by the studio literally every day—except Shabbos, naturally—even if only for a few minutes, just to let Uncle Chaim know that someone besides Aunt Rifke was concerned about him. Of course, obviously, a whole lot of other people would have been, from family to gallery owners to friends like Jules and Ruthie; but I was ten years old, and feeling like my uncle's only guardian, and a private detective to boot. A guardian against *what*? An angel? Detecting *what*? A portrait? I couldn't have said for a minute, but a ten-year-old boy with a sense of mission definitely qualifies as a dangerous flying object.

Uncle Chaim didn't talk to me anymore while he was working, and I really missed that. To this day, almost everything I know about painting—about *being* a painter, every day, all day—I learned from him, grumbled out of the side of his mouth as he sized a canvas, touched up a troublesome corner, or stood back, scratching his head, to reconsider a composition or a subject's expression, or simply to study the stoop of a shadow. Now he worked in bleak near-total silence; and since the blue angel never spoke unless addressed directly, the studio had become a far less inviting place than my three-year-old self had found it. Yet I felt that Uncle Chaim still liked having me there, even if he didn't say anything, so I kept going, but it was an effort some days, mission or no mission.

His only conversation was with the angel—Uncle Chaim always chatted with his models; paradoxically, he felt that it helped them to concentrate—and while I honestly wasn't trying to eavesdrop (except sometimes), I couldn't help overhearing their talk. Uncle Chaim would ask the angel to lift a wing slightly, or to alter her stance somewhat: as I've said, sitting remained uncomfortable and unnatural for her, but she had finally been able to manage a sort of semi-recumbent posture, which made her look curiously vulnerable, almost like a tired child after an adult party, playing at being her mother, with the grownups all asleep upstairs. I can close my eyes today and see her so.

One winter afternoon, having come tired, and stayed late, I was half-asleep on a padded rocker in a far corner when I heard Uncle Chaim saying, "You ever think that maybe we might both be dead, you and me?"

"We angels do not die," the blue angel responded. "It is not in us to die."

"I told you, lift your chin," Uncle Chaim grunted. "Well, it's built into *us,* believe me, it's mostly what we do from day one." He looked up at her from the easel. "But I'm trying to get you into a painting, and I'll never be able to do it, but it doesn't matter, got to keep trying. The head a *little* bit to the left—no, that's too much, I said a *little.*" He put down his brush and walked over to the angel, taking her chin in his hand. He said, "And you... whatever you're after, you're not going to get that right, either, are you? So it's like we're stuck here together—and if we *were* dead, maybe this is hell. Would we know? You ever think about things like that?"

"No." The angel said nothing further for a long time, and I was dozing off again when I heard her speak. "You would not speak so lightly of hell if you had seen it. I have seen it. It is not what you think."

"*Nu?*" Uncle Chaim's voice could raise an eyebrow itself. "So what's it like?"

"*Cold.*" The words were almost inaudible. "So cold... so lonely... so *empty.* God is not there... no one is there. No one, no one, no one... no one..."

It was that voice, that other voice that I had heard once before, and I have never again been as frightened as I was by the murmuring terror in her words. I actually grabbed my books and got up to leave, already framing some sort of gotta-go to Uncle Chaim, but just then Aunt Rifke walked into the studio for the first time, with Rabbi Shulevitz trailing behind her, so I stayed where I was. I don't know a thing about ten-year-olds today; but in those times one of the major functions of adults was to supply drama and mystery to our lives, and we took such things where we found them.

Rabbi Stuart Shulevitz was the nearest thing my family had to an actual regular rabbi. He was Reform, of course, which meant that he had no beard, played the guitar, performed Bat Mitzvahs and interfaith marriages, invited local priests and imams to lead the Passover ritual, and put up perpetually with all the jokes told, even by his own congregation, about young, beardless, terminally tolerant Reform rabbis. Uncle Chaim, who allowed Aunt Rifke to drag him to *shul* twice a year, on the High Holidays, regarded him as being somewhere between a mild head cold and mouse droppings in the pantry. But Aunt Rifke always defended Rabbi Shulevitz, saying, "He's smarter than he looks, and anyway he can't help being blond. Also, he smells good."

Uncle Chaim and I had to concede the point. Rabbi Shulevitz's immediate predecessor, a huge, hairy, bespectacled man from Riga, had smelled mainly of rancid hair oil and cheap peach *schnapps*. And he couldn't sing "Red River Valley," either.

Aunt Rifke was generally a placid-appearing, *hamishe* sort of woman, but now her plump face was set in lines that would have told even an angel that she meant business. The blue angel froze in position in a different way than she usually held still as required by the pose. Her strange eyes seemed almost to change their shape, widening in the center and somehow *lifting* at the corners, as though to echo her wings. She stood at near-attention, silently regarding Aunt Rifke and the rabbi.

Uncle Chaim never stopped painting. Over his shoulder he said, "Rifke, what do you want? I'll be home when I'm home."

"So who's rushing you?" Aunt Rifke snapped back. "We didn't come about you. We came the rabbi should take a look at your *model* here." The word burst from her mouth trailing blue smoke.

"What look? I'm working, I'm going to lose the light in ten, fifteen minutes. Sorry, Rabbi, I got no time. Come back next week, you could say a *barucha* for the whole studio. Goodbye, Rifke."

But my eyes were on the Rabbi, and on the angel, as he slowly approached her, paying no heed to the quarreling voices of Uncle Chaim and Aunt Rifke. Blond or not, "Red River Valley" or not, he was still magic in my sight, the official representative of a power as real as my disbelief. On the other hand, the angel could fly. The Chassidic wonder-*rebbes* of my parents' Eastern Europe could fly up to heaven and share the Shabbos meal with God, when they chose. Reform rabbis couldn't fly.

As Rabbi Shulevitz neared her, the blue angel became larger and more stately, and there was now a certain menacing aspect to her divine radiance, which set me shrinking into a corner, half-concealed by a dusty drape. But the rabbi came on.

"Come no closer," the angel warned him. Her voice sounded deeper, and slightly distorted, like a phonograph record when the Victrola hasn't been wound tight enough. "It is not for mortals to lay hands on the Lord's servant and messenger."

"I'm not touching you," Rabbi Shulevitz answered mildly. "I just want to look in your eyes. An angel can't object to that, surely."

"The full blaze of an angel's eyes would leave you ashes, impudent man." Even I could hear the undertone of anxiety in her voice.

"That is foolishness." The rabbi's tone continued gentle, almost playful. "My friend Chaim paints your eyes full of compassion, of sorrow for the world and all its creatures, every one. Only turn those eyes to me for a minute, for a very little minute, where's the harm?"

Obediently he stayed where he was, taking off his hat to reveal the black *yarmulke* underneath. Behind him, Aunt Rifke made as though to take Uncle Chaim's arm, but he shrugged her away, never taking his own eyes from Rabbi Shulevitz and the blue angel. His face was very pale. The glass of Scotch in his left hand, plainly as forgotten as the brush in his right, was beginning to slosh over the rim with his trembling, and I was distracted with fascination, waiting for him to drop it. So I wasn't quite present, you might say, when the rabbi's eyes looked into the eyes of the blue angel.

But I heard the rabbi gasp, and I saw him stagger backwards a couple of steps, with his arm up in front of his eyes. And I saw the angel turning away, instantly; the whole encounter couldn't have lasted more than five seconds, if that much. And if Rabbi Shulevitz looked stunned and frightened—which he did—there is no word that I know to describe the expression on the angel's face. No words.

Rabbi Shulevitz spoke to Aunt Rifke in Hebrew, which I didn't know, and she answered him in swift, fierce Yiddish, which I did, but only insofar as it pertained to things my parents felt were best kept hidden from me, such as money problems, family gossip and sex. So I missed most of her words, but I caught anyway three of them. One was *shofar*, which is the ram's horn blown at sundown on the High Holidays, and about which I already knew two good dirty jokes. The second was *minyan*, the number of adult Jews needed to form a prayer circle on special occasions. Reform *minyanim* include women, which Aunt Rifke always told me I'd come to appreciate in a couple of years. She was right.

The third word was *dybbuk*.

I knew the word, and I didn't know it. If you'd asked me its meaning, I would have answered that it meant some kind of bogey, like the Invisible Man, or just maybe the Mummy. But I learned the real meaning fast, because Rabbi Shulevitz had taken off his glasses and was wiping his forehead, and whispering, "*No. No. Ich vershtaye nicht…*"

Uncle Chaim was complaining, "What the hell *is* this? See now, we've lost the light already, I *told* you." No one—me included—was paying any attention.

Aunt Rifke—who was never entirely sure that Rabbi Shulevitz *really* understood Yiddish—burst into English. "It's a *dybbuk*, what's not to understand? There's a *dybbuk* in that woman, you've got to get rid of it! You get a *minyan* together, right now, you get rid of it! Exorcise!"

Why on earth did she want the rabbi to start doing pushups or jumping-jacks in this moment? I was still puzzling over that when he said, "That woman, as you call her, is an angel. You cannot… Rifke, you do not exorcise an angel." He was trembling—I could see that—but his voice was steady and firm.

"You do when it's possessed!" Aunt Rifke looked utterly exasperated with everybody. "I don't know how it could happen, but Chaim's angel's got a *dybbuk* in her—" she whirled on her husband—"which is why she makes you just keep painting her and painting her, day and night. You finish—really finish, it's done, over—she might have to go back out where it's not so nice for a *dybbuk*, you know about that? Look at her!" and she pointed an orange-nailed finger straight in the blue angel's face. "*She* hears me, *she* knows what I'm talking about. You know what I'm talking, don't you, Miss Angel? Or I should say, Mister *Dybbuk*? You tell me, okay?"

I had never seen Aunt Rifke like this; she might have been possessed herself. Rabbi Shulevitz was trying to calm her, while Uncle Chaim fumed at the intruders disturbing his model. To my eyes, the angel looked more than disturbed—she looked as terrified as a cat I'd seen backed against a railing by a couple of dogs, strays, with no one to call them away from tearing her to pieces. I was anxious for her, but much more so for my aunt and uncle, truly expecting them to be struck by lightning, or turned to salt, or something on that order. I was scared for the rabbi as well, but I figured he could take care of himself. Maybe even with Aunt Rifke.

"A *dybbuk* cannot possibly possess an angel," the rabbi was saying. "Believe me, I majored in Ashkenazic folklore—wrote my thesis on Lilith, as a matter of fact—and there are no accounts, no legends, not so much as a single *bubbemeise* of such a thing. *Dybbuks* are wandering spirits, some of them good, some malicious, but all houseless in the universe. They cannot enter heaven, and Gehenna won't have them, so they take refuge within the first human being they can reach, like any parasite. But an angel? Inconceivable, take my word. Inconceivable."

"In the mind of God," the blue angel said, "nothing is inconceivable."

Strangely, we hardly heard her; she had almost been forgotten in the dispute over her possession. But her voice was that other voice—I could see Uncle Chaim's eyes widen as he caught the difference. That voice said now, "She is right. I am a *dybbuk*."

In the sudden absolute silence, Aunt Rifke, serenely complacent, said, "Told you."

I heard myself say, "Is she bad? I thought she was an angel."

Uncle Chaim said impatiently, "What? She's a model."

Rabbi Shulevitz put his glasses back on, his eyes soft with pity behind the heavy lenses. I expected him to point at the angel, like Aunt Rifke, and thunder out stern and stately Hebrew maledictions, but he only said, "Poor thing, poor thing. Poor creature."

Through the angel's mouth, the *dybbuk* said, "Rabbi, go away. Let me alone, let me be. I am warning you."

I could not take my eyes off her. I don't know whether I was more fascinated by what she was saying, and the adults having to deal with its mystery, or by the fact that all the time I had known her as Uncle Chaim's winged and haloed model, someone else was using her the way I played with my little puppet theatre at home—moving her, making up things for her to say, perhaps even putting her away at night when the studio was empty. Already it was as though I had never heard her strange, shy voice asking a child's endless questions about the world, but only this grownup voice, speaking to Rabbi Shulevitz. "You cannot force me to leave her."

"I don't want to force you to do anything," the rabbi said gently. "I want to help you."

I wish I had never heard the laughter that answered him. I was too young to hear something like that, if anyone could ever be old enough. I cried out and doubled up around myself, hugging my stomach, although what I felt was worse than the worst bellyache I had ever wakened with in the night. Aunt Rifke came and put her arms around me, trying to soothe me, murmuring, half in English, half in Yiddish, "Shh, shh, it's all right, *der rebbe* will make it all right. He's help-ing the angel, he's getting rid of that thing inside her, like a doctor. Wait, wait, you'll see, it'll be all right." But I went on crying, because I had been visited by a monstrous grief not my own, and I was only ten.

The *dybbuk* said, "If you wish to help me, Rabbi, leave me alone. I will not go into the dark again."

Rabbi Shulevitz wiped his forehead. He asked, his tone still gentle and wonder-ing, "What did you do to become... what you are? Do you remember?"

The *dybbuk* did not answer him for a long time. Nobody spoke, except for Uncle Chaim muttering unhappily to himself, "Who needs this? Try to get your work done, it turns into a *ferkockte* party. Who needs it?" Aunt Rifke shushed him, but she reached for his arm, and this time he let her take it.

The rabbi said, "You are a Jew."

"I was. Now I am nothing."

"No, you are still a Jew. You must know that we do not practice exorcism, not as others do. We heal, we try to heal both the person possessed and the one possess-ing. But you must tell me what you have done. Why you cannot find peace."

The change in Rabbi Shulevitz astonished me as much as the difference between Uncle Chaim's blue angel and the spirit that inhabited her and spoke through her. He didn't even look like the crewcut, blue-eyed, guitar-playing, basketball-playing (well, he tried) college-student-dressing young man whose idea of a good time was getting people to sit in a circle and sing "So Long, It's Been Good to Know You" or "Dreidel, Dreidel, Dreidel" together. There was a power of his own inhabiting him, and clearly the *dybbuk* recognized it. It said slowly, "You cannot help me. You cannot heal."

"Well, we don't know that, do we?" Rabbi Shulevitz said brightly. "So, a bargain.

You tell me what holds you here, and I will tell you, honestly, what I can do for you. *Honestly.*"

Again the *dybbuk* was slow to reply. Aunt Rifke said hotly, "What is this? What *help*? We're here to expel, to get rid of a demon that's taken over one of God's angels, if that's what she really is, and enchanted my husband so it's all he can paint, all he can think about painting. Who's talking about *helping* a demon?"

"The rabbi is," I said, and they all turned as though they'd forgotten I was there. I gulped and stumbled along, feeling like I might throw up. I said, "I don't think it's a demon, but even if it is, it's given Uncle Chaim a chance to paint a real angel, and everybody loves the paintings, and they buy them, which we wouldn't have had them to sell if the—the *thing*—hadn't made her stay in Uncle Chaim's studio." I ran out of breath, gas and show-business ambitions all at pretty much the same time, and sat down, grateful that I had neither puked nor started to cry. I was still grandly capable of both back then.

Aunt Rifke looked at me in a way I didn't recall her ever doing before. She didn't say anything, but her arm tightened around me. Rabbi Shulevitz said quietly, "Thank you, David." He turned back to face the angel. In the same voice, he said, "Please. Tell me."

When the *dybbuk* spoke again, the words came one by one—two by two, at most. "A girl… There was a girl… a young woman…"

"*Ai*, how not?" Aunt Rifke's sigh was resigned, but not angry or mocking, just as Uncle Chaim's, "*Shah*, Rifkela" was neither a dismissal nor an order. The rabbi, in turn, gestured them to silence.

"She wanted us to marry," the *dybbuk* said. "I did too. But there was time. There was a world… there was my work… there were things to see… to taste and smell and do and *be*… It could wait a little. She could wait. She could wait…"

"Uh-huh. Of course. You could *die* waiting around for some damn man!"

"*Shah*, Rifkela!"

"But this one did not wait around," Rabbi Shulevitz said to the *dybbuk*. "She did not wait for you, am I right?"

"She married another man," came the reply, and it seemed to my ten-year-old imagination that every tortured syllable came away tinged with blood. "They had been married for two years when he beat her to death."

It was my Uncle Chaim who gasped in shock. I don't think anyone else made a sound.

The *dybbuk* said, "She sent me a message. I came as fast as I could. I *did* come," though no one had challenged his statement. "But it was too late."

This time we were the ones who did not speak for a long time. Rabbi Shulevitz finally asked, "What did you do?"

"I looked for him. I meant to kill him, but he killed himself before I found him. So I was too late again."

"What happened then?" That was me, once more to my own surprise. "When you didn't get to kill him?"

"I lived. I wanted to die, but I lived."

From Aunt Rifke—how not? "You ever got married?"

"No. I lived alone, and I grew old and died. That is all."

"Excuse me, but that is *not* all." The rabbi's voice had suddenly, startlingly, turned probing, almost harsh. "That is only the beginning." Everyone looked at him. The rabbi said, "So, after you died, what did happen? Where did you go?"

There was no answer. Rabbi Shulevitz repeated the question. The *dybbuk* responded finally, "You have said it yourself. Houseless in the universe I am, and how should it be otherwise? The woman I loved died because I did not love her enough—what greater sin is there than that? Even her murderer had the courage to atone, but I dared not offer my own life in payment for hers. I chose to live, and living on has been my punishment, in death as well as in life. To wander back and forth in a cold you cannot know, shunned by heaven, scorned by purgatory… do you wonder that I sought shelter where I could, even in an angel? God himself would have to come and cast me out again, Rabbi—you never can."

I became aware that my aunt and uncle had drawn close around me, as though expecting something dangerous and possibly explosive to happen. Rabbi Shulevitz took off his glasses again, ran his hand through his crewcut, stared at the glasses as though he had never seen them before, and put them back on.

"You are right," he said to the *dybbuk*. "I'm a rabbi, not a *rebbe*—no Solomonic wisdom, no magical powers, just a degree from a second-class seminary in Metuchen, New Jersey. You wouldn't know it." He drew a deep breath and moved a few steps closer to the blue angel. He said, "But this *gornisht* rabbi knows anyway that you would never have been allowed this refuge if God had not taken pity on you. You must know this, surely?" The *dybbuk* did not answer. Rabbi Shulevitz said, "And if God pities you, might you not have a little pity on yourself? A little forgiveness?"

"Forgiveness…" Now it was the *dybbuk* who whispered. "Forgiveness may be God's business. It is not mine."

"Forgiveness is everyone's business. Even the dead. On this earth or under it, there is no peace without forgiveness." The rabbi reached out then, to touch the blue angel comfortingly. She did not react, but he winced and drew his hand back instantly, blowing hard on his fingers, hitting them against his leg. Even I could see that they had turned white with cold.

"You need not fear for her," the *dybbuk* said. "Angels feel neither cold nor heat. You have touched where I have been."

Rabbi Shulevitz shook his head. He said, "I touched you. I touched your shame and your grief—as raw today, I know, as on the day your love died. But the cold… the cold is yours. The loneliness, the endless guilt over what you should have done, the endless turning to and fro in empty darkness… none of that comes from God. You must believe me, my friend." He paused, still flexing his frozen fingers. "And you must come forth from God's angel now. For her sake and your own."

The *dybbuk* did not respond. Aunt Rifke said, far more sympathetically than she had before, "You need a *minyan,* I could make some calls. We'd be careful, we wouldn't hurt it."

Uncle Chaim looked from her to the rabbi, then back to the blue angel. He opened his mouth to say something, but didn't.

The rabbi said, "You have suffered enough at your own hands. It is time for you to surrender your pain." When there was still no reply, he asked, "Are you afraid to be without it? Is that your real fear?"

"It has been my only friend!" the *dybbuk* answered at last. "Even God cannot understand what I have done so well as my pain does. Without the pain, there is only me."

"There is heaven," Rabbi Shulevitz said. "Heaven is waiting for you. Heaven has been waiting a long, long time."

"*I am waiting for me!*" It burst out of the *dybbuk* in a long wail of purest terror, the kind you only hear from small children trapped in a nightmare. "You want me to abandon the one sanctuary I have ever found, where I can huddle warm in the consciousness of an angel and sometimes—for a little—even forget the thing I am. You want me to be naked to myself again, and I am telling you *no, not ever, not ever, not ever.* Do what you must, Rabbi, and I will do the only thing I can." It paused, and then added, somewhat stiffly, "Thank you for your efforts. You are a good man."

Rabbi Shulevitz looked genuinely embarrassed. He also looked weary, frustrated and older than he had been when he first recognized the possession of Uncle Chaim's angel. Looking vaguely around at us, he said, "I don't know—maybe it *will* take a *minyan.* I don't want to, but we can't just…" His voice trailed away sadly, too defeated even to finish the sentence.

Or maybe he didn't finish because that was when I stepped forward, pulling away from my aunt and uncle, and said, "He can come with me, if he wants. He can come and live in me. Like with the angel."

Uncle Chaim said, "*What?*" and Aunt Rifke said, "*No!*" and Rabbi Shulevitz said, "*David!*" He turned and grabbed me by the shoulders, and I could feel him wanting to shake me, but he didn't. He seemed to be having trouble breathing. He said, "David, you don't know what you're saying."

"Yes, I do," I said. "He's scared, he's so scared. I know about scared."

Aunt Rifke crouched down beside me, peering hard into my face. "David, you're ten years old, you're a little boy. This one, he could be a thousand years, he's been hiding from God in an angel's body. How could you know what he's feeling?"

I said, "Aunt Rifke, I go to school. I wake up every morning, and right away I think about the boys waiting to beat me up because I'm small, or because I'm Jewish, or because they just don't like my face, the way I look at them. Every day I want to stay home and read, and listen to the radio, and play my All-Star Baseball game, but I get dressed and I eat breakfast, and I walk to school. And every day I have to think how I'm going to get through recess, get through gym class, get home without running into Jay Taffer, George DiLucca. Billy Kronish. I know all about not wanting to go outside."

Nobody said anything. The rabbi tried several times, but it was Uncle Chaim who finally said loudly, "I got to teach you to box. A little Archie Moore, a little Willie Pep, we'll take care of those *mamzers*." He looked ready to give me my first lesson right there.

When the *dybbuk* spoke again, its voice was somehow different: quiet, slow, wondering. It said, "Boy, you would do that?" I didn't speak, but I nodded.

Aunt Rifke said, "Your mother would *kill* me! She's hated me since I married Chaim."

The *dybbuk* said, "Boy, if I come… outside, I cannot go back. Do you understand that?"

"Yes," I said. "I understand."

But I was shaking. I tried to imagine what it would be like to have someone living inside me, like a baby, or a tapeworm. I was fascinated by tapeworms that year. Only this would be a spirit, not an actual physical thing—that wouldn't be so bad, would it? It might even be company, in a way, almost like being a comic-book superhero and having a secret identity. I wondered whether the angel had even known the *dybbuk* was in her, as quiet as he had been until he spoke to Rabbi Shulevitz. Who, at the moment, was repeating over and over, "No, I can't permit this. This is *wrong*, this can't be allowed. No." He began to mutter prayers in Hebrew.

Aunt Rifke was saying, "I don't care, I'm calling some people from the *shul*, I'm getting some people down here right *away!*" Uncle Chaim was gripping my shoulder so hard it hurt, but he didn't say anything. But there was really no one in the room except the *dybbuk* and me. When I think about it, when I remember, that's all I see.

I remember being thirsty, terribly thirsty, because my throat and my mouth were so dry. I pulled away from Uncle Chaim and Aunt Rifke, and I moved past Rabbi Shulevitz, and I croaked out to the *dybbuk*, "Come on, then. You can come out of the angel, it's safe, it's okay." I remember thinking that it was like trying to talk a cat down out of a tree, and I almost giggled.

I never saw him actually leave the blue angel. I don't think anyone did. He was simply standing right in front of me, tall enough that I had to look up to meet his eyes. Maybe he wasn't a thousand years old, but Aunt Rifke hadn't missed by much. It wasn't his clothes that told me—he wore a white turban that looked almost square, a dark red vest sort of thing and white trousers, under a gray robe that came all the way to the ground—it was the eyes. If blackness is the absence of light, then those were the blackest eyes I'll ever see, because there was no light in those eyes, and no smallest possibility of light ever. You couldn't call them sad: *sad* at least knows what *joy* is, and grieves at being exiled from joy. However old he really was, those eyes were a thousand years past sad.

"Sephardi," Rabbi Shulevitz murmured. "Of course he'd be Sephardi."

Aunt Rifke said, "You can see through him. Right through."

In fact he seemed to come and go: near-solid one moment, cobweb and smoke the next. His face was lean and dark, and must have been a proud face once. Now it was just weary, unspeakably weary—even a ten-year-old could see that. The lines down his cheeks and around the eyes and mouth made me think of desert pictures I'd seen, where the earth gets so dry that it pulls apart, cracks and pulls away from itself. He looked like that.

But he smiled at me. No, he smiled *into* me, and just as I've never seen eyes like his again, I've never seen a smile as beautiful. Maybe it couldn't reach his eyes, but it must have reached mine, because I can still see it. He said softly, "Thank you. You are a kind boy. I promise you, I will not take up much room."

I braced myself. The only invasive procedures I'd had any experience with then were my twice-monthly allergy shots and the time our doctor had to lance an infected finger that had swollen to twice its size. Would possession be anything like that? Would it make a difference if you were sort of inviting the possession, not being ambushed and taken over, like in *Invasion of the Body Snatchers?* I didn't mean to close my eyes, but I did.

Then I heard the voice of the blue angel.

"There is no need." It sounded like the voice I knew, but the *breath* in it was different—I don't know how else to put it. I could say it sounded stronger, or clearer, or maybe more musical; but it was the breath, the free breath. Or maybe that isn't right either, I can't tell you—I'm not even certain whether angels breathe, and I knew an angel once. There it is.

"Manassa, there is no need," she said again. I turned to look at her then, when she called the *dybbuk* by his name, and she was smiling herself, for the first time. It wasn't like his; it was a faraway smile at something I couldn't see, but it was real, and I heard Uncle Chaim catch his breath. To no one in particular, he said, "*Now* she smiles. Never once, I could never once get her to smile."

"Listen," the blue angel said. I didn't hear anything but my uncle grumbling, and Rabbi Shulevitz's continued Hebrew prayers. But the *dybbuk*—Manassa—lifted his head, and the endlessly black eyes widened, just a little.

The angel said again, "Listen," and this time I did hear something, and so did everyone else. It was music, definitely music, but too faint with distance for me to make anything out of it. But Aunt Rifke, who loved more kinds of music than you'd think, put her hand to her mouth and whispered, "*Oh.*"

"Manassa, listen," the angel said for the third time, and the two of them looked at each other as the music grew stronger and clearer. I can't describe it properly: it wasn't harps and psalteries—whatever a psaltery is, maybe you use it singing psalms—and it wasn't a choir of soaring heavenly voices, either. It was almost a little scary, the way you feel when you hear the wild geese passing over in the autumn night. It made me think of that poem of Tennyson's, with that line about *the horns of Elfland faintly blowing.* We'd been studying it in school.

"It is your welcome, Manassa," the blue angel said. "The gates are open for you. They were always open."

But the *dybbuk* backed away, suddenly whimpering. "I cannot! I am afraid! They will see!"

The angel took his hand. "They see now, as they saw you then. Come with me, I will take you there."

The *dybbuk* looked around, just this side of panicking. He even tugged a bit at the blue angel's hand, but she would not let him go. Finally he sighed very deeply—lord, you could feel the dust of the tombs in that sigh, and the wind between the stars—and nodded to her. He said, "I will go with you."

The blue angel turned to look at all of us, but mostly at Uncle Chaim. She said to him, "You are a better painter than I was a muse. And you taught me a great deal about other things than painting. I will tell Rembrandt."

Aunt Rifke said, a little hesitantly, "I was maybe rude. I'm sorry." The angel smiled at her.

Rabbi Shulevitz said, "Only when I saw you did I realize that I had never believed in angels."

"Continue not to," the angel replied. "We rather prefer it, to tell you the truth. We work better that way."

Then she and the *dybbuk* both looked at me, and I didn't feel even ten years old; more like four or so. I threw my arms around Aunt Rifke and buried my face in her skirt. She patted my head—at least I guess it was her, I didn't actually see her. I heard the blue angel say in Yiddish, "*Sei gesund*, Chaim's Duvidl. You were always courteous to me. Be well."

I looked up in time to meet the old, old eyes of the *dybbuk*. He said, "In a thousand years, no one has ever offered me freely what you did." He said something else, too, but it wasn't in either Hebrew or Yiddish, and I didn't understand.

The blue angel spread her splendid, shimmering wings one last time, filling the studio—as, for a moment, the mean winter sky outside seemed to flare with a sunset hope that could not have been. Then she and Manassa, the *dybbuk,* were gone, vanished instantly, which makes me think that the wings aren't really for flying. I don't know what other purpose they could serve, except they did seem somehow to enfold us all and hold us close. But maybe they're just really decorative. I'll never know now.

Uncle Chaim blew out his breath in one long, exasperated sigh. He said to Aunt Rifke, "I never did get her right. You know that."

I was trying to hear the music, but Aunt Rifke was busy hugging me, and kissing me all over my face, and telling me not ever, *ever* to do such a thing again, what was I thinking? But she smiled up at Uncle Chaim and answered him, "Well, she got *you* right, that's what matters." Uncle Chaim blinked at her. Aunt Rifke said, "She's probably telling Rembrandt about you right now. Maybe Vermeer, too."

"You think so?" Uncle Chaim looked doubtful at first, but then he shrugged and began to smile himself. "Could be."

I asked Rabbi Shulevitz, "He said something to me, the *dybbuk*, just at the end.

I didn't understand."

The rabbi put his arm around me. "He was speaking in old Ladino, the language of the Sephardim. He said, '*I will not forget you.*'" His smile was a little shaky, and I could feel him trembling himself, with everything over. "I think you have a friend in heaven, David. Extraordinary Duvidl."

The music was gone. We stood together in the studio, and although there were four of us, it felt as empty as the winter street beyond the window where the blue angel had posed so often. A taxi took the corner too fast, and almost hit a truck; a cloud bank was pearly with the moon's muffled light. A group of young women crossed the street, singing. I could feel everyone wanting to move away, but nobody did, and nobody spoke, until Uncle Chaim finally said, "Rabbi, you got time for a sitting tomorrow? Don't wear that suit."

# FIXING HANOVER

## JEFF VANDERMEER

World Fantasy Award winner Jeff VanderMeer grew up in the Fiji Islands and has had fiction published in over twenty countries. His books, including the bestselling *City of Saints & Madmen*, have made the year's best lists of *Publishers Weekly, LA Weekly, Amazon, the San Francisco Chronicle*, and many more. He has worked with rock band The Church, *30 Days of Night* creator Ben Templesmith, Dark Horse Comics, and PlayStation Europe on various projects including music soundtracks and short films. With his wife Ann (they have been cited by Boing Boing as a literary "power couple"), he is also an award-winning editor whose books include the iconic *Steampunk* anthology. Current projects include noir fantasy novel *Finch*. He currently lives in Tallahassee, Florida, and serves as assistant director for Wofford College's Shared Worlds writing camp for teens (Spartanburg, South Carolina).

When Shyver can't lift it from the sand, he brings me down from the village. It lies there on the beach, entangled in the seaweed, dull metal scoured by the sea, limpets and barnacles stuck to its torso. It's been lost a long time, just like me. It smells like rust and oil still, but only a tantalizing hint.

"It's good salvage, at least," Shyver says. "Maybe more."

"Or maybe less," I reply. Salvage is the life's blood of the village in the off-season, when the sea's too rough for fishing. But I know from past experience, there's no telling what the salvagers will want and what they discard. They come from deep in the hill country abutting the sea cliffs, their needs only a glimmer in their savage eyes.

To Shyver, maybe the thing he's found looks like a long box with a smaller box on top. To me, in the burnishing rasp of the afternoon sun, the last of the winter winds lashing against my face, it resembles a man whose limbs have been torn off. A man made of metal. It has lamps for eyes, although I have to squint hard to imagine there ever being an ember, a spark, of understanding. No expression defiles the broad pitted expanse of metal.

As soon as I see it, I call it "Hanover," after a character I had seen in an old movie back when the projector still worked.

"Hanover?" Shyver says with a trace of contempt.

"Hanover never gave away what he thought," I reply, as we drag it up the gravel track toward the village. Sandhaven, they call it, simply, and it's carved into the side of cliffs that are sliding into the sea. I've lived there for almost six years, taking on odd jobs, assisting with salvage. They still know next to nothing about me, not really. They like me not for what I say or who I am, but for what I do: anything mechanical I can fix, or build something new from poor parts. Someone reliable in an isolated place where a faulty water pump can be devastating. That means something real. That means you don't have to explain much.

"Hanover, whoever or whatever it is, has given up on more than thoughts," Shyver says, showing surprising intuition. It means he's already put a face on Hanover, too. "I think it's from the Old Empire. I think it washed up from the Sunken City at the bottom of the sea."

Everyone knows what Shyver thinks, about everything. Brown-haired, green-eyed, gawky, he's lived in Sandhaven his whole life. He's good with a boat, could navigate a cockleshell through a typhoon. He'll never leave the village, but why should he? As far as he knows, everything he needs is here.

Beyond doubt, the remains of Hanover are heavy. I have difficulty keeping my grip on him, despite the rust. By the time we've made it to the courtyard at the center of Sandhaven, Shyver and I are breathing as hard as old men. We drop our burden with a combination of relief and self-conscious theatrics. By now, a crowd has gathered, and not just stray dogs and bored children.

First law of salvage: what is found must be brought before the community. Is it scrap? Should it be discarded? Can it be restored?

John Blake, council leader, all unkempt black beard, wide shoulders, and watery turquoise eyes, stands there. So does Sarah, who leads the weavers, and the blacksmith Growder, and the ethereal captain of the fishing fleet: Lady Salt as she is called—she of the impossibly pale, soft skin, the blonde hair in a land that only sees the sun five months out of the year. Her eyes, ever-shifting, never settling—one is light blue and one is fierce green, as if to balance the sea between calm and roiling. She has tiny wrinkles in the corners of those eyes, and a wry smile beneath. If I remember little else, fault the eyes. We've been lovers the past three years, and if I ever fully understand her, I wonder if my love for her will vanish like the mist over the water at dawn.

With the fishing boats not launching for another week, a host of broad-faced fisher folk, joined by lesser lights and gossips, has gathered behind us. Even as the light fades: shadows of albatross and gull cutting across the horizon and the roofs of the low houses, huddled and glowing a deep gold-and-orange around the edges, framed by the graying sky.

Blake says, "Where?" He's a man who measures words as if he had only a few given to him by Fate; too generous a syllable from his lips, and he might fall over dead.

"The beach, the cove," Shyver says. Blake always reduces him to a similar terseness.

"What is it?"

This time, Blake looks at me, with a glare. I'm the fixer who solved their well problems the season before, who gets the most value for the village from what's sold to the hill scavengers. But I'm also Lady Salt's lover, who used to be his, and depending on the vagaries of his mood, I suffer more or less for it.

I see no harm in telling the truth as I know it, when I can. So much remains unsaid that extra lies exhaust me.

"It is part of a metal man," I say.

A gasp from the more ignorant among the crowd. My Lady Salt just stares right through me. I know what she's thinking: in scant days she'll be on the open sea. Her vessel is as sleek and quick and buoyant as the water, and she likes to call it *Seeker*, or sometimes *Mist*, or even just *Cleave*. Salvage holds little interest for her.

But I can see the gears turning in Blake's head. He thinks awhile before he says more. Even the blacksmith and the weaver, more for ceremony and obligation than their insight, seem to contemplate the rusted bucket before them.

A refurbished water pump keeps delivering from the aquifers; parts bartered to the hill people mean only milk and smoked meat for half a season. Still, Blake knows that the fishing has been less dependable the past few years, and that if we do not give the hill people something, they will not keep coming back.

"Fix it," he says.

It's not a question, although I try to treat it like one.

Later that night, I am with the Lady Salt, whose whispered name in these moments is Rebecca. "Not a name men would follow," she said to me once. "A land-ish name."

In bed, she's as shifting as the tides, beside me, on top, and beneath. Her mouth is soft but firm, her tongue curling like a question mark across my body. She makes little cries that are so different from the orders she barks out ship-board that she might as well be a different person. We're all different people, depending.

Rebecca can read. She has a few books from the hill people, taught herself with the help of an old man who remembered how. A couple of the books are even from the Empire—the New Empire, not the old. Sometimes I want to think she is not the Lady Salt, but the Lady Flight. That she wants to leave the village. That she seeks so much more. But I look into those eyes in the dimness of half-dawn, so close, so far, and realize she would never tell me, no matter how long I live here. Even in bed, there is a bit of Lady Salt in Rebecca.

When we are finished, lying in each other's arms under the thick covers, her hair against my cheek, Rebecca asks me, "Is that thing from your world? Do you know what it is?"

I have told her a little about my past, where I came from—mostly bed-time stories when she cannot sleep, little fantasies of golden spires and a million thronging people, fables of something so utterly different from the village that it must exist only in dream. *Once upon a time there was a foolish man. Once upon a time there was an Empire.* She tells me she doesn't believe me, and there's freedom in that. It's a strange pillow talk that can be so grim.

I tell her the truth about Hanover: "It's nothing like what I remember." If it came from Empire, it came late, after I was already gone.

"Can you really fix it?" she asks.

I smile. "I can fix anything," and I really believe it. If I want to, I can fix anything. I'm just not sure yet I want Hanover fixed, because I don't know what he is.

But my hands can't lie—they tremble to *have at it*, to explore, impatient for the task even then and there, in bed with Blake's lost love.

I came from the same sea the Lady Salt loves. I came as salvage, and was fixed. Despite careful preparation, my vessel had been damaged first by a storm, and then a reef. Forced to the surface, I managed to escape into a raft just before my creation drowned. It was never meant for life above the waves, just as I was never meant for life below them. I washed up near the village, was found, and eventually accepted into their community; they did not sell me to the hill people.

I never meant to stay. I didn't think I'd fled far enough. Even as I'd put distance between me and Empire, I'd set traps, put up decoys, sent out false rumors. I'd done all I could to escape that former life, and yet some nights, sleepless, restless, it feels as if I am just waiting to be found.

Even failure can be a kind of success, my father always said. But I still don't know if I believe that.

Three days pass, and I'm still fixing Hanover, sometimes with help from Shyver, sometimes not. Shyver doesn't have much else to do until the fishing fleet goes out, but that doesn't mean he has to stay cooped up in a cluttered workshop with me. Not when, conveniently, the blacksmithy is next door, and with it the lovely daughter of Growder, who he adores.

Blake says he comes in to check my progress, but I think he comes to check on me. After the Lady Salt left him, he married another—a weaver—but she died in childbirth a year ago, and took the baby with her. Now Blake sees before him a different past: a life that might have been, with the Lady Salt at his side.

I can still remember the generous Blake, the humorous Blake who would stand on a table with a mug of beer made by the hill people and tell an amusing story about being lost at sea, poking fun at himself. But now, because he still loves her, there is only me to hate. Now there is just the brambly fence of his beard to hide him, and the pressure of his eyes, the pursed, thin lips. *If I were a different man. If I loved the Lady Salt less. If she wanted him.*

But instead it is him and me in the work room, Hanover on the table, surrounded by an autopsy of gears and coils and congealed bits of metal long past their purpose. Hanover up close, over time, smells of sea grasses and brine along with the oil. I still do not *know* him. Or what he does. Or why he is here. I think I recognize some of it as the work of Empire, but I can't be sure. Shyver still thinks Hanover is merely a sculpture from beneath the ocean. But no one makes a sculpture with so many moving parts.

"Make it work," Blake says. "You're the expert. Fix it."

*Expert?* I'm the only one with any knowledge in this area. For hundreds, maybe thousands, of miles.

"I'm trying," I say. "But then what? We don't know what it does."

This is the central question, perhaps of my life. It is why I go slow with Hanover. My hands already know where most of the parts go. They know most of what is broken, and why.

"Fix it," Blake says, "or at the next council meeting, I will ask that you be sent to live with the hill people for a time."

There's no disguising the self-hatred in his gaze. There's no disguising that he's serious.

"For a time? And what will that prove? Except to show I can live in caves with shepherds?" I almost want an answer.

Blake spits on the wooden floor. "No use to us, why should we feed you? House you…"

*Even if I leave, she won't go back to you.*

"What if I fix it and all it does is blink? Or all it does is shed light, like a whale lamp? Or talk in nonsense rhymes? Or I fix it and it kills us all."

"Don't care," Blake says. "Fix it."

The cliffs around the village are low, like the shoulders of a slouching giant, and caulked with bird shit and white rock, veined through with dark green bramble. Tough, thick lizards scuttle through the branches. Tiny birds take shelter there, their dark eyes staring out from shadow. A smell almost like mint struggles through. Below is the cove where Shyver found Hanover.

Rebecca and I walk there, far enough beyond the village that we cannot be seen, and we talk. We find the old trails and follow them, sometimes silly, sometimes serious. We don't need to be who we are in Sandhaven.

"Blake's getting worse," I tell her. "More paranoid. He's jealous. He says he'll exile me from the village if I don't fix Hanover."

"Then fix Hanover," Rebecca says.

We are holding hands. Her palm is warm and sweaty in mine, but I don't care. Every moment I'm with her feels like something I didn't earn, wasn't looking for, but don't want to lose. Still, something in me rebels. It's tiring to keep proving myself.

"I can do it," I say. "I know I can. But…"

"Blake can't exile you without the support of the council," Lady Salt says. I know it's her, not Rebecca, because of the tone, and the way her blue eye flashes when she looks at me. "But he can make life difficult if you give him cause." A pause, a tightening of her grip. "He's in mourning. You know it makes him not himself. But we need him. We need him back."

A twinge as I wonder how she means that. But it's true: Blake has led Sandhaven through good times and bad, made tough decisions and cared about the village.

Sometimes, though, leadership is not enough. What if what you really need is the instinct to be fearful? And the thought as we make our way back to the village: *What if Blake is right about me?*

So I begin to work on Hanover in earnest. There's a complex balance to him that I admire. People think engineering is about practical application of science, and that might be right, if you're building something. But if you're fixing something, something you don't fully understand—say, you're fixing a Hanover—you have no access to a schematic, to a helpful context. Your work instead becomes a kind of detection. You become a kind of detective. You track down clues—cylinders that fit into holes in sheets of steel, that slide into place in grooves, that lead to wires, that lead to understanding.

To do this, I have to stop my ad hoc explorations. Instead, with Shyver's reluctant help, I take Hanover apart systematically. I document where I find each part, and if I think it truly belongs there, or has become dislodged during the trauma that resulted in his "death." I note gaps. I label each part by what I believe it contributed to his overall function. In all things, I remember that Hanover has been made to look like a man, and therefore his innards roughly resemble those of a man in form or function, his makers consciously or subconsciously unable to ignore the implications of that form, that function.

Shyver looks at the parts lying glistening on the table, and says, "They're so different out of him." So different cleaned up, greased with fresh fish oil. Through the window, the sun's light sets them ablaze. Hanover's burnished surface, whorled with a patina of greens, blues, and rust red. The world become radiant.

When we remove the carapace of Hanover's head to reveal a thousand wires, clockwork gears, and strange fluids, even Shyver cannot think of him as a statue anymore.

"What does a machine like this *do?*" Shyver says, who has only rarely seen anything more complex than a hammer or a watch.

I laugh. "It does whatever it wants to do, I imagine."

By the time I am done with Hanover, I have made several leaps of logic. I have made decisions that cannot be explained as rational, but in their rightness set my head afire with the absolute certainty of Creation. The feeling energizes me and horrifies me all at once.

It was long after my country became an Empire that I decided to escape. And still I might have stayed, even knowing what I had done. That is the tragedy of everyday life: when you are in it, you can never see yourself clearly.

Even seven years in, Sandhaven having made the Past the past, I still had nightmares of gleaming rows of airships. I would wake, screaming, from what had once been a blissful dream, and the Lady Salt and Rebecca both would be there to comfort me.

Did I deserve that comfort?

Shyver is there when Hanover comes alive. I've spent a week speculating on ways to bypass what look like missing parts, missing wires. I've experimented with a hundred different connections. I've even identified Hanover's independent power source and recharged it using a hand-cranked generator.

Lady Salt has gone out with the fishing fleet for the first time and the village is deserted. Even Blake has gone with her, after a quick threat in my direction once again. If the fishing doesn't go well, the evening will not go any better for me.

Shyver says, "Is that a spark?"

A spark?

"Where?"

I have just put Hanover back together again for possibly the twentieth time and planned to take a break, to just sit back and smoke a hand-rolled cigarette, compliments of the enigmatic hill people.

"In Hanover's... eyes."

Shyver goes white, backs away from Hanover, as if something monstrous has occurred, even though this is what we wanted.

It brings memories flooding back—of the long-ago day steam had come rushing out of the huge iron bubble and the canvas had swelled, and held, and everything I could have wished for in my old life had been attained. That feeling had become addiction—I wanted to experience it again and again—but now it's bittersweet, something to cling to and cast away.

My assistant then had responded much as Shyver is now: both on some instinctual level knowing that something unnatural has happened.

"Don't be afraid," I say to Shyver, to my assistant.

"I'm not afraid," Shyver says, lying.

"You should be afraid," I say.

Hanover's eyes gain more and more of a glow. A clicking sound comes from him. *Click, click, click.* A hum. A slightly rumbling cough from deep inside, a hum again. We prop him up so he is no longer on his side. He's warm to the touch.

The head rotates from side to side, more graceful than in my imagination.

A sharp intake of breath from Shyver. "It's alive!"

I laugh then. I laugh and say, "In a way. It's got no arms or legs. It's harmless."

*It's harmless.*

Neither can it speak—just the click, click, click. But no words.

Assuming it is trying to speak.

John Blake and the Lady Salt come back with the fishing fleet. The voyage seems to have done Blake good. The windswept hair, the salt-stung face—he looks relaxed as they enter my workshop.

As they stare at Hanover, at the light in its eyes, I'm almost jealous. Standing side by side, they almost resemble a King and his Queen, and suddenly I'm acutely aware they were lovers, grew up in the village together. Rebecca's gaze is distant; thinking of Blake or of me or of the sea? They smell of mingled brine and fish and salt, and somehow the scent is like a knife in my heart.

"What does it do?" Blake asks.

Always, the same kinds of questions. Why should everything have to have a function?

"I don't know," I say. "But the hill folk should find it pretty and perplexing, at least."

Shyver, though, gives me away, makes me seem less and less from this place: "He thinks it can talk. We just need to fix it *more*. It might do all kinds of things for us."

"It's fixed," I snap, looking at Shyver as if I don't know him at all. We've drunk together, talked many hours. I've given him advice about the blacksmith's daughter. But now that doesn't matter. He's from here and I'm from *there*. "We should trade it to the hill folk and be done with it."

*Click, click, click.* Hanover won't stop. And I just want it over with, so I don't slide into the past.

Blake's calm has disappeared. I can tell he thinks I lied to him. "Fix it," he barks. "I mean really fix it. Make it talk."

He turns on his heel and leaves the workshop, Shyver behind him.

Lady Salt approaches, expression unreadable. "Do as he says. Please. The fishing… there's little enough out there. We need every advantage now."

Her hand on the side of my face, warm and calloused, before she leaves.

Maybe there's no harm in it. If I just do what they ask, this one last time—the last of many times—it will be over. Life will return to normal. I can stay here. I can still find a kind of peace.

Once, there was a foolish man who saw a child's balloon rising into the sky and thought it could become a kind of airship. No one in his world had ever created such a thing, but he already had ample evidence of his own genius in the things he had built before. Nothing had come close to challenging his engineering skills. No one had ever told him he might have limits. His father, a biology teacher, had taught him to focus on problems and solutions. His mother, a caterer, had shown him the value of attention to detail and hard work.

He took his plans, his ideas, to the government. They listened enough to give him some money, a place to work, and an assistant. All of this despite his youth, because of his brilliance, and in his turn he ignored how they talked about their enemies, the need to thwart external threats.

When this engineer was successful, when the third prototype actually worked, following three years of flaming disaster, he knew he had created something that had never before existed, and his heart nearly burst with pride. His wife had left him because she never saw him except when he needed sleep, the house was a junk yard, and yet he didn't care. He'd done it.

He couldn't know that it wouldn't end there. As far as he was concerned, they could take it apart and let him start on something else, and his life would have been good because he knew when he was happiest.

But the government's military advisors wanted him to perfect the airship. They asked him to solve problems that he hadn't thought about before. How to add weight to the carriage without it serving as undue ballast, so things could be dropped from the airship. How to add "defensive" weapons. How to make them work without igniting the fuel that drove the airship. A series of challenges that appealed to his pride, and maybe, too, he had grown used to the rich life he had now. Caught up in it all, he just kept going, never said no, and focused on the gears, the wires, the air ducts, the myriad tiny details that made him ignore everything else.

This foolish man used his assistants as friends to go drinking with, to sleep with, to be his whole life, creating a kind of cult there in his workshop that had become a gigantic hangar, surrounded by soldiers and barbed wire fence. He'd become a national hero.

But I still remembered how my heart had felt when the prototype had risen into the air, how the tears trickled down my face as around me men and women literally danced with joy. How I was struck by the image of my own success, almost as if I were flying.

The prototype wallowed and snorted in the air like a great golden whale in a harness, wanting to be free: a blazing jewel against the bright blue sky, the dream made real.

I don't know what the Lady Salt would have thought of it. Maybe nothing at all.

One day, Hanover finally speaks. I push a button, clean a gear, move a circular bit into place. It is just me and him. Shyver wanted no part of it.

He says, "Command water the sea was bright with the leavings of the fish that there were now going to be."

Clicks twice, thrice, and continues clicking as he takes the measure of me with his golden gaze and says, "Engineer Daniker."

The little hairs on my neck rise. I almost lose my balance, all the blood rushing to my head.

"How do you know my name?"

"You are my objective. You are why I was sent."

"Across the ocean? Not likely."

"I had a ship once, arms and legs once, before your traps destroyed me."

I had forgotten the traps I'd set. I'd almost forgotten my true name.

"You will return with me. You will resume your duties."

I laugh bitterly. "They've found no one to replace me?"

Hanover has no answer—just the clicking—but I know the answer. Child prodigy. Unnatural skills. An unswerving ability to focus in on a problem and solve it. Like... building airships. I'm still an asset they cannot afford to lose.

"You've no way to take me back. You have no authority here," I say.

Hanover's bright eyes dim, then flare. The clicking intensifies. I wonder now if it is the sound of a weapons system malfunctioning.

"Did you know I was here, in this village?" I ask.

A silence. Then: "Dozens were sent for you—scattered across the world."

"So no one knows."

"I have already sent a signal. They are coming for you."

Horror. Shock. And then anger—indescribable rage, like nothing I've ever experienced.

When they find me with Hanover later, there isn't much left of him. I've smashed his head in and then his body, and tried to grind that down with a pestle. I didn't know where the beacon might be hidden, or if it even mattered, but I had to try.

They think I'm mad—the soft-spoken blacksmith, a livid Blake, even Rebecca. I keep telling them the Empire is coming, that I am the Empire's chief engineer. That I've been in hiding. That they need to leave now—into the hills, into the sea. *Anywhere but here...*

But Blake can't see it—he sees only me—and whatever the Lady Salt thinks, she hides it behind a sad smile.

"I said to fix it," Blake roars before he storms out. "Now it's no good for anything!"

Roughly I am taken to the little room that functions as the village jail, with the bars on the window looking out on the sea. As they leave me, I am shouting, "I created their airships! They're coming for me!"

The Lady Salt backs away from the window, heads off to find Blake, without listening.

After dark, Shyver comes by the window, but not to hear me out—just to ask why I did it.

"We could at least have sold it to the hill people," he whispers. He sees only the village, the sea, the blacksmith's daughter. "We put so much work into it."

I have no answer except for a story that he will not believe is true.

Once, there was a country that became an Empire. Its armies flew out from the center and conquered the margins, the barbarians. Everywhere it inflicted itself on the world, people died or came under its control, always under the watchful, floating gaze of the airships. No one had ever seen anything like them before. No one had any defense for them. People wrote poems about them and cursed them and begged for mercy from their attentions.

The chief engineer of this atrocity, the man who had solved the problems, sweated the details, was finally called up by the Emperor of the newly minted Empire fifteen years after he'd seen a golden shape float against a startling blue sky. The Emperor was on the far frontier, some remote place fringed by desert where the people built their homes into the sides of hills and used tubes to spit fire up into the sky.

They took me to His Excellency by airship, of course. For the first time, except for excursions to the capital, I left my little enclave, the country I'd created for myself. From on high, I saw what I had helped create. In the conquered lands, the people looked up at us in fear and hid when and where they could. Some, beyond caring, threw stones up at us: an old woman screaming words I could not hear from that distance, a young man with a bow, the arrows arching below the carriage until the airship commander opened fire, left a red smudge on a dirt road as we glided by from on high.

This vision I had not known existed unfurled like a slow, terrible dream, for we were like languid Gods in our progress, the landscape revealing itself to us with a strange finality.

On the fringes, war still was waged, and before we reached the Emperor I saw my creations clustered above hostile armies, raining down *my* bombs onto stick figures who bled, screamed, died, were mutilated, blown apart... all as if in a silent film, the explosions deafening us, the rest reduced to distant pantomime narrated by the black-humored cheer of our airship's officers.

A child's head resting upon a rock, the body a red shadow. A city reduced to rubble. A man whose limbs had been torn from him. All the same.

By the time I reached the Emperor, received his blessing and his sword, I had nothing to say; he found me more mute than any captive, his instrument once more. And when I returned, when I could barely stand myself anymore, I found a way to escape my cage.

Only to wash up on a beach half a world away.

*Out of the surf, out of the sand, dripping and half-dead, I stumble and the Lady Salt and Blake stand there, above me. I look up at them in the half-light of morning, arm raised against the sun, and wonder whether they will welcome me or kill me or just cast me aside.*

*The Lady Salt looks doubtful and grim, but Blake's broad face breaks into a smile. "Welcome stranger," he says, and extends his hand.*

*I take it, relieved. In that moment, there's no Hanover, no pain, no sorrow, nothing but the firm grip, the arm pulling me up toward them.*

They come at dawn, much faster than I had thought possible: ten airships, golden in the light, the humming thrum of their propellers audible over the crash of the sea. From behind my bars, I watch their deadly, beautiful approach across the slate-gray sky, the deep-blue waves, and it is as if my children are returning to me. If there is no mercy in them, it is because I never thought of mercy when I created the bolt and canvas of them, the fuel and gears of them.

Hours later, I sit in the main cabin of the airship *Forever Triumph*. It has mahogany tables and chairs, crimson cushions. A platter of fruit upon a dais. A telescope on a tripod. A globe of the world. The scent of snuff. All the debris of the real world. We sit on the window seat, the Lady Salt and I. Beyond, the rectangular windows rise and fall just slightly, showing cliffs and hills and sky; I do not look down.

Captain Evans, aping civilized speech, has been talking to us for several minutes. He is fifty and rake-thin and has hooded eyes that make him mournful forever. I don't really know what he's saying; I can't concentrate. I just feel numb, as if I'm not really there.

Blake insisted on fighting what could not be fought. So did most of the others. I watched from behind my bars as first the bombs came and then the troops. I heard Blake die, although I didn't see it. He was cursing and screaming at them; he didn't go easy. Shyver was shot in the leg, dragged himself off moaning. I don't know if he made it.

I forced myself to listen—to all of it.

They had orders to take me alive, and they did. They found the Lady Salt with a gutting knife, but took her too when I told the captain I'd cooperate if they let her live.

Her presence at my side is something unexpected and horrifying. What can she be feeling? Does she think I could have saved Blake but chose not to? Her eyes are dry and she stares straight ahead, at nothing, at no one, while the captain continues with his explanations, his threats, his flattery.

"Rebecca," I say. "Rebecca," I say.

The whispered words of the Lady Salt are everything, all, the chief engineer could have expected: *"Someday I will kill you and escape to the sea."*

I nod wearily and turn my attention back to the captain, try to understand what he is saying.

Below me, the village burns as all villages burn, everywhere, in time.

> *"Suffering's going to come to everyone someday."*
> — The Willard Grant Conspiracy

*for Jay Lake*

# THE GAMBLER

## PAOLO BACIGALUPI

Paolo Bacigalupi is a freelance writer who lives and works in Colorado. He has written about his travels in China for *Salon,* and is the online editor/webmaster for *High Country News.* His first story, "A Pocketful of Dharma," appeared in *The Magazine of Fantasy & Science Fiction* in 1999. It was followed by a handful of dark science fiction stories including Theodore Sturgeon Memorial Award nominee "The Fluted Girl," Hugo Award nominee "The People of Sand and Slag," "The Pasho," "The Calorie Man" and the tale that follows. His first short story collection, *Pump Six,* appeared to widespread acclaim in 2008. Upcoming are two new books, young adult SF novel *Ship Breaker* and adult SF novel *The Windup Girl.*

My father was a gambler. He believed in the workings of karma and luck. He hunted for lucky numbers on license plates and bet on lotteries and fighting roosters. Looking back, I think perhaps he was not a large man, but when he took me to the muy thai fights, I thought him so. He would bet and he would win and laugh and drink laolao with his friends, and they all seemed so large. In the heat drip of Vientiane, he was a lucky ghost, walking the mirror-sheen streets in the darkness.

Everything for my father was a gamble: roulette and blackjack, new rice variants and the arrival of the monsoons. When the pretender monarch Khamsing announced his New Lao Kingdom, my father gambled on civil disobedience. He bet on the teachings of Mr. Henry David Thoreau and on whisper sheets posted on lampposts. He bet on saffron-robed monks marching in protest and on the hidden humanity of the soldiers with their well-oiled AK-47s and their mirrored helmets.

My father was a gambler, but my mother was not. While he wrote letters to the editor that brought the secret police to our door, she made plans for escape. The old Lao Democratic Republic collapsed, and the New Lao Kingdom blossomed with tanks on the avenues and tuk-tuks burning on the street corners. Pha That Luang's shining gold chedi collapsed under shelling, and I rode away on a UN evacuation helicopter under the care of kind Mrs. Yamaguchi.

From the open doors of the helicopter, we watched smoke columns rise over the city like nagas coiling. We crossed the brown ribbon of the Mekong with its jeweled belt of burning cars on the Friendship Bridge. I remember a Mercedes floating in the water like a paper boat on Loi Kratong, burning despite the water all around.

Afterward, there was silence from the land of a million elephants, a void into which light and Skype calls and email disappeared. The roads were blocked. The telecoms died. A black hole opened where my country had once stood.

Sometimes, when I wake in the night to the swish and honk of Los Angeles traffic, the confusing polyglot of dozens of countries and cultures all pressed together in this American melting pot, I stand at my window and look down a boulevard full of red lights, where it is not safe to walk alone at night, and yet everyone obeys the traffic signals. I look down on the brash and noisy Americans in their many hues, and remember my parents: my father who cared too much to let me live under the self-declared monarchy, and my mother who would not let me die as a consequence. I lean against the window and cry with relief and loss.

Every week I go to temple and pray for them, light incense and make a triple bow to Buddha, Damma, and Sangha, and pray that they may have a good rebirth, and then I step into the light and noise and vibrancy of America.

My colleagues' faces flicker gray and pale in the light of their computers and tablets. The tap of their keyboards fills the newsroom as they pass content down the workflow chain and then, with a final keystroke and an obeisance to the "publish" button, they hurl it onto the net.

In the maelstrom, their work flares, tagged with site location, content tags, and social poke data. Blooms of color, codes for media conglomerates: shades of blue and Mickey Mouse ears for Disney-Bertelsmann. A red-rimmed pair of rainbow O's for Google's AOL News. Fox News Corp. in pinstripes gray and white. Green for us: Milestone Media—a combination of NTT DoCoMo, the Korean gaming consortium Hyundai-Kubu, and the smoking remains of the New York Times Company. There are others, smaller stars, Crayola shades flaring and brightening, but we are the most important. The monarchs of this universe of light and color.

New content blossoms on the screen, bathing us all in the bloody glow of a Google News content flare, off their WhisperTech feed. They've scooped us. The posting says that new ear bud devices will be released by Frontal Lobe before Christmas: terabyte storage with Pin-Line connectivity for the Oakley microresponse glasses. The technology is next-gen, allowing personal data control via Pin-Line scans of a user's iris. Analysts predict that everything from cell phones to digital cameras will become obsolete as the full range of Oakley features becomes available. The news flare brightens and migrates toward the center of the maelstrom as visitors flock to Google and view stolen photos of the iris-scanning glasses.

Janice Mbutu, our managing editor, stands at the door to her office, watching with a frown. The maelstrom's red bath dominates the newsroom, a pressing reminder that Google is beating us, sucking away traffic. Behind glass walls, Bob and Casey, the heads of the Burning Wire, our own consumer technology feed, are screaming at their reporters, demanding they do better. Bob's face has turned almost as red as the maelstrom.

The maelstrom's true name is LiveTrack IV. If you were to go downstairs to the fifth floor and pry open the server racks, you would find a sniper sight logo and the words SCRY GLASS—KNOWLEDGE IS POWER stamped on their chips in metallic orange, which would tell you that even though Bloomberg rents us the machines, it is a Google-Nielsen partnership that provides the proprietary algorithms for analyzing the net flows—which means we pay a competitor to tell us what is happening with our own content.

LiveTrack IV tracks media user data—Web site, feed, VOD, audiostream, TV broadcast—with Google's own net statistics gathering programs, aided by Nielsen hardware in personal data devices ranging from TVs to tablets to ear buds to handsets to car radios. To say that the maelstrom keeps a finger on the pulse of media is an understatement. Like calling the monsoon a little wet. The maelstrom is the pulse, the pressure, the blood-oxygen mix; the count of red cells and white, of T-cells and BAC, the screening for AIDS and hepatitis G... It is reality.

Our service version of the maelstrom displays the performance of our own content and compares it to the top one hundred user-traffic events in real-time. My own latest news story is up in the maelstrom, glittering near the edge of the screen, a tale of government incompetence: the harvested DNA of the check-erspot butterfly, already extinct, has been destroyed through mismanagement at the California Federal Biological Preserve Facility. The butterfly—along with sixty-two other species—was subjected to improper storage protocols, and now there is nothing except a little dust in vials. The samples literally blew away. My coverage of the story opens with federal workers down on their knees in a two-billion-dollar climate-controlled vault, with a dozen crime scene vacuums that they've borrowed from LAPD, trying to suck up a speck of butterfly that they might be able to reconstitute at some future time.

In the maelstrom, the story is a pinprick beside the suns and pulsing moons of traffic that represent other reporters' content. It doesn't compete well with news of Frontal Lobe devices, or reviews of Armored Total Combat, or live feeds of the Binge-Purge championships. It seems that the only people who are reading my story are the biologists I interviewed. This is not surprising. When I wrote about bribes for subdivision approvals, the only people who read the story were county planners. When I wrote about cronyism in the selection of city water recycling technologies, the only people who read were water engineers. Still, even though no one seems to care about these stories, I am drawn to them, as though poking at the tiger of the American government will somehow make up for not being able to poke at the little cub of New Divine Monarch Khamsing. It is a foolish thing, a sort of Don Quixote crusade. As a consequence, my salary is the smallest in the office.

"Whoooo!"

Heads swivel from terminals, look for the noise: Marty Mackley, grinning.

"You can thank me..." He leans down and taps a button on his keyboard. "Now."

A new post appears in the maelstrom, a small green orb announcing itself on the Glamour Report, Scandal Monkey blog, and Marty's byline feeds. As we watch, the post absorbs pings from software clients around the world, notifying the millions of people who follow his byline that he has launched a new story.

I flick my tablet open, check the tags:

Double DP,

Redneck HipHop,

Music News,

Schadenfreude,

underage,

pedophilia...

According to Mackley's story, Double DP the Russian mafia cowboy rapper—who, in my opinion, is not as good as the Asian pop sensation Kulaap, but whom half the planet likes very much—is accused of impregnating the fourteen-year-old daughter of his face sculptor. Readers are starting to notice, and with their attention Marty's green-glowing news story begins to muscle for space in the maelstrom. The content star pulses, expands, and then, as though someone has thrown gasoline on it, it explodes. Double DP hits the social sites, starts getting recommended, sucks in more readers, more links, more clicks... and more ad dollars.

Marty does a pelvic grind of victory, then waves at everyone for their attention. "And that's not all, folks." He hits his keyboard again, and another story posts: live feeds of Double's house, where... it looks as though the man who popularized Redneck Russians is heading out the door in a hurry. It is a surprise to see video of the house, streaming live. Most freelance paparazzi are not patient enough to sit and hope that maybe, perhaps, something interesting will happen. This looks as though Marty has stationed his own exclusive papcams at the house, to watch for something like this.

We all watch as Double DP locks the door behind himself. Marty says, "I thought DP deserved the courtesy of notification that the story was going live."

"Is he fleeing?" Mikela Plaa asks.

Marty shrugs. "We'll see."

And indeed, it does look as if Double is about to do what Americans have popularized as an "OJ." He is into his red Hummer. Pulling out.

Under the green glow of his growing story, Marty smiles. The story is getting bigger, and Marty has stationed himself perfectly for the development. Other news agencies and blogs are playing catch-up. Follow-on posts wink into existence in the maelstrom, gathering a momentum of their own as newsrooms scramble to hook our traffic.

"Do we have a helicopter?" Janice asks. She has come out of her glass office to watch the show.

Marty nods. "We're moving it into position. I just bought exclusive angel view with the cops, too, so everyone's going to have to license our footage."

"Did you let Long Arm of the Law know about the cross-content?"

"Yeah. They're kicking in from their budget for the helicopter."

Marty sits down again, begins tapping at his keyboard, a machine-gun of data entry. A low murmur comes from the tech pit, Cindy C. calling our telecom providers, locking down trunklines to handle an anticipated data surge. She knows something that we don't, something that Marty has prepared her for. She's bringing up mirrored server farms. Marty seems unaware of the audience around him. He stops typing. Stares up at the maelstrom, watching his glowing ball of content. He is the maestro of a symphony.

The cluster of competing stories is growing as Gawker and Newsweek and Throb all organize themselves and respond. Our readers are clicking away from us, trying to see if there's anything new in our competitor's coverage. Marty smiles, hits his "publish" key, and dumps a new bucket of meat into the shark tank of public interest: a video interview with the fourteen-year-old. On-screen, she looks very young, shockingly so. She has a teddy bear.

"I swear I didn't plant the bear," Marty comments. "She had it on her own."

The girl's accusations are being mixed over Double's run for the border, a kind of synth loop of accusations:

"And then he…"

"And I said…"

"He's the only one I've ever…"

It sounds as if Marty has licensed some of Double's own beats for the coverage of his fleeing Humvee. The video outtakes are already bouncing around YouTube and MotionSwallow like Ping-Pong balls. The maelstrom has moved Double DP to the center of the display as more and more feeds and sites point to the content. Not only is traffic up, but the post is gaining in social rank as the numbers of links and social pokes increase.

"How's the stock?" someone calls out.

Marty shakes his head. "They locked me out from showing the display."

This, because whenever he drops an important story, we all beg him to show us the big picture. We all turn to Janice. She rolls her eyes, but she gives the nod. When Cindy finishes buying bandwidth, she unlocks the view. The maelstrom slides aside as a second window opens, all bar graphs and financial landscape: our stock price as affected by the story's expanding traffic—and expanding ad revenue.

The stock bots have their own version of the maelstrom; they've picked up the reader traffic shift. Buy and sell decisions roll across the screen, responding to the popularity of Mackley's byline. As he feeds the story, the beast grows.

More feeds pick us up, more people recommend the story to their friends, and every one of them is being subjected to our advertisers' messages, which means more revenue for us and less for everyone else. At this point, Mackley is bigger than the Super Bowl. Given that the story is tagged with Double DP, it will have a targetable demographic: thirteen- to twenty-four-year-olds who buy lifestyle gadgets, new music, edge clothes, first-run games, boxed hairstyles, tablet skins, and ringtones: not only a large demographic, a valuable one.

Our stock ticks up a point. Holds. Ticks up another. We've got four different screens running now. The papcam of Double DP, chase cycles with views of the cops streaking after him, the chopper lifting off, and the window with the four-teen-year-old interviewing. The girl is saying, "I really feel for him. We have a connection. We're going to get married," and there's his Hummer screaming down Santa Monica Boulevard with his song "Cowboy Banger" on the audio overlay.

A new wave of social pokes hits the story. Our stock price ticks up again. Daily bonus territory. The clicks are pouring in. It's got the right combination of content, what Mackley calls the "Three S's": sex, stupidity, and schadenfreude. The stock ticks up again. Everyone cheers. Mackley takes a bow. We all love him. He is half the reason I can pay my rent. Even a small newsroom bonus from his work is enough for me to live. I'm not sure how much he makes for himself when he creates an event like this. Cindy tells me that it is "solid seven, baby." His byline feed is so big he could probably go independent, but then he would not have the resources to scramble a helicopter for a chase toward Mexico. It is a symbiotic relationship. He does what he does best, and Milestone pays him like a celebrity.

Janice claps her hands. "All right, everyone. You've got your bonus. Now back to work."

A general groan rises. Cindy cuts the big monitor away from stocks and bonuses and back to the work at hand: generating more content to light the maelstrom, to keep the newsroom glowing green with flares of Milestone coverage—everything from reviews of Mitsubishi's 100 mpg Road Cruiser to how to choose a perfect turkey for Thanksgiving. Mackley's story pulses over us as we work. He spins off smaller additional stories, updates, interactivity features, encouraging his vast audience to ping back just one more time.

Marty will spend the entire day in conversation with this elephant of a story that he has created. Encouraging his visitors to return for just one more click. He'll give them chances to poll each other, discuss how they'd like to see DP punished, ask whether you can actually fall in love with a fourteen-year-old. This one will have a long life, and he will raise it like a proud father, feeding and nurturing it, helping it make its way in the rough world of the maelstrom.

My own little green speck of content has disappeared. It seems that even gov-ernment biologists feel for Double DP.

When my father was not placing foolish bets on revolution, he taught agronomy at the National Lao University. Perhaps our lives would have been different if he had been a rice farmer in the paddies of the capital's suburbs, instead of surrounded by intellectuals and ideas. But his karma was to be a teacher and a researcher, and so while he was increasing Lao rice production by 30 percent, he was also filling himself with gambler's fancies: Thoreau, Gandhi, Martin Luther King, Sakharov, Mandela, Aung Sung Kyi. True gamblers, all. He would say that if white South Africans could be made to feel shame, then the pretender monarch must right his ways. He claimed that Thoreau must have been Lao, the way he protested so politely.

In my father's description, Thoreau was a forest monk, gone into the jungle for enlightenment. To live amongst the banyan and the climbing vines of Massachusetts and to meditate on the nature of suffering. My father believed he was undoubtedly some arhat reborn. He often talked of Mr. Henry David, and in my imagination this falang, too, was a large man like my father.

When my father's friends visited in the dark—after the coup and the countercoup, and after the march of Khamsing's Chinese-supported insurgency—they would often speak of Mr. Henry David. My father would sit with his friends and students and drink black Lao coffee and smoke cigarettes, and then he would write carefully worded complaints against the government that his students would then copy and leave in public places, distribute into gutters, and stick onto walls in the dead of night.

His guerrilla complaints would ask where his friends had gone, and why their families were so alone. He would ask why monks were beaten on their heads by Chinese soldiers when they sat in hunger strike before the palace. Sometimes, when he was drunk and when these small gambles did not satisfy his risk-taking nature, he would send editorials to the newspapers.

None of these were ever printed, but he was possessed with some spirit that made him think that perhaps the papers would change. That his stature as a father of Lao agriculture might somehow sway the editors to commit suicide and print his complaints.

It ended with my mother serving coffee to a secret police captain while two more policemen waited outside our door. The captain was very polite: he offered my father a 555 cigarette—a brand that already had become rare and contraband—and lit it for him. Then he spread the whisper sheet onto the coffee table, gently pushing aside the coffee cups and their saucers to make room for it. It was rumpled and torn, stained with mud. Full of accusations against Khamsing. Unmistakable as one of my father's.

My father and the policeman both sat and smoked, studying the paper silently.

Finally, the captain asked, "Will you stop?"

My father drew on his cigarette and let the smoke out slowly as he studied the whisper sheet between them. The captain said, "We all respect what you have done for the Lao kingdom. I myself have family who would have starved if not for your work in the villages." He leaned forward. "If you promise to stop writing these whispers and complaints, everything can be forgotten. Everything."

Still, my father didn't say anything. He finished his cigarette. Stubbed it out. "It would be difficult to make that sort of promise," he said.

The captain was surprised. "You have friends who have spoken on your behalf. Perhaps you would reconsider. For their sake."

My father made a little shrug. The captain spread the rumpled whisper sheet, flattening it out more completely. Read it over. "These sheets do nothing," he said. "Khamsing's dynasty will not collapse because you print a few complaints. Most of these are torn down before anyone reads them. They do nothing. They are pointless." He was almost begging. He looked over and saw me watching at the door. "Give this up. For your family, if not your friends."

I would like to say that my father said something grand. Something honorable about speaking against tyranny. Perhaps invoked one of his idols. Aung Sung Kyi or Sakharov, or Mr. Henry David and his penchant for polite protest. But he didn't say anything. He just sat with his hands on his knees, looking down at the torn whisper sheet. I think now that he must have been very afraid. Words always came easily to him, before. Instead, all he did was repeat himself. "It would be difficult."

The captain waited. When it became apparent that my father had nothing else to say, he put down his coffee cup and motioned for his men to come inside. They were all very polite. I think the captain even apologized to my mother as they led him out the door.

We are into day three of the Double DP bonanza, and the green sun glows brightly over all of us, bathing us in its soothing, profitable glow. I am working on my newest story with my Frontal Lobe ear buds in, shutting out everything except the work at hand. It is always a little difficult to write in one's third language, but I have my favorite singer and fellow countryperson Kulaap whispering in my ear that "Love Is a Bird," and the work is going well. With Kulaap singing to me in our childhood language, I feel very much at home.

A tap on my shoulder interrupts me. I pull out my ear buds and look around. Janice, standing over me. "Ong, I need to talk to you." She motions me to follow.

In her office, she closes the door behind me and goes to her desk. "Sit down, Ong." She keys her tablet, scrolls through data. "How are things going for you?"

"Very well. Thank you." I'm not sure if there is more that she wants me to say, but it is likely that she will tell me. Americans do not leave much to guesswork.

"What are you working on for your next story?" she asks.

I smile. I like this story; it reminds me of my father. And with Kulaap's soothing voice in my ears I have finished almost all of my research. The bluet, a flower made famous in Mr. Henry David Thoreau's journals, is blooming too early to be pollinated. Bees do not seem to find it when it blooms in March. The scientists I interviewed blame global warming, and now the flower is in danger of extinction. I have interviewed biologists and local naturalists, and now I would like to go to Walden Pond on a pilgrimage for this bluet that may soon also be bottled in a Federal Reserve laboratory with its techs in clean suits and their crime scene vacuums.

When I finish describing the story, Janice looks at me as if I am crazy. I can tell that she thinks I am crazy, because I can see it on her face. And also because she tells me.

"You're fucking crazy!"

Americans are very direct. It's difficult to keep face when they yell at you. Sometimes, I think that I have adapted to America. I have been here for five years now, ever since I came from Thailand on a scholarship, but at times like this, all I can do is smile and try not to cringe as they lose their face and yell and rant. My father was once struck in the face with an official's shoe, and he did not show his anger. But Janice is American, and she is very angry.

"There's no way I'm going to authorize a junket like that!"

I try to smile past her anger, and then remember that the Americans don't see an apologetic smile in the same way that a Lao would. I stop smiling and make my face look... something. Earnest, I hope.

"The story is very important," I say. "The ecosystem isn't adapting correctly to the changing climate. Instead, it has lost..." I grope for the word. "Synchronicity. These scientists think that the flower can be saved, but only if they import a bee that is available in Turkey. They think it can replace the function of the native bee population, and they think that it will not be too disruptive."

"Flowers and Turkish bees."

"Yes. It is an important story. Do they let the flower go extinct? Or try to keep the famous flower, but alter the environment of Walden Pond? I think your readers will think it is very interesting."

"More interesting than that?" She points through her glass wall at the maelstrom, at the throbbing green sun of Double DP, who has now barricaded himself in a Mexican hotel and has taken a pair of fans hostage.

"You know how many clicks we're getting?" she asks. "We're exclusive. Marty's got Double's trust and is going in for an interview tomorrow, assuming the Mexicans don't just raid it with commandos. We've got people clicking back every couple minutes just to look at Marty's blog about his preparations to go in."

The glowing globe not only dominates the maelstrom's screen, it washes everything else out. If we look at the stock bots, everyone who doesn't have protection under our corporate umbrella has been hurt by the loss of eyeballs. Even the Frontal Lobe/Oakley story has been swallowed. Three days of completely dominating the maelstrom has been very profitable for us. Now Marty's showing his viewers how he will wear a flak jacket in case the Mexican commandos attack while he is discussing the nature of true love with DP. And he has another exclusive interview with the mother ready to post as well. Cindy has been editing the footage and telling us all how disgusted she is with the whole thing. The woman apparently drove her daughter to DP's mansion for a midnight pool party, alone.

"Perhaps some people are tired of DP and wish to see something else," I suggest.

"Don't shoot yourself in the foot with a flower story, Ong. Even Pradeep's cooking journey through Ladakh gets more viewers than this stuff you're writing."

She looks as though she will say more, but then she simply stops. It seems as if she is considering her words. It is uncharacteristic. She normally speaks before her thoughts are arranged.

"Ong, I like you," she says. I make myself smile at this, but she continues. "I hired you because I had a good feeling about you. I didn't have a problem with clearing the visas to let you stay in the country. You're a good person. You write well. But you're averaging less than a thousand pings on your byline feed." She looks down at her tablet, then back up at me. "You need to up your average. You've got almost no readers selecting you for Page One. And even when they do subscribe to your feed, they're putting it in the third tier."

"Spinach reading," I supply.

"What?"

"Mr. Mackley calls it spinach reading. When people feel like they should do something with virtue, like eat their spinach, they click to me. Or else read Shakespeare."

I blush, suddenly embarrassed. I do not mean to imply that my work is of the same caliber as a great poet. I want to correct myself, but I'm too embarrassed. So instead I shut up, and sit in front of her, blushing.

She regards me. "Yes. Well, that's a problem. Look, I respect what you do. You're obviously very smart." Her eyes scan her tablet. "The butterfly thing you wrote was actually pretty interesting."

"Yes?" I make myself smile again.

"It's just that no one wants to read these stories."

I try to protest. "But you hired me to write the important stories. The stories about politics and the government, to continue the traditions of the old newspapers. I remember what you said when you hired me."

"Yeah, well." She looks away. "I was thinking more about a good scandal."

"The checkerspot is a scandal. That butterfly is now gone."

She sighs. "No, it's not a scandal. It's just a depressing story. No one reads a depressing story, at least, not more than once. And no one subscribes to a depressing byline feed."

"A thousand people do."

"A thousand people." She laughs. "We aren't some Laotian community weblog, we're Milestone, and we're competing for clicks with them." She waves outside, indicating the maelstrom. "Your stories don't last longer than half a day; they never get social-poked by anyone except a fringe." She shakes her head. "Christ,

I don't even know who your demographic is. Centenarian hippies? Some federal bureaucrats? The numbers just don't justify the amount of time you spend on stories."

"What stories do you wish me to write?"

"I don't know. Anything. Product reviews. News you can use. Just not any more of this 'we regret to inform you of bad news' stuff. If there isn't something a reader can do about the damn butterfly, then there's no point in telling them about it. It just depresses people, and it depresses your numbers."

"We don't have enough numbers from Marty?"

She laughs at that. "You remind me of my mother. Look, I don't want to cut you, but if you can't start pulling at least a fifty thousand daily average, I won't have any choice. Our group median is way down in comparison to other teams, and when evaluations come around, we look bad. I'm up against Nguyen in the Tech and Toys pool, and Penn in Yoga and Spirituality, and no one wants to read about how the world's going to shit. Go find me some stories that people want to read."

She says a few more things, words that I think are meant to make me feel inspired and eager, and then I am standing outside the door, once again facing the maelstrom.

The truth is that I have never written popular stories. I am not a popular story writer. I am earnest. I am slow. I do not move at the speed these Americans seem to love. Find a story that people want to read. I can write some follow-up to Mackley, to Double DP, perhaps assist with sidebars to his main piece, but somehow, I suspect that the readers will know that I am faking it.

Marty sees me standing outside of Janice's office. He comes over.

"She giving you a hard time about your numbers?"

"I do not write the correct sort of stories."

"Yeah. You're an idealist."

We both stand there for a moment, meditating on the nature of idealism. Even though he is very American, I like him because he is sensitive to people's hearts. People trust him. Even Double DP trusts him, though Marty blew his name over every news tablet's front page. Marty has a good heart. Jai dee. I like him. I think that he is genuine.

"Look, Ong," he says. "I like what you do." He puts his hand around my shoulder. For a moment, I think he's about to try to rub my head with affection and I have to force myself not to wince, but he's sensitive and instead takes his hand away. "Look, Ong. We both know you're terrible at this kind of work. We're in the news business, here. And you're just not cut out for it."

"My visa says I have to remain employed."

"Yeah. Janice is a bitch for that. Look." He pauses. "I've got this thing with Double DP going down in Mexico. But I've got another story brewing. An exclusive. I've already got my bonus, anyway. And it should push up your average."

"I do not think that I can write Double DP sidebars."

He grins. "It's not that. And it's not charity; you're actually a perfect match."

"It is about government mismanagement?"

He laughs, but I think he's not really laughing at me. "No." He pauses, smiles. "It's Kulaap. An interview."

I suck in my breath. My fellow countryperson, here in America. She came out during the purge as well. She was doing a movie in Singapore when the tanks moved, and so she was not trapped. She was already very popular all over Asia, and when Khamsing turned our country into a black hole, the world took note. Now she is popular here in America as well. Very beautiful. And she remembers our country before it went into darkness. My heart is pounding.

Marty goes on. "She's agreed to do an exclusive with me. But you even speak her language, so I think she'd agree to switch off." He pauses, looks serious. "I've got a good history with Kulaap. She doesn't give interviews to just anyone. I did a lot of exposure stories about her when Laos was going to hell. Got her a lot of good press. This is a special favor already, so don't fuck it up."

I shake my head. "No. I will not." I press my palms together and touch them to my forehead in a nop of appreciation. "I will not fuck it up." I make another nop.

He laughs. "Don't bother with that polite stuff. Janice will cut off your balls to increase the stock price, but we're the guys in the trenches. We stick together, right?"

In the morning, I make a pot of strong coffee with condensed milk; I boil rice noodle soup and add bean sprouts and chiles and vinegar, and warm a loaf of French bread that I buy from a Vietnamese bakery a few blocks away. With a new mix of Kulaap's music from DJ Dao streaming in over my stereo, I sit down at my little kitchen table, pour my coffee from its press pot, and open my tablet.

The tablet is a wondrous creation. In Laos, the paper was still a paper, physical, static, and empty of anything except the official news. Real news in our New Divine Kingdom did not come from newspapers, or from television, or from handsets or ear buds. It did not come from the net or feeds unless you trusted your neighbor not to look over your shoulder at an Internet cafe and if you knew that there were no secret police sitting beside you, or an owner who would be able to identify you when they came around asking about the person who used that workstation over there to communicate with the outside world.

Real news came from whispered rumor, rated according to the trust you accorded the whisperer. Were they family? Did they have long history with you? Did they have anything to gain by the sharing? My father and his old classmates trusted one another. He trusted some of his students, as well. I think this is why the security police came for him in the end. One of his trusted friends or students also whispered news to official friends. Perhaps Mr. Inthachak, or Som Vang. Perhaps another. It is impossible to peer into the blackness of that history and guess at who told true stories and in which direction.

In any case, it was my father's karma to be taken, so perhaps it does not matter who did the whispering. But before then—before the news of my father flowed up to official ears—none of the real news flowed toward Lao TV or the *Vientiane Times*. Which meant that when the protests happened and my father came through the door with blood on his face from baton blows, we could read as much as we wanted about the three thousand schoolchildren who had sung the national anthem to our new divine monarch. While my father lay in bed, delirious with pain, the papers told us that China had signed a rubber contract that would triple revenue for Luang Namtha province and that Nam Theun Dam was now earning BT 22.5 billion per year in electricity fees to Thailand. But there were no bloody batons, and there were no dead monks, and there was no Mercedes-Benz burning in the river as it floated toward Cambodia.

Real news came on the wings of rumor, stole into our house at midnight, sat with us and sipped coffee and fled before the call of roosters could break the stillness. It was in the dark, over a burning cigarette that you learned Vilaphon had disappeared or that Mr. Saeng's wife had been beaten as a warning. Real news was too valuable to risk in public.

Here in America, my page glows with many news feeds, flickers at me in video windows, pours in at me over broadband. It is a waterfall of information. As my personal news page opens, my feeds arrange themselves, sorting according to the priorities and tag categories that I've set, a mix of Meung Lao news, Lao refugee blogs, and the chatting of a few close friends from Thailand and the American college where I attended on a human relief scholarship.

On my second page and my third, I keep the general news, the arrangements of Milestone, the Bangkok Post, the Phnom Penh Express—the news chosen by editors. But by the time I've finished with my own selections, I don't often have time to click through the headlines that these earnest news editors select for the mythical general reader.

In any case, I know far better than they what I want to read, and with my keyword and tag scans, I can unearth stories and discussions that a news agency would never think to provide. Even if I cannot see into the black hole itself, I can slip along its edges, divine news from its fringe.

I search for tags like Vientiane, Laos, Lao, Khamsing, China-Lao friendship, Korat, Golden Triangle, Hmong independence, Lao PDR, my father's name… Only those of us who are Lao exiles from the March Purge really read these blogs. It is much as when we lived in the capital. The blogs are the rumors that we used to whisper to one another. Now we publish our whispers over the net and join mailing lists instead of secret coffee groups, but it is the same. It is family, as much as any of us now have.

On the maelstrom, the tags for Laos don't even register. Our tags bloomed brightly for a little while, while there were still guerrilla students uploading content from their handsets, and the images were lurid and shocking. But then the phone lines went down and the country fell into its black hole and now it is just us, this small network that functions outside the country.

A headline from Jumbo Blog catches my eye. I open the site, and my tablet fills with the colorful image of the three-wheeled taxi of my childhood. I often come here. It is a node of comfort.

Laofriend posts that some people, maybe a whole family, have swum the Mekong and made it into Thailand. He isn't sure if they were accepted as refugees or if they were sent back.

It is not an official news piece. More, the idea of a news piece. SomPaBoy doesn't believe it, but Khamchanh contends that the rumor is true, heard from someone who has a sister married to an Isaan border guard in the Thai army. So we cling to it. Wonder about it. Guess where these people came from, wonder if, against all odds, it could be one of ours: a brother, a sister, a cousin, a father....

After an hour, I close the tablet. It's foolish to read anymore. It only brings up memories. Worrying about the past is foolish. Lao PDR is gone. To wish otherwise is suffering.

The clerk at Novotel's front desk is expecting me. A hotel staffer with a key guides me to a private elevator bank that whisks us up into the smog and heights. The elevator doors open to a small entryway with a thick mahogany door. The staffer steps back into the elevator and disappears, leaving me standing in this strange airlock. Presumably, I am being examined by Kulaap's security.

The mahogany door opens, and a smiling black man who is forty centimeters taller than I and who has muscles that ripple like snakes smiles and motions me inside. He guides me through Kulaap's sanctuary. She keeps the heat high, almost tropical, and fountains rush everywhere around. The flat is musical with water. I unbutton my collar in the humidity. I was expecting air-conditioning, and instead I am sweltering. It's almost like home. And then she's in front of me, and I can hardly speak. She is beautiful, and more. It is intimidating to stand before someone who exists in film and in music but has never existed before you in the flesh. She's not as stunning as she is in the movies, but there's more life, more presence; the movies lose that quality about her. I make a nop of greeting, pressing my hands together, touching my forehead.

She laughs at this, takes my hand and shakes it American-style. "You're lucky Marty likes you so much," she says. "I don't like interviews."

I can barely find my voice. "Yes. I only have a few questions."

"Oh no. Don't be shy." She laughs again, and doesn't release my hand, pulls me toward her living room. "Marty told me about you. You need help with your ratings. He helped me once, too."

She's frightening. She is of my people, but she has adapted better to this place than I have. She seems comfortable here. She walks differently, smiles differently; she is an American, with perhaps some flavor of our country, but nothing of our roots. It's obvious. And strangely disappointing. In her movies, she holds herself so well, and now she sits down on her couch and sprawls with her feet kicked out in front of her. Not caring at all. I'm embarrassed for her, and I'm glad I don't have my camera set up yet. She kicks her feet up on the couch. I can't help but be shocked. She catches my expression and smiles.

"You're worse than my parents. Fresh off the boat."

"I am sorry."

She shrugs. "Don't worry about it. I spent half my life here, growing up; different country, different rules."

I'm embarrassed. I try not to laugh with the tension I feel. "I just have some interview questions," I say.

"Go ahead." She sits up and arranges herself for the video stand that I set up.

I begin. "When the March Purge happened, you were in Singapore."

She nods. "That's right. We were finishing The Tiger and the Ghost."

"What was your first thought when it happened? Did you want to go back? Were you surprised?"

She frowns. "Turn off the camera."

When it's off she looks at me with pity. "This isn't the way to get clicks. No one cares about an old revolution. Not even my fans." She stands abruptly and calls through the green jungle of her flat. "Terrell?"

The big black man appears. Smiling and lethal. Looming over me. He is very frightening. The movies I grew up with had falang like him. Terrifying large black men whom our heroes had to overcome. Later, when I arrived in America, it was different, and I found out that the falang and the black people don't like the way we show them in our movies. Much like when I watch their Vietnam movies, and see the ugly way the Lao freedom fighters behave. Not real at all, portrayed like animals. But still, I cannot help but cringe when Terrell looks at me.

Kulaap says, "We're going out, Terrell. Make sure you tip off some of the pap-cams. We're going to give them a show."

"I don't understand," I say.

"You want clicks, don't you?"

"Yes, but—"

She smiles. "You don't need an interview. You need an event." She looks me over. "And better clothes." She nods to her security man. "Terrell, dress him up."

A flashbulb frenzy greets us as we come out of the tower. Papcams everywhere. Chase cycles revving, and Terrell and three others of his people guiding us through the press to the limousine, shoving cameras aside with a violence and power that are utterly unlike the careful pity he showed when he selected a Gucci suit for me to wear.

Kulaap looks properly surprised at the crowd and the shouting reporters, but not nearly as surprised as I am, and then we're in the limo, speeding out of the tower's roundabout as papcams follow us.

Kulaap crouches before the car's onboard tablet, keying in pass codes. She is very pretty, wearing a black dress that brushes her thighs and thin straps that caress her smooth bare shoulders. I feel as if I am in a movie. She taps more keys. A screen glows, showing the taillights of our car: the view from pursuing papcams.

"You know I haven't dated anyone in three years?" she asks.

"Yes. I know from your Web site biography."

She grins. "And now it looks like I've found one of my countrymen."

"But we're not on a date," I protest.

"Of course we are." She smiles again. "I'm going out on a supposedly secret date with a cute and mysterious Lao boy. And look at all those papcams chasing after us, wondering where we're going and what we're going to do." She keys in another code, and now we can see live footage of the paparazzi, as viewed from the tail of her limo. She grins. "My fans like to see what life is like for me."

I can almost imagine what the maelstrom looks like right now: there will still be Marty's story, but now a dozen other sites will be lighting up, and in the center of that, Kulaap's own view of the excitement, pulling in her fans, who will want to know, direct from her, what's going on. She holds up a mirror, checks herself, and then she smiles into her smartphone's camera.

"Hi everyone. It looks like my cover's blown. Just thought I should let you know that I'm on a lovely date with a lovely man. I'll let you all know how it goes. Promise." She points the camera at me. I stare at it stupidly. She laughs. "Say hi and good-bye, Ong."

"Hi and good-bye."

She laughs again, waves into the camera. "Love you all. Hope you have as good a night as I'm going to have." And then she cuts the clip and punches a code to launch the video to her Web site.

It is a bit of nothing. Not a news story, not a scoop even, and yet, when she opens another window on her tablet, showing her own miniversion of the maelstrom, I can see her site lighting up with traffic. Her version of the maelstrom isn't as powerful as what we have at Milestone, but still, it is an impressive window into the data that is relevant to Kulaap's tags.

"What's your feed's byline?" she asks. "Let's see if we can get your traffic bumped up."

"Are you serious?"

"Marty Mackley did more than this for me. I told him I'd help." She laughs. "Besides, we wouldn't want you to get sent back to the black hole, would we?"

"You know about the black hole?" I can't help doing a double-take.

Her smile is almost sad. "You think just because I put my feet up on the furniture that I don't care about my aunts and uncles back home? That I don't worry about what's happening?"

"I—"

She shakes her head. "You're so fresh off the boat."

"Do you use the Jumbo Cafe—" I break off. It seems too unlikely.

She leans close. "My handle is Laofriend. What's yours?"

"Littlexang. I thought Laofriend was a boy—"

She just laughs.

I lean forward. "Is it true that the family made it out?"

She nods. "For certain. A general in the Thai army is a fan. He tells me everything. They have a listening post. And sometimes they send scouts across."

It's almost as if I am home.

We go to a tiny Laotian restaurant where everyone recognizes her and falls over her and the owners simply lock out the paparazzi when they become too intrusive. We spend the evening unearthing memories of Vientiane. We discover that we both favored the same rice noodle cart on Kaem Khong. That she used to sit on the banks of the Mekong and wish that she were a fisherman. That we went to the same waterfalls outside the city on the weekends. That it is impossible to find good dum mak hoong anywhere outside of the country. She is a good companion, very alive. Strange in her American ways, but still, with a good heart. Periodically, we click photos of one another and post them to her site, feeding the voyeurs. And then we are in the limo again and the paparazzi are all around us. I have the strange feeling of fame. Flashbulbs everywhere. Shouted questions. I feel proud to be beside this beautiful intelligent woman who knows so much more than any of us about the situation inside our homeland.

Back in the car, she has me open a bottle of champagne and pour two glasses while she opens the maelstrom and studies the results of our date. She has reprogrammed it to watch my byline feed ranking as well.

"You've got twenty thousand more readers than you did yesterday," she says.

I beam. She keeps reading the results. "Someone already did a scan on your face." She toasts me with her glass. "You're famous."

We clink glasses. I am flushed with wine and happiness. I will have Janice's average clicks. It's as though a bodhisattva has come down from heaven to save my job. In my mind, I offer thanks to Marty for arranging this, for his generous nature. Kulaap leans close to her screen, watching the flaring content. She opens another window, starts to read. She frowns.

"What the fuck do you write about?"

I draw back, surprised. "Government stories, mostly." I shrug. "Sometimes environment stories."

"Like what?"

"I am working on a story right now about global warming and Henry David Thoreau."

"Aren't we done with that?"

I'm confused. "Done with what?"

The limo jostles us as it makes a turn, moves down Hollywood Boulevard, letting the cycles rev around us like schools of fish. They're snapping pictures at the side of the limo, snapping at us. Through the tinting, they're like fireflies, smaller flares than even my stories in the maelstrom.

"I mean, isn't that an old story?" She sips her champagne. "Even America is reducing emissions now. Everyone knows it's a problem." She taps her couch's armrest. "The carbon tax on my limo has tripled, even with the hybrid engine. Everyone agrees it's a problem. We're going to fix it. What's there to write about?"

She is an American. Everything that is good about them: their optimism, their willingness to charge ahead, to make their own future. And everything that is bad about them: their strange ignorance, their unwillingness to believe that they must behave as other than children.

"No. It's not done," I say. "It is worse. Worse every day. And the changes we make seem to have little effect. Maybe too little, or maybe too late. It is getting worse."

She shrugs. "That's not what I read."

I try not to show my exasperation. "Of course it's not what you read." I wave at the screen. "Look at the clicks on my feed. People want happy stories. Want fun stories. Not stories like I write. So instead, we all write what you will read, which is nothing."

"Still—"

"No." I make a chopping motion with my hand. "We newspeople are very smart monkeys. If you will give us your so lovely eyeballs and your click-throughs we will do whatever you like. We will write good news, and news you can use, news you can shop to, news with the 'Three S's.' We will tell you how to have better sex or eat better or look more beautiful or feel happier and or how to meditate—yes, so enlightened." I make a face. "If you want a walking meditation and Double DP, we will give it to you."

She starts to laugh.

"Why are you laughing at me?" I snap. "I am not joking!"

She waves a hand. "I know, I know, but what you just said 'double'—" She shakes her head, still laughing. "Never mind."

I lapse into silence. I want to go on, to tell her of my frustrations. But now I am embarrassed at my loss of composure. I have no face. I didn't used to be like this. I used to control my emotions, but now I am an American, as childish and unruly as Janice. And Kulaap laughs at me.

I control my anger. "I think I want to go home," I say. "I don't wish to be on a date anymore."

She smiles and reaches over to touch my shoulder. "Don't be that way."

A part of me is telling me that I am a fool. That I am reckless and foolish for walking away from this opportunity. But there is something else, something about this frenzied hunt for page views and click-throughs and ad revenue that suddenly feels unclean. As if my father is with us in the car, disapproving. Asking if he posted his complaints about his missing friends for the sake of clicks.

"I want to get out," I hear myself say. "I do not wish to have your clicks."

"But—"

I look up at her. "I want to get out. Now."

"Here?" She makes a face of exasperation, then shrugs. "It's your choice."

"Yes. Thank you."

She tells her driver to pull over. We sit in stiff silence.

"I will send your suit back to you," I say.

She gives me a sad smile. "It's all right. It's a gift."

This makes me feel worse, even more humiliated for refusing her generosity, but still, I get out of the limo. Cameras are clicking at me from all around. This is my fifteen minutes of fame, this moment when all of Kulaap's fans focus on me for a few seconds, their flashbulbs popping.

I begin to walk home as paparazzi shout questions.

Fifteen minutes later I am indeed alone. I consider calling a cab, but then decide I prefer the night. Prefer to walk by myself through this city that never walks anywhere. On a street corner, I buy a pupusa and gamble on the Mexican Lottery because I like the tickets' laser images of their Day of the Dead. It seems an echo of the Buddha's urging to remember that we all become corpses.

I buy three tickets, and one of them is a winner: one hundred dollars that I can redeem at any TelMex kiosk. I take this as a good sign. Even if my luck is obviously gone with my work, and even if the girl Kulaap was not the bodhisattva that I thought, still, I feel lucky. As though my father is walking with me down this cool Los Angeles street in the middle of the night, the two of us together again, me with a pupusa and a winning lottery ticket, him with an Ah Daeng cigarette and his quiet gambler's smile. In a strange way, I feel that he is blessing me.

And so instead of going home, I go back to the newsroom.

My hits are up when I arrive. Even now, in the middle of the night, a tiny slice of Kulaap's fan base is reading about checkerspot butterflies and American government incompetence. In my country, this story would not exist. A censor would kill it instantly. Here, it glows green; increasing and decreasing in size as people click. A lonely thing, flickering amongst the much larger content flares of Intel processor releases, guides to low-fat recipes, photos of lol-cats, and episodes of Survivor! Antarctica. The wash of light and color is very beautiful.

In the center of the maelstrom, the green sun of the Double DP story glows—surges larger. DP is doing something. Maybe he's surrendering, maybe he's murdering his hostages, maybe his fans have thrown up a human wall to protect him. My story snuffs out as reader attention shifts.

I watch the maelstrom a little longer, then go to my desk and make a phone call. A rumpled hairy man answers, rubbing at a sleep-puffy face. I apologize for the late hour, and then pepper him with questions while I record the interview.

He is silly looking and wild-eyed. He has spent his life living as if he were Thoreau, thinking deeply on the forest monk and following the man's careful paths through what woods remain, walking amongst birch and maple and bluets. He is a fool, but an earnest one.

"I can't find a single one," he tells me. "Thoreau could find thousands at this time of year; there were so many he didn't even have to look for them."

He says, "I'm so glad you called. I tried sending out press releases, but…" He shrugs. "I'm glad you'll cover it. Otherwise, it's just us hobbyists talking to each other."

I smile and nod and take notes of his sincerity, this strange wild creature, the sort that everyone will dismiss. His image is bad for video; his words are not good for text. He has no quotes that encapsulate what he sees. It is all couched in the jargon of naturalists and biology. With time, I could find another, someone who looks attractive or who can speak well, but all I have is this one hairy man, disheveled and foolish, senile with passion over a flower that no longer exists.

I work through the night, polishing the story. When my colleagues pour through the door at 8 a.m. it is almost done. Before I can even tell Janice about it, she comes to me. She fingers my clothing and grins. "Nice suit." She pulls up a chair and sits beside me. "We all saw you with Kulaap. Your hits went way up." She nods at my screen. "Writing up what happened?"

"No. It was a private conversation."

"But everyone wants to know why you got out of the car. I had someone from the Financial Times call me about splitting the hits for a tell-all, if you'll be interviewed. You wouldn't even need to write up the piece."

It's a tempting thought. Easy hits. Many click-throughs. Ad-revenue bonuses. Still, I shake my head. "We did not talk about things that are important for others to hear."

Janice stares at me as if I am crazy. "You're not in the position to bargain, Ong. Something happened between the two of you. Something people want to know about. And you need the clicks. Just tell us what happened on your date."

"I was not on a date. It was an interview."

"Well then publish the fucking interview and get your average up!"

"No. That is for Kulaap to post, if she wishes. I have something else."

I show Janice my screen. She leans forward. Her mouth tightens as she reads. For once, her anger is cold. Not the explosion of noise and rage that I expect. "Bluets." She looks at me. "You need hits and you give them flowers and Walden Pond."

"I would like to publish this story."

"No! Hell, no! This is just another story like your butterfly story, and your road contracts story, and your congressional budget story. You won't get a damn click. It's pointless. No one will even read it."

"This is news."

"Marty went out on a limb for you—" She presses her lips together, reining in her anger. "Fine. It's up to you, Ong. If you want to destroy your life over Thoreau and flowers, it's your funeral. We can't help you if you won't help yourself. Bottom line, you need fifty thousand readers or I'm sending you back to the third world."

We look at each other. Two gamblers evaluating one another. Deciding who is betting, and who is bluffing.

I click the "publish" button.

The story launches itself onto the net, announcing itself to the feeds. A minute later a tiny new sun glows in the maelstrom.

Together, Janice and I watch the green spark as it flickers on the screen. Readers turn to the story. Start to ping it and share it amongst themselves, start to register hits on the page. The post grows slightly.

My father gambled on Thoreau. I am my father's son.

# THE DUST ASSASSIN

## IAN MCDONALD

Ian McDonald was born in 1960 in Manchester and moved to Northern Ireland in 1965. He is the author of ten novels, most notably *Desolation Road*, *Out on Blue Six*, Philip K. Dick Award winner *King of Morning, Queen of Day*, *Chaga*, and *Ares Express*. His most acclaimed novel is British SF Award winner and Hugo and Arthur C. Clarke award nominee, *River of Gods*. His short fiction has won the Sturgeon and British Science Fiction awards, been nominated for the Nebula, World Fantasy, and Tiptree awards, and is collected in *Empire Dreams* and *Speaking in Tongues*. His most recent novel is *Brasyl*, and a new short story collection, *Cyberabad Days*, is due in early 2009.

When I was small a steel monkey would come into my room. My ayah put me to bed early, because a growing girl needed sleep, big sleep. I hated sleep. The world I heard beyond the carved stone jali screens of my verandah was too full of things for sleep. My ayah would set the wards, but the steel monkey was one of my own security robots and invisible to them. As I lay on my side in the warmth and perfume of dusk, I would see first its little head, then one hand, then two appear over the lip of my balcony, then all of it. It would crouch there for a whole minute, then slip down into the night shadows filling up my room. As my eyes grew accustomed to the dark I would see it watching me, turning its head from one side to the other. It was a handsome thing: metal shell burnished as soft as skin (for in time it came close enough for me to slip a hand through my mosquito nets to stroke it) and adorned with the symbol of my family and make and serial number. It was not very intelligent, less smart than the real monkeys that squabbled and fought on the rooftops, but clever enough to climb and hunt the assassin robots of the Azads along the ledges and turrets and carvings of the Jodhra Palace. And in the morning I would see them lining the ledges and rooftops with their solar cowls raised and then they did not seem to me like monkeys at all, but cousins of the sculpted gods and demons among which they sheltered, giving salutation to the sun.

You never think your life is special. Your life is just your life, your world is just your world, even lived in a Rajput palace defended by machine monkeys against

97

an implacable rival family. Even when you are a weapon.

Those four words are my memory of my father: his face filling my sight like the Marwar moon, his lips, full as pomegranates, saying down to me, *You are a weapon, Padmini, our revenge against the Azads.* I never see my mother's face there: I never knew her. She lived in seclusion in the zenana, the women's quarters. The only woman I ever saw was my ayah, mad Harpal, who every morning drank a steaming glass of her own piss. Otherwise, only men. And Heer, the khidmutgar, our steward. Not man, not woman: other. A *nute*. As I said, you always think your life is normal.

Every night, the monkey-robot watched me, turning its head this way, that way. Then one night it slipped away on its little plastic paws and I slid out of my nets in my silk pajamas after it. It jumped up on the balcony, then in two leaps it was up the vine that climbed around my window. Its eyes glittered in the full moon. I seized two handfuls of tough, twisted vine, thick as my thigh, and was up after it. Why did I follow that steel monkey? Maybe because of that moon on its titanium shell. Maybe because that was the moon of the great kite festival, which we always observed by flying a huge kite in the shape of a man with a bird's tail and outstretched wings for arms. My father kept all the festivals and rituals, the feasts of the gods. It was what made us different from, better than, the Azads. That man with wings for arms, flying up out of the courtyard in front of my apartment with the sun in his face, could see higher and further than I, the only daughter of the Jodhras, ever could. By the moonlight in the palace courtyard I climbed the vine, like something from one of ayah's fairy tales of gods and demons. The steel monkey led on, over balconies, along ledges, over carvings of heroes from legends and full-breasted apsara women. I never thought how high I was: I was as light and luminous as the bird-man. Now the steel monkey beckoned me, squatting on the parapet with only the stars above it. I dragged myself up onto the roof. Instantly an army of machine monkeys reared up before me like Hanuman's host. Metal gleamed, they bared their anti-personnel weapons: needle throwers tipped with lethal neurotoxins. My family has always favoured poison. I raised my hand and they melted away at the taste of my body chemistry, all but my guide. It skipped and bounded before me. I walked barefoot through a moonlit world of domes and turrets, with every step drawn closer to the amber sky-glow of the city outside. Our palace presented a false front of bays and windows and jharokas to the rude people in the street: I climbed the steps behind the façade until I stood on the very top, the highest balcony. A gasp went out of me. Great Jaipur lay before me, a hive of streetlights and pulsing neons, the reds and whites and blinking yellows of vehicles swarming along the Johan Bazaar, the trees hung with thousands of fairy lights, like stars fallen from the night, the hard fluorescent shine of the open shop fronts, the glowing waver of the tivi screens, the floodlight pools all along the walls of the old city: all, all reflected in the black water of the moat my father had built around his palace. A moat, in the middle of a drought.

The noise swirled up from the street: traffic, a hundred musics, a thousand voices. I swayed on my high perch but I was not afraid. Softness brushed against my leg, my steel monkey pressed close, clinging to the warm pink stone with plastic fingers. I searched the web of light for the sharp edges of the Jantar Mantar, the observatory my ancestors had built three hundred years before. I made out the great wedge of the Samrat Yantra, seven stories tall, the sundial accurate to two seconds; the floodlit bowls of the Jai Prakash Yantra, mapping out the heavens on strips of white marble. The hot night wind tugged at my pajamas; I smelled biodiesel, dust, hot fat, spices carried up from the thronged bazaar. The steel monkey fretted against my leg, making a strange keening sound, and I saw out on the edge of the city: a slash of light down the night, curved like a sail filled with darkness. A tower, higher than any of the others of the new industrial city on the western edges of Jaipur. The glass tower of the Azads, our enemies, as different as could be from our old-fashioned Rajput-style palace: glowing from within with blue light. And I thought, *I am to bring that tower to the ground.*

Then, voices. Shouts. *Hey, you. Up there. Where? There. See that? What is it? Is it a man? I don't know. Hey, you, show yourself.* I leaned forwards, peered carefully down. Light blinded me. At the end of the flashlight beams were two palace guards in combat armour, weapons trained on me. *It's all right, it's all right, don't shoot, for gods' sake, it's the girl.*

"Memsahb," a solider called up. "Memsahb, stay exactly where you are, don't move a muscle, we're coming to get you."

I was still staring at the glowing scimitar of the Azad tower when the roof door opened and the squad of guards came to bring me down.

Next morning I was taken to my father in his audience Diwan. Climate-mod fields held back the heat and the pollution; the open, stone-pillared hall was cool and still. My father sat on his throne of cushions between the two huge silver jars, taller than two of me, that were always filled with water from the holy River Ganga. My father drank a glass at every dawn every morning. He was a very traditional Rajput. I saw the plastic coil of his lighthoek behind his ear. To him his Diwan was full of attendants: his virtual aeai staff, beamed through his skull into his visual centres, busy busy busy on the affairs of Jodhra Water.

My brothers had been summoned and sat uncomfortably on the floor, pulling at their unfamiliar, chafing old-fashioned costumes. This was to be a formal occasion. Heer knelt behind him, hands folded in yts sleeves. I could not read yts eyes behind yts polarised black lenses. I could never read anything about Heer. Not man, not woman—*yt*—yts muscles lay in unfamiliar patterns under yts peach-smooth skin. I always felt that yt did not like me.

The robot lay on its back, deactivated, limbs curled like the dry dead spiders I found in the corners of my room where ayah Harpal was too lazy to dust.

"That was a stupid, dangerous thing to do," my father said. "What would have happened if our jawans had not found you?"

I set my jaw and flared my nostrils and rocked on my cushions.

"I just wanted to see. That's my right, isn't it? It's what you're educating me for, that world out there, so it's my right to see it."

"When you are older. When you are a…woman. The world is not safe, for you, for any of us."

"I saw no danger."

"You don't need to. All danger has to do is see you. The Azad assassins—"

"But I'm a weapon. That's what you always tell me, I'm a weapon, so how can the Azads harm me? How can I be a weapon if I'm not allowed to see what I'm to be used against?"

But the truth was I didn't know what that meant, what I was meant to do to bring that tower of blue glass collapsing down into the pink streets of Jaipur.

"Enough. This unit is defective."

My father made a gesture with his fingers and the steel monkey sprang up, released. It turned its head in its this-way, that-way gesture I knew so well, confused. In the same instant, the walls glittered with light reflecting from moving metal as the machines streamed down the carved stonework and across the pink marble courtyard. The steel monkey gave a strange, robot cry and made to flee but the reaching plastic paws seized it and pulled it down and turned it on its back and circuit by circuit, chip by chip, wire by wire, took it to pieces. When they had finished there was no part of my steel monkey left big enough to see. I felt the tightness in my chest, my throat, my head of about-to-cry, but I would not, I would never, not in front of these men. I glanced again at Heer. Yts black lenses gave nothing, as ever. But the way the sun glinted from those insect eyes told me yt was looking at me.

My life changed that day. My father knew that something between us had been taken apart like the artificial life of the steel monkey. But I had seen beyond the walls of my life, so I was allowed out from the palace a little way into the world. With Heer, and guards, in armoured German cars to bazaars and malls; by tilt-jet to relatives in Jaisalmer and Delhi; to festivals and melas and pujas in the Govind temple. I was still schooled in the palace by tutors and aeai artificial intelligences, but I was presented with my new friends, all the daughters of high-ranking, high-caste company executives, carefully vetted and groomed. They wore all the latest fashions and makeup and jewellery and shoes and tech. They dressed me and styled me and wove brass and amber beads into my hair; they took me to shops and pool parties—in the heart of a drought—and cool summer houses up in the mountains, but they were never comfortable like friends, never free, never friends at all. They were afraid of me. But there were clothes and trips and Star Asia tunes and celebrity gupshup and so I forgot about the steel monkey that I once pretended was my friend and was taken to pieces by its brothers.

Others had not forgotten.

They remembered the night after my fourteenth birthday. There had been a puja by the Govind priest in the Diwan. It was a special age, fourteen, the age I became a woman. I was blessed with fire and ash and light and water and given a sari, the dress of a woman. My friends wound it around me and decorated my hands with mehndi, intricate patterns in dark henna. They set the red bindi of the Kshatriya caste over my third eye and led me out through the rows of applauding company executives and then to a great party. There were gifts and kisses, the food was laid out the length of the courtyard, and there were press reporters and proper French champagne that I was allowed to drink because I was now a woman. My father had arranged a music set by MTV-star Anila—real, not artificial intelligence—and in my new woman's finery I jumped up and down and screamed like any other of my teenage girlfriends. At the very end of the night, when the staff took the empty silver plates away and Anila's roadies folded up the sound system, my father's jawans brought out the great kite of the Jodhras, the winged man-bird the colour of fire, and sent him up, shining, into the night above Jaipur, up towards the hazy stars. Then I went to my new room, in the zenana, the women's quarter, and old disgusting ayah Harpal locked the carved wooden door to my nursery.

It was that that saved me, when the Azads struck.

I woke an instant before Heer burst through the door, but in that split second was all the confusion of waking in an unfamiliar bed, in a strange room, in an alien house, in a body you do not fully know as your own.

Heer. Here. Not Heer. Dressed in street clothes. Men's clothes. Heer, with a gun in yts hand. The big gun with the two barrels, the one that killed people and the one that killed machines.

"Memsahb, get up and come with me. You must come with me."

"Heer—"

"Now, memsahb."

Mouth working for words, I reached for clothes, bag, shoes, things. Heer threw me across the room to crash painfully against the Rajput chest.

"How dare—" I started and, as if in slow motion, I saw the gun fly up. A flash, like lightning in the room. A metallic squeal, a stench of burning, and the smoking steel shell of a defence robot went spinning across the marble floor like a burning spider. Its tail was raised, its stinger erect. Not knowing if this was some mad reality or I was still in a dream, I reached my hand towards the dead machine. Heer snatched me away.

"Do you want to die? It may still be operational."

Yt pushed me roughly into the corridor, then turned to fire a final e-m charge into the room. I heard a long keening wail like a cork being turned in a bottle that faded into silence. In that silence I heard for the first time the sounds. Gunfire, men shouting, men roaring, engines revving, aircraft overhead, women crying. Women wailing. And everywhere, above and below, the clicking scamper of small plastic feet.

"What's going on?" Suddenly I was chilled and trembling with dread. "What's happened?"

"The House of Jodhra is under attack," Heer said.

I pulled away from yts soft grip.

"Then I have to go, I have to fight, I have to defend us. I am a weapon."

Heer shook yts head in exasperation and with yts gun hand struck me a ring-ing blow on the side of my head.

"Stupid stupid! Understand! The Azads, they are killing everything! Your father, your brothers, they are killing everyone. They would have killed you, but they forgot you moved to a new room."

"Dadaji? Arvind, Kiran?"

Heer tugged me along, still reeling, still dizzy from the blow but more dazed, more stunned by what the nute had told me. My father, my brothers…

"Mamaji?" My voice was three years old.

"Only the geneline."

We rounded a corner. Two things happened at the same time. Heer shouted, "Down!" and as I dived for the smooth marble I glimpsed a swarm of monkey-machines bounding towards me, clinging to walls and ceiling. I covered my head and cried out with every shot as Heer fired and fired and fired until the gas-cell canister clanged to the floor.

"They hacked into them and reprogrammed them. Faithless, betraying things. Come *on*." The smooth, manicured hand reached for me and I remember only shards of noise and light and dark and bodies until I found myself in the back seat of a fast German car, Heer beside me, gun cradled like a baby. I could smell hot electricity from the warm weapon. Doors slammed. Locks sealed. Engine roared.

"Where to?"

"The Hijra Mahal."

As we accelerated through the gate more monkey-robots dropped from the naqqar khana. I heard their steel lives crack and burst beneath our wheels. One clung to the door, clawing at the window frame until the driver veered and scraped it off on a streetlight.

"Heer…"

Inside it was all starting to burst, to disintegrate into the colours and visions and sounds and glances of the night. My father my head my brothers my head my mother my family my head my head my head.

"It's all right," the nute said, taking my hand in yts. "You're safe. You're with us now."

The House of Jodhra, which had endured for a thousand years, fell, and I came to the house of the nutes. It was pink, as all the great buildings of Jaipur were pink, and very discreet. In my life *before*, as I now thought of it, I must have driven past its alleyway a hundred times without ever knowing the secret it concealed: cool marble rooms and corridors behind a façade of orioles and turrets and intricately carved windows, courts and tanks and water-gardens open only to the sky and the birds. But then the Hijra Mahal had always been a building apart. In another age it had been the palace of the hijras, the eunuchs. The un-men, shunned yet essential to the ritual life of Rajput Jaipur, living in the very heart of the old city, yet apart.

There were six of them: Sul, the janampatri seer, astrologer to celebs as far away as the movie boulevards of Mumbai; Dahin, the plastic surgeon, who worked on faces on the far side of the planet through remote machines accurate to the width of an atom; Leel, the ritual dancer, who performed the ancient Nautch traditions and festival dances; Janda, the writer, whom half of India knew as Queen Bitch of gupshup columnists; Suleyra, whose parties and events were the talk of society from Srinagar to Madurai; and Heer, once khidmutgar to the House of Jodhra. My six guardians bundled me from the car wrapped in a heavy chador like a Muslim woman and took me to a domed room of a hundred thousand mirror fragments. Their warm, dry hands gently held me on the divan—I was thrashing, raving, as the shock hit me—and Dahin the face surgeon deftly pressed an efuser to my arm.

"Hush. Sleep now."

I woke among the stars. For an instant I wondered if I was dead, stabbed in my sleep by the poison needle of an Azad assassin robot that had scaled the hundred windows of the Jodhra Mahal. Then I saw that they were the mirror shards of the ceiling, shattering the light of a single candle into a hundred thousand pieces. Heer sat cross-legged on a dhurrie by my low bedside.

"How long…"

"Two days, child."

"Are they…"

"Dead. Yes. I cannot lie. Every one."

But even as the House of Jodhra fell, it struck back like a cobra, its back broken by a stick. Homing missiles, concealed for years, clinging like bats under shop eaves and bus shelters, unfolded their wings and lit their engines and sought out the pheromone profiles of Azad vehicles. Armoured Lexuses went up in fireballs in the middle of Jaipur's insane traffic as they hooted their way towards the safety of the airport. No safety even there: a Jodhra missile locked on to the company tilt-jet as it lifted off, hooked into the engine intake with its titanium claws until the aircraft reached an altitude at which no one could survive. The blast cast momentary shadows across the sundials of the Jantar Mantar, marking the moment of Jodhra revenge. Burning debris set fires all across the slums.

"Are they…"

"Jahangir and the Begum Azad died in the tilt-jet attack and our missiles took out much of their board, but their countermeasures held off our attack on their headquarters."

"Who survived?"

"Their youngest son, Salim. The line is intact."

I sat up in my low bed that smelled of sandalwood. The stars were jewels around my head.

"It's up to me then."

"Memsahb—"

"Don't you remember what he said, Heer? My father? *You are a weapon, never forget that.* Now I know what I am a weapon for."

"Memsahb… Padmini." The first time yt had ever spoken my name. "You are still shocked, you don't know what you're saying. Rest. You need rest. We'll talk in the morning." Yt touched yts forefinger to yts full lips, then left. When I could no longer hear soft footfalls on cool marble, I went to the door. Righteousness, rage, and revenge were one song inside me. Locked. I heaved, I beat, I screamed. The Hijra Mahal did not listen. I went to the balcony that hung over the alley. Even if I could have shattered the intricate stone jali, it was a ten-metre drop to street level where the late-night hum of phatphat autorickshaws and taxis was giving way to the delivery drays and cycle-vans of the spice merchants. Light slowly filled up the alley and crept across the floor of my bedroom: by its gathering strength I could read the headlines of the morning editions. WATER WARS: DOZENS DEAD IN CLASH OF THE RAJAS. JAIPUR REELS AS JODHRAS ANNIHILATED. POLICE POWERLESS AGAINST BLOODY VENDETTA.

In Rajputana, now as always, water is life, water is power. The police, the judges, the courts: we owned them. Us, and the Azads. In that we were alike. When gods fight, what mortal would presume to judge?

"A ride in triumph, a fall through a window into love, a marriage, and a mourning?" I asked. "That's it?"

Sul the astrologer nodded slowly. I sat on the floor of yts observatory. Incense rose on all sides of me from perforated brass censors. At first glance, the room was so simple and bare that even a saddhu would have been uncomfortable, but as my eyes grew accustomed to the shadow in which it must be kept to work as a prediction machine, I saw that every centimetre of the bare pink marble was covered in curving lines and Hindi inscriptions, so small and precise they might be the work of tiny gods. The only light came from a star-shaped hole in the domed ceiling: Sul's star chamber was in the topmost turret of the Hijra Mahal, closest to heaven. As yt worked with yts palmer and made the gestures in the air of the janampatri calculations, I watched a star of dazzling sunlight crawl along an arc etched in the floor, measuring out the phases of the House of Meena. Sul caught me staring at yt, but I had only been curious to see what another nute looked like, close up. I had only ever known Heer. I had not known there could be as many as six nutes in the whole of India, let alone Jaipur. Sul was fat and had unhealthy yellow skin and eyes and shivered a lot as yt pulled yts shawl around yt, though the turret room directly under the sun was stifling hot. I looked for clues to what yt had been before: woman, man. *Woman,* I thought. I had always thought of Heer as a man—an ex-man, though yt never mentioned the subject. I had always known it was taboo. When you Stepped Away, you never looked back.

"No revenge, no justice?"

"If you don't believe me, see for yourself."

Fingers slipped the lighthoek behind my ear and the curving lines on the floor leaped up into mythical creatures studded with stars. Makara the crocodile, Vrishaba the bull, the twin fishes of Meena; the twelve rashi. Kanya the dutiful daughter. Between them the twenty-seven nakshatars looped and arced, each of them subdivided into four padas; wheels within wheels within wheels, spinning around my head like blades as I sat on Sul's marble floor.

"You know I can't make any sense out of this," I said, defeated by the whirling numbers. Sul leaned forwards and gently touched my hand.

"A ride in triumph, a fall through a window into love, a marriage, and a mourning. Window to widow. Trust me."

"Young girls are truly beautiful on the inside." Dahin the dream doctor's voice came from beyond the bank of glaring surgical lights as the bed on which I lay tilted back. "No pollution, no nasty dirty hormones. Everything clean and fresh and lovely. Most of the women who come here, I never see any deeper than their skin. It is a rare privilege to be allowed to look inside someone."

It was midnight in the chrome and plastic surgery in the basement of the Hijra Mahal, a snatched half-hour between the last of the consultations (society ladies swathed in veils and chadors to hide their identities) and Dahin hooking into the global web, settling the lighthoek over the visual centre in yts brain and pulling on the manipulator gloves connected to surgical robots in theatres half a world away. So gentle, so deft; too agile for any man. Dahin of the dancing hands.

"Have you found it yet?" I asked. My eyes were watering from the lights. Something in them, something beyond them, was looking into my body and displaying it section by section, organ by organ, on Dahin's inner vision. Traditionally, the hijras were the only ones allowed to examine the bodies of the zenana women and reported their findings to the doctors outside.

"Found what? Finger lasers? Retractable steel claws? A table-top nuke wired into your tummy?"

"My father said over and over, I'm a weapon, I'm special... I will destroy the House of Azad."

"Cho chweet, if there's anything there, this would have shown it to me."

My eyes were watering. I pretended it was the brightness of the light.

"Maybe there's something... smaller, something you can't see, like... bugs. Like a disease."

I heard Dahin sigh and imagined the waggle of yts head.

"It'll take a day or two but I can run a diagnostic." Tippy-tapping by my ear. I turned my head and froze as I saw a spider robot no bigger than my thumb move towards my throat. It was a month since *the night*, but still I was distrustful of robots. I imagined I always would be. I felt a little flicking needle pain in the side of my neck, then the robot moved over my belly. I cringed at the soft spiking of its sharp, precise feet. I said, "Dahin, do you mind me asking—did you do this?"

A short jab of pain in my belly.

"Oh yes, baba. All this, and more. Much much more. I only work on the outside, the externals. To be like me—to become one of us—you have to go deep, right down into the cells."

Now the robot was creeping over my face. I battled the urge to sweep it away and crush it on the floor. I was a weapon, I was special. This machine would show me how.

"Woman, man, that's not a thing easily undone. They take you apart, baba. Everything, hanging there in a tank of fluid. Then they put you back together again. Different. Neither. Better."

*Why*, I wanted to ask, *why do this thing to yourself?* But then I felt a tiny scratch in the corner of my eye as the robot took a scrape from my optic nerve.

"Three days for the test results, baba."

Three days, and Dahin brought the results to me as I sat in the Peacock Pavilion overlooking the bazaar. The wind was warm and smelled of ashes of roses as it blew through the jali and turned the delicately handwritten sheets. No implants. No special powers or abilities. No abnormal neural structures, no tailored combat viruses. I was a completely normal fourteen-year-old Kshatriya girl.

I leaped over the swinging stick. While still in the air, I brought my own staff up in a low arc, catching the Azad's weapon between his hands. It flew from his grasp, clattered across the wooden floor of the hall. He threw a kick at me, rolled to pick up his pole, but my swinging tip caught him hard against the temple, sending him down to the floor like dropped laundry. I vaulted over him, swung my staff high to punch its brass-shod tip into the nerve cluster under the ear. Instant death.

"And finish."

I held the staff millimetres away from my enemy's brain. Then I slipped the lighthoek from behind my ear and the Azad vanished like a djinn. Across the practice floor, Leel set down yts staff and unhooked yts 'hoek. In yts inner vision yts representation of me—enemy, sparring partner, pupil—likewise vanished. As ever at these practice sessions, I wondered what shape Leel's avatar took. Yt never said. Perhaps yt saw me.

"All fighting is dance, all dance is fighting." That was Leel's first lesson to me on the day yt agreed to train me in Silambam. For weeks I had watched yt from a high balcony as yt practised the stampings and head movements and delicate hand gestures of the ritual dances. Then one night after yt had dismissed yts last class, something told me, *Stay on*, and I saw yt strip down to a simple dhoti and take out the bamboo staff from the cupboard and leap and whirl and stamp across the floor, the attacks and defences of the ancient Keralan martial art.

"Since it seems I was not born a weapon, then I must become a weapon."

Leel had the dark skin of a southerner and I always felt that yt was very much older than yt appeared. I also felt—again with no evidence—that yt was the oldest inhabitant of the Hijra Mahal, that yt had been there long before any of the others came. I felt that yt might once have been a hijra and that the dance moves it practised and taught were from the days when no festival or wedding was complete without the outrageous, outcast eunuchs.

"Weapon, so? Cut anyone tries to get close to you, then when you've cut everyone, you cut yourself. Better things for you to be than a weapon."

I asked Leel that same question every day until one evening thick with smog and incense from the great Govind festival yt came to me as I sat in my window reading the chati channels on my lighthoek.

"So. The stick fighting."

That first day, as I stood barefoot on the practice floor in my Adidas baggies and stretchy sports top trying to feel the weight and heft of the fighting staff in my hands, I had been surprised when Leel fitted the lighthoek behind my ear. I had assumed I would spar against the guru ytself.

"Vain child. With what I teach you, you can kill. With one blow. Much safer to fight your image, in here." Yt tapped yts forehead. "As you fight mine. Or whatever you make me."

All that season I learned the dance and ritual of Silambam; the leaps and the timings and the sweeps and the stabs. The sharp blows and the cries. I blazed across the practice floor yelling Kerala battle hymns, my staff a blur of thrusts and parries and killing strokes.

"Heavy child, heavy. Gravity has no hold on you, you must fly. Beauty is everything. See?" And Leel would vault on yts staff and time seemed to freeze around yt, leaving yt suspended there, like breath, in midair. And I began to understand about Leel, about all the nutes in this house of hijras. Beauty was everything, a beauty not male, not female; something else. A third beauty.

The hard, dry winter ended and so did my training. I went down in my Adidas gear and Leel was in yts dance costume, bells ringing at yts ankles. The staffs were locked away.

"This is so unfair."

"You can fight with the stick, you can kill with a single blow, how much more do you need to become this weapon you so want to be?"

"But it takes years to become a master."

"You don't need to become a master. And that is why I have finished your training today, because you should have learned enough to understand the perfect uselessness of what you want to do. If you can get close, if you ever learn to fly, perhaps you might kill Salim Azad, but his soldiers will cut you apart. Realise this, Padmini Jodhra. It's over. They've won."

In the morning, when the sun cast pools of light in the shapes of birds onto the floor of the little balcony, Janda would drink coffee laced with paan and, lazily lifting a finger to twirl away another page in yts inner vision, survey the papers the length and breadth of India, from the Rann of Kutch to the Sundarbans of Bengal.

"Darling, how can you be a bitch if you don't *read?*"

In the afternoon over tiffin, Janda would compose yts scandalous gossip columns: who was doing what with whom where and why, how often and how much and what all good people should think. Yt never did interviews. Reality got in the way of creativity.

"They love it, sweetie. Gives them an excuse to get excited and run to their lawyers. First real emotion some of them have felt in years."

At first I had been scared of tiny, monkey-like Janda, always looking, checking, analysing from yts heavily kohled eyes, seeking weaknesses for yts acid tongue. Then I saw the power that lay in yts cuttings and clippings and entries, taking a rumour here, a whisper there, a suspicion yonder, and putting them together into a picture of the world. I began to see how I could use it as a weapon. Knowledge was power. So as dry winter gave way to thirsty spring and the headlines in the streets clamoured MONSOON SOON? and RAJPUTANA DEHYDRATES, Janda helped me build a picture of Salim Azad and his company. Looking beyond those sensationalist headlines to the business sections I grew to recognise his face beneath the headlines: AZAD PLUNDERS CORPSE OF RIVALS. SALIM AZAD: REBUILDER OF A DYNASTY. AZAD WATER IN FIVE RIVERS PROJ-ECT. In the society section I saw him at weddings and parties and premiers. I saw him skiing in Nepal and shopping in New York and at the races in Paris. In the stock-market feeds I watched the value of Azad Water climb as deals were struck, new investments announced, takeovers and buyouts made public. I learned Salim Azad's taste in pop music, restaurants, tailors, designers, filmi stars, fast fast cars. I could tell you the names of the people who hand-sewed his shoes, who wrote the novel on his bedside table, who massaged his head and lit cones of incense along his spine, who flew his private tilt-jets and programmed his bodyguard robots.

One smoggy, stifling evening as Janda cleared away the thalis of sweetmeats yt gave me while I worked ("Eat, darling, eat and act.") I noticed the lowlight illuminate two ridges of shallow bumps along the inside of yts forearm. I remembered seeing them on Heer all my life and had always known they were as much a part of a nute as the absence of any sexual organs, as the delicate bones and the long hands and the bare skull. In the low, late light they startled me because I had never asked, *What are they for?*

"For? Dear girl." Janda clapped yts soft hands together. "For love. For making love. Why else would we bear these nasty, ugly little goose bumps? Each one generates a different chemical response in our brains. We touch, darling. We play each other like instruments. We feel… things you cannot. Emotions for which you have no name, for which the only name is to experience them. We Step Away to somewhere not woman, not man; to the nute place."

Yt turned yts arm wrist-upwards to me so that yts wide sleeve fell away. The two rows of mosquito-bite mounds were clear and sharp in the yellow light. I thought of the harmonium the musicians would play in the old Jodhra Palace, fingers running up and down the buttons, the other hand squeezing the bellows. Play any tune on it. I shuddered. Janda saw the look on my face and snatched yts arm back into yts sleeve. And then, laid on in the newspaper in front of me was an emotion for which I had no name, which I could only know by experiencing it. I thought no one knew more than I about Salim Azad, but here was a double spread of him pushing open the brass-studded gates of the Jodhra Mahal, my old home, where his family annihilated mine, under the screaming headline: AZAD BURIES PAST, BUYS PALACE OF RIVALS. Below that, Salim Azad standing by the pillars of the Diwan, shading his eyes against the sun, as his staff ran our burning sun-man-bird kite up above the turrets and battlements into the hot yellow sky.

In the costume and makeup of Radha, divine wife of Krishna, I rode the painted elephant through the pink streets of Jaipur. Before me the band swung and swayed, its clarinets and horns rebounding from the buildings. Around and through the players danced Leel and the male dancer in red, swords flashing and clashing, skirts whirling, bells ringing. Behind me came another twenty elephants, foreheads patterned with the colours of Holi, howdahs streaming pennons and gold umbrellas. Above me robot aircraft trailed vast, gossamer-light banners bearing portraits of the Holy Pair and divine blessings. Youths and children in red wove crimson patterns with smoke-sticks and threw handfuls of coloured powder into the crowd. *Holi Hai! Holi Hai!* Reclining beside me on the golden howdah, Suleyra waved yts flute to the crowd. Jaipur was an endless tunnel of sound: people cheering, holiday shouts, the hooting of phatphat horns.

"Didn't I tell you you needed to get out of that place, cho chweet?"

In the blur of days inside the Hijra Mahal, I had not known that a year had passed without me setting foot outside its walls. Then Suleyra, the fixer, the jester, the party-maker, had come skipping into my room, pointed yts flute at me, and said, "Darling, you simply must be my wife," and I had realised that it was Holi, the Elephant Festival. I had always loved Holi, the brightest, maddest of festivals.

"But someone might see me—"

"Baba, you'll be blue all over. And anyway, no one can touch the bride of a god on her wedding day."

And so, blue from head to toe, I reclined on gilded cushions beside Suleyra, who had been planning this public festival for six months, equally blue and not remotely recognisable as anything human, man, woman, or nute. The city was clogged with people, the streets stifling hot, the air so thick with hydrocarbon fumes that the elephants wore smog goggles and I loved every bit of it. I was set free from the Hijra Mahal.

A wave of Suleyra/Krishna's blue hand activated the chips in the elephant's skull and turned it left through the arched gateway to the Old City, behind the boogying band and the leaping, sword-wielding dancers. The crowds spilled off the arcades onto the street, ten, twenty deep. Every balcony was lined; women and children threw handfuls of colour down on us. Ahead I could see a platform and a canopy. The band was already marching in place while Leel and yts partner traded mock blows.

"Who is up there?" I asked, suddenly apprehensive.

"A most important dignitary," said Suleyra, taking the praise of the spectators. "A very rich and powerful man."

"Who is he, Suleyra?" I asked. Suddenly, I was cold in the stinking heat of Jaipur. "*Who is he?*"

But the dancers and the band had moved on and now our elephant took their place in front of the podium. A tap from Suleyra's Krishna-flute: the elephant wheeled to face the dais and bent its front knees in a curtsey. A tall, young man in a Rajput costume with a flame-red turban stood up to applaud, face bright with delight.

I knew that man's shoe size and star sign. I knew the tailor who had cut his suit and the servant who wound his turban. I knew everything about him, except that he would be here, reviewing the Holi parade. I tensed myself to leap. One blow; Suleyra's Krishna-flute would suffice as a weapon. But I did nothing, for I saw a thing more incredible. Behind Salim Azad, bending forwards, whispering in his ear, eyes black as obsidian behind polarising lenses, was Heer.

Salim Azad clapped his hands in delight.

"Yes, yes, this is the one! Bring her to me. Bring her to my palace."

So I returned from the Palace of the Hijras to the Palace of the Jodhras, which was now the Palace of the Azads. I came through the brass gates under the high tower from which I had first looked out across Jaipur on the night of the steel monkey, across the great courtyard. The silver jars of holy Ganga water still stood on either side of the Diwan where my father had managed his water empire. Beneath the gaze of the gods and the monkeys on the walls, I was dragged out of the car by Azad jawans who carried me, screaming and kicking, up the stairs to the zenana. "My brother lay there, so and so died there, my father died there," I shouted at them as they dragged me along that same corridor down which I had fled a year before. The marble floors were pristine, polished. I could not remember where the blood had been. Women retainers waited for me at the entrance to the zenana, for men could not enter the women's palace, but I flew and kicked and punched at them with all the skills Leel had taught me. They fled shrieking, but all that happened was the soldiers held me at gunpoint until house robots arrived. I could kick and punch all I liked and never lay a scratch on their spun-diamond carapaces.

In the evening I was brought to the Hall of Conversations, an old and lovely room where women could talk and gossip with men across the delicate stone jali that ran the length of the hall. Salim Azad walked the foot-polished marble. He was dressed as a Rajput, in the traditional costume. I thought he looked like a joke. Behind him was Heer. Salim Azad paced up and down for five minutes, studying me. I pressed myself to the jali and tried to stare him down.

Finally he said, "Do you have everything you want? Is there anything you need?"

"Your heart on a thali," I shouted. Salim Azad took a step back.

"I'm sorry about the necessity of this… But please understand, you're not my prisoner. We are the last. There has been enough death. The only way I can see to finish this feud is to unite our two houses. But I won't force you, that would be… impolite. Meaningless. I have to ask and you have to answer me." He came as close to the stonework as was safe to avoid my Silambam punch. "Padmini Jodhra, will you marry me?"

It was so ridiculous, so stupid and vain and so impossible, that in my shock, I felt the word *yes* in the back of my throat. I swallowed it down, drew back my head, and spat long and full at him. The spit struck a moulding and ran down the carved sandstone.

"Understand I have nothing but death for you, murderer."

"Even so, I shall ask every day, until you say yes," Salim Azad said. With a whisk of robes, he turned and walked away. Heer, hands folded in yts sleeves, eyes pebbles of black, followed.

"And you, hijra," I yelled, reaching a clawing hand through the stone jali to seize, to rip. "You're next, traitor."

That night I thought about starving myself to death, like the great Gandhiji when he battled the British to make India free and their Empire had stepped aside for one old, frail, thin, starving man. I shoved my fingers down my throat and puked up the small amount of food I had forced myself to eat that evening. Then I realised that starved and dead I was no weapon. The House of Azad would sail undisturbed into the future. It was the one thing that kept me alive, kept me sane in those first days in the zenana—my father's words: *You are a weapon.* All I had to discover was what kind.

In the night a small sweeper came and cleaned away my puke.

It was as he said. Every evening as the sun touched the battlements of the Nahargarh Fort on the hill above Jaipur, Salim Azad came to the Hall of Conversations. He would talk to me about the history of his family; back twenty generations to central Asia, from where they had swept down into the great river plains of Hindustan to build an empire of unparalleled wealth and elegance and beauty. They had not been warriors or rulers. They had been craftsmen and poets, makers of exquisite fine miniatures and jewel-like verses in Urdu, the language of poets. As the great Mughals erected their forts and palaces and fought their bloody civil wars, they had advanced from court painters and poets to court advisors, then to viziers and khidmutgars, not just to the Mughals, but to the

Rajputs, the Marathas, and later to the East India Company and the British Raj. He told me tales of illustrious ancestors and stirring deeds; of Aslam, who rode out between the armies of rival father and son Emperors and saved the Panjab; of Farhan, who carried love notes between the English Resident of Hyderabad and the daughter of the Nizam and almost destroyed three kingdoms; of Shah Hussain, who had struggled with Gandhi against the British for India, who had been approached by Jinnah to support partition and the creation of Pakistan but who had refused, though his family had all but been annihilated in the ethnic holocaust following Independence. He told me of Elder Salim, his grandfather, founder of the dynasty, who had come to Jaipur when the monsoon failed the first terrible time in 2008 and set up village water reclamation schemes that over the decades became the great water empire of the Azads. Strong men, testing times, thrilling stories. And every night, as the sun dipped behind Nahargarh Fort, he said, "Will you marry me?" Every night I turned away from him without a word. But night by night, story by story, ancestor by ancestor, he chipped away at my silence. These were people as real, as vital as my own family. Now their stories had all ended. We two were the last.

I tried to call Janda at the Hijra Mahal, to seek wisdom and comfort from my sister/brothers, to find out if they knew why Heer had turned and betrayed me but mostly to hear another voice than the sat channels or Salim Azad. My calls bounced. White noise: Salim had my apartments shielded with a jamming field. I flung the useless palmer against the painted wall and ground it under the heel of my jewelled slipper. I saw endless evenings reaching out before me. Salim would keep coming, night after night, until he had his answer. He had all the time in the world. Did he mean to drive me mad to marry him?

*Marry him.* This time I did not push the thought away. I turned it this way, that way, studied it, felt out its implications. Marry him. It was the way out of this marble cage.

In the heat of midday, a figure in voluminous robes came hurrying down the cool corridor to the zenana. Heer. I had summoned yt. Because yt was not a man yt could enter the zenana, like the eunuchs of the Rajput days. Yt did not fear the skills Leel had taught me. Yt knew. Yt namasted.

"Why have you done this to me?"

"Memsahb, I have always been, and remain, a loyal servant of the House of Jodhra."

"You've given me into the hands of my enemies."

"I have saved you from the hands of your enemies, Padmini. It would not just be the end of this stupid, pointless, bloody vendetta. He would make you a partner. Padmini, listen to what I am saying: you would be more than just a wife. Azad Jodhra. A name all India would learn."

"Jodhra Azad."

Heer pursed yts rosebud lips.

"Padmini Padmini, always, this pride."

And yt left without my dismissal.

That night in the blue of the magic hour Salim Azad came again to the zenana, a pattern of shadows beyond the jali. I saw him open his lips. I put a finger up to mine.

"Ssh. Don't speak. Now it's time for me to tell you a story, my story, the story of the House of Jodhra."

So I did, for one hundred and one nights, like an old Muslim fairy tale, seated on cushions leaning up against the jali, whispering to Salim Azad in his Rajput finery wonderful tales of dashing Kshatriya cavalry charges and thousand-cannon sieges of great fortresses, of handsome princes with bold moustaches and daring escapes with princesses in disguise in baskets over battlements, of princedoms lost over the fall of a chessman and Sandhurst-trained sowar officers more British than the British themselves and air-cav raids against Kashmiri insurgents and bold antiterrorist strikes; of great polo matches and spectacular durbars with a hundred elephants and the man-bird-sun kite of the Jodhras sailing up into the sky over Jaipur; for a thousand years our city. For one hundred nights I bound him with spells taught to me by the nutes of the Hijra Mahal, then on the one hundred and first night I said, "One thing you've forgotten."

"What?"

"To ask me to marry you."

He gave a little start, then waggled his head in disbelief and smiled. He had very good teeth.

"So, will you marry me?"

"Yes," I said. "Yes."

The day was set three weeks hence. Sul had judged it the most propitious for a wedding of dynasties. Suleyra had been commissioned to stage the ceremony: Muslim first, then Hindu. Janda had been asked to draw on yts celebrity inside knowledge to invite all India to the union of the houses of Azad and Jodhra. *This is the wedding of the decade,* yt cried in yts gupshup columns, *come or I will bad-mouth you.* Schedules of the great and glorious were rearranged, aeai soapi stars prepared avatars to attend, as did those human celebs who were unavoidably out of the subcontinent. From the shuttered jharokas of the zenana I watched Salim order his staff and machines around the great court, sending architects here, fabric designers there, pyrotechnicians yonder. Marquees and pavilions went up, seating was positioned, row upon row, carpet laid, patterns drawn in sand to be obliterated by the feet of the processional elephants. Security robots circled among the carrion-eating black kites over the palace, camera drones flitted like bats around the great court, seeking angles. Feeling my eyes on him, Salim would glance up at me, smile, lift his hand in the smallest greeting. I glanced away, suddenly shy, a girl-bride. This was to be a traditional, Rajputana wedding. I would emerge from purdah only to meet my husband. For those three weeks, the zenana was not a marble cage but an egg from which I would hatch. Into what? Power, unimaginable wealth, marriage to a man who had been my enemy. I still did not know if I loved him or not. I still saw the ghost shadows on the marble where his family had destroyed mine. He still came every night to read me Urdu poetry I could not understand. I smiled and laughed but I still did not know if what I felt was love, or just my desperation to be free. I still doubted it on the morning of my wedding.

Women came at dawn to bathe and dress me in wedding yellow and make up my hair and face and anoint me with turmeric paste. They decked me with jewels and necklaces, rings and bangles. They dabbed me with expensive perfume from France and gave me good-luck charms and advice. Then they threw open the brass-studded doors of the zenana and, with the palace guard of robots, escorted me along the corridors and down the stairs to the great court. Leel danced and somersaulted before me; no wedding could be lucky without a hijra, a nute.

All of India had been invited and all of India had come, in flesh and in avatar. People rose, applauding. Cameras swooped on ducted fans. My nutes, my family from the Hijra Mahal, had been given seats at row ends.

"How could I improve on perfection?" said Dahin the face doctor as my bare feet trod rose petals towards the dais.

"The window, the wedding!" said Sul. "And, pray the gods, many many decades from now, a very old and wise widow."

"The setting is nothing without the jewel," exclaimed Suleyra Party Arranger, throwing pink petals into the air.

I waited with my attendants under the awning as Salim's retainers crossed the courtyard from the men's quarters. Behind them came the groom on his pure white horse, kicking up the rose petals from its hooves. A low, broad *ooh* went up from the guests then more applause. The maulvi welcomed Salim onto the platform. Cameras flocked for angles. I noticed that every parapet and carving was crowded with monkeys—flesh and machine—watching. The maulvi asked me most solemnly if I wished to be Salim Azad's bride.

"Yes," I said, as I had said the night when I first accepted his offer. "I do, yes."

He asked Salim the same question, then read from the Holy Quran. We exchanged contracts, our assistants witnessed. The maulvi brought the silver plate of sweetmeats. Salim took one, lifted my gauze veil, and placed it on my tongue. Then the maulvi placed the rings upon our fingers and proclaimed us husband and wife. And so were our two warring houses united, as the guests rose from their seats cheering and festival crackers and fireworks burst over Jaipur and the city returned a roaring wall of vehicle horns. Peace in the streets at least. As we moved towards the long, cool pavilions for the wedding feast, I tried to catch Heer's eye as yt paced behind Salim. Yts hands were folded in the sleeves of yts robes, yts head thrust forwards, lips pursed. I thought of a perching vulture.

We sat side by side on golden cushions at the head of the long, low table. Guests great and good took their places, slipping off their Italian shoes, folding their legs and tucking up their expensive Delhi frocks as waiters brought vast thalis of festival food. In their balcony overlooking the Diwan, musicians struck up, a Rajput piece older than Jaipur itself. I clapped my hands. I had grown up to this tune. Salim leaned back on his bolster.

"And look."

Where he pointed, men were running up the great sun-bird-man kite of the Jodhras. As I watched, it skipped and dipped on the erratic winds in the court, then a stronger draught took it soaring up into the blue sky. The guests went *oooh* again.

"You have made me the happiest man in the world," Salim said.

I lifted my veil, bent to him, and kissed his lips. Every eye down the long table turned to me. Everyone smiled. Some clapped.

Salim's eyes went wide. Tears suddenly streamed from them. He rubbed them away and when he put his hands down, his eyelids were two puffy, blistered boils of flesh, swollen shut. He tried to speak but his lips were bloated, cracked, seeping blood and pus. Salim tried to stand, push himself away from me. He could not see, could not speak, could not breathe. His hands fluttered at the collar of his gold-embroidered sherwani.

"Salim!" I cried. Leel was already on yts feet, ahead of all the guest doctors and surgeons as they rose around the table. Salim let out a thin, high-pitched wail, the only scream that would form in his swollen throat. Then he went down onto the feast table.

The pavilion was full of screaming guests and doctors shouting into palmers and security staff locking the area down. I stood useless as a butterfly in my makeup and wedding jewels and finery as doctors crowded around Salim. His face was like a cracked melon, a tight bulb of red flesh. I swatted away an intrusive hovercam. It was the best I could do. Then I remember Leel and the other nutes taking me out into the courtyard where a tilt-jet was settling, engines sending the rose petals up in a perfumed blizzard. Paramedics carried Salim out from the pavilion on a gurney. He wore an oxygen rebreather. There were tubes in his arms. Security guards in light-scatter armour pushed the great and the celebrated aside. I struggled with Leel as the medics slid Salim into the tilt-jet but yt held me with strange, withered strength.

"Let me go, let me go, that's my husband—"

"Padmini, Padmini, there is nothing you can do."

"What do you mean?"

"Padmini, he is dead. Salim your husband is dead."

Yt might have said that the moon was a great mouse in the sky.

"Anaphylactic shock. Do you know what that is?"

"Dead?" I said simply, quietly. Then I was flying across the court towards the tilt-jet as it powered up. I wanted to dive under its engines. I wanted to be scattered like the rose petals. Security guards ran to cut me off but Leel caught me first and brought me down. I felt the nip of an efuser on my arm and everything went soft as the tranquilizer took me.

After three weeks I called Heer to me. For the first week the security robots had kept me locked back in the zenana while the lawyers argued. I spent much of that time out of my head, part grief-stricken, part insane at what had happened. Just one kiss. A widow no sooner than I was wed. Leel tended to me; the lawyers and judges reached their legal conclusions. I was the sole and lawful heir of Azad–Jodhra Water. The second week I came to terms with my inheritance: the biggest water company in Rajputana, the third largest in the whole of India. There were contracts to be signed, managers and executives to meet, deals to be set up. I waved them away, for the third week was my week, the week in which I understood what I had lost. And I understood what I had done, and how, and what I was. Then I was ready to talk to Heer.

We met in the Diwan, between the great silver jars that Salim, dedicated to his new tradition, had kept topped up with holy Ganga water. Guard-monkeys kept watch from the rooftops. My monkeys. My Diwan. My palace. My company, now. Heer's hands were folded in yts sleeves. Yts eyes were black marble. I wore widow's white—a widow, at age fifteen.

"How long had you planned it?"

"From before you were born. From before you were even conceived."

"I was always to marry Salim Azad."

"Yes."

"And kill him."

"You could not do anything but. You were designed that way."

*Always remember*, my father had said, here among these cool, shady pillars, *you are a weapon.* A weapon deeper, subtler than I had ever imagined, deeper even than Dahin's medical machines could look. A weapon down in the DNA: designed from conception to cause a fatal allergic reaction in any member of the Azad family. An assassin in my every cell, in every pore and hair, in every fleck of dust shed from my deadly skin.

I killed my beloved with a kiss.

I felt a huge, shuddering sigh inside me, a sigh I could never, must never utter.

"I called you a traitor when you said you had always been a loyal servant of the House of Jodhra."

"I was, am, and will remain so, please God." Heer dipped yts hairless head in a shallow bow. Then yt said, "When you become one of us, when you Step Away, you step away from so much: from your own family, from the hope of ever having children… You are my family, my children. All of you, but most of all you, Padmini. I did what I had to for my family, and now you survive, now you have all that is yours by right. We don't live long, Padmini. Our lives are too intense, too bright, too brilliant. There's been too much done to us. We burn out early. I had to see my family safe, my daughter triumph."

"Heer…"

Yt held up a hand, glanced away, I thought I saw silver in the corners of those black eyes.

"Take your palace, your company, it is all yours."

That evening I slipped away from my staff and guards. I went up the marble stairs to the long corridor where my room had been before I became a woman, and a wife, and a widow, and the owner of a great company. The door unlocked to my thumbprint; I swung it open into dust-hazy golden sunlight. The bed was still made, mosquito nets neatly knotted up. I crossed to the balcony. I expected the vines and creepers to have grown to a jungle; with a start I realized it was just over a year since I had slept here. I could still pick out the handholds and footholds where I had followed the steel monkey up onto the roof. I had an easier way there now. A door at the end of the corridor, previously locked to me, now opened onto a staircase. Sentry robots immediately bounced up as I stepped out onto the roof, crests raised, dart-throwers armed. A mudra from my hand sent them back into watching mode.

Once again I walked between the domes and turrets to the balcony at the very top of the palace façade. Again, Great Jaipur at my bare feet took my breath away. The pink city kindled and burned in the low evening light. The streets still roared with traffic; I could smell the hot oil and spices of the bazaar. I now knew how to find the domes of the Hijra Mahal among the confusion of streets and apartment buildings. The dials and half-domes and buttresses of the Jantar Mantar threw huge shadows over each other, a confusion of clocks. Then I turned towards the glass scimitar of the Azad Headquarters—my headquarters now, my palace as much as this dead old Rajput pile. I had brought that house crashing down, but not in any way I had imagined. I wanted to apologise to Salim as he had apologised to me, every night when he came to me in the zenana, for what his family had done. *They always told me I was a weapon. I thought I must become one; I never thought they had made me into one.*

How easy to step out over the traffic, step away from it all. Let it all end, Azad and Jodhra. Cheat Heer of yts victory. Then I saw my toes with their rings curl over the edge and I knew I could not, must not. I looked up and there, at the edge of vision, along the bottom of the red horizon, was a line of dark. The monsoon, coming at last. My family had made me one kind of weapon, but my other family, the kind, mad, sad, talented family of the nutes, had taught me, in their various ways, to be another weapon. The streets were dry but the rains were coming. I had reservoirs and canals and pumps and pipes in my power. I was Maharani of the Monsoon. Soon the people would need me. I took a deep breath and imagined I could smell the rain. Then I turned and walked back through the waiting robots to my kingdom.

# VIRGIN

## HOLLY BLACK

Holly Black is the author of the bestselling "The Spiderwick Chronicles." Her first story appeared in 1997, but she first garnered attention with her debut novel, *Tithe: A Modern Faerie Tale*. She has written six Spiderwick novels and two novels in her "Modern Faerie Tale" sequence, including Andre Norton Award winner *Valiant: A Modern Tale of Faerie*. Black's most recent book is the first in a second series of Spiderwick novels, *The Nixie's Song*. Upcoming is her first short story collection, *The Poison Eaters and Other Stories*.

Let me tell you something about unicorns—they're faeries and faeries aren't to be trusted. Read your storybooks. But maybe you can't get past the rainbows and pastels crap. That's your problem.

Zachary told me once why the old stories say that mortals who eat faerie food can't leave Faerie. That's a bunch of rot too, but at least there's some truth in it. You see, they *can* leave—they just won't ever be able to find another food they'll want to eat. Normal food tastes like ashes, so they starve. Zachary should have listened to his own stories.

I met him the summer I was squatting in an old building with my friend Tanya and her boyfriend. I'd run away from my last foster family, mostly because there didn't seem to be any point in staying. I was humoring myself into thinking I could live indefinitely like this.

Tanya had one prosthetic leg made from this shiny pink plastic stuff, so she looked like she was part Barbie doll, part girl. She loved to wear short, tight skirts and platform shoes to show her leg off. She knew the name of every boy who hung out in LOVE park—so called for the sculpture of the word, but best known for all the skaters that hung around. It was Tanya who introduced us.

My first impression of Zachary was that he was a beautiful junkie. He wasn't handsome; he was pretty, the kind of boy that girls draw obsessively in the corners of their notebooks. Tall, great cheekbones, and reddish black hair rolling down the sides of his face in fat curls. He was juggling a tennis ball, a fork, and three spoons. A cardboard sign next to his feet had "will juggle anything for food" written on it in an unsteady hand. *Anything* had been underlined shakily, twice. Junkie, I thought. I wondered if Tanya had ever slept with him. I wanted to ask her what it was like.

After he was done and had collected a little cash in a paper cup, he walked around with us for a while, mostly listening to Tanya tell him about her band. He had a bag over his shoulder and walked solemnly, hands in the pockets of his black jeans. He didn't look at her, although sometimes he nodded along with what she was saying, and he didn't look at me. He bought us ginger beer with the coins people had thrown at him, and that's when I knew he wasn't a junkie, because no junkie who looked as hard up as he did would spend his last quarters on anything but getting what he needed.

The next time I saw Zachary, it was at the public library. All us street kids would go there when we got cold. Sometimes I would go alone to read sections of *The Two Towers*, jotting down the page where I stopped on the inside hem of my jeans. I found him sitting on the floor between the mythology and psychiatry shelves. He looked up when I started walking down the aisle and we just stared at one another for a moment, like we'd been found doing something illicit. Then he grinned and I grinned. I sat down on the floor next to him.

"Just looking," I said. "What are you reading?" I had just run half the way to the library and could feel the sweat on my scalp. I knew I looked really awful. He looked dry, even cold. His skin was pale, as if he had never spent a day in the park.

He lifted up the book spread open across his lap: *Faerie Folktales of Europe*.

I was used to people who wouldn't shut up. I wasn't used to making conversation.

"You're Zachary, right?" I asked like an ass.

He looked up again. "Mmhmm. You're Jen, Tanya's friend."

"I didn't think you'd remember," I said, then felt stupid. He just smiled at me.

"What are you reading?" I stumbled over the words, realizing halfway through the sentence I'd already asked that. "I mean, what *part* are you reading?"

"I'm reading about unicorns," he said, "but there's not much here."

"They like virgins," I volunteered.

He sighed. "Yeah. They'd send out girls into the woods in front of the hunts to lure out the unicorn, get it to lie down, to sleep. Then they'd ride up and shoot it or stab it or slice off its horn. Can you imagine how that girl must have felt? The sharp horn pressing against her stomach, her ears straining to listen for the hounds."

I shifted uncomfortably. I didn't know anyone who talked like that. "You looking for something else about them?"

"I don't even know." He tucked some curls behind one ear. Then he grinned at me again.

All that summer was a fever dream, restless and achy. He was a part of it, meeting me in the park or at the library. I told him about my last foster home and

about the one before that, the one that had been really awful. I told him about
the boys I met and where we went to drink—up on rooftops. We talked about
where pigeons spent their winters and where we were going to spend ours. When
it was his turn to talk, he told stories. He told me ones I knew and old-sounding
ones I had never heard. It didn't matter that I spent the rest of the time begging
for cigarettes and hanging with hoodlums. When I was with Zachary, everything
seemed different.

Then one day, when it was kind of rainy and cold and we were scrounging in
our pockets for money for hot tea, I asked him where he slept.

"Outside the city, near the zoo."

"It must stink." I found another sticky dime in the folds of my backpack and
put it on the concrete ledge with our other change.

"Not so much. When the wind's right."

"So how come you live all the way out there? Do you live with someone?" It
felt strange that I didn't know.

He put some lint-encrusted pennies down and looked at me hard. His mouth
parted a little and he looked so intent that for a moment, I thought he was going to kiss me.

Instead he said, "Can I tell you something crazy? I mean totally insane."

"Sure. I've told you weird stuff before."

"Not like this. Really not like this."

"OK," I said.

And that's when he told me about her—a unicorn. His unicorn, whom he
lived with in a forest between two highways just outside the city, who waited
for him at night, and who ran free, hanging out with the forest animals or doing whatever it is unicorns do all day long, while Zachary told me stories and
scrounged for tea money.

"My mother . . . she was pretty screwed up. She sold drugs for some guys and
then she sold information on those guys to the cops. So one day when this car
pulled up and told us to get in, I guess I wasn't all that surprised. Her friend,
Gina, was already sitting in the back and she looked like she'd been crying. The
car smelled bad, like old frying oil.

"Mom kept begging them to drop me off and they kept silent, just driving. I
don't think I was really scared until we got on the highway.

"They made us get out of the car near some woods and then walk for a really
long time. The forest was huge. We were lost. I was tired. My mother dragged me
along by my hand. I kept falling over branches. Thorns wiped along my face.

"Then there was a loud pop and I started screaming from the sound even
before my mother fell. Gina puked."

I didn't know what to do, so I put my hand on his shoulder. His body was warm
underneath his thin T-shirt. He didn't even look at me as he talked.

"There isn't much more. They left me alone there with my dead mom in the
dark. Her eyes glistened in the moonlight. I wailed. You can imagine. It was awful.

I guess I remember a lot, really. I mean, it's vivid but trivial.

"After a long time, I saw this light coming through the trees. At first I thought it was the men coming back. Then I saw the horn—like bleached bone. Amazing, Jen. So amazing. I lifted up my hand to pet her side and blood spread across her flank. I forgot everything but that moment, everything but the white pelt, for a long, long while. It was like the whole world went white."

His face was flushed. We bought one big cup of tea with tons of honey and walked in the rain, passing the cup between us. He moved more restlessly than usual, but was quieter too.

"Tell me some more, Zachary," I said.

"I shouldn't have said what I did."

We walked silently for a while 'til the rain got too hard and we had to duck into the foyer of a church to wait it out.

"I believe you," I said.

He frowned. "What's wrong with you? What kind of idiot believes a story like that?"

I hadn't really considered whether I believed him or not. Sometimes people just tell you things and you have to accept that *they* believe them. It doesn't always matter if the stories are true.

I turned away and lit a cigarette. "So you lied?"

"No, of course not. Can we just talk about something else for a while?" he asked.

"Sure," I said, searching for something good. "I've been thinking about going home."

"To your jerk of a foster father and your slutty foster sisters?"

"The very ones. Where am I going to stay come winter otherwise?"

He mulled that over for a few minutes, watching the rain pound some illegally parked cars.

"How 'bout you squat libraries?" he said, grinning.

I grinned back. "I could find an elderly, distinguished, gentlemanly professor and totally throw myself at him. Offer to be his Lolita."

We stood awhile more before I said, "Maybe you should hang with people, even if they're assholes. You could stay with me tonight."

He shook his head, looking at the concrete.

And that was that.

I told Tanya about Zachary and the unicorn that night while we waited for Bobby Diablo to come over. Telling it, the story became a lot funnier than it had been with Zachary's somber black eyes on mine. Tanya and I laughed so hard that I started to choke.

"Look," she said. "Zach's entertainingly crazy. Everybody loves him. But he's craz-*az*-azy. Like last summer, he said that he could tell if it was going to rain by how many times he dropped stuff." She grinned. "Besides, he looks like a girl."

"And he's into unicorns." I thought about how I'd felt when I thought he was about to kiss me. "Maybe I like girly."

She pointed to a paperback of *The Hobbit* with a dragon on the torn remains of the cover. "Maybe you like crazy."

I rolled my eyes.

"Seriously," she said. "Reading that stuff would depress me. People like us, we're not in those kinds of books. They're not *for* us."

I stared at her. It might have been the worst thing anybody had ever said to me, because no matter how much I thought about it, I couldn't make it feel any less true.

But when I was around Zachary, it had seemed possible that those stories were for me, as if it didn't matter where I came from, as if there were something heroic and special and magical about living on the street. Right then, I hated him for being crazy—hated him more than I hated Tanya, who was just pointing out the obvious.

"What do you think really happened?" I asked finally, because I had to say something eventually. "With his mom? Why would he tell me a story about a *unicorn?*"

She shrugged. She wasn't big on introspection. "He just needs to get laid."

Later on, while Bobby Diablo tried to put his hands up Tanya's halter top before her boyfriend came back from the store and I tried to pretend I didn't hear her giggling yelps, while the whiskey burned my throat raw and smooth, I had a black epiphany. There were rules to things, even to delusions. And if you broke those rules, there were consequences. I lay down on the stinking rug and breathed in cigarette smoke and incense, measuring out my miracle.

The next afternoon, I left Tanya and her boyfriend tangled around one another. The cold gray sky hung over me. Zachary was going to hate me, I thought, but that only made me walk faster through the gates to the park. When I finally found him, he was throwing bits of bread to some wet rats. The rodents scattered when I got close.

"I thought those things were bold as hustlers," I said.

"No, they're shy." He tossed the remaining pieces in the air, juggling them. Each throw was higher than the last.

"You're a virgin, aren't you?"

He looked at me like I'd hit him. The bits of bread kept moving though, as if his hands were separate from the rest of him.

That night I followed Zachary home through the winding urine-stained tunnels of the subway and the crowded trains themselves. I was always one car behind, watching him through the milky, scratched glass between the cars. I followed him as he changed trains, hiding behind a newspaper like a cheesy TV cop. I followed him all the way from the park through the edge of a huge cemetery where the stink of the zoo carried in the breeze. By then, I couldn't understand how he didn't hear me rustling behind him, what with the newspaper long gone and me hiking up my backpack every ten minutes. But Zachary doesn't exactly live in the here and now, and for once I had to be glad for that.

Then we came to a patch of woods and I hesitated. It reminded me of where my foster family lived, where the trees always seemed a menacing border to every strip mall. There were weird sounds all around and it was impossible to walk quietly. I forced myself to crunch along behind him in the very dark dark.

Finally, we stopped. A canopy of thick branches hung in front of him, their leaves dragging on the forest floor. I couldn't see anything much there, but it did seem like there was a slight light. He turned, either reflexively or because he had heard me after all, but his face stayed blank. He parted the branches with his hands and ducked under them. My heart was beating madly in my chest, that too-much-caffeine drumming. I crept up and tried not to think too hard, because right then I wished I were in Tanya's apartment watching her snort whatever, the way you're supposed to wish for Mom's apple pie.

I wasn't cold; I had brought Tanya's boyfriend's thick jacket. I fumbled around in the pocket and found a big, dirty knife, which I opened and closed to make myself feel safer. I thought about walking back, but if I got lost I would absolutely freak out. I thought about going under the branches into Zachary's house, but I didn't know what to expect, and for some reason that scared me more than the darkness.

He came out then, looked around, and whispered, "Jen."

I stood up. I was so relieved that I didn't even hesitate. His eyes were red-rimmed, as if he had been crying. He extended one hand to me.

"God, it's scary out here," I said.

He put one finger to his lips.

He didn't ask me why I'd followed him; he just took my hand and led me farther into the forest. When we stopped, he just looked at me. He swallowed as if his throat were sore. This was my idea, I reminded myself.

"Sit down," I said, and smiled.

"You want me to sit?" He sounded reassuringly like himself.

"Well, take off your pants first."

He looked at me incredulously, but he started to do it.

"Underwear too," I said. I was nervous. Oh boy, was I nervous. Mostly I had been drunk all the times before, or I had done what was expected of me. Never, never had I seduced a boy. I started to unlace my work boots.

"I can't," he said, looking toward the faint light.

"You don't want to?" I took one of his hands and set it on my hip.

His fingers dug into my skin, pulling me closer.

"Why are you doing this?" His voice sounded husky.

I didn't answer. I couldn't. It didn't seem to matter anyway. His hands—those juggling hands that didn't seem to care what he was thinking—fumbled with the buttons of my jeans. We didn't kiss. He didn't close his eyes.

Leaves rustled and I could smell that rich, wet storm smell in the air. The wind picked up around us.

Zachary looked up at me and then past my face. His features stiffened. I turned and saw a white horse with muddy hooves. For a moment, it seemed funny. It was just a horse. Then she bolted. She cut through the forest so fast that all I could see was a shape—a cutout of white paper—still running.

I could feel his breath on my mouth. It was the closest our faces had ever been. His eyes stared at nothing, watching for another flash of white.

"Do you want to get your stuff?" I asked, stepping back from him.

He shook his head.

"What about your clothes?"

"It doesn't matter."

"I'll get them," I said, starting for the tree.

"No, don't," he said, so I didn't.

"Let's go back." I said.

He nodded, but he was still looking after where she had run.

We walked back, through the forest, and then the graveyard, back, back to the comforting stink of urine and cigarettes. Back to the sulfur of buses that run all night. Back to people who hassle you because you forgot your work boots in the enchanted forest where you cursed your best friend to live a life as small as your own.

I brought Zachary back to Tanya's. She was used to extra people crashed out there, so she didn't pay us any mind. Besides, Bobby was over. That night Zachary couldn't eat much, and what he did eat wouldn't stay down. I watched him, bent over her toilet, puking his guts out. After, he sat by the window, watching the swirling patterns of traffic while I huddled in the corner, letting numbness overtake me. Bobby and Tanya were rolling on the floor, wrestling. Finally Bobby pulled off Tanya's shorts right in front of the both of us. Zachary watched them in horrified fascination. He just stared. Then he started to cry, just a little, in his fist.

I fell asleep sometime around that.

When I woke up, he was juggling books, making them seem like they were flying. Tanya came in and gave him a tiny, plastic unicorn.

"Juggle this," she said.

He dropped the books. One hit me on the shin, but I didn't make a sound. When he looked at me, his face was empty, as if he wasn't even surprised to be betrayed. I felt sick.

Three days he lived there with me. Bobby taught him how to roll a joint perfectly and smoke without coughing. Tanya's boyfriend let him borrow his old guitar and Zachary screwed around with it all that second day. He laughed when we did, but always a little late, as though it were an afterthought. The next night, he told me he was leaving.

"But the unicorn's gone," I said.

"I'll find her."

"You're going to hunt her? Like one of those guys in the unicorn tapestries?" I tried to keep my voice from shaking. "She doesn't want you anymore."

He shook his head, but he didn't look at me, as if I were the crazy one, the one with the problem.

I took a deep breath. "Unicorns don't exist. I saw her. She was a horse. A white horse. She didn't have a horn."

"Of course she did," he said and kissed me. It was a quick kiss, an awful kiss really—his teeth bumped mine and his lips were chapped—but I still remember every bit of it.

That fall, I took my stuff and went back to my foster home. They yelled at me and demanded to know where I'd been, but in the end they let me stay. I didn't tell them anything.

I went back to school sometime around Halloween. I still read a lot, but now I'm careful about the books I choose. I don't let myself think about Zachary. I turn on the television. I turn it up loud. I force my dinner out of cardboard boxes and swallow it down. Never mind that it turns to ash in my mouth.

# PRIDE AND PROMETHEUS

## JOHN KESSEL

John Kessel was born in Buffalo, New York, in 1950 and lives in Raleigh, North Carolina, where he is professor of American literature at North Carolina State University. A writer of erudite short fiction that often make reference to, or are pastiches of, popular culture, Kessel made his first sale in 1975, and is best known for early stories "Another Orphan" and "Buffalo." He has published a series of constantly impressive short fiction, including a series of screwball comedies featuring series character Detlev Gruber, the most recent of which is "It's All True," and a series of science fiction stories set in the same world as recent Sturgeon Award nominee "The Juniper Tree." Kessel's short fiction has been collected in three volumes: *Meeting In Infinity*, *The Pure Product*, and *The Baum Plan for Financial Independence and Other Stories*, and he has published three novels: *Freedom Beach* (with James Patrick Kelly), *Good News from Outer Space*, and *Corrupting Dr. Nice*.

Had both her mother and her sister Kitty not insisted upon it, Miss Mary Bennet, whose interest in Nature did not extend to the Nature of Society, would not have attended the ball in Grosvenor Square. This was Kitty's season. Mrs. Bennet had despaired of Mary long ago, but still bore hopes for her younger sister, and so had set her determined mind on putting Kitty in the way of Robert Sidney of Detling Manor, who possessed a fortune of six thousand pounds a year, and was likely to be at that evening's festivities. Being obliged by her unmarried state to live with her parents, and the whims of Mrs. Bennet being what they were, although there was no earthly reason for Mary to be there, there was no good excuse for her absence.

So it was that Mary found herself in the ballroom of the great house, trussed up in a silk dress with her hair piled high, bedecked with her sister's jewels. She was neither a beauty, like her older and happily married sister Jane, nor witty, like her older and happily married sister Elizabeth, nor flirtatious, like her younger and less happily married sister Lydia. Awkward and nearsighted, she had never cut an attractive figure, and as she had aged she had come to see herself as others saw her. Every time Mrs. Bennet told her to stand up straight, she felt despair. Mary had seen how Jane and Elizabeth had made good lives for themselves by finding appropriate mates. But there was no air of grace or mystery about Mary, and no man ever looked upon her with admiration.

Kitty's card was full, and she had already contrived to dance once with the distinguished Mr. Sidney, then whom Mary could not imagine a being more tedious. Hectically glowing, Kitty was certain that this was the season she would get a husband. Mary, in contrast, sat with her mother and her Aunt Gardiner, whose good sense was Mary's only respite from her mother's silliness. After the third minuet Kitty came flying over.

"Catch your breath, Kitty!" Mrs. Bennet said. "Must you rush about like this? Who is that young man you danced with? Remember, we are here to smile on Mr. Sidney, not on some stranger. Did I see him arrive with the Lord Mayor?"

"How can I tell you what you saw, Mother?"

"Don't be impertinent."

"Yes. He is an acquaintance of the Mayor. He's from Switzerland! Mr. Clerval, on holiday."

The tall, fair-haired Clerval stood with a darker, brooding young man, both impeccably dressed in dove-gray breeches, black jackets, and waistcoats, with white tie and gloves.

"Switzerland! I would not have you marry any Dutchman—though 'tis said their merchants are uncommonly wealthy. And who is that gentleman with whom he speaks?"

"I don't know, Mother—but I can find out."

Mrs. Bennet's curiosity was soon to be relieved, as the two men crossed the drawing room to the sisters and their chaperones.

"Henry Clerval, madame," the fair-haired man said, "and this is my good friend Mr. Victor Frankenstein."

Mr. Frankenstein bowed but said nothing. He had the darkest eyes that Mary had ever encountered, and an air of being there only on obligation. Whether this was because he was as uncomfortable in these social situations as she, Mary could not tell, but his diffident air intrigued her. She fancied his reserve might bespeak sadness rather than pride. His manners were faultless, as was his command of English, though he spoke with a slight French accent. When he asked Mary to dance she suspected he did so only at the urging of Mr. Clerval; on the floor, once the orchestra of pianoforte, violin, and cello struck up the quadrille, he moved with some grace but no trace of a smile.

At the end of the dance, Frankenstein asked whether Mary would like some refreshment, and they crossed from the crowded ballroom to the sitting room, where he procured for her a cup of negus. Mary felt obliged to make some conversation before she should retreat to the safety of her wallflower's chair.

"What brings you to England, Mr. Frankenstein?"

"I come to meet with certain natural philosophers here in London, and in Oxford—students of magnetism."

"Oh! Then have you met Professor Langdon, of the Royal Society?"

Frankenstein looked at her as if seeing her for the first time. "How is it that you are acquainted with Professor Langdon?"

"I am not personally acquainted with him, but I am, in my small way, an enthusiast of the sciences. You are a natural philosopher?"

"I confess that I can no longer countenance the subject. But yes, I did study with Mr. Krempe and Mr. Waldman in Ingolstadt."

"You no longer countenance the subject, yet you seek out Professor Langdon."

A shadow swept over Mr. Frankenstein's handsome face. "It is unsupportable to me, yet pursue it I must."

"A paradox."

"A paradox that I am unable to explain, Miss Bennet."

All this said in a voice heavy with despair. Mary watched his sober black eyes, and replied, "'The heart has its reasons of which reason knows nothing.'"

For the second time that evening he gave her a look that suggested an understanding. Frankenstein sipped from his cup, then spoke: "Avoid any pastime, Miss Bennet, that takes you out of the normal course of human contact. If the study to which you apply yourself has a tendency to weaken your affections, and to destroy your taste for simple pleasures, then that study is certainly unlawful."

The purport of this extraordinary speech Mary was unable to fathom. "Surely there is no harm in seeking knowledge."

Mr. Frankenstein smiled. "Henry has been urging me to go out into London society; had I known that I might meet such a thoughtful person as yourself I would have taken him up on it long 'ere now."

He took her hand. "But I spy your aunt at the door," he said. "No doubt she has been dispatched to protect you. If you will, please let me return you to your mother. I must thank you for the dance, and even more for your conversation, Miss Bennet. In the midst of a foreign land, you have brought me a moment of sympathy."

And again Mary sat beside her mother and aunt as she had half an hour before. She was nonplused. It was not seemly for a stranger to speak so much from the heart to a woman he had never previously met, yet she could not find it in herself to condemn him. Rather, she felt her own failure in not keeping him longer.

A cold March rain was falling when, after midnight, they left the ball. They waited under the portico while the coachman brought round the carriage. Kitty began coughing. As they stood there in the chill night, Mary noticed a hooded man, of enormous size, standing in the shadows at the corner of the lane. Full in the downpour, unmoving, he watched the town house and its partiers without coming closer or going away, as if this observation were all his intention in life. Mary shivered.

In the carriage back to Aunt Gardiner's home near Belgravia, Mrs. Bennet insisted that Kitty take the lap robe against the chill. "Stop coughing, Kitty. Have a care for my poor nerves." She added, "They should never have put the supper at the end of that long hallway. The young ladies, flushed from the dance, had to walk all that cold way."

Kitty drew a ragged breath and leaned over to Mary. "I have never seen you so taken with a man, Mary. What did that Swiss gentleman say to you?"

"We spoke of natural philosophy."

"Did he say nothing of the reasons he came to England?" Aunt Gardiner asked.

"That was his reason."

"That's not so!" said Kitty. "He came to forget his grief! His little brother William was murdered, not six months ago, by the family maid!"

"How terrible!" said Aunt Gardiner.

Mrs. Bennet asked in open astonishment, "Could this be true?"

"I have it from Lucy Copeland, the Lord Mayor's daughter," Kitty replied. "Who heard it from Mr. Clerval himself. And there is more! He is engaged to be married—to his cousin. Yet he has abandoned her, left her in Switzerland and come here instead."

"Did he say anything to you about these matters?" Mrs. Bennet asked Mary.

Kitty interrupted. "Mother, he's not going to tell the family secrets to strangers, let alone reveal his betrothal at a dance."

Mary wondered at these revelations. Perhaps they explained Mr. Frankenstein's odd manner. But could they explain his interest in her? "A man should be what he seems," she said.

Kitty snorted, and it became a cough.

"Mark me, girls," said Mrs. Bennet, "that engagement is a match that he does not want. I wonder what fortune he would bring to a marriage?"

In the days that followed, Kitty's cough became a full-blown catarrh, and it was decided against her protest that, the city air being unhealthy, they should cut short their season and return to Meryton. Mr. Sidney was undoubtedly unaware of his narrow escape. Mary could not honestly say that she regretted leaving, though the memory of her half hour with Mr. Frankenstein gave her as much regret at losing the chance of further commerce with him as she had ever felt from her acquaintance with a man.

Within a week Kitty was feeling better, and repining bitterly their remove from London. In truth, she was only two years younger than Mary and had made none of the mental accommodations to approaching spinsterhood that her older sister had attempted. Mr. Bennet retreated to his study, emerging only at mealtimes to cast sardonic comments about Mrs. Bennet and Kitty's marital campaigns. Perhaps, Mrs. Bennet said, they might invite Mr. Sidney to visit Longbourn when Parliament adjourned. Mary escaped these discussions by practicing the pianoforte and, as the advancing spring brought warm weather, taking walks in the countryside, where she would stop beneath an oak and read, indulging her passion for Goethe and German philosophy. When she tried to engage her father in speculation, he warned her, "I am afraid, my dear, that your understanding is too dependent on books and not enough on experience of the world. Beware, Mary. Too much learning makes a woman monstrous."

What experience of the world had they ever allowed her? Rebuffed, Mary wrote to Elizabeth about the abrupt end of Kitty's latest assault on marriage, and her subsequent ill temper, and Elizabeth wrote back inviting her two younger sisters to come visit Pemberley.

Mary was overjoyed to have the opportunity to escape her mother and see something more of Derbyshire, and Kitty seemed equally willing. Mrs. Bennet was not persuaded when Elizabeth suggested that nearby Matlock and its baths might be good for Kitty's health (no man would marry a sickly girl), but she was persuaded by Kitty's observation that, though it could in no way rival London, Matlock did attract a finer society than sleepy Meryton, and thus offered opportunities for meeting eligible young men of property. So in the second week of May, Mr. and Mrs. Bennet tearfully loaded their last unmarried daughters into a coach for the long drive to Derbyshire. Mrs. Bennet's tears were shed because their absence would deprive Kitty and Mary of her attentions, Mr. Bennet's for the fact that their absence would assure him of Mrs. Bennet's.

The two girls were as ever delighted by the grace and luxury of Pemberley, Mr. Darcy's ancestral estate. Darcy was kindness itself, and the servants attentive, if, at the instruction of Elizabeth, less indulgent of Kitty's whims and more careful of her health than the thoroughly cowed servants at home. Lizzy saw that Kitty got enough sleep, and the three sisters took long walks in the grounds of the estate. Kitty's health improved, and Mary's spirits rose. Mary enjoyed the company of Lizzy and Darcy's eight-year-old son William, who was attempting to teach her and Darcy's younger sister Georgiana to fish. Georgiana pined after her betrothed, Captain Broadbent, who was away on crown business in the Caribbean, but after they had been there a week, Jane and her husband Mr. Bingley came for an extended visit from their own estate thirty miles away, and so four of the five Bennet sisters were reunited. They spent many cordial afternoons and evenings. Both Mary and Georgiana were accomplished at the pianoforte, though Mary had come to realize that her sisters tolerated more than enjoyed her playing. The reunion of Lizzy and Jane meant even more time devoted to Kitty's improvement, with specific attention to her marital prospects, and left Mary feeling invisible. Still, on occasion she would join them and drive into Lambton or Matlock to shop and socialize, and every week during the summer a ball was held in the assembly room of the Old Bath Hotel, with its beeswax polished floor and splendid chandeliers.

On one such excursion to Matlock, Georgiana stopped at the milliners while Kitty pursued some business at the butcher's shop—Mary wondered at her sudden interest in Pemberley's domestic affairs—and Mary took William to the museum and circulating library, which contained celebrated cabinets of natural history. William had told her of certain antiquities unearthed in the excavation for a new hotel and recently added to the collection.

The streets, hotels, and inns of Matlock bustled with travelers there to take the waters. Newly wedded couples leaned on one another's arms, whispering secrets that no doubt concerned the alpine scenery. A crew of workmen was breaking up the cobblestone street in front of the hall, swinging pickaxes in the bright sun. Inside she and Will retreated to the cool quiet of the public exhibition room.

Among the visitors to the museum Mary spied a slender, well-dressed man at one of the display cases, examining the artifacts contained there. As she drew near, Mary recognized him. "Mr. Frankenstein!"

The tall European looked up, startled. "Ah—Miss Bennet?"

She was pleased that he remembered. "Yes. How good to see you."

"And this young man is?"

"My nephew, William."

At the mention of this name, Frankenstein's expression darkened. He closed his eyes. "Are you not well?" Mary asked.

He looked at her again. "Forgive me. These antiquities call to mind sad associations. Give me a moment."

"Certainly," she said. William ran off see the hall's steam clock. Mary turned and examined the contents of the neighboring cabinet.

Beneath the glass was a collection of bones that had been unearthed in the local lead mines. The card lettered beside them read: *Bones, resembling those of a fish, made of limestone.*

Eventually Frankenstein came to stand beside her. "How is it that you are come to Matlock?" he inquired.

"My sister Elizabeth is married to Mr. Fitzwilliam Darcy, of Pemberley. Kitty and I are here on a visit. Have you come to take the waters?"

"Clerval and I are on our way to Scotland, where he will stay with friends, while I pursue—certain investigations. We rest here a week. The topography of the valley reminds me of my home in Switzerland."

"I have heard it said so," she replied. Frankenstein seemed to have regained his composure, but Mary wondered still at what had awakened his grief. "You have an interest in these relics?" she asked, indicating the cabinets.

"Some, perhaps. I find it remarkable to see a young lady take an interest in such arcana." Mary detected no trace of mockery in his voice.

"Indeed, I do," she said, indulging her enthusiasm. "Professor Erasmus Darwin has written of the source of these bones:

"Organic life beneath the shoreless waves
Was born and nurs'd in ocean's pearly caves;
First forms minute, unseen by spheric glass,
Move on the mud, or pierce the watery mass;
These, as successive generations bloom,
New powers acquire and larger limbs assume;

Whence countless groups of vegetation spring,
And breathing realms of fin and feet and wing.

"People say this offers proof of the great flood. Do you think, Mr. Frankenstein, that Matlock could once have been under the sea? They say these are creatures that have not existed since the time of Noah."

"Far older than the flood, I'll warrant. I do not think that these bones were originally made of stone. Some process has transformed them. Anatomically, they are more like those of a lizard than a fish."

"You have studied anatomy?"

Mr. Frankenstein tapped his fingers upon the glass of the case. "Three years gone by it was one of my passions. I no longer pursue such matters."

"And yet, sir, you met with men of science in London."

"Ah—yes, I did. I am surprised that you remember a brief conversation, more than two months ago."

"I have a good memory."

"As evidenced by your quoting Professor Darwin. I might expect a woman such as yourself to take more interest in art than science."

"Oh, you may rest assured that I have read my share of novels. And even more, in my youth, of sermons. Elizabeth is wont to tease me for a great moralizer. 'Evil is easy,' I tell her, 'and has infinite forms.'"

Frankenstein did not answer. Finally he said, "Would that the world had no need of moralizers."

Mary recalled his warning against science from their London meeting. "Come, Mr. Frankenstein. There is no evil in studying God's handiwork."

"A God-fearing Christian might take exception to Professor Darwin's assertion that life began in the sea, no matter how poetically stated." His voice became distant. "Can a living soul be created without the hand of God?"

"It is my feeling that the hand of God is everywhere present." Mary gestured toward the cabinet. "Even in the bones of this stony fish."

"Then you have more faith than I, Miss Bennet—or more innocence."

Mary blushed. She was not used to bantering in this way with a gentleman. In her experience, handsome and accomplished men took no interest in her, and such conversations as she had engaged in offered little of substance other than the weather, clothes, and town gossip. Yet she saw that she had touched Frankenstein, and felt something akin to triumph.

They were interrupted by the appearance of Georgiana and Kitty, entering with Henry Clerval. "There you are!" said Kitty. "You see, Mr. Clerval, I told you we would find Mary poring over these heaps of bones!"

"And it is no surprise to find my friend here as well," said Clerval.

Mary felt quite deflated. The party moved out of the town hall and in splendid sunlight along the North Parade. Kitty proposed, and the visitors acceded to, a stroll on the so-called Lover's Walk beside the river. As they walked along the gorge, vast ramparts of limestone rock, clothed with yew trees, elms, and limes, rose up on either side of the river. William ran ahead, and Kitty, Georgiana, and Clerval followed, leaving Frankenstein and Mary behind. Eventually they came in sight of the High Tor, a sheer cliff rearing its brow on the east bank of the Derwent. The lower part was covered with small trees and foliage. Massive boulders that had fallen from the cliff broke the riverbed below into foaming rapids. The noise of the waters left Mary and Frankenstein, apart from the others, as isolated as if they had been in a separate room. Frankenstein spent a long time gazing at the scenery. Mary's mind raced, seeking some way to recapture the mood of their conversation in the town hall.

"How this reminds me of my home," he said. "Henry and I would climb such cliffs as this, chase goats around the meadows and play at pirates. Father would walk me though the woods and name every tree and flower. I once saw a lightning bolt shiver an old oak to splinters."

"Whenever I come here," Mary blurted out, "I realize how small I am, and how great time is. We are here for only seconds, and then we are gone, and these rocks, this river, will long survive us. And through it all we are alone."

Frankenstein turned toward her. "Surely you are not so lonely. You have your family, your sisters. Your mother and father."

"One can be alone in a room of people. Kitty mocks me for my 'heaps of bones.'"

"A person may marry."

"I am twenty-eight years old, sir. I am no man's vision of a lover or wife."

What had come over her, to say this aloud, for the first time in her life? Yet what did it matter what she said to this foreigner? There was no point in letting some hope for sympathy delude her into greater hopes. They had danced a single dance in London, and now they spent an afternoon together; soon he would leave England, marry his cousin, and Mary would never see him again. She deserved Kitty's mockery.

Frankenstein took some time before answering, during which Mary was acutely aware of the sound of the waters, and of the sight of Georgiana, William, and Clerval playing in the grass by the river bank, while Kitty stood pensive some distance away.

"Miss Bennet, I am sorry if I have made light of your situation. But your fine qualities should be apparent to anyone who took the trouble truly to make your acquaintance. Your knowledge of matters of science only adds to my admiration."

"You needn't flatter me," said Mary. "I am unused to it."

"I do not flatter," Frankenstein replied. "I speak my own mind."

William came running up. "Aunt Mary! This would be an excellent place to fish! We should come here with Father!"

"That's a good idea, Will."

Frankenstein turned to the others. "We must return to the hotel, Henry," he told Clerval. "I need to see that new glassware properly packed before shipping it ahead."

"Very well."

"Glassware?" Georgiana asked.

Clerval chuckled. "Victor has been purchasing equipment at every stop along our tour—glassware, bottles of chemicals, lead and copper disks. The coachmen threaten to leave us behind if he does not ship these things separately."

Kitty argued in vain, but the party walked back to Matlock. The women and William met the carriage to take them back to Pemberley. "I hope I see you again, Miss Bennet," Frankenstein said. Had she been more accustomed to reading the emotions of others she would have ventured that his expression held sincere interest—even longing.

On the way back to Pemberley William prattled with Georgiana, Kitty, subdued for once, leaned back with her eyes closed, while Mary puzzled over every moment of the afternoon. The fundamental sympathy she had felt with Frankenstein in their brief London encounter had been only reinforced. His sudden dark moods, his silences, bespoke some burden he carried. Mary was almost convinced that her mother was right—that Frankenstein did not love his cousin, and that he was here in England fleeing from her. How could this second meeting with him be chance? Fate had brought them together.

At dinner that evening, Kitty told Darcy and Elizabeth about their encounter with the handsome Swiss tourists. Later, Mary took Lizzy aside and asked her to invite Clerval and Frankenstein to dinner.

"This is new!" said Lizzy. "I expected this from Kitty, but not you. You have never before asked to have a young man come to Pemberley."

"I have never met someone quite like Mr. Frankenstein," Mary replied.

"Have you taken the Matlock waters?" Mary asked Clerval, who was seated opposite her at the dinner table. "People in the parish say that a dip in the hot springs could raise the dead."

"I confess that I have not," Clerval said. "Victor does not believe in their healing powers."

Mary turned to Frankenstein, hoping to draw him into discussion of the matter, but the startled expression on his face silenced her.

The table, covered with a blinding white damask tablecloth, glittered with silver and crystal. A large epergne, studded with lit beeswax candles, dominated its center. In addition to the family members, and in order to even the number of guests and balance female with male, Darcy and Elizabeth had invited the vicar, Mr. Chatsworth. Completing the dinner party were Bingley and Jane, Georgiana, and Kitty.

The footmen brought soup, followed by claret, turbot with lobster and Dutch sauce, oyster pâté, lamb cutlets with asparagus, peas, a fricandeau a l'oseille, venison, stewed beef a la jardinière, with various salads, beetroot, French and

English mustard. Two ices, cherry water and pineapple cream, and a chocolate cream with strawberries. Champagne flowed throughout the dinner, and Madeira afterward.

Darcy inquired of Mr. Clerval's business in England, and Clerval told of his meetings with men of business in London, and his interest in India. He had even begun the study of the language, and for their entertainment spoke a few sentences in Hindi. Darcy told of his visit to Geneva a decade ago. Clerval spoke charmingly of the differences in manners between the Swiss and the English, with witty preference for English habits, except, he said, in the matter of boiled meats. Georgiana asked about women's dress on the continent. Elizabeth allowed as how, if they could keep him safe, it would be good for William's education to tour the continent. Kitty, who usually dominated the table with bright talk and jokes, was unaccustomedly quiet. The vicar spoke amusingly of his travels in Italy.

Through all of this, Frankenstein offered little in the way of response or comment. Mary had put such hopes on this dinner, and now she feared she had misread him. His voice warmed but once, when he spoke of his father, a counselor and syndic, renowned for his integrity. Only on inquiry would he speak of his years in Ingolstadt.

"And what did you study in the university?" Bingley asked.

"Matters of no interest," Frankenstein replied.

An uncomfortable silence followed. Clerval gently explained, "My friend devoted himself so single-mindedly to the study of natural philosophy that his health failed. I was fortunately able to bring him back to us, but it was a near thing."

"For which I will ever be grateful to you," Frankenstein mumbled.

Lizzy attempted to change the subject. "Reverend Chatsworth, what news is there of the parish?"

The vicar, unaccustomed to such volume and variety of drink, was in his cups, his face flushed and his voice rising to pulpit volume. "Well, I hope the ladies will not take it amiss," he boomed, "if I tell about a curious incident that occurred last night!"

"Pray do."

"So, then—last night I was troubled with sleeplessness—I think it was the trout I ate for supper, it was not right—Mrs. Croft vowed she had purchased it just that afternoon, but I wonder if perhaps it might have been from the previous day's catch. Be that as it may, lying awake some time after midnight, I thought I heard a scraping out my bedroom window—the weather has been so fine of late that I sleep with my window open. It is my opinion, Mr. Clerval, that nothing aids the lungs more than fresh air, and I believe that is the opinion of the best continental thinkers, is it not? The air is exceedingly fresh in the alpine meadows, I am told?"

"Only in those meadows where the cows have not been feeding."

"The cows? Oh, yes, the cows—ha, ha!— very good! The cows, indeed! So, where was I? Ah, yes. I rose from my bed and looked out the window, and what did I spy but a light in the churchyard. I threw on my robe and slippers and hurried out to see what might be the matter.

"As I approached the churchyard I saw a dark figure wielding a spade. His back was to me, silhouetted by a lamp which rested beside Nancy Brown's grave. Poor Nancy, dead not a week now, so young, only seventeen."

"A man?" said Kitty.

The vicar's round face grew serious. "You may imagine my shock. 'Halloo!' I shouted. At that the man dropped his spade, seized the lantern, and dashed 'round the back of the church. By the time I had reached the corner he was out of sight. Back at the grave I saw that he had been on a fair way to unearthing poor Nancy's coffin!"

"My goodness!" said Jane.

"Defiling a grave?" asked Bingley. "I am astonished."

Darcy said nothing, but his look demonstrated that he was not pleased by the vicar bringing such an uncouth matter to his dinner table. Frankenstein, sitting next to Mary, put down his knife and took a long draught of Madeira.

The vicar lowered his voice. He was clearly enjoying himself. "I can only speculate on what motive this man might have had. Could it have been some lover of hers, overcome with grief?"

"No man is so faithful," Kitty said.

"My dear vicar," said Lizzy. "You have read too many of Mrs. Radcliffe's novels."

Darcy leaned back in his chair. "Gypsies have been seen in the woods about the quarry. It was no doubt their work. They were seeking jewelry."

"Jewelry?" the vicar said. "The Browns had barely enough money to see her decently buried."

"Which proves that whoever did this was not a local man."

Clerval spoke. "At home, fresh graves are sometimes defiled by men providing cadavers to doctors. Was there not a spate of such grave robbings in Ingolstadt, Victor?"

Frankenstein put down his glass. "Yes," he said. "Some anatomists, in seeking knowledge, will abandon all human scruple."

"I do not think that is likely to be the cause in this instance," Darcy observed. "Here there is no university, no medical school. Doctor Phillips, in Lambton, is no transgressor of civilized rules."

"He is scarcely a transgressor of his own threshold," said Lizzy. "One must call him a day in advance to get him to leave his parlor."

"Rest assured, there are such men," said Frankenstein. "I have known them. My illness, as Henry has described to you, was in some way my spirit's rebellion against the understanding that the pursuit of knowledge will lead some men into mortal peril."

Here was Mary's chance to impress Frankenstein. "Surely there is a nobility in risking one's life to advance the claims of one's race. With how many things are we upon the brink of becoming acquainted, if cowardice or carelessness did not restrain our inquiries?"

"Then I thank God for cowardice and carelessness, Miss Bennet," Frankenstein said, "One's life, perhaps, is worth risking, but not one's soul."

"True enough. But I believe that science may demand our relaxing the strictures of common society."

"We have never heard this tone from you, Mary," Jane said.

Darcy interjected, "You are becoming quite modern, sister. What strictures are you prepared to abandon for us tonight?" His voice was full of the gentle condescension with which he treated Mary at all times.

How she wished to surprise them! How she longed to show Darcy and Lizzy, with their perfect marriage and perfect lives, that she was not the simple old maid they thought her. "Anatomists in London have obtained the court's permission to dissect the bodies of criminals after execution. Is it unjust to use the body of a murderer, who has already forfeited his own life, to save the lives of the innocent?"

"My uncle, who is on the bench, has spoken of such cases," Bingley said.

"Not only that," Mary added. "Have you heard of the experiments of the Italian scientist Aldini? Last summer in London at the Royal College of Surgeons he used a powerful battery to animate portions of the body of a hanged man. According to the *Times*, the spectators genuinely believed that the body was about to come to life!"

"Mary, please!" said Lizzy.

"You need to spend less time on your horrid books," Kitty laughed. "No suitor is going to want to talk with you about dead bodies."

And so Kitty was on their side, too. Her mockery only made Mary more determined to force Frankenstein to speak. "What do you say, sir? Will you come to my defense?"

Frankenstein carefully folded his napkin and set it beside his plate. "Such attempts are not motivated by bravery, or even curiosity, but by ambition. The pursuit of knowledge can become a vice deadly as any of the more common sins. Worse still, because even the most noble of natures are susceptible to such temptations. None but he who has experienced them can conceive of the enticements of science."

The vicar raised his glass. "Mr. Frankenstein, truer words have never been spoken. The man who defiled poor Nancy's grave has placed himself beyond the mercy of a forgiving God."

Mary felt charged with contradictory emotions. "You have experienced such enticements, Mr. Frankenstein?"

"Sadly, I have."

"But surely there is no sin that is beyond the reach of God's mercy? 'To know all is to forgive all.'"

The vicar turned to her. "My child, what know you of sin?"

"Very little, Mr. Chatsworth, except of idleness. Yet I feel that even a wicked person can have the veil lifted from his eyes."

Frankenstein looked at her. "Here I must agree with Miss Bennet. I have to believe that even the most corrupted nature is susceptible to grace. If I did not think this were possible, I could not live."

"Enough of this talk," insisted Darcy. "Vicar, I suggest you mind your parishioners, including those in the churchyard, more carefully. But now I for one am eager to hear Miss Georgiana play the pianoforte. And perhaps Miss Mary and Miss Catherine will join her. We must uphold the accomplishments of English maidenhood before our foreign guests."

On Kitty's insistence, the next morning, despite lowering clouds and a chill in the air that spoke more of March than late May, she and Mary took a walk along the river.

They walked along the stream that ran from the estate toward the Derwent. Kitty remained silent. Mary's thoughts turned to the wholly unsatisfying dinner of the previous night. The conversation in the parlor had gone no better than dinner. Mary had played the piano ill, showing herself to poor advantage next to the accomplished Georgiana. Under Jane and Lizzy's gaze she felt the folly of her intemperate speech at the table. Frankenstein said next to nothing to her for the rest of the evening; he almost seemed wary of being in her presence.

She was wondering how he was spending this morning when, suddenly turning her face from Mary, Kitty burst into tears.

Mary touched her arm. "Whatever is the matter, Kitty?"

"Do you believe what you said last night?"

"What did I say?"

"That there is no sin beyond the reach of God's mercy?"

"Of course I do! Why would you ask?"

"Because I have committed such a sin!" She covered her eyes with her hand. "Oh, no, I mustn't speak of it!"

Mary refrained from pointing out that, having made such a provocative admission, Kitty could hardly remain silent—and undoubtedly had no intention of doing so. But Kitty's intentions were not always transparent to Mary.

After some coaxing and a further walk along the stream, Kitty was prepared finally to unburden herself. It seemed that, from the previous summer, she had maintained a secret admiration for a local man from Matlock, Robert Piggot, son of the butcher. Though his family was quite prosperous and he stood to inherit the family business, he was in no way a gentleman, and Kitty had vowed never to let her affections overwhelm her sense.

But, upon their recent return to Pemberley, she had encountered Robert on her first visit to town, and she had been secretly meeting with him when she went into Matlock on the pretext of shopping. Worse still, the couple had allowed their passion to get the better of them, and Kitty had given way to carnal love.

The two sisters sat on a fallen tree in the woods as Kitty poured out her tale. "I want so much to marry him." Her tears flowed readily. "I do not want to be alone, I don't want to die an old maid! And Lydia—Lydia told me about—about the act of love, how wonderful it was, how good Wickham makes her feel. She boasted of it! And I said, why should vain Lydia have this, and me have nothing, to waste my youth in conversation and embroidery, in listening to Mother prattle and Father throw heavy sighs. Father thinks me a fool, unlikely ever to find a husband. And now he's right!" Kitty burst into wailing again. "He's right! No man shall ever have me!" Her tears ended in a fit of coughing.

"Oh, Kitty," Mary said.

"When Darcy spoke of English maidenhood last night, it was all I could do to keep from bursting into tears. You must get Father to agree to let me marry Robert."

"Has he asked you to marry him?"

"He shall. He must. You don't know how fine a man he is. Despite the fact that he is in trade, he has the gentlest manners. I don't care if he is not well born."

Mary embraced Kitty. Kitty alternated between sobs and fits of coughing. Above them the thunder rumbled, and the wind rustled the trees. Mary felt Kitty's shivering body. She needed to calm her, to get her back to the house. How frail, how slender her sister was.

She did not know what to say. Once Mary would have self-righteously condemned Kitty. But much that Kitty said was the content of her own mind, and Kitty's fear of dying alone was her own fear. As she searched for some answer, Mary heard the sound of a torrent of rain hitting the canopy of foliage above them. "You have been foolish," Mary said, holding her. "But it may not be so bad."

Kitty trembled in her arms, and spoke into Mary's shoulder. "But will you ever care for me again? What if Father should turn me out? What will I do then?"

The rain was falling through now, coming down hard. Mary felt her hair getting soaked. "Calm yourself. Father would do no such thing. I shall never forsake you. Jane would not, nor Lizzy."

"What if I should have a child!"

Mary pulled Kitty's shawl over her head. She looked past Kitty's shoulder to the dark woods. Something moved there. "You shan't have a child."

"You can't know! I may!"

The woods had become dark with the rain. Mary could not make out what lurked there. "Come, let us go back. You must compose yourself. We shall speak with Lizzy and Jane. They will know—"

Just then a flash of lightning lit the forest, and Mary saw, beneath the trees not ten feet from them, the giant figure of a man. The lightning illuminated a face of monstrous ugliness: Long, thick, tangled black hair. Yellow skin the texture of dried leather, black eyes sunken deep beneath heavy brows. Worst of all, an expression hideous in its cold, inexpressible hunger. All glimpsed in a split second; then the light fell to shadow.

Mary gasped, and pulled Kitty toward her. A great peal of thunder rolled across the sky.

Kitty stopped crying. "What is it?"

"We must go. Now." Mary seized Kitty by the arm. The rain pelted down on them, and the forest path was already turning to mud.

Mary pulled her toward the house, Kitty complaining. Mary could hear nothing over the drumming of the rain. But when she looked over her shoulder, she caught a glimpse of the brutish figure, keeping to the trees, but swiftly, silently moving along behind them.

"Why must we run?" Kitty gasped.

"Because we are being followed!"

"By whom?"

"I don't know!"

Behind them, Mary thought she heard the man croak out some words: "Halt! Bitter!"

They had not reached the edge of the woods when figures appeared ahead of them, coming from Pemberley. "Miss Bennet! Mary! Kitty!"

The figures resolved themselves into Darcy and Mr. Frankenstein. Darcy carried a cloak, which he threw over them. "Are you all right?" Frankenstein asked.

"Thank you!" Mary gasped. "A man. He's there," she pointed, "following us."

Frankenstein took a few steps beyond them down the path. "Who was it?" Darcy asked.

"Some brute. Hideously ugly," Mary said.

Frankenstein came back. "No one is there."

"We saw him!"

Another lightning flash, and crack of thunder. "It is very dark, and we are in a storm," Frankenstein said.

"Come, we must get you back to the house," Darcy said. "You are wet to the bone."

The men helped them back to Pemberley, trying their best to keep the rain off the sisters.

Darcy went off to find Bingley and Clerval, who had taken the opposite direction in their search. Lizzy saw that Mary and Kitty were made dry and warm. Kitty's cough worsened, and Lizzy insisted she must be put to bed. Mary sat with Kitty, whispered a promise to keep her secret, and waited until she slept. Then she went down to meet the others in the parlor.

"This chill shall do her no good," Jane said. She chided Mary for wandering off in such threatening weather. "I thought you had developed more sense, Mary. Mr. Frankenstein insisted he help to find you, when he realized you had gone out into the woods."

"I am sorry," Mary said. "You are right." She was distracted by Kitty's plight, wondering what she might do. If Kitty were indeed with child, there would be no helping her.

Mary recounted her story of the man in the woods. Darcy said he had seen no one, but allowed that someone might have been there. Frankenstein, rather than engage in the speculation, stood at the tall windows staring across the lawn through the rain toward the tree line.

"This intruder was some local poacher, or perhaps one of those gypsies," said Darcy. "When the rain ends I shall have Mr. Mowbray take some men to check the grounds. We shall also inform the constable."

"I hope this foul weather will induce you to stay with us a few more days, Mr. Frankenstein," Lizzy ventured. "You have no pressing business in Matlock, do you?"

"No. But we were to travel north by the end of this week."

"Surely we might stay a while longer, Victor," said Clerval. "Your research can wait for you in Scotland."

Frankenstein struggled with his answer. "I don't think we should prevail on these good people any more."

"Nonsense," said Darcy. "We are fortunate for your company."

"Thank you," Frankenstein said uncertainly. But when the conversation moved elsewhere, Mary noticed him once again staring out the window. She moved to sit beside him. On an impulse, she said to him, *sotto voce*, "Did you know this man we came upon in the woods?"

"I saw no one. Even if someone was there, how should I know some English vagabond?"

"I do not think he was English. When he called after us, it was in German. Was this one of your countrymen?"

A look of impatience crossed Frankenstein's face, and he lowered his eyes. "Miss Bennet, I do not wish to contradict you, but you are mistaken. I saw no one in the woods."

Kitty developed a fever, and did not leave her bed for the rest of the day. Mary sat with her, trying, without bringing up the subject of Robert Piggot, to quiet her.

It was still raining when Mary retired, to a separate bedroom from the one she normally shared with Kitty. Late that night, Mary was wakened by the opening of her bedroom door. She thought it might be Lizzy to tell her something about Kitty. But it was not Lizzy.

Rather than call out, she watched silently as a dark figure entered and closed the door behind. The remains of her fire threw faint light on the man as he approached her. "Miss Bennet," he called softly.

Her heart was in her throat. "Yes, Mr. Frankenstein."

"Please do not take alarm. I must speak with you." He took two sudden steps toward her bed. His handsome face was agitated. No man, in any circumstances remotely resembling these, had ever broached her bedside. Yet the racing of her heart was not entirely a matter of fear.

"This, sir, is hardly the place for polite conversation," she said. "Following on your denial of what I saw this afternoon, you are fortunate that I do not wake the servants and have you thrown out of Pemberley."

"You are right to chide me. My conscience chides me more than you ever could, and should I be thrown from your family's gracious company it would be less than I deserve. And I am afraid that nothing I have to say to you tonight shall qualify as polite conversation." His manner was greatly changed; there was a sound of desperation in his whisper. He wanted something from her, and he wanted it a great deal.

Curious, despite herself, Mary drew on her robe and lit a candle. She made him sit in one of the chairs by the fire and poked the coals into life. When she had settled herself in the other, she said, "Go on."

"Miss Bennet, please do not toy with me. You know why I am here."

"Know, sir? What do I know?"

He leaned forward, earnestly, hands clasped and elbows on his knees. "I come to beg you to keep silent. The gravest consequences would follow your revealing my secret."

"Silent?"

"About—about the man you saw."

"You *do* know him!"

"Your mockery at dinner convinced me that, after hearing the vicar's story, you suspected. Raising the dead, you said to Clerval—and then your tale of Professor Aldini. Do not deny it."

"I don't pretend to know what you are talking about."

Frankenstein stood from his chair and began to pace the floor before the hearth. "Please! I saw the look of reproach in your eyes when we found you in the forest. I am trying to make right what I put wrong. But I will never be able to do so if you tell." To Mary's astonishment, she saw, in the firelight, that his eyes glistened with tears.

"Tell me what you did."

And with that the story burst out of him. He told her how, after his mother's death, he longed to conquer death itself, how he had studied chemistry at the university, how he had uncovered the secret of life. How, emboldened and driven on by his solitary obsession, he had created a man from the corpses he had stolen from graveyards and purchased from resurrection men. How he had succeeded, through his science, in bestowing it with life.

Mary did not know what to say to this astonishing tale. It was the raving of a lunatic—but there was the man she had seen in the woods. And the earnestness with which Frankenstein spoke, his tears and desperate whispers, gave every proof that, at least in his mind, he had done these things. He told of his revulsion at his accomplishment, how he had abandoned the creature, hoping it would die, and how the creature had, in revenge, killed his brother William and caused his family's ward Justine to be blamed for the crime.

"But why did you not intervene in Justine's trial?"

"No one should have believed me."

"Yet I am to believe you now?"

Frankenstein's voice was choked. "You have seen the brute. You know that these things are possible. Lives are at stake. I come to you in remorse and penitence, asking only that you keep this secret." He fell to his knees, threw his head into her lap, and clutched at the sides of her gown.

Frankenstein was wholly mistaken in what she knew; he was a man who did not see things clearly. Yet if his story were true, it was no wonder that his judgment was disordered. And here he lay, trembling against her, a boy seeking forgiveness. No man had ever come to her in such need.

She tried to keep her senses. "Certainly the creature I saw was frightening, but to my eyes he appeared more wretched than menacing."

Frankenstein lifted his head. "Here I must warn you—his wretchedness is mere mask. Do not let your sympathy for him cause you ever to trust his nature. He is the vilest creature that has ever walked this earth. He has no soul."

"Why then not invoke the authorities, catch him, and bring him to justice?"

"He cannot be so easily caught. He is inhumanly strong, resourceful, and intelligent. If you should ever be so unlucky as to speak with him, I warn you not to listen to what he says, for he is immensely articulate and satanically persuasive."

"All the more reason to see him apprehended!"

"I am convinced that he can be dealt with only by myself." Frankenstein's eyes pleaded with her. "Miss Bennet—Mary—you must understand. He is in some ways my son. I gave him life. His mind is fixed on me."

"And, it seems, yours on him."

Frankenstein looked surprised. "Do you wonder that is so?"

"Why does he follow you? Does he intend you harm?"

"He has vowed to glut the maw of death with my remaining loved ones, unless I make him happy." He rested his head again in her lap.

Mary was touched, scandalized, and in some obscure way aroused. She felt his trembling body, instinct with life. Tentatively, she rested her hand on his head. She stroked his hair. He was weeping. She realized that he was a physical being, a living animal, that would eventually, too soon, die. And all that was true of him was true of herself. How strange, frightening, and sad. Yet in this moment she felt herself wonderfully alive.

"I'll keep your secret," she said.

He hugged her skirts. In the candle's light, she noted the way his thick, dark hair curled away from his brow.

"I cannot tell you," he said softly, "what a relief it is to share my burden with another soul, and to have her accept me. I have been so completely alone. I cannot thank you enough."

He rose, kissed her forehead, and was gone.

Mary paced her room, trying to grasp what had just happened. A man who had conquered death? A monster created from corpses? Such things did not happen, certainly not in her world, not even in the world of the novels she read. She climbed into bed and tried to sleep, but could not. The creature had vowed to kill all whom Frankenstein loved. Mary remembered the weight of his head upon her lap.

The room felt stiflingly hot. She got up, stripped off her nightgown, and climbed back between the sheets, where she lay naked, listening to the rain on the window.

Kitty's fever worsened in the night, and before dawn Darcy sent to Lambton for the doctor. Lizzy dispatched an urgent letter to Mr. and Mrs. Bennet, and the sisters sat by Kitty's bedside through the morning, changing cold compresses from her brow while Kitty labored to breathe.

When Mary left the sick room, Frankenstein approached her. His desperation of the previous night was gone. "How fares your sister?"

"I fear she is gravely ill."

"She is in some danger?"

Mary could only nod.

He touched her shoulder, lowered his voice. "I will pray for her, Miss Bennet. I cannot thank you enough for the sympathy you showed me last night. I have never told anyone—"

Just then Clerval approached them. He greeted Mary, inquired after Kitty's condition, then suggested to Frankenstein that they return to their hotel in Matlock rather than add any burden to the household and family. Frankenstein agreed. Before Mary could say another word to him in private, the visitors were gone.

Doctor Phillips arrived soon after Clerval and Frankenstein left. He measured Kitty's pulse, felt her forehead, examined her urine. He administered some medicines, and came away shaking his head. Should the fever continue, he said, they must bleed her.

Given how much thought she had spent on Frankenstein through the night, and how little she had devoted to Kitty, Mary's conscience tormented her. She spent the day in her sister's room. That night, after Jane had retired and Lizzy fallen asleep in her chair, she still sat up, holding Kitty's fevered hand. She had matters to consider. Was Kitty indeed with child, and if so, should she tell the doctor? Yet even as she sat by Kitty's bedside, Mary's mind cast back to the feeling of Frankenstein's lips on her forehead.

In the middle of the night, Kitty woke, bringing Mary from her doze. Kitty tried to lift her head from the pillow, but could not. "Mary," she whispered. "You must send for Robert. We must be married immediately."

Mary looked across the room at Lizzy. She was still asleep.

"Promise me," Kitty said. Her eyes were large and dark.

"I promise," Mary said.

"Prepare my wedding dress," Kitty said. "But don't tell Lizzy."

Lizzy awoke then. She came to the bedside and felt Kitty's forehead. "She's burning up. Get Doctor Phillips."

Mary sought out the doctor, and then, while he went to Kitty's room, pondered what to do. Kitty clearly was not in her right mind. Her request ran contrary to both sense and propriety. If Mary sent one of the footmen to Matlock for Robert, even if she swore her messenger to silence, the matter would soon be the talk of the servants, and probably the town.

It was the sort of dilemma that Mary would have had no trouble settling, to everyone's moral edification, when she was sixteen. She hurried to her room and took out paper and pen:

*I write to inform you that one you love, residing at Pemberley House, is gravely ill. She urgently requests your presence. Simple human kindness, which from her description of you I do not doubt you possess, let alone the duty incumbent upon you owing to the compact that you have made with her through your actions, assure me that we shall see you here before the night is through.*

*Miss Mary Bennet*

She sealed the letter and sought out one of the footmen, whom she dispatched immediately with the instruction to put the letter into the hand of Robert Piggot, son of the Matlock butcher.

Doctor Phillips bled Kitty, with no improvement. She did not regain consciousness through the night. Mary waited. The footman returned, alone, at six in the morning. He assured Mary that he had ridden to the Piggot home and given the letter directly to Robert. Mary thanked him.

Robert did not come. At eight in the morning Darcy sent for the priest. At nine-thirty Kitty died.

On the evening of the day of Kitty's passing, Mr. and Mrs. Bennet arrived, and a day later Lydia and Wickham—it was the first time Darcy had allowed Wickham to cross the threshold of Pemberley since they had become brothers by marriage. In the midst of her mourning family, Mary felt lost. Jane and Lizzy supported each other in their grief. Darcy and Bingley exchanged quiet, sober conversation. Wickham and Lydia, who had grown fat with her three children, could not pass a word between them without sniping, but in their folly they were completely united.

Mrs. Bennet was beyond consoling, and the volume and intensity of her mourning was exceeded only by the degree to which she sought to control every detail of Kitty's funeral. There ensued a long debate over where Kitty should be buried. When it was pointed out that their cousin Mr. Collins would eventually inherit the house back in Hertfordshire, Mrs. Bennet fell into despair: Who, when she was gone, would tend to her poor Kitty's grave? Mr. Bennet suggested that Kitty be laid to rest in the churchyard at Lambton, a short distance from Pemberley, where she might also be visited by Jane and Bingley. But when Mr. Darcy offered the family vault at Pemberley, the matter was quickly settled to the satisfaction of both tender hearts and vanity.

Though it was no surprise to Mary, it was still a burden for her to witness that even in the gravest passage of their lives, her sisters and parents showed themselves to be exactly what they were. And yet, paradoxically, this did not harden her heart toward them. The family was together as they had not been for many years, and she realized that they should never be in the future except on the occasion of further losses. Her father was grayer and quieter than she had ever seen him, and on the day of the funeral even her mother put aside her sobbing and exclamations long enough to show a face of profound grief, and a burden of age that Mary had never before noticed.

The night after Kitty was laid to rest, Mary sat up late with Jane and Lizzy and Lydia. They drank Madeira and Lydia told many silly stories of the days she and Kitty had spent in flirtations with the regiment. Mary climbed into her bed late that night, her head swimming with wine, laughter, and tears. She lay awake, the moonlight shining on the counterpane through the opened window, air carrying the smell of fresh earth and the rustle of trees above the lake. She drifted into a dreamless sleep. At some point in the night she was half awakened by the barking of the dogs in the kennel. But consciousness soon faded and she fell away.

In the morning it was discovered that the vault had been broken into and Kitty's body stolen from her grave.

Mary told the stablemaster that Mrs. Bennet had asked her to go to the apothecary in Lambton, and had him prepare the gig for her. Then, while the house was in turmoil and Mrs. Bennet being attended by the rest of the family, she drove off to Matlock. The master had given her the best horse in Darcy's stable; the creature was equable and quick, and despite her inexperience driving, Mary was able to reach Matlock in an hour. All the time, despite the splendid summer morning and the picturesque prospects which the valley of the Derwent continually unfolded before her, she could not keep her mind from whirling through a series of distressing images—among them the sight of Frankenstein's creature as she had seen him in the woods.

When she reached Matlock she hurried to the Old Bath Hotel and inquired after Frankenstein. The concierge told her that he had not seen Mr. Frankenstein since dinner the previous evening, but that Mr. Clerval had told him that morning that the gentlemen would leave Matlock later that day. She left a note asking Frankenstein, should he return, to meet her at the inn, then went to the butcher shop.

Mary had been there once before, with Lizzy, some years earlier. The shop was busy with servants purchasing joints of mutton and ham for the evening meal.

Behind the counter Mr. Piggot senior was busy at his cutting board, but helping one of the women with a package was a tall young man with thick brown curls and green eyes. He flirted with the house servant as he shouldered her purchase, wrapped in brown paper, onto her cart.

On the way back into the shop, he spotted Mary standing unattended. He studied her for a moment before approaching. "May I help you, miss?"

"I believe you knew my sister."

His grin vanished. "You are Miss Mary Bennet."

"I am."

The young man studied his boots. "I am so sorry what happened to Miss Catherine."

Not so sorry as to bring you to her bedside before she died, Mary thought. She bit back a reproach and said, "We did not see you at the service. I thought perhaps the nature of your relationship might have encouraged you to grieve in private, at her graveside. Have you been there?"

He looked even more uncomfortable. "No. I had to work. My father—"

Mary had seen enough already to measure his depth. He was not a man to defile a grave, in grief or otherwise. The distance between this small-town lothario—handsome, careless, insensitive—and the hero Kitty had praised, only deepened Mary's compassion for her lost sister. How desperate she must have been. How pathetic.

As Robert Piggot continued to stumble through his explanation, Mary turned and departed.

She went back to the inn where she had left the gig. The barkeep led her into a small ladies' parlor separated from the tap room by a glass partition. She ordered tea, and through a latticed window watched the people come and go in the street and courtyard, the draymen with their Percherons and carts, the passengers waiting for the next van to Manchester, and inside, the idlers sitting at tables with pints of ale. In the sunlit street a young bootblack accosted travelers, most of whom ignored him. All of these people alive, completely unaware of Mary or her lost sister. Mary ought to be back with their mother, though the thought turned her heart cold. How could Kitty have left her alone? She felt herself near despair.

She was watching through the window as two draymen struggled to load a large square trunk onto their cart when the man directing them came from around the team of horses, and she saw it was Frankenstein. She rose immediately and went out into the inn yard. She was at his shoulder before he noticed her. "Miss Bennet!"

"Mr. Frankenstein. I am so glad that I found you. I feared that you had already left Matlock. May we speak somewhere in private?"

He looked momentarily discommoded. "Yes, of course," he said. To the draymen he said. "When you've finished loading my equipment, wait here."

"This is not a good place to converse," Frankenstein told her. "I saw a churchyard nearby. Let us retire there."

He walked Mary down the street to the St. Giles Churchyard. They walked through the rectory garden. In the distance, beams of afternoon sunlight shone through a cathedral of clouds above the Heights of Abraham. "Do you know what has happened?" she asked.

"I have heard reports, quite awful, of the death of your sister. I intended to write you, conveying my condolences, at my earliest opportunity. You have my deepest sympathies."

"Your creature! That monster you created—"

"I asked you to keep him a secret."

"I have kept my promise—so far. But it has stolen Kitty's body."

He stood there, hands behind his back, clear eyes fixed on her. "You find me astonished. What draws you to this extraordinary conclusion?"

She was hurt by his diffidence. Was this the same man who had wept in her bedroom? "Who else might do such a thing?"

"But why? This creature's enmity is reserved for me alone. Others feel its ire only to the extent that they are dear to me."

"You came to plead with me that night because you feared I knew he was responsible for defiling that town girl's grave. Why was he watching Kitty and me in the forest? Surely this is no coincidence."

"If, indeed, the creature has stolen your sister's body, it can be for no reason I can fathom, or that any god-fearing person ought to pursue. You know I am determined to see this monster banished from the world of men. You may rest assured that I will not cease until I have seen this accomplished. It is best for you and your family to turn your thoughts to other matters." He touched a strand of ivy growing up the side of the garden wall, and plucked off a green leaf, which he twirled in his fingers.

She could not understand him. She knew him to be a man of sensibility, to have a heart capable of feeling. His denials opened a possibility that she had tried to keep herself from considering. "Sir, I am not satisfied. It seems to me that you are keeping something from me. You told me of the great grief you felt at the loss of your mother, how it moved you to your researches. If, as you say, you have uncovered the secret of life, might you—have you taken it upon yourself to restore Kitty? Perhaps a fear of failure, or of the horror that many would feel at your trespassing against God's will, underlies your secrecy. If so, please do not keep the truth from me. I am not a girl."

He let the leaf fall from his fingers. He took her shoulders, and looked directly into her eyes. "I am sorry, Mary. To restore your sister is not in my power. The soulless creature I brought to life bears no relation to the man from whose body I fashioned him. Your sister has gone on to her reward. Nothing—nothing I can do would bring her back."

"So you know nothing about the theft of her corpse?"

"On that score, I can offer no consolation to you or your family."

"My mother, my father—they are inconsolable."

"Then they must content themselves with memories of your sister as she lived. As I must do with my dear, lost brother William, and the traduced and dishonored Justine. Come, let us go back to the inn."

Mary burst into tears. He held her to him and she wept on his breast. Eventually she gathered herself and allowed him to take her arm, and they slowly walked back down to the main street of Matlock and the inn. She knew that when they reached it, Frankenstein would go. The warmth of his hand on hers almost made her beg him to stay, or better still, to take her with him.

They came to the busy courtyard. The dray stood off to the side, and Mary saw the cartmen were in the taproom. Frankenstein, agitated, upbraided them. "I thought I told you to keep those trunks out of the sun."

The older of the two men put down his pint and stood, "Sorry, Gov'nor. We'll see to it directly."

"Do so now."

As Frankenstein spoke the evening coach drew up before the inn and prepared for departure. "You and Mr. Clerval leave today?" Mary asked.

"Yes. As soon Henry arrives from the Old Bath, we take the coach to the Lake District. And thence to Scotland."

"They say it is very beautiful there."

"I am afraid that its beauty will be lost on me. I carry the burden of my great crime, not to be laid down until I have made things right."

She felt that she would burst if she did not speak her heart to him. "Victor. Will I ever see you again?"

He avoided her gaze. "I am afraid, Miss Bennet, that this is unlikely. My mind is set on banishing that vile creature from the world of men. Only then can I hope to return home and marry my betrothed Elizabeth."

Mary looked away from him. A young mother was adjusting her son's collar before putting him on the coach. "Ah, yes. You are affianced. I had almost forgotten."

Frankenstein pressed her hand. "Miss Bennet, you must forgive me the liberties I have taken with you. You have given me more of friendship than I deserve. I wish you to find the companion you seek, and to live your days in happiness. But now, I must go."

"God be with you, Mr. Frankenstein." She twisted her gloved fingers into a knot.

He bowed deeply, and hurried to have a few more words with the draymen. Henry Clerval arrived just as the men climbed to their cart and drove the baggage away. Clerval, surprised at seeing Mary, greeted her warmly. He expressed his great sorrow at the loss of her sister, and begged her to convey his condolences to the rest of her family. Ten minutes later the two men climbed aboard the coach and it left the inn, disappearing down the Matlock high street.

Mary stood in the inn yard. She did not feel she could bear to go back to

Pemberley and face her family, the histrionics of her mother. Instead she re-entered the inn and made the barkeep seat her in the ladies' parlor and bring her a bottle of port.

The sun declined and shadows stretched over the inn yard. The evening papers arrived from Nottingham. The yard boy lit the lamps. Still, Mary would not leave. Outside on the pavements, the bootblack sat in the growing darkness with his arms draped over his knees and head on his breast. She listened to the hoofs of the occasional horse striking the cobbles. The innkeeper was solicitous. When she asked for a second bottle, he hesitated, and wondered if he might send for someone from her family to take her home.

"You do not know my family," she said.

"Yes, miss. I only thought—"

"Another port. Then leave me alone."

"Yes, miss." He went away. She was determined to become intoxicated. How many times had she piously warned against young women behaving as she did now? *Virtue is her own reward.* She had an apothegm for every occasion, and had tediously produced them in place of thought. *Show me a liar, and I'll show thee a thief. Marry in haste, repent at leisure. Men should be what they seem.*

She did not fool herself into thinking that her current misbehavior would make any difference. Perhaps Bingley or Darcy had been dispatched to find her in Lambton. But within an hour or two she would return to Pemberley, where her mother would scold her for giving them an anxious evening, and Lizzy would caution her about the risk to her reputation. Lydia might even ask her, not believing it possible, if she had an assignation with some man. The loss of Kitty would overshadow Mary's indiscretion, pitiful as it had been. Soon all would be as it had been, except Mary would be alive and Kitty dead. But even that would fade. The shadow of Kitty's death would hang over the family for some time, but she doubted that anything of significance would change.

As she lingered over her glass, she looked up and noticed, in the now empty taproom, a man sitting at the table farthest from the lamps. A huge man, wearing rough clothes, his face hooded and in shadow. Mary rose, left the parlor for the taproom, and crossed toward him. On the table in front of him was a tankard of ale and a few coppers.

He looked up, and the faint light from the ceiling lamp caught his black eyes, sunken beneath heavy brows. He was hideously ugly. "May I sit with you?" she asked. She felt slightly dizzy.

"You may sit where you wish." The voice was deep, but swallowed, unable to project. It was almost a whisper.

Trembling only slightly, she sat. His wrists and hands, resting on the table, stuck out past the ragged sleeves of his coat. His skin was yellowish brown, and the fingernails livid white. He did not move. "You have some business with me?"

"I have the most appalling business." Mary tried to look him in the eyes, but her gaze kept slipping. "I want to know why you defiled my sister's grave, why you have stolen her body, and what you have done with her."

"Better you should ask Victor. Did he not explain all to you?"

"Mr. Frankenstein explained who—what—you are. He did not know what had become of my sister."

The thin lips twitched in a sardonic smile. "Poor Victor. He has got things all topsy-turvy. Victor does not know what I am. He is incapable of knowing, no matter the labors I have undertaken to school him. But he does know what became, and is to become, of your sister." The creature tucked the thick black hair behind his ear, a sudden unconscious gesture that made him seem completely human for the first time. He pulled the hood further forward to hide his face.

"So tell me."

"Which answer do you want? Who I am, or what happened to your sister?"

"First, tell me what happened to—to Kitty."

"Victor broke into the vault and stole her away. He took the utmost care not to damage her. He washed her fair body in diluted carbolic acid, and replaced her blood with a chemical admixture of his own devising. Folded up, she fit neatly within a cedar trunk sealed with pitch, and is at present being shipped to Scotland. You witnessed her departure from this courtyard an hour ago."

Mary's senses rebelled. She covered her face with her hands. The creature sat silent. Finally, without raising her head, she managed, "Victor warned me that you were a liar. Why should I believe you?"

"You have no reason to believe me."

"*You* took her!"

"Though I would not have scrupled to do so, I did not. Miss Bennet, I do not deny I have an interest in this matter. Victor did as I have told you at my bidding."

"At your bidding? Why?"

"Kitty—or not so much Kitty, as her remains—is to become my wife."

"Your wife! This is insupportable! Monstrous!"

"Monstrous." Suddenly, with preternatural quickness, his hand flashed out and grabbed Mary's wrist.

Mary thought to call for help, but the bar was empty and she had driven the innkeeper away. Yet his grip was not harsh. His hand was warm, instinct with life. "Look at me," he said. With his other hand he pushed back his hood.

She took a deep breath. She looked.

His noble forehead, high cheekbones, strong chin, and wide set eyes might have made him handsome, despite the scars and dry yellow skin, were it not for his expression. His ugliness was not a matter of lack of proportion—or rather, the lack of proportion was not in his features. Like his swallowed voice, his face was submerged, as if everything was hidden, revealed only in the eyes, the twitch of a cheek or lip. Every minute motion showed extraordinary animation. Hectic sickliness, but energy. This was a creature who had never learned to associate with civilized company, who had been thrust into adulthood with the passions of a wounded boy. Fear, self-disgust, anger. Desire.

The force of longing and rage in that face made her shrink. "Let me go," she whispered.

He let go her wrist. With bitter satisfaction, he said, "You see. If what I demand is insupportable, that is only because your kind has done nothing to support me. Once, I falsely hoped to meet with beings, who, pardoning my outward form, would love me for the excellent qualities which I was capable of bringing forth. Now I am completely alone. More than any starving man on a deserted isle, I am cast away. I have no brother, sister, parents. I have only Victor who, like so many fathers, recoiled from me the moment I first drew breath. And so, I have commanded him to make of your sister my wife, or he and all he loves will die at my hand."

"No. I cannot believe he would commit this abomination."

"He has no choice. He is my slave."

"His conscience could not support it, even at the cost of his life."

"You give him too much credit. You all do. He does not think. I have not seen him act other than according to impulse for the last three years. That is all I see in any of you."

Mary drew back, trying to make some sense of this horror. Her sister, to be brought to life, only to be given to this fiend. But would it be her sister, or another agitated, hungry thing like this?

She still retained some scraps of skepticism. The creature's manner did not bespeak the isolation which he claimed. "I am astonished at your grasp of language," Mary said. "You could not know so much without teachers."

"Oh, I have had many teachers." The creature's mutter was rueful. "You might say that, since first my eyes opened, mankind has been all my study. I have much yet to learn. There are certain words whose meaning has never been proved to me by experience. For example: *Happy*. Victor is to make me happy. Do you think he can do it?"

Mary thought of Frankenstein. Could he satisfy this creature? "I do not think it is in the power of any other person to make one happy."

"You jest with me. Every creature has its mate, save me. I have none."

She recoiled at his self-pity. Her fear faded. "You put too much upon having a mate."

"Why? You know nothing of what I have endured."

"You think that having a female of your own kind will insure that she will accept you?" Mary laughed. "Wait until you are rejected, for the most trivial of reasons, by one you are sure has been made for you."

A shadow crossed the creature's face. "That will not happen."

"It happens more often than not."

"The female that Victor creates shall find no other mate than me."

"That has never prevented rejection. Or if you should be accepted, then you may truly begin to learn."

"Learn what?"

"You will learn to ask a new question: Which is worse, to be alone, or to be wretchedly mismatched?" Like Lydia and Wickham, Mary thought. Like Collins and his poor wife Charlotte. Like her parents.

The creature's face spasmed with conflicting emotions. His voice gained volume. "Do not sport with me. I am not your toy."

"No. You only seek a toy of your own."

The creature was not, apparently, accustomed to mockery. "You must not say these things!" He lurched upward, awkwardly, so suddenly that he upended the table. The tankard of beer skidded across the top and spilled on Mary, and she fell back.

At that moment the innkeeper entered the bar room with two other men. They saw the tableau and rushed forward. "Here! Let her be!" he shouted. One of the other men grabbed the creature by the arm. With a roar the creature flung him aside like an old coat. His hood fell back. The men stared in horror at his face. The creature's eyes met Mary's, and with inhuman speed he whirled and ran out the door.

The men gathered themselves together. The one whom the creature had thrown aside had a broken arm. The innkeeper helped Mary to her feet. "Are you all right, miss?"

Mary felt dizzy. Was she all right? What did that mean?

"I believe so," she said.

When Mary returned to Pemberley, late that night, she found the house in an uproar over her absence. Bingley and Darcy both had been to Lambton, and had searched the road and the woods along it throughout the afternoon and evening. Mrs. Bennet had taken to bed with the conviction that she had lost two daughters in a single week. Wickham condemned Mary's poor judgment, Lydia sprang to Mary's defense, and this soon became a row over Wickham's lack of an income and Lydia's mismanagement of their children. Mr. Bennett closed himself up in the library.

Mary told them only that she had been to Matlock. She offered no explanation, no apology. Around the town the story of her conflict with the strange giant in the inn was spoken of for some time, along with rumors of Robert Piggot the butcher's son, and the mystery of Kitty's defiled grave—but as Mary was not a local, and nothing of consequence followed, the talk soon passed away.

That winter, Mary came upon the following story in the Nottingham newspaper.

Ghastly Events
in Scotland

Our northern correspondent files the following report. In early November, the body of a young foreigner, Mr. Henry Clerval of Geneva, Switzerland, was found upon the beach near the far northern town of Thurso. The body, still warm, bore marks of strangulation. A second foreigner, Mr. Victor Frankstone, was taken into custody, charged with the murder, and held for two months. Upon investigation, the magistrate Mr. Kirwan determined that Mr. Frankstone was in the Orkney Islands at the time of the killing. The accused was released in the custody of his father, and is assumed to have returned to his home on the continent.

A month after the disposition of these matters, a basket, weighted with stones and containing the body of a young woman, washed up in the estuary of the River Thurso. The identity of the woman is unknown, and her murderer undiscovered, but it is speculated that the unfortunate may have died at the hands of the same person or persons who murdered Mr. Clerval. The woman was given Christian burial in the Thurso Presbyterian churchyard.

The village has been shaken by these events, and prays God to deliver it from evil.

Oh, Victor, Mary thought. She remembered the pressure of his hand, through her dressing gown, upon her thigh. Now he had returned to Switzerland, there, presumably, to marry his Elizabeth. She hoped that he would be more honest with his wife than he had been with her, but the fate of Clerval did not bode well. And the creature still had no mate.

She clipped the newspaper report and slipped it into the drawer of her writing table, where she kept her copy of Samuel Galton's *The Natural History of Birds, Intended for the Amusement and Instruction of Children*, and the *Juvenile Anecdotes* of Priscilla Wakefield, and a Dudley locust made of stone, and a paper fan from the first ball she had ever attended, and a dried wreath of flowers that had been thrown to her, when she was nine years old, from the top of a tree by one of the town boys playing near Meryton common.

After the death of her parents, Mary lived with Lizzy and Darcy at Pemberley for the remainder of her days. Under a pen name, she pursued a career as a writer of philosophical speculations, and sent many letters to the London newspapers. Aunt Mary, as she was called at home, was known for her kindness to William, and to his wife and children. The children teased Mary for her nearsightedness, her books, and her piano. But for a woman whose experience of the world was so slender, and whose soul it seemed had never been touched by any passion, she came at last to be respected for her understanding, her self-possession, and her wise counsel on matters of the heart.

# THE THOUGHT WAR

## PAUL MCAULEY

Paul McAuley was born in England in 1955 and currently lives in London. He worked as a researcher in biology at various universities before lecturing in botany at St. Andrew's University for six years, before becoming a full-time writer.

His first novel, *Four Hundred Billion Stars,* was published in 1988 and was followed by a string of cutting edge science fiction novels, including *Red Dust, Pasquale's Angel,* the Confluence trilogy, *Fairyland,* and *Cowboy Angels.* Earlier ths decade McAuley focused more on sophisticated science thrillers like *The Secret of Life, Whole Wide World,* and *Mind's Eye,* but had recently returned to widescreen SF with new novel *The Quiet War.* He has won the Philip K. Dick Memorial Award, the Arthur C. Clarke Award, and the John W. Campbell Memorial Award. His short fiction has been collected in *The King of the Hill, The Invisible Country,* and *Little Machines.*

Listen:
Don't try to speak. Don't try to move. Listen to me. Listen to my story.
Everyone remembers their first time. The first time they saw a zombie and knew it for what it was. But my first time was one of the first times ever. It was so early in the invasion that I wasn't sure what was happening. So early we didn't yet call them zombies.
It was in the churchyard of St Pancras Old Church, in the fabulous, long lost city of London. Oh, it's still there, more or less; it's one of the few big cities that didn't get hit in the last, crazy days of global spasm. But it's lost to us now because it belongs to them.
Anyway, St Pancras Old Church was one of the oldest sites of Christian worship in Europe. There'd been a church there, in one form or another, for one and a half thousand years; and although the railway lines to St Pancras station ran hard by its north side it was an isolated and slightly spooky place, full of history and romance. Mary Wollstonecraft Godwin was buried there, and it was at her graveside that her daughter, who later wrote *Frankenstein,* first confessed her love to the poet Shelley, and he to her. In his first career as an architect's assistant, the

novelist Thomas Hardy supervised the removal of bodies when the railway was run through part of the churchyard, and set some of the displaced gravestones around an ash tree that was later named after him.

I lived nearby. I was a freelance science journalist then, and when I was working at home and the weather was good I often ate my lunch in the churchyard. That's where I was when I saw my first zombie.

I can see that you don't understand much of this. It's all right. You are young. Things had already changed when you were born and much that was known then is unknowable now. But I'm trying to set a mood. An emotional tone. Because it's how you respond to the mood and emotions of my story that's important. That's why you have to listen carefully. That's why you are gagged and bound, and wired to my machines.

Listen:

It was a hot day in June in that ancient and hallowed ground. I was sitting on a bench in the sun-dappled shade of Hardy's ash tree and eating an egg-and-cress sandwich and thinking about the article I was writing on cosmic rays when I saw him. It looked like a man, anyway. A ragged man in a long black raincoat, ropy hair down around his face as he limped towards me with a slow and stiff gait. Halting and raising his head and looking all around, and then shambling on, the tail of his black coat dragging behind.

I didn't pay much attention to him at first. I thought he was a vagrant. We are all of us vagrants now, but in the long ago most of us had homes and families and only the most unfortunate, slaves to drink or drugs, lost souls brought down by misfortune or madness, lived on the streets. Vagrants were drawn to churchyards by the quietness and sense of ancient sanctuary, and there was a hospital at the west end of the churchyard of Old St Pancras where they went to fill their prescriptions and get treatment for illness or injury. So he wasn't an unusual sight, shambling beneath the trees in a slow and wavering march past Mary Godwin's grave towards Hardy's ash and the little church.

Then a dog began to bark. A woman with several dogs on leads and several more trotting freely called to the little wire-haired terrier that was dancing around the vagrant in a fury of excitement. Two more dogs ran up to him and began to bark too, their coats bristling and ears laid flat. I saw the vagrant stop and shake back the ropes from his face and look all around, and for the first time I saw his face.

It was dead white and broken. Like a vase shattered and badly mended. My first thought was that he'd been in a bad accident, something involving glass or industrial acids. Then I saw that what I had thought were ropes of matted hair were writhing with slow and awful independence like the tentacles of a sea creature; saw that the tattered raincoat wasn't a garment. It was his skin, falling stiff and black around him like the wings of a bat.

The dog woman started screaming. She'd had a clear look at the vagrant too. Her dogs pranced and howled and whined and barked. I was on my feet. So were the handful of other people who'd been spending a lazy lunch hour in the warm and shady churchyard. One of them must have had the presence of mind to call the police, because almost at once, or so it seemed, there was the wail of a siren and a prickle of blue lights beyond the churchyard fence and two policemen in yellow stab vests came running.

They stopped as soon as they saw the vagrant. One talked into the radio clipped to his vest; the other began to round everyone up and lead us to the edge of the churchyard. And all the while the vagrant stood at the centre of a seething circle of maddened dogs, looking about, clubbed hands held out in a gesture of supplication. A hole yawned redly in his broken white face and shaped hoarse and wordless sounds of distress.

More police came. The road outside the churchyard was blocked off. A helicopter clattered above the tops of the trees. The men in hazmat suits entered the park. One of them carried a rifle. By this time everyone who had been in the park was penned against a police van. The police wouldn't answer our questions and we were speculating in a fairly calm and English way about terrorism. That was the great fear, in the long ago. Ordinary men moving amongst us, armed with explosives and hateful certainty.

We all started when we heard the first shot. The chorus of barks doubled, redoubled. A dog ran pell-mell out of the churchyard gate and a marksman shot it there in the road and the woman who still held the leashes of several dogs cried out. Men in hazmat suits separated us and made us walk one by one through a shower frame they'd assembled on the pavement and made us climb one by one in our wet and stinking clothes into cages in the backs of police vans.

I was in quarantine for a hundred days. When I was released, the world had changed forever. I had watched it change on TV and now I was out in it. Soldiers everywhere on the streets. Security checks and sirens and a constant low-level dread. Lynch mobs. Public hangings and burnings. Ten or twenty menezesings in London alone, each and every day. Quarantined areas cleared and barricaded. Invaders everywhere.

By now, everyone was calling them zombies. We knew that they weren't our own dead come back to walk the Earth, of course, but that's what they most looked like. More and more of them were appearing at random everywhere in the world, and they were growing more and more like us. The first zombies had been only approximations. Barely human in appearance, with a brain and lungs and a heart but little else by way of internal organs, only slabs of muscle that stored enough electrical energy to keep them alive for a day or so. But they were changing. Evolving. Adapting. After only a hundred days, they were almost human. The first had seemed monstrous and pitiful. Now, they looked like dead men walking. Animated showroom dummies. Almost human, but not quite.

After I was released from quarantine, I went back to my trade. Interviewing scientists about the invasion, writing articles. There were dozens of theories, but no real evidence to support any of them. The most popular was that we had been targeted for invasion by aliens from some far star. That the zombies were like the robot probes we had dispatched to other planets and moons in the Solar System, growing ever more sophisticated as they sent back information to their controllers. It made a kind of sense, although it didn't explain why, although they had plainly identified us as the dominant species, their controllers didn't try to contact us. Experiments of varying degrees of cruelty showed that the zombies were intelligent and self-aware, yet they ignored us unless we tried to harm or kill them. Otherwise they simply walked amongst us, and no matter how many were detected and destroyed, there were always more of them.

The most unsettling news came from an old and distinguished physicist, a Nobel laureate, who told me that certain of the fundamental physical constants seemed to be slowly and continuously changing. He had been trying to convey the urgent importance of this to the government but as I discovered when I tried to use my contacts to bring his findings to the attention of ministers and members of parliament and civil servants, the government was too busy dealing with the invasion and the consequences of the invasion.

There was an old and hopeful lie that an alien invasion would cause the nations of Earth to set aside their differences and unite against the common enemy. It didn't happen. Instead, global paranoia and suspicion ratcheted up daily. The zombies were archetypal invaders from within. Hatreds and prejudices that once had been cloaked in diplomatic evasions were now nakedly expressed. Several countries used the invasion as an excuse to attack troublesome minorities or to accuse old enemies of complicity with the zombies. There were genocidal massacres and brush fire wars across the globe. Iran attacked Iraq and Israel with nuclear weapons and what was left of Israel wiped out the capital cities of its neighbours. India attacked Pakistan. China and Russia fought along their long border. The United States invaded Cuba and Venezuela, tried to close its borders with Canada and Mexico, and took sides with China against Russia. And so on, and so on. The zombies didn't have to do anything to destroy us. We were tearing ourselves apart. We grew weaker as we fought each other and the zombies grew stronger by default.

In Britain, everyone under thirty was called up for service in the armed forces. And then everyone under forty was called up too. Three years after my first encounter, I found myself in a troop ship at the tail end of a convoy wallowing through the Bay of Biscay towards the Mediterranean. Huge columns of zombies were straggling out of the Sahara Desert. We were supposed to stop them. Slaughter them. But as we approached the Straits of Gibraltar, someone, it was never clear who, dropped a string of nuclear bombs on zombies massing in Algeria, Tunisia, Libya, and Egypt. On our ships, we saw the flashes of the bombs light the horizon. An hour later we were attacked by the remnants of the Libyan and Egyptian air forces. Half our fleet were sunk; the rest limped home. Britain's government was still intact, more or less, but everyone was in the armed forces now. Defending ourselves from the zombies and from waves of increasingly desperate refugees from the continent. There was a year without summer. Snow in July. Crops failed and despite rationing millions died of starvation and cold. There were biblical plagues of insects and all the old sicknesses came back.

And still the zombies kept appearing.

They looked entirely human now, but it was easy to tell what they were because they weren't starving, or haunted, or mad.

We kept killing them and they kept coming.

They took our cities from us and we fled into the countryside and regrouped and they came after us and we broke into smaller groups and still they came after us.

We tore ourselves apart trying to destroy them. Yet we still didn't understand them. We didn't know where they were coming from, what they were, what they wanted. We grew weaker as they grew stronger.

Do you understand me? I think that you do. Your pulse rate and pupil dilation and skin conductivity all show peaks at the key points of my story. That's good. That means that you might be human.

Listen:

Let me tell you what the distinguished old physicist told me. Let me tell you about the observer effect and Boltzmann brains.

In the nineteenth century, the Austrian physicist Ludwig Boltzmann developed the idea that the universe could have arisen from a random thermal fluctuation. Like a flame popping into existence. An explosion from nowhere. Much later, other physicists suggested that similar random fluctuations could give rise to anything imaginable, including conscious entities in any shape or form: Boltzmann brains. It was one of those contra-intuitive and mostly theoretical ideas that helped cosmologists shape their models of the universe, and how we fit into it. It helped to explain why the universe was hospitable to the inhabitants of an undistinguished planet of an average star in a not very special galaxy in a group of a million such, and that group of galaxies one of millions more. We are typical. Ordinary. And because we are ordinary, our universe is ordinary too, because there is no objective reality beyond that which we observe. Because, according to quantum entanglement, pairs of particles share information about each other's quantum states even when distance and timing means that no signal can pass between them. Because observation is not passive. Because our measurements influence the fundamental laws of the universe. They create reality.

But suppose other observers outnumbered us? What would happen then?

The probability of even one Boltzmann brain appearing in the fourteen billion years of the universe's history is vanishingly small. But perhaps something changed the local quantum field and made it more hospitable to them. Perhaps the density of our own consciousness attracted them, as the mass of a star changes the gravitation field and attracts passing comets. Or perhaps the inhabitants of another universe are interfering with our universe. Perhaps the zombies are their avatars: Boltzmann brains that pop out of the energy field and change our universe to suit their masters simply because they think differently and see things differently.

This was what the old physicist told me, in the long ago. He had evidence, too. Simple experiments that measured slow and continuous changes in the position of the absorption lines of calcium and helium and hydrogen in the sun's spectrum, in standards of mass and distance, and in the speed of light. He believed that the fundamental fabric of the universe was being altered by the presence of the zombies, and that those changes were reaching back into the past and forward into the future, just as a pebble dropped into a pond will send ripples spreading out to either side. Every time he checked the historical records of the positions of those absorption lines, they agreed with his contemporaneous measurements, even though those measurements were continuously changing. We are no longer what we once were, but we are not aware of having changed because our memories have been changed too.

Do you see why this story is important? It is not just a matter of my survival, or even the survival of the human species. It is a matter of the survival of the entire known universe. The zombies have already taken so much from us. The few spies and scouts who have successfully mingled with them and escaped to tell the tale say that they are demolishing and rebuilding our cities. Day and night they ebb and flow through the streets in tidal masses, like army ants or swarming bees, under the flickering auroras of strange energies. They are as unknowable to us as we are to them.

Listen:

This is still our world. That it is still comprehensible to us, that we can still survive in it, suggests that the zombies have not yet won an outright victory. It suggests that the tide can be turned. We have become vagrants scattered across the face of the Earth, and now we must come together and go forward together. But the zombies have become so like us that we can't trust any stranger. We can't trust someone like you, who stumbled out of the wilderness into our sanctuary. That's why you must endure this test. Like mantids or spiders, we must stage fearful courtship rituals before we can accept strangers as our own.

I want you to survive this. I really do. There are not many of us left and you are young. You can have many children. Many little observers.

Listen:

This world can be ours again. It has been many years since the war, and its old beauty is returning. Now that civilisation has been shattered, it has become like Eden again. Tell me: Is a world as wild and clean and beautiful as this not worth saving? Was the sky never so green, or grass never so blue?

# BEYOND THE SEA GATES OF THE SCHOLAR PIRATES OF SARSKÖE

## GARTH NIX

Garth Nix was born in 1963 in Melbourne, Australia, and grew up in Canberra. When he turned nineteen he left to drive around the UK in a beat-up Austin with a boot full of books and a Silver-Reed typewriter. Despite a wheel literally falling off the car, he survived to return to Australia and study at the University of Canberra. He has since worked in a bookshop, as a book publicist, a publisher's sales representative, an editor, a literary agent, and as a public relations and marketing consultant. He was also a part-time soldier in the Australian Army Reserve, but now writes full-time.

His first story was published in 1984 and was followed by novels *The Ragwitch*, *Sabriel*, *Shade's Children*, *Lirael*, *Abhorsen*, the six-book YA fantasy series "The Seventh Tower," and most recently the seven-book "The Keys to the Kingdom" series. He lives in Sydney with his wife and their two children.

"Remind me why the pirates won't sink us with cannon fire at long range," said Sir Hereward as he lazed back against the bow of the skiff, his scarlet-sleeved arms trailing far enough over the side to get his twice-folded-back cuffs and hands completely drenched, with occasional splashes going down his neck and back as well. He enjoyed the sensation, for the water in these eastern seas was warm, the swell gentle, and the boat was making a good four or five knots, reaching on a twelve knot breeze.

"For the first part, this skiff formerly belonged to Annim Tel, the pirate's agent in Kerebad," said Mister Fitz. Despite being only three feet, six and a half inches tall and currently lacking even the extra height afforded by his favourite hat, the puppet was easily handling both tiller and main sheet of their small craft. "For the second part, we are both clad in red, the colour favoured by the pirates of this archipelagic trail, so they will account us as brethren until proven otherwise. For the third part, any decent perspective glass will bring close to their view the chest that lies lashed on the thwart there, and they will want to examine it, rather than blow it to smithereens."

163

"Unless they're drunk, which is highly probable," said Hereward cheerfully. He lifted his arms out of the water and shook his hands, being careful not to wet the tarred canvas bag at his feet that held his small armoury. Given the mission at hand, he had not brought any of his usual, highly identifiable weapons. Instead the bag held a mere four snaphance pistols of quite ordinary though serviceable make, an oiled leather bag of powder, a box of shot, and a blued steel main gauche in a sharkskin scabbard. A sheathed mortuary sword lay across the top of the bag, its half-basket hilt at Hereward's feet.

He had left his armour behind at the inn where they had met the messenger from the Council of the Treaty for the Safety of the World, and though he was currently enjoying the light air upon his skin, and was optimistic by nature, Hereward couldn't help reflect that a scarlet shirt, leather breeches and sea boots were not going to be much protection if the drunken pirates aboard the xebec they were sailing towards chose to conduct some musketry exercise.

Not that any amount of leather and proof steel would help if they happened to hit the chest. Even Mister Fitz's sorcery could not help them in that circumstance, though he might be able to employ some sorcery to deflect bullets or small shot from both boat and chest.

Mister Fitz looked, and was currently dressed in the puffy-trousered raiment of one of the self-willed puppets that were made long ago in a gentler age to play merry tunes, declaim epic poetry and generally entertain. This belied his true nature and most people or other beings who encountered the puppet other than casually did not find him entertaining at all. While his full sewing desk was back at the inn with Hereward's gear, the puppet still had several esoteric needles concealed under the red bandanna that was tightly strapped on his pumpkin-sized papier-mâché head, and he was possibly one of the greatest practitioners of his chosen art still to walk—or sail—the known world.

"We're in range of the bow-chasers," noted Hereward. Casually, he rolled over to lie on his stomach, so only his head was visible over the bow. "Keep her head on."

"I have enumerated three excellent reasons why they will not fire upon us," said Mister Fitz, but he pulled the tiller a little and let out the main sheet, the skiff's sails billowing as it ran with the wind, so that it would bear down directly on the bow of the anchored xebec, allowing the pirates no opportunity for a full broadside. "In any case, the bow-chasers are not even manned."

Hereward squinted. Without his artillery glass he couldn't clearly see what was occurring on deck, but he trusted Fitz's superior vision.

"Oh well, maybe they won't shoot us out of hand," he said. "At least not at first. Remind me of my supposed name and title?"

"Martin Suresword, Terror of the Syndical Sea."

"Ludicrous," said Hereward. "I doubt I can say it, let alone carry on the pretense of being such a fellow."

"There is a pirate of that name, though I believe he was rarely addressed by his preferred title," said Mister Fitz. "Or perhaps I should say there was such a pirate, up until some months ago. He was large and blond, as you are, and the Syndical Sea is extremely distant, so it is a suitable cognomen for you to assume."

"And you? Farnolio, wasn't it?"

"Farolio," corrected Fitz. "An entertainer fallen on hard times."

"How can a puppet fall on hard times?" asked Hereward. He did not look back, as some movement on the bow of the xebec fixed his attention. He hoped it was not a gun crew making ready.

"It is not uncommon for a puppet to lose their singing voice," said Fitz. "If their throat was made with a reed, rather than a silver pipe, the sorcery will only hold for five or six hundred years."

"Your throat, I suppose, is silver?"

"An admixture of several metals," said Fitz. "Silver being the most ordinary. I stand corrected on one of my earlier predictions, by the way."

"What?"

"They *are* going to fire," said Fitz, and he pushed the tiller away, the skiff's mainsail flapping as it heeled to starboard. A few seconds later, a small cannon ball splashed down forty or fifty yards to port.

"Keep her steady!" ordered Hereward. "We're as like to steer into a ball as not."

"I think there will only be the one shot," said the puppet. "The fellow who fired it is now being beaten with a musket stock.

Hereward shielded his eyes with his hand to get a better look. The sun was hot in these parts, and glaring off the water. But they were close enough now that he could clearly see a small red-clad crowd gathered near the bow, and in the middle of it, a surprisingly slight pirate was beating the living daylights out of someone who was now crouched—or who had fallen—on the deck.

"Can you make out a name anywhere on the vessel?" Hereward asked.

"I cannot," answered Fitz. "But her gun ports are black, there is a remnant of yellow striping on the rails of her quarterdeck and though the figurehead has been partially shot off, it is clearly a rampant sea-cat. This accords with Annim Tel's description, and is the vessel we seek. She is the *Sea-Cat,* captained by one Romola Fury. I suspect it is she who has clubbed the firer of the bow-chaser to the deck."

"A women pirate," mused Hereward. "Did Annim Tel mention whether she is comely?"

"I can see for myself that you would think her passing fair," said Fitz, his tone suddenly severe. "Which has no bearing on the task that lies ahead."

"Save that it may make the company of these pirates more pleasant," said Hereward. "Would you say we are now close enough to hail?"

"Indeed," said Fitz.

Hereward stood up, pressed his knees against the top strakes of the bow to keep his balance, and cupped his hands around his mouth.

"Ahoy *Sea-Cat!*" he shouted. "Permission for two brethren to come aboard?"

There was a brief commotion near the bow, most of the crowd moving purposefully to the main deck. Only two pirates remained on the bow: the slight figure, who now they were closer they could see was female and so was almost certainly Captain Fury, and a tub-chested giant of a man who stood behind her. A crumpled body lay at their feet.

The huge pirate bent to listen to some quiet words from Fury, then filling his lungs to an extent that threatened to burst the buttons of his scarlet waistcoat, answered the hail with a shout that carried much farther than Hereward's.

"Come aboard then, cullies! Port-side if you please."

Mister Fitz leaned on the tiller and hauled in the main sheet, the skiff turning wide, the intention being to circle in off the port-side of the xebec and then turn bow-first into the wind and drop the sail. If properly executed, the skiff would lose way and bump gently up against the pirate ship. If not, they would run into the vessel, damage the skiff and be a laughing stock.

This was the reason Mister Fitz had the helm. Somewhere in his long past, the puppet had served at sea for several decades, and his wooden limbs were well-salted, his experience clearly remembered and his instincts true.

Hereward, for his part, had served as a gunner aboard a frigate of the Kahlian Mercantile Alliance for a year when he was fifteen and though that lay some ten years behind him, he had since had some shorter-lived nautical adventures and was thus well able to pass himself off as a seaman aboard a fair-sized ship. But he was not a great sailor of small boats and he hastened to follow Mister Fitz's quiet commands to lower sail and prepare to fend off with an oar as they coasted to a stop next to the anchored *Sea-Cat*.

In the event, no fending off was required, but Hereward took a thrown line from the xebec to make the skiff fast alongside, while Fitz secured the head- and main-sail. With the swell so slight, the ship at anchor, and being a xebec low in the waist, it was then an easy matter to climb aboard, using the gun ports and chain-plates as foot- and hand-holds, Hereward only slightly hampered by his sword. He left the pistols in the skiff.

Pirates sauntered and swaggered across the deck to form two rough lines as Hereward and Fitz found their feet. Though they did not have weapons drawn, it was very much a gauntlet, the men and women of the *Sea-Cat* eyeing their visitors with suspicion. Though he did not wonder at the time, presuming it the norm among pirates, Hereward noted that the men in particular were ill-favoured, disfigured, or both. Fitz saw this too, and marked it as a matter for further investigation.

Romola Fury stepped down the short ladder from the forecastle deck to the waist and stood at the open end of the double line of pirates. The red waist-coated bully stood behind, but Hereward hardly noticed him. Though she was sadly lacking in the facial scars necessary for him to consider her a true beauty, Fury was indeed comely, and there was a hint of a powder burn on one high cheek-bone that accentuated her natural charms. She wore a fine blue silk coat embroidered with leaping sea-cats, without a shirt. As her coat was only loosely buttoned, Hereward found his attention very much focussed upon her. Belatedly, he remembered his instructions, and gave a flamboyant but unstructured wave of his open hand, a gesture meant to be a salute.

"Well met, Captain! Martin Suresword and the dread puppet Farolio, formerly of the *Anodyne Pain*, brothers in good standing of the chapter of the Syndical Sea."

Fury raised one eyebrow and tilted her head a little to the side, the long reddish hair on the unshaved half of her head momentarily catching the breeze. Hereward kept his eyes on her, and tried to look relaxed, though he was ready to dive aside, headbutt a path through the gauntlet of pirates, circle behind the mizzen, draw his sword and hold off the attack long enough for Fitz to wreak his havoc…

"You're a long way from the Syndical Sea, Captain Suresword," Fury finally replied. Her voice was strangely pitched and throaty, and Fitz thought it might be the effects of an acid or alkaline burn to the tissues of the throat. "What brings you to these waters, and to the *Sea-Cat*? In Annim Tel's craft, no less, with a tasty-looking chest across the thwarts?"

She made no sign, but something in her tone or perhaps in the words themselves made the two lines of pirates relax and the atmosphere of incipient violence ease.

"A proposition," replied Hereward. "For the mutual benefit of all."

Fury smiled and strolled down the deck, her large enforcer at her heels. She paused in front of Hereward, looked up at him, and smiled a crooked smile, provoking in him the memory of a cat that always looked just so before it sat on his lap and trod its claws into his groin.

"Is it riches we're talking about, Martin Sure… sword? Gold treasure and the like? Not slaves, I trust? We don't hold with slaving on the *Sea-Cat*, no matter what our brothers of the Syndical Sea may care for."

"Not slaves, Captain," said Hereward. "But treasure of all kinds. More gold and silver than you've ever seen. More than anyone has ever seen."

Fury's smile broadened for a moment. She slid a foot forward like a dancer, moved to Hereward's side and linked her arm through his, neatly pinning his sword-arm.

"Do tell, Martin," she said. "Is it to be an assault on the Ingmal Convoy? A cutting-out venture in Hryken Bay?"

Her crew laughed as she spoke, and Hereward felt the mood change again. Fury was mocking him, for it would take a vast fleet of pirates to carry an assault on the fabulous biennial convoy from the Ingmal saffron fields, and Hryken Bay was dominated by the guns of the justly famous Diamond Fort and its red-hot shot.

"I do not bring you dreams and fancies, Captain Fury," said Hereward quietly.

"What I offer is a prize greater than even a galleon of the Ingmal."

"What then?" asked Fury. She gestured at the sky, where a small turquoise disc was still visible near the horizon, though it was faded by the sun. "You'll bring the blue moon down for us to plunder?"

"I offer a way through the Secret Channels and the Sea Gate of the Scholar-Pirates of Sarsköe," said Hereward, speaking louder with each word, as the pirates began to shout, most in angry disbelief, but some in excited greed.

Fury's hand tightened on Hereward's arm, but she did not speak immediately. Slowly, as her silence was noted, her crew grew quiet, such was her power over them. Hereward knew very few others who had such presence, and he had known many kings and princes, queens and high priestesses. Not for the first time, he felt a stab of doubt about their plan, or more accurately Fitz's plan. Fury was no cat's-paw, to be lightly used by others.

"What is this way?" asked Fury, when her crew was silent, the only sound the lap of the waves against the hull, the creak of the rigging, and to Hereward at least, the pounding of his own heart.

"I have a dark rutter for the channels," he said. "Farolio here, is a gifted navigator. He will take the star sights."

"So the Secret Channels may be traveled," said Fury. "If the rutter is true."

"It is true, madam," piped up Fitz, pitching his voice higher than usual. He sounded childlike, and harmless. "We have journeyed to the foot of the Sea Gate and returned, this past month."

Fury glanced down at the puppet, who met her gaze with his unblinking, blue-painted eyes, the sheen of the sorcerous varnish upon them bright. She met the puppet's gaze for several seconds, her eyes narrowing once more, in a fashion reminiscent of a cat that sees something it is not sure whether to flee or fight. Then she slowly looked back at Hereward.

"And the Sea Gate? It matters not to pass the channels if the gate is shut against us."

"The Sea Gate is not what it once was," said Hereward. "If pressure is brought against the correct place, then it will fall."

"Pressure?" asked Fury, and the veriest tip of her tongue thrust out between her lips.

"I am a Master Gunner," said Hereward. "In the chest aboard out skiff is a mortar shell of particular construction—and I believe that not a week past you captured a Harker-built bomb vessel, and have yet to dispose of it."

He did not mention that this ship had been purchased specifically for his command, and its capture had seriously complicated their initial plan.

"You are well-informed," said Fury. "I do have such a craft, hidden in a cove beyond the strand. I have my crew, none better in all this sea. You have a rutter, a navigator, a bomb, and the art to bring the Sea Gate down. Shall we say two-thirds to we Sea-Cats and one-third to you and your puppet?"

"Done," said Hereward.

"Yes," said Fitz.

Fury unlinked her arm from Hereward's, held up her open hand and licked her palm most daintily, before offering it to him. Hereward paused, then spat mostly air on his own palm, and they shook upon the bargain.

Fitz held up his hand, as flexible as any human's, though it was dark brown and grained like wood, and licked his palm with a long blue-stippled tongue that was pierced with a silver stud. Fury slapped more than shook Fitz's hand, and she did not look at the puppet.

"Jabez!" instructed Fury, and her great hulking right-hand man was next to shake on the bargain, his grip surprisingly light and deft, and his eyes warm with humour, a small smile on his battered face. Whether it was for the prospect of treasure or some secret amusement, Hereward could not tell, and Jabez did not smile for Fitz. After Jabez came the rest of the crew, spitting and shaking till the bargain was sealed with all aboard. Like every ship of the brotherhood, the Sea-Cats were in theory a free company, and decisions made by all.

The corpse on the forecastle was an indication that this was merely a theory and that in practice, Captain Fury ruled as she wished. The spitting and handshaking was merely song and dance and moonshadow, but it played well with the pirates, who enjoyed pumping Hereward's hand till his shoulder hurt. They did not take such liberties with Fitz, but this was no sign they had discerned his true nature, but merely the usual wariness of humans towards esoteric life.

When all the hand-clasping was done, Fury took Hereward's arm again and led him towards the great cabin in the xebec's stern. As they strolled along the deck, she called over her shoulder, "Make ready to sail, Jabez. Captain Suresword and I have some matters to discuss."

Fitz followed at Hereward's heels. Jabez's shouts passed over his head, and he had to weave his way past pirates rushing to climb the ratlines or man the capstan that would raise the anchor.

Fury's great cabin was divided by a thick curtain that separated her sleeping quarters from a larger space that was not quite broad enough to comfortably house both the teak-topped table and the two twelve-pounder guns. Fury had to let go of Hereward to slip through the space between the breech of one gun and the table corner, and he found himself strangely relieved by the cessation of physical proximity. He was no stranger to women, and had dallied with courtesans, soldiers, farm girls, priestesses and even a widowed empress, but there was something about Fury that unsettled him more than any of these past lovers.

Consequently he was even more relieved when she did not lead him through the curtain to her sleeping quarters, but sat at the head of the table and gestured for him to sit on one side. He did so, and Fitz hopped up on to the table.

"Drink!" shouted Fury. She was answered by a grunt from behind a half-door in the fore bulkhead that Hereward had taken for a locker. The door opened a fraction and a scrawny, tattooed, handless arm was thrust out, the stump through the leather loop of a wineskin which was unceremoniously thrown up to the table.

"Go get the meat on the forecastle," added Fury. She raised the wineskin and daintily directed a jet of a dark, resinous wine into her mouth, licking her lips most carefully when she finished. She passed the skin to Hereward, who took the merest swig. He was watching the horribly mutilated little man who was crawling across the deck. The pirate's skin was so heavily and completely tattooed that it took a moment to realize he was an albino. He had only his left hand, his right arm ending at the wrist. Both of his legs were gone from the knee, and he scuttled on his stumps like a tricorn beetle.

"M' steward," said Fury, as the fellow left. She took another long drink. "Excellent cook."

Hereward nodded grimly. He had recognized some of the tattoos on the man, which identified him as a member of one of the cannibal societies that infested the decaying city of Coradon, far to the south.

"I'd invite you to take nuncheon with me," said Fury, with a sly look. "But most folk don't share my tastes."

Hereward nodded. He had in fact eaten human flesh, when driven to extremity in the long retreat from Jeminero. It was not something he wished to partake of again, should there be any alternative sustenance.

"We are all but meat and water, in the end," said Fury. "Saving your presence, puppet."

"It is a philosophic position that I find unsurprising in one of your past life," said Fitz. "I, for one, do not think it strange for you to eat dead folk, particularly when there is always a shortage of fresh meat at sea."

"What do you know of my 'past life'?" asked Fury, and she smiled just a little, so her sharp eye teeth protruded over her lower lip.

"Only what I observe," remarked Fitz. "Though the mark is faded, I perceive a Lurquist slave brand in that quarter of the skin above your left breast and below your shoulder. You also have the characteristic scar of a Nagolon manacle on your right wrist. These things indicate you have been a slave at least twice, and so must have freed yourself or been freed, also twice. The Nagolon cook the flesh of their dead rowers to provide for the living, hence your taste—"

"I think that will do," interrupted Fury. She looked at Hereward. "We all need our little secrets, do we not? But there are others we must share. It is enough for the crew to know no more than the song about the Scholar-Pirates of Sarsköe and the dangers of the waters near their isle. But I would know the whole of it. Tell me more about these Scholar-Pirates and their fabled fortress. Do they still lurk behind the Sea Gate?"

"The Sea Gate has been shut fast these last two hundred years or more," Hereward said carefully. He had to answer before Fitz did, as the puppet could not always be trusted to sufficiently skirt the truth, even when engaged on a task that required subterfuge and misdirection. "The Scholar-Pirates have not been seen since that time and most likely the fortress is now no more than a dark and silent tomb."

"If it is not now, we shall make it so," said Fury. She hesitated for a second, then added, "For the Scholar-Pirates," and tapped the table thrice with the bare iron ring she wore on the thumb of her left hand. This was an ancient gesture, and told Fitz even more about the captain.

"The song says they were indeed as much scholars as pirates," said Fury. "I have no desire to seize a mound of dusty parchment or rows of books. Do you know of anything more than legend that confirms their treasure?"

"I have seen inside their fortress," said Fitz. "Some four hundred years past, before the Sea Gate was... permanently raised. There were very few true scholars among them even then, and most had long since made learning secondary to the procurement of riches... and riches there were, in plenty."

"How old are you, puppet?"

Fitz shrugged his little shoulders and did not answer, a forbearance that Hereward was pleased to see. Fury was no common pirate, and anyone who knew Fitz's age and a little history could put the two together in a way that might require adjustment, and jeopardize Hereward's current task.

"There will be gold enough for all," Hereward said hastily. "There are four or five accounts extant from ransomed captives of the Scholar-Pirates, and all mention great stores of treasure. Treasure for the taking."

"Aye, after some small journey through famously impassable waters and a legendary gate," said Fury. "As I said, tell me the whole."

"We will," said Hereward. "Farolio?"

"If I may spill a little wine, I will sketch out a chart," said Fitz.

Fury nodded. Hereward poured a puddle of wine on the corner of the table for the puppet, who crouched and dipped his longest finger in it, which was the one next to his thumb, then quickly sketched a rough map of many islands. Though he performed no obvious sorcery, the wet lines were quite sharp and did not dry out as quickly as one might expect.

"The fortress itself is built wholly within a natural vastness inside this isle, in the very heart of the archipelago. The pirates called both island and fortress Cror Holt, though its proper name is Sarsköe, which is also the name of the entire island group."

Fitz made another quick sketch, an enlarged view of the same island, a roughly circular land that was split from its eastern shore to its centre by a jagged, switch-backed line of five turns.

"The sole entry to the Cror Holt cavern is from the sea, through this gorge which cuts a zigzag way for almost nine miles through the limestone. The gorge terminates at a smooth cliff, but here the pirates bored a tunnel through to their cavern. The entrance to the tunnel is barred by the famed Sea Gate, which measures one hundred and seven feet wide and one hundred and ninety-seven feet high. The sea abuts it at near forty feet at low water and sixty-three at the top of the tide.

"The gorge is narrow, only broad enough for three ships to pass abreast, so it is not possible to directly fire upon the Sea Gate with cannon. However, we have devised a scheme to fire a bomb from the prior stretch of the gorge, over the intervening rock wall and into the top of the gate.

"Once past the gate, there is a harbour pool capacious enough to host a dozen vessels of a similar size to your *Sea-Cat*, with three timber wharves built out from a paved quay. The treasure- and store-houses of the Scholar-Pirates are built on an inclined crescent above the quay, along with residences and other buildings of no great note."

"You are an unusual puppet," said Fury. She took the wineskin and poured another long stream down her throat. "Go on."

Fitz nodded, and returned to his first sketch, his finger tracing a winding path between the islands.

"To get to the Cror Holt entry in the first place, we must pick our way through the so-called Secret Channels. There are close to two hundred islands and reefs arrayed around the central isle, and the only passage through is twisty indeed. Adding complication to difficulty, we must pass these channels at night, a night with a clear sky, for we have only the dark rutter to guide us through the channels, and the path contained therein is detailed by star sights and soundings.

"We will also have to contend with most difficult tides. This is particularly so in the final approach to the Sea-Gate, where the shape of the reefs and islands—and I suspect some sorcerous tinkering—funnel two opposing tidewashes into each other. The resultant *eagre*, or bore as some call it, enters the mouth of the gorge an hour before high water and the backwash returns some fifteen minutes later. The initial wave is taller than your top-masts and very swift, and will destroy any craft caught in the gorge.

"Furthermore, we must also be in the Cror Holt gorge just before the turn of the tide, in order to secure the bomb vessel ready for firing during the slack water. With only one shot, He… Martin, that is, will need the most stable platform possible. I have observed the slack water as lasting twenty-three minutes and we must have the bomb vessel ready to fire.

"Accordingly we must enter after the *eagre* has gone in and come out, anchor and spring the bomb vessel at the top of the tide, fire on the slack and then we will have some eight or nine hours at most to loot and be gone before the *eagre* returns, and without the Sea Gate to block it, floods the fortress completely and drowns all within."

Fury looked from the puppet to Hereward, her face impassive. She did not speak for at least a minute. Hereward and Fitz waited silently, listening to the sounds of the crew in deck and rigging above them, the creak of the vessel's timbers and above all that, the thump of someone chopping something up in the captain's galley that lay somewhat above them and nearer the waist.

"It is a madcap venture, and my crew would mutiny if they knew what lies ahead," said Fury finally. "Nor do I trust either of you to have told me the half of it. But… I grow tired of the easy pickings on this coast. Perhaps it is time to test my luck again. We will join with the bomb vessel, which is called *Strongarm*, by nightfall and sail on in convoy. You will both stay aboard the *Sea-Cat*. How long to gain the outer archipelago, master navigator puppet?"

"Three days with a fair wind," said Fitz. "If the night then is clear, we shall have two of three moons sufficiently advanced to light our way, but not so much they will mar my star sights. Then it depends upon the wind. If it is even passing fair, we should reach the entrance to the Cror Holt gorge two hours after midnight, as the tide nears its flood."

"Madness," said Fury again, but she laughed and slapped Fitz's sketch, a spray of wine peppering Hereward's face. "You may leave me now. Jabez will find you quarters."

Hereward stood and almost bowed, before remembering he was a pirate. He turned the bow into a flamboyant wipe of his wine-stained face and turned away, to follow Fitz, who had jumped down from the table without any attempt at courtesy.

As they left, Fury spoke quietly, but her words carried great force.

"Remember this, Captain Suresword. I eat my enemies—and those that betray my trust I eat alive."

That parting comment was still echoing in Hereward's mind four days later, as the *Sea-Cat* sailed cautiously between two lines of white breakers no more than a mile apart. The surf was barely visible in the moonlight, but all aboard could easily envision the keel-tearing reefs that lay below.

*Strongarm* wallowed close behind, its ragged wake testament to its inferior sailing properties, much of this due to the fact that it had a huge mortar sitting where it would normally have a foremast. But though it would win no races, *Strongarm* was a beautiful vessel in Hereward's eyes, with her massively reinforced decks and beams, chain rigging and, of course, the great iron mortar itself.

Though Fury had not let him stay overlong away from the *Sea-Cat*, and Fitz had been required to stay on the xebec, Hereward had spent nearly all his daylight hours on the bomb vessel, familiarizing himself with the mortar and training the crew he had been given to serve it. Though he would only have one shot with the special bomb prepared by Mister Fitz, and he would load and aim that himself, Hereward had kept his gunners busy drilling. With a modicum of luck, the special shot would bring the Sea Gate down, but he thought there could well be an eventuality where even commonplace bombs might need to be rained down upon the entrance to Cror Holt.

A touch at Hereward's arm brought his attention back to Fitz. Both stood on the quarterdeck, next to the helmsman, who was peering nervously ahead. Fury was in her cabin, possibly to show her confidence in her chosen navigator—and in all probability, dining once more on the leftovers of the unfortunate pirate who had taken it on himself to fire the bow-chaser.

"We are making good progress," said Fitz. He held a peculiar device at his side that combined a small telescope and a tiny, ten-line abacus of screw-thread beads. Hereward had never seen any other navigator use such an instrument, but by taking sights on the moons and the stars and with the mysterious aid of the silver chronometric egg he kept in his waistcoat, Fitz could and did fix their position most accurately. This could then be checked against the directions contained with the salt-stained leather bindings of the dark rutter.

"Come to the taffrail," whispered Fitz. More loudly, he said, "Keep her steady, helm. I shall give you a new course presently."

Man and puppet moved to the rail at the stern, to stand near the great lantern that was the essential beacon for the following ship. Hereward leaned on the rail and looked back at the *Strongarm* again. In the light of the two moons the bomb vessel was a pallid, ghostly ship, the great mortar giving it an odd silhouette.

Fitz, careless of the roll and pitch of the ship, leaped to the rail. Gripping Hereward's arm, he leaned over and looked intently at the stern below.

"Stern windows shut—we shall not be overheard," whispered Fitz.

"What is it you wish to say?" asked Hereward.

"Elements of our plan may need re-appraisal," said Fitz. "Fury is no easy dupe and once the Sea Gate falls, its nature will be evident. Though she must spare me to navigate our return to open water, I fear she may well attempt to slay you in a fit of pique. I will then be forced into action, which would be unfortunate as we may well need the pirates to carry the day."

"I trust you would be 'forced into action' before she killed me... or started eating me alive," said Hereward.

Fitz did not deign to answer this sally. They both knew Hereward's safety was of *almost* paramount concern to the puppet.

"Perchance we should give the captain a morsel of knowledge," said Fitz. "What do you counsel?"

Hereward looked down at the deck and thought of Fury at her board below, carving off a more literal morsel.

"She is a most uncommon woman, even for a pirate," he said slowly.

"She is that," said Fitz. "On many counts. You recall the iron ring, the three-times tap she did on our first meeting below? That is a grounding action against some minor forms of esoteric attack. She used it as a ward against ill-saying, which is the practice of a number of sects. I would think she was a priestess once, or at least a novice, in her youth."

"Of what god?" asked Hereward. "A listed entity? That might serve us very ill."

"Most probably some benign and harmless godlet," said Fitz. "Else she could not have been wrested from its service to the rowing benches of the Nagolon. But there is something about her that goes against this supposition... it would be prudent to confirm which entity she served."

"If you wish to ask, I have no objection..." Hereward began. Then he stopped and looked at the puppet, favouring his long-time comrade with a scowl.

"I have to take many more star sights," said Fitz. He jumped down from the rail and turned to face the bow. "Not to mention instruct the helmsman on numerous small points of sail. I think it would be in our interest to grant Captain Fury some further knowledge of our destination, and also endeavour to discover which godlet held the indenture of her youth. We have some three or four hours before we will reach the entrance to the gorge."

"I am not sure—" said Hereward.

"Surely that is time enough for such a conversation," interrupted Fitz. "Truly, I have never known you so reluctant to seek private discourse with a woman of distinction."

"A woman who feasts upon human flesh," protested Hereward as he followed Fitz.

"She merely does not waste foodstuffs," said Fitz. "I think it commendable. You have yourself partaken of—"

"Yes, yes, I remember!" said Hereward. "Take your star sight! I will go below and speak to Fury."

The helmsman looked back as Hereward spoke, and he realized he was no longer whispering.

"Captain Fury, I mean. I will speak with you anon, Mister... Farolio!"

Captain Fury was seated at her table when Hereward entered, following a cautious knock. But she was not eating and there were no recognizable human portions upon the platter in front of her. It held only a dark glass bottle and a small silver cup, the kind used in birthing rights or baptismal ceremonies. Fury drank from it, flicking her wrist to send the entire contents down her throat in one gulp. Even from a few paces distant, Hereward could smell the sharp odour of strong spirits.

"Arrack," said Fury. "I have a taste for it at times, though it does not serve me as well as once it did. You wish to speak to me? Then sit."

Hereward sat cautiously, as far away as he dared without giving offence, and angled his chair so as to allow a clean draw of the main gauche from his right hip. Fury appeared less than sober, if not exactly drunk, and Hereward was very wary of the trouble that might come from the admixture of a pirate with cannibalistic tendencies and a powerfully spirituous drink.

"I am not drunk," said Fury. "It would take three bottles of this stuff to send me away, and a better glass to sup it with. I am merely wetting down my powder before we storm the fortress."

"Why?" asked Hereward. He did not move any closer.

"I am cursed," said Fury. She poured herself another tot. "Did you suppose 'Fury' is my birth name?"

Hereward shook his head slowly.

"Perhaps I am blessed," continued the woman. She smiled her small, toothy smile again, and drank. "You will see when the fighting starts. Your puppet knows, doesn't it? Those blue eyes… it will be safe enough, but you'd best keep your distance. It's the tall men and the well-favoured that she must either bed or slay, and it's all I can do to point her towards the foe…"

"Who is she?" asked Hereward. It took some effort to keep his voice calm and level. At the same time he let his hand slowly fall to his side, fingers trailing across the hilt of his parrying dagger.

"What I become," said Fury. "A fury indeed, when battle is begun."

She made a sign with her hand, her fingers making a claw. Her nails had grown, Hereward saw, but not to full talons. Not yet. More discoloured patches—spots— had also appeared on her face, making it obvious the permanent one near her eye was not a powder-burn at all.

"You were a sister of Chelkios, the Leoparde," stated Hereward. He did not have Fitz's exhaustive knowledge of cross-dimensional entities, but Chelkios was one of the more prominent deities of the old Kvarnish Empire. Most importantly from his point of view, at least in the longer term, it was not proscribed.

"I was taken from Her by slavers when I was but a novice, a silly little thing who disobeyed the rules and left the temple," said Fury. She took another drink. "A true sister controls the temper of the beast. I must manage with rum, for the most part, and the occasional…"

She set her cup down, stood up and held her hand out to Hereward and said, "Distraction."

Hereward also stood, but did not immediately take her hand. Two powerful instincts warred against each other, a sensuous thrill that coursed through his whole body versus a panicked sense of self-preservation that emanated from a more rational reckoning of threat and chance.

"Bed or slay, she has no middle course," said Fury. Her hand trembled and the nails on her fingers grew longer and began to curve.

"There are matters pertaining to our task that you must hear," said Hereward, but as he spoke all his caution fell away and he took her hand to draw her close. "You should know that the Sea Gate is now in fact a wall…"

He paused as cool hands found their way under his shirt, muscles tensing in anticipation of those sharp nails upon his skin. But Fury's fingers were soft pads now, and quick, and Hereward's own hands were launched upon a similar voyage of discovery.

"A wall," gulped Hereward. "Built two hundred years ago by the surviving Scholar-Pirates… to… to keep in something they had originally summoned to aid them… the treasure is there… but it is guarded…"

"Later," crooned Fury, close to his ear, as she drew him back through the curtain to her private lair. "Tell me later…"

Many hours later, Fury stood on the quarterdeck and looked down at Hereward as he took his place aboard the boat that was to transfer him to the *Strongarm*.

She gave no sign that she viewed him with any particular affection or fondness, or indeed recalled their intimate relations at all. However, Hereward was relieved to see that though the lanterns in the rigging cast shadows on her face, there was only the one leoparde patch there and her nails were of a human dimension.

Fitz stood at her side, his papier-mâché head held at a slight angle so that he might see both sky and boat. Hereward had managed only a brief moment of discourse with him, enough to impart Fury's nature and to tell him that she had seemed to take the disclosure of their potential enemy with equanimity. Or possibly had not heard him properly, or recalled it, having been concerned with more immediate activities.

Both *Sea-Cat* and *Strongarm* were six miles up the gorge, its sheer, grey-white limestone walls towering several hundred feet above them. Only the silver moon was high enough to light their way, the blue moon left behind on the horizon of the open sea. Even so, it was a bright three-quarter moon, and the sky clear and full of stars, so on one score at least the night was ideal for the expedition.

But the wind had been dropping by the minute, and now the air was still, and what little sail the *Sea-Cat* had set was limp and useless. *Strongarm*'s poles were bare, as she was already moored in the position Fitz had chosen on their preliminary exploration a month before, with three anchors down and a spring on each mooring line. Hereward would adjust the vessel's lie when he got aboard, thus training the mortar exactly on the Sea Gate, which lay out of sight on the other side of the northern wall, in the next turn of the gorge.

In consequence of the calm, recourse had to be made to oars, so a longboat, two gigs and Annim Tel's skiff were in line ahead of the *Sea-Cat*, ready to tow her the last mile around the bend in the gorge. Hereward would have preferred to undertake the assault entirely in the small craft, but they could not deliver sufficient force. There were more than a hundred and ninety pirates aboard the xebec, and he suspected they might need all of them and more.

"High water," called out someone from near the bow of the *Sea-Cat*. "The flow has ceased."

"Give way!" ordered Hereward, and his boat surged forward, six pirates bending their strength upon the oars. With the gorge so narrow it would only take a few minutes to reach the *Strongarm*, but with the tide at its peak and slack water begun, Hereward had less than a quarter-hour to train, elevate and fire the mortar.

Behind him, he heard Jabez roar, quickly followed by the splash of many oars in the water as the boats began the tow. It would be a slow passage for the *Sea-Cat*, and Hereward's gig would easily catch them up.

The return journey out of the gorge would be just as slow, Hereward thought, and entailed much greater risk. If they lost too many rowers in battle, and if the wind failed to come up, they might well not make it out before the *eagre* came racing up the gorge once more.

He tried to dismiss images of the great wave roaring down the gorge as he climbed up the side of the bomb vessel and quickly ran to the mortar. His crew had everything ready. The chest was open to show the special bomb, the charge bags were laid on oil-cloth next to it and his gunner's quadrant and fuses were laid out likewise on the opposite side.

Hereward looked up at the sky and at the marks Fitz had sorcerously carved into the cliff the month before, small things that caught the moonlight and might be mistaken for a natural pocket of quartz. Using these marks, he ordered a minor adjustment of the springs to warp the bomb vessel around a fraction, a task that took precious minutes as the crew heaved on the lines.

While they heaved, Hereward laid the carefully calculated number and weight of charge bags in the mortar. Then he checked and cut the fuse, measuring it three times and checking it again, before pushing it into the bomb. This was a necessary piece of misdirection for the benefit of the pirates, for in fact Fitz had put a sorcerous trigger in the bomb so that it would explode exactly as required.

"Load!" called Hereward. The six pirates who served the mortar leaped into action, two carefully placing the wadding on the charge bags while the other four gingerly lifted the bomb and let it slide back into the mortar.

"Prepare for adjustment," came the next command. Hereward laid his gunner's quadrant in the barrel and the crew took a grip on the two butterfly-shaped handles that turned the cogs that would raise the mortar's inclination. "Up six turns!"

"Up six turns!" chorused the hands as they turned the handles, bronze cogs ticking as the teeth interlocked with the thread of the inclination screws. The barrel of the mortar slowly rose, till it was pointing up at the clear sky and was only ten degrees from the vertical.

"Down one quarter turn!"

"Down one quarter turn!"

The barrel came down. Hereward checked the angle once more. All would depend upon this one shot.

"Prime her and ready matches!"

The leading hand primed the touch-hole with fine powder from a flask, while his second walked back along the deck to retrieve two linstocks, long poles that held burning lengths of match cord.

"Stand ready!"

Hereward took one linstock and the leading gunner the other. The rest of the gun crew walked aft, away from the mortar, increasing their chances of survival should there be some flaw in weapon or bomb that resulted in early detonation.

"One for the sea, two for the shore, three for the match," Hereward chanted. On three he lit the bomb's fuse and strode quickly away, still chanting, "four for the gunner and five for the bore!"

On "bore" the gunner lit the touch-hole.

Hereward already had his eyes screwed shut and was crouched on the deck fifteen feet from the mortar, with his back to it and a good handhold. Even so, the flash went through his eyelids and the concussion and thunderous report that followed sent him sprawling across the deck. The *Strongarm* pitched and rolled too, so that he was in some danger of going over the side, till he found another handhold.

Hauling himself upright, Hereward looked up to make sure the bomb had cleared the rim of the gorge, though he knew that if it hadn't there would already be broken rock falling all around. Blinking against the spots and luminous blurring that were the after-effects of the flash, he stared up at the sky and a few seconds later, was rewarded by the sight of another, even brighter flash and, hard on its heels, a deep, thunderous rumble.

"A hit, a palpable hit!" cried the leading gunner, who was an educated man who doubtless had some strange story of how he had become a pirate. "Well done, sir!"

"It hit something, sure enough," said Hereward, as the other gunners cheered. "But has it brought the Sea Gate down? We shall see. Gunners, swab out the mortar and stand ready. Crew, to the boat. We must make haste."

As expected, Hereward's gig easily caught the *Sea-Cat* and its towing boats, which were making slow progress, particularly as a small wave had come down from farther up the gorge, setting them momentarily aback, but heartening Hereward as it indicated a major displacement of the water in front of the Sea Gate.

This early portent of success was confirmed some short time later as his craft came in sight of the gorge's terminus. Dust and smoke still hung in the air, and there was a huge dark hole in the middle of what had once been a great wall of pale green bricks.

"Lanterns!" called Hereward as they rowed forward, and his bowman held a lantern high in each hand, the two beams catching spirals of dust and blue-grey gunsmoke which were still twisting their way up towards the silver moon.

The breach in the wall was sixty feet wide, Hereward reckoned, and though bricks were still tumbling on either side, there were none left to fall from above. The *Sea-Cat* could be safely towed inside, to disgorge the pirates upon the wharves or, if they had rotted and fallen away, to the quay itself.

Hereward looked aft. The xebec was some hundred yards behind, its lower yardarms hung with lanterns so that it looked like some strange, blazing-eyed monster slowly wading up the gorge, the small towing craft ahead of it low dark shapes, lesser servants lit by duller lights.

"Rest your oars," said Hereward, louder than he intended. His ears were still damped from the mortar blast. "Ready your weapons and watch that breach."

Most of the pirates hurried to prime pistols or ease dirks and cutlasses in scabbards, but one woman, a broad-faced bravo with a slit nose, laid her elbows on her oars and watched Hereward as he reached into his boot and removed the brassard he had placed there. A simple armband, he had slid it up his arm before he noticed her particular attention, which only sharpened as she saw that the characters embroidered on the brassard shone with their own internal light, far brighter than could be obtained by any natural means.

"What's yon light?" she asked. Others in the crew also turned to look.

"So you can find me," answered Hereward easily. "It is painted with the guts of light-bugs. Now I must pray a moment. If any of you have gods to speak to, now is the time."

He watched for a moment, cautious of treachery or some reaction to the brassard, but the pirates had other concerns. Many of them did bend their heads, or close one eye, or touch their knees with the backs of their hands, or adopt one of the thousands of positions of prayer approved by the godlets they had been raised to worship.

Hereward did none of these things, but spoke under his breath, so that none might hear him.

"In the name of the Council of the Treaty for the Safety of the World, acting under the authority granted by the Three Empires, the Seven Kingdoms, the Palatine Regency, the Jessar Republic and the Forty Lesser Realms, I declare myself an agent of the Council. I identify the godlet manifested in this fortress of Cror Holt as Forjill-Um-Uthrux, a listed entity under the Treaty. Consequently the said godlet and all those who assist it are deemed to be enemies of the World, and the Council authorizes me to pursue any and all actions necessary to banish, repel or exterminate the said godlet."

"Captain Suresword! Advance and clear the channel!"

It was Fury calling, no longer relying on the vasty bellow of Jabez. The xebec was closing more rapidly, the towing craft rowing faster, the prospect of gold reviving tired pirates. Hereward could see Fury in the bow of the *Sea-Cat*, and Fitz beside her, his thin arm a-glow from his own brassard.

Hereward touched the butts of the two pistols in his belt and then the hilt of his mortuary sword. The entity that lay in the darkness within could not be harmed by shot or steel, but it was likely served by those who could die as readily as any other mortal. Hereward's task was to protect Fitz from such servants, while the puppet's sorcery dealt with the god.

"Out oars!" he shouted, loud as he could this time. "Onwards to fortune! Give way!"

Oars dipped, the boat surged forward and they passed the ruins of the Sea Gate into the black interior of Cror Holt.

Out of the moonlight the darkness was immediate and disturbing, though the tunnel was so broad and high and their lantern-light of such small consequence that they had no sense of being within a confined space. Indeed, though Hereward knew the tunnel itself was short, he could only tell when they left it and entered the greater cavern by the difference in the sound of their oar-splashes, immediate echoes being replaced by more distant ones.

"Keep her steady," he instructed, his voice also echoing back across the black water. "Watch for the wharves or submerged piles. It can't be far."

"There, Captain!"

It was not a wharf, but the spreading rings of some disturbance upon the surface of the still water. Something big had popped up and sank again, off the starboard quarter of the boat.

"Pull harder!" instructed Hereward. He drew a pistol and cocked the lock. The *Sea-Cat* was following, and from its many lanterns he could see the lower outline of the tunnel around it.

"I see the wharf!" cried the bowman, his words immediately followed by a sudden thump under the hull, the crack of broken timber and a general falling about in the boat, one of the lanterns going over the side into immediate extinguishment.

"We've struck!" shouted a pirate. He stood as if to leap over the side, but paused and looked down.

Hereward looked too. They had definitely hit something hard and the boat should be sinking beneath them. But it was dry. He looked over the side and saw that the boat was at rest on stony ground. There was no water beneath them at all. Another second of examination, and a backward look confirmed that rather than the boat striking a reef, the ground below them had risen up. There was a wharf some ten yards away but its deck was well above them, and the harbour wall a barrier behind it, that they would now need to climb to come to the treasure houses.

"What's that?" asked the gold-toothed pirate uncertainly.

Hereward looked and fired in the same moment, at a seven-foot-tall yellow starfish that was shuffling forward on two points. The bullet took it in the midsection, blasting out a hole the size of a man's fist, but the starfish did not falter.

"Shoot it!" he shouted. There were starfish lurching upright all around and he knew there would be even more beyond the lantern-light. "*Sea-Cat*, ware shallows and enemy!"

The closer starfish fell a second later, its lower points shot to pulp. Pirates swore as they reloaded, all of them clustering closer to Hereward as if he might ward them from this sudden, sorcerous enemy.

Louder gunfire echoed in from the tunnel. Hereward saw flashes amid the steady light of the xebec's lanterns. The *Sea-Cat*'s bow-chasers and swivel guns were being fired, so they too must be under attack. He also noted that the ship was moving no closer and in fact, might even be receding.

"Cap'n, the ship! She's backing!" yelled a panicked pirate. He snatched up the remaining lantern and ran from the defensive ring about the boat, intent on the distant lights of the *Sea-Cat*. A few seconds later the others saw pirate and lantern go under a swarm of at least a dozen starfish, and then it was dark once more, save for the glow of the symbols on Hereward's arm.

"Bowman, get a line over the wharf!" shouted Hereward. The mortuary sword was in his hand now, though he could not recall drawing it, and he hacked at a starfish whose points were reaching for him. The things were getting quicker, as if, like battlemounts, they needed to warm their blood. "We must climb up! Hold them back!"

The six of them retreated to the piles of the wharf, the huge, ambulatory starfish pressing their attack. With no time to reload, Hereward and the pirates had to hack and cut at them with sword, cutlasses and a boarding axe, and kick away the pieces that still writhed and sought to fasten themselves on their enemies. Within a minute, all of them had minor wounds to their lower legs, where the rough suckers of the starfish's foul bodies had rasped away clothing and skin.

"Line's fast!" yelled the bowman, and he launched himself up it, faster than any topman had ever climbed a ratline. Two of the other pirates clashed as they tried to climb together, one kicking the other in the face as he wriggled above. The lower pirate fell and was immediately smothered by a starfish that threw itself over him. Muffled screams came from beneath the writhing, yellow five-armed monster, and the pirate's feet drummed violently on the ground for several seconds before they stilled.

"Go!" shouted Hereward to the remaining pirate, who needed no urging. She was halfway up the rope as Hereward knelt down, held his sword with both hands and whirled on his heel in a complete circle, the fine edge of his blade slicing through the lower points of half a dozen advancing starfish. As they fell over, Hereward threw his sword up to the wharf, jumped on the back of the starfish that was hunched over the fallen pirate, leaped to the rope and swarmed up it as starfish points tugged at his heels, rasping off the soles of his boots.

The woman pirate handed Hereward his sword as he reached the deck of the wharf. Once again the surviving quartet huddled close to him, eager to stay within the small circle of light provided by his brassard.

"Watch the end of the wharf!" instructed Hereward. He looked over the side. The huge starfish were everywhere below, but they were either unable or unwilling to climb up, so unless a new enemy presented itself there was a chance of some respite.

"She's gone," whispered one of his crew.

The *Sea-Cat* was indeed no longer visible in the tunnel, though there was still a great noise of gunfire, albeit more distant than before.

"The ground rising up has set her aback," said Hereward. "But Captain Fury will land a reinforcement, I'm sure."

"There are so many of them evil stars," whispered the same man.

"They can be shot and cut to pieces," said Hereward sternly. "We will prevail, have no fear."

He spoke confidently, but was not so certain himself. Particularly as he could see the pieces of all the cut-up starfish wriggling together into a pile below, joining together to make an even bigger starfish, one that could reach up to the wharf.

"We'll move back to the quay," he announced, as two of the five points of the assembling giant starfish below began to flex. "Slow and steady, keep your wits about you."

The five of them moved back along the wharf in a compact huddle, with weapons facing out, like a hedgehog slowly retreating before a predator. Once on the quay, Hereward ordered them to reload, but they had all dropped their pistols, and Hereward had lost one of his pair. He gave his remaining gun to the gold-toothed pirate.

"There are stone houses above," he said, gesturing into the dark. "If we must retreat, we shall find a defensible position there."

"Why wait? Let's get behind some walls now."

"We wait for Captain Fury and the others," said Hereward. "They'll be here any—"

The crack of a small gun drowned out his voice. It was followed a second later by a brilliant flash that lit up the whole cavern and then hard on the heels of the flash came a blinding horizontal bolt of forked lightning that spread across the whole harbour floor, branching into hundreds of lesser jolts that connected with the starfish in a crazed pattern of blue-white sparks.

A strong, nauseatingly powerful stench of salt and rotted meat washed across the pirates on the quay as the darkness returned. Hereward blinked several times and swallowed to try and clear his ears, but neither effort really worked. He knew from experience that both sight and sound would return in a few minutes, and he also knew that the explosion and lightning could only be the work of Mister Fitz. Nevertheless he had an anxious few minutes till he could see enough to make out the fuzzy globes that must be lanterns held by approaching friendly forces, and hear his fellows well enough to know that he would also hear any enemy on the wharf or quay.

"It's the captain!" cried a pirate. "She's done those stars in."

The starfish had certainly been dealt a savage blow. Fury and Fitz and a column of lantern-bearing pirates were making their way through a charnel field of thousands of pieces of starfish meat, few of them bigger than a man's fist.

But as the pirates advanced, the starfish pieces began to move, pallid horrors wriggling across the stony ground, melding with other pieces to form more mobile gobbets of invertebrate flesh, all of them moving to a central rendezvous somewhere beyond the illumination of the lanterns.

Hereward did not pause to wonder exactly what these disgusting starfish remnants were going to do in the darker reaches of the harbour. He ran along the wharf and took Fitz's hand, helping the puppet to climb the boarding nets that Fury's crew were throwing up. Before Fitz was on his feet, pirates raced past them both, talking excitedly of treasure, the starfish foe forgotten. Hereward's own boat crew, who might have more reason than most to be more thoughtful, had already been absorbed into this flood of looters.

"The starfish are growing back," said Hereward urgently, as he palmed off a too-eager pirate who nearly trod on Fitz.

"Not exactly," corrected Fitz. "Forjill-Um-Uthrux is manifesting itself more completely here. It will use its starfish minions to craft a physical shape. And possibly more importantly—"

"Captain Suresword!" cried Fury, clapping him on the back. Her eyes were bright, there were several dark spots on her face and her ears were long and furred, but she evidently had managed to halt or slow the full transformation. "On to the treasure!"

She laughed and ran past him, with many pirates behind her. Up ahead, the sound of ancient doors being knocked down was already being replaced by gleeful and astonished cries as many hundredweight of loose gold and silver coinage poured out around the looter's thighs.

"More importantly perhaps, Um-Uthrux is doing something to manipulate the sea," continued Fitz. "It has tilted the harbour floor significantly and I can perceive energistic tendrils extending well beyond this island. I fear it raising the tide ahead of time and with it—"

"The *eagre*," said Hereward. "Do we have time to get out?"

"No," said Fitz. "It will be at the mouth of the gorge within minutes. We must swiftly deal with Um-Uthrux and then take refuge in one of the upper buildings, the strongest possible, where I will spin us a bubble of air."

"How big a bubble?" asked Hereward, as he took a rapid glance around. There were lanterns bobbing all around the slope above the quay, and it looked like all two hundred odd of Fury's crew were in amongst the Scholar-Pirates' buildings.

"A single room, sufficient for a dozen mortals," said Fitz. "Ah, Um-Uthrux has made its host. Please gather as many pirates as you can to fire on it, Hereward. I will require some full minutes of preparation."

The puppet began to take off his bandanna and Hereward shielded his face with his hand. A terrible, harsh light filled the cavern as Fitz removed an esoteric needle that had been glued to his head, the light fading as he closed his hand around it. Any mortal that dared to hold such a needle unprotected would no longer have hand or arm, but Fitz had been specifically made to deal with such things.

In the brief flash of light, Hereward saw a truly giant starfish beginning to stand on its lower points. It was sixty feet wide and at least that tall, and was not pale yellow like its lesser predecessors, but a virulent colour like infected pus, and its broad surface was covered not in a rasping, lumpy structure of tiny suckers but in hundreds of foot-wide puckered mouths that were lined with sharp teeth.

"Fury!" roared Hereward as he sprinted back along the wharf, ignoring the splinters in his now bare feet, his ruined boots flapping about his ankles. "Fury! Sea-Cats! To arms, to arms!"

He kept shouting, but he could not see Fury, and the pirates in sight were gold-drunk, bathing uproariously in piles of coin and articles of virtu that had spilled out of the broken treasure houses and into the cobbled streets between the buildings.

pushed it forward, timber flying as it bulled its way to the quay. Then with
veep of a middle point, it swept up a dozen pirates and, rolling the point
n a tight circle, held them while its many mouths went to work.
e and fall back!" shouted Fury. "Fire and fall back!"
fired a long-barrelled pistol herself, but it too had no effect. Um-Uthrux
several more pirates as they tried to flee, wrapping around them, bones
oody fragments falling upon shocked companions who were snatched up
elves by another point seconds later.
eward and Fury ran back to the corner of one of the treasure houses.
ard tripped over a golden salt-boat and a pile of coins and would have
had not Fury dragged him on even as the tip of a starfish point crashed
where he had been, flattening the masterwork of some long-forgotten
iith.
r sorcerer-puppet had best do something," said Fury.
will," panted Hereward. But he could not see Fitz, and Um-Uthrux was
ending over the quay with its central torso as well as its points, so its reach
be greater. The quay was crumbling under its assault, and the stones were
with the blood of many pirates. "We must go higher up!"
k Sea-Cats!" shouted Fury. "Higher up!"
treasure house that had sheltered them was pounded into dust and frag-
as they struggled up the steep, cobbled street. Panicked pirates streamed
em, most without their useless weapons. There was no screaming now,
groans and panting of the tired and wounded, and the sobbing of those
nerve was entirely gone.
ward pointed to a door at the very top of the street. It had already been
in by some pirate, but the building's front appeared to be a mere façade
ver a chamber dug into the island itself, and so would be stronger than
er.
 here!" he shouted, but the pirates were running down the side alleys as
Um-Uthrux's points slammed down directly behind, sending bricks,
y and treasure in all directions. Hereward pushed Fury towards the door,
ned back to see if he could see Fitz.
ere was only the vast starfish in view. It had slid its lower body up on to
and was reaching forth with three of its points, each as large as an angled
bastion. First it brought them down to smash the buildings, then it used
ends to pluck out any pirates, like an anteater digging out its lunch.
" shouted Hereward. "Fitz!"
f Um-Uthrux's points rose up, high above Hereward. He stepped back,
pped as the godlet suddenly reared back, its upper points writhing in
nd lower points staggering. A tiny, glowing hole appeared in its middle,
w larger. The godlet lurched back still farther and reached down with its
lawing at itself as the glowing void in its guts yawned wider still. Then,
ack that rocked the cavern and knocked Hereward over again, the giant

"To arms! The enemy!" Hereward shouted again. He r
of pirates and dragged one away from a huge gold-chas
near as big as he was. "Form line on the quay!"

The pirate shrugged him off and clutched his cup.

"It's mine!" he yelled. "You'll not have it!"

"I don't want it!" roared Hereward. He pointed bacl
enemy! Look, you fools!"

The nearer pirates stared at him blankly. Hereward tur
but darkness.

"Fitz! Light the cursed monster up!"

He was answered by a blinding surge of violet light th
and washed across the giant starfish, which was now
lifting one point to march forwards.

There was silence for several seconds, the silence of th
carrying voice snatched order from the closing jaws of

"Sea-Cats! First division form line on the quay, right
load behind them! Move, you knaves! The loot will wai

Fury emerged from behind a building, a necklace of go
around her neck. She marched to Hereward and plac
and together they walked to the quay as if they had not
pirates ran past them.

"You have not become a leoparde," said Hereward.
couldn't help but look up at the manifested godlet. Li
was becoming quicker with every movement, and Fitz
the end of the wharf. There was a nimbus of sorcerous
indicating that he was working busily with one or more
stitching something otherworldly together or unpick
was commonly considered to be reality.

"Cold things from the sea, no matter their size, do r
Fury. "Or perhaps it is the absence of red blood… Sta

The last words were for the hundred pirates who sto
sporting a wide array of muskets, musketoons, blund
some crossbows. Behind them, the second division kn
ready to pass on, and the necessaries for reloading lai

"Fire!" shouted Fury. A ragged volley rang out and a
back across Hereward and drifted up towards the tre
struck home, but their effect was much less than on th
visible holes being torn in the strange stuff of Um-U

"Firsts, fire as you will!" called Fury. "Seconds, relo
Though the shots appeared to have no affect, the
pirates shooting and reloading did attract Um-Uth
and took a step towards the quay, one huge point cra
wharf to the left of Mister Fitz. Rather than pulling th

starfish's points were sucked through the hole, it turned inside out and the hole closed taking with it all evidence of Um-Uthrux's existence upon the earth and with it most of the light.

"Your puppet has done well," said Fury. "Though I perceive it is called Fitz and not Farolio."

"Yes," said Hereward. He did not look at her, but waved his arm, the brassard leaving a luminous trail in the air. "Fitz! To me!"

"It has become a bloody affair after all," said Fury. Her voice was a growl and now Hereward did look. Fury still stood on two legs, but she had grown taller and her proportions had changed. Her skin had become spotted fur, and her skull transformed, her jaw thrust out to contain savage teeth, including two incisors as long as Hereward's thumbs. Long curved nails sprouted from her rounded hands, her eyes had become bright with a predatory gleam, and a tail whisked the ground behind.

"Fury," said Hereward. He looked straight at her and did not back away. "We have won. The fight is done."

"I told you that I ate my enemies," said Fury huskily. Her tail twitched and she bobbed her head in a manner no human neck could mimic. Hereward could barely understand her, human speech almost lost in growls and snarls.

"You did not tell me your name, or your true purpose."

"My name is Hereward," said Hereward, and he raised his open hands. If she attacked, his only chance would be to grip her neck and break it before those teeth and nails did mortal damage. "I am not your enemy."

Fury growled, speech entirely gone, and began to crouch.

"Fury! I am not your—"

The leoparde sprang. He caught her on his forearms and felt the nails rake his skin. Fending her off with his left hand, he seized hold of the necklace of yellow diamonds with his right and twisted it hard to cut off her air. But before he could apply much pressure, the beast gave a sudden, human gasp, strange and sad from that bestial jaw. The leoparde's bright eyes dulled as if by sea-mist, and Hereward felt the full weight of the animal in his hands.

The necklace broke, scattering diamonds, as the beast slid down Hereward's chest. Fitz rode on the creature's shoulders all the way down, before he withdrew the stiletto that he had thrust with inhuman strength up through the nape of her neck into her brain.

Hereward closed his hand on the last diamond. He held it just for a second, before he let that too slip through his fingers.

"Inside!" called Fitz, and the puppet was at his companion's knees, pushing Hereward through the door. The knight fell over the threshold as Fitz turned and gestured with an esoteric needle, threads of blinding white whipping about faster than any weaver's shuttle.

His work was barely done before the wave hit. The ground shook and the sorcerous bubble of air bounced to the ceiling and back several times, tumbling

Hereward and Fitz over in a mad crush. Then as rapidly as it had come, the wave receded.

Fitz undid the bubble with a deft twitch of his needle and cupped it in his hand. Hereward lay back on the sodden floor and groaned. Blood trickled down his shredded sleeves, bruises he had not even suspected till now made themselves felt, and his feet were unbelievably sore.

Fitz crouched over him and inspected his arms.

"Scratches," he proclaimed. He carefully put the esoteric needle away inside his jerkin and took off his bandanna, ripping it in half to bind the wounds. "Bandages will suffice."

When the puppet was finished, Hereward sat up. He cupped his face in his hands for a second, but his burned palms made him wince and drop them again.

"We have perhaps six hours to gather materials, construct a raft and make our way out the gorge," said Fitz. "Presuming the *eagre* comes again at the usual time, in the absence of Um-Uthrux. We'd best hurry."

Hereward nodded and lurched upright, holding the splintered doorframe for support. He could see nothing beyond Fitz, who stood a few paces away, but he could easily envision the many corpses that would be floating in the refilled harbour pool, or drifting out to the gorge beyond.

"She was right," he said.

Fitz cocked his head in question.

"Meat and water," replied Hereward. "I suppose that *is* all we are, in the end."

Fitz did not answer, but still looked on, his pose unchanged.

"Present company excepted," added Hereward.

# THE SMALL DOOR

## HOLLY PHILLIPS

Holly Phillips lives in a small city on a big island off of Canada's western coast. She is a full-time writer, but has recently decided to call herself a "professional fantasist." It probably won't cut down on the number of blank looks she gets when she's introduced to strangers at a dinner party, but the subsequent conversation might be a lot more fun. Holly's most recent novel, *The Engine's Child*, was released by Del Rey in November 2008.

Only two more months to the end of school, and like a tantalizing forerunner to summer, the fair came to town. Sal saw the carnies setting up rides as the bus crawled by the arena parking lot that Thursday morning. The Sizzler, the Tumbler, the Tilt-a-Whirl. The Ferris Wheel, unlit and seatless, leaning on its crane. Sal imagined it busting loose and rolling off down the highway, across the bridge, up the hill past the school and on out of town. She knew exactly how it would sound, a hollow steel-on-concrete rumble, louder than the river that ran so smoothly in its banks. She kept her face pressed to the window until the parking lot was out of sight, but the Wheel only raised itself a little closer to vertical.

After school everyone walked past the bus stop, a chain of kids like a clumsy bead necklace, bunches and pairs strolling down, even the cool kids, even the rebels who might plan to get stoned first, but who were still going to ride the rides. Sal, remembering the sideways swoop and crush of the Sizzler, the jangle of rock music and yelling kids, the smells of burnt sugar and hot oil and cigarettes—the expansion of the parking lot into a convoluted world that could seem to go on forever as long as you took the long way around every ride and that only got brighter and louder and hotter as the day fell into evening and evening into night—Sal, remembering all this, stood alone at the bus stop and waited for the bus that would take her past the fair and home.

Her mom was in the kitchen, crushing garlic into a bowl of soya sauce.

"What are we having?" Sal said.

"How was school? Did you do okay on the math test?"

"Sure, I guess." The test had been last week. "What are we having?"

"Baked chicken. Macey said she might be hungry tonight."

"Oh." Sal picked up a garlic clove and peeled the papery skin.

189

"Wash your hands."

Sal peeled another clove. "Is she awake?"

"She had a good sleep this afternoon. You might go up and see."

Sal brushed the garlic papers into the garbage and rinsed her hands, debating whether to mention the fair. Probably she shouldn't. Probably her mom wouldn't appreciate the reminder of the passage of time. Anyway, it wasn't like Sal could go, even if she wanted to. Which she didn't.

Macey lay propped up on big pillows, her face turned to the window. She looked like a fragile bone doll these days, all the flesh under her skin eaten up by fever, and when she lay still Sal always found it hard to believe she would move again. She didn't stir when Sal opened her door, but she wasn't asleep. She said, "The Weirdo has another cat."

"Really?" Sal shut the door and toed off her shoes. The bed had been pushed up close to the big window so Macey could look out over the back yard to the alley and the houses on the other side. Sal climbed up, careful of her sister's feet, so she could look out too. "Is it hurt?"

"I think it's maybe pregnant."

Sal contemplated the gruesome possibilities of kittens in the Weirdo's hands. She could just see over the high fence to the roofed chicken-wire pens in the Weirdo's yard. It was impossible to know what was in any of those pens until you saw what the Weirdo took out of one. Cats, raccoons, crows, even a puppy once, taken out of a pen and carried inside and *never seen again*. Three days ago it had been another raccoon. Macey was keeping a log.

Sal said, "Do you think he'll wait until the kittens are born?"

"Gross."

Neither knew what the Weirdo did with his captives, but it was hard to think of a possibility that wasn't horrible. Not when you saw that figure, with its thatched gray hair, lumpy shoulders and white hands as big as baseball gloves, carry some hapless creature into the house with the broken drainpipes and curtained windows. Even *cooking* and *eating* seemed too simple, too close to human.

"Sal," Macey said, "we've got to find out."

"You keep saying that." Sal picked fuzzies off the bedspread, her mind drifting to the candy-bright commotion of the fair.

"But now I have a plan."

Sal's eyes slid to her sister's face. Despite being twins, they'd never looked that much alike. Now, with Macey gone all skinny and white, her eyes shiny with fever and her hair dull and thin, they hardly seemed to belong to the same species. Sal glared at her own robust health when she brushed her teeth in the mornings, seeing ugliness in the flesh of her face, the color of her skin. Macey's mind, too, had changed, as if, riding a tide of febrile blood, it had entered a realm that Sal could not even see.

"What kind of plan?" she said warily.

Macey finally moved. She rolled her head on the rainbow pillowcase and gave Sal a glittering look. The late light of afternoon shone on the sweat that beaded her hairline. Not the worst fever, Sal knew. The worst fever baked her sister dry, and sounded like ambulance men rattling their stretcher up the stairs.

The smell of garlicky chicken wafted into the room as Macey gave Sal her instructions.

Friday was garbage day.

There was no way in the world to do it casually. Maybe if she was old enough to drive, and had a car… But no. Sal didn't think in ifs. If led to *If only Macey wasn't sick*, and even *If only Sal's bone marrow was a match*. If never did anybody any good at all.

There was no way to do it casually, so she just did it. She left the house like she was going to school, walked around the block to the front of the Weirdo's house, lifted the lid of his trash can, hoisted out the sack, dropped the lid and walked away. She didn't look at the Weirdo's windows. If he saw her, he saw her, that was all. She stashed the trash bag, neatly closed with a yellow twist tie, inside the unused garden shed at the side of her house, and then ran, legs and lungs strong from PE, for the bus.

When she got home from school, her parents were in the living room having The Discussion: mortgages, private donor lists, tissue matches, travel costs, hospital fees, time. Time sliced into months, into weeks. Seven weeks to summer holidays. Sal drifted past them to the kitchen, ran cold tap water into a glass, and carried it up the stairs.

Macey hardly seemed to dent her pillows anymore. Her hands lay on the sheet's hem, her head canted toward the window. Sunlight filtered cool through spring clouds and gauze curtains, the same sunlight that dulled the lights at the parking lot fair. Sal had kept her eyes on her book as the half-empty bus trundled past, but the smells—hot dog, caramel, cigarette, machine—had billowed in the open windows and made her hungry. She stood in the doorway until she was sure Macey was asleep, then drank the cold water in one smooth series of gulps and carried the glass back down. The Discussion continued. Even Sal knew the end result would be the same: wait and see. Months, weeks, days. The fair was in town until Monday. She put the glass in the sink and went out the back door.

The garden shed had been there when they moved into the new house. The small house, was how Sal and Macey spoke of it, as it was actually a lot older than the old house, older and smaller, and with neighbors tucked in all around. The people who had lived here before had kept a square patch of lawn and planted irises and other things Sal didn't know between the grass and the weathered wooden fence. Sal's mother had said how nice it would be to have flowers and a "manageable" yard, but Sal noticed she never came out back, and the garden tools and lawn furniture all lurked in the back of the shed collecting spiders.

Inside was dark and smelled like mold, but Sal lingered a moment, the Weirdo's trash unacknowledged by her foot. She could almost imagine setting up the lawn chairs inside, hanging the hammock from corner to corner, using one of those collapsible lanterns like they used to have for camping. A tiny house beside the small one. Except Macey could never come in. Sal picked up the trash bag and took it outside.

Look for fur, Macey had said. And bones, and bloody rags, and burnt candles, especially black ones. And incense and chalk.

What Sal shook out onto the shaggy grass was rinsed-out milk cartons, clean dog food cans and cottage cheese containers, and a week's worth of newspapers. The creepiest item was a toilet paper roll that she nudged back into the plastic bag with her toe. She didn't know what to feel about this lack of discovery, but Macey would be disappointed. Or rather, Macey would write another mystery into her log, and then come up with some other assignment for Sal, something a little bit harder, a little bit scarier. She always used to win the contest of dares, back when Sal could dare her to do anything. As Sal shuffled the Weirdo's trash back into its bag, she had to admit to herself that, sooner or later, she was going over the fence into the Weirdo's back yard. She was tempted to get it over with, but that would deprive Macey of her share in the adventure. Sal had to comb the grass with her fingers before she found the yellow twist tie, and then she didn't know what to do with the Weirdo's trash. After a moment's thought, she tossed the bag back in the garden shed and went into the kitchen to wash her hands. Next week she could put the bag in their can for the garbage men to haul away.

Macey was on the IV again when Sal went up after dinner. The drip always made Macey cold, so she had a fluffy blanket wrapped around her arm, a pink one sewn with butterflies that didn't quite match the rainbow sheets. Their mom was convinced that bright colors would keep Macey's spirits up, and even Macey was too kind to tell her she'd rather have something cool and calm, like sand or stone. Against the gaudy stripes, Macey's face was a dry yellowy white, with patches of red in the hollows of her cheeks. She gave Sal a cross look.

"It's too dark to look at the evidence now."

"I already looked." Sal was not surprised when her sister looked more cross, not less.

"Why didn't you say so? What did you find?"

Sal told her, as accurately as she could remember.

Macey rocked her head on the pillow. "You must have missed something. Did the newspapers have any bits cut out of them?"

Sal hadn't thought to look. She hesitated, then decided on a simple, "No."

Macey made an old lady tsk of annoyance. "He's too smart for that. I should have known." She looked out the window, where dusk was fattening into dark.

A light showed through the curtained window of one of the Weirdo's back rooms. His kitchen, Sal guessed. All the houses in this neighborhood were variations on the one they lived in. She sat waiting for her instructions on the end of Macey's bed, and it was a while before she realized Macey was asleep. She went on sitting, listening to her sister breathe. Somewhere close, a cat softly meowed.

Saturday mornings Sal would carry the TV into Macey's room and they'd watch cartoons together, like when they were kids and they'd sneak downstairs while their mom and dad slept in and muffle their laughter in sofa cushions. Not that she had to sneak to do it now. Sometimes their dad would even move the TV for them before heading off to a weekend consultation. But this Saturday the morning nurse told her Macey'd had a bad night and needed peace and quiet, which would drive Macey up the wall unless she was really bad, but you couldn't argue about things like that with the nurse. So Sal wrestled one of the lawn chairs out of the garden shed and set it up in a patch of sunlight by the back fence where she could keep an eye on the alley, at least, and pretend to be doing her homework and getting a suntan at the same time. Macey could look down from her bedroom window and know Sal was on the job.

She was working on another senseless problem about the farmer who didn't know how big any of his fields were (she imagined a city guy with romantic notions about getting back to the land, and neighbors that laughed at him behind his back) when she heard the unmistakable scuffling and whispers of kids trying to be sneaky. She dropped her pencil in the crack of her textbook and leaned over the arm of her canvas-slung chair to press her face against a crack in the fence.

Three boys, probably about ten years old: too tall to be little, but still children to Sal's thirteen-year-old eye. They wore T-shirts and premature shorts and were elbowing each other into some daring deed. They stood outside the Weirdo's tall fence, and Sal felt a hollow open up inside her chest even before the tallest boy shrugged off the other two and with a gesture commanded a hand stirrup for his foot. The next tallest boy lofted him to the top of the fence... there was a thump-scuffle-scrape... and then he was over and out of sight. Like the boys in the alley, Sal waited, breathless, for whatever would come next. The boy might have fallen down a hole for all the noise he made.

Her ribs hurt where the arm of the chair dug into her side. Her neck and shoulder creaked. She tried to shift position without losing her line of sight and the chair almost tipped, and she caught herself with her fingertips on the fence, and wondered if Macey was awake and watching, or if Macey was too sick to care.

Then sudden furious meowing, loose rattle of chicken wire, thumps and scrapes, and a bundle fell from the top of the fence—only half in Sal's view but from the caterwaul she deduced it was a cat wrapped in the tall boy's shirt. The two boys in the alley scrabbled to keep the animal contained, while the tall boy appeared, shirtless, scratched, and triumphant, at the top of the fence. He swung a leg over and posed for a second before hopping down.

The hollow in Sal's chest swelled until her breath came short. The cat was meowing, more frantic than angry, now. The boys were laughing. She dropped her books to the grass, got up, and fumbled open the gate.

"Hey!"

The boys, in the act of departing, froze.

"Let go of that cat." Even Sal could hear how lame that sounded.

The shirtless boy looked her over and sneered. "Make us," he said.

The other two, prisoning the bundled cat between them, looked unsure but excited at the possibilities.

Sal swallowed, and thought of Macey maybe watching. She took two fast steps forward and gave the boy a shove. He wasn't much shorter than she was, and was all wiry boy muscle under the scratched skin. He shoved back and kicked her hard in the shin. Then it was all stupid and confused, kicking and clutching, and someone's fist in the back of her shirt, until, in the midst of scuffing feet and angry breathing, came the unmistakable grate of a key turned in a lock.

The fight stopped so suddenly Sal found herself leaning for balance against her adversary. He shrugged her off, and they stood, staring, the four of them, while the Weirdo's gate creaked partway open on rusted hinges.

The smallest boy dropped the shirt-wrapped cat and bolted.

The cat bolted, too, between the Weirdo's feet and the fence post, back into his yard.

Then the other boys were running, too, whooping insults to cover their retreat, and Sal was left standing in the alley with the Weirdo peering at her through the cracked-open gate. He had small pale defenseless eyes blinking in the shadow of his gray thatch of hair. One huge white hand shook with palsy on the side of the fence. As it registered with Sal that he was as frightened as she was, she heard the mewing of fearful kittens.

She gulped a "Sorry" at him and scurried back into her yard, slamming the gate behind her.

Macey was furious. Furious, though only someone who knew her as well as Sal did would be able to tell. Her hands lay as if abandoned on the covers, and her voice was a thin warble, as if she lacked the strength to control its ups and downs. But she had indeed been awake and watching, and she thought Sal had done everything wrong.

"Those boys could have been allies. Why'd you fight?"

"I don't think they were going to take the cat home and feed her cream," Sal said.

"It wasn't even a good fight. You fought like a girl."

Sal shrugged. Her legs were black with bruises, and she was rather proud of the swelling of her lower lip.

"And now the cat's back where it started."

"She went back on her own," Sal pointed out.

"You said it had kittens. It probably thought it had to protect them."

"She was more scared of those boys. Way more scared."

"That's just because it doesn't know, yet."

"Know what?"

"What's in store."

Sal prodded her swollen lip. "We don't know what's in store, either."

"*Yes we do.*"

All Macey's strength seemed to go into those three words. When she closed her glittering eyes, her hands, her whole body, seemed more abandoned than ever. Sal sat on the end of her bed and watched her closely until she was sure her breathing was regular, then dropped her chin into her palm and gazed outside. The morning sun had been swallowed by clouds. It might even rain. She looked down at her math books, still open on the grass by the tipped-over chair, and thought about going down to bring them in. There was no sign of the Weirdo.

"You know," she said quietly, in case Macey was asleep, "he might just take them out the front door. He might just take them out and let them go."

Silence for so long she thought Macey must be sleeping. But then her sister said, "Doesn't."

"How do you know?"

"Brings them in the back. Would take them out the same way."

Sal had to concede there was a certain logic to this. Silence gathered again, while the clouds closed in a little tighter, a little darker. Sal thought of the kids at the fair, wondered how many parents had thought to bring rain gear along.

"I have to go get my books before it rains," she said.

Macey didn't say anything. Sal got up and went to the door. She was almost in the hall when she heard her sister's voice, thin as a thread.

"You're just scared," Macey said. "You just don't want to find out."

Sal bit her swollen lip and winced. Having seen those fearful, blinking eyes, those shaking hands, she found she had nothing to say. She slipped out and went downstairs to put on her shoes.

That night she cracked her bedroom window open and listened to the rustle of the rain. It followed her in and out of sleep, the same way her parents' footsteps did as they took turns to check on Macey. Every hour. Then, starting at 1:33 by Sal's digital alarm clock, every half hour. Then, when the red numbers shone 3:41, they were both up and about. She dimly knew that she did sleep, but it seemed as if she didn't. It seemed as if she were already wide awake when she heard the ambulance grumble to a stop on the street outside, and the tinny whicker of the radio as the paramedics reported their arrival. She lay still and comfortable while the gurney came rattling up the stairs, while the hallway became full of movement, while the calm professional voices moved into Macey's room. Then she got up and opened her bedroom door. The bright light made her squint.

She couldn't see past her parents, but from the crunch-and-rustle sound the paramedics were tucking Macey in with cold packs. They were almost ready to go. She went back in her room and traded her pajamas for sweats and running shoes. The paramedics rolled Macey out and down the hall. Sal and Macey's parents, already dressed, followed. Sal trailed after. Her dad only noticed her when he turned to close the front door.

"Oh, sweetheart," he said sadly. "You don't have to come."

Sal shrugged. Of course she didn't *have* to.

Her mom came over and gave her a one-armed hug. "Macey's going to be all right. They just need to get the fever down. We'll call first thing and let you know when she'll be home."

Sal didn't say anything. She couldn't. The paramedics were lifting Macey into the ambulance. One climbed in with her. The other was hurrying around to the cab when Sal's dad shut the front door, cutting off her view. The living room window filled with red and blue light, like the lights of a carnival fairway. Then the ambulance pulled away, followed by her parents' car, leaving darkness behind.

It was still raining in the morning. Sal waited until her parents had called before she headed out the kitchen door.

*Doctor Helleran wants to keep Macey in for a few days, just to make sure… Mom will be home to pick up some things this afternoon… Dad will be home to make dinner… Be sure you finish your homework… Everything's going to be all right…*

The Weirdo's fence was taller than she was, but she could hook her fingers over the top, just. The rubber toes of her sneakers skidded on the damp wood, so it was by the strength of her arms that she lifted herself over. Her hands ached and stung with splinters, and she dropped quickly, more clumsily than she might have. Cement paving stones were a shock to her feet. At her right hand a cat growled, low and angry, and she started.

The huts were in two rows that faced each other across the small yard, six in each row. They had tin roofs pattering under the last of the rain, and wire fronts, and were otherwise made of plywood and boards, sturdy but not elegant. Sal was surprised at how big they were, four feet to a side and on short legs. She was also surprised at the smell of clean straw that came from the bales tucked under the Weirdo's eaves. Macey must have seen him cleaning the huts, laying new straw and bundling up the old, but she'd never mentioned it. Sal bent over to peer into the nearest hut and could just make out the angry black mask of the mother cat glaring from her corner nest. The cat gave another warning snarl.

"It's okay," Sal whispered. "Your kittens are safe."

*From me*, she added silently, creeping up the row.

Most of the huts seemed empty, though with the heaps of straw it was hard to tell. But the fourth one on the left had an occupant that was more than willing to be seen. Beady eyes in a lone ranger mask, damp twitching nose, and delicate finger-paws hooked through the chicken wire of the door: the raccoon, small enough that Sal could have tucked him under her arm like a nerf football, chittered happily at the sight of company. She hunkered down before the hut, then registered the shaved patch on the creature's haunch, the coarse stitching, the missing foot. She bit her lip, and winced when her tooth hit the sore reminder of yesterday's tussle.

"Poor little guy."

The raccoon snuffled at her through three different holes. In his excitement he planted one forepaw in the plastic water dish wired to the front of the hut. With a look of disgust he shook his paw, then settled down to lick it dry, keeping a bright eye on Sal between laps of his pink tongue.

Sal rocked back on her heels and turned her head to stare over the fence and up at the back of her own house. At the wide dark rectangle of the window to Macey's room.

"Excuse me," said a rusty voice, "but you shouldn't be here."

Sal rocketed to her feet. For one fleeting instant, she'd actually forgotten.

"This is private, you see, private property."

The Weirdo stood on his back step, the door to his house open behind him. He wore the same navy blue polyester jacket zipped up to his chin, the same gray pants baggy at the knees, the same blinking look of fright. Except this time the fear was mixed with a tenuous look of dignity. Sal felt herself start to blush.

"I'm sorry," she said stupidly. "I was just, uh, just—" What could she possibly say? "checking to see how the cat was." She twitched her head and shoulder toward the mother cat's hut. "From yesterday? I thought those boys, uh, might have…" She ran out of steam, though the blood in her ears was hot enough to boil water.

The Weirdo's blinking slowed to a less frantic tempo. "But you aren't the defender. Are you?"

"Well, yeah." Sal shrugged, her hands creeping into the pockets of her jeans. "I mean, I guess."

"You could have knocked. You see, on the door."

Sal wasn't sure if this was reproach or simply information. "Sorry," she mumbled again.

The Weirdo, unbelievably, smiled. A funny, scrunching quirk of a smile that disappeared his eyes and didn't reveal any teeth, but a smile nevertheless. "You want to see the kittens." He stepped down from the back stair and shuffled towards her.

Sal, indoctrinated against the man who offers to show little girls his kitten or puppy or whatever-it-might-be tucked away in the back of his van (just around the corner, the teacher won't even notice you're gone), scuttled crab-wise until her shoulder bumped the gate. The Weirdo, with his lumpy shoulders and shaking hands, lowered himself with care to kneel before the mother cat's hut, apparently blind to Sal's skittishness. Looking down at his stiff hair thatch, Sal wondered what she was doing here. Wondered, confusingly, if she wouldn't have preferred to have been run off by some harrowing Freddy-like creature, chased back over the fence and home. But instead of razor blades, his hands had only trimmed yellow nails and a tremor that she was beginning to realize wasn't fear, or at least not only fear, but some nervous disorder, or possibly even age. The big pale shaking hands reached through the hut's open front and emerged a moment later with a squeaking palmful of black and white.

"Here. Here." The Weirdo lifted the kitten towards Sal. "You mustn't let her get cold, you see."

Impossible to take the kitten without touching his hand. Impossible not to take the kitten, even though the rain had dripped to an end. Almost shivering herself, Sal scooped the tiny beast from his palm (warm and dry) and cupped her under her chin.

Squeak, said the kitten, blindly nuzzling her thumb.

"Hello," whispered Sal, ruffling the soft fur with her breath.

The Weirdo reached with a rustle of straw to reassure the mother.

What would Macey say to this? Sal wondered. *Get out while you can?*

No.

*Find out where they go.*

The kitten was nestled in with her siblings, the wire door shut on their nest, the Weirdo raising himself to his feet.

"My sister," Sal blurted, then choked.

The Weirdo blinked at her.

"My sister's in the hospital." God, how dumb. "She's sick." Dumber. "She might die." Dumbest. Sal could taste the salt reservoir swelling in her throat.

The Weirdo blinked some more. He seemed oddly patient and, despite the hands that still trembled at his sides, as if contact with the animals had soothed his fear. "Your sister. Is she the child who watches?" He glanced over her head at Macey's window.

Child. Macey would hate that. Sal took a breath. "My sister sees you take the animals in your house, but she doesn't see you bring them out again." She took another breath, but there she stuck.

The old man waited.

The rain started to drip again.

Sal started to shiver. "My sister wonders. Where they go."

The Weirdo's blinks seemed to beat sad time with the rain. "Your sister is in the hospital?"

Sal nodded.

"So you came to see."

Sal nodded again, though that wasn't it at all.

The Weirdo closed his eyes to commune with himself while the rain fell into a steady patter and the raccoon chirruped for attention. The Weirdo drew in a slow breath, let it out quietly, and nodded, before he opened his eyes. "Yes," he said. "Yes," and then, "perhaps." He looked at her doubtfully.

Sal swallowed. "It isn't anything bad. Is it?"

He blinked, flit, flit, flit. "No. It isn't anything bad."

But she would be crazy if she believed him.

Crazy stupid dumb. So Sal told herself as she followed the old man inside.

But Macey would have dared her. Macey *had* dared her. So she stayed while the Weirdo opened the raccoon's hut and tucked the little animal against his chest, and closed the door, and led the way into his kitchen.

The room was dim, dusty '70s-orange curtains half-drawn against the rain, or the prying eyes of the neighbor's children. Every surface was cluttered with such a dense, organic jumble of stuff Sal could hardly make out individual elements. Bags of dog food, screwdrivers, oily rags, cookie jars, coffee cans full of nails. The only bare surface was the wooden table which bore just a small first aid kit and a bottle of what looked to be peroxide. The Weirdo sat in the one clear chair and placed the raccoon before him, holding him still while he rummaged in the kit for a cotton ball. Sal stood against the kitchen door, trying not to breathe the Weirdo's air. It was heavy with smells as jumbled and unrecognizable as the mess, not nasty, but *his*.

His hands, forever trembling, were surprisingly deft in the dull sepia light. He swabbed the bare patch on the raccoon's haunch, then reached for tiny scissors. The raccoon curled around his restraining hand like a furry meal bug, sharp teeth nibbling his knuckles, unconcerned by the twitch of the stitches' removal.

"It isn't so much that they have to, you see, be healed," the Weirdo said, "but they have to be unafraid." He swabbed the points of blood, dropped the cotton ball, looked up at Sal. "It's important they aren't afraid."

The hackles all down Sal's back rose and prickled beneath her clothes.

The Weirdo stood and lifted the three-legged raccoon against his shoulder. There was a door in the corner by the rattling old fridge. A cupboard, Sal thought, but it opened on a black doorway and narrow stairs going down. The Weirdo started down without looking at Sal. Sal moved after. Macey had always found a way to make her wimp out before, always found the one thing Sal couldn't bring herself to do, but this time, this dare, she had to see it through.

She had to see it through.

The odors were stronger here, compounded by the smell of damp basement and mold dust. It was very dark before Sal's eyes adjusted, but she refrained from reaching out for a banister or wall. She didn't want to touch anything here. Groping for the way down—the flight seemed impossibly long—her damp runners squeaked on bare boards, while the old man's feet padded almost silent on the stairs.

The young raccoon peered over his shoulder at her, black-button eyes inexpressibly cheerful and inquisitive.

*It's important they aren't afraid.*

Was Sal afraid? She wasn't sure. Her skin tingled and the back of her eyes stung, and her heart was beating quick and light, and her hands wanted to crawl up inside her sleeves. But it wasn't the same feeling as when she heard the ambulance arrive. It was more like when she stepped out on the high platform above the deep pool at the aquatic center, and looked down to see the thin hiss of spray that was the only clue to where the surface lay, and curled her toes over the edge of damp concrete (knowing that even Macey wouldn't jump, she hated heights, the one dare Sal would never put to her) and lifted her arms, in her head already flying and ready for the cold.

The basement was warm, filled by a pervasive furnace hum.

The old man groped above his head, a weird gesture that stopped Sal on the bottom step, until his hand found a string and a light came on, a forty-watt bulb that shone on his thatch of hair, the raccoon's eyes, the claustrophobic clutter all around. The mess of the kitchen was writ large here, rusty bikes and wheelbarrows and garden tools, cardboard boxes stained and warped by damp, glass jars filled with cobwebs and bugs. The dim yellow light was brightest on the ceiling of rough, web-hung joists, dimmest in the narrow passage that disappeared between walls of junk. The Weirdo paused under the bulb, looked at Sal, blinking a little. Sal looked back. His big pale hands cradled the little raccoon.

"It's a secret, you know, a secret thing."

Sal swallowed. "I won't tell."

"But your sister wants to know?"

Sal was shocked, then remembered she had told him as much. "She's sick." As if that explained, or excused.

The old man hesitated, nodded. Moved down the passage without looking back.

Sal followed, robot-like, numb, as if she operated her body from a distance, mental thumbs on the remote control.

There was a room at the end of the passage. Or maybe it was just a clear space, defined not by walls but by piled junk. Rocking chair, step-ladder, storm window, bookshelf, doll-house, glass vase, all of them broken, all of them smeared with dust and mold and time, locked together like bricks in a wall. They sprang into being when the old man pulled another string, lighting another weak bulb. He shuffled forward and Sal saw, set into the junk wall like it was just another bit of trash, a door. A small door. The size of a door that might admit a cat or a puppy or a crow or a young three-legged raccoon, but nothing larger. Nothing like big enough for a person, even if the person was a kid no bigger than Sal, who was not tall for her age, or Macey, who had become so thin. It was made of bare boards held together by brass screws, and had no proper doorknob, just a pull like on a cupboard or a drawer.

The old man knelt on the rough, damp-stained cement floor with the same care he'd shown outside, gently containing the raccoon that wriggled with excitement. Then he looked up at Sal, who still stood just inside the room. "You can open it, if you want. Then you'll see."

Like a diver in mid-flight, Sal could not back out now. Flying, falling, numb, she walked over, her shoes no longer squeaking, and knelt beside him. Her bruised shins hurt, distantly. The pain reminded her of Macey. She had almost forgotten why she was here.

At close quarters, the old man smelled like his house only sweeter, perfumed by straw and rain.

Sal reached for the little knob, closed finger and thumb, pulled. The door stuck a bit, then jerked and swung open onto a gurgle of running water.

Drains, Sal thought. Storm drain, sewer, something. Then she cocked her head and looked inside.

Outside.

The small door opened onto a forest clearing. A stream of rocks and pools burbled almost within arm's reach of the threshold. Beyond, above, big trees raised a canopy against a blue evening sky. There were stars pale between leaves, birds singing on their nests, grasshoppers fiddling, a draft that smelled of water and earth and green.

"It always opens," the old man's rusty voice said, "on the place they'd most like to go. That's why they can't be afraid. You see, it's magic."

He set the raccoon down, and the young animal skitter-hopped to the threshold, where he paused and sniffed. Then, as if it were the most natural thing in the world, he skitter-hopped over and headed down to the stream for a wash, and maybe to poke about for a dinner of frogs. And as he went, his injured leg grew fur, and a paw, and toes and claws, and he was whole.

The old man shut the door. They knelt together side by side before the crooked wall of junk.

Sal cleared her throat. "My sister."

"I'm sorry," the old man said. "It's, you see, it's such a small door."

"Yes," Sal said. "I see."


Her father came home in time to heat up leftover chicken for dinner. Macey's fever was down, he said. The bleeding had stopped almost as soon as they were at the hospital. She would be home in a few days. Sally looked pretty tired. Maybe she should go to bed early tonight.

Sal agreed, she was pretty tired.

As the school bus trundled past the arena parking lot on Monday morning, she saw that, early as it was, the carnies had been hard at work for hours. The game stalls and concession stands and rides were nearly all dismantled and loaded into the big rigs that would drive them to the next town. Only the Ferris Wheel still hung, captive, on its axle.

# TURING'S APPLES

## STEPHEN BAXTER

Stephen Baxter is one of the most important science fiction writers to emerge from Britain in the past thirty years. His "Xeelee" sequence of novels and short stories is arguably the most significant work of future history in modern science fiction. Baxter is the author of more than forty books and over 100 short stories. His most recent book is the major SF novel, *Flood*. Upcoming is sequel, *Ark*.

Near the centre of the Moon's far side there is a neat, round, well-defined crater called Daedalus. No human knew this existed before the middle of the twentieth century. It's a bit of lunar territory as far as you can get from Earth, and about the quietest.

That's why the teams of astronauts from Europe, America, Russia and China went there. They smoothed over the floor of a crater ninety kilometres wide, laid sheets of metal mesh over the natural dish, and suspended feed horns and receiver systems on spidery scaffolding. And there you had it, an instant radio telescope, by far the most powerful ever built: a super-Arecibo, dwarfing its mother in Puerto Rico. Before the astronauts left they christened their telescope Clarke.

Now the telescope is a ruin, and much of the floor of Daedalus is covered by glass, Moon dust melted by multiple nuclear strikes. But, I'm told, if you were to look down from some slow lunar orbit you would see a single point of light glowing there, a star fallen to the Moon. One day the Moon will be gone, but that point will remain, silently orbiting Earth, a lunar memory. And in the further future, when the Earth has gone too, when the stars have burned out and the galaxies fled from the sky, still that point of light will shine.

My brother Wilson never left the Earth. In fact he rarely left England. He was buried, what was left of him, in a grave next to our father's, just outside Milton Keynes. But he *made* that point of light on the Moon, which will be the last legacy of all mankind.

Talk about sibling rivalry.

### 2020

It was at my father's funeral, actually, before Wilson had even begun his SETI searches, that the Clarke first came between us.

There was a good turnout at the funeral, at an old church on the outskirts of Milton Keynes proper. Wilson and I were my father's only children, but as well as his old friends there were a couple of surviving aunts and a gaggle of cousins mostly around our age, mid-twenties to mid-thirties, so there was a good crop of children, like little flowers.

I don't know if I'd say Milton Keynes is a good place to live. It certainly isn't a good place to die. The city is a monument to planning, a concrete grid of avenues with very English names like Midsummer, now overlaid by the new monorail. It's so *clean* it makes death seem a social embarrassment, like a fart in a shopping mall. Maybe we need to be buried in ground dirty with bones.

Our father had remembered, just, how the area was all villages and farmland before the Second World War. He had stayed on even after our mother died twenty years before he did, him and his memories made invalid by all the architecture. At the service I spoke of those memories—for instance how during the war a tough Home Guard had caught him sneaking into the grounds of Bletchley Park, not far away, scrumping apples while Alan Turing and the other geniuses were labouring over the Nazi codes inside the house. "Dad always said he wondered if he picked up a mathematical bug from Turing's apples," I concluded, "because, he would say, for sure Wilson's brain didn't come from him."

"Your brain too," Wilson said when he collared me later outside the church. He hadn't spoken at the service; that wasn't his style. "You should have mentioned that. I'm not the only mathematical nerd in the family."

It was a difficult moment. My wife and I had just been introduced to Hannah, the two-year-old daughter of a cousin. Hannah had been born profoundly deaf, and we adults in our black suits and dresses were awkwardly copying her parents' bits of sign language. Wilson just walked through this lot to get to me, barely glancing at the little girl with the wide smile who was the centre of attention. I led him away to avoid any offence.

He was thirty then, a year older than me, taller, thinner, edgier. Others have said we were more similar than I wanted to believe. He had brought nobody with him to the funeral, and that was a relief. His partners could be male or female, his relationships usually destructive; his companions were like unexploded bombs walking into the room.

"Sorry if I got the story wrong," I said, a bit caustically.

"Dad and his memories, all those stories he told over and over. Well, it's the last time I'll hear about Turing's apples!"

That thought hurt me. "We'll remember. I suppose I'll tell it to Eddie and Sam someday." My own little boys.

"They won't listen. Why should they? Dad will fade away. Everybody fades away. The dead get deader." He was talking about his own father, whom we had just buried. "Listen, have you heard they're putting the Clarke through its acceptance test run?…" And, there in the churchyard, he actually pulled a handheld computer out of his inside jacket pocket and brought up a specification. "Of course you understand the importance of it being on Farside." For the millionth time in my life he had set his little brother a pop quiz, and he looked at me as if I was catastrophically dumb.

"Radio shadow," I said. To be shielded from Earth's noisy chatter was particularly important for SETI, the search for extraterrestrial intelligence to which my brother was devoting his career. SETI searches for faint signals from remote civilisations, a task made orders of magnitude harder if you're drowned out by very loud signals from a nearby civilisation.

He actually applauded my guess, sarcastically. He often reminded me of what had always repelled me about academia—the barely repressed bullying, the intense rivalry. A university is a chimp pack. That was why I was never tempted to go down that route. That, and maybe the fact that Wilson had gone that way ahead of me.

I was faintly relieved when people started to move out of the churchyard. There was going to be a reception at my father's home, and we had to go.

"So are you coming for the cakes and sherry?"

He glanced at the time on his handheld. "Actually I've somebody to meet."

"He or she?"

He didn't reply. For one brief moment he looked at me with honesty. "You're better at this stuff than me."

"What stuff? Being human?"

"Listen, the Clarke should be open for business in a month. Come on down to London; we can watch the first results."

"I'd like that."

I was lying, and his invitation probably wasn't sincere either. In the end it was over two years before I saw him again.

By then he'd found the Eagle signal, and everything had changed.

2022

Wilson and his team quickly established that their brief signal, first detected just months after Clarke went operational, was coming from a source six thousand five hundred light years from Earth, somewhere beyond a starbirth cloud called the Eagle nebula. That's a long way away, on the other side of the Galaxy's next spiral arm in, the Sagittarius.

And to call the signal "brief" understates it. It was a second-long pulse, faint and hissy, and it repeated just once a *year*, roughly. It was a monument to robotic patience that the big lunar ear had picked up the damn thing at all.

Still it was a genuine signal from ET, the scientists were jumping up and down, and for a while it was a public sensation. Within days somebody had rushed out a pop single inspired by the message: called "Eagle Song," slow, dreamlike, littered with what sounded like sitars, and very beautiful. It was supposedly based on a Beatles master lost for five decades. It made number two.

But the signal was just a squirt of noise from a long way off. When there was no follow-up, when no mother ship materialised in the sky, interest moved on. That song vanished from the charts.

The whole business of the signal turned out to be your classic nine-day wonder. Wilson invited me in on the tenth day. That was why I was resentful, I guess, as I drove into town that morning to visit him.

The Clarke Institute's ground station was in one of the huge glass follies thrown up along the banks of the Thames in the profligate boom-capitalism days of the noughties. Now office space was cheap enough even for academics to rent, but central London was a fortress, with mandatory crawl lanes so your face could be captured by the surveillance cameras. I was in the counter-terror business myself, and I could see the necessity as I edged past St. Paul's, whose dome had been smashed like an egg by the Carbon Cowboys' bomb of 2018. But the slow ride left me plenty of time to brood on how many more *important* people Wilson had shown off to before he got around to his brother. Wilson never was loyal that way.

Wilson's office could have been any modern data-processing installation, save for the all-sky projection of the cosmic background radiation painted on the ceiling. Wilson sat me down and offered me a can of warm Coke. An audio transposition of the signal was playing on an open laptop, over and over. It sounded like waves lapping at a beach. Wilson looked like he hadn't shaved for three days, slept for five, or changed his shirt in ten. He listened, rapt.

Even Wilson and his team hadn't known about the detection of the signal for a year. The Clarke ran autonomously; the astronauts who built it had long since packed up and come home. A year earlier the telescope's signal processors had spotted the pulse, a whisper of microwaves. There was structure in there, and evidence that the beam was collimated—it looked artificial. But the signal faded after just a second.

Most previous SETI searchers had listened for strong, continuous signals, and would have given up at that point. But what about a lighthouse, sweeping a microwave beam around the Galaxy like a searchlight? That, so Wilson had explained to me, would be a much cheaper way for a transmitting civilisation to send to a lot more stars. So, based on that economic argument, the Clarke was designed for patience. It had waited a whole year. It had even sent requests to other installations, asking them to keep an electronic eye out in case the Clarke, stuck in its crater, happened to be looking the other way when the signal recurred. In the end it struck lucky and found the repeat pulse itself, and at last alerted its human masters.

"We're hot favourites for the Nobel," Wilson said, matter of fact.

I felt like having a go at him. "Probably everybody out there has forgotten about your signal already." I waved a hand at the huge glass windows; the office, meant for fat-cat hedge fund managers, had terrific views of the river, the Houses of Parliament, the tangled wreck of the London Eye. "Okay, it's proof of existence, but that's all."

He frowned at that. "Well, that's not true. Actually we're looking for more data in the signal. It is very faint, and there's a lot of scintillation from the interstellar medium. We're probably going to have to wait for a few more passes to get a better resolution."

"A few more passes? A few more years!"

"But even without that there's a lot we can tell just from the signal itself." He pulled up charts on his laptop. "For a start we can deduce the Eaglets' technical capabilities and power availability, given that we believe they'd do it as cheaply as possible. This analysis is related to an old model called Benford beacons." He pointed to a curve minimum. "Look—we figure they are pumping a few hundred megawatts through an array kilometres across, probably comparable to the one we've got listening on the Moon. Sending out pulses around the plane of the Galaxy, where most of the stars lie. We can make other guesses." He leaned back and took a slug of his Coke, dribbling a few drops to add to the collection of stains on his shirt. "The search for ET was always guided by philosophical principles and logic. Now we have this one data point, the Eaglets six thousand light years away, we can test those principles."

"Such as?"

"The principle of plenitude. We believed that because life and intelligence arose on this Earth, they ought to arise everywhere they can. Here's one validation of that principle. Then there's the principle of mediocrity."

I remembered enough of my studies to recall that. "We aren't at any special place in space and time."

"Right. Turns out, given this one data point, it's not likely to hold too well."

"Why do you say that?"

"Because we found these guys in the direction of the centre of the Galaxy…"

When the Galaxy was young, star formation was most intense at its core. Later a wave of starbirth swept out through the disc, with the heavy elements necessary for life baked in the hearts of dead stars and driven on a wind of supernovas. So the stars inward of us are older than the sun, and are therefore likely to have been harbours for life much longer.

"We would expect to see a concentration of old civilisations towards the centre of the Galaxy. This one example validates that." He eyed me, challenging. "We can even guess how many technological, transmitting civilisations there are in the Galaxy."

"From this one instance?" I was practiced at this kind of contest between us. "Well, let's see. The Galaxy is a disc a hundred thousand light years across, roughly. If all the civilisations are an average of six thousand light years apart—divide the area of the Galaxy by the area of a disc of diameter six thousand light years—around three hundred?"

He smiled. "Very *good*."

"So we're not typical," I said. "We're young, and out in the suburbs. All that from a single microwave pulse."

"Of course most ordinary people are too dumb to be able to appreciate logic like that. That's why they aren't rioting in the streets." He said this casually. Language like that always made me wince, even when we were undergraduates.

But he had a point. Besides, I had the feeling that most people had already believed in their gut that ET existed; this was a confirmation, not a shock. You might blame Hollywood for that, but Wilson sometimes speculated that we were looking for our lost brothers. All those other hominid species, those other kinds of mind, that we killed off one by one, just as in my lifetime we had destroyed the chimps in the wild—sentient tool-using beings, hunted down for bushmeat. We evolved on a crowded planet, and we missed them all.

"A lot of people are speculating about whether the Eaglets have souls," I said. "According to Saint Thomas Aquinas—"

He waved away Saint Thomas Aquinas. "You know, in a way our feelings behind SETI were always theological, explicitly or not. We were looking for God in the sky, or some technological equivalent. Somebody who would care about *us*. But we were never going to find Him. We were going to find either emptiness, or a new category of being, between us and the angels. The Eaglets have got nothing to do with us, or our dreams of God. That's what people don't see. And that's what people will have to deal with, ultimately."

He glanced at the ceiling, and I guessed he was looking towards the Eagle nebula. "And they won't be much like us. Hell of a place they live. Not like here. The Sagittarius arm wraps a whole turn around the Galaxy's core, full of dust and clouds and young stars. Why, the Eagle nebula itself is lit up by stars only a few million years old. Must be a tremendous sky, like a slow explosion—not like our sky of orderly wheeling pinpoints, which is like the inside of a computer. No wonder we began with astrology and astronomy. How do you imagine their thinking will be different, having evolved under such a different sky?"

I grunted. "We'll never know. Not for six thousand years at least."

"Maybe. Depends what data we find in the signal. You want another Coke?"

But I hadn't opened the first.

That was how that day went. We talked of nothing but the signal, not how he was, who he was dating, not about my family, my wife and the boys—all of us learning sign, incidentally, to talk to little Hannah. The Eagle signal was inhuman, abstract. Nothing you could see or touch; you couldn't even hear it without fancy signal processing. But it was all that filled his head. That was Wilson all over.

This was, in retrospect, the happiest time of his life. God help him.

2026

"You want my help, don't you?"

Wilson stood on my doorstep, wearing a jacket and shambolic tie, every inch the academic. He looked shifty. "How do you know?"

"Why else would you come here? You *never* visit." Well, it was true. He hardly ever even mailed or called. I didn't think my wife and kids had seen him since our father's funeral six years earlier.

He thought that over, then grinned. "A reasonable deduction, given past observation. Can I come in?"

I took him through the living room on the way to my home study. The boys, then twelve and thirteen, were playing a hologram boxing game, with two wavering foot-tall prize fighters mimicking the kids' actions in the middle of the carpet. I introduced Wilson. They barely remembered him and I wasn't sure if he remembered *them*. I hurried him on. The boys signed to each other: *What a dork*, roughly translated.

Wilson noticed the signing. "What are they doing? Some kind of private game?"

I wasn't surprised he wouldn't know. "That's British Sign Language. We've been learning it for years—actually since Dad's funeral, when we hooked up with Barry and his wife, and we found out they had a little deaf girl. Hannah, do you remember? She's eight now. We've all been learning to talk to her. The kids find it fun, I think. You know, it's an irony that you're involved in a billion-pound project to talk to aliens six thousand light years away, yet it doesn't trouble you that you can't speak to a little girl in your own family."

He looked at me blankly. I was mouthing words that obviously meant nothing to him, intellectually or emotionally. That was Wilson.

He just started talking about work. "We've got six years' worth of data now—six pulses, each a second long. There's a *lot* of information in there. They use a technique like our own wave-length division multiplexing, with the signal divided into sections each a kilohertz or so wide. We've extracted gigabytes…"

I gave up. I went and made a pot of coffee, and brought it back to the study. When I returned he was still standing where I'd left him, like a switched-off robot. He took a coffee and sat down.

I prompted, "Gigabytes?"

"Gigabytes. By comparison the whole *Encyclopaedia Britannica* is just one gigabyte. The problem is we can't make sense of it."

"How do you know it's not just noise?"

"We have techniques to test for that. Information theory. Based on experiments to do with talking to dolphins, actually." He dug a handheld out of his pocket and showed me some of the results.

The first was simple enough, called a "Zipf graph." You break your message up into what look like components—maybe words, letters, phonemes in English. Then you do a frequency count: how many letter As, how many Es, how many Rs. If you have random noise you'd expect roughly equal numbers of the letters, so you'd get a flat distribution. If you have a clean signal without information content, a string of identical letters, A, A, A, you'd get a graph with a spike. Meaningful information gives you a slope, somewhere in between those horizontal and vertical extremes.

"And we get a beautiful log-scale minus one power law," he said, showing me. "There's information in there all right. But there is a lot of controversy over identifying the elements themselves. The Eaglets did *not* send down neat binary code. The data is frequency modulated, their language full of growths and decays. More like a garden growing on fast-forward than any human data stream. I wonder if it has something to do with that young sky of theirs. Anyhow, after the Zipf, we tried a Shannon entropy analysis."

This is about looking for relationships between the signal elements. You work out conditional probabilities: Given pairs of elements, how likely is it that you'll see U following Q? Then you go on to higher-order "entropy levels," in the jargon, starting with triples: How likely is it to find G following I and N?

"As a comparison, dolphin languages get to third- or fourth-order entropy. We humans get to eighth or ninth."

"And the Eaglets?"

"The entropy level breaks our assessment routines. We think it's around order thirty." He regarded me, seeing if I understood. "It is information, but much more complex than any human language. It might be like English sentences with a fantastically convoluted structure—triple or quadruple negatives, overlapping clauses, tense changes." He grinned. "Or triple entendres. Or quadruples."

"They're smarter than us."

"Oh, yes. And this is proof, if we needed it, that the message isn't meant specifically for us."

"Because if it were, they'd have dumbed it down. How smart do you think they are? Smarter than us, certainly, but—"

"Are there limits? Well, maybe. You might imagine that an older culture would plateau, once they've figured out the essential truths of the universe, and a technology optimal for their needs... There's no reason to think progress need be onward and upward forever. Then again perhaps there are fundamental limits to information processing. Perhaps a brain that gets too complex is prone to crashes and overloads. There may be a trade-off between complexity and stability."

I poured him more coffee. "I went to Cambridge. I'm used to being with entities smarter than I am. Am I supposed to feel demoralised?"

He grinned. "That's up to you. But the Eaglets are a new category of being for us. This isn't like the Incas meeting the Spaniards, a mere technological gap. They had a basic humanity in common. We may find the gulf between us and the Eaglets is *forever* unbridgeable. Remember how Dad used to read *Gulliver's Travels* to us?"

The memory made me smile.

"Those talking horses used to scare the wits out of me. They were genuinely smarter than us. And how did Gulliver react to them? He was totally overawed. He tried to imitate them, and even after they kicked him out he always despised his own kind, because they weren't as good as the horses."

"The revenge of Mister Ed," I said.

But he never was much good at that kind of humour. "Maybe that will be the way for us—we'll ape the Eaglets or defy them. Maybe the mere knowledge that a race smarter than your own exists is death."

"Is all this being released to the public?"

"Oh, yes. We're affiliated to NASA, and they have an explicit open-book policy. Besides the Institute is as leaky as hell. There's no point even trying to keep it quiet. But we're releasing the news gradually and soberly. Nobody's noticing much. You hadn't, had you?"

"So what do you think the signal is? Some kind of super-encyclopaedia?"

He snorted. "Maybe. That's the fond hope among the contact optimists. But when the European colonists turned up on foreign shores, their first impulse wasn't to hand over encyclopaedias or histories, but—"

"Bibles."

"Yes. It could be something less disruptive than that. A vast work of art, for instance. Why would they send such a thing? Maybe it's a funeral pyre. Or a pharaoh's tomb, full of treasure. Look: we were here, this is how good we became."

"So what do you want of me?"

He faced me. I thought it was clear he was trying to figure out, in his clumsy way, how to get me to do whatever it was he wanted. "Well, what do you think? This makes translating the most obscure human language a cakewalk, and we've got nothing like a Rosetta stone. Look, Jack, our information processing suites at the Institute are pretty smart theoretically, but they are limited. Running off processors and memory store not much beefier than this." He waved his handheld. "Whereas the software brutes that do your data mining are an order of magnitude more powerful."

The software I developed and maintained mined the endless torrents of data culled on every individual in the country, from your minute-to-minute movements on private or public transport to the porn you accessed and how you hid it from your partner. We tracked your patterns of behaviour, and deviations from those patterns. "Terrorist" is a broad label, but it suited to describe the modern phenomenon we were looking for. The terrorists were needles in a haystack, of which the rest of us were the millions of straws.

This continual live data mining took up monstrous memory storage and processing power. A few times I'd visited the big Home Office computers in their hardened bunkers under New Scotland Yard: giant superconducting neural nets suspended in rooms so cold your breath crackled. There was nothing like it in the private sector, or in academia.

Which, I realised, was why Wilson had come to me today.

"You want me to run your ET signal through my data mining suites, don't you?" He immediately had me hooked, but I wasn't about to admit it. I might have rejected the academic life, but I think curiosity burned in me as strongly as it ever did in Wilson. "How do you imagine I'd get permission for that?"

He waved that away as a technicality of no interest. "What we're looking for is patterns embedded deep in the data, layers down, any kind of recognisable starter for us in decoding the whole thing… Obviously software designed to look for patterns in the way I use my travel cards is going to have to be adapted to seek useful correlations in the Eaglet data. It will be an unprecedented challenge.

"In a way that's a good thing. It will likely take generations to decode this stuff, if we ever do, the way it took the Renaissance Europeans generations to make sense of the legacy of antiquity. The sheer time factor is a culture-shock prophylactic.

"So are you going to bend the rules for me, Jack? Come on, man. Remember what Dad said. Solving puzzles like this is what we do. We both ate Turing's apples…"

He wasn't entirely without guile. He knew how to entice me. He turned out to be wrong about the culture shock, however.

2029

Two armed coppers escorted me through the Institute building. The big glass box was entirely empty save for me and the coppers and a sniffer dog. The morning outside was bright, a cold spring day, the sky a serene blue, elevated from Wilson's latest madness.

Wilson was sitting in the Clarke project office, beside a screen across which data displays flickered. He had big slabs of Semtex strapped around his waist, and some kind of dead man's trigger in his hand. My brother, reduced at last to a cliché suicide bomber. The coppers stayed safely outside.

"We're secure." Wilson glanced around. "They can see us but they can't hear us. I'm confident of that. My firewalls—" When I walked towards him he held up his hands. "No closer. I'll blow it, I swear."

"Christ, Wilson." I stood still, shut up, and deliberately calmed down.

I knew that my boys, now in their teens, would be watching every move on the spy-hack news channels. Maybe nobody could hear us, but Hannah, now a beautiful eleven-year-old, had plenty of friends who could read lips. That would never occur to Wilson. If I was to die today, here with my lunatic of a brother, I wasn't going to let my boys remember their father broken by fear.

I sat down, as close to Wilson as I could get. I tried to keep my head down, my lips barely moving when I spoke. There was a six-pack of warm soda on the bench. I think I'll always associate warm soda with Wilson. I took one, popped the tab and sipped; I could taste nothing. "You want one?"

"No," he said bitterly. "Make yourself at home."

"What a fucking idiot you are, Wilson. How did it ever come to this?"

"You should know. You helped me."

"And by God I've regretted it ever since," I snarled back at him. "You got me sacked, you moron. And since France, every nut job on the planet has me targeted, and my kids. We have police protection."

"Don't blame me. You chose to help me."

I stared at him. "That's called loyalty. A quality which you, entirely lacking it yourself, see only as a weakness to exploit."

"Well, whatever. What does it matter now? Look, Jack, I need your help."

"This is turning into a pattern."

He glanced at his screen. "I need you to buy me time, to give me a chance to complete this project."

"Why should I care about your project?"

"It's not *my* project. It never has been. Surely you understand that much. It's the Eaglets'…"

Everything had changed in the three years since I had begun to run Wilson's message through the big Home Office computers under New Scotland Yard—all under the radar of my bosses; they'd never have dared risk exposing their precious supercooled brains to such unknowns. Well, Wilson had been right. My data mining had quickly turned up recurring segments, chunks of organised data differing only in detail.

And it was Wilson's intuition that these things were bits of executable code: programs you could run. Even as expressed in the Eaglets' odd flowing language, he thought he recognised logical loops, start and stop statements. Mathematics may or may not be universal, but computing seems to be—my brother had found Turing machines, buried deep in an alien database.

Wilson translated the segments into a human mathematical programming language, and set them to run on a dedicated processor. They turned out to be like viruses. Once downloaded on almost any computer substrate they organised themselves, investigated their environment, started to multiply, and quickly grew, accessing the data banks that had been downloaded from the stars with them. Then they started asking questions of the operators: simple yes-no, true-false exchanges that soon built up a common language.

"The Eaglets didn't send us a message," Wilson had whispered to me on the phone in the small hours; at the height of it he worked twenty-four seven. "They downloaded an AI. And now the AI is learning to speak to us."

It was a way to resolve a ferocious communications challenge. The Eaglets were sending their message to the whole Galaxy; they knew nothing about the intelligence, cultural development, or even the physical form of their audiences. So they sent an all-purpose artificial mind embedded in the information stream itself, able to learn and start a local dialogue with the receivers.

This above all else proved to me how smart the Eaglets must be. It didn't comfort me at all that some commentators pointed out that this "Hoyle strategy" had been anticipated by some human thinkers; it's one thing to anticipate, another to build. I wondered if those viruses found it a challenge to dumb down their message for creatures capable of only ninth-order Shannon entropy, as we were.

We were soon betrayed. For running the Eaglet data through the Home Office mining suites I was sacked, arrested, and bailed on condition I went back to work on the Eaglet stuff under police supervision.

And of course the news that there was information in the Eaglets' beeps leaked almost immediately. A new era of popular engagement with the signal began; the chatter became intense. But because only the Clarke telescope could pick up the signal, the scientists at the Clarke Institute and the consortium of governments they answered to were able to keep control of the information itself. And that information looked as if it would become extremely valuable.

The Eaglets' programming and data compression techniques, what we could make of them, had immediate commercial value. When patented by the UK government and licensed, an information revolution began that added a billion euros to Britain's balance of payments in the first year. Governments and corporations outside the loop of control jumped up and down with fury.

And then Wilson and his team started to publish what they were learning of the Eaglets themselves.

We don't know anything about what they look like, how they live—or even if they're corporeal or not. But they are old, vastly old compared to us. Their cultural records go back a million years, maybe ten times as long as we've been human, and even then they built their civilisation on the ruins of others. But they regard themselves as a young species. They live in awe of older ones, whose presence they have glimpsed deep in the turbulent core of the Galaxy.

Not surprisingly, the Eaglets are fascinated by time and its processes. One of Wilson's team foolishly speculated that the Eaglets actually made a religion of time, deifying the one universal that will erode us all in the end. That caused a lot of trouble. Some people took up the time creed with enthusiasm. They looked for parallels in human philosophies, the Hindu and the Mayan. If the Eaglets really were smarter than us, they said, they must be closer to the true god, and we should follow them. Others, led by the conventional religions, moved sharply in the opposite direction. Minor wars broke out over a creed that was entirely unknown to humanity five years before, and which nobody on Earth understood fully.

Then the economic dislocations began, as those new techniques for data handling made whole industries obsolescent. That was predictable; it was as if the aliens had invaded cyberspace, which was economically dominant over the physical world. Luddite types began sabotaging the software houses turning out the new-generation systems, and battles broke out in the corporate universe, themselves on the economic scale of small wars.

"This is the danger of speed," Wilson had said to me, just weeks before he wired himself up with Semtex. "If we'd been able to take it slow, unwrapping the message would have been more like an exercise in normal science, and we could have absorbed it. Grown with it. Instead, thanks to the viruses, it's been like a revelation, a pouring of holy knowledge into our heads. Revelations tend to be destabilising. Look at Jesus. Three centuries after the Crucifixion Christianity had taken over the whole Roman empire."

Amid all the economic, political, religious and philosophical turbulence, if anybody had dreamed that knowing the alien would unite us around our common humanity, they were dead wrong.

Then a bunch of Algerian patriots used pirated copies of the Eaglet viruses to hammer the electronic infrastructure of France's major cities. As everything from sewage to air traffic control crashed, the country was simultaneously assaulted with train bombs, bugs in the water supply, a dirty nuke in Orleans. It was a force-multiplier attack, in the jargon; the toll of death and injury was a shock, even by the standards of the third decade of the bloody twenty-first century. And our counter-measures were useless in the face of the Eaglet viruses.

That was when the governments decided the Eaglet project had to be shut down, or at the very least put under tight control. But Wilson, my brother, wasn't having any of that.

"None of this is the fault of the Eaglets, Jack," he said now, an alien apologist with Semtex strapped to his waist. "They didn't mean to harm us in any way."

"Then what do they want?"

"Our help…"

And he was going to provide it. With, in turn, my help.

"Why me? I was sacked, remember."

"They'll listen to you. The police. Because you're my brother. You're useful."

"Useful?…" At times Wilson seemed unable to see people as anything other than useful robots, even his own family. I sighed. "Tell me what you want."

"Time," he said, glancing at his screen, the data and status summaries scrolling across it. "The great god of the Eaglets, remember? Just a little more time."

"How much?"

He checked. "Twenty-four hours would let me complete this download. That's an outside estimate. Just stall them. Keep them talking, stay here with me. Make them think you're making progress in talking me out of it."

"While the actual progress is being made by *that*." I nodded at the screen. "What are you doing here, Wilson? What's it about?"

"I don't know all of it. There are hints in the data. Subtexts sometimes…" He was whispering.

"Subtexts about what?"

"About what concerns the Eaglets. Jack, what do you imagine a long-lived civilisation *wants*? If you could think on very long timescales you would be concerned about threats that seem remote to us."

"An asteroid impact due in a thousand years, maybe? If I expected to live that long, or my kids—"

"That kind of thing. But that's not long enough, Jack, not nearly. In the data there are passages—poetry, maybe—that speak of the deep past and furthest future, the Big Bang that is echoed in the microwave background, the future that will be dominated by the dark energy expansion that will ultimately throw all the other galaxies over the cosmological horizon… The Eaglets think about these things, and not just as scientific hypotheses. They *care* about them. The dominance of their great god time. 'The universe has no memory.'"

"What does that mean?"

"I'm not sure. A phrase in the message."

"So what are you downloading? And to where?"

"The Moon," he said frankly. "The Clarke telescope, on Farside. They want us to build something, Jack. Something physical, I mean. And with the fabricators and other maintenance gear at Clarke there's a chance we could do it. I mean, it's not the most advanced offworld robot facility; it's only designed for maintenance and upgrade of the radio telescope—"

"But it's the facility you can get your hands on. You're letting these Eaglet agents out of their virtual world and giving them a way to build something real. Don't you think that's dangerous?"

"Dangerous how?" And he laughed at me and turned away.

I grabbed his shoulders and swivelled him around in his chair. "Don't you turn away from me, you fucker. You've been doing that all our lives. You know what I mean. Why, the Eaglets' software alone is making a mess of the world. What if this is some kind of Trojan horse—a Doomsday weapon they're getting us suckers to build ourselves?"

"It's hardly likely that an advanced culture—"

"Don't give me that contact-optimist bullshit. You don't believe it yourself. And even if you did, you don't *know* for sure. You can't."

"No. All right." He pulled away from me. "I can't know. Which is one reason why I set the thing going up on the Moon, not Earth. Call it a quarantine. If we don't like whatever it is, there's at least a *chance* we could contain it up there. Yes, there's a risk. But the rewards are unknowable, and huge." He looked at me, almost pleading for me to understand. "We have to go on. This is the Eaglets' project, not ours. Ever since we unpacked the message, this story has been about them, not us. That's what dealing with a superior intelligence means. It's like those religious nuts say. We *know* the Eaglets are orders of magnitude smarter than us. Shouldn't we trust them? Shouldn't we help them achieve their goal, even if we don't understand precisely what it is?"

"This ends now." I reached for the keyboard beside me. "Tell me how to stop the download."

"No." He sat firm, that trigger clutched in his right hand.

"You won't use that. You wouldn't kill us both. Not for something so abstract, inhuman—"

"*Superhuman*," he breathed. "Not inhuman. Superhuman. Oh, I would. You've known me all your life, Jack. Look into my eyes. *I'm not like you.* Do you really doubt me?"

And, looking at him, I didn't.

So we sat there, the two of us, a face-off. I stayed close enough to overpower him if he gave me the slightest chance. And he kept his trigger before my face.

Hour after hour.

In the end it was time that defeated him, I think, the Eaglets' invisible god. That and fatigue. I'm convinced he didn't mean to release the trigger. Only seventeen hours had elapsed, of the twenty-four he asked for, when his thumb slipped.

I tried to turn away. That small, instinctive gesture was why I lost a leg, a hand, an eye, all on my right side.

And I lost a brother.

But when the forensics guys had finished combing through the wreckage, they were able to prove that the seventeen hours had been enough for Wilson's download.

### 2033

It took a month for NASA, ESA and the Chinese to send up a lunar orbiter to see what was going on. The probe found that Wilson's download had caused the Clarke fabricators to start making stuff. At first they made other machines, more specialised, from what was lying around in the workshops and sheds. These in turn made increasingly tiny versions of themselves, heading steadily down to the nano scale. In the end the work was so fine only an astronaut on the ground might have had a chance of even seeing it. Nobody dared send in a human.

Meanwhile the machines banked up Moon dust and scrap to make a high-energy facility—something like a particle accelerator or a fusion torus, but not.

Then the real work started.

The Eaglet machines took a chunk of Moon rock and crushed it, turning its mass-energy into a spacetime artefact—something like a black hole, but not. They dropped it into the body of the Moon, where it started accreting, sucking in material, like a black hole, and budding off copies of itself, unlike a black hole.

Gradually these objects began converting the substance of the Moon into copies of themselves. The glowing point of light we see at the centre of Clarke is leaked radiation from this process.

The governments panicked. A nuclear warhead was dug out of cold store and dropped plumb into Daedalus Crater. The explosion was spectacular. But when the dust subsided that pale, unearthly spark was still there, unperturbed.

As the cluster of nano artefacts grows, the Moon's substance will be consumed at an exponential rate. Centuries, a millennium tops, will be enough to consume it all. And Earth will be orbited, not by its ancient companion, but by a spacetime artefact, like a black hole, but not. That much seems well established by the physicists.

There is less consensus as to the purpose of the artefact. Here's my guess.

The Moon artefact will be a recorder.

Wilson said the Eaglets feared the universe has no memory. I think he meant that, right now, in our cosmic epoch, we can still see relics of the universe's birth, echoes of the Big Bang, in the microwave background glow. And we also see evidence of the expansion to come, in the recession of the distant galaxies. We discovered both these basic features of the universe, its past and its future, in the twentieth century.

There will come a time—the cosmologists quote hundreds of billions of years—when the accelerating recession will have taken *all* those distant galaxies over our horizon. So we will be left with just the local group, the Milky Way and Andromeda and bits and pieces, bound together by gravity. The cosmic expansion will be invisible. And meanwhile the background glow will have become so attenuated you won't be able to pick it out of the faint glow of the interstellar medium.

So in that remote epoch you wouldn't be able to repeat the twentieth-century discoveries; you couldn't glimpse past or future. That's what the Eaglets mean when they say the universe has no memory.

And I believe they are countering it. They, and those like Wilson that they co-opt into helping them, are carving time capsules out of folded spacetime. At some future epoch these will evaporate, maybe through something like Hawking radiation, and will reveal the truth of the universe to whatever eyes are there to see it.

Of course it occurs to me—this is Wilson's principle of mediocrity—that ours might not be the only epoch with a privileged view of the cosmos. Just after the Big Bang there was a pulse of "inflation," superfast expansion that homogenised the universe and erased details of whatever came before. Maybe we should be looking for other time boxes, left for our benefit by the inhabitants of those early realms.

The Eaglets are conscious entities trying to give the universe a memory. Perhaps there is even a deeper purpose: it may be intelligence's role to shape the ultimate evolution of the universe, but you can't do that if you've forgotten what went before.

Not every commentator agrees with my analysis, as above. The interpretation of the Eaglet data has always been uncertain. Maybe even Wilson wouldn't agree. Well, since it's my suggestion he would probably argue with me by sheer reflex.

I suppose it's possible to care deeply about the plight of hypothetical beings a hundred billion years hence. In one sense we ought to; their epoch is our inevitable destiny. Wilson certainly did care, enough to kill himself for it. But this is a project so vast and cold that it can engage only a semi-immortal supermind like an Eaglet's—or a modern human who is functionally insane.

What matters most to me is the now. The sons who haven't yet aged and crumbled to dust, playing football under a sun that hasn't yet burned to a cinder. The fact that all this is transient makes it more precious, not less. Maybe our remote descendants in a hundred billion years will find similar brief happiness under their black and unchanging sky.

If I could wish one thing for my lost brother it would be that I could be sure he felt this way, this alive, just for one day. Just for one minute. Because, in the end, that's all we've got.

# THE NEW YORK TIMES AT SPECIAL BARGAIN RATES

## STEPHEN KING

Stephen King is arguably the most famous writer of popular fiction of his generation. He has sold over 350 million copies of his books. He is best known for his horror fiction, which demonstrates a thorough knowledge of the genre's history. He has also written science fiction, fantasy, short-fiction, non-fiction, screenplays, teleplays, and stageplays. Many of his stories have been adapted for other media, including movies, television series, and comic books. King has written a number of books using the pen name Richard Bachman and one short story where he was credited as John Swithen. In 2003 he received The National Book Foundation's Medal for Distinguished Contribution to American Letters.

She's fresh out of the shower when the phone begins to ring, but although the house is still full of relatives—she can hear them downstairs, it seems they will never go away, it seems she never had so many—no one picks up. Nor does the answering machine, as James programmed it to do after the fifth ring.

Anne goes to the extension on the bed-table, wrapping a towel around herself, her wet hair thwacking unpleasantly on the back of her neck and bare shoulders. She picks it up, she says hello, and then he says her name. It's James. They had thirty years together, and one word is all she needs. He says *Annie* like no one else, always did.

For a moment she can't speak or even breathe. He has caught her on the ex-hale and her lungs feel as flat as sheets of paper. Then, as he says her name again (sounding uncharacteristically hesitant and unsure of himself), the strength slips from her legs. They turn to sand and she sits on the bed, the towel falling off her, her wet bottom dampening the sheet beneath her. If the bed hadn't been there, she would have gone to the floor.

Her teeth click together and that starts her breathing again.

"James? Where *are* you? *What happened?*" In her normal voice, this might have come out sounding shrewish—a mother scolding her wayward eleven-year-old who's come late to the supper-table yet again—but now it emerges in a kind of horrified growl. The murmuring relatives below her are, after all, planning his funeral.

James chuckles. It is a bewildered sound. "Well, I tell you what," he says. "I don't exactly know where I am."

Her first confused thought is that he must have missed the plane in London, even though he called her from Heathrow not long before it took off. Then a clearer idea comes: although both the *Times* and the TV news say there were no survivors, there was at least one. Her husband crawled from the wreckage of the burning plane (and the burning apartment building the plane hit, don't forget that, twenty-four more dead on the ground and the number apt to rise before the world moved on to the next tragedy) and has been wandering around Brooklyn ever since, in a state of shock.

"Jimmy, are you all right? Are you...are you burned?" The truth of what that would mean occurs after the question, thumping down with the heavy weight of a dropped book on a bare foot, and she begins to cry. "Are you in the hospital?"

"Hush," he says, and at his old kindness—and at that old word, just one small piece of their marriage's furniture—she begins to cry harder. "Honey, hush."

"But I don't *understand!*"

"I'm all right," he says. "Most of us are."

"Most—? There are *others?*"

"Not the pilot," he says. "He's not so good. Or maybe it's the co-pilot. He keeps screaming, 'We're going down, there's no power, oh my God.' Also 'This isn't my fault, don't let them blame it on me.' He says that, too."

She's cold all over. "Who is this really? Why are you being so horrible? I just lost my husband, you asshole!"

"Honey—"

"Don't call me that!" There's a clear strand of mucus hanging from one of her nostrils. She wipes it away with the back of her hand and then flings it into the wherever, a thing she hasn't done since she was a child. "Listen, mister—I'm going to star-sixty-nine this call and the police will come and slam your ass...your ignorant, unfeeling *ass....*"

But she can go no further. It's his voice. There's no denying it. The way the call rang right through—no pick-up downstairs, no answering machine—suggests this call was just for her. And...*Honey, hush.* Like in the old Carl Perkins song.

He has remained quiet, as if letting her work these things through for herself. But before she can speak again, there's a beep on the line.

"James? *Jimmy?* Are you still there?"

"Yeah, but I can't talk long. I was trying to call you when we went down, and I guess that's the only reason I was able to get through at all. Lots of others have been trying, we're lousy with cell phones, but no luck." That beep again. "Only now my phone's almost out of juice."

"Jimmy, did you know?" This idea has been the hardest and most terrible part for her—that he might have known, if only for an endless minute or two. Others might picture burned bodies or dismembered heads with grinning teeth; even light-fingered first responders filching wedding rings and diamond ear-clips, but what has robbed Annie Driscoll's sleep is the image of Jimmy looking out his window as the streets and cars and the brown apartment buildings of Brooklyn swell closer. The useless masks flopping down like the corpses of small yellow animals. The overhead bins popping open, carry-ons starting to fly, someone's Norelco razor rolling up the tilted aisle.

"Did you know you were going down?"

"Not really," he says. "Everything seemed all right until the very end—maybe the last thirty seconds. Although it's hard to keep track of time in situations like that, I always think."

*Situations like that.* And even more telling: *I always think.* As if he has been aboard half a dozen crashing 767s instead of just the one.

"In any case," he goes on, "I was just calling to say we'd be early, so be sure to get the FedEx man out of bed before I got there."

Her absurd attraction for the FedEx man has been a joke between them for years. She begins to cry again. His cell utters another of those beeps, as if scolding her for it.

"I think I died just a second or two before it rang the first time. I think that's why I was able to get through to you. But this thing's gonna give up the ghost pretty soon."

He chuckles as if this is funny. She supposes that in a way it is. She may see the humor in it herself, eventually. *Give me ten years or so,* she thinks.

Then, in that just-talking-to-myself voice she knows so well: "Why didn't I put the tiresome motherfucker on charge last night? Just forgot, that's all. Just forgot."

"James…honey…the plane crashed two days ago."

A pause. Mercifully with no beep to fill it. Then: "Really? Mrs. Corey *said* time was funny here. Some of us agreed, some of us disagreed. I was a disagreer, but looks like she was right."

"Hearts?" Annie asks. She feels now as if she is floating outside and slightly above her plump damp middle-aged body, but she hasn't forgotten Jimmy's old habits. On a long flight he was always looking for a game. Cribbage or canasta would do, but hearts was his true love.

"Hearts," he agrees. The phone beeps, as if seconding that.

"Jimmy…." She hesitates long enough to ask herself if this is information she really wants, then plunges with that question still unanswered. "Where *are* you, exactly?"

"Looks like Grand Central Station," he says. "Only bigger. And emptier. As if it wasn't really Grand Central at all but only…mmm…a movie set of Grand Central. Do you know what I'm trying to say?"

"I…I think so.…"

"There certainly aren't any trains…and we can't hear any in the distance…but there are doors going everywhere. Oh, and there's an escalator, but it's broken. All dusty, and some of the treads are gone." He pauses, and when he speaks again he does so in a lower voice, as if afraid of being overheard. "People are leaving. Some climbed the escalator—I saw them—but most are using the doors. I guess I'll have to leave, too. For one thing, there's nothing to eat. There's a candy machine, but that's broken, too."

"Are you…honey, are you hungry?"

"A little. Mostly what I'd like is some water. I'd *kill* for a cold bottle of Dasani."

Annie looks guiltily down at her own legs, still beaded with water. She imagines him licking off those beads and is horrified to feel a sexual stirring.

"I'm all right, though," he adds hastily. "For now, anyway. But there's no sense staying here. Only…"

"What? What, Jimmy?"

"I don't know which door to use."

Another beep.

"I wish I knew which one Mrs. Corey took. She's got my damn cards."

"Are you…" She wipes her face with the towel she wore out of the shower; then she was fresh, now she's all tears and snot. "Are you scared?"

"Scared?" he asks thoughtfully. "No. A little worried, that's all. Mostly about which door to use."

*Find your way home*, she almost says. *Find the right door and find your way home.* But if he did, would she want to see him? A ghost might be all right, but what if she opened the door on a smoking cinder with red eyes and the remains of jeans (he always traveled in jeans) melted into his legs? And what if Mrs. Corey was with him, his baked deck of cards in one twisted hand?

*Beep.*

"I don't need to tell you to be careful about the FedEx man anymore," he says. "If you really want him, he's all yours."

She shocks herself by laughing.

"But I did want to say I love you—"

"Oh honey I love you t—"

"—and not to let the McCormack kid do the gutters this fall, he works hard but he's a risk-taker, last year he almost broke his fucking neck. And don't go to the bakery anymore on Sundays. Something's going to happen there, and I know it's going to be on a Sunday, but I don't know which Sunday. Time really *is* funny here."

The McCormack kid he's talking about must be the son of the guy who used to be their caretaker in Vermont…only they sold that place ten years ago, and the kid must be in his mid-twenties by now. And the bakery? She supposes he's talking about Zoltan's, but what on *Earth*—

*Beep.*

"Some of the people here were on the ground, I guess. That's very tough, because they don't have a clue how they got here. And the pilot keeps screaming. Or maybe it's the co-pilot. I think he's going to be here for quite a while. He just wanders around. He's very confused."

The beeps are coming closer together now.

"I have to go, Annie. I can't stay here, and the phone's going to shit the bed any second now, anyway." Once more in that I'm-scolding-myself voice (impossible to believe she will never hear it again after today; impossible *not* to believe), he mutters, "It would have been so simple just to…well, never mind. I love you, sweetheart."

"Wait! Don't go!"

"I c—"

"I love you, too! Don't go!"

But he already has. In her ear there is only black silence.

She sits there with the dead phone to her ear for a minute or more, then breaks the connection. The non-connection. When she opens the line again and gets a perfectly normal dial-tone, she touches star-sixty-nine after all. According to the robot who answers her page, the last incoming call was at nine o'clock that morning. She knows who that one was: her sister Nell, calling from New Mexico. Nell called to tell Annie that her plane had been delayed and she wouldn't be in until tonight. Nell told her to be strong.

All the relatives who live at a distance—James's, Annie's—flew in. Apparently they feel that James used up all the family's Destruction Points, at least for the time being.

There is no record of an incoming call at—she glances at the bedside clock and sees it's now 3:17 PM—at about ten past three, on the third afternoon of her widowhood.

Someone raps briefly on the door and her brother calls, "Anne? Annie?"

"Dressing!" she calls back. Her voice sounds like she's been crying, but unfortunately, no one in this house would find that strange. "Privacy, please!"

"You okay?" he calls through the door. "We thought we heard you talking. And Ellie thought she heard you call out."

"Fine!" she calls, then wipes her face again with the towel. "Down in a few!"

"Okay. Take your time." Pause. "We're here for you." Then he clumps away.

"Beep," she whispers, then covers her mouth to hold in laughter that is some emotion even more complicated than grief trying to find the only way out it has. "Beep, beep. Beep, beep, beep." She lies back on the bed, laughing, and above her cupped hands her eyes are large and awash with tears that overspill down her cheeks and run all the way to her ears. "Beep-fucking-beepity-beep."

She laughs for quite a while, then dresses and goes downstairs to be with her relatives, who have come to mingle their grief with hers. Only they feel apart from her, because he didn't call any of them. He called her. For better or worse, he called her.

During the autumn of that year, with the blackened remains of the apartment building the jet crashed into still closed off from the rest of the world by yellow police tape (although the taggers have been inside, one leaving a spray-painted message reading CRISPY CRITTERS LAND HERE), Annie receives the sort of e-blast computer-addicts like to send to a wide circle of acquaintances. This one comes from Gert Fisher, the town librarian in Tilton, Vermont. When Annie and James summered there, Annie used to volunteer at the library, and although the two women never got on especially well, Gert has included Annie in her quarterly updates ever since. They are usually not very interesting, but halfway through the weddings, funerals, and 4-H winners in this one, Annie comes across a bit of news that makes her catch her breath. Jason McCormack, the son of old Hughie McCormack, was killed in an accident on Labor Day. He fell from the roof of a summer cottage while cleaning the gutters and broke his neck.

"He was only doing a favor for his dad, who as you may remember had a stroke the year before last," Gert wrote before going on to how it rained on the library's end-of-summer lawn sale, and how disappointed they all were.

Gert doesn't say in her three-page compendium of breaking news, but Annie is quite sure Jason fell from the roof of what used to be their cottage. In fact, she is positive.

Five years after the death of her husband (and the death of Jason McCormack not long after), Annie remarries. And although they relocate to Boca Raton, she gets back to the old neighborhood often. Craig, the new husband, is only semi-retired, and his business takes him to New York every three or four months. Annie almost always goes with him, because she still has family in Brooklyn and on Long Island. More than she knows what to do with, it sometimes seems. But she loves them with that exasperated affection that seems to belong, she thinks, only to people in their fifties and sixties. She never forgets how they drew together for her after James's plane went down, and made the best cushion for her that they could. So she wouldn't crash, too.

When she and Craig go back to New York, they fly. About this she never has a qualm, but she stops going to Zoltan's Family Bakery on Sundays when she's home, even though their raisin bagels are, she is sure, served in heaven's waiting room. She goes to Froger's instead. She is actually there, buying doughnuts (the doughnuts are at least passable), when she hears the blast. She hears it clearly even though Zoltan's is eleven blocks away. LP gas explosion. Four killed, including the woman who always passed Annie her bagels with the top of the bag rolled down, saying, "Keep it that way until you get home or you lose the freshness."

People stand on the sidewalks, looking east toward the sound of the explosion and the rising smoke, shading their eyes with their hands. Annie hurries past them, not looking. She doesn't want to see a plume of rising smoke after a big bang; she thinks of James enough as it is, especially on the nights when she can't sleep. When she gets home she can hear the phone ringing inside. Either everyone has gone down the block to where the local school is having a sidewalk art sale, or no one can hear that ringing phone. Except for her, that is. And by the time she gets her key turned in the lock, the ringing has stopped.

Sarah, the only one of her sisters who never married, *is* there, it turns out, but there is no need to ask her why she didn't answer the phone; Sarah Bernicke, the one-time disco queen, is in the kitchen with the Village People turned up, dancing around with the O-Cedar in one hand, looking like a chick in a TV ad. She missed the bakery explosion, too, although their building is even closer to Zoltan's than Froger's.

Annie checks the answering machine, but there's a big red zero in the MESSAGES WAITING window. That means nothing in itself, lots of people call without leaving a message, but—

Star-sixty-nine reports the last call at eight-forty last night. Annie dials it anyway, hoping against hope that somewhere outside the big room that looks like a Grand Central Station movie set he found a place to re-charge his phone. To him it might seem he last spoke to her yesterday. Or only minutes ago. *Time really is funny here*, he said. She has dreamed of that call so many times it now almost seems like a dream itself, but she has never told anyone about it. Not Craig, not even her own mother, now almost ninety but alert and with a firmly held belief in the afterlife.

In the kitchen, the Village People advise that there is no need to feel down. There isn't, and she doesn't. She nevertheless holds the phone very tightly as the number she has star-sixty-nined rings once, then twice. Annie stands in the living room with the phone to her ear and her free hand touching the brooch above her left breast, as if touching the brooch could still the pounding heart beneath it. Then the ringing stops and a recorded voice offers to sell her *The New York Times* at special bargain rates that will not be repeated.

# FIVE THRILLERS

## ROBERT REED

Robert Reed was born in Omaha, Nebraska, in 1956. He has a Bachelor of Science in Biology from Nebraska Wesleyan University, and has worked as a lab technician. He became a full-time writer in 1987, the same year he won the L. Ron Hubbard Writers of the Future Contest, and has published eleven novels, including *The Leeshore*, *The Hormone Jungle*, and far future science fiction novels *Marrow* and *The Well of Stars*. An extraordinarily prolific writer, Reed has published over 140 short stories, mostly in *The Magazine of Fantasy & Science Fiction* and *Asimov's Science Fiction*, which have been nominated for the Hugo, James Tiptree Jr. Memorial, Locus, Nebula, Seiun, Theodore Sturgeon Memorial, and World Fantasy awards, and have been collected in *The Dragons of Springplace* and *The Cuckoo's Boys*. His novella "A Billion Eves" won the Hugo Award last year. Nebraska's only SF writer, Reed lives in Lincoln with his wife and daughter, and is an ardent long-distance runner.

### I. The Ill-Fated Mission

Their situation was dire. A chunk of primordial iron had slashed its way through the *Demon Dandy*, crippling the engines and pushing life support to the brink of failure. Even worse, a shotgun blast of shrapnel had shredded one of the ship's two life-pods. The mission engineer, a glum little man who had spent twenty years mining Earth-grazing asteroids, studied the wreckage with an expert eye. There was no sane reason to hope that repairs could be made in time. But on the principle of keeping his staff busy, he ordered the robots and his new assistant to continue their work on the useless pod. Then after investing a few moments cursing God and Luck, the engineer dragged himself to the remnants of the bridge to meet with the *Dandy*'s beleaguered captain.

His assistant was a young fellow named Joseph Carroway.

Handsome as a digital hero, with green eyes and an abundance of curly blond hair, Joe was in his early twenties, born to wealthy parents who had endowed their only child with the earliest crop of synthetic human genes. He was a tall, tidy fellow, and he was a gifted athlete as graceful as any dancer, on the Earth or in freefall. According to a dozen respected scales, Joe was also quite intelligent. With an impressed shake of the head, the company psychiatrist had confided that his bountiful talents made him suitable for many kinds of work. But by the same token, that supercharged brain carried certain inherent risks.

Dipping his head in the most charming fashion, he said, "Risks?"

"And I think you know what I'm talking about," she remarked, showing a wary, somewhat flirtatious smile.

"But I don't know," Joe lied.

"And I believe you do," she countered. "Without exception, Mr. Carroway, you have been telling me exactly what I want to hear. And you're very believable, I should add. If I hadn't run the T-scan during our interview, I might have come away believing that you are the most kind, most decent gentleman in the world."

"But I am decent," he argued.

Joe sounded, and looked, exceptionally earnest.

The psychiatrist laughed. A woman in her early fifties, she was an overqualified professional doing routine tasks for a corporation larger and more powerful than most nations. The solar system was being opened to humanity—humanity in all of its forms, old and new. Her only task was to find qualified bodies to do exceptionally dangerous work. The vagaries of this young man's psyche were factors in her assessment. But they weren't the final word. After a moment's reflection, she said, "God. The thing is, you're beautiful."

Joe smiled and said, "Thank you."

Then with a natural smoothness, he added, "And you are an exceptionally lovely woman."

She laughed, loudly and with a trace of despair, as if aware that she would never again hear such kind words from a young man.

Joe leaned forward and, wearing the perfect smile—a strong winning grin—he told the psychiatrist, "I am a very good person."

"No," she said. "No, Joe, you are not."

Then she sat back in her chair, and with a finger twirling her mousy-brown hair, she confessed, "But dear God, my boy, I really would just love to have you for dinner."

That was five months ago, and now Joe was on board a ship that had been devastated by a mindless piece of iron.

As soon as the engineer left for the bridge, Joe kicked away from the battered escape pod. Both robots quietly reminded him of their orders. Dereliction of duty would leave a black mark on the mission report. But their assignment had no purpose except to keep them busy and Joe distracted. And since arguing with machines served no role, he said nothing, focusing on the only rational course available to him.

The com-line to the bridge was locked, but that was a puzzle easily solved. For the next few minutes, Joe concentrated on a very miserable conversation between the ship's top officers. The best launch window was only a little more than three hours from now. The surviving pod had finite fuel and oxygen. Kilograms and the time demanded by any return voyage were the main problems. Thirty precious seconds were wasted when the captain announced that she would remain behind, forcing the engineer to point out that she was a small person, which meant they would need to find another thirty kilos of mass, at the very least.

Of course both officers could play the hero role, sacrificing themselves to save their crew. But neither mentioned what was painfully obvious. Instead, what mattered was the naming and discarding of a string of increasingly unworkable fixes.

Their conversation stopped when Joe drifted into the bridge.

"I've got two options for you," he announced. "And when it comes down to it, you'll take my second solution."

The captain glanced at her engineer, as if to ask, "Should we listen to this kid?"

In despair, the engineer said, "Tell us, Joe. Quick."

"The fairest answer? We chop off everybody's arms and legs." He smiled and dipped his head as he spoke, pretending to be squeamish. "We'll use the big field laser, since that should cauterize the wounds. Then our robots dope everybody up and shove us onboard the pod. With the robots remaining behind, of course."

Neither officer had considered saving their machines.

"We chop off our own arms?" the engineer whined. "And our legs too?"

"Prosthetics do wonders," Joe pointed out. "Or the company can grow us new limbs. They won't match the originals, but they'll be workable enough."

The officers traded nervous looks.

"What else do you have?" the captain asked.

"One crewmember remains behind."

"We've considered that," the engineer warned. "But there's no decent way to decide who stays and who goes."

"Two of us have enough mass," Joe pointed out. "If either one stays, everybody else escapes."

At six foot and ninety kilos, Joe was easily the largest crewman.

"So you're volunteering?" asked the captain, hope brightening her tiny brown face.

Joe said, "No," with a flat, unaffected voice. "I'm sorry. Did I say anything about volunteers?"

Suddenly the only sound was the thin wind caused by a spaceship suffering a thousand tiny leaks.

One person among the crew was almost as big as Joe.

The engineer whispered, "Danielle."

Both officers winced. Their colleague was an excellent worker and a dear friend, and Danielle also happened to be attractive and popular. Try as they might, they couldn't accept the idea that they would leave her behind, and without her blessing, at that.

Joe had anticipated their response. "But if you had a choice between her and me, you'd happily abandon me. Is that right?"

They didn't answer. But Joe was new to the crew, and when their eyes dropped, they were clearly saying, "Yes."

He took no offense.

With a shrug and a sigh, Joe gave his audience time enough to feel ashamed. Then he looked at the captain, asking, "What about Barnes? He's only ten, maybe eleven kilos lighter than me."

That name caused a brief exchange of glances.

"What are you planning?" asked the engineer.

Joe didn't respond.

"No," the captain told him.

"No?" asked Joe. "'No' to what?"

Neither would confess what they were imagining.

Then Joe put on a horrified expression. "Oh, God," he said. "Do you really believe I would consider *that?*"

The engineer defended himself with soft mutters.

Joe's horror dissolved into a piercing stare.

"There are codes to this sort of thing," the captain reminded everybody, including herself. "Commit violence against a fellow crewmember, I don't care who it is…and you won't come home with us, Mr. Carroway. Is that clear enough for you to understand?"

Joe let her fume. Then with a sly smile, he said, "I'm sorry. I thought we wanted the best way to save as many lives as possible."

Again, the officers glanced at each other.

The young man laughed in a charming but very chilly fashion—a moment that always made empathic souls uneasy. "Let's return to my first plan," he said. "Order everybody into the machine shop, and we'll start carving off body parts."

The captain said, "No," and then looked for a good reason.

The engineer just shrugged, laughing nervously.

"We don't know if that would work," the captain decided. "People could be killed by the trauma."

"And what if we had to fly the pod manually?" the engineer asked. "Without hands, we're just cargo."

An awful option had been excluded, and they could relax slightly.

"Okay," said Joe. "This is what I'm going to do: I'll go talk to Barnes. Give me a few minutes. And if I don't get what we want, then I will stay behind."

"You?" the captain said hopefully.

Joe offered a firm, trustworthy, "Sure."

But when he tallied up everyone's mass, the engineer found trouble. "Even with Barnes gone, we're still five kilos past our limit. And I'd like to give us a bigger margin of error, if I can."

"So," said Joe. "The rest of us give blood."

The captain stared at this odd young man, studying that dense blond hair and those bright hazel eyes.

"Blood," Joe repeated. "As much as we can physically manage. And we can also enjoy a big chemically induced shit before leaving this wreck."

The engineer began massaging the numbers.

Joe matter-of-factly dangled his leg between the officers. "And if we're pressed, I guess I could surrender one of these boys. But my guess is that it won't come to that."

And in the end, it did not.

Three weeks later, Joe Carroway was sitting in the psychiatrist's office, calmly discussing the tragedy.

"I've read everyone's report," she admitted.

He nodded, and he smiled.

Unlike their last meeting, the woman was striving to maintain a strict professional distance. She couldn't have foreseen what would happen to the *Demon Dandy* or how this employee would respond. But there was the possibility that blame would eventually settle on her, and to save her own flesh, she was determined to learn exactly what Joe and the officers had decided on the bridge.

"Does your face hurt?" she inquired.

"A little bit."

"How many times did he strike you?"

"Ten," Joe offered. "Maybe more."

She winced. "The weapon?"

"A rough piece of iron," he said. "Barnes had a souvenir from the first asteroid he helped work."

Infrared sensors and the hidden T-scanner were observing the subject closely. Examining the telemetry, she asked, "Why did you pick Mr. Barnes?"

"That's in my report."

"Remind me, Joe. What were your reasons?"

"He was big enough to matter."

"And what did the others think about the man?"

"You mean the crew?" Joe shrugged. "He was one of us. Maybe he was quiet and kept to himself—"

"Bullshit."

When he wanted, Joe could produce a shy, boyish grin.

"He was different from the rest of you," the psychiatrist pointed out. "And I'm not talking about his personality."

"You're not," Joe agreed.

She produced images of the dead man. The oldest photograph showed a skinny, homely male in his middle twenties, while the most recent example presented a face that was turning fat—a normal consequence that came with the most intrusive, all-encompassing genetic surgery.

"Your colleague was midway through some very radical genetic surgery."

"He was," Joe agreed.

"He belonged to the Rebirth Movement."

"I'm sorry. What does this have to do with anything?" Joe's tone was serious. Perhaps even offended. "Everybody is human, even if they aren't *sapiens* anymore. Isn't that the way our laws are written?"

"You knew exactly what you were doing, Joe."

He didn't answer.

"You selected Barnes. You picked him because you understood that nobody would stand in your way."

Joe's only response was the trace of a grin at the corners of his mouth.

"Where did you meet with Barnes?"

"In his cabin."

"And what did you say to him?"

"That I loved him," Joe explained. "I told him that I was envious of his courage and vision. Leaving our old species was noble. Was good. I thought that he was intriguing and very beautiful. And I told him that to save his important life, as well as everybody else, I was going to sacrifice myself. I was staying behind with the robots."

"You lied to him."

"Except Barnes believed me."

"Are you sure?"

"Yes."

"When you told him you loved him...did you believe he was gay?"

"He wasn't."

"But if he had been? What would you have done if he was flattered by your advances?"

"Oh, I could have played that game too."

The psychiatrist hesitated. "What do you mean?"

"If Barnes preferred guys, then I would have seduced him. If I'd thought there was enough time, I mean. I would have convinced him to remain behind and save my life. Really, the guy was pretty easy to manipulate, all in all. It wouldn't have taken much to convince him that being the hero was his idea in the first place."

"You could have managed all that?"

Joe considered hard before saying, "If I'd had a few days to work with, sure. Easy. But you're probably right. A couple hours wasn't enough time."

The psychiatrist had stopped watching the telemetry, preferring to stare at the creature sitting across from her.

Quietly, she said, "Okay."

Joe waited patiently.

"What did Mr. Barnes say to you?" she asked. "After you professed your love, how did he react?"

"'You're lying.'" Joe didn't just quote the man, but he sounded like him too. The voice was thick and a little slow, wrapped around vocal chords that were slowly changing their configuration. "'You've slept with every damn woman on this ship,' he told me. 'Except our dyke captain.'"

The psychiatrist's face stiffened slightly.

"Is that true?" she muttered.

Joe gave her a moment. "Is what true?"

"Never mind." She found a new subject to pursue. "Mr. Barnes's cabin was small, wasn't it?"

"The same as everybody's."

"And you were at opposite ends of that room. Is that right?"

"Yes."

By birth, Barnes was a small man, but his Rebirth had given him temporary layers of fat that would have eventually been transformed into new tissues and bones, and even two extra fingers on each of his long, lovely hands. The air inside that cubbyhole had smelled of biology—raw and distinctly strange. But it wasn't an unpleasant odor. Barnes had been drifting beside his bed, and next to him was the image of the creature he wanted to become—a powerful, fur-draped entity with huge golden eyes and a predator's toothy grin. The cabin walls were covered with his possessions, each lashed in place to keep them out of the way. And on the surface of what was arbitrarily considered to be the ceiling, Barnes had painted the motto of the Rebirth movement:

TO BE TRULY HUMAN IS TO BE DIFFERENT.

"Do you want to know what I told him?" asked Joe. "I didn't put this in my report. But after he claimed I was sleeping with those women…do you know what I said that got him to start pounding on me…?"

The psychiatrist offered a tiny, almost invisible nod.

"I said, 'I'm just playing with those silly bitches. They're toys to me. But you, you're nothing like them. Or like me. You're going to be a spectacular creature. A vision of the future, you lucky shit. And before I die, please, let me blow you. Just to get the taste of another species.'"

She sighed. "All right."

"And that's when I reached for him—"

"You're heterosexual," she complained.

"I was saving lives," Joe responded.

"You were saving your own life."

"And plenty of others, too," he pointed out. Then with a grin, he added, "You don't appreciate what I was prepared to do, Doctor. If it meant saving the rest of us, I was capable of anything."

She once believed that she understood Joe Carroway. But in every possible way, she had underestimated the man sitting before her, including his innate capacity to measure everybody else's nature.

"The crew was waiting in the passageway outside," he mentioned. "With the captain and engineer, they were crowding in close, listening close, trying to hear what would happen. All these good decent souls, holding their breaths, wondering if I could pull this trick off."

She nodded again.

"They heard the fight, but it took them a couple minutes to force the door's lock. When they got inside, they found Barnes all over me and that lump of iron in his hand." Joe paused before asking, "Do you know how blood looks in space? It forms a thick mist of bright red drops that drift everywhere, sticking to every surface."

"Did Mr. Barnes strike you?"

Joe hesitated, impressed enough to show her an appreciative smile. "What does it say in my report?"

"But it seems to me...." Her voice trailed away. "Maybe you were being honest with me, Joe. When you swore that you would have done anything to save yourself, I should have believed you. So I have to wonder now—what if you grabbed that piece of asteroid and turned it on yourself? Mr. Barnes would have been surprised. For a minute or so, he might have been too stunned to do anything but watch you strike yourself in the face. Then he heard the others breaking in, and he naturally kicked over to you and pulled the weapon from your hand."

"Now why would I admit to any of that?" Joe replied.

Then he shrugged, adding, "But really, when you get down to it, the logistics of what happened aren't important. What matters is that I gave the captain a very good excuse to lock that man up, which was how she cleared her conscience before we could abandon ship."

"The captain doesn't look at this as an excuse," the psychiatrist said.

"No?"

"Barnes was violent, and her conscience rests easy."

Joe asked, "Who ordered every com-system destroyed before we abandoned the *Demon Dandy*? Who left poor Barnes with no way even to call home?"

"Except by then, your colleague was a prisoner, and according to our corporate laws, the captain was obligated to silence the criminal to any potential lawsuits." The woman kept her gaze on Joe. "Somebody had to be left behind, and in the captain's mind, you weren't as guilty as Mr. Barnes."

"I hope not."

"But nobody was half as cold or a tenth as ruthless as you were, Joe."

His expression was untroubled, even serene.

"The captain understands what you are. But in the end, she had no choice but to leave the other man behind."

Joe laughed. "Human or not, Barnes wasn't a very good person. He was mean-spirited and distant, and even if nobody admits it, I promise you: Nobody on the ship has lost two seconds' sleep over what happened there."

The psychiatrist nearly spoke, then hesitated.

Joe leaned forward. "Do you know how it is, Doctor? When you're a kid, there's always something that you think you're pretty good at. Maybe you're the best on your street, or you're the best at school. But you never know how good you really are. Not until you get out into the big world and see what other people can do. And in the end, we aren't all that special. Not extra clever or pretty or strong. But for a few of us, a very few, there comes a special day when we realize that we aren't just a little good at something. We are great.

"Better than anybody ever, maybe.

"Do you know how that feels, ma'am?"

She sighed deeply. Painfully. "What are you telling me, Joe?"

He leaned back in his chair, absently scratching at the biggest bandage on his iron-battered face. "I'm telling you that I am excellent at sizing people up. Even better than you, and I think you're beginning to appreciate that. But what you call being a borderline psychopath is to me just another part of my bigger, more important talent."

"You're not borderline anything," she said.

He took no offense from the implication. "Here's what we can learn from this particular mess: Most people are secretly bad. Under the proper circumstances, they will gladly turn on one of their own and feel nothing but good about it afterward. But when the stakes are high and the world's going to shit, I can see exactly what needs to be done. Unlike everybody else, I will do the dirtiest work. Which is a rare and rich and remarkable gift, I think."

She took a breath. "Why are you telling me this, Joe?"

"Because I don't want to be a mechanic riding clunky spaceships," he confessed. "And I want your help, Doctor. All right? Will you find me new work…something that's closer to my talents? Closer to my heart.

"Would you do that for me, pretty lady?"

### II. Natural Killer

At four in the morning, the animals slept—which was only reasonable since this was a zoo populated entirely by synthetic organisms. Patrons didn't pay for glimpses of furry lumps, formerly wild and now slumbering in some shady corner. What they wanted were spectacular, one-of-a-kind organisms doing breathtaking feats, and doing them in daylight. But high metabolisms had their costs, and that's why the creatures now lay in their cages and grottos, inside glass boxes and private ponds, beautiful eyes closed while young minds dreamed about who-could-say-what.

For the moment, privacy was guaranteed, and that was one fine reason why desperate men would agree to meet in that public place.

Slipping into the zoo unseen brought a certain ironic pleasure too.

But perhaps the most important, at least for Joe, were the possibilities inherent with that unique realm.

A loud, faintly musical voice said, "Stop, Mr. Carroway. Stop where you are, sir. And now please…lift your arms for us and dance in a very slow circle.…"

Joe was in his middle thirties. His rigorously trained body was clad in casual white slacks and a new gray shirt. His face had retained its boyish beauty, a prominent scar creasing the broad forehead and a several-day growth of beard lending a rough, faintly threadbare quality to his otherwise immaculate appearance. Arms up, he looked rather tired. As he turned slowly, he took deep breaths, allowing several flavors of radiation to wash across his body, reaching into his bones.

"I see three weapons." The voice came from no particular direction. "One at a time, please, lower the weapons and kick each of them toward the fountain. If you will, Mr. Carroway."

A passing shower had left the plaza wet and slick. Joe dropped the Ethiopian machine pistol first, followed by the matching Glocks. Each time he kicked one of the guns, it would spin and skate across the red bricks, each one ending up within a hand's length of the fountain—an astonishing feat, considering the stakes and his own level of exhaustion.

Unarmed, Joe stood alone in the empty plaza.

The fountain had a round black-granite base, buried pumps shoving water up against a perfect sphere of transparent crystal. The sphere was a monstrous, stylized egg. Inside the egg rode a never-to-be-born creature—some giant beast with wide black eyes and gill slits, its tail half-formed and the stubby little limbs looking as though they could turn into arms or legs, or even tentacles. Joe knew the creature was supposed to be blind, but he couldn't shake the impression that the eyes were watching him. He watched the creature slowly roll over and over again, its egg suspended on nothing but a thin chilled layer of very busy water.

Eventually five shapes emerged from behind the fountain.

"Thank you, Mr. Carroway," said the voice. Then the sound system was deactivated, and with a hand to the mouth, one figure shouted, "A little closer, sir. If you will."

That familiar voice accompanied the beckoning arm.

Two figures efficiently disabled Joe's weapons. They were big men, probably Rebirth Neanderthals or some variation on that popular theme. A third man looked like a Brilliance-Boy, his skull tall and deep, stuffed full with a staggering amount of brain tissue. The fourth human was small and slight, held securely by the Brilliance-Boy; even at a distance, she looked decidedly female.

Joe took two steps and paused.

The fifth figure, the one that spoke, approached near enough to show his face. Joe wasn't surprised, but he pretended to be. "Markel? What are you doing here?" He laughed as if nervous. "You're not one of them, are you?"

The man looked as *sapien* as Joe.

With a decidedly human laugh, Markel remarked, "I'm glad to hear that you were fooled, Mr. Carroway. Which of course means that you killed Stanton and Humphrey for no good reason."

Joe said nothing.

"You did come here alone, didn't you?"

"Yes."

"Because you took a little longer than I anticipated."

"No I didn't."

"Perhaps not. I could be mistaken."

Markel never admitted to errors. He was a tall fellow, as bald as an egg and not particularly handsome. Which made his disguise all the more effective. The new *Homo* species were always physically attractive, and they were superior athletes, more often than not. Joe had never before met a Rebirth who had gone through the pain and expense and then not bothered to grow some kind of luxurious head of hair as a consequence.

"You have my vial with you, Joseph. Yes?"

"Joe. That's my name." He made a show of patting his chest pocket.

"And the sealed recordings too?"

"Everything you asked for." Joe looked past Markel. "Is that the girl?"

Something about the question amused Markel. "Do you honestly care if she is?"

"Of course I care."

"Enough to trade away everything and earn her safety?"

Joe said nothing.

"I've studied your files, Joseph. I have read the personality evaluations, and I know all about your corporate security work, and even all those wicked sealed records covering the last three years. It is a most impressive career. But nothing about you, sir—nothing in your nature or your history—strikes me as being sentimental. And I cannot believe that this girl matters enough to convince you to make this exchange."

Joe smiled. "Then why did I come here?"

"That's my question too."

Joe waited for a moment, then suggested, "Maybe it's money?"

"Psychopaths always have a price," Markel replied. "Yes, I guessed it would be something on those lines."

Joe reached into his shirt pocket. The vial was diamond, smaller than a pen and only halfway filled with what looked to be a plain white powder. But embossed along the vial's length were the ominous words: NATURAL KILLER.

"How much do you want for my baby, Joseph?"

"Everything," he said.

"And what does that mean?"

"All the money."

"My wealth? Is that what you're asking for?"

"I'm not asking," Joe said. "Don't be confused, Markel. This is not a negotiation. I am demanding that you and your backers give me every last cent in your coffers. And if not, I will ruin everything that you've worked to achieve. You sons-of-bitches."

Markel had been born *sapien* and gifted, and his minimal and very secret steps to leave his species behind had served to increase both his mind and his capacity for arrogance. But he was stunned to hear the ultimatum. To make such outrageous demands, and in these circumstances! He couldn't imagine anybody with that much gall. Standing quite still, his long arms at his side, Markel tried to understand why an unarmed man in these desperate circumstances would have any power over him. What wasn't he seeing? No reinforcements were coming; he was certain of that. Outside this tiny circle, nobody knew anything. This *sapien* was bluffing, Markel decided. And with that, he began to breathe again, and he relaxed, announcing, "You're right, this is not a negotiation. And I'm telling you no."

Inside the same shirt pocket was a child's toy—a completely harmless lump of luminescent putty stolen from a passing giftbot. Joe shoved the vial into the bright red plaything, and before Markel could react, he flung both the putty and vial high into the air.

Every eye watched that ruddy patch of light twirl and soften, and then plunge back to the earth.

Beside the plaza was a deep acid-filled moat flanked by a pair of high fences, electrified and bristling with sensors. And on the far side were woods and darkness, plus the single example of a brand new species designed to bring huge crowds through the zoo's front gate.

The Grendel.

"You should not have done that," Markel said with low, furious voice. "I'll just have you killed now and be done with you."

Joe smiled, lifting his empty hands over his head. "Maybe you should kill me. If you're so positive that you can get your precious Killer back."

That's when Joe laughed at the brilliant bastard.

But it was the girl who reacted first, squirming out of the Brilliance-Boy's hands to run straight for her lover.

No one bothered to chase her down.

She stopped short and slapped Joe.

"You idiot," she spat.

He answered her with a tidy left hook.

Then one of the big soldiers shot a tacky round into Joe's chest, pumping in enough current to drop him on the wet bricks, leaving him hovering between consciousness and white-hot misery.

"You idiot."

The girl repeated herself several times, occasionally adding a dismissive, "Moron," or "Fool," to her invectives. Then as the electricity diminished, she leaned close to his face. "Don't you understand? We were never going to use the bug. We don't want to let it loose. It's just one more way to help make sure you *sapiens* won't declare war on us. Natural Killer is our insurance policy, and that's it."

The pain diminished to a lasting ache. Wincing, Joe struggled to sit up. While he was down, smart-cuffs had wrapped themselves around his wrists and ankles. The two soldiers and the Brilliance-Boy were standing before the Grendel's large enclosure. They had donned night goggles and were studying the schematics of the zoo, tense voices discussing how best to slip into the cage and recover the prize.

"Joe," she said, "how can you be this stupid?"

"Comes naturally, I guess."

To the eye, the girl was beautiful and purely *sapien*. The long black hair and rich brown skin sparkled in the plaza's light. The word "natural" was a mild insult among the Rebirths. She sat up, lips pouting. Like Markel, the young woman must have endured major revisions of her genetics—far more involved than a few synthetic genes sprinkled about the DNA. Extra pairs of chromosomes were standard among the new humans. But despite rumors that some of the Rebirths were hiding among the naturals, this was the first time Joe had knowingly crossed paths with them.

"I am stupid," he admitted. Then he looked at Markel, adding, "Both of you had me fooled. All along."

That was a lie, but it made Markel smile. Of course he was clever, and of course no one suspected the truth. Behind that grim old face was enough self-esteem to keep him believing that he would survive the night.

The idiot.

Markel and his beautiful assistant glanced at each other.

Then the Brilliance-Boy called out. "We'll use the service entrance to get in," he announced. "Five minutes to circumvent locks and cameras, I should think."

"Do it," Markel told them.

"You'll be all right here?"

The scientist lifted a pistol over his head. "We're fine. Just go. Get my child out of that cage, now!"

That left three people on the plaza, plus the monster locked inside the slowly revolving crystal egg.

"The plague is just an insurance policy, huh?"

Joe threw out the question, and waited.

After a minute, the girl said, "To protect us from people like you, yes."

He put on an injured expression. "Like me? What's that mean?"

She glanced at Markel. In an acid tone, she said, "He showed me your history, Joe. After our first night together...."

"And what did it tell you?"

"When you were on the *Demon Dandy*, you saved yourself by leaving a Rebirth behind. And you did it in a cold, calculating way."

He shrugged, smiled. "What else?"

"After joining the security arm of the corporation, you distinguished yourself as a soldier. Then you went to work for the U.N., as a contractor, and your expertise has been assassinations."

"Bad men should be killed," Joe said flatly. "Evil should be removed from the world. Get the average person to be honest, and he'll admit that he won't lose any sleep, particularly if the monster is killed with a single clean shot."

"You are horrible," she maintained.

"If I'm so horrible," said Joe, "then do the world a favor. Shoot me in the head."

She began to reach behind her back, then thought better of it.

Markel glanced at both of them, pulling his weapon closer to his body. But nothing seemed urgent, and he returned to keeping watch over the Grendel's enclosure.

"I suppose you noticed," Joe began.

The girl blinked. "Noticed what?"

"In my career, I've killed a respectable number of Rebirths."

The dark eyes stared at him. Very quietly, with sarcasm, she said, "I suppose they were all bad people."

"Drug lords and terrorists, or hired guns in the service of either." Joe shook his head, saying, "Legal murder is easy. Clean, clear-cut. A whole lot more pleasant than the last few weeks have been, I'll admit."

Markel looked at him. "I am curious, Joseph. Who decided you were the ideal person to investigate our little laboratory?"

"You don't have a little lab," said Joe. "There aren't ten or twelve better-equipped facilities when it comes to high-end genetic research."

"There aren't even twelve," the man said, bristling slightly. "Perhaps two or three."

"Well, you wouldn't have found this item in any official file," Joe said. "But a couple months ago, I was leading a team that hit a terror cell in Alberta. Under interrogation, the Rebirth boss started making threats about unleashing something called Natural Killer on us. On the poor helpless *sapiens*. He claimed that we'd be wiped out of existence, and the new species could then take over. Which is their right, he claimed, and as inevitable as the next sunrise."

His audience exchanged looks.

"But that hardly explains how you found your way to me," Markel pointed out.

"There was a trail. Bloody in places, but every corpse pointing in your general direction."

Markel almost spoke. But the creak of a heavy door being opened interrupted him. Somewhere in the back of the Grendel's enclosure, three pairs of goggled eyes were peering out into the jungle and shadow.

"It's an amazing disease," Joe stated. "Natural Killer is."

"Quiet," Markel warned.

But the girl couldn't contain herself. She bent low, whispering, "It is," while trying to burn him with her hateful smile.

"The virus targets old, outmoded stretches of the human genome," Joe continued. "From what I can tell—and I'm no expert in biology, of course—but your extra genes guarantee you wouldn't get anything worse than some wicked flu symptoms out of the bug. Is that about right?"

"A tailored pox phage," she said. "Rapidly mutating, but always fatal to *sapiens* genome."

"So who dreamed up the name?" Joe glanced at Markel and then winked at her. "It was you, wasn't it?"

She sat back, grinning.

"And it's going to save you? From bastards like me, is it?"

"You won't dare lift a hand against us," she told Joe. "As soon as you realize we have this weapon, and that it could conceivably wipe your entire species off the face of the Earth...."

"Smart," he agreed. "Very smart."

From the Grendel enclosure came the sharp soft noise of a gun firing. One quick burst and then two single shots from the same weapon. Then, silence.

Markel lifted his pistol reflexively.

"So when do you Rebirths make your official announcement?" Joe asked. "And how do you handle this kind of event? Hold a news conference? Unless you decide on a demonstration, I suppose. You know, murder an isolated village, or devastate one of the orbital communities. Just to prove to the idiots in the world that you can deliver on your threats."

A voice called from the enclosure: "I have it."

Joe turned in time to see the reddish glow rise off the ground, partly obscured by the strong hand holding it. But as the arm cocked, ready to throw the prize back into the plaza, there was a grunt, almost too soft to be heard. A terrific amount of violence occurred in an instant, without fuss. Then the red glow appeared on a different portion of the jungle floor, and the only sound was the slow lapping of a broad happy tongue.

Markel cursed.

The girl stood up and looked.

Markel called out a name, and nobody answered. And then somebody else fired their weapon in a spray pattern, cutting vegetation and battering the high fence on the far side of the moat.

"I killed it," the second soldier declared. "I'm sure."

The Brilliance-Boy offered a few cautionary words.

"I do feel exceptionally stupid," Joe said. "Tell me again: Why exactly do you need Natural Killer?"

The girl stared at him and then stepped back.

"I didn't know we were waging a real war against you people," he continued. "I guess we keep that a secret, what with our political tricks and PR campaigns. Like when we grant you full citizenship. And the way we force you to accept the costs and benefits of all the laws granted to human beings everywhere—"

"You hate us," she interrupted. "You despise every last one of us."

Quietly, Joe assured her, "You don't know what I hate."

She stiffened, saying nothing.

"This is the situation. As I see it." Joe paused for a moment. "Inside that one vial, you have a bug that could wipe out your alleged enemies. And by enemies, I mean people that look at you with suspicion and fear. You intend to keep your doomsday disease at the ready, just in case you need it."

"Of course."

"Except you'll have to eventually grow more of it. If you want to keep it as a credible, immediate threat. And you'll have to divide your stocks and store them in scattered, secure locations. Otherwise assholes like me are going to throw the bugs in a pile and burn it all with a torch."

She watched Joe, her sore jaw clamped tight.

"But having stockpiles of Natural Killer brings a different set of problems. Who can trust who not to use it without permission? And the longer this virus exists, the better the chance that the Normals will find effective fixes to keep themselves safe. Vaccines. Quarantine laws. Whatever we need to weather the plague, and of course, give us our chance to take our revenge afterward."

The red glow had not moved. For a full minute, the little jungle had been perfectly, ominously silent.

Markel glanced at Joe and then back at the high fence. He was obviously fighting the urge to shout warnings to the others. That could alert the Grendel. But it took all his will to do nothing.

"You have a great, great weapon," Joe allowed. "But your advantage won't last."

The girl was breathing faster now.

"You know what would be smart? Before the Normals grow aware of your power, you should release the virus. No warnings, no explanations. Do it before we know what hit us, and hope you kill enough of us in the first week that you can permanently gain the upper hand."

"No," Markel said, taking two steps toward the enclosure. "We don't have more than a sample of the virus, and it is just a virus."

"Meaning what?"

"Diseases are like wildfires," he explained. "You watch them burn, and you can't believe that anything would survive the blaze. But afterward there are always islands of green surrounded by scorched forest." The man had given this considerable thought. "Three or four billion *sapiens* might succumb. But that would still leave us in the minority, and we wouldn't be able to handle the retribution."

The girl showed a satisfied smile.

But then Joe said, "Except," and laughed quietly.

The red glow had not moved, and the jungle stood motionless beneath the stars. But Markel had to look back at his prisoner, a new terror pushing away the old.

"What do you mean?" the girl asked. "Except what?"

"You and your boss," Joe said. "And who knows how many thousands of others too. Each one of you looks exactly like us. You sound like us." Then he grinned and smacked his lips, adding, "And you taste like us, too. Which means that your particular species, whatever you call yourselves…you'll come out of this nightmare better than anybody.…"

The girl's eyes opened wide; a pained breath was taken and then held deep.

"Which of course is the central purpose of this gruesome exercise," Joe said. "I'm sure Dr. Markel would have eventually let you in on his dirty secret. The real scheme hiding behind the first, more public plan."

Too astonished to react, Markel stared at the cuffed, unarmed man sitting on the bricks.

"Is this true?" the girl whispered.

There was a moment of hesitation, and then the genius managed to shake his head, lying badly when he said, "Of course not. The man is telling you a crazy wild story, dear."

"And you know why he never told you?" Joe asked.

"Shut up," Markel warned.

The girl was carrying a weapon, just as Joe had guessed. From the back of her pants, she pulled out a small pistol, telling Markel, "Let him talk."

"Darling, he's trying to poison you—"

"Shut up," she snapped.

Then to Joe, she asked, "Why didn't he tell me?"

"Because you're a good decent person, or at least you like to think so. And because he knew how to use that quality to get what he wants." Showing a hint of compassion, Joe sighed. "Markel sure knows how to motivate you. First, he makes you sleep with me. And then he shows you my files, convincing you that I can't be trusted or ignored. Which is why you slept with me three more times. Just to keep a close watch over me."

The girl lowered her pistol, and she sobbed and then started to lift the pistol again.

"Put that down," Markel said.

She might have obeyed, given another few moments to think. But Markel shot her three times. He did it quickly and lowered his weapon afterward, astonished that he had done this very awful thing. It took his great mind a long sloppy moment to wrap itself around the idea that he could murder in that particular fashion, that he possessed such brutal, prosaic power. Then he started to lift his gun again, searching for Joe.

But Joe, wrists and feet bound, was already rolling to the dead girl's body. And with her little gun, he put a bullet into Markel's forehead.

The blind, unborn monster watched the drama from inside its crystal egg.

A few moments later, a bloody Brilliance-Boy ran up to the Grendel's fence, and with a joyous holler flung the red putty and diamond vial back onto the plaza. Then he turned and fired twice at shadows before something monstrous lifted him high, shook him once, and folded him backward before neatly tearing him in two.

### III. The Ticking Bomb

"Goodness," the prisoner muttered. "It's the legend himself."

Joe said nothing.

"Well, now I feel especially terrified." She laughed weakly before coughing, a dark bubble of blood clinging to the split corner of her mouth. Then she closed her eyes for a moment, suppressing her pain as she turned her head to look straight at him. "You must be planning all kinds of horrors," she said. "Savage new ways to break my spirit. To bare my soul."

Gecko slippers gripped the wall. Joe watched the prisoner. He opened his mouth as if to speak but then closed it again, one finger idly scratching a spot behind his left ear.

"I won't be scared," she decided. "This is an honor, having someone this famous assigned to my case. I must be considered an exceptionally important person."

He seemed amused, if just for a moment.

"But I'm not a person, am I? In your eyes, I'm just another animal."

What she was was a long, elegant creature—the ultimate marriage between human traditions and synthetic chromosomes. Four bare arms were restrained with padded loops and pulled straight out from the shockingly naked body. Because hair could be a bother in space, she had none. Because dander was an endless source of dirt in freefall, her skin would peel away periodically, not unlike the worn skin of a cobra. She was smart, but not in the usual ways that the two or three thousand species of Rebirths enhanced their minds. Her true genius lay in social skills. Among the Antfolk, she could instantly recognize every face and recall each name, knowing at least ten thousand nest-mates as thoroughly as two *sapiens* who had been life-long pals. Even among the alien faces of traditional humans, she was a marvel at reading faces, deciphering postures. Every glance taught her something more about her captors. Each careless word gave her room to maneuver. That's why the first team—a pair of low-ranking interrogators, unaware of her importance—was quickly pulled from her case. She had used what was obvious, making a few offhand observations, and in the middle of their second session, the two officers had started to trade insults and then punches.

"A Carroway-worthy moment," had been the unofficial verdict.

A second, more cautious team rode the skyhook up from Quito, and they were wise enough to work their prisoner without actually speaking to her. Solitude and sensory deprivation were the tools of choice. Without adequate stimulation, an Antfolk would crumble. And the method would have worked, except that three or four weeks would have been required. But time was short: Several intelligence sources delivered the same ominous warning. This was not just another low-level prisoner. The Antfolk, named Glory, was important. Maybe essential. Days mattered now, even hours. Which was why a third team went to work immediately, doing their awful best from the reassuring confines of a U.N. bunker set two kilometers beneath the Matterhorn.

That new team consisted of AIs and autodocs with every compassion system deleted. Through the careful manipulation of pain and hallucinogenic narcotics, they managed to dislodge a few nuggets of intelligence as well as a level of hatred and malevolence that they had never before witnessed.

"The bomb is mine," she screamed. "I helped design it, and I helped build it. Antimatter triggers the fusion reaction, and it's compact and efficient, and shielded to where it's nearly invisible. I even selected our target. Believe me…when my darling detonates, everything is going to change!"

At that point, their prisoner died.

Reviving her wasted precious minutes. But that was ample time for the machines to discuss the obvious possibilities and then calculate various probabilities. In the time remaining, what could be done? And what was impossible? Then without a shred of ego or embarrassment, they contacted one of the only voices that they considered more talented than themselves.

And now Joe stood before the battered prisoner.

Again, he scratched at his ear.

Time hadn't touched him too roughly. He was in his middle forties, but his boyish good looks had been retained through genetics and a sensible indifference to sunshine. Careful eyes would have noticed the fatigue in his body, his motions. A veteran soldier could have recognized the subtle erosion of spirit. And a studied gaze of the kind that an Antfolk would employ would detect signs of weakness and doubt that didn't quite fit when it came to one of the undisputed legends of this exceptionally brutal age.

Joe acted as if there was no hurry. But his heart was beating too fast, his belly roiling with nervous energy. And the corners of his mouth were a little too tight, particularly when he looked as if he wanted to speak.

"What are you going to do with me?" his prisoner inquired.

And again, he scratched at his scalp, something about his skin bothering him to distraction.

She was puzzled, slightly.

"Say something," Glory advised.

"I'm a legend, am I?" The smile was unchanged, bright and full; but behind the polished teeth and bright green eyes was a quality…some trace of some subtle emotion that the prisoner couldn't quite name.

She was intrigued.

"I know all about you," Glory explained. "I know your career in detail, successes and failures both."

For an instant, Joe looked at the lower pair of arms, following the long bones to where they met within the reconfigured hips.

"Want to hear something ironic?" she asked.

"Always."

"The asteroid you were planning to mine? Back during your brief, eventful career as an astronaut, I mean. It's one of ours now."

"Until your bomb goes boom," he said. "And then that chunk of iron and humanity is going to be destroyed. Along with every other nest of yours, I would guess."

"Dear man. Are you threatening me?"

"You would be the better judge of that."

She managed to laugh. "I'm not particularly worried."

He said nothing.

"Would we take such an enormous risk if we didn't have the means to protect ourselves?"

Joe stared at her for a long while. Then he looked beyond her body, at a random point on the soft white wall. Quietly he asked, "Who am I?"

She didn't understand the question.

"You've seen some little digitals of me. Supposedly you've peeked at my files. But do you know for sure who I am?"

She nearly laughed. "Joseph Carroway."

He closed his eyes.

"Security," he said abruptly. "I need you here. Now."

Whatever was happening, it was interesting. Despite the miseries inflicted on her mind and aching body, the prisoner twisted her long neck, watching three heavily armed soldiers kick their way into her cell.

"This is an emergency," Joe announced. "I need everybody. Your full squad in here now."

The ranking officer was a small woman with the bulging muscles of a steroid hopper. A look of genuine admiration showed in her face. She knew all about Joe Carroway. Who didn't? But her training and regulations held sway. This man might have saved the Earth, on one or several occasions, but she still had the fortitude to remind him, "I can't bring everybody in here. That's against regulations."

Joe nodded.

Sighing, he said, "Then we'll just have to make do."

In an instant, with a smooth, almost beautiful motion, he grabbed the officer's face and broke her jaw and then pulled a weapon from his pocket, shoving the stubby barrel into the nearest face.

The pistol made a soft, almost negligible sound.

The remains of the skull were scattered into the face of the next guard.

He shot that soldier twice and then killed the commanding officer before grabbing up her weapon, using his security code to override its safety and then leaping into the passageway. The prisoner strained at her bonds. Mesmerized, she counted the soft blasts and the shouts, and she stared, trying to see through the spreading fog of blood and shredded brain matter. Then a familiar figure reappeared, moving with commendable grace despite having a body designed to trek across the savannas of Africa.

"We have to go," said Joe. "Now." He was carrying a fresh gun and jumpsuit.

"I don't believe this," she managed.

He cut her bonds and said, "Didn't think you would." Then he paused, just for an instant. "Joe Carroway was captured and killed three years ago, during the Tranquility business. I'm the lucky man they spliced together to replace that dead asshole."

"You're telling me—?"

"Suit up. Let's go, lady."

"You can't be." She was numb, fighting to understand what was possible, no matter how unlikely. "What species of Rebirth are you?"

"I was an Eagle," he said.

She stared at the face. Never in her life had she tried so hard to slice through skin and eyes, fighting to decipher what was true.

"Suit up," he said again.

"But I don't see—?"

Joe turned suddenly, launching a recoilless bundle out into the hall. The detonation was a soft crack, smart-shards aiming only for armor and flesh. Sparing the critical hull surrounding them.

"We'll have to fight our way to my ship," he warned.

Slowly, with stiff clumsy motions, she dressed herself. As the suit retailored itself to match her body, she said again, "I don't believe you. I don't believe any of this."

Now Joe stared at her.

Hard.

"What do you think, lady?" he asked. "You rewrote your own biology in a thousand crazy ways. But one of your brothers—a proud Eagle—isn't able to reshape himself? He can't take on the face of your worst enemy? He can't steal the dead man's memories? He is allowed this kind of power, all in a final bid to get revenge for what that miserable shit's done to us?"

She dipped her head.

No, she didn't believe him.

But three hours later, as they were making the long burn out of Earth orbit, a flash of blue light announced the abrupt death of fifty million humans and perhaps half a million innocents.

"A worthy trade," said the man strapped into the seat beside her.

And that was the moment when Glory finally offered two of her hands to join up with one of his, and after that, her other two hands as well.

Her nest was the nearest Antfolk habitat. Waiting at the moon's L5 Lagrange point, the asteroid was a smooth blackish ball, heat-absorbing armor slathered deep over the surface of a fully infested cubic kilometer—a city where thousands of bodies squirmed about in freefall, thriving inside a maze of warm tunnels and airy rooms. Banks of fusion reactors powered factories and the sun-bright lights. Trim, enduring ecosystems created an endless feast of edible gruel and free oxygen. The society was unique, at least within the short rich history of the Rebirths. Communal and technologically adept, this species had accomplished much in a very brief period. That's why it was so easy for them to believe that they alone now possessed the keys to the universe.

Joe was taken into custody. Into quarantine. Teams drawn from security and medical castes tried to piece together the truth, draining off his blood and running electrodes into his skull, inflicting him with induced emotions and relentless urges to be utterly, perfectly honest.

The Earth's counterassault arrived on schedule—lasers and missiles followed by robot shock troops. But the asteroid's defense network absorbed every blow. Damage was minor, casualties light, and before larger attacks could be organized, the Antfolk sent an ultimatum to the U.N.: One hundred additional fusion devices had been smuggled to the Earth's surface, each now hidden and secured, waiting for any excuse to erupt.

For the good of humankind, the Antfolk were claiming dominion over everything that lay beyond the Earth's atmosphere. Orbital facilities and the lunar cities would be permitted, but only if reasonable rents were paid. Other demands included nationhood status for each of the Rebirth species, reimbursements for all past wrongs, and within the next year, the total and permanent dismantling of the United Nations.

Both sides declared a ragged truce.

Eight days later, Joe was released from his cell, guards escorting him along a tunnel marked by pheromones and infrared signatures. Glory was waiting, wearing her best gown and a wide, hopeful smile. The Antfolk man beside her seemed less sure. He was a giant hairless creature. Leader of the nest's political caste, he glared at the muscular *sapien*, and with a cool smooth voice said, "The tunnel before you splits, Mr. Carroway. Which way will you travel?"

"What are my choices?" asked the prisoner.

"Death now," the man promised. "Or death in some ill-defined future."

"I think I prefer the future," he said. Then he glanced at Glory, meeting her worried smile with a wink and slight nod.

The look that Glory shot her superior was filled with meaning and hope.

"I don't relish the idea of trusting you," the man confessed. "But every story you've told us, with words and genetics, has been confirmed by every available source. You were once a man named Magnificent. We see traces of your original DNA inside what used to be Joseph Carroway. It seems that our old enemy was indeed taken prisoner during the Luna Revolt. The Eagles were a talented bunch. They may well have camouflaged you inside Mr. Carroway's body and substance. A sorry thing that the species was exterminated—save for you, of course. But once this new war is finished, I promise you: my people will reconstitute yours as well as your culture, to the best of our considerable abilities."

Joe dipped his head. "I can only hope to see that day, sir."

The man had giant white eyes and tiny blond teeth. Watching the prisoner did no good; he could not read this man's soul. So he turned to Glory, prompting her with the almost invisible flick of a finger.

She told Joe, "The U.N. attack was almost exactly as you expected it to be, and your advice proved extremely useful. Thank you."

Joe showed a smug little smile.

"And you've told us a lot we didn't know," Glory continued. "Those ten agents on Pallas. The Deimos booby trap. And how the U.N. would go about searching for the rest of our nuclear devices."

"Are your bombs safe?"

She glanced at her superior, finding encouragement in some little twitch of the face. Then she said, "Yes."

"Do you want to know their locations?" the man asked Joe.

"No."

Then in the next breath, Joe added, "And I hope you don't know that either, sir. You're too much of a target, should somebody grab you up."

"More good advice," the man replied.

That was the instant when Joe realized that he wouldn't be executed as a precaution. More than three years of careful preparation had led to this: The intricate back-story and genetic trickery were his ideas. Carrying off every aspect of this project, from the Eagle's identity to his heightened capacity to read bodies and voices, was the end result of hard training. Hundreds of specialists, all AIs, had helped produce the new Joseph Carroway. And then each one of those machines was wiped stupid and melted to an anonymous slag.

On that day when he dreamed up this outrageous plan, the Antfolk were still just one of a dozen Rebirths that might or might not cause trouble someday.

Nobody could have planned for these last weeks.

Killing the guards to free the woman was an inspiration and a necessity, and he never bothered to question it. One hundred fusion bombs were scattered across a helpless, highly vulnerable planet, and setting them off would mean billions dead, and perhaps civilization too. Sacrificing a few soldiers to protect the rest of the world was a plan born of simple, pure mathematics.

The Antfolk man coughed softly. "From this point on, Joe…or should I call you Magnificent?"

With an appealing smile, he said, "I've grown attached to Joe."

The other two laughed gently. Then the man said, "For now, you are my personal guest. And except for security bracelets and a bomblet planted inside your skull, you will be given the freedoms and responsibilities expected of all worthy visitors."

"Then I am grateful," said Joe. "Thank you to your nation and to your good species, sir. Thank you so much."

The truce was shattered with one desperate assault—three brigades of shock troops riding inside untested star-drive boosters, supported by every weapon system and reconfigured com-laser available to the U.N. The cost was twenty thousand dead *sapiens* and a little less than a trillion dollars. One platoon managed to insert itself inside Joe's nest, but when the invaders grabbed the nursery and a thousand young hostages, he distinguished himself by helping plan and then lead the counterstrike. All accounts made him the hero. He killed several of the enemy, and alone, he managed to disable the warhead that would have shattered their little world. But even the most grateful mother insisted on looking at their savior with detached pleasure. Trust was impossible. Joe's face was too strange, his reputation far too familiar. Pheromones delivered the mandatory thanks, and there were a few cold gestures wishing the hero well. But there were insults too, directed at him and at the long lovely woman who was by now sleeping with him.

In retribution for that final attack, the Antfolk detonated a second nuclear weapon, shearing off one slope of the Hawai'i volcano and killing eight million with the resulting tsunami.

Nine days later, the U.N. collapsed, reformed from the wreckage and then shattered again before the next dawn. What rose from that sorry wreckage enjoyed both the laws to control every aspect of the mother world and the mandate to beg for their enemies' mercy.

The giants in the sky demanded, and subsequently won, each of their original terms.

For another three months, Joe lived inside the little asteroid, enduring a never-subtle shunning.

Then higher powers learned of his plight and intervened. For the next four years, he traveled widely across the new empire, always in the company of Glory, the two of them meeting an array of leaders, scientists, and soldiers—that last group as suspicious as any, but ever eager to learn whatever little tricks the famous Carroway might share with them.

To the end, Joe remained under constant observation. Glory made daily reports about his behaviors and her own expert impressions. Their relationship originally began under orders from Pallas, but when she realized that they might well remain joined until one or both died, she discovered, to her considerable surprise, that she wasn't displeased with her fate.

In the vernacular of her species, she had floated into love…and so what if the object of her affections was an apish goon?

During their journey, they visited twenty little worlds, plus Pallas and Ceres and Vesta. The man beside her was never out of character. He was intense and occasionally funny, and he was quick to learn and astute with his observations about life inside the various nests. Because it would be important for the last member of a species, Joe pushed hard for the resurrection of the fabled Eagles.

Final permission came just as he and Glory were about to travel to outer moons of Jupiter. Three tedious, painful days were spent inside the finest biogenic lab in the solar system. Samples of bone and marrow and fat and blood were cultured, and delicate machines rapidly separated what had been Joe from the key traces of the creature that had been dubbed Magnificent.

A long voyage demands large velocities, which was why the transport ship made an initial high-gee burn. The crew and passengers were strapped into elaborate crash seats, their blood laced with comfort drugs, eyes and minds distracted by immersion masks. Six hours after they leaped clear of Vesta, Joe disabled each of his tracking bracelets and the bomblet inside his head, and then he slipped out of his seat, fighting the terrific acceleration as he worked his way to the bridge.

The transport was an enormous, utterly modern spaceship. The watch officer was on the bridge, stretched out in his own crash seat. Instantly suspicious and without even the odor of politeness, he demanded that his important passenger leave at once. Joe smiled for a moment. Then he turned without complaint or hesitation, showing his broad back to the spidery fellow before he climbed out of view.

What killed the officer was a fleck of dust carrying microchines—a fleet of tiny devices that attacked essential genes found inside the Antfolk metabolism, causing a choking sensation, vomiting and soon death.

Joe returned to the bridge and sent a brief, heavily coded message to the Earth. Then he did a cursory job of destroying the ship's security systems. With luck, he had earned himself a few hours of peace. But when he returned to his cabin, Glory was gone. She had pulled herself out her seat, or somebody had roused her. For a moment, he touched the deep padding, allowing the sheets to wrap around his arm and hand, and he carefully measured the heat left behind by her long, lovely body.

"Too bad," he muttered.

The transport carried five fully equipped lifepods. Working fast, Joe killed the hangar's robots and both of the resident mechanics. He dressed in the only pressure suit configured for his body and crippled all but one of the pods. His plan was to flee without fuss. The pods had potent engines and were almost impossible to track. There was no need for more corpses and mayhem. But he wanted a back-up plan, that's what he was working on when the ship's engines abruptly cut out.

A few minutes later, an armed team crawled into the hangar through a random vent.

There was no reason to fight, since Joe was certain to lose.

Instead he surrendered his homemade weapons and looked past the nervous crew, finding the lovely hairless face that he knew better than his own.

"What did you tell them?" Glory asked.

"Tell who?"

"Your people," she said. "The Earth."

Glory didn't expect answers, much less any honest words. But the simple fact was that whatever he said now and did now was inconsequential: Joe would survive or die in this cold realm, but what happened next would change nothing that was about to happen elsewhere.

"Your little home nest," he began.

She drifted forward, and then hesitated.

"It will be dead soon," he promised. "And nothing can be done to save it."

"Is there a bomb?"

"No," he said. "A microchine plague. I brought it with me when I snatched you away, Glory. It was hiding inside my bones."

"But you were tested," she said.

"Not well enough."

"We hunted for diseases," she insisted. "Agents. Toxins. We have the best minds anywhere, and we searched you inside and out…and found nothing remotely dangerous."

He watched the wind leak out of her. Then very quietly, Joe admitted, "You might have the best minds. And best by a long ways. But we have a lot more brains down on the Earth, and I promise, a few of us are a good deal meaner than even you could ever be."

Enduring torture, Glory never looked this frail or sad.

Joe continued. "Every world you've taken me to is contaminated. I made certain of that. And since you managed to set off two bombs on my world, the plan is to obliterate two of your worlds. After that, if you refuse to surrender, it's fair to guess that every bomb and disease on both sides is going be set free. Then in the end, nobody wins. Ever."

Glory could not look at him.

Joe laughed, aiming to humiliate.

He said, "I don't care how smart or noble you are. Like everybody else, you're nothing but meat and scared brains. And now you've been thrown into a dead-end tunnel, and I am Death standing at the tunnel's mouth.

"The clock is ticking. Can you make the right decision?"

Glory made a tiny, almost invisible motion with her smallest finger, betraying her intentions.

Joe leaped backward. The final working lifepod was open, and he dove inside as its hatch slammed shut, moments before the doomed could manage one respectable shot. Then twenty weapons were firing at a hull designed to shrug off the abuse of meteors and *sapien* weapons. Joe pulled himself into the pilot's ill-fitting chair, and once he was strapped down, he triggered his just-finished booby trap.

The fuel onboard two other pods exploded.

With a silent flash of light, the transport shattered, spilling its contents across the black and frigid wilderness.

IV. The Assassin

"Eat," the voice insisted. "Don't our dead heroes deserve their feast?"

"So that's what I am?"

"A hero? Absolutely, my friend!"

"I meant that I'm dead." Joe looked across the table, measuring his host—an imposing Chinese-Indian male wearing the perfect suit and a face conditioned to convey wisdom and serene authority. "I realize that I got lost for a time," he admitted. "But I never felt particularly deceased."

"Perhaps that's how the dead perceive their lot. Yes?"

Joe nodded amiably, and using his stronger arm, stabbed at his meal. Even in lunar gravity, every motion was an effort.

"Are your rehabilitations going well?"

"They tell me that I'm making some progress."

"Modesty doesn't suit you, my friend. My sources assure me that you are amazing your trainers. And I think you know that perfectly well."

The meat was brown and sweet, like duck, but without the grease.

"Presently you hold the record, Joe."

Joe looked up again.

"Five and a half years in freefall," said Mr. Li, slowly shaking his head. "Assumed dead, and in your absence, justly honored for the accomplishments of an intense and extremely successful life. I'm sorry no one was actively searching for you, sir. But no Earth-based eye saw the Antfolks' spaceship explode, much less watched the debris scatter. So we had no starting point, and to make matters worse, your pod had a radar signature little bigger than a fist. You were very fortunate to be where you happened to be, drifting back into the inner solar system. And you were exceptionally lucky to be noticed by that little mining ship. And just imagine your reception if that ship's crew had been anyone but *sapiens....*"

The billionaire let his voice trail away.

Joe had spent years wandering through the solar system, shepherding his food and riding roughshod over his recycling systems. That the lifepod was designed to carry a dozen bodies was critical; he wouldn't have lasted ten months inside a lesser bucket. But the explosion that destroyed the transport damaged the pod, leaving it dumb and deaf. Joe had soon realized that nobody knew where he was, or even that he was. After the first year, he calculated that he might survive for another eight, but it would involve more good luck and hard focus than even he might have been able to summon.

"I want to tell you, Joe. When I learned about your survival, I was thrilled. I turned to my dear wife and my children and told everybody, 'This man is a marvel. He is a wonder. A one-in-a-trillion kind of *sapien.*'"

Joe laughed quietly.

"Oh, I'm well-studied in Joseph Carroway's life," his host boasted. "After the war, humanity wanted to know who to thank for saving the Earth. That's why the U.N. released portions of your files. Millions of us became amateur scholars.

I myself acquired some of the less doctored accounts of your official history. I've also read your five best biographies, and just like every other *sapien*, I have enjoyed your immersion drama—*Warrior on the Ramparts*. As a story, it takes dramatic license with your life. Of course. But *Warrior* was and is a cultural phenomenon, Joe. A stirring tale of courage and bold skill in the midst of wicked, soulless enemies."

Joe set his fork beside the plate.

"After all the misery and death of these last two decades," said Mr. Li, "the world discovered the one man who could be admired, even emulated. A champion for the people."

He said the word "People" with a distinct tone.

Then Mr. Li added, "Even the Rebirths paid to see *Warrior*. Paid to read the books and the sanitized files. Which is nicely ironic, isn't it? Your actions probably saved millions of them. Without your bravery, how many species would be ash and bone today?"

Joe lifted his fork again. A tenth of his life had been spent away from gravity and meaningful exercise. His bones as well as the connecting muscles had withered to where some experts, measuring the damage, cautioned their patient to expect no miracles. It didn't help that cosmic radiation had slashed through the pod's armor and through him. Even now, the effects of malnutrition could be seen in the spidery hands and forearms, and how his own lean meat hung limp on his suddenly ancient bones.

Mr. Li paused for a moment, an observant smile building. Whatever he said next would be important.

Joe interrupted, telling him, "Thank you for the meal, sir."

"And thank you for being who you are, sir."

When Joe left the realm of the living, this man was little more than an average billionaire. But the last five years had been endlessly lucrative for Li Enterprises. Few had more money, and when ambition was thrown into the equation, perhaps no other private citizen wielded the kind of power enjoyed by the man sitting across the little table.

Joe stabbed a buttery carrot.

"Joe?"

He lowered the carrot to the plate.

"Can you guess why I came to the moon? Besides to meet you over dinner, of course."

Joe decided on a shy, self-deprecating smile.

This encouraged his host. "And do you have any idea what I wish to say to you? Any intuitions at all?"

Six weeks ago, Joe had abruptly returned to the living. But it took three weeks to rendezvous with a hospital ship dispatched just for him, and that vessel didn't touch down on the moon until the day before yesterday. Those two crews and his own research had shown Joe what he meant to the human world. He was a hero and a rich but controversial symbol. And he was a polarizing influence in a great debate that still refused to die—an interspecies conflict forever threatening to bring on another terrible war.

Joe knew exactly what the man wanted from him, but he decided to offer a lesser explanation.

"You're a man with enemies," he mentioned.

Mr. Li didn't need to ask, "Who are my enemies?" Both men understood what was being discussed.

"You need somebody qualified in charge of your personal security," Joe suggested.

The idea amused Mr. Li. But he laughed a little too long, perhaps revealing a persistent unease in his own safety. "I have a fine team of private bodyguards," he said at last. "A team of *sapiens* who would throw their lives down to protect mine."

Joe waited.

"Perhaps you aren't aware of this, sir. But our recent tragedies have changed our government. The U.N. presidency now commands a surprising amount of authority. But he, or she, is still elected by adult citizens. A pageant that maintains the very important illusion of a genuine, self-sustaining democracy."

Joe leaned across the table, nodding patiently.

"Within the next few days," said Mr. Li, "I will announce my candidacy for that high office. A few months later, I will win my party's primary elections. But I'm a colorless merchant with an uneventful life story. I need to give the public one good reason to stand in my camp. What I have to find is a recognizable name that will inspire passions on both sides of the issues."

"You need a dead man," Joe said.

"And what do you think about that, sir?"

"That I'm still trapped in that damned pod." Leaning back in his chair, Joe sighed. "I'm starving to death, bored to tears, and dreaming up this insanity just to keep me a little bit sane."

"Sane or not, do you say yes?"

He showed his host a thoughtful expression. Then very quietly, with the tone of a joke, Joe asked, "So which name sits first on the ballot?"

As promised, Mr. Li easily won the Liberty Party's nomination, and with a force-fed sense of drama, the candidate announced his long-secret choice for running mate. By then Joe had recovered enough to endure the Earth's relentless tug. He was carried home by private shuttle, and with braces under his trouser legs and a pair of lovely and strong women at his side, the celebrated war hero strode into an auditorium/madhouse. Every motion had been practiced, every word scripted, yet somehow the passion and heart of the event felt genuine. Supporters and employees of the candidate pushed against one another, fighting for a better look at the running mate. With a natural sense for when to pause and how to wave at the world, Joe's chiseled, scarred face managed to portray that essential mixture of fearlessness and sobriety. Li greeted him with open arms—the only time the two men would ever embrace. Buoyed by the crowd's energy, Joe felt strong, but when he decided to sit, he almost collapsed into his chair. Li was a known quantity; everyone kept watch over the new man. When Joe studied his boss, he used an expression easily confused for admiration. The acceptance speech was ten minutes of carefully crafted theater designed to convey calm resolve wrapped around coded threats. For too long, Li said, their old honorable species had allowed its traditions to be undercut and diluted. When unity mattered, people followed every path. When solidarity was a virtue, evolution and natural selection were replaced by whim and caprice. But the new leadership would right these past wrongs. Good men and good women had died in the great fight, and new heroes were being discovered every day. (Li glanced at his running mate, winning a burst of applause; and Joe nodded at his benefactor, showing pride swirled with modesty.) The speech concluded with a promise for victory in the general election, in another six weeks, and Joe applauded with everyone else. But he stood slowly, as if weak, shaking as an old man might shake.

He was first to offer his hand of congratulations to the candidate.

And he was first to sit again, feigning the aching fatigue that he had earned over these last five years.

Three days later, a lone sniper was killed outside the arena where the controversial running mate was scheduled to appear. Joe's security detail was led by a career police officer, highly qualified and astonishingly efficient. Using a quiet, unperturbed tone, he explained what had happened, showing his boss images of the would-be assassin.

"She's all *sapien*," he mentioned. "But with ties to the Rebirths. A couple lovers, and a lot of politics."

Joe scanned the woman's files as well the pictures. "Was the lady working alone?"

"As far as I can tell, yes. Sir."

"What's this gun?"

"Homemade," the officer explained. "An old Czech design grown in a backyard nano-smelter. She probably thought it would make her hard to trace. And I suppose it would have: An extra ten minutes to track her down through the isotope signatures and chine-marks."

Joe asked, "How accurate?"

"The rifle? Well, with that sight and in competent hands—"

"Her hands, I mean. Was she any good?"

"We don't know yet, sir." The officer relished these occasional conversations. After all, Joe Carroway had saved humanity on at least two separate occasions, and always against very long odds. "I suppose she must have practiced her marksmanship somewhere. But the thing is...."

"What?"

"This barrel isn't as good as it should be. Impurities in the ceramics, and the heat of high-velocity rounds had warped it. Funny as it sounds, the more your killer practiced, the worse her gun would have become."

Joe smiled and nodded.

The officer nodded with him, waiting for the legend to speak.

"It might have helped us," Joe mentioned. "If we'd let her take a shot or two, I mean."

"Help us?"

"In the polls."

The officer stared at him for a long moment. The dry Carroway humor was well known. Was this a worthy example? He studied the man whom he was sworn to defend, and after considerable reflection, the officer decided to laugh weakly and shrug his shoulders. "But what if she got off one lucky shot?"

Joe laughed quietly. "I thought that's what I was saying."


To be alone, Joe took a lover.

The young woman seemed honored and more than a little scared. After passing through security, they met inside his hotel room, and when the great man asked to send a few messages through her links, she happily agreed. Nothing about those messages would mean anything to anybody. But when they reached their destinations, other messages that had waited for years were released, winding their way to the same secure e-vault. Afterward Joe had sex with her, and then she let him fix her a drink that he laced with sedatives. Once she was asleep, he donned arm and leg braces designed for the most demanding physical appearances. Then Joe opened a window, and ten stories above the bright cold city, he climbed out onto the narrow ledge and slipped through the holes that he had punched in the security net.

Half an hour later, shaking from exhaustion, Joe was standing at the end of a long alleyway.

"She was a mistake," he told the shadows.

There was no answer.

"A blunder," he said.

"Was she?" a deep voice asked.

"But you were always a little too good at inspiring others," Joe continued. "Getting people to be eager, making them jump before they were ready."

In the darkness, huge lungs took a deep, lazy breath.

Then the voice mentioned, "I could kill you myself. I could kill you now." It was deep and slow, and the voice always sounded a little amused. Just a little. "No guards protecting you, and from what I see, you aren't carrying more than a couple baby pistols."

Joe said, "That's funny."

Silence.

"I'm not the one you want," he said. "You'd probably settle for me. But think about our history, friend. Look past all the public noise. And now remember everything that's happened between you and me."

Against an old brick wall, a large body stirred. Then the voice said, "Remind me."

Joe mentioned, "Baltimore."

"Yes."

"And Singapore."

"We helped each other there."

"And what about Kiev?"

"I was in a gracious mood. A weak mood, looking back."

Joe smiled. "Regardless of moods, you let me live."

The voice seemed to change, rising from a deeper part of the unseen body. It sounded wetter and very warm, admitting, "I knew what you were, Joe. I understood how you thought, and between us, I felt we had managed an understanding."

"We had that, yes."

"You have always left my species alone."

"No reason not to."

"We weren't any threat to you."

"You've never been in trouble, until now."

"But this man you are helping…this Li monster…he is an entirely different kind of creature, I believe…."

Joe said nothing.

"And you are helping him. Don't deny it."

"I won't."

A powerful sigh came from the dark, carrying the smell of raw fish and peppermint.

"Two days from now…," Joe began.

"That would be the Prosperity Conference."

"The monster and I will be together, driving through São Paulo. Inside a secure vehicle, surrounded by several platoons of soldiers."

"I would imagine so."

"Do you know our route?"

"No, as it happens. Do you?"

"Not yet."

The shadows said nothing, and they didn't breathe, and they held themselves still enough that it was possible to believe that they had slipped away entirely.

Then very softly, the voice asked, "When will you learn the route?"

"Tomorrow night."

"But as you say, the level of protection will be considerable."

"So you want things to be easy? Is that it?"

The laugh was smooth, unhurried. "I want to know your intentions, Joe.

Having arranged this collision of forces, what will you do? Pretend to fall ill at the last moment? Stand on the curb and offer a hearty ·wave as your benefactor rolls off to his doom?"

"Who says I won't ride along?"

This time the laugh was louder, confident and honestly amused. "Suppose you learn the route and share it with me. And imagine that despite my logistical nightmares, I have time enough to assemble the essential forces. Am I to understand that you will be riding into that worst kind of trouble?"

"I've survived an ambush or two."

"When you were young. And you still had luck to spend."

Joe said nothing.

"But you do have a reasonable point," the voice continued. "If you aren't riding with the monster, questions will be asked. Doubts will rise. Your character might have to endure some rather hard scrutiny."

"Sure, that's one fine reason to stay with him."

"And another is?"

"You fall short. You can't get to Li in the end. So don't you want to have a second option in place, just in case?"

"What option?"

"Me."

That earned a final long laugh.

"Point taken, my friend. Point taken."

The limousine could have been smaller and less pretentious, but the man strapped into its safest seat would accept nothing less than a rolling castle. And following the same kingly logic, the limousine's armor and its plasma weapons were just short of spectacular. The AI driver was capable of near-miracles, if it decided to flee. But in this vehicle, in most circumstances, the smart tactic would be to stand its ground and fight. One hundred *sapien* soldiers and ten times as many mechanicals were traveling the same street, sweeping for enemies and the possibility of enemies. In any battle, they would count for quite a lot, unless of course some of them were turned, either through tricks or bribery. Which was as much consideration as Joe gave to the problem of attacking the convoy. Effort wasted was time lost. What mattered was the next ten or eleven minutes and how he handled himself and how he managed to control events within his own limited reach.

Li and two campaign wizards were conferring at the center of the limousine. Polls were a painful topic. They were still critical points behind the frontrunners, and the propaganda wing of his empire was getting worried. Ideas for new campaigns were offered, and then buried. Finally the conversation fell into glowering silences and hard looks at a floor carpeted with cultured white ermine.

That was when Joe unfastened his harness and approached.

Li seemed to notice him. But his assistant—a cold little Swede named

Hussein—took the trouble to ask, "What do you need, Mr. Carroway?"

"Just want to offer my opinion," he said.

"Opinion? About what?"

Joe made a pistol with his hand and pointed it at Hussein, and then he jerked so suddenly that the man flinched.

"What is it, Joe?" asked Li.

"People are idiots," Joe said.

The candidate looked puzzled, but a moment later, something about those words intrigued him. "In what way?"

"We can't see into the future."

"We can't?"

"None of us can," said Joe. He showed a smile, a little wink. "Not even ten seconds ahead, in some cases."

"Yet we do surprisingly well despite our limitations." The candidate leaned back, trying to find the smoothest way to dismiss this famous name.

"We can't see tomorrow," said Joe, "but we are shrewd."

"People, you mean?"

"Particularly when ten billion of us are thinking hard about the same problem. And that's why you aren't going to win this race. Nobody sees what will happen, but in this case, it's very easy to guess how the Li presidency will play out."

Hussein bristled.

But Li told him and everyone else to let the man speak.

"You're assuming that I hate these other species," Joe told him. "In fact, you've counted on it from the start. But the truth is…I don't have any compelling attachment to *sapiens*. By and large, I am a genuinely amoral creature. While you, sir…you are a bigot and a genocidal asshole. And should you ever come to power, the solar system has a respectable chance of collapsing into full-scale civil war."

Li took a moment. Then he pointed out, "In my life, I have killed no one. Not a single Rebirth, or for that matter, a *sapien*."

"Where I have slaughtered thousands," Joe admitted. "And stood aside while millions more died."

"Maybe you are my problem. Perhaps we should drop you from the ticket."

"That is an option," Joe agreed.

"Is this what you wanted to say to me? That you wish to quit?"

Joe gave the man a narrow, hard-to-read smile.

"My life," he said.

"Pardon?" Li asked.

"Early in life, I decided to live as if I was very important. As if I was blessed in remarkable ways. In my hand, I believed, were the keys to a door that would lead to a worthy future, and all that was required of me was that I make hard calculations about matters that always seem to baffle everyone else."

"I'm sorry, Joe. I'm not quite sure—"

"I have always understood that I am the most important person there is, on the Earth or any other world within our reach. And I have always been willing to do or say anything that helps my climb to the summit."

"But how can you be that special? Since that's my place to be!"

Li laughed, and his assistants heartily joined in.

Again, Joe made a pistol with his hand, pointing his index finger at the candidate's face.

"You are a scary individual," Li remarked. Then he tried to wave the man back, looking at no one when he said, "Perhaps a medical need needs to be diagnosed. A little vacation for our dear friend, perhaps."

Hussein gave an agreeable nod.

In the distance, a single soft pop could be heard.

Joe slipped back to his seat.

His security man was sitting beside him. Bothered as well as curious, he asked, "What was that all about?"

"Nothing," said Joe. "Never mind."

Another mild pop was followed by something a little louder, a little nearer.

Just in case, the security man reached for his weapon. But he discovered that his holster was empty now.

Somehow his gun had found its way into Joe's hand.

"Stay close to me," Joe said.

"You know I will," the man muttered weakly.

Then came the flash of a thumb-nuke, followed by the sharp wail of people screaming, begging with Fortune to please show mercy, to please save their glorious, important lives.


### V. World's End

Three terms as President finally ended with an assortment of scandals—little crimes and large ones, plus a series of convenient nondisclosures—and those troubles were followed by the sudden announcement that Joseph Carroway would slide gracefully into retirement. After all that, there was persistent talk about major investigations and unsealing ancient records. Tired allegations refused to die. Could the one-time leader of humanity be guilty of even one tenth of the crimes that he was rumored to have committed? In judicial circles, wise minds discussed the prospects of charging and convicting the Old Man on the most egregious insults to common morality. Politicians screamed for justice without quite defining what justice required. Certain species were loudest in their complaints, but that was to be expected.

What was more surprising, perhaps, were the numbers of pure *sapiens* who blamed the President for every kind of ill. But most of the pain and passion fell on one-time colleagues and allies. Unable to sleep easily, they would sit at home, secretly considering their own complicities in old struggles and more recent deeds, as well as non-deeds and omissions that seemed brilliant at the moment, but now, in different light, looked rather ominous.

In the end, nothing substantial happened.

In the end, the Carroway Magic continued to hold sway.

His successor was a talented and noble soul. No one doubted her passion for peace or the decency of her instincts. And she was the one citizen of the Inhabited Worlds who could sit at a desk and sign one piece of parchment, forgiving crimes and transgressions and mistakes and misjudgments. And then she showed her feline face to the cameras, winning over public opinion by pointing out that trials would take decades, verdicts would be contested for centuries, and every last one of the defendants had been elected and then served every citizen with true skill.

The new president served one six-year term before leaving public life.

Joseph Carroway entered the next race at the last moment, and he won with a staggering seventy percent mandate. But by then the Old Man was exactly that: A slowed, sorry image of his original self, dependent on a talented staff and the natural momentum of a government that achieved the ordinary without fuss or too much controversy.

Fifteen months into Joe's final term, an alien starship entered the solar system. In physical terms, it was a modest machine: Twenty cubic kilometers of metal and diamond wrapped around empty spaces. There seemed to be no crew or pilot. Nor was there a voice offering to explain itself. But its course was clear from the beginning. Moving at nearly one percent of light speed, the Stranger, as it had been dubbed, missed the moon by a few thousand kilometers. Scientists and every telescope studied its configuration, and two nukes were set off in its vicinity—neither close enough to cause damage, it was hoped, but both producing EM pulses that helped create a detailed portrait of what lay inside. Working separately, teams of AI savants found the same awful hypothesis, and a single Antfolk nest dedicated to the most exotic physics proved that hypothesis to everyone's grim satisfaction. By then, the Stranger was passing through the sun's corona, its hull red-hot and its interior awakening. What might have been a hundred-thousand-year sleep was coming to an end. In less than a minute, this very unwelcome guest had vanished, leaving behind a cloud of ions and a tiny flare that normally would trouble no one, much less spell doom for humankind.

They told Joe what would happen.

His science advisor spoke first, and when there was no obvious reaction on that perpetually calm face, two assistants threw their interpretations of these events at the Old Man. Again, nothing happened. Was he losing his grip finally? This creature who had endured and survived every kind of disaster—was he suddenly lost, at wit's end and such?

But no, he was just letting his elderly mind assemble the puzzle that they had given him.

"How much time?" he asked.

"Ten, maybe twelve minutes," the science advisor claimed. "And then another eight minutes before the radiation and scorching heat reach us."

Others were hoping for a longer delay. As if twenty or thirty minutes would offer some kind of help.

Joe looked out the window, and with a wry smile pointed out, "It is a beautiful day."

In other words, the sun was up, and they were dead.

"How far will the damage extend?" he asked.

Nobody replied.

The Antfolk ambassador was watching from her orbital embassy, tied directly into the President's office. For a multitude of reasons, she despised this *sapien*. But he was the ruler of the Great Nest, and in awful times, she was willing to do or say anything to help him, even if that meant telling him the full, undiluted truth.

"Our small worlds will be vaporized. The big asteroids will melt and seal in the deepest parts of our nests." With a sad gesture of every hand, she added, "Mars is worse off than Earth, what with the terraforming only begun. And soon there won't be any solid surfaces on the Jovian moons."

Joe turned back to his science advisor. "Will the Americas survive?"

"In places, maybe." The man was nearly sobbing. "The flares will finish before the sun rises, and even with the climate shifts and the ash falls, there's a fair chance that the atmosphere will remain breathable."

Joe nodded.

Quietly, firmly, he told everyone, "I want an open line to every world. In thirty seconds."

Before anyone could react, the youngest assistant screamed out, "Why? Why would aliens do this awful thing to us?"

Joe laughed, just for a moment.

Then with a grandfatherly voice, he said, "Because they can. That's why."


"It has been an honor to serve as your President," Joe told an audience of two and then three and then four billion. But most citizens were too busy to watch this unplanned speech—an important element in his gruesome calculations. "But my days are done. The sun has been infiltrated, its hydrogen stolen to use in the manufacture of an amazing bomb, and virtually everybody in the range of my voice will be dead by tomorrow.

"If you are listening to me, listen carefully.

"The only way you will survive in the coming hell is to find those very few people whom you trust most. Do it now. Get to your families, hold hands with your lovers. Whoever you believe will watch your back always. And then you need to search out those who aren't aware of what I am telling you to do.

"Kill those other people.

"Whatever they have of value, take it.

"And store their corpses, if you can. In another week or two, you might relish the extra protein and fat."

He paused, just for a moment.

Then Joe said, "For the next ten generations, you will need to think only about yourselves. Be selfish. Be vicious. Be strong, and do not forget:

"Kindness is a luxury.

"Empathy will be a crippling weakness.

"But in another fifty generations, we can rebuild everything that we have lost here today. I believe that, my friends. Goodness can come again. Decency can flower in any rubble. And in fifty more generations after that, we will reach out to the stars together.

"Keep that thought close tonight, and always.

"One day, we will punish the bastards who did this awful thing to us. But to make that happen, a few of you must find the means to survive!"

# THE MAGICIAN'S HOUSE

## MEGHAN MCCARRON

*Meghan McCarron's stories have recently appeared in* Strange Horizons, Clarkesworld Magazine, *and* Lady Churchill's Rosebud Wristlet. *She has been an action
movie researcher, a Hollywood assistant, a boarding school English teacher, and,
briefly, a typist for an experimental philosopher. She lives in Brooklyn.*

The magician's house looked like every other house in our neighborhood on
the inside, except it had more doors. There were three doors in the foyer, two
under the stairs, four in the hallway, one next to the fireplace, and another hidden behind the sofa. They were the builder's standard issue, painted the same
blank white color as the walls. I pictured each one leading to a room in another
house that looked exactly like this one. This house was the ur-house, the house
that allowed all other houses in the development to exist.

We didn't go through any of those doors, like I had been expecting. Instead,
the magician led me into the kitchen, opened the oven, and crawled inside. The
oven seemed too small for a man that tall, let alone for me. I peered inside; there
were no racks or walls or heat sources. There was nothing but darkness. I glanced
up at the control knobs. They were turned to "OFF."

"Well?" said the magician's voice from inside. It echoed, as if coming from
below ground.

I ducked my head into the oven; inside was strangely humid, and the air smelled
warm and yeasty. There were no walls I could make out, only receding darkness.
Taking a deep breath, I placed one hand inside, then another. I banged my shin
on the oven's edge as I pulled my legs up. I crawled forward into the pitch black,
the hard metal floor warming beneath my hands. Suddenly, this seemed like a
terrible idea. But before I could turn around, the darkness enveloped me, and
I slid down.

Inside the oven, a gas lamp flickered over upholstered chairs that I had seen in
a dumpster a few months ago. I remembered them because they were lime green,
and I had thought about hauling them home for my pink-and-floral bedroom
to piss off my mom. The magician was already seated, waiting for me. He looked
bored. I wiped the nervous sweat from my face, took a deep breath, and sat.

The magician was a tall, spindly man with surprisingly thick hands and dark, graying hair. He folded into the chair like a marionette. To meet me, he wore black stretch pants, a silk pajama shirt, a burgundy cardigan, and decaying black flip-flops. If I had seen him on the street, I would have laughed, but in the oven room he looked right at home, whereas I felt ridiculous in my khaki shorts and pre-faded T-shirt. I had even blow-dried my hair. For the first time, instead of feeling invisible in my prepster clothes, I felt exposed.

The magician stared at me for an uncomfortable moment. Finally, he leaned forward and said, "Tell me what you see when you see the color black."

I thought of the lightless oven tunnel. "I see... black?" I said.

The magician sighed. "What do you see," he repeated. "Black."

I closed my eyes. In the darkness, I saw a smooth, shimmering surface, taut against a woman's hip. Little black dress. Satin.

"Um," I said. I didn't want to tell him what I saw; it felt secret. "Um. Like, um, I see space. You know, outer space?"

The magician jerked forward and slapped me.

I yelped and pulled away. I pressed my hand to my stinging cheek. The magician gave me a knowing, angry look.

"Liar," he said. "You see a woman's body."

My eyes hazed over with tears.

"What did the woman look like?" he said.

I sniffled hard. "I just saw... her hip. She was reclining, in a black satin dress."

There was a strange light in his eyes when he heard this. Later, much later, he would tell me that when his master asked him this question, he saw the exact same thing.

"Why do you want to learn magic?" he said.

I blinked the tears out of my eyes. It was a stupid question. My mother had wanted me to find a hobby. She threw out suggestions: horseback riding, dance, music—I blurted out magic as a joke. But she'd had a thing for tarot cards at my age, and the suggestion delighted her. Since calling the magician, she kept recounting weird stories of things I did as a kid that suggested, in her mind, miraculous abilities. As far as I could tell, they were all about me eating dirt. I don't think she expected oven rooms.

But I didn't want to blurt out the lame, "My mother made me come." The magician had clearly already written me off, and I didn't like it. I said, "Because I want to know something real."

The magician sat back in his chair a little bit and glowered at me. "Come back next week," he said finally. "Dress like a human being. And bring a shovel."

I came back in ripped jeans and an old band T-shirt of my dad's. It felt like just another costume, but the magician nodded when he saw me, pleased. My dad had done the same thing when I asked to borrow the shirt.

The magician took me to his backyard and told me to dig. He gave me no other instructions, just a shovel (the one I had brought was "too puny"), and permission to destroy his yard.

At first, I dug shallow, lazy holes, and the magician made me fill them all back in. Then he told me to stop digging like a girl. I told him that it wasn't a bad thing to be female, but when I went back to digging I jabbed the shovel into the earth, hard and angry, like I imagined boys to be.

My next holes were narrow, deep, mysterious things. I dug them all over the yard, turning up rich, dark dirt that used to grow corn, back when this development was a farm. I turned up the occasional rusted can, too, lids hanging off in a lewd way. I sweated through my dad's T-shirt and covered my jeans with dirty handprints. As time wore on, the digging started to feel a little like dancing, or a little like making music, with the rhythmic bite of the shovel, and the flow of my body. I found my holes very beautiful.

At the end of the day, the magician came out to inspect my work. He stuck his leg in a few holes to see how deep they went. He tasted the dirt. Then, he sent me home.

When I came back the next week, the holes were gone; I stared at the grassy, unblemished yard with something like grief. The magician wasn't home; instead, a diagram waited for me on his kitchen table, which overlooked the flat, hole-less yard.

The next hole I dug was sinewy and undulating. I thought of it as a drawing of a heart, taken apart and bent. The digging had grown easier, the magician said because the earth knew me better. I was pretty sure it was the arm muscles, but I didn't argue. I liked his idea more. While I dug, the magician played blues records out of a second floor window. Howlin' Wolf, Lightnin' Hopkins, Son House, Robert Johnson, Mississippi John Hurt, Blind Willie McTell. Men with names that told you something about them, all except Robert Johnson, whose name was a black hole, a mystery. When the records ended, the magician would lean out his window and lecture me about these men, their genius and strangeness. They understood the earth, according to him. They understood where they were from.

As soon as I finished my hole, the magician jumped down into it with me. I was covered with dirt and sweat, and my arms were still shaking. The magician guided me by my shoulders, eyes closed, through the twists and turns of my labyrinth. His breath blew against my neck, and his hands were warm on my skin. When we reached the end, he took his shovel and told me not to come back until he called.

The magician didn't call until December, when he sent me a text message at two A.M. that read, "Come over." I squinted at the message and wondered if I was dreaming. But the phone beeped again, and I stumbled out of bed. I crawled out through the dog door so my parents wouldn't hear me sneaking out. The magician was waiting for me on his front lawn, bundled up in a blue and orange ski jacket from the eighties. He wore a red hat with a pom-pom. He looked like a tall, skinny bear dressed up in clown clothes. Cute at first glance, but ultimately sinister.

"Do you know what today is?" he said.

"The solstice?" I said.

The magician patted me on the head, so I guessed I had the right answer.

"Tonight the earth is in her deepest sleep. We will go learn some secrets. Then we will do our part to wake her up."

We tramped through the woods in silence, passing abandoned Boy Scout cabins, a rusting Coke machine, and a massive sign that said MILK. The woods used to be the trash heap for the farm—somewhere a whole car was buried. The magician picked his way along the path ahead of me, a blare of orange over invisible legs. I pretended I was tracking him.

We climbed to the highest point, where there was some exposed rock and a tiny cave. Kids went up there to drink, and when the magician climbed inside on his hands and knees I heard the clatter of empty beer cans. Inside was pitch black and freezing; it smelled faintly of cigarettes and dirt. I shivered against the frozen rock.

"Turn your face to the rock and whisper your question," the magician said to me across the darkness.

"My question?" I said.

His clothing rustled as he turned, and his voice hissed against the rock as he whispered things I couldn't hear. I sat with my cheek against the cold stone, silent, listening to the magician's breath move against the cave wall. I couldn't just rattle off questions to a rock at two o'clock in the morning. If he had warned me, I'd have thought of the perfect questions, the questions that would tell me everything I needed to know about my life, but instead I was sitting here silent and alone—

The magician's whispers stopped, and he crawled towards me in the dark. His hand found my shoulder.

"What do you want?" he said.

"What?"

"What do you want in this world?"

I pressed my cheek against the rock and thought.

"You don't have to tell me," he said. "Just ask."

He crawled out with another clatter of empties, and the silence in the cave lulled me. The rock was freezing my cheek, so I lifted my head and whispered, "How do I become a magician?"

Images cascaded into my head, too many too fast, like I had asked a question too big to be answered. I gasped for breath. When it was over, all I had left was my desire, sharper than before, more focused. I hadn't even realized until then how much I wanted it, but now it was desperately clear.

While I had been in the cave, the magician had built a fire on top of the hill.

When he saw me crawl out, he smiled. I wondered if now we were friends.

When I opened my mouth to say something, however, the magician turned back to the fire. He held out his hands to warm them, then stuffed them back in his mittens. In one quick, violent movement, he threw his head back and shouted, "WAKE UP!"

He began to dance around the fire, a funny, undignified dance, lots of flailing arms and bent knees and shuffling. I couldn't stop myself from giggling.

He ignored me. He threw his head back again and shouted, "WAKE UP!"

He didn't invite me over, and at first I was too scared to join. Instead, I lingered at the edge, just outside the fire's halo of heat. When I finally joined in, it was as much about the warmth of the fire as the ritual. I ducked in the dance right after him, but I danced better than he did. I moved my arms up and out like a rising sun. I shook my hips to remind the earth of the pleasures of spring. When he threw his head back, I threw mine back too, and together we shouted, "WAKE UP!"

We danced and shouted until dawn, then put out the fire and tramped back through the woods. He cracked some eggs and made omelets, filled the room with the smell of coffee. While we ate, his wife came in the front door, fresh from her own magic's solstice. The magician had told me she was bound to fire; maybe that was why her face was flushed in an athletic, almost sexy way. She was tall and elegant and graceful when she kissed her husband on the cheek. I found her terrifying.

"Good solstice?" she asked.

"Oh yes," the magician said.

She faced me and smiled a big hostess smile.

"Nice to see you again, dear," she said. "Good solstice?"

I smiled and nodded.

When it was time for me to leave, the magician walked me to the door, then swooped in to kiss me on the cheek, a dry, awkward peck. I made, belatedly, a kissing noise in the air near his own cheek, but I was too shocked by the gesture to get the timing right, so I air-kissed his neck instead of his face. His wife called from the kitchen, "Is she too tired to drive?"

"She's fine," he called back. "She had coffee."

I nodded along, as if his wife could see me.

"Happy solstice," the magician said.

He stood in the door as I left and watched me drive away.

In the spring, I began to have tasks. Not like the hole digging, which had been more of a test. Real magicians have deeds, but to learn to have deeds, first you must have tasks. To be honest, I was a little fuzzy on the distinction, but I guessed you got more credit for one than the other.

The magician sometimes talked about other students he had. They were all boys and, in his opinion, dull. When I asked him if they had tasks, the magician gave me a secret look. "No, none of them are ready for tasks," he said, waving a hand as if brushing them aside. Then he smiled at me again and said, "None of them are like you."

I carried those words around with me for days, shivering with pleasure when I replayed them in my head. The magician believed I was like him. He believed I would be great, like him. I would be nothing like the person I'd thought I was.

My first task was to connect two places that had yet to be connected. I couldn't feel the earth through the wheels of my car, so I went for walks. I quickly discovered, to my dismay, that most places were already connected in the suburbs, albeit in terrible ways. Thoughtless roads linked houses to strip malls, churches, synagogues, schools. Trees clung for dear life to other trees by the roads of their roots. Animals left roads with their scents, roads that faded over time, but provided all the connecting they needed. I could connect houses to other houses, but people put up wardings to frustrate me: wooden fences, electric fences, stakes marking exactly where their property ended, even in the middle of the woods.

I explained these problems to the magician, and he laughed at me. "You're being very literal," he said, like it was cute.

I walked on the cul-de-sacs and main roads and driveways and unfinished dirt tracks in the development the magician and I shared, feeling the way the earth groaned and strained against the ill-placed swaths of asphalt. The people who didn't drive around the neighborhood—children—zigzagged in all directions, flying past property markers, hopping fences (much to the consternation of family dogs), and avoiding the roads whenever possible. The only things that hemmed them in were the big busy roads that surrounded the development, when clearly all they wanted was to run, on and on and on.

A four-lane road separated us from a farm that sold ice cream. Children crashed against the barrier like waves on a cliff, looking longingly at the freshly plowed cornfields and dairy cows and signs announcing *Cho-co Mint Chip!* At first I thought about building them a bridge, but I didn't know the mechanics of air, even if a road was involved. A crosswalk was a silly idea, but I considered anyway; I drew scale diagrams and observed the road late at night, to see if the cars disappeared for long enough to paint (they didn't). I already knew how to dig. A tunnel it was.

There was an undeveloped lot across from the cornfield, so I started digging there, at the edge of the road. I dug at night, and dumped the dirt in the lot next door, where they were digging the foundation of a house. The earth was wet and heavy from the spring rain, and at night I could still see my breath. It was exhausting work, and by the third day, I wasn't sure I could go on. But when I arrived the next night, I found a little boy waiting for me, holding a plastic shovel. I let him help. The next night there was another child, then three more, then ten. Thirteen children dug along with me using sandbox shovels, garden trowels, and even a real shovel or two. Bikes were rigged with buckets and hitched to wheeled trashcans, and the children hid the dirt in their playhouses, in their parents' mulch piles, or out in the dry, grassless plain of the undeveloped lots. On the twelfth night, we finished digging and planted mailboxes on each end of the tunnel, though there were no houses in sight. On the thirteenth, I slept in the center of the tunnel alone and asked the earth to remember what it was like to be a hard and sturdy stone as the cars rumbled above me.

The next afternoon we were together, the magician and I walked across the development to see my handiwork. We had spent so many hours together in the basement that the sight of him in the sunlight was shocking—he was so strange looking, tall and translucently pale, with his too-big T-shirt and long, skinny pants. I was embarrassed that someone might see him loping beside me; I was ashamed to feel that way, but I still hid my face from passing cars.

We crossed the scrubby, vacant lot to the lone mailbox. It was shaped like a goose in flight, flying towards its sister mailbox. I had given in to a little bit of silliness and bought another one shaped like a swan, also in flight, so it looked like they were heading for an epic battle. Goose vs. Swan.

I made this joke, but the magician didn't smile.

"So?" he said, nodding at my twin mailboxes. "What is it?"

"Pull the goose's beak towards you," I said.

The magician reached out a long wiry arm and pulled. The whole mailbox came with it, as well as the piece of earth the mailbox was rooted in, revealing a ladder that glinted in the sunlight, and a dark tunnel below.

"Ha!" the magician said. He climbed down, and I followed, closing the trap-door behind us.

I had instructed the kids to leave a stash of flashlights at the foot of each ladder, but they hadn't done it yet, and the tunnel was pitch dark. I had dug it, dreamt it, but this perfect blackness paralyzed me. The magician breathed next to me.

"Do you have to stoop?" I whispered. It seemed wrong to speak normally.

"A bit," he said.

"Follow me," I said, and fumbled backwards for his hand. He took mine loosely, leaving it up to me to hold on. His fingers fidgeted over the back of my hand.

It took us only a minute or two to cross the tunnel, but every second felt essential as our two bodies moved through the cold, clammy dark. Even the sound of cars overhead disappeared. The magician bumped his head twice, and once he inhaled sharply, as if something surprising had occurred to him. His hand continued to fidget over mine; the space between our palms grew warm.

"This is remarkable," he said. "Just remarkable."

He squeezed my hand when he said this, and then held on tight. I shivered.

"Cold?" he said with an odd urgency.

"No!" I said, equally jumpy. "No, no, I'm fine."

I walked right into the ladder with a deafening clank. I giggled and released his hand. After a brief hesitation, he let go too, and laughed.

I put a foot on the ladder, ascended a rung.

"This really is remarkable," the magician said again. "You have real talent."

I paused mid-climb to bask in his praise, and the magician's chest brushed against my arm; we were closer than I realized. "Thank you?" I said. My chest was tight.

The magician reached for my hand again. In the darkness, his breath brushed my neck. The sensation was delicious, but my stomach felt sick.

I took back my hand and climbed.

I busied myself with brushing the dirt off my clothes in the sunshine as the magician emerged from the tunnel. The field beneath my feet was a dark, wet brown, freshly turned and rich. Green shoots rose in rows all around me, fresh and alive in the sunshine. The magician set the mailbox back in place and laughed to himself in a high, odd way. I kept my back to him. I didn't want to see what an absurd figure he cut in the sunlight, what an ugly person made my heart hammer, my skin sweat.

"You made a lovely road," the magician said behind me. I turned around; he was running a finger along the edge of the swan mailbox, taking it in. He looked up at the roaring cars between us and home. "Should we . . . go back down?"

My stomach jumped. "I'll just run across," I said.

He had been holding my eyes, and when I said this, his face crumbled.

"All right. Run away," he said with a small laugh. "I'm going to take another look."

For a long, tense moment he hesitated, while I waited for a space to open between cars. Finally, he pulled the trap door open and disappeared below ground. A second, maybe two, of space opened between the cars, and I ran. When I got across, I forced myself to slow to a walk, but I walked hard, like I knew someone was following me. My fists balled at my sides, and a steady stream of *fuck you fuck you fuck you* ran through my head. But all my skin could feel was the caress of his thumb across my palm, the rush of his breath, and the thick, humid feeling of his warmth underground.

I did not see the magician for a few weeks after that. I had some legitimate excuses, a few fabricated ones. Family vacation, Easter, "sick" with the "flu." I wasn't leaving forever, but I didn't want to go back until I was more anchored in the real world. I had decided it was time for me to become a real teenage girl again.

My mom was thrilled to take me shopping for bright T-shirts and flowery flip-flops at the mall. My dad was equally thrilled when I joined the stage crew for the spring play (to put my building skills to use)—he called it "a *healthy* hobby." In school, I sat with old friends at lunch for the first time in months and started cracking jokes in class. I said nothing about magic, and no one asked. When I went back to the magician, we sat a respectable distance apart and were back to holes and blues records. He didn't offer a new task, and I didn't ask.

Then I started dreaming.

I couldn't remember the dreams at first. Images would bubble to the surface, ruined cities, swollen rivers, skyscraper trees, but I didn't know why I woke at dawn drained, disoriented, sometimes aroused, sometimes afraid. I finally put a notebook by my bed, and when I woke put pen to paper. My hand moved on the paper; I read what I was writing.

*I had a sister, and we had to build a house. The house was also an ark—it would keep us safe from catastrophe. We made it out of stones, a dome. But when I went inside it was my parents' house, white carpets and sand-colored walls. I opened doors, looking for my dome house, but the rooms were burnt out. Charred, crumbled furniture. Horrible stains on the floor. I found my house in the oven. It was one empty room, dirt floor, with stone walls rising around me. Sunshine fell through an opening. A naked woman waited for me in the pool of light. She had gray hair, large beautiful breasts. I was ashamed. I kept staring at the triangle of hair between her thighs. I wanted her to kiss me, but when she did, my mouth filled with dirt. I stumbled onto my mother's flowered couch, choking because—*

I didn't know how to finish this sentence. I slid my hand beneath my underwear and felt between my legs. I was wet and swollen like—like I wanted someone. But the dreams had left me terrified. Or, the choking left me terrified.

I went down to the magician's basement that week with my heart thumping. I could barely stay awake in school anymore, because I woke up every morning gasping for breath. Clearly, I had to ask him for help. But this dream felt too personal, too true, to share even with him.

The magician waited for me on his orange couch, fiddling with his guitar. I sat down on the opposite end of the couch, my butt on the armrest, and leaned forward, elbows on my knees.

The magician didn't look up from his guitar when he said, "What would you like to tell me?"

"How did you know?" I said.

The magician put the guitar aside and smiled at me in a way he hadn't since the tunnel expedition. "You look very intent."

I looked down at my feet, trying to find the words I needed. "I've been having dreams," I said. "A dream. About a stone house with a secret room." I trailed off, and the magician nodded at me, prompting me for more. "And . . . there's a naked woman. When she . . . when she kisses me, my mouth fills with dirt, and I choke."

The magician jumped when I said this. "Why didn't you tell me?"

"I—I'm sorry," I said.

He looked down at his fingers, which were thrumming against his bony knees. He looked like a little boy thinking over a difficult problem. His fingers stopped thrumming, and he reached out for me—the only thing he could reach was my foot perched on the cushion. He held it.

"How much do you want to know about magic?" he said.

He was nervous, watching me carefully like I might bolt.

"Everything," I said without thinking.

He shifted in his seat; his slick magician pants made a swishing noise against the couch.

"There are a lot of ways to—manage surges in power, which is what that dream is showing you," he said. "Some ways are faster and more demanding. Others are slower, and safer. The time has come for you to—choose one."

The moment crystallized—the look in his eyes, his hand on my foot, my shaking legs—and I gazed at the scene impartially, as if from high above. I'd read all the standard texts, heard all the rumors, read my sensational novels. This was what always came next. But in real life, it felt unnatural and unreal.

The magician started talking again, like the silence spooked him. "Your dream is telling you that your magic—well, that your magic is tied to sex. Earth magicians, they get like that, especially as adolescents, with all the hormones, when I was your age I had dreams and the power and desire that pumped through me made me miserable. Because I couldn't focus it. I—I could help you get through this. Help you ground it, otherwise you'll continue to have these dreams. I understand if this makes you nervous because of the way you've been brought up, but I—"

I couldn't speak. I just nodded.

"Yes?" he said. "Yes to what?"

I had an urge to curl up on the couch and giggle like a twelve-year-old when someone says "sex." I hid my face in my hands.

"I want you to help me," I said into my palms.

He leaned towards me. "How?"

He drew my hands down from my face and rubbed his thumbs against the insides of my wrists. He was so beautiful in that moment, and his face seemed to have layers, like I could see him through time, my handsome old teacher, my hungry young man. I felt ill, I couldn't tell if it was with fear or desire. He had said I might be afraid.

He looked at me, waiting.

I kissed him, right on the mouth. He gathered me in his arms and pulled me down on top of him, straddling me across his lap. Our hips aligned, and he was hard against me.

Fear shot through me again, and I buried my face in his neck. I couldn't look at him. "You can't get tied up in this," he said into my ear. "This is about the work, not me. I'm a married man."

As he said this, he stroked my head, then slid his hand over my neck, down my back, and held my hip. No one had ever touched me like that, so softly, with such confidence. I saw him howling at the moon on the solstice, that freedom, that crack in the ice. His neck was dry and smelled like clay.

"I want to," I said, and pulled away from his neck. "I want to be a magician."

He took my face in his hand and stroked it. "You and I are very much alike," he said, and slid his other hand between my thighs.

* * *

Once the magician and I started having sex, I gave up on being a normal teenager. All I wanted to talk about was magic, and the magician, and no one wanted to hear that. My friends nicknamed me Silent Bob in the cafeteria, stopped calling me on weekends. My parents said polite things about my renewed enthusiasm for magic, but in insincere tones, so I would know they actually disapproved. A girl I had been close with on stage crew finally asked me, bluntly, "What's your deal?" and I told her what the magician and I were doing. She rolled her eyes and said, "Of course you are."

It wasn't "of course you are." It was dangerous and exhilarating. Our time together was full of color, where everything else in my life was grays and beiges. I'd had sex before, exactly twice, with a boy I'd liked so little I'd blocked his last name from my memory. It was fast and painful and existentially disappointing—*This is it? This is what makes the world go round?* He took more care tying the condom into a knot afterwards and tossing it, ceremonially, out the car window.

The magician held me like I was a precious thing. He kissed me deeply, brushed his fingers along my face. He buried his mouth between my legs and stayed there until I sweated, screamed, cried. He put himself inside me and told me to concentrate. "What do you see?" he said, over and over, moving inside me. "What do you see?"

I saw his face, his ear, his arms, his shoulder, his chest. I smelled rich and fertile things. We didn't do magic; maybe we were magic. When I walked home afterwards, the earth lit up beneath my footsteps.

I stopped dreaming about the house, the dirt, and the woman. Instead, in my dreams I was underground. Beside me were seeds, and corpses. When I woke up, I believed I was one of the seeds, but I thought of those dreams with dread.


A week before the winter solstice, I found the magician sitting upstairs in his kitchen with his wife. There was a cup of coffee waiting for me.

I wanted to bolt back out the door. But the magician looked calm, and his wife smiled at me. I looked down at my clothes, as if there were something that would give me away. If she didn't already know that I was sleeping with her husband—maybe magicians understood this kind of thing?

When I sat, the magician's wife announced that she would like to invite me to a women's solstice celebration. She and her husband had agreed that it would be good for me to experience a more traditional rite.

I looked over at the magician; his face was still blank. His wife still smiled at me. I had no idea what a "traditional rite" was, and that did, with reflection, seem like a flaw in my education. Most of the rites I knew involved messing around with her husband.

"Sure," I said. Somehow, my voice came out smooth and even.

"Great!" the magician's wife said.

Then the magician and I retreated downstairs and began to remove our clothes, as if this were the most natural thing in the world.

"Does she, um, know?" I asked as he kissed my neck.

"Please don't discuss it," he said, and kissed me on the mouth, to seal the deal. This didn't answer my question, but I knew enough to let it drop. His hands were already fumbling for my bra.

"You're warm," he said.

I smiled against his shoulder. "So are you."

The solstice ritual took place in a park that had once been a battlefield. Cannons from the Revolutionary War pointed at me as I drove in the main entrance, the heat blasting in my little car. I hadn't had to sneak out this year; my parents had liked the sound of "a traditional rite." I had bundled myself in my thickest ski jacket and snow boots, though there was only a white film of frost on the ground. It had been dark since four thirty that afternoon, and now the dark was so complete that my headlights could not penetrate more than a few feet in front of me.

My car wound through dark, narrow roads up to a summit Washington's army had once seized from the British. Now it was nothing but frozen grass and hibernating trees, not a hint of ghosts or bloodshed. There was a single other car parked in the spot where I'd been told to leave mine, and a number of bicycles, which seemed like relics of another era on such a cold night. My feet crunched on the frost as I ascended the rest of the way to the hilltop, where a massive bonfire burned. At least ten other women clustered around another cannon; they were removing their clothes and draping them over the cannon's snout.

The magician's wife, about to pull her sweater over her head, spotted me and waved.

The women were greeting each other like old friends. They ranged from twenties to eighties, though most were middle-aged. There were a few girls my age, too; some of the women were introducing them as their students. The magician's wife put her arm around me possessively and introduced me to the group as her husband's student.

"She works with the earth, then?" one of the women said.

"She does," the magician's wife said, in a way that suggested she wasn't sure how that would go over.

A few of the women giggled, and one or two gave me uncomfortable looks. Another smiled at me, in a half-knowing, half-embarrassed way.

The magician's wife rolled her eyes and turned to me. "We do this ritual naked. You okay with that?"

"Of course she is," one woman whispered to another.

"Sure?" I said, not understanding anything.

"Go ahead and undress, then," the magician's wife said, and turned back to the cannon where she'd draped her coat. She pulled her sweater over her head, revealing breasts that spilled out of her black bra. I didn't realize I was staring until the woman who'd caught my eye caught it again and smirked. I crouched down to untie my shoe.

"She's *cute*," a naked woman said to the magician's wife, making it sound like a strike against me.

"You're lucky to have an earthy husband," another added.

"No, she's just lucky his students will never be interested in *him*," the first woman said with a laugh.

The magician's wife cast an uncomfortable glance back at me; I pretended to be engrossed in the mechanics of unbuttoning my pants. There was some reason I shouldn't be attracted to the magician?

"She's a talented kid," the magician's wife said. "It's been good for him to have a student like that again."

The rest of the women drifted towards the heat of the fire as I struggled out of my layers of clothes. My legs shook and pimpled with goosebumps as soon as I slid off my pants. I ripped the rest of my layers off as fast as I could and sprinted for the fire, expecting relief. Instead, the heat of the fire hit me like a wall. I felt trapped between two walls, the fire-heat wall in front of me, and the ice-cold wall at my back. The women around me stood comfortably, laughing and chatting. They were warm. Again, I was on the outside of their society. The magician was probably just crawling out of bed right now, getting ready to go out to the cave and learn secrets. It seemed much more dignified than public nudity and women talking about me like I wasn't even there.

"This ritual is hardest for people like us," a voice said next to me. It was the woman who had caught my eye. Her arms were crossed over her breasts, like mine, and she shivered with cold. "Our element is too asleep to warm us. But we're the most important. You've never done this before, have you?"

I felt like a kid on the first day of school, whose mom had dressed her and given her all the wrong advice. "Last year I went into a cave, with my teacher," I said.

"He is a private man," the woman said thoughtfully. "It's good you're here this year, even if you're cold and confused and . . . distracted."

"Distracted?" I said.

"Oh, you know. Earth women. Our blood runs hot, even when we're freezing."

She smiled when she said that, but she wasn't looking at me anymore; she was embarrassed. I looked around the circle at all the naked women, orange and beautiful in the firelight. Heat flushed me as I gazed at them, a familiar, latent feeling; I wanted to hold them, to kiss them and see if my mouth still filled with dirt. Is this what the women had been talking about? How looking at them made me feel?

The magician's wife lit herself on fire.

"Come on," the other earth woman said, yanking me out of my daze. "We're starting."

She crouched and dug at the cold, frozen earth. She worked it with her hands until it softened and spread it over her body in messy handfuls. I crouched and followed her lead. The dirt was grainy and dry in my hands, but it stuck to my skin as if I were the other side of a magnet.

Time jittered. My hands pulled up dirt, but didn't spread it. I dug, and then dug again. The magician's wife lit herself on fire once, twice, too many times. She was consumed. She was extinguished. She burned steady, like a wick. Time blurred completely. I spent days spreading dirt on my shoulder, my thigh, my cheek. Every grain of dirt worked into my skin, mingling with it, transforming me. The circle joined hands and rotated around the fire. I had the earth woman's clay hand in my left, and a wet, icy hand in my right. The air women blew counterclockwise, driving the circle; they floated in the air and pulled the fire and water women with them. But the earth woman and I had stone feet, and we kept the circle bound to the frozen ground.

At the same moment, the earth woman and I were crouched on the ground, whispering our questions, hopes, and fears through our dirty fingers. Questions flowed out of me, and insight flowed in with perfect clarity. I understood roads, I understood rocks, I understood dirt and plants and even dared to ask about the hot, rushing lava beneath. The water women slept on their backs, arms splayed as if floating. The air women had climbed trees. And the magician's wife, still aflame, stared at me with eyes full of disbelief, or perhaps anger, or perhaps sorrow, or the peculiar mixture of the three that comes when you discover the impossible thing you suspected was actually true.

Before I could react to her stare, I was back in the circle, and it turned faster and faster, the fire was driving it now, burning the ice off the water women, making the air women float to the sky, melting our stone feet to clay.

The water women's ice melted, and now the circle moved so fast it flowed. We rushed around the fire, moving from creek to river to ocean to rain, my feet broke and I fell from high above—

The circle stomped its feet, STOMP STOMP STOMP. Wherever my feet fell, shoots of green sprung up; they would only die again in the cold; it was cruel and beautiful. We no longer moved, or flowed, or fell; we shook the ground and shouted with one voice, "WAKE UP! WAKE UP! WAKE UP!"

This was not just a dance around a fire. The earth woman and I pulled the whole world around. We were the earth, and all these women shouted our name.

When the first line of light appeared on the horizon, the circle broke apart. The sun burned the magic off like a fog, and in the light of day we were sweaty, sooty, winded and undressed. The women hurried to douse the fire, to clean their bodies, to put on clothes. I stood stock-still as everyone else normalized around me, my thoughts racing, my heart crashing from an enormous high. The sky glowed blue in the east, and the earth opened its eyes.

Finally, the earth woman took my shoulder, and invited me to meet up with them at the local diner for pancakes and coffee. That reminder of the real world—coffee, breakfast, shiny red booths—shook me out of my trance. I shuffled back to the cannon and pulled clothes on, trying to put together what had just happened.

As I pulled my frozen hat off the cannon, the magician's wife approached me. Fear filled me, though I couldn't remember why. Something about fire. The sun was about to rise, and the light filled her singed, blackened hair. I could barely see her face.

"What did you think?" she said in a tone impossible to read.

I worked the hat in my hands, breaking off the frost. "It was—it was like nothing else."

The magician's wife crossed her arms. "Is that a good thing?"

"Yes!" I said. "I'd like to do . . . more magic, like this."

"What kind *have* you been doing—" she began, then trailed off.

The answer to the question—sweaty limbs, coursing energy—leapt to mind, and I saw her staring at me across the fire again, that devastated look on her face. I took a step backwards before I remembered that I couldn't run.

"Can I ask you a question?" she said.

*Please don't*, I thought. "Sure," I said.

She sighed, like she hadn't thought up the question yet. Finally she said, "When my husband interviewed you, what did you see?"

I was overcome by the urge to lie, but I knew she expected me to. "A woman's hip, under a dress," I said.

The magician's wife nodded. "And when you dream, what do you dream about?"

"Being underground," I said.

This threw her. "Well, I don't know what to make of that dream, but—"

"Before that," I interrupted. "I dreamed about a house, and a naked woman who kissed me and choked my mouth with dirt."

She fell silent, and looked at me. I wondered if I'd confessed too much. "Did you tell my husband about that dream?" his wife said.

"Yes," I said.

"What did he tell you, after you told him?"

Again, an urge to lie; I pushed it away. "That it was . . . about sex."

The magician's wife laughed once, hard and sharp. "You hadn't picked up on that on your own, had you?" she said.

Her words were a slap, both to me and to him. I grew angry. "Those dreams were terrifying," I said. "He said he could help me."

The magician's wife looked at me. "Magic is supposed to be terrifying."

The sun broke the horizon and the light, in one moment, changed. The magician's wife gave me another look, then walked away, to catch a ride to the diner. I waited until she was gone, and then I drove to the magician's house.

The magician answered the door in his robe, his hair wet from the shower. It was so warm inside that I started to sweat under my coat. I stripped off layers in his kitchen, draping them over the counter across from the oven. I wondered what would happen if we opened it now.

He watched me peel off my winter clothes. His eyes were red from the smoke of the fire, and his shoulders hunched more than usual. I wondered what he'd asked the earth last night. I asked for some coffee.

Coffee, the drink for talking over. I had questions, and I was going to ask them. He pressed a mug into my hands and stood too close as I sipped it.

"Good solstice?" he said.

"Um. Yeah," I said.

"I missed you last night," he said.

*Missed me!* my brain sighed. I smothered the thought. "Look, I—" I began.

He pushed my coffee aside and kissed me. He pressed my hand against his bare chest, slid it down between the folds of his robe. His skin was warm and moist beneath my palm.

I dropped the mug on the counter, because otherwise I would throw it. I tore myself out of his arms and turned away.

"I'm pissed!" I said, clenching my arms around myself.

"What—what's the matter?" he said.

"Are you really—helping me?"

The magician took a step towards me, then two. He put his hands on my shoulders. "I think you know that better than I do."

I shook my head, then turned and buried my face in his shoulder. "I don't."

He stroked my hair, and I leaned into him. He tilted my face up to his and kissed me tentatively. When I returned the kiss, he put his hand behind my head and pressed me to him. His hands tangled with my shirt, the waist of my jeans; he slid the clothes from my body, then let his robe fall on the floor. He held me naked for a moment, the warmth of the sunlight on our skin. Then he led me down to the basement, where we were safe. He bent me over the couch and slid himself inside of me, fucked me hard as I braced my hands against the scratchy fabric. Then I was on my back, and he kissed my face as he climbed on top of me. I started to wrap my legs around him but he pushed them away and sat up as he fucked me, watching me from above with a face I couldn't read. As he got closer, he doubled over me, moving his sweaty body against mine. I felt buried, underground. His breath was too hot on my shoulder as he came in a spurt on my stomach. He wiped it off and settled on top of me. I stroked his gray hair.

Before I could chicken out, I said, "I love you." I wasn't sure if I meant it, but I'd been wanting to say it for so long that I didn't want to miss my chance.

"Don't say that," he murmured, and kissed my ear.

After I left, I drove in circles around our town. I traced all the gray, groaning streets linking my neighborhood to the supermarket, the big box store, the pizza delivery place, the gas station, my high school. The parking lots were deserted this early in the morning, and the empty, anonymous buildings looked sinister without people. I didn't want to stare at these places, but I didn't know where to go. My house? Back to his? California? Where did you go, when you felt like this? I couldn't put a name to the panic filling me; I couldn't see straight.

The mailboxes still marked my tunnel, though the cornfield was frozen and the empty lot had a huge hole where the basement of a new house would be. Inside the tunnel, I found several flashlights, all of them dusty; I took the one shaped like a cartoon superhero. Its battery was low, but I could scry crumpled candy wrappers, gutted stuffed animals, a broken bicycle, a heap of frozen crayons. I had forgotten how disgusting kids were. I curled up on a pile of smudged dinosaur sheets, put my head on a lion leaking stuffing, and shut off the light.

No advice came to me from the just-woken earth, no visionary dreams. I cried, and the sleeve of my coat chafed my nose. A stash of fun-sized Halloween candy became dinner. In my sleep, a girl just like me threw up, over and over, into a hole in the ground.

When I pulled myself back above ground, it was already the middle of the morning. My cell phone was frozen from its night in the car; no missed calls. The magician's number was at the top of my recently dialed; I called it.

The speech I had rehearsed underground flew out of my head as the phone rang once, twice, three, four times. I had steeled myself to leave a dignified message when the magician's voice said, "Hello?"

"Hey," I said. My voice was so rough I coughed, and then repeated, "Hey."

"Hey," he said.

Silence stretched out.

"I want to come over," I said.

"Where are you?" he said. His voice was full of expectation. Maybe his wife still hadn't come home.

"Look, I can't—I don't want to—I can't, um, make out with you, okay?" I spat. I took a deep breath. "Can I just come over to talk?"

"Today isn't good," the magician said. "I'll see you at our usual time. Call me later in the week."

I was too shocked to respond. "Um. Okay," I said.

He hung up, and I stared at my phone's screen, as if an answer would appear to explain what had just happened. Nothing happened.

The car's engine took several tries before it turned over and slid into gear with a groan. I wasn't going to call him. I wasn't going back at my usual time. I didn't know what I was going to do. The car and I were moving; I hadn't noticed. I had exhumed myself, or sprouted. Farm land rolled by outside my window. The cornfields were dead and frozen, but in the corner of my eye they were seething beneath the frost. The earth was awake. So was I.

# GOBLIN MUSIC

## JOAN AIKEN

Joan Aiken was one of the great English fantasists. Born in Rye, East Sussex, into a family of writers, including her father, Conrad Aiken (who won a Pulitzer Prize for his poetry), and her sister, Jane Aiken Hodge, Aiken worked for the BBC and the UNIC, before she started writing professionally, mainly children's books and thrillers including classics like *The Wolves of Willoughby Chase, Black Hearts in Battersea,* and many, many others. For her books she received the Guardian Award (1969) and the Edgar Allan Poe Award (1972). Aiken died in 2004. Her most recent book is the posthumously published, *The Serial Garden: The Complete Armitage Family Stories.*

The Armitage family had been to Cornwall for a week at the end of April. They did this every year, for April 30 was old Miss Thunderhurst's birthday. Miss Thunderhurst lived next door to the Armitages and the celebrations of her birthday grew louder and wilder every year. This year was her hundredth birthday and, as Mr. Armitage said, staying at home through the festivities was not to be thought of. So the Armitages went off to their usual rented seaside cottage in the little port of Gwendreavy where, if you wanted to buy a loaf of bread, you had to row across the estuary to South-the-Water on the other side. There was a wonderful secondhand bookshop in South-the-Water; when they were sent across for the bread Mark and Harriet put in a lot of time browsing there and came back with battered copies of treasures such as *What Katie Knew, The Herr of Poynton, Eric or Little Women, More About Rebecca of Manderley Farm,* and *Simple Peter Rabbit.* The family took their cat Walrus along with them on these holidays and he had a fine time catching fish.

So it was decidedly puzzling, when the family returned home after a five-hour drive, arriving in the middle of the night, to find a line of muddy cat footprints on the white paint of the front door, leading straight upwards, from the doorstep to the lintel.

"Cats don't walk up vertical walls," said Mr. Armitage indignantly, rummaging for the front door key.

"Here it is," said his wife, getting it out of her handbag. And she added, "I *have* seen Walrus bounce upwards off a wall when the jump to the top was a bit more

283

than he reckoned he could manage."

"Granted, but not *walk up the whole wall*."

Walrus was sniffing suspiciously at the lowest of the footprints, and he let out a loud and disapproving noise between a hiss and a growl.

"Let's go in," said Mrs. Armitage hastily in case Walrus's challenge received an answer. "They are only kitten prints. And I'm dying for a cup of tea and bed."

"I'm surprised to see that marquee still there," grumbled her husband, carrying bags into the house.

Since Miss Thunderhurst's party had been planned for an extra big one this year, she had rented a marquee for the occasion, and got permission to put it in farmer Beezeley's field across the road. The car's headlights had caught the great grey-white canvas shape as the Armitages turned into their own driveway.

"So we still have all that nuisance ahead, poles clanking and trucks blocking the road while they take it down," growled Mr. Armitage, as ruffled as Walrus.

"Oh I expect they do that tomorrow while we're still getting unpacked," said his wife. "Here's your tea, dear. I'm going up."

But when Mrs. Armitage was halfway up the stairs, the most amazing noise started up outside the house. It seemed to be piano music played by giants. It was a fugue—the same tune played again and again, overlapping like tiles on a roof, in different keys, some high, some low.

"It's rather terrific," said Mark, impressed in spite of himself.

"Terrific? It's the most ear-splitting racket I ever heard! At three minutes to one a.m.? Are they out of their flagrant minds? I'm going across to give them what-for!"

"Oh, Gilbert! Do you think that's neighbourly? We don't want to be on bad terms with Miss Thunderhurst."

"How long does she expect her birthday to last? It's the fourth of May, dammit."

Mr. Armitage strode out of the front door, down the steps, across the road, and Mark followed him, curious to see what instruments produced that astonishing sound.

The door-flaps of the marquee were folded back. A dim glow inside was just enough to show that the big tent was completely packed with people—far more, surely, than even Miss Thunderhurst would have invited to her birthday celebrations—and Miss Thunderhurst knew every soul in the village.

"Where is Miss Thunderhurst? I want to speak to her," Mr. Armitage said to a shortish, stoutish person who met him in the entrance.

"Miss Thunderhurst has long since departed to her own place of residence."

"Oh, *indeed!*—well, who's in charge here? You are making a devilish rumpus and it has to stop. At once!"

"Oh, no, sir. That is not quite possible."

"Not possible? I should just about think it *is* possible! You are making an ear-splitting row. It has to stop. At once!"

"No, sir. To make music is our right."

"*Right?* Who the deuce do you think you are?"

"We are the Niffel people. Our own place of residence—Niffelheim-under-Lyme—has been rendered unfit for occupation. They set light to an opencast coal mine on top of our cave habitation, and the roof collapsed. Luckily there was no loss of life, but many were injured. Much damage. So we appealed to the County Council and they have found us this dwelling for the time. We are sadly cramped but it must serve until we find a more suitable home."

"Oh! I see! Very well. If the Council settled you here, that's different. I suppose you don't know how long you'll be here? … But you must, *immediately*, stop making that atrocious row. People need to sleep."

"No, sir. To make the music is our right. Is our need."

"Not at this time of night, dammit!"

"Sir, we are nocturnal people. Earthfolk. Gloam Goblins. Our work is done at nighttime. By day we sleep. Dark is our day. Day is our dark. Music is our stay."

"Who is in charge here? Who is your president—or whatever you have? Your head person?"

"I am the Spokesman. My name is Albrick," The small man said with dignity. "Our First Lady—our Sovereign—is the Lady Holdargh."

"Well let me speak to her."

"She is not here at this time. She travels. She seeks a place for us."

"Oh. Well—won't you, in the meantime, *please* stop making this hideous din!"

"No, sir. That we cannot do. It is our must." And as Mr. Armitage looked at him in incredulous outrage, he repeated with dignity, "It is our must."

"Come on, Dad." Mark plucked his father's arm. "We can't make a fuss if they are here by permission of the Council. I'll lend you a pair of earplugs."

Very unwillingly and reluctantly Mr. Armitage allowed himself to be led back across the road to his own house. There he was supplied with earplugs by Mark (who used them when practising with his Group) and a sleeping-pill by his wife.

Harriet, during this interval, had opened a tin of sardines for Walrus, who was upset and nervous at the traces of an intruder around his home. Mark and his father came back just as she was about to go out in search of them. Mr. Armitage stomped off gloomily upstairs, muttering, "Niffel people indeed!"

"What's going on?" Harriet asked Mark. "Couldn't Dad get them to stop?"

"No, he couldn't. They aren't Miss Thunderhurst's guests at all. They are goblins—displaced goblins."

"Goblins? I've never met a goblin. Who displaced them?"

"A burning coal mine. Coal is burned underground these days to make gas. The goblins were obliged to shift. They didn't seem unfriendly. Their spokesman was quite reasonable. They are nocturnal. They work at night. And they need music to work."

"I wonder what sort of work they do? Could you see? Were they doing it?"

"No, I couldn't see. There were a whole lot of them in the tent—several hundred at least. All crammed together in a very dim light."

"Well!" said Harriet. "Fancy having a group of hardworking goblins across the road. I can't wait to see what they make. I'll go across after breakfast."

"They'll all be asleep," her brother pointed out.

"Bother! So they will. But I suppose they start to get active after sunset, about half past seven. I'll go and call on them then. Now I'm off to bed. Come on, Walrus."

But Walrus was going out, to watch for Goblin cats, and, if necessary, beat them up.

The full moon had just worked its way round the corner of the house, and was blazing in at Harriet's bedroom window, throwing a great square of white light across her bedroom wall.—Harriet had once sat in a train opposite two women who were evidently sisters in some religious order. They wore black habits and white wimples. They were laughing a great deal and talking to each other nonstop in some foreign language that was full of s's and k's. Harriet could not at all understand what they were saying, but she somehow took a great liking to them and, when she got home, drew a picture of them from memory and hung it up on her bedroom wall. Two or three months later she noticed an interesting phenomenon: when the moon shone on her picture, she could see the two women's hands move about and sometimes catch a little of what they were saying. Now, too, she could partly understand the language, but one of the two women, the spectacled one, had a bad stammer, and Harriet only caught a word here and a word there.

"Refugees—immigrants—l-l-look after them somehow—p-p-poor d-d-dears—"

Tonight the moonlight was fully on the picture, and the two women were deeply engrossed in what they were saying.

"Hardworking—industrious—deserving."

"No place for them here—"

"Only l-l-lead to t-t-trouble—"

Harriet went and stood in front of the picture. "Excuse me—" she began politely. Then she realised that she was blocking off the moonlight from the picture and the ladies stopped talking and moving their hands.

"I'm so sorry, I didn't mean to interrupt," said Harriet, and stepped to one side. But now a cloud had drifted across the moon and the ladies remained silent. Harriet waited for ten minutes, but by the time the cloud had floated away, the moon had moved also, and no longer shone in at the window.

"I'll try again tomorrow," thought Harriet, and went to bed, for she was tired.

In the morning, as soon as breakfast was over, Mark and Harriet raced across the road to inspect the new occupants of farmer Beezeley's meadow.

The Gloam Goblins were packing up their work materials and preparing their evening meal. They were evidently smiths and potters. They had portable kilns and forges.

"They seem to use solar heat," said Mark. "It's very adaptable of them! If they lived underground up to now they must have changed their habits very quickly."

"Oh look," said Harriet. "There are stalls with things for sale."

The things for sale were lace made of filigree iron, exquisitely fine and light; also iron jewellry, and pottery—bowls, plates, cups, jugs, also very light and delicate, ornamented with a dark-green and white glazed pattern resembling the foam on a wave crest.

"Ma would like these," said Harriet. Mrs. Armitage collected china and had brought back from Cornwall an enormous blue-and-white platter with a romantic landscape on it which she had found in a junk shop in South-the-Water.

"I'll come back later with some money and buy one of these," Harriet told the little woman behind the stall, who smiled and nodded.

The Goblins were about half the size of humans. Their skin was brown and weather-worn as if at sometime they had lived out of doors for centuries. Their faces were rugged, rather plain but friendly and honest-looking. Their manners were somewhat abrupt, as if all they wanted was to be left alone to get on with what they were doing. Mark and Harriet now felt rather embarrassed and apologetic at their plan to inspect the new arrivals like creatures in a zoo. They retreated from the doorway, taking in as quickly and unobtrusively as possible all the activities that were going on: pots of vegetable stew being stirred over small fires, bedding rolls pulled out of sacks and spread on the ground, children's faces being washed in basins of water. There were cats and dogs, too, of a size to match their owners.

"You don't mind us just looking?" Mark said to Albrick, the man who had talked to his father. Albrick was evidently a smith; he was packing up a small anvil and a portable forge and cooling off his tools in a pail of water.

"Very well cannot stop you, can I?" said Albrick gruffly. But he added, "You are alright. But some folk do more than just look—they want us to go. Where we stopped before here, we needed guards with swords and pistols. And the young ones needed to go out with guards. Folk in this village not bad—but not welcoming. What can we expect?"

"I expect—if it weren't for the music at night—"

"Ah, the music. It is our must." Albrick glanced toward the interior of the tent and Mark and Harriet, following the direction of his eyes, had a glimpse of a massive structure—a portable organ?—which a party of Goblins were wrapping up in layers of thick felt.

"Our must," Albrick repeated. "Work and music."

"Oh!" said Mark. "Is it an organ? Oh, I'd love to play it. Could I? *Could* I?"

Mark had piano lessons from Professor Johansen in the village and was understood to show promise. He was certainly very keen and practised a great deal.

"You wish to play our keyboard?" Albrick said doubtfully. "You do nothing foolish?"

"Oh *no!*"

"He does play quite well," Harriet put in hopefully.

"We see. We see. Not now. I put my child to bed. Goodbye. We talk again."

Albrick nodded in a dismissive manner and called, "Dwine! Dwiney! Bed-time!"

"Here, Father!" A small tousle-headed Goblin child came rushing towards him followed by a Goblin kitten. "Come, Fryxse!" she called to the cat. But Fryxse was small, wayward, and playful. He clawed and scampered his way up the side of the marquee and disappeared. On his way, no doubt, to go and tease Walrus.

Mark and Harriet strolled along the village street to find how the rest of the neighbours were reacting to having a community of Gloam Goblins deposited on their doorstep.

Mr. Budd the blacksmith said, "They're not bad. Decent enough. The chair-person, that Albrick, he's a sensible chap. Good workman too. Knows what's what. He comes round to my forge for a chat now and then. There's not much I can tell him about iron."

"But what about their music?"

Mr. Budd gave a half grin, rubbing his bristly jaw.

"Don't worrit me none. I'm deaf, see? All blacksmiths are deaf, 'count of the hammering. I pulls the covers over me head, nights, and sleep through the lot. And little Dwiney, his kid, she'd be in here all evening long, with her cat, if I didn't chase her home to bed. Taken a fair shine to her, I have. Sharp as a tack, she be."

Mrs. Case, at the village shop, was not so enthusiastic.

"Only middling customers, see? Grow a lot of their own stuff, they do, in pots and trays. Vegetarians, like. I will say, they pay up promptly for what they do buy—but at first they wanted to pay in gold coins. 'Gold?' I say to them, 'I'm not having any of that fancy stuff. You'll have to go and change it at Mr. Watson's bank.' Which they did, I'm bound to say. A lot of them never heard of a bank before. The music? Drives me up the wall, that do. Shouldn't be allowed."

"They need it for their work," Mark said.

"Well, they oughta do their work somewhere else, where they won't drive honest day-biding folk clean balmy. That's what I say! And so do lots of neighbours."

Half the village shared Mrs. Case's feelings. If the newcomers had to make such an ear-splitting row in order to do their work, why then they must move to a place where nobody could hear them. Else why couldn't they alter their habits to fit in with their new neighbours?

Mrs. Owlet, a witch, the Chair Person of the Parish Council, threatened to stage a protest about the new arrivals.

"And it will be terribly inconvenient if she does," worried Mrs. Armitage, who was secretary to the Council. "Last time she protested it was about the plan for a bypass running through Titania Copse; never shall I forget the trouble."

"The cows were all giving sour milk for eight weeks," remembered Mr. Armitage. "Mind, she was quite right about the bypass. What is she threatening to do this time?"

"Put up a pillar in the middle of the village green and stand on it till somebody gives way. Like Saint Simeon the Stylites."

"I should think the pillar would collapse. Mrs. Owlet must weigh as much as the Statue of Liberty. Ask her round for a drink, and I'll see if I can't persuade her to think of some other form of protest."

"What in the world can we offer her to drink?"

"She likes low-calorie poison," Harriet said. "Sue Case told me her mother orders it specially for Mrs. Owlet and they deliver four cases a week.

"Oh well, we'd better get some. And some wolfsbane-flavoured cheese straws."

"I'll make those," Harriet offered. "And little Dwiney Albrick can help."

Little Dwiney Albrick, that sociable child, had taken a great fancy to the Armitage family and spent a lot of time in their house, unless her father came and fetched her.

"Don't let her be a nuisance to ye, ma'am," he said to Mrs. Armitage.

"No, we're very fond of her, Mr. Albrick. Her and that crazy kitten of hers…"

The Armitage house contained a room which was simply known as the Top Room. In it were kept all the things that members of the family had acquired in one way or another, but had no plans for just at present: the huge blue-and-white platter that Mrs. Armitage had bought in Cornwall; a spinning-wheel for llama's wool that was waiting for Harriet to collect enough wool from Hebdons' llama farm; a fishing-rod for when Mr. Armitage had a spare day from the office to visit his carp pools; several thousand empty egg-boxes stacked against the wall which Mark intended to make into a launching-pad for the flint-powered space-craft that he was in the process of constructing.

Mark spent more time than the rest of the family in this pleasant attic, with its skylight looking out over the village green, and little Dwiney and her kitten liked to come and keep him company. Dwiney was a quiet and untroublesome companion; she drew pictures, using a box of crayons that Harriet had given her, arranged little chips of flint into patterns, and sang to herself in a soft, true little voice while Mark played on the shallow, tinkling old piano that also lived up there.

Dwiney's kitten was something else. It was not that he was badly behaved—after a tendency to tease Walrus had been firmly dealt with by that character—but he was so interested in everything and so inquisitive that it was not safe to leave him unobserved for more than a very few minutes.

On the evening that Mrs. Owlet was invited for a drink, Mark was working on his space-craft and chose to stay upstairs; he was never particularly fond of adult company and he thought Mrs. Owlet was an old bore anyway; always carrying on about the human race and their habit of hurting and killing one another.

"Can't we persuade you to try some other form of protest?" suggested Mr. Armitage hopefully when the lady guest had been provided with a plateful of wolfsbane cheese straws and a brimming beaker of low-calorie poison.

"Why, pray?" snapped Mrs. Owlet. She was a large, commanding lady; Harriet imagined her on top of an eighty-foot column on the village green and decided that it would be an impressive sight.

"Well—I don't want to discourage you—but those young tearaways on their motorbikes—not from our village, I'm thankful to say, they come over from Trottenworth—I don't like to think what they might get up to if they arrived one evening and saw you on your column—what's it going to be made of, by the way?"

"Fuel containers," snapped Mrs. Owlet, "threaded together on a ship's mast I purchased from the United Sorcerer's Supply Stores; they are erecting it now, on the green. It will be a most superior addition to the village—I expect photographers from the national press, and our Member of Parliament has been sent an invitation; he has half promised to come down on Sunday—and of course representatives from the National Trust and Downlands Heritage will certainly come—I expect a sculpture award, it will certainly put our village on the map."

"But it is on the map already," said Mrs. Armitage plaintively. "We surely don't want a lot of tourists and day-trippers coming and rubbernecking—do we?—and I'm sure the poor Goblins don't either. They hate being stared at. It would probably be at times when they would be asleep—"

Mr. Armitage saw that their guest was displeased by these remarks, and made haste to change the subject.

"How do you plan to get to the top of the pillar?" he inquired, thinking of cranes and hoists.

Mrs. Owlet was affronted.

"To someone with my qualifications that presents no problem at all," she said shortly. "I merely levitate. In fact"—she looked at her watch—"I should be on my way now."

And, nodding perfunctory thanks, she drained her glass and left the room and the house.

At this moment, upstairs, little Dwiney's kitten Fryxse was sitting in the middle of the Top Room, eying Mark's massive rampart of egg-boxes stacked against the wall. Mark, at the piano, was playing a tune which he had christened "Dwiney's Night Song." He hoped to play it to Mr. Albrick, to persuade him to let Mark have a try on the organ.

Dwiney was listening with total attention. When Mark had finished she gave a sigh of pure happiness. "Oh, that was nice, Mark! Play it again!"

But, at that moment, Fryxse finished his calculations, and sprang to the top of the egg-box mountain, bouncing lightly halfway to give himself extra launching-power.

Mark and his father argued for years afterwards about whether the fact that, by sheer unfortunate accident, one of the egg-boxes was *not* empty but contained six eggs and a use-by label that was five years old made any difference to the ultimate outcome.

There was a thunderous crash, followed by the slithering sound of a torrent of egg-boxes cascading down the attic stairs to the bedroom floor. This was accompanied, simultaneously, by the powerful smell of six five-year-old eggs, which poured through the house like poison gas and caused the Armitage parents to run into the garden in case it *was* poison gas.

Poor Fryxse, the cause of this cataclysm, was terrified, and rushed from the room, down the stairs, and out through the front door, which Mrs. Owlet had left open behind her.

"Fryxse! Come back! It's alright! Come *back!*"

Dwiney rushed after him—out the front door, through the garden, across the road—straight into the path of the young tearaways from Trottenworth on their motor-bikes come to laugh at the lady balancing on top of her pillar.

Both Dwiney and her kitten were killed instantly.

That night, when the square of moonlight slipped round the wall to the picture of the two Sisters, Harriet addressed them.

"Please listen! Things are in a very bad way here. The Goblins are terribly unhappy. Mrs. Owlet is threatening to jump down off her pillar in protest at the Goblins being here if they don't leave and go somewhere else. They say they don't care if she does jump. But they have nowhere to go…"

A black cloud drifted across the sky and blotted out the picture of the Sisters.

Harriet went unhappily to bed. Since the house still reeked of five-year-old eggs she packed a lavender-bag under her pillow. But it made very little difference.

Next day was little Dwiney's funeral.

One or two people (including Mrs. Owlet from her pillar) raised objections to little Dwiney being buried in the village churchyard, but the Vicar responded so fiercely that they soon backed down.

Everybody was at the ceremony except Mrs. Owlet. The funeral had been held at twilight so as not to interfere with anybody's habits. The villagers were just coming home from work, the Goblins just waking up. A huge mass of flowers had been brought by different people and laid in the corner of the churchyard where the new small grave had been dug for Dwiney and her kitten.

Harriet arrived just as the service was about to begin. An enormous Hunter's Moon had recently risen and was floating above the churchyard wall, competing with the setting sun. Harriet had been in her bedroom, consulting with the pictured Sisters.

And this time she had obtained a reply.

The Vicar, ending his short sad talk by the small grave said:

"And I'm sure that none of us would wish or expect our good neighbours the Goblins to move away from our village now, since they must leave this sad token behind them. We were all fond of little Dwiney—she was like our own child—we would never dream of asking them to leave—"

"Yes we would!" shouted Mrs. Owlet from the top of her pillar. "If they don't agree to get away from here by the end of this week, I'm going to jump from my pillar! And that will make a heap of trouble for them!"

"So jump, you old bag!" shouted one of the Goblins—not Albrick, who was standing wrapped in silence by the grave.

Mrs. Owlet jumped.

Her landing was not at all spectacular, for Mark and some of his friends had piled all the empty egg-boxes under the column in a massive, rustling heap which also contained the fragments of Mrs. Armitage's blue platter and Harriet's spinning wheel. And smelt of five-year-old eggs. So the landing was soft, if untidy.

But meanwhile, at the graveside, Harriet had come forward, and was saying, "I have a message for the Goblin people from their Lady Holdargh. She has talked to the two Sisters who live on my bedroom wall, and she wishes to tell you that she has found a good place underground for you all to live, in a cave in southern Tasmania. Plenty of room for all, and there will be no problem about the music. She will be expecting you there tomorrow by E-Travel."

"Tasmania!" whispered some of the crowd. "That be a long way sure-lye!"

"Don't worry about little Dwiney's grave, Mr. Albrick," whispered Harriet to the man beside her. "Mark and I will look after it very carefully, I promise!"

Next day the Goblins were gone and there was no trace of them left. The huge tent was clean and tidy as if it had just been put up. Only on the Armitages' doorstep were two parcels, containing a very beautiful iron lace-work necklace and an elegant green-and-white bowl.

Mark said sadly, "I never did get a chance to play on their organ." And Harriet sighed as they looked at the last book saved from their Cornish trip—*Elizabeth and Her Secret German Garden*—somehow at the moment she had no wish to read it.

Every year on Dwiney's grave they found a very uncommon flower, a beautiful white star, not like any product of English fields or gardens. "*Actinotus helianthi*," the Vicar said. It could only have come from Tasmania.

# MACHINE MAID

## MARGO LANAGAN

Margo Lanagan was born in Newcastle, New South Wales, Australia, and has a BA in History from Sydney University. She spent ten years as a freelance book editor and currently makes a living as a technical writer. Lanagan wrote teenage romances under various pseudonyms before publishing junior and teenage fiction novels under her own name, including fantasies *WildGame*, *The Tankermen*, and *Walking Through Albert*. She has also written an installment in a shared-world YA fantasy series, The Quentaris Chronicles: *Treasure Hunters of Quentaris*, and three acclaimed original story collections: *White Time*, World Fantasy Award winner *Black Juice*, and *Red Spikes*. Her latest book is a fantasy novel for young adults, *Tender Morsels*. Lanagan currently lives in Sydney with her partner and their two children.

We came to Cuttajunga through the goldfields; Mr Goverman was most eager to show me the sites of his successes.

They were impressive only in being so very unprepossessing. How could such dusty earth, such quantities of it piled up discarded by the road and all up and down the disembowelled hills, have yielded anything of value? How did this devastated place have any connection with the metal of crowns and rings and chains of office, and with the palaces and halls where such things were worn and wielded, on the far side of the globe?

Well, it must, I said to myself, as I stood obediently at the roadside, feeling the dust stain my hems and spoil the shine of my Pattison's shoes. See how much attention is being paid it, by this over-layer of dusty men shoveling, crawling, winching up buckets or baskets of broken rock, or simply standing, at rest from their labours as they watch one of their number return, proof in his carriage and the cut of his coat that they are not toiling here for nothing. There must be something of value here.

"This hill is fairly well dug out," said Mr Goverman, "and there was only ever wash-gold from ancient watercourses here in any case. 'Tis good for nobody but Chinamen now." And indeed I saw several of the creatures, in their smockish clothing and their umbrella-ish hats, each with his long pigtail, earnestly working at a pile of tailings in the gully that ran by the road.

The town was hardly worthy of the name, it was such a collection of sordid drinking-palaces, fragile houses and luckless miners lounging about the lanes. Bowling alleys there were, and a theatre, and stew-houses offering meals for so little, one wondered how the keepers turned a profit. And all blazed and fluttered and showed its patches and cracks in the unrelenting sunlight.

The only woman I saw leaned above the street on a balcony railing that looked set to give way beneath her generous arms. She was dressed with profound tastelessness and she smoked a pipe, as a gypsy or a man would, surveying the street below and having no care that it saw her so clearly. I guessed her to be Mrs Bawden, there being a painted canvas sign strung between the veranda posts beneath her feet: "MRS HUBERT BAWDEN/Companions Live and Electric." Her gaze went over us as my husband drew my attention to how far one could see across the wretched diggings from this elevation. I felt as if the creature had raked me into disarray with her nails. *She* would know exactly the humiliations Mr Goverman had visited on me in the night; she would be smiling to herself at my prim and upright demeanour now, at the thought of what had been pushed at these firm-closed lips while the animal that was my husband pleaded and panted above.

On we went, thank goodness, and soon we were viewing a panorama similar to that of the dug-out hill, only the work here involved larger machinery than the human body. Parties of men trooped in and out of several caverns dug into the hillside, pushing roughly made trucks along rails between the mines and the precarious, thundering houses where the stamping-machines punished the gold from the obdurate quartz. My husband had launched into a disquisition on the geological feature that resulted in this hill's having borne him so much fruit, and if truth be told it gave me some pleasure to imagine the forces he described at their work in their unpeopled age, heaving and pressing, breaking and slicing and finally resting, their uppermost layers washed and smoothed by rains, while the quartz-seam underneath, split away and forced upward from its initial deposition, held secret in its cracks and crevices its gleamless measure of gold.

But we must move on, to reach our new home before dark. The country grew ever more desolate, dry as a whisper and grey, grey under cover of this grey, disorderly forest. Unearthly birds the size of men stalked among the ragged tree-trunks, and others, lurid, shrieking, flocked to the boughs. In places the trees were cut down and their bodies piled into great windrows; set alight, and with an estate's new house rising half-built from the hill or field beyond, they presented a scene more suggestive of devastation by war than of the hopefulness and ambition of a youthful colony.

Cuttajunga when we reached it was not of such uncomfortable newness; Mr Goverman had bought it from a gentleman pastoralist who had tamed and tended his allotment of this harsh land, but in the end had not loved it enough to be buried in it, and had returned to Sussex to live out his last years. The house had a settled look, and ivy, even, covered the shady side; the garden was a miracle of

Home plants watered by an ingenious system of runnels brought up by electric pump from the stream, and the fields on which our fortune grazed in the form of fat black cattle were free of the stumps and wreckage that marked other properties as having so recently been torn from the primeval Bush.

"I hope you will be very happy here," said my husband, handing me down from the sulky.

The smile I returned him felt very wan from within, for now there would be nothing in the way of society or culture to diminish, or to compensate me for, the ghastly rituals of married life, now there would only be Mr Goverman and me, marooned on this island of wealth and comfort, amid the fields and cattle, bordered on all sides by the tattered wilderness.

Cuttajunga was all as he had described it to me during the long grey miles: the kitchen anchored by its weighty stove and ornamented with shining pans, the orchard and the vegetable garden, which Mr Goverman immediately set the electric yard-man watering, for they were parched after his short absence. There was a farm manager, Mr Fredericks, who appeared not to know how to greet and converse with such a foreign creature as a woman, but instead droned to my husband about stock movements and water and feed until I thought he must be some kind of lunatic. The housekeeper, Mrs Sanford, was a blowsy, bobbing, distractible woman who behaved as if she were accustomed to being slapped or shouted into line rather than reasoned with. The maid Sarah Poplin was of the poorest material. "She has some native blood in her," Mr Goverman told me *sotto voce* when she had flounced away from his introductions. "You will be a marvellously civilising influence on her, I am sure."

"I can but try to be," I murmured. I had been forewarned, by Melbourne matrons as well as by Mr Goverman himself, of the difficulty of finding and retaining staff, what with the goldfields promising any man or woman an independent fortune, should they happen to kick over the right pebble "up north" or "out west."

The other maid, the mechanical one Mr Goverman had promised me, lived seated in a little cabinet attached to a charging chamber under the back stairs. Her name was Clarissa—I did not like to call such creatures by real names, but she would not recognise commands without their being prefaced by that combination of guttural and sibilant. She was of unnervingly fine quality, and beautiful with it; except for the rigidity of her face I would say she was undoubtedly more comely than I was. Her eyes were the most realistic I had seen, blue-irised and glossy between thickly lashed lids; her hair sprang dark from her clear brow without the clumping that usually characterises an electric servant's hair; each strand must be set individually. She would have cost a great deal, both to craft and to import from her native France; I had never seen so close a simulacrum of a real person, myself.

Mr Goverman, seeing how impressed I was, insisted on commanding Clarissa upright and showing me her interior workings. I hardly knew where to rest my eyes as my husband's hands unlaced the automaton's dress behind with such practised motions, but once he had removed the panels from her back and head, the intricate machine-scape that gleamed and whirred within as Clarissa enacted his simple commands so fascinated me that I was able to forget the womanliness of this figure and the maleness of my man as he explained how this impeller drove this shaft to turn this cam and translate into the lifting of Clarissa's heavy, strong arms *this* way, and the bowing of her body *that* way, all the movements smooth, balanced and, again, the subtlest and most realistic I had witnessed in one of these creatures.

"Does she speak, then?" I said, peering into the back of her head.

"No, no," he said. "There is not sufficient room with all her other functions to allow for speaking."

"Why then are her mouth-parts so carefully made?" I moved my own head to allow more window-light into Clarissa's head-workings; the red silk-covered cavity that was the doll's mouth enlivened the brass and steel scenery, and I could discern some system of rings around it, their inner edges clothed with India-rubber, which seemed purpose-built for producing the movements of speech.

"Oh, she once spoke," said my husband. "She once sang. She is adapted from her usage as an entertainer on the Paris stage. I was impressed by the authenticity of her movements. But, alas, my dear, if you are to have your carpets beaten you must forgo her lovely singing."

He fixed her head-panel back into place. "She interests you," he said. "Have I taken an engineer for a wife?" He spoke in an amused tone, but I heard the edge in it of my mother's anxiety, felt the vacancy in my hands where she had snatched away the treatise on artificial movement I had taken from my brother Artie's bookshelf. *So unbecoming, for a girl to know such things.* She clutched the book to herself and looked me up and down as if I were some kind of electrically powered creature, and malfunctioning into the bargain. *For your pretty head to be full of… of cog-wheels and machine-oil,* she said disgustedly. *I will find you some more suitable reading.* My husband officiously buttoning the doll-dress; my mother sweeping from the parlour with the fascinating book—I recognised this dreary feeling. As soon as I evinced a budding interest in some area of worldly affairs, people inevitably began working to keep it from blossoming. I was meant to be vapid and colourless like my mother, a silent helpmeet in the shadows of Father and my brothers; I was not to engage with the world myself, but only to witness and encourage the men's engagement, to be a decorative background to it, like the parlour wallpaper, like the draped window against which my mother smiled and sat mute as Father discoursed to our dinner-guests, the window that was obscured by impressive velvet at night, that in daytime prettified the world outside with its cascade of lace foliage.

I had barely had time to accustom myself to my new role as mistress of Cuttajunga when Mr Goverman informed me that he would be absent for a period of weeks, riding the boundaries of his estate and perhaps venturing further up country in the company of his distant neighbour Captain Jollyon and some of that gentleman's stockmen and tamed natives.

"Perhaps you will appreciate my leaving you," he said, the night before he left, as he withdrew himself from me after having completed the marriage act. "You need not endure the crudeness of my touching you, for a little while."

My face was locked aside, stiff as a doll's on the pillow, and my entire body was motionless with revulsion, with humiliation. Still I did feel relief, firstly that he was done, and would not require to emit himself at my face or onto my bosom, and secondly, yes, that the nightmare of our congress would not recur for at least two full weeks and possibly more. I turned from him, and waited—not long—for his breathing to deepen and lengthen into sleep, before I rose to wash the slime of him, the smell of him, from my person.

After the riding-party left, my staff waited a day or two before deserting me. Sarah Poplin disappeared in the night, without a word. The following afternoon, as I was contemplating which of her tasks I should next instruct Mrs Sanford to take up, that woman came into my parlour and announced that she and Mr Fredericks had married and now intended to leave my service, Mr Fredericks to try his luck on the western goldfields. Direct upon her quitting the room, she said, she would be quitting the house for the wider world.

"But Mrs Sanf—Mrs Fredericks," I said. "You leave me quite solitary and help-less. Whatever shall I do?"

"You have that machine-woman, at least, I tell myself. She's the strength of two of me."

"But no intelligence," I said. "She cannot accomplish half the tasks you can, with a quarter the subtlety. But you are right, she will never leave me, at least. She will stay out of stupidity, if not loyalty."

At the sound of that awkward word "loyalty" the new Mrs Fredericks blushed, and soon despite my protestations she was gone, walking off without a backward glance along the western road. Her *inamorata* walked beside her, curved like a wilting grass-stalk over her stout figure, droning who knew what passionate promises into that pitiless ear? The house, meaningless, unattended around me, echoed with the fact that I was not the kind of woman servants felt compelled either to obey or to protect. Not under these conditions, at any rate, so remote from society and opinion.

I stood watching her go, keeping myself motionless rather than striding up and down as I wished to in my distress; should either of them turn, I did not want them to see the state of terror to which they had reduced me.

I was alone. My nearest respectable neighbour was Captain Jollyon's wife, a pretty, native-born chatterer with a house-party of Melbourne friends currently gathered around her, a day's ride from here. I could not abide the thought of throwing myself on the mercies of so inconsequential a person.

And I was not quite alone, was I? I was not quite helpless. I had electric servants—the yard-man and Clarissa. And I had... I pressed my hands to my waist and sat rather heavily in a woven cane chair, heedless for the moment of the afternoon sun shafting in under the veranda roof. I was almost certain by now that I carried Cuttajunga's heir in my womb. All my washing, all my shrinking from my husband's advances, had not been sufficient to stop his seed taking root in me. He had "covered" me as a stallion covers a mare, and in time I would bring forth a Master Goverman, who would complete my banishment into utter obscurity behind my family of menfolk.

But for now—I straightened in the creaking, ticking chair, focusing again on the two diminishing figures as they flickered along the shade-dappled road between the bowing, bleeding, bark-shedding eucalypt trees—for now, I had Master Goverman tucked away neatly inside me, all his needs met, much as Clarissa's and the yard-man's were by their respective electrification chambers. He required no more action from me than that I merely continue, and sustain His Little Lordship by sustaining my own self.

I did not ride to Captain Jollyon's; I did not take the sulky into the town to send the police after my disloyal servants, or to hire any replacements for them. I decided that I would manage, with Clarissa and the yard-man. I had more than three months' stores; I had a thriving vegetable garden; and I did not long for human company so strongly that stupid company would suffice, or uncivilised. If the truth be told, the more I considered my situation, the greater I felt it suited me, and the more relieved I was to have been abandoned by that sly Poplin girl, by Mr Droning Fredericks and his resentful-seeming wife. I felt, indeed, that I was well rid of them, that I might enjoy this short season where I prevailed, solitary, in this gigantic landscape, before life and my husband returned, crowding around me, bidding me this way and that, interfering with my body, and my mind, and my reputation, in ways I could neither control nor rebuff.

And so I lived a few days proudly independent, calling my mechanical servants out, the yard-man from his charging shed and Clarissa from her cupboard under the stairs, only when I required them to undertake the more tedious and strenuous tasks of watering, or sweeping, or stirring the copper. And I returned them thence when those were completed; I kept neither of them sitting about the place to give the illusion of a resident population. I was quite comfortable walking from room to empty room, and striding or riding about my husband's empty property unaccompanied.

After several days, despite fully occupying myself as my own housekeeper and chambermaid, I began to feel restless when evening came and it was time to retire to my parlour and occupy myself with ladylike pursuits. Needlework of the decorative kind had always infuriated me; nothing in my new house was sufficiently worn to require mending yet; I had never sung well, or played the piano or the violin as my cousins did and my brother James; I could sketch, but if the choice was between reproducing the drear landscapes I moved in by day, and stretching my heartstrings by re-creating remembered scenes of London and the surrounding countryside, I felt disinclined to exercise that talent. My husband had bought me a library, but I found it to contain nothing but fashionable novels, most of which gave me the same sense of irritation, of having my mind and my being confined to meaningless matters, as conversation with that gentleman did, or with women such as Mrs Jollyon, and it was a great freedom to cease attempting to occupy my time with them.

Then, one afternoon, I set Clarissa to sweeping the paved paths around the house, and I sat myself at a corner of the veranda ready to redirect her when she reached me. I was labouring on a letter to Mother—a daughterly letter, full of lies and optimism, telling the news of my own impending motherhood as if it were wonderful, as if it were ordinary. I looked up from my duties at the automaton as she trundled and swept, thorough and inhumanly regular and pauseless in her sweeping. My disinclination to continue my letter, and the glimpse I had had of Clarissa's workings through the opening of her back combined with the fragmented memory of a diagram I had examined in Artie's treatise—which I had borrowed many times in secret after Mother had forbidden it me, which I had wrestled to understand. In something like a stroke of mental lightning I saw the full chain of causes and effects that produced one movement, her turning from the left side to the right at the limit of her sweeping. I could not have described it; I could not even recall it fully, a moment later. But the flash was sufficient to make me forget my letter, my mother. Intently I watched Clarissa progress down the path, hoping for another such insight. None came, and she reached me, and I turned her with a command to the right so that she would sweep the path down to the hedge, and still I watched her, as dutifully she went on. And then, in the bottom half of my written page, I drew some lines, the shape of one of the cams I had seen, that had something of a duckbill-like projection from its edge, a length of thin cable coming up to a pulley. The marks were hardly more than traces of idle movements; they were barely identifiable as mechanical parts, but as they streaked and ghosted up out of the paper I knew that I had found myself an occupation for my long and lonely days. It was more purposeless than embroidery; it would produce nothing of beauty; it would not make me a better daughter, wife or mother, but it would satisfy me utterly.

She never failed to unnerve me, smiling out in her vague way when I opened the door of the cabinet under the stairs. Her toes would move in her shoes, her fingers splay and crook and enact the last other movements of the lubrication sequence. Her beautiful mouth, too, pursed and stretched and made moues, subtle and unnatural. Un-mouthlike sounds came from behind the India-rubber lips, inside the busy mechanical head. Her ears were cupped themselves slightly for the sound of my commands.

"Clarissa: Stand," I would say, and step back to make room for her.

She would bend forward and push herself upright, using her hands on the rim of the cabinet.

"Clarissa: Forward. Two steps," I would command, and she would perform them.

Now I could see the loosened back of the garment, the wheels and workings coming to a stop inside her. I left them visible now, unless I was putting her to work outside, so that I would not have the same troubles over and over, removing the panel from her back. I brought the lamp nearer, my gaze already on the parts I had been mis-drawing in my tiredness at the end of the day before. I would already be absorbed in her labyrinthine structure; even as I followed her to the study I would be checking her insides against the fistful of drawings I had made—the "translations," as I liked to think of them. She was a marvellous thing, which I was intent on reducing to mere mechanics; by the end of my project it would no longer disturb me to lock her away in her cabinet as into a coffin; I would know her seeming aliveness for the illusion it was; I would have diagrammed all the person-ness, all her apparent humanity, out of her. She would unnerve me no longer; I would know her for exactly what she was.

By the time Mr Goverman returned home I had discovered much more than I wished to. I made my first unwelcome finding one breathlessly hot afternoon perhaps three days before he arrived, when I had brought Clarissa to the study, commanded her to kneel and opened the back of her head, and was busy drawing what I could see of her mouth-parts behind the chutes and membrane-discs and tuning-forks of her hearing apparatus. Soft gusts of hot wind ventured in through the window from time to time, the gentlest buffetings, which did nothing to refresh me, but only moved my looser hair or vaguely rippled the buttoned edge of Clarissa's gown.

It was frustrating, attempting to draw this mouth. I do not know what ex-clamation I loosed in my annoyance, but it must have included a guttural and a sibilant at some point and further sounds the doll mistook for a command, for suddenly, smoothly, expensively, she lifted her arms from her sides where she knelt, manipulated her lovely fingers, her beautifully engineered elbow and shoulder joints, and drew her loosened bodice down from her shoulders, so that her bosom, so unbodily and yet so naked-seeming, was exposed to the hot study air. I heard in the momentarily still air the muted clicks and slidings within her head—I saw, indistinctly in the shadows, partly behind other workings, the movements of her mouth readying itself for something.

I rose and stood before her; she remained kneeling, straight-backed and shame-less, presenting her shining breasts, gazing without embarrassment or any other emotion at my belly. The seam of her lips glistened a little with exuded oil, and the shiftings in her weighty head ceased.

I crouched before her awful readiness. I knew how tall my husband was; I knew what this doll was about. Like one girl confiding in another, like a tiny child in play with its mother or nurse, I reached out and touched Clarissa's lower lip. It yielded—not exactly as if it welcomed my touch and expectations, but with a bland absence of resistance, an emotionless acceptance that I knew I could not muster in my own marriage-bed.

I pushed my forefinger against the meeting-place of the automaton's lips. They gave, a little; they allowed my fingertip to push them apart. Slowly my finger sank in, touching the porcelain teeth. They too moved aside, following pad and joint of my finger as if learning its shape as it intruded.

Her tongue—what cloth was it, so slippery smooth? And how so wet? I pulled out my finger and rubbed the wetness with my thumb; it was a clear kind of oil or gel; I could not quite say what it was. It smelled of nothing, not perfumed, not bodily, not as machine-oil should. It must be very refined.

I put the finger back in, all the way to the knuckle. I thought I might be able to reach to the back of the cavity as I had seen it from within, the clothy, closed-off throat with its elaborate mechanical corsetry. Inside her felt disconcertingly like a real mouth; I expected the doll at any moment to release my finger and ask, with this tongue, with this palate and throat and teeth, what I thought I was about. But she only held to my finger, closely all around like living tissue, living muscle.

And then some response was triggered in her, by the very tip of my finger in her throat. Her lips clasped my knuckle somewhat tighter, and her mouth moved against the rest of my finger. Oh, it was strange! It reminded me of a caterpillar, the concertina-like way they convey themselves across a leaf, along a branch; the rippling. Back and forth along my finger the ripples ran, combining the movements of her resisting my intrusive finger with those of attempting to milk it, massaging it root to tip with a firm and varied persuasiveness. How was such seeming randomness generated? I must translate that, I must account for it in my drawings. Yet at the same time I wanted to know nothing of it; there was something in the sensations that made my own throat clench, my stomach rebel, and every part of me below the waist solidify in a kind of horror.

What horrified me worst was that I knew, as a married woman, how to put an end to the rippling. Yet the notion of doing so, and in that way imitating the most repellent, the most beast-like movements of my husband, when, blinded, stupid with his lust he… emptied himself into me, as if I were a spittoon or the pit of a privy, stilled my hand amid the awful mouth-movements. I was on the point of spasm myself, spasms of revulsion, near-vomiting. Before they should overtake me I jabbed the automaton several times in her lubricious silken throat, my knuckle easily pushing her lips and teeth aside, my finger inside her mouth-workings cold, and bonily slender, and passionless—unless curiosity is a passion, unless disgust is.

Clarissa clamped that cold finger tightly, and some workings braced her neck against what should follow upon such prodding: my husband's convulsions in his ecstasy. It was as if the man was in the room with us, I imagined his exclamations so clearly. I shuddered there myself, a shudder so rich with feeling that my own eyes were sightless with it a moment. Then the doll relaxed her grip on me, and my arm's weight drew my forefinger from her mouth, slack as my husband's member would be slack, gleaming as that would gleam with her lubricants. Quietly, dutifully, she began a mouthish process; her lips parted slightly to allow the stuff of him, the mess of him, the man-spittle, to flow forth, to fall to her bosom. Some of her oil welled out eventually onto her pillowy, rosy lower lip. I watched the whole sequence with a stony attentiveness. When the oil dripped to her shining décolletage, such pity afflicted me at what this doll had been created to undergo that I stood and, using my own handkerchief bordered with Irish lace, cleaned the poor creature's bosom, wiped her mouth as a nurse wipes a child's, and when I was certain no further oils would come forth I restored her the modesty of her bodice; I raised her from her kneeling and took her, I hardly knew why, to sit in her cabinet. I did not close her in, then—I only stood, awkward, regarding her serene face. I felt as if I ought to say something—to apologise, perhaps; perhaps to accuse. Then—and I moved with such certainty that I must have noticed-without-noticing this before—my hand went to a pleat of the velvet lining of the lid of the cabinet, and a dry *pop* sounded under my fingertips, and I drew forth a folded slip of creamy writing paper, which matched that on which Clarissa's domestic commands were written. I opened and glanced down it, the encoded list of Clarissa's tortures, the list of my own.

Revulsion attacked me then, and hurriedly I refolded and replaced the paper, and shut the doll away, and went and stood at the study window gazing out over the green lawn and the dark hedge to the near-featureless landscape beyond, the green-gold fields a-glare in the unforgiving sunlight.

Clarissa's other activities—I began to study and translate them next morning—were more obviously, comically, hideously calculated to meet a man's needs. She could be made to suffer two ways, lying like an upturned frog with her legs and her arms crooked around her torturer—without an actual man within them they contracted tightly enough to hold a very slight man indeed—or propped on all fours like any number of other beasts. In both positions she maintained continuous subtle rotations and rockings of her hips, and I could hear within her similar silky-wet movements to those her mouth had made about my finger, working studiedly upon my husband's intangible member.

To prevent her drawers becoming soaked with the lubricant oil and betraying to Mr Goverman that I had discovered his unfaithfulness with the doll, I was forced to remove them. When I exposed her marriage parts my whole body flushed hot with mortification, and this heat afflicted me periodically throughout the course of her demonstration. Studiously applying myself to my drawing, and to the intellectual effort of translating the doll's mechanisms into her movements, was all I could do to cool myself.

If they had not been what they were, one would have considered her underparts fine examples of the seamstress's craft, or perhaps the upholsterer's. A softly heart-shaped area of wiry dark hairs formed something of a welcome or an announcement that this was no child's doll, with all such private features erased and denied. Then such padded folds, cream-velvety without, red-purple and beaded with moisture within, eventuated behind these hairs, between these heavy legs, that I shook and burned examining them. My own such parts I had no more than washed with haste and efficiency; my husband's incursions within them had been utterly surprising to me, that I should be shaped so, and for such abominable usages. Now I could see them, and on another, one constructed never to feel a whisper of embarrassment. That I should be so curious, so fascinated, disgusted me; I told myself this was all in the spirit of scientific enquiry, this was all to assist in a complete translation of the doll's movements, but the sensations that gripped me—the hot shame; the excruciating awareness, as I examined her fore and aft, of the corresponding places on my own body; the sudden exquisite sensitivity of my fingertips to her softness and her slickness and the differing textures of the fleshy doors into her; the stiffness in my neck and jaw from my rage and repugnance—these were anything but scientific.

In a shaking voice I commanded her, from the secret list. The room's atmosphere was now entirely strange, and I shivered to picture some person walking in, and I made Clarissa pause in her clasping, in her undulations, several times, so that I could circle the house and reassure myself that the country around was as deserted as ever. For what was anyone to make of the scene, of the half-clothed automaton whirring and squirming in her mechanical pleasure, of the cold-faced human seated on the ottoman watching, of the list dropped to the floor so as not to be crumpled in those tight-clenched fists?

Mr Goverman's return woke me from the state I had plunged into by the end of the week, wherein I barely ate and did not bother to dress, but at first light went in my night-dress to the study where Clarissa stood, and all day drew, surely and intricately and in a blistering cold rage, the working innards of the doll. Something warned me—some far distant jingle of harness carried to my ears on the breeze, some hoofstrike beyond the hills echoing through the earth and up through the foundations of the homestead and into my pillow—and I rose and bathed and clothed myself properly and hid my translations away and was well engaged in housekeeperly activities by the time my husband's party approached across the fields.

Then duties crowded in on me: to be hostess, to cook and prepare rooms; to apologise for the makeshiftness of our hospitality, and the absence of servants; to inform Mr Goverman of the presence of his heir; to submit to his embraces that night. My season of solitude vanished like a frightened bird, and the days filled up so fully with words and work, with negotiations and the maintaining of various appearances, that I scarcely had time to recall how I had occupied myself before, let alone determine any particular action to take arising from my discoveries.

Days and then weeks and then months passed, and little Master Goverman began at last to be evident to the point where I was forced to withdraw again from society, such as it was. And I was also forced—because my husband conceived a sudden dislike of visiting the vestibule of his son's little palace—to endure close visitings at my face and bosom of the most grotesque parts of Mr Goverman's anatomy, during which he would seem to lose the powers of articulate speech and even, sometimes, of rational thought. His early reticence and acceptance of my refusals to have him near in that way were transformed now; he no longer apologised, but seemed to delight in my resistance, to take extra pleasure in grasping my head and restraining me in his chosen position, to exult, almost, in his final befoulment of me. I would watch him with our guests, or conferring with Mr Brightwell the new manager, and marvel at this well-dressed man of manners. Could he have any connection with the lamplit or moonlit assortment of limbs and hairiness and animal odours that assaulted me in the nights? I hardly knew which I hated worst, his savagery then or his expertise in disguising it now. What a sleight-of-hand marriage was, how fraudulent the social world! I despised every matron that she did not complain, every new bride as she sank from the glow and glory of betrothal and wedding to invisible compliant wifeliness, every man that he took these concealments and these changes as his due, that he took what he took, in exchange for what he gave a woman, which we called—fools that we were!—respectability.

By the time Mr Goverman left for the city in the sixth month of my pregnancy, I will concede that I was no longer quite myself. Only a thin layer of propriety concealed my rage at my imprisonment—in this savage land, in this brute institution, in this swelling body dominated by the needs and nudgings of my little master within. I will plead, if ever I am called to account, that it was insanity kept me up during those nights, at first studying my translations (What certain hand had drawn these? Why, they looked almost authentic, almost the work of an engineer!) and then (What leap into the darkness was this?) re-translating them, some of them, into new drawings, devising how this part could be substituted for that, or a spring from the mantel-clock in a spare room could be added here, how a rusted saw-blade could be thinned and polished and given an edge and inserted there, out of sight within existing mechanisms, how this cam could be pared away a little there, and this whole arm of the apparatus adjusted higher to allow for the fact that I could not resort to actual metal casting for my lunatic enterprise.

Once the plans were before me, and Mr Goverman still away arranging the terms of his investment in the mining consortium, to the accompaniment, no doubt, of a great deal of roast meat and brandy, cigars and theatre attendances, there remained no more for me to do—lamplit, lumbering, discreet in the sounds I made, undisturbed through the nights—but piece by piece to dismantle and reassemble Clarissa's head according to those sure-handed drawings. I went about in the days like a thief, collecting a tool here, something that could be fashioned into a component there. I tested, I adjusted, I perfected. I was very happy. And then one early morning Lilty Meddows, my maid, knocked uncertainly at the study door to offer me tea and porridge, and there I was, as brightly cheerful as if I had only just risen from my sleep, stirring the just-burnt ashes of my translations, and with Clarissa demure in the armchair opposite, sealed up and fully clothed, betraying nothing of what I had accomplished on her.

Life, I discovered, is always more complex than it seems. The ground on which one bases one's beliefs, and actions arising from those beliefs, is sand, is quicksand, or reveals itself instead to be water. Circumstances change; madnesses end, or lessen, or begin inexorable transformations into new madnesses.

Mr Goverman returned. I greeted him warmly. I was very frightened of what I had done, at the same time as, with the influx of normality that came with his return, with the bolstering of the sense of people watching me, so that I could not behave oddly or poorly, often I found my own actions impossible to credit. I only knew that each morning I greeted my husband more cordially; each night that I accepted him into my bed I did so with less dread and even with a species of amiable curiosity; I attended very much more closely to what he enjoyed in the marriage bed, and he in turn, in his surprise, in his ignorance, ventured to try and discover ways by which I might perhaps experience pleasures approaching the intensity of his own.

My impending maternity ended these experiments before they had progressed very far, however, and I left Cuttajunga for Melbourne and Holmegrange, a large, pleasant house by the wintry sea, where wealthy country ladies were sent by their solicitous husbands to await the birth of the colony's heirs and learn the arts and rituals of motherhood.

There I surprised myself very much by giving birth to a daughter, and there Mr Goverman surprised me when very soon upon the birth he visited, by being more than delighted to welcome little Mary Grace into the world.

"She is *exactly* her mother," he said, looking up from the bundle of her in his arms, and I was astonished to see the glisten of tears in his eyes. Did he love me, then? Was this what love was? Was this, then, also affection, that I felt in return, this tortuous knot of puzzlements and awareness somewhere in my chest, somewhere above and behind my head? Had I birthed more than a child during that long day and night?

Certainly I loved Mary Grace—complete and unqualified, my love surprised me with its certainty when the rest of me was so awash with conflicting emotions, like an iron stanchion standing firm in a rushing current. I had only to look on her puzzling wakefulness, her innocent sleep, to know that region of my own heart clearly. And perhaps a little of my enchantment with my daughter puffed out—like wattle blossom!—and gilded Mr Goverman too. Was that how it went, then, that wifely attachment grew from motherly? Why had my own mother not told me, when I had not the wit to ask her myself?

Mr Goverman returned to Cuttajunga to ready it for Her Little Ladyship, and in his absence, through the milky, babe-ruled days of my lying-in, I wondered and I floundered and I feared, in all the doubt that surrounded my one iron-hard, iron-firm attachment in the world. I did not have leisure or privacy to draw, but in my mind I resurrected the drawings I had burnt in the study at the homestead, and laboured on the adjustments that would be necessary to restore Clarissa to her former state, or near it. If only he loved me and was loyal to me enough; if only he could control his urges until I returned.

Lilty was at my side; Mary Grace was in my arms; train-smoke and train-steam, all around, warmed us momentarily before delivering us up to the winter air, to the view of the ravaged country that was to be my daughter's home.

"Where is he?" said Lilty. "I cannot see him. I thought he would be here."

"Of course he will be." I strode forward through the smoke.

Four tall men, in long black coats, stood by the station gate, watching me in solemnity and some fear, I thought. Captain Jollyon stepped out from among them, but his customary jauntiness had quite deserted him. There was a man who by his headgear must be a policeman; a collared man, a reverend; and Dr Stone, my husband's physician. I did not know what to think, or feel. I must not turn and run; that was all I knew.

The train, which had been such a comforting, noisome, busy wall behind me, slid away, leaving a vastness out there, with Lilty twittering against it, senseless. The gentlemen ushered me, expected me to move with them. They made Lilty take Mary Grace from me. They made me sit, in the station waiting room, and then they sat either side of me, and Captain Jollyon sat on one heel before me, and they delivered their tidings.

It is easy to look bewildered when you have killed a man and are not suspected. It is easy to seem innocent, when all believe you to be so.

It must have been the maid Abigail, they said, from the blood in the kitchen, and the fact that she had disappeared. Mrs Hodds, the housekeeper? She was at Cuttajunga now, but she had been at the Captain's, visiting her cousin Esther on their night off, when the deed was done. Mrs Hodds it was who had found the master in the morning, bled to death in his bed, lying just as if asleep. She had called Dr Stone here, who had discovered the dreadful crime.

I went with them, silent, stunned that it all had happened just as I wished. The sky opened up so widely above the carriage, I feared we would fall out into it, these four black-coated crows of men and me lace-petticoated among them, like a bit of cloud, like a puff of train-steam disappearing. Now that they had cluttered up my clear knowledge with their stories, they respected my silence; only the reverend, who could not be suspected of impropriety, occasionally glanced at my stiff face and patted my gloved hand.

At Cuttajunga Mrs Hodds ran at me weeping, and Mr Brightwell turned his hat in his hands and covered it with muttered condolences. Then that was over, and Mrs Hodds did more cluttering, more exclaiming, and told me what she had had to clean, until one of the black coats sharply interrupted her laundry listing: "Mrs Goverman hardly wants to hear this, woman."

I did not require sedating; I had not become hysterical; I had not shed a tear. But then Mary Grace became fretful, and I took her and Lilty into the study—"But you must not say a word, Lilty, not a *word*," I told her. And as I fed my little daughter, there looking down into her soft face, her mouth working so busy and greedily, her eyes closed in supreme confidence that the milk would continue, forever if it were required—that was when the immense loneliness of my situation hollowed out around me, and of my pitiable husband's, who had retired to the room now above us, and in his horror—for he must have realised what I had done, and who I therefore was—felt his lifeblood ebb away.

Still I did not weep, but my throat and my chest hardened with occluded tears, and I thought—I welcomed the thought—that my heart might stop from the strain of containing them.

Abigail, Abigail: the name kept flying from people's mouths like an insect, distracting me from my thoughts. The pursuit of Abigail preoccupied everyone. I let it, for it prevented them asking other questions; it prevented them seeing through my grief to my guilt.

In the night I rose from my bed. Lilty was asleep on the bedchamber couch, on the doctor's advice and the reverend's, in case I should need her in the state of confusion into which my sudden widowhood had plunged me. I took the candle downstairs, and along the hall to the back of the house.

I should have brought a rag, I thought. A damp rag. But in any case, she will be so bloodied, her bodice, her skirts—it will have all run down. Did he leave the piece in her mouth? I wondered. Will I find it there? Or did he retrieve it and have it with him, in his handkerchief, or in his bed, bound against him with the wrappings nearer where it belonged? It was not a question one could ask Captain Jollyon, or even Dr Stone.

I opened the door of the charging chamber. There was no smudge or spot on or near the cabinet door that I could see on close examination by candle-light.

I opened the cabinet. "Clarissa?" I said in my surprise, and she began her initiation-lubrication sequence, almost as if in pleasure at seeing me and being greeted, almost the way Mary Grace's limbs came alive when she heard my voice, her smoky-grey eyes seeking my face above her cradle. The chamber buzzed and crawled with the sounds of the doll's coming to life, and I could identify each one, as you recognise the gait of a familiar, or the cough he gives before knocking on your parlour door, or his cry to the stable boy as he rides up out of the afternoon, after weeks away.

"Clarissa: Stand," I said, and I made her turn, a full circle so that I could assure myself that not a single drop of blood was on any part of her clothing; then, that her garments had not been washed, for there was the tea-drop I had spilt upon her bodice myself during my studies. I might have unbuttoned her; I might have brought the candle close to scrutinise her breasts, her teeth, for blood not quite cleansed away, but I was prevented, for here came Lilty down the stairs, rubbing her sleepy eyes.

"Oh, ma'am! I was frightened for you! Come, you'd only to wake me, ma'am. You've no need to resort to mechanical people. What is it you were wanting? She's no good warming milk for you, that one—you know that."

And on she scolded, so fierce and gentle in the midnight, so comforting to my confusion—which was genuine now, albeit not sourced where she thought, not where any of them thought—that I allowed her to put the doll away, to lead me to the kitchen, to murmur over me as she warmed and honeyed me some milk.

"The girl Abigail," I said when I was calmer, into the steam above the cup. "Is there any news of her?"

"Don't you worry, Mrs Goverman." Lilty clashed the pot into the wash basin, slopped some water in. Then she sat opposite me, her jaw set, her fists red and white on the table in front of her. "They will find that Abigail. There is only so many people in this country yet, that she can hide among. And most of them would sell their mothers for a penny or a half-pint. Don't you worry." She leaned across and squeezed my cold hand with her hot, damp one. "They will track that girl down. They will bring her to justice."

# THE ART OF ALCHEMY

## TED KOSMATKA

Ted Kosmatka is a twenty-first-century writer. His first stories appeared in 2003, and he has published a small handful of thoughtful, challenging science fiction tales like "The God Engine" and "Bitterseed" in venues like *Asimov's Science Fiction*. According to his website, he lives not far from the dunes of Lake Michigan in a house shaped, vaguely, like a ship.

Sometimes when I came over, Veronica would already be naked. I'd find her spread out on a lawn chair behind the fence of her townhome, several sinewy yards of black skin visible to second story windows across the park. She'd scissor her long legs, raising a languid eyelid.

"You have too many clothes on," she'd say.

And I'd sit. Run a hand along smooth, dark curves. Curl pale fingers into hers.

The story of Veronica is the story of this place. These steel mills, and the dying little city-states around them, have become a part of it somehow—Northwest Indiana like some bizarre, composite landscape we've all consented to believe in. Cornfields and slums and rich, gated communities. National parkland and industrial sprawl.

It is a place of impossible contrasts.

Let it stand for the rest of the country. Let it stand for everything.

On cold days, the blast furnaces assemble huge masses of white smoke across the Lake Michigan shoreline. You can still see it mornings, driving I90 on the way to work—a broad cumulous mountain range billowing from the northern horizon, like we are an alpine community, nestled beneath shifting peaks.

Veronica was twenty-five when we met—just a few years younger than me. She was brilliant, and beautiful, and broken. Her townhome sat behind gates on the expensive side of Ridge Road and cost more than I made in five years. Her neighbors were doctors and lawyers. From the courtyard where she lay naked, you could see a church steeple, the beautiful, dull green of oxidized copper, rising over distant rooftops.

The story of Veronica is also the story of boundaries. And that's what I think about most when I think of her now. The exact line where one thing becomes another. The exact point where an edge becomes sharp enough to cut you.

* * *

We might have been talking about her work. Or maybe she was just making conversation, trying to cover her nervousness; I don't remember. But I remember the rain and the hum of her BMW's engine. And I remember her saying, as she took the Randolph Street exit, "His name is Voicheck."

"Is that his first name, or last?"

"It's the only one he gave me."

We took Randolph down to the loop, and the Chicago skyline reared up at us. Veronica knew the up-town streets. The restaurant on Dearborne had been her choice of location—a nice $60 a plate Kazuto bar that stayed open till two A.M. Trendy, clubby, dark. Big-name suppliers sometimes brought her there for business dinners, if they were also trying to sleep with her. It was the kind of place wealthy people went to get drunk with other wealthy people.

"He claims he's from Poland," she said. "But the accent isn't quite right. More Baltic than Slavic."

I wondered at that. At how she knew the difference.

"Where's he based out of?" I asked.

"Ukraine, formerly, but he sure as hell can't go back now. Had a long list of former this, former that. Different think tanks and research labs. Lots of burned bridges."

"Is he the guy, or just the contact?"

"He's playing like the guy, but I don't know."

She hit her signal and made a left. The rain came down harder, Chicago slick-bright with streetlights and traffic. Green lions on the right, and at some point, we crossed the river.

"Is he bringing it with him?" I asked.

"I don't know."

"But he said he was actually bringing it?"

"Yeah." She looked at me. "He said."

"Jesus."

Her face wore a strange expression in the red glow of dashboard light. It took me a moment to place it. Then it hit me; in the year and a half I'd known her, this was the first time I'd ever seen her scared.

I first met her at the lab. I say "lab" and people imagine white walls and sterile test tubes, but it's not like that. It's mostly math I do, and something close to metallurgy. All of it behind glass security walls. I check my work with a scanning electron microscope, noting crystalline lattices and surface structure micro-abrasions.

She walked through the door behind Hal, the lab's senior supervisor.

"This is the memory metals lab," Hal told her, gesturing as he entered.

The girl nodded. She was young and slender, smooth dark skin, a face that seemed, at first glance, to be more mouth than it should. That was my initial impression of her—some pretty new-hire the bosses were showing around. That's it. And then she was past me, following the supervisor deeper into the lab. At the time, I had no idea.

I heard the supervisor's voice drone on as he showed her the temper ovens and the gas chromatograph in the next room. When they returned, the super was following her.

I looked up from the lab bench and she was staring at me. "So you're the genius," she said.

That was the first time she pointed it at me. The look. The way she could look at you with those big dark eyes, and you could almost see the gears moving—her full mouth pulled into a sensuous smile that wanted to be more than it was. A smile like she knew something you didn't.

There were a dozen things I could have said, but the nuclear wind behind those eyes blasted my words away until all that was left was a sad kind of truth. "Yeah," I said. "I guess that's me."

She turned to the supervisor. "Thank you for your time."

Hal nodded and left. It took me a moment to realize what had just happened. The laboratory supervisor—my direct boss—had been dismissed.

"Tell me," she said. "What do you do here?"

I paused for three seconds before I spoke, letting myself process the seismic shift. Then I explained it.

She smiled while I talked. I'd done it for an audience a dozen times, these little performances. It was practically a part of my job description since the last corporate merger made Uspar-Nagoi the largest steel company in the world. I'd worked for three different corporations in the last two years and hadn't changed offices once. The mill guys called them white-hats, these management teams that flew in to tour the facilities, shaking hands, smiling under their spotless white hardhats, attempting to fit their immediate surroundings into the flowchart of the company's latest international acquisitions. Research was a prime target for the tours, but here in the lab, they were harder to spot—just another suit come walking through. It was hard to know who you were talking to, really. But two things were certain. The management types were usually older than the girl standing in front of me. And they'd always, up till now, been male.

But I explained it like I always did. Or maybe I put a little extra spin on it; maybe I showed off. I don't know. "Nickel-titanium alloys," I said. I opened the desiccator and pulled out a small strip of steel. It was long and narrow, cut into almost the exact dimensions of a ruler.

"First you take the steel," I told her, holding out the dull strip of metal. "And you heat it." I lit the Bunsen burner and held the steel over the open flame. Nothing happened for ten, twenty seconds. She watched me. I imagined what I must look like to her at that moment—blue eyes trained on the warming steel, short brown hair jutting at wild angles around the safety goggles I wore on my forehead. Just another technophile lost in his obsession. It was a type. Flame licked the edges of the dull metal.

Then all at once, the metal moved.

It contracted muscularly, like a living thing, twisting itself into a ribbon, a curl, a spring.

"It's caused by micro- and nano-scale surface restructuring," I told her. "The change in shape results from phase transformations. Martensite when cool; austenite when heated. The steel remembers its earlier configurations. The different phases want to be in different shapes."

"Memory metal," she said. "I've always wanted to see this. What applications does it have?"

The steel continued to flex, winding itself tighter. "Medical, structural, automotive. You name it."

"Medical?"

"For broken bones. The shape memory alloy has a transition temp near body temp. You attach a plate to the break site, and body heat causes the alloy to contract, thereby creating a compressive force on the bone at both ends of the fracture."

"Interesting."

"They're also investigating the alloy's use in heart stents. A cool-crushed alloy tube can be inserted into narrow arteries where it'll expand and open once it's heated to blood temperature."

"You mentioned automotive."

I nodded. Automotive. The big money. "Imagine that you've put a small dent in your fender," I said. "Instead of taking it to the shop, you pull out your hairdryer. The steel pops right back in shape."

She stayed at the lab for another hour, asking intelligent questions, watching the steel cool and straighten itself. Before she left, she shook my hand politely and thanked me for my time. She never once told me her name. I watched the door close behind her as she left.

Two weeks later she was back. This time, without Hal.

She drifted into the lab like a ghost near the end of my shift.

In the two weeks since I'd seen her, I'd learned a little about her. I'd learned her name, and that her corporate hat wasn't just management; but upper management. She had an engineering degree from out east, then Ivy League grad school by age twenty. She gave reports to men who ran a corporate economy larger than most countries. She was somebody's golden-child, fast-tracked to the upper circles. The company based her out of the East Chicago regional headquarters but occasionally flew her to Korea, India, South Africa, to the latest corporate takeovers and the steady flow of new facilities that needed integration. She was an organizational savant, a voice in the ear of the global acquisition market. The transglobals had long since stopped pretending they were about actually making things; it was so much more Darwinian than that now. The big fish ate the little fish, and Uspar-Nagoi, by anyone's standards, was a whale. You grow fast enough, long enough, and pretty soon you need an army of gifted people to understand what you own, and how it all fits together. She was part of that army.

"So what else have you been working on?" she asked.

When I heard her voice, I turned. Veronica: her smooth, pretty face utterly emotionless, the smile gone from her full mouth.

"Okay," I said. And this time I showed her my real tricks. I showed her what I could really do. Because she'd asked.

Martensite like art. A gentle flame—a slow, smooth origami unfolding.

We watched it together. Metal and fire, a thing I'd never shown anyone before.

"This is beautiful," she said.

I showed her the butterfly, my little golem—its only movement a slow flexing of its delicate steel wings as it passed through phase changes.

"You made this?"

I nodded. "There are no mechanical parts," I told her. "Just a single solid sheet of steel."

"It's like magic," she said. She touched it with a slender index finger.

"Just science," I said. "Sufficiently advanced."

We watched the butterfly cool, wings flapping slowly. Finally, it began folding in on itself, cocooning, the true miracle. "The breakthrough was micro-degree shifting," I said. "It gives you more design control."

"Why this design?"

I shrugged. "You heat it slow, an ambient rise, and it turns into a butterfly."

"What happens if you heat it fast?"

I looked at her. "It turns into a dragon."

That night at her townhome, she took her clothes off slow—her mouth prehensile and searching. Although I was half a head taller, I found her legs were as long as mine. Strong, lean runner's legs, calf muscles bunched high like fists. Afterward we lay on her dark sheets, a distant streetlight filtering through the blinds, drawing a pattern on the wall.

"Are you going to stay the night?" she asked.

"Do you want me to?"

She was silent for a moment. "Yeah, I want you to."

"Then I'll stay."

The ceiling fan above her bed hummed softly, circulating the air, cooling the sweat on my bare skin.

"I've been doing research on you for the last week," she said. "On what you do."

"Checking up on me?"

She ignored the question and draped a slick arm across my shoulder. "Nagoi has labs in Asia running parallel to yours. Did you know that?"

"No."

"From years before the Uspar merger. Smart alloys with chemical triggers instead of heat; and stranger things, too. A special copper-aluminum-nickel alloy that's supposed to be triggered by remote frequency. Hit a button on a transmitter, and you get phase change by some kind of resonance. I didn't understand most of it. More of your magic steel."

"Not magic," I said.

"Modern chemistry grew out of the art of alchemy. At what point does it start being alchemy again?"

"It's always been alchemy, at the heart of it. We're just getting better at it now."

"I should tell you," she said, curling her fingers into my hair. "I don't believe in interracial relationships." That was the first time she said it—a thing she'd repeat often during the next year and a half, usually when we were in bed.

"You don't believe in them?"

"No," she said.

In the darkness she was a silhouette, a complication of shadows against the window light. She wasn't looking at me, but at the ceiling. I studied her profile—the rounded forehead, the curve of her jaw, the placement of her mouth, positioned not just between her nose and lips, but also forward of them, as if something in the architecture of her face were straining outward. She wore a steel-gray necklace, Uspar-Nagoi logo glinting between the dark curve of her full breasts. I traced her bottom lip with my finger.

"You're wrong," I said.

"How's that?'

"I've seen them. They exist."

I closed my eyes and slept.

The rain was still coming down, building puddles across the Chicago streets. We pulled onto Dearborne and parked the car in a twenty-dollar lot. Veronica squeezed my hand as we walked toward the restaurant.

Voicheck was standing near the door; you couldn't miss him. Younger than I expected—pale and broad-faced, with a shaved head, dark glasses. He stood outside the restaurant, bare arms folded in front of his chest. He looked more like a bouncer than a scientist.

"You must be Voicheck," Veronica said, extending her hand.

He hesitated for a moment. "I didn't expect you to be black."

She accepted this with only a slight narrowing of her eyes. "Certain people never do. This is my associate, John."

I nodded and shook his hand, thinking, *Typical Eastern European lack of tact.* It wasn't racism. It was just that people didn't come to this country knowing what *not* to say; they didn't understand the racial context. On the floor of the East Chicago steel plant, I'd once had a Russian researcher ask me, loudly, how I could tell the Mexican workers from the Puerto Ricans. He was honestly curious. "You don't," I told him. "Ever."

A hostess walked us down dark carpet, past rows of potted bamboo, and seated us at a table near the back. The waitress brought us our drinks. Voicheck took his glasses off and rubbed the bridge of his nose. The lenses were prescription, I noticed. Over the last decade, surgery had become so cheap and easy in the States that glasses had become rare. Only anachronists and foreigners wore glasses anymore. Voicheck took a long swig of his Goose Island and got right to the point. "We need to discuss price."

Veronica shook her head. "First, we need to know how it is made."

"That information is what you'll be paying for." His accent was thick, but he spoke slowly enough to be understood. He opened his hand and showed us a small, gray flash drive, the kind you'd pay thirty dollars for at Best Buy. His fingers curled back into a fist. "This is data you'll understand."

"And you?" Veronica asked.

He smiled. "I understand enough to know what it is worth."

"Where is it from?"

"Donets'k, originally. After that, Chisinau laboratory, until about two years ago. Now the work is owned by a publicly traded company which shall, for the time being, remain nameless. The work is top secret. Only a few people at the company even know about the breakthrough. I have all the files saved. Now we discuss price."

Veronica was silent. She knew better than to make the first offer.

Voicheck let the silence draw out. "One hundred thirteen thousand," he said.

"That's a pretty exact number," Veronica said.

"Because that's exactly twice what I'll entertain as a first counter offer."

Veronica blinked. "So you'll take half that?"

"You offer fifty-six thousand five hundred? My answer is no, I am sorry. But here is where I rub my chin; and because I'm feeling generous, I tell you we can split the difference. We are negotiating, no? Then one of us does the math, and it comes out to eighty-five thousand. Is that number round enough for you?"

"I liked the fifty-six thousand better."

"Eighty-five minimum."

"That is too much."

"What, I should let you steal from me? You talked me down from one hundred thirteen already. I can go no further."

"There's no way we—"

Voicheck held up his hand. "Eighty-five in three days."

"I don't know if we can get it in three days."

"If no, then I disappear. It is simple."

Veronica glanced at me.

I spoke for the first time. "How do we even know what we'd be paying for? You expect us to pay eighty-five grand for what's on some flash drive?"

Voicheck looked at me and frowned. "No, of course not." He opened his other fist. "For this, too." He dropped something on the table. Something that looked like a small red wire.

"People have died for this." He gestured toward the red wire. "You may pick it up."

I looked closely. It wasn't one wire; it was two. Two rubber-coated wires, like what you'd find behind a residential light switch. He noticed our confusion.

"The coating is for protection and to make it visible," he said.

"Why does it need protection?"

"Not it. You. The coating protects you."

Veronica stood and looked at me. "Let's go. He's been wasting our time."

"No, wait," he said. "Look." He picked up one of the wires. He lifted it delicately by one end—and the other wire lifted, too, rising from the table's surface like some magician's illusion.

I saw then that I'd been wrong; it was not two wires after all, but one.

"The coating was stripped from ten centimeters in the middle," Voicheck said. "So you could see what was underneath."

But in the dim light, there was nothing to see. I bent close. Nothing at all. In the spot where the coating had been removed, the strand inside was so fine that it lacked a cross-section. There was only the hint of something—a thing that might or might not be there, at the very edge of perception.

"What is it?" I asked.

"An allotrope of carbon, Fullerene structural family. You take it," he said. "Do tests to confirm. But remember, is just a neat toy without this." He held out the flash drive. "This explains how the carbon nanotubes are manufactured. How they can be woven into sheets, what lab is developing the technique, and more."

I stared at him. "The longest carbon nanotubes anybody has been able to make are just over a centimeter."

"Until now," he said. "Now they can be miles. In three days you come back. You give me the eighty-five thousand, I give you the data and information about where the graphene rope is being developed."

Veronica picked up the wire. "All right," she said. "Three days."

Iron and fire and dark, cool water. The mills jut for miles out into the lake, black structures built on mounds of slag.

My father had been a steelworker, as had his father before him. And now I, too, work in steel. My great-grandfather, though, had been here before the mills. He'd been a builder. He was here when the Lake Michigan shoreline was unbroken sand from Illinois to St. Joseph. He'd built Bailey Cemetery around the turn of the century—a great stone mausoleum in which some of the area's earliest settlers were buried. Tourists visit the place now. It's on some list of historic sites, and once a summer, I take my sister's daughters to see it, careful to pick up the brochure.

There is a street in Porter named after him, my great-grandfather. Not because he was important, but because he was the only person who lived there. It was the road to his house, so they gave it his name. Now bi-levels crowd the street. He was here before the cities, before the kingdoms of rust and fire. Before the mills came and ate the beaches.

I try to imagine what this part of Indiana must have looked like then. Woods, and wetlands, and rolling dunes. It must have been beautiful.

Sometimes I walk out to the pier at night and watch the ore boats swing through the darkness. From the water, the mill looks like any city. Any huge, sprawling city. You can see the glow of a thousand lights; you hear the trains and the rumble of heavy machines. Then the blast furnace taps a heat, a false-dawn glow of red and orange—flames making dragon's fire on the rolling Lake Michigan waves, lighting up the darkness like hell itself.

The drive back to Indiana was quiet. The rain had stopped. We drove with the windows half-open, letting the wind flutter in, both of us lost in thought.

The strand—that's what we'd call it later—was tucked safely into her purse.

"Do you think it's for real?" she asked.

"We'll know tomorrow."

"You can do the testing at your lab?"

"Yeah," I said.

"Do you think he is who he says he is?"

"No, he's not even trying."

"He called it a graphene rope, which isn't quite right."

"So?" I said.

"Clusters of the tubes *do* naturally aggregate into ropes linked together by Van der Waals forces. It's the kind of slip only somebody familiar with the theory would make."

"So he's more familiar with it than he lets on?"

"Maybe, but there's no way to know," she said.

The next day I waited until the other researchers had gone home, and then I took the strand out of my briefcase and laid it on the lab bench. I locked the door to the materials testing lab and energized the tensile machine. The fluorescent lights flickered. It was a small thing, the strand. It seemed insignificant as it rested there on the bench. A scrap of insulated wiring from an electrician's tool box. Yet it was a pivot point around which the world would change, if it was what it was supposed to be. If it was what it was supposed to be, the world had changed already. We were just finding out about it.

The testing took most of the night. When I finished, I walked back to my office and opened a bottle I kept in the bottom drawer of a filing cabinet. I sat and sipped.

It's warm in my office. My office is a small cubby in the back room of the lab, a thrown-together thing made by wall dividers and shelves. It's an office because my desk and computer sit there. Otherwise it might be confused with a closet or small storage room. File cabinets line one side. There are no windows. To my left, a hundred sticky notes feather the wall. The other wall is metal, white, magnetic. A dozen refrigerator magnets hold calendars, pictures, papers. There is a copy of the lab's phone directory, a copy of the lab's quality policy, and a sheet of paper on which the geometry of crystal systems is described. The R&D directory of services is there, held to the wall by a magnetic clip. All the phone numbers I might need. A picture of my sister, blonde, unsmiling, caught in the act of speaking to me over a paper plate of fried chicken, the photo taken at a summer party three years ago. There is an Oxford Instruments periodic table. There's also a picture of a sailboat. Blue waves. And a picture of the Uspar-Nagoi global headquarters, based out of London.

Veronica finally showed up a few minutes past midnight. I was watching the butterfly as she walked through the door.

"Well?" she asked.

"I couldn't break it."

"What do you mean?"

"I couldn't get a tensile strength because I couldn't get it to fail. Without failure, there's no result."

"What about the other tests?"

"It took more than 32,000 pounds per square inch without shearing. It endured 800 degrees Fahrenheit without a measurable loss of strength or conductivity. Transmission electron microscopy allowed for direct visualization. I took these pictures." I handed her the stack of printed sheets. She went through them one by one.

Veronica blinked. She sat. "What does this mean?"

"It means that I think they've done it," I said. "Under impossibly high pressures, nanotubes can link, or so the theory holds. Carbon bonding is described by quantum chemistry orbital hybridization, and they've swapped some sp2 bonds for the sp3 bonds of diamond."

She looked almost sad. She kissed me. The kiss was sad. "What are its uses?"

"Everything. Literally, almost everything. A great many things steel can do, these carbon nanotubes will do better. It's super-light and super-strong, perfect for aircraft. This material moves the fabled space elevator into the realm of possibility."

"There'd still be a lot of R&D necessary—"

"Yes, of course, it will be years down the road, but eventually the sky's the limit. There's no telling what this material will do, if it's manufactured right. It could be used for everything from suspension bridges to spacecraft. It could open our way to the stars. We're at the edge of a revolution."

I looked down at the strand. After a long time, I finally said what had been bothering me for the last sixteen hours. "But why did Voicheck come to you?" I said. "Of all places, why bring this to a steel company?"

She looked at me. "If you invent an engine that runs on water, why offer it to an oil company?" She picked up the strand. "Only one reason to do that, John."

She glanced down at the red wire in her hand. "Because the oil company is certain to buy it."

That night we drank. I stood at the window on the second story of her town-home and looked out at her quiet neighborhood, watching the expensive cars roll by on Ridge Road. The Ridge Road which neatly bisects Lake County. Land on the south, higher; the land to the north, low, easing toward urban sprawl, and the marshes, and Lake Michigan. That long, low ridge of land on which the road was built represented the glacial maxim—the exact line where the glacier stopped during the last ice age, pushing all that dirt and stone in front of it like a plow, before it melted and receded and became the Great Lakes—and thousands of years later, road builders would stand on that ridge and think to themselves how easy it would be to follow the natural curve of the land; and so they built what they came to build and called it the only name that would fit: Ridge Road. The exact line, in the region, where one thing became another.

I wrapped the naked strand around my finger, watching the bright red blood well up from where it contacted my skin—because in addition to being strong and thin, the strand had the property of being *sharp*. For the tests, I'd stripped away most of the rubber coating, leaving only a few inches of insulation at the ends. The rest was exposed strand. Nearly invisible.

"You cut yourself," Veronica said. She parted her full lips and drew my finger into her mouth.

The first time I'd told her I loved her, it was an accident. In bed, half asleep, I'd said it. Good night, I love you. A thing that was out of my mouth before I even realized it—a habit from an old relationship come rising up out of me, the way every old relationship lives just under the skin of every new one. All the promises. All the possibilities. Right there under the skin. I'd felt her stiffen beside me, and an hour later, she nudged me awake. She was sitting up, arms folded across her bare breasts, as defensive as I'd ever seen her. I realized she hadn't slept at all. "I heard what you said." There was anger in her voice, and whole complex layers of pain.

But I denied it. "You're hearing things."

Though of course it was true. What I'd said. Even if saying it was an accident. It had been true for a while.

The night after I tested the strand, I lay in bed and watched her breathing, blankets kicked to the floor. Light through the window glinted off her necklace, a thin herringbone pattern—some shiny new steel, Uspar-Nagoi emblem across her beautiful dark skin. I caressed the herringbone plate with my finger, such an odd interlinking of metal.

"They gave this to you?"

She fingered the necklace, still half awake. "They gave one to all of us," she said. "Management perk. Supposed to be worth a mint."

"The logo ruins it," I said. "Like a tag."

"Everything is tagged, one way or another," she said. "I met him once."

"Who?"

"The name on the necklace."

"Nagoi? You met him?"

"At a facility in Brussels. He came through with his group. Shook my hand. He was taller than I thought, but his handshake was this flaccid, aqueous thing, straight fingered, like a flipper. It was obvious he loathed the Western tradition. I was prepared to like him, prepared to be impressed, or to find him merely ordinary."

She was silent for so long I thought she might have fallen asleep. "I've never been one of those people who judged a person by their handshake," she said. "But still…I can't remember a handshake that gave me the creeps like that. They paid sixty-six billion for the Uspar acquisition. Can you imagine that much money? That many employees? That much power? When his daughter went through her divorce, the company stock dropped by two percent. His daughter's divorce did that. Can you believe that? Do you know how much two percent is?"

"A lot."

"They have billions invested in infrastructure alone. More in hard assets and research facilities, not to mention the mills themselves. Those assets are quantifiable and linked to actuarial tables that translate into real dollars. Real dollars which can be used to leverage more takeovers, and the monster keeps growing. If Nagoi's daughter's divorce dipped the share price by two percent, what do you think would happen if a new carbon-product competitor came to market?"

I ran a finger along her necklace. "You think they'll try to stop it?"

"Nagoi's money is in steel. If a legitimate alternative reached market, then each mill, each asset all across the world, would suddenly be worth less. Billions of dollars would blink out of existence."

"So what happens?"

"We get the data. I write my report. I give my presentation. The board suddenly gets interested in buying a certain company in Europe that just happens to be working in carbon research. If they won't sell, Uspar-Nagoi buys all the stock and owns them anyway. Then shuts them down."

"Suppression won't work. The Luddites never win in the long run."

She smiled. "The three richest men in the world have as much money as the poorest forty-nine nations," she said. "Combined."

I watched her face.

She continued. "The yearly gross product of the planet is something like fifty-five trillion dollars, and yet there are millions of people who are still trying to live on less than three dollars a day. You trust business to do the right thing?"

"No, but I trust the market. A better product will always find its way to the consumer. Even Uspar-Nagoi can't stop that."

"You only say that because you don't understand how it really works. That might have been true a long time ago. The Uspar-Nagoi board does hostile takeovers for a living, and they're not going to release a technology that will devalue their core assets."

Veronica was silent.

"Why did you get into steel?" I asked. "What brought you here?"

"Money," she said. "Just money."

"Then why haven't you told your bosses about Voicheck?"

"I don't know."

"Are you going to tell them?"

She was silent.

"Are you going to tell them?"

"No," she said. "I don't think I am."

There was a long pause.

"What are you going to do?"

"Buy it," she said. "Buy the data."

"And then what? After you've bought it."

"After I've bought it, I'm going to post it on the internet."

The drive to meet Voicheck seemed to take forever. The traffic was stop and go until we reached Halsted, and it took us nearly an hour to reach downtown Chicago.

We parked in the same twenty-dollar lot and Veronica squeezed my hand again as we walked toward the restaurant.

But this time, Voicheck wasn't standing outside looking like a bouncer. He wasn't looking like anything, because he wasn't there. We waited a few minutes and went inside. We asked for the same table. We didn't speak. There was no reason to speak.

After a few moments, a man in a suit came and sat. He was a gray man in a gray suit. He wore black leather gloves. He was in his fifties, but he was in his fifties the way certain breeds of athletes enter their fifties—broad, and solid, and blocky-shouldered. He had a lantern jaw and thin, sandy hair receding from a broad forehead. The waitress came and asked if he needed anything to drink.

"Yes, please," the man said. "Bourbon. And oh, for my friends here, a Bailey's for him, and what was it?" He looked at Veronica. "A Coke, right?"

Veronica didn't respond. The man's accent was British.

"A Coke," the man told the waitress. "Thank you."

He smiled and turned toward us. "Did you know that bourbon was the official spirit of the U.S. by act of Congress?"

We were silent.

"That's why I always used to make a point of drinking it when I came to the States. I wanted to enjoy the authentic American experience. I wanted to drink bourbon like American's drink bourbon. But then I discovered an unsettling secret in my travels." The man took something from the inside pocket of his suit jacket and set it on the table. Glasses. Voicheck's glasses, one of the prescription lenses shattered.

The man caressed the bent frames with his finger. "I discovered that American's don't really drink bourbon. A great many American's have never so much as tasted it. So then why is it the official spirit of your country?"

We had no opinion. We were without opinion.

"Would you like to hear what I think?" The man asked. He bent close and spoke low across the table. "I've developed a theory. I think it was a lie all along. I think someone in your Congress probably had his hand in the bourbon business all those years ago, and sales were flagging; so they came up with the idea to make bourbon the official spirit of the country as a way to line their own pockets. Would you like to hear something else I discovered in my travels? No? Well, I'll tell you anyway. I discovered that I don't care much, one way or the other. I discovered that I *like* bourbon. And I feel like I'm drinking the most American drink of them all, because your Congress said so, lie or not. The ability to believe a lie can be an important talent. You're probably wondering who I am."

"No," Veronica said.

"Good, then you're smart enough to realize it doesn't matter. You're smart enough to realize that if I'm here, it means that your friend isn't coming back."

"Where is he?" Veronica asked.

"I can't say, but rest assured that wherever he is, he sends his regrets."

"Are you here for the money?"

"The money? I couldn't care less about your money."

"Where's the flash drive?" Veronica asked.

"You mean this?" The man held the gray flash drive between leathered finger and thumb, then returned it to the breast pocket of his neat gray suit. "This is the closest you're going to get to it, I'm afraid. Your friend seemed to think it belonged to him. I disabused him of that misconception."

"What do you want?" Veronica asked.

"I want what everyone wants, my dear. But what I'm here for today—what I'm being paid to do—is to tie up some loose ends. You can help me."

Silence.

"Where is the strand?" he asked.

"He never gave it to us."

The man's gray eyes looked pained. Like a father with a wayward child. "I'm disappointed," he said. "I thought we were developing some trust here. Do you know what loyalty is?"

"Yes."

"No, I don't think you do. Loyalty to your company. Loyalty to the cause. You have shown that you have no loyalty at all. You had some very important people who looked after you, Veronica. You had some important friends."

"You're from Uspar-Nagoi?"

"Who did you think?"

"I…"

"You have embarrassed certain people who have invested their trust in you. You have embarrassed some very important people."

"That wasn't my intention."

"In my experience, it never is." He spread his hands. "Yet here we are. What were you planning on doing with the data once you obtained it?"

Veronica was silent for a moment, then, "I don't know what you're talking about."

The pain returned to the man's eyes. He shook his head sadly. "I'm going to ask you a question in a moment. If you lie to me again, I promise you." He leaned forward. "I promise you that I will make you regret it. Do you believe that?"

Veronica nodded.

"Good. Do you have the strand with you?"

"No."

"Then this is what is going to happen now," he said. "We're going to leave. We're going to drive to where the strand is, and you're going to give it to me."

"If I did have it somewhere, and if I did give it to you, what happens then?"

"Probably you'll have to look for another job. I can't say for sure." He leaned back in his chair, taking on a pleasant expression again. "That's between you and your company. I'm just here to obtain the strand."

The man stood. He laid a hundred-dollar bill on the table and grabbed Veronica's arm. The way he grabbed her arm, he could have been a prom date—just a gentleman walking his lady out the door. Only I could see his fingers dug deep into her flesh.

I followed them out. Walking behind them. When we got near the front door, I picked up one of the trendy bamboo pots and brought it down on the man's head with everything I had.

The crash was shocking. Every head in the restaurant swiveled toward us. I bent and fished the flash drive from his breast pocket. "Run," I told her.

We hit the night air sprinting.

"What the fuck are you doing?" she screamed.

"Voicheck is dead," I told her. "We were next."

Veronica climbed behind the wheel and sped out of the parking lot just as the gray man stumbled out the front door of the restaurant.

The BMW was fast. Faster than anything I would have suspected. Veronica drove with the pedal to the floor, weaving in and out of traffic. Pools of light ticked past.

"They'll still come after us," she said.

"Yeah."

"What are we going to do?"

"We have to stay ahead of them."

"How do we do that? Where do we go?"

"We get through tonight, and then we worry about the rest."

"We can hop a flight somewhere."

"No, what happens tonight decides everything. That strand is our only insurance. Without the strand, we're dead."

Her hands tightened on the steering wheel.

"Where is it?" I asked.

"I left it at the house."

Veronica kept the accelerator floored. "I'm sorry I got you into this," she said.

"Don't be."

We were almost to her house when Veronica's forehead creased. She took the turn onto Ridge, frowning. She looked confused for a second, then surprised. Her hand went to her neck. It happened so quickly.

I had time to notice her necklace, gone flat-gray. There was an instant of recognition in her eyes before the alloy phase-changed—an instant of panic, and then the necklace shifted, writhed, herringbone plate tightening like razor wire. She gasped and let go of the wheel, clutching at her throat. I grabbed the wheel with one hand, trying to grab her necklace with the other. But already it was gone, tightened through her skin, blood spilling from her jugulars as she shrieked. Then even her shrieks changed, gurgling, as the blade cut through her voice box.

I screamed and the car spun out of control. The sound of squealing tires, and we hit the curb hard, sideways—the crunch of metal and glass, world trading places with black sky, rolling three times before coming to a stop.

Sirens. The creak of a spinning wheel. I looked over, and Veronica was dead. Dead. That look, gone forever—gears in her eyes gone silent and still. The Uspar-Nagoi logo slid from her wound as the necklace phase changed again, expanding to its original size. I thought of labs in Asia and parallel projects, Veronica saying, *They gave one to all of us.*

I climbed out of the wreck and stood swaying. The sirens closer now. I sprinted the remaining few blocks to her house.

When I got to her front door, I tried the knob. Locked. I stood, panting. When I caught my breath, I kicked the door in. I walked inside, up the stairs. The strand was in Veronica's jewelry box on her dresser. I glanced around the room; it was the last time I'd stand there, I knew, the last time I'd be in her bedroom. I saw the four-poster bed where we'd lain so often, and the grief came down on me like a freight train. I did my best to push it away. Later, I thought. Later, I'd deal with it. When there was time. I closed my eyes and saw Veronica's face.

Coming back down the stairs, I stopped. The front door was closed. I didn't remember closing it.

I stood silent, listening.

The first blow knocked me over the chair.

The gray man came again, open hands extended, smiling. "I was going to be nice," the man said. "I was going to be quick. But then you hit me with a pot."

Some flash of movement, and his leg swung, connecting with the side of my head. "Now I'm going to take my time and enjoy this."

I tried to climb to my feet, but the world swam away, off to the side. He kicked me under my armpit, and I felt ribs break.

"Come on, stand up," he said. I tried to breathe. Another kick. Another.

I pulled myself up the side of the couch. He caught me with a chipping blow to the face. My lip split wide open, blood pouring onto Veronica's white carpet. His leg came up, connecting with my ribs again. I felt another snap. I collapsed onto my back, writhing in agony. His leg rose and fell as I tried to curl in on myself—an instinct to protect my vital organs. He landed a solid kick to my face and my head snapped back. The world went black.

He was crouching over me when I opened my eyes. That smile.

"Come on," he said. "Stand up."

He dragged me to my feet and slammed me against the wall. A right hand like iron pinned me to the wall by my throat.

"Where is the strand?"

I tried to speak, but my voice pinched shut. He smiled wider, turning an ear toward me. "What's that?" he said. "I can't hear you."

A flutter of movement and his other hand came up. He laid the straight razor against my cheek. Cold steel. "I'm going to ask you one more time," he said. "And then I'm going to start cutting slices down your face. I'm going to do it slowly, so you can feel it." He eased up on my windpipe just enough for me to draw a breath.

"Now tell me," he said, "where is the strand?"

I looped the strand around his forearm. "Right here," I said, and pulled.

There was little resistance, just a slight snag when it parted bone. The man's hand came off with a thump, spurting blood in a fountain. The razor dropped to the carpet. He had time to look confused before the pain hit. Then surprised. Like Veronica. He bent for the razor, reaching to pick it up with his other hand, and this time I hooked my arm around his neck, looping the chord tight—and pulled again. Warmth. Like bathwater on my face. He slumped to the floor.

I picked up the razor and limped out the front door.

Eighty-five grand buys you a lot of distance. It'll take you places. It'll take you across continents, if you need it to. It will introduce you to the right people.

There is no carbon-tube industry. Not yet. No monopoly to pay or protect. And the data I downloaded onto the internet is just starting to make news. Nagoi still comes for me—in my dreams, and in my waking paranoia. A man with a razor. A man with steel in his fist.

Already Uspar-Nagoi stock has started to slide as those long thinkers in the international investment markets gaze into their crystal balls and see a future that might, just maybe, be made of different stuff. Uspar-Nagoi made a grab for that European company, but it cost them more than they ever expected to pay. And the carbon project was buried, just as Veronica said it would be. Only now the data is on the net, for anyone to see.

Carbon has this property: it bonds powerfully and promiscuously to itself. In one form, carbon is diamond. In another, it builds itself into structures we are just beginning to understand. We are not smarter than the ones who came before us—the ones who built the pyramids and navigated oceans by the stars. If we've done more, it's because we've had better materials. What would da Vinci have done with polycarbon? Seven billion people in the world. Maybe now we find out.

I think of what I said to Veronica about alchemy. The art of turning one thing into another. That maybe it's been alchemy all along.

# 26 MONKEYS, ALSO THE ABYSS

## KIJ JOHNSON

Kij Johnson sold her first short story in 1987, and has subsequently appeared regularly in *Analog*, *Asimov's Science Fiction*, the *Magazine of Fantasy & Science Fiction*, and *Realms of Fantasy*. She has won the Theodore Sturgeon Memorial Award and the International Association for the Fantastic in the Art's Crawford Award. Her short story "The Evolution of Trickster Stories among the Dogs of North Park After the Change" was placed on the final ballot for the 2007 Nebula Award and the 2007 World Fantasy Award, and it was a nominee for the Sturgeon and Hugo awards.

Her novels include *The Fox Woman* and *Fudoki*. She is currently researching a third novel set in Heian Japan. Johnson divides her time between the Midwest and the West Coast.

1.

Aimee's big trick is that she makes twenty-six monkeys vanish onstage.

2.

She pushes out a claw-foot bathtub and asks audience members to come up and inspect it. The people climb in and look underneath, touch the white enamel, run their hands along the little lion's feet. When they're done, four chains are lowered from the proscenium stage's fly space. Aimee secures them to holes drilled along the tub's lip and gives a signal, and the bathtub is hoisted ten feet into the air.

She sets a stepladder next to it. She claps her hands and the twenty-six monkeys onstage run up the ladder one after the other and jump into the bathtub. The bathtub shakes as each monkey thuds in among the others. The audience can see heads, legs, tails; but eventually every monkey settles and the bathtub is still again. Zeb is always the last monkey up the ladder. As he climbs into the bathtub, he makes a humming boom deep in his chest. It fills the stage.

And then there's a flash of light, two of the chains fall off, and the bathtub swings down to expose its interior.

Empty.

### 3.

They turn up later, back at the tour bus. There's a smallish dog door, and in the hours before morning, the monkeys let themselves in, alone or in small groups, and get themselves glasses of water from the tap. If more than one returns at the same time, they murmur a bit among themselves, like college students meeting in the dorm halls after bar time. A few sleep on the sofa, and at least one likes to be on the bed, but most of them wander back to their cages. There's a little grunting as they rearrange their blankets and soft toys, and then sighs and snoring. Aimee doesn't really sleep until she hears them all come in.

Aimee has no idea what happens to them in the bathtub, or where they go, or what they do before the soft click of the dog door opening. This bothers her a lot.

### 4.

Aimee has had the act for three years now. She was living in a month-by-month furnished apartment under a flight path for the Salt Lake City airport. She was hollow, as if something had chewed a hole in her body and the hole had grown infected.

There was a monkey act at the Utah State Fair. She felt a sudden and totally out-of-character urge to see it, and afterward, with no idea why, she walked up to the owner and said, "I have to buy this."

He nodded. He sold it to her for a dollar, which he told her was the price he had paid four years before.

Later, when the paperwork was filled out, she asked him, "How can you leave them? Won't they miss you?"

"You'll see, they're pretty autonomous," he said. "Yeah, they'll miss me and I'll miss them. But it's time, they know that."

He smiled at his new wife, a small woman with laugh lines and a vervet hanging from one hand. "We're ready to have a garden," she said.

He was right. The monkeys missed him. But they also welcomed her, each monkey politely shaking her hand as she walked into what was now her bus.

### 5.

Aimee has: a nineteen-year-old tour bus packed with cages that range in size from parrot-sized (for the vervets) to something about the size of a pickup bed (for all the macaques); a stack of books on monkeys ranging from *All About Monkeys* to *Evolution and Ecology of Baboon Societies*; some sequined show costumes, a sewing machine, and a bunch of Carhartts and tees; a stack of show posters from a few years back that say 24 MONKEYS! FACE THE ABYSS; a battered sofa in a virulent green plaid; and a boyfriend who helps with the monkeys.

She cannot tell you why she has any of these, not even the boyfriend, whose name is Geof, whom she met in Billings seven months ago. Aimee has no idea where anything comes from any more: she no longer believes that anything makes sense, even though she can't stop hoping.

The bus smells about as you'd expect a bus full of monkeys to smell; though after a show, after the bathtub trick but before the monkeys all return, it also smells of cinnamon, which is the tea Aimee sometimes drinks.

6.

For the act, the monkeys do tricks, or dress up in outfits and act out hit movies—*The Matrix* is very popular, as is anything where the monkeys dress up like little orcs. The maned monkeys, the lion-tails and the colobuses, have a lion-tamer act, with the old capuchin female, Pango, dressed in a red jacket and carrying a whip and a small chair. The chimpanzee (whose name is Mimi, and no, she is not a monkey) can do actual sleight-of-hand; she's not very good, but she's the best Chimp Pulling A Coin From Someone's Ear in the world.

The monkeys also can build a suspension bridge out of wood chairs and rope, make a four-tier champagne fountain, and write their names on a white-board.

The monkey show is very popular, with a schedule of 127 shows this year at fairs and festivals across the Midwest and Great Plains. Aimee could do more, but she likes to let everyone have a couple months off at Christmas.

7.

This is the bathtub act:

Aimee wears a glittering purple-black dress designed to look like a scanty magician's robe. She stands in front of a scrim lit deep blue and scattered with stars. The monkeys are ranged in front of her. As she speaks they undress and fold their clothes into neat piles. Zeb sits on his stool to one side, a white spotlight shining straight down to give him a shadowed look.

She raises her hands.

"These monkeys have made you laugh, and made you gasp. They have created wonders for you and performed mysteries. But there is a final mystery they offer you—the strangest, the greatest of all."

She parts her hands suddenly, and the scrim goes transparent and is lifted away, revealing the bathtub on a raised dais. She walks around it, running her hand along the tub's curves.

"It's a simple thing, this bathtub. Ordinary in every way, mundane as breakfast. In a moment I will invite members of the audience up to let you prove this for yourselves.

"But for the monkeys it is also a magical object. It allows them to travel—no one can say where. Not even I—" she pauses "—can tell you this. Only the monkeys know, and they share no secrets.

"Where do they go? Into heaven, foreign lands, other worlds—or some dark abyss? We cannot follow. They will vanish before our eyes, vanish from this most ordinary of things."

And after the bathtub is inspected and she has told the audience that there will be no final spectacle in the show—"It will be hours before they return from their secret travels"—and called for applause for them, she gives the cue.

8.

Aimee's monkeys:

2 siamangs, a mated couple

2 squirrel monkeys, though they're so active they might as well be twice as many

2 vervets

a guenon, who is probably pregnant, though it's still too early to tell for sure. Aimee has no idea how this happened

3 rhesus monkeys. They juggle a little

an older capuchin female named Pango

a crested macaque, 3 snow monkeys (one quite young), and a Java macaque. Despite the differences, they have formed a small troop and like to sleep together

a chimpanzee, who is not actually a monkey

a surly gibbon

2 marmosets

a golden tamarin; a cotton-top tamarin

a proboscis monkey

red and black colobuses

Zeb

9.

Aimee thinks Zeb might be a de Brazza's guenon, except that he's so old that he has lost almost all his hair. She worries about his health but he insists on staying in the act. By now all he's really up for is the final rush to the bathtub, and for him it is more of a stroll. The rest of the time, he sits on a stool that is painted orange and silver and watches the other monkeys, looking like an aging impresario watching his *Swan Lake* from the wings. Sometimes she gives him things to hold, such as a silver hoop through which the squirrel monkeys jump.

10.

No one knows how the monkeys vanish or where they go. Sometimes they return holding foreign coins or durian fruit, or wearing pointed Moroccan slippers. Every so often one returns pregnant, or accompanied by a new monkey. The number of monkeys is not constant.

"I just don't get it," Aimee keeps asking Geof, as if he has any idea. Aimee never knows anything any more. She's been living without any certainties, and this one thing—well, the whole thing, the fact the monkeys get along so well and know how to do card tricks and just turned up in her life and vanish from the bathtub; *everything*—she coasts with that most of the time, but every so often, when she feels her life is wheeling without brakes down a long hill, she starts poking at this again.

Geof trusts the universe a lot more than Aimee does, trusts that things make sense and that people can love, and therefore he doesn't need the same proofs. "You could ask them," he says.

11.

Aimee's boyfriend:

Geof is not at all what Aimee expected from a boyfriend. For one thing, he's fifteen years younger than Aimee, twenty-eight to her forty-three. For another, he's sort of quiet. For a third, he's gorgeous, silky thick hair pulled into a shoulder-length ponytail, shaved sides showing off his strong jaw line. He smiles a lot, but he doesn't laugh very often.

Geof has a degree in history, which means that he was working in a bike-repair shop when she met him at the Montana Fair. Aimee never has much to do right after the show, so when he offered to buy her a beer she said yes. And then it was four A.M. and they were kissing in the bus, monkeys letting themselves in and getting ready for bed; and Aimee and Geof made love.

In the morning over breakfast, the monkeys came up one by one and shook his hand solemnly, and then he was with the band, so to speak. She helped him pick up his cameras and clothes and the surfboard his sister had painted for him one year as a Christmas present. There's no room for the surfboard so it's suspended from the ceiling. Sometimes the squirrel monkeys hang out there and peek over the side.

Aimee and Geof never talk about love.

Geof has a class-C driver's license, but this is just lagniappe.

12.

Zeb is dying.

Generally speaking, the monkeys are remarkably healthy and Aimee can handle their occasional sinus infections and gastrointestinal ailments. For anything more difficult, she's found a couple of communities online and some helpful specialists.

But Zeb's coughing some, and the last of his fur is falling out. He moves very slowly and sometimes has trouble remembering simple tasks. When the show was in St. Paul six months ago, a Como Zoo biologist came to visit the monkeys, complimented her on their general health and well-being, and at her request looked Zeb over.

"How old is he?" the biologist, Gina, asked.

"I don't know," Aimee said. The man she bought the show from hadn't known either.

"*I'll* tell you then," Gina said. "He's old. I mean, seriously old."

Senile dementia, arthritis, a heart murmur. No telling when, Gina said. "He's a happy monkey," she said. "He'll go when he goes."

### 13.

Aimee thinks a lot about this. What happens to the act when Zeb's dead? Through each show he sits calm and poised on his bright stool. She feels he is somehow at the heart of the monkeys' amiability and cleverness. She keeps thinking that he is somehow the reason the monkeys all vanish and return.

Because there's always a reason for everything, isn't there? Because if there isn't a reason for even *one* thing, like how you can get sick, or your husband stops loving you or people you love die—then there's no reason for anything. So there must be reasons. Zeb's as good a guess as any.

### 14.

What Aimee likes about this life:

It doesn't mean anything. She doesn't live anywhere. Her world is thirty-eight feet and 127 shows long and currently twenty-six monkeys deep. This is manageable.

Fairs don't mean anything, either. Her tiny world travels within a slightly larger world, the identical, interchangeable fairs. Sometimes the only things that cue Aimee to the town she's in are the nighttime temperatures and the shape of the horizon: badlands, mountains, plains, or city skyline.

Fairs are as artificial as titanium knees: the carnival, the animal barns, the stock-car races, the concerts, the smell of burnt sugar and funnel cakes and animal bedding. Everything is an overly bright symbol for something real, food or pets or hanging out with friends. None of this has anything to do with the world Aimee used to live in, the world from which these people visit.

She has decided that Geof is like the rest of it: temporary, meaningless. Not for loving.

### 15.

These are some ways Aimee's life might have come apart:

She might have broken her ankle a few years ago, and gotten a bone infection that left her on crutches for ten months, and in pain for longer.

Her husband might have fallen in love with his admin and left her.

She might have been fired from her job in the same week she found out her sister had colon cancer.

She might have gone insane for a time and made a series of questionable choices that left her alone in a furnished apartment in a city she picked out of the atlas.

Nothing is certain. You can lose everything. Eventually, even at your luckiest, you will die and then you *will* lose it all. When you are a certain age or when you have lost certain things and people, Aimee's crippling grief will make a terrible poisoned dark sense.

### 16.

Aimee has read up a lot, so she knows how strange all this is.

There aren't any locks on the cages. The monkeys use them as bedrooms, places to store their special possessions and get away from the others when they want some privacy. Much of the time, however, they are loose in the bus or poking around in the worn grass around it.

Right now, three monkeys are sitting on the bed playing a game where they match colored cards. Others are playing with a Noah's ark, or rolling around on the floor, or poking at a piece of wood with a screwdriver, or climbing on Aimee and Geof and the battered sofa. Some of the monkeys are crowded around the computer watching kitten videos on a pirated wireless connection.

The black colobus is stacking children's wooden blocks on the kitchenette's table. He brought them back one night a couple of weeks ago, and since then he's been trying to make an arch. After two weeks and Aimee's showing him repeatedly how a keystone works, he still hasn't figured it out, but he's still patiently trying.

Geof's reading a novel out loud to the capuchin Pango, who watches the pages as if she's reading along. Sometimes she points to a word and looks up at him with her bright eyes, and he repeats it to her, smiling, and then spells it out.

Zeb is sleeping in his cage: he crept in there at dusk, fluffed up his toys and his blanket, and pulled the door closed behind him. He does this a lot lately.

### 17.

Aimee's going to lose Zeb, and then what? What happens to the other monkeys? Twenty-six monkeys is a lot of monkeys, but they all like each other. No one except maybe a zoo or a circus can keep that many monkeys, and she doesn't think anyone else will let them sleep wherever they like or watch kitten videos. And if Zeb's not there, where will they go, those nights when they can no longer drop through the bathtub and into their mystery? And she doesn't even know whether it *is* Zeb, whether he is the cause of this, or that's just her flailing for reasons again.

And Aimee? She'll lose her safe artificial world: the bus, the identical fairs, the meaningless boyfriend. The monkeys. And then what?

### 18.

Just a few months after she bought the act, when she didn't care much about whether she lived or died, she followed the monkeys up the ladder in the closing act. Zeb raced up the ladder, stepped into the bathtub and stood, lungs filling for his great call. And she ran up after him. She glimpsed the bathtub's interior, the monkeys tidily sardined in, scrambling to get out of her way as they realized what she was doing. She hopped into the hole they made for her, curled up tight.

This only took an instant. Zeb finished his breath, boomed it out. There was a flash of light, she heard the chains release, and felt the bathtub swing down, monkeys shifting around her.

She fell the ten feet alone. Her ankle twisted when she hit the stage but she managed to stay upright. The monkeys were gone again.

There was an awkward silence. It wasn't one of her more successful performances.

### 19.

Aimee and Geof walk through the midway at the Salina Fair. She's hungry and doesn't want to cook, so they're looking for somewhere that sells $4.50 hotdogs and $3.25 Cokes, and suddenly Geof turns to Aimee and says, "This is bullshit. Why don't we go into town? Have real food. Act like normal people."

So they do: pasta and wine at a place called Irina's Villa. "You're always asking why they go," Geof says, a bottle and a half in. His eyes are an indeterminate blue-gray, but in this light they look black and very warm. "See, I don't think we're ever going to find out what happens. But I don't think that's the real question, anyway. Maybe the question is, why do they come back?"

Aimee thinks of the foreign coins, the wood blocks, the wonderful things they bring home. "I don't know," she says. "Why *do* they come back?"

Later that night, back at the bus, Geof says, "Wherever they go, yeah, it's cool. But see, here's my theory." He gestures to the crowded bus with its clutter of toys and tools. The two tamarins have just come in, and they're sitting on the kitchenette counter, heads close as they examine some new small thing. "They like visiting wherever it is, sure. But this is their home. Everyone likes to come home sooner or later."

"If they have a home," Aimee says.

"Everyone has a home, even if they don't believe in it," Geof says.

### 20.

That night, when Geof's asleep curled up around one of the macaques, Aimee kneels by Zeb's cage. "Can you at least show me?" she asks. "Please? Before you go?"

Zeb is an indeterminate lump under his baby-blue blanket, but he gives a little sigh and climbs slowly out of his cage. He takes her hand with his own hot leathery paw, and they walk out the door into the night.

The back lot where all the trailers and buses are parked is quiet, only a few voices still audible from behind curtained windows. The sky is blue-black and scattered with stars. The moon shines straight down on them, shadowing Zeb's face. His eyes when he looks up seem bottomless.

The bathtub is backstage, already on its wheeled dais waiting for the next show. The space is nearly pitch dark, lit by some red EXIT signs and a single sodium-vapor away off to one side. Zeb walks her up to the tub, lets her run her hands along its cold curves and the lion's paws, and shows her the dimly lit interior.

And then he heaves himself onto the dais and over the tub lip. She stands beside him, looking down. He lifts himself upright and gives a boom. And then he drops flat and the bathtub is empty.

She saw it, him vanishing. He was there and then he was gone. But there was nothing to see, no gate, no flickering reality or soft pop as air snapped in to fill the vacated space. It still doesn't make sense, but it's the answer that Zeb has.

He's already back at the bus when she gets there, already buried under his blanket and wheezing in his sleep.

21.

Then one day:

Everyone is backstage. Aimee is finishing her makeup, and Geof is double-checking everything. The monkeys are sitting neatly in a circle in the dressing room, as if trying to keep their bright vests and skirts from creasing. Zeb sits in the middle, Pango beside him in her little green sequined outfit. They grunt a bit, then lean back. One after the other, the rest of the monkeys crawl forward and shake his hand, and then hers. She nods, like a small queen at a flower show.

That night, Zeb doesn't run up the ladder. He stays on his stool and it's Pango who is the last monkey up the ladder, who climbs into the bathtub and gives a screech. Aimee has been wrong to think Zeb had to be the reason for what is happening with the monkeys, but she was so sure of it that she missed all the cues. But Geof didn't miss a thing, so when Pango screeches, he hits the flash powder. The flash, the empty bathtub.

Zeb stands on his stool, bowing like an impresario called onstage for the curtain call. When the curtain drops for the last time, he reaches up to be lifted. Aimee cuddles him as they walk back to the bus, Geof's arm around them both.

Zeb falls asleep with them that night, between them in the bed. When she wakes up in the morning, he's back in his cage with his favorite toy. He doesn't wake up. The monkeys cluster at the bars peeking in.

Aimee cries all day. "It's okay," Geof says.

"It's not about Zeb," she sobs.

"I know," he says. "It's okay. Come home, Aimee."

But she's already there. She just hadn't noticed.

22.

Here's the trick to the bathtub trick. There is no trick. The monkeys pour across the stage and up the ladder and into the bathtub and they settle in and then they vanish. The world is full of strange things, things that make no sense, and maybe this is one of them. Maybe the monkeys choose not to share, that's cool, who can blame them.

Maybe this is the monkeys' mystery, how they found other monkeys that ask questions and try things, and figured out a way to all be together to share it.

Maybe Aimee and Geof are really just houseguests in the monkeys' world: they are there for a while and then they leave.

23.

Six weeks later, a man walks up to Aimee as she and Geof kiss after a show. He's short, pale, balding. He has the shell-shocked look of a man eaten hollow from the inside. She knows the look.

"I need to buy this," he says.

Aimee nods. "I know you do."

She sells it to him for a dollar.

Three months later, Aimee and Geof get their first houseguest in their apartment in Bellingham. They hear the refrigerator close and come out to the kitchen to find Pango pouring orange juice from a carton.

They send her home with a pinochle deck.

# MARRY THE SUN

## RACHEL SWIRSKY

Rachel Swirsky holds a Masters degree in Fiction from the University of Iowa, and is a graduate of the Clarion West Writers Workshop. Her fiction and poetry has appeared in a number of magazines and anthologies, including *Subterranean Magazine, Weird Tales, Interzone, Best American Fantasy*, and *Fantasy: The Best of the Year 2008*. She edits *PodCastle,* the world's first audio fantasy magazine, which puts up readings of great fantasy stories every week at http://podcastle.org.

The wedding went well until the bride caught fire.

Bridget's pretty white dress went up in a whoosh, from train-length veil to taffeta skirt to rose-embroidered bodice and Juliet cap with ferronière of pearls. The fabric burned so hot and fast that it went up without igniting Bridget's skin, leaving her naked, singed, embarrassed, and crying.

Of these problems, nudity was easiest to cope with. Bridget pulled the silk drape off the altar and tied it around her chest like a toga.

"That is it," she said. She pried the engagement ring off her finger and threw it at the groom. The grape-sized diamond sparkled as it arced through the air.

Gathering up the drape's hem, Bridget ran back down the aisle. She flung open the double doors, letting in the moonlight, and fled into the night.

The groom sighed. He opened his palm and stared down at the glittering diamond, which reflected his fiery nimbus in shades of crimson, ginger, and gold. His best man patted him on the shoulder—cautiously. The bride's father gave a manly nod of sympathy, but kept his distance. Like his daughter, he was mortal.

"Too bad, Helios," said Apollo.

The groom shrugged. "I gave it my best shot. I can't keep my flame on low all the time. What did the woman want? Sometimes a man's just got to let himself shine."

Apollo clapped him on the back. "You said it, brother."

Bridget went down to the reception hall. She let the hotel clerk gawk at her knotted drape, and then told him they'd be cancelling.

"The hall or the honeymoon suite?"

337

"Both," said Bridget.

The clerk rapped a few keys on the keyboard. "I'm sorry, but we can't accept cancellations this late. I'll have the staff take down the decorations in the hall, but we'll have to charge you."

Bridget felt too drained to argue. "Fine."

She went down the corridor to the reception hall. She at least wanted to see the chocolate fondue fountain and the ice sculptures, even if they were going to waste. Caterers and hotel staff ran back and forth, clearing away cups of fresh summer fruit and floral arrangements of birds of paradise and yellow tulips.

Bridget approached the six-tiered cake with the tiny bride figurine standing next to a brass sun. She plucked the bride out of the butter cream frosting. "What was I thinking?" she asked the little painted face.

"Don't we all wish we knew the answer to that question?"

Bridget looked up. Her matchmaker, the goddess of childbirth Eilethyia, leaned against the wine bar, tidy in a burgundy pantsuit and three-inch heels.

"I heard what happened," said Eilethyia.

"He couldn't hold it in, even on our wedding day?"

"Isn't that what you wanted? Someone dazzling, someone out of the ordinary, someone who could light a dark room with his smile?"

"But being dazzling isn't just what he is, it's something he does *to* other people. He can't just shine, he has to consume."

Eilethyia sipped her 1998 Chablis. "Good thing you found out before your vows, at least. The pre-nup you signed's a bitch."

Helios and Apollo settled in at the hotel bar. Floor-length windows overlooked the river where streetlights cast golden ripples on dark water. The scene was twinned in the mirror behind the bar.

Apollo improvised a sonnet about the cocktail waitress and got a free drink. Not to be outdone, Helios earned a shower of applause by lighting a vixen's cigarette from across the room.

Helios still wore his tuxedo, untied ascot draped across his chest like a scarf. He spun on his barstool to face his drink. "I thought she was different," he said.

Apollo had stopped to change into dress shirt and slacks, chic and metrosexual. He waved Helios's point away, marquise cut topaz and agate rings sparkling on his fingers. "They're all the same. I could have told you that."

"How helpful and droll," said Helios.

"It's true. It's the beauty of mortal women. Sure, they're unique, like snowflakes are unique, but who catches a snowflake to marvel over geodesic ice crystals? That's missing the point of snowflakes."

"Which is?"

"All the power and loveliness of the snow birthing this intricate, astonishing thing that's gone in an instant." Apollo winked at the brunette by the piano. "And they melt on your tongue, too."

Helios lifted his index finger, inspiring a tuft of flame on the brunette's bosom. As she beat it out with her cocktail napkin, Helios shaped the smoke above to spell out the phrase *Hot Stuff*. The brunette giggled, averting her eyes coquettishly.

Helios turned back to his friend. "That's not why I go with mortal women."

"Pray tell."

"They have a better understanding of things like joy and grief because their lives are difficult. They appreciate what they get. They make you feel real."

"Be honest, you just like having all the power in the relationship."

"That's not true!"

"If you say so."

Helios went on, "I like being with mortal women because of how different we are. Fire and water is more interesting than fire and fire."

"Interesting if you're fire. Fatal if you're water."

"Fire and earth, then." Helios lit a flame in his palm. He shifted its composition so that it burned rose and then gold and then iris. "The problem is, most mortal women don't get that. They think being with a god is going to make them more than human. They want to be special. They want to be anointed. I thought Bridget was different than that. She was grounded. She knew she was just an ordinary girl. I thought she was happy with who both of us were. But it turns out she wanted me to be just as dishwater dull as she is."

"We should turn them all into laurel trees," said Apollo, draining his drink. He rose from his barstool and ran his fingers through the loose wheat-colored curls of his Caesar cut. "Come on. If we can't find any nymphs, let's at least get us a couple nymphomaniacs."

Bridget remembered the day she realized the world was populated with gods. Really, it was an old suspicion, stemming from playground hierarchies and high school lunchrooms. Some people just seemed more *there* than others. They gleamed, they glittered. While Bridget and her peers stumbled through adolescence with scrapes and bruises, *they* floated through life without so much as a detention slip.

Wasn't it something everyone sensed? People watched the godly among them raise waves with a pitchfork, inspire love with an arrow, win track meets in winged sandals. Later they were remembered in a jeweled blur, details fuzzy but gist intact: the dare devil surfer, the counselor who saved my marriage, the kid who could run like nothing you ever saw.

But Bridget didn't really figure it out until she was finishing the fifth year of her Ph.D., tabulating data on a thesis few people outside her field could really understand.

Bridget was one of the world's foremost experts on the sun. Parts of the sun, at least. She studied sunspots, the patches of relative cold that blot the sun's surface like tears. She spent her hours in the laboratory, calculating the frequency of coronal loops, and checking them against the predicted occurrence of solar flares.

"The sun is a romantic metaphor," she was fond of telling friends over drinks, back when she had friends, and went out for drinks. "These little dark patches are caused by intense magnetic activity. It's all about attraction and repulsion. It can make the sun burn hot, or blow cold, or eject solar flares so vast they leave traces in Greenland."

Bridget had the kind of mind that thrived on solitude and data, or so she convinced herself in the absence of anything but solitude and data to thrive upon. By the fifth year of her Ph.D., the last of her undergraduate friends had gotten jobs and moved away, not that she had much in common with them any longer anyway. Her father lived in a rental house three states away with two bachelor friends, and while he claimed he wanted updates on Bridget's life, Bridget heard the flat grieved tone of his voice when he picked up the telephone. Bridget had her mother's dark, sunken eyes, and hair the hue of corn sheaves. She knew that, to her father, she was one more reminder of her mother's illness and death. It had been hard on him, being a widower. He dealt with grief by making himself a new life. Bridget was part of the old one. She mostly stayed away.

Daily, Bridget woke at dawn. She showered and brushed her teeth and rode her bike onto campus where she grabbed a cup of coffee from a vendor in the student union. She sat in her lab, watching the sun's arc through the office's high window that let in baking heat during midafternoon, until the sun sank and the room grew dark, and then she sat there some more. She rode her bicycle home around two in the morning, and went to bed in her clothes.

One afternoon, as Bridget sat in her lab on a day when heavy snow had piled on the campus's hills, sparkling under a bright but distant sun that lacked the power to melt it, Bridget looked down at her keyboard and realized she couldn't feel her fingers. They'd been typing for an hour without her conscious command. They felt more like part of the machine than part of her.

Red and blue lines criss-crossed the screen, mapping her data. Bridget recognized none of it. She pulled her hands away from the keyboard and fanned her fingers in front of her eyes. Slowly, she began to feel the ache of her cold, unheated office settle in her fingertips.

She tried to remember the last time she'd spoken to anyone for more than two sentences. It had been over three weeks. She was twenty-nine years old and she couldn't fathom why she'd ever thought that mapping sunspots was worth the utter lack of human company.

She fled the office early, ignoring the queries of professors and students as she unlocked her bike from the rack outside the building and rode away down the snowy road. When she reached her house, she found an unfamiliar woman standing there, her outfit and coiffure so immaculate that at first Bridget thought she was selling Avon.

"I've been sent by a secret admirer," said the woman, introducing herself as Eilethyia.

Bridget couldn't imagine any student or professor, the only two groups of people she interacted with, hiring this elegant woman to make a suit on their behalf. "Oh, yes?" she asked.

"Indeed," said Eilethyia, unruffled. "My client prefers to woo via a mediator, someone who understands human culture better than he does."

"Human culture?" asked Bridget, wondering what prank was being pulled on her. "Tell this admirer, whoever he is, that I don't go on blind dates."

"It's not a blind date, exactly," said Eilethyia. "You've met before."

"Who is he?" asked Bridget.

A sly smile crossed Eilethyia's lips. She turned and pointed toward the summit of the noontime sky where the sun blazed through the cold air, dazzling. Somehow, Bridget was unsurprised.

"I daresay you're as enamored of him as he is of you," said Eilethyia. "That's probably what he likes about you. Never forget that gods are narcissists. Why do you think we want everyone to worship us?"

Bridget laughed, not at the fact of her admirer's godhood, for that she had already strangely come to accept. She laughed at the frank and unabashed admission of narcissism. At the time, she thought it was a joke.

Most gods dabbled with mortals the way most mortals dabbled with self-love. It was entertaining, it was convenient, it was a way of releasing tension when nothing better presented itself. The chief deity himself liked to season his love life by seducing mortal maidens as a white bull or swan. But it was like an hors d'oeuvre to a gourmet meal. Once the champagne framboise and lobster bisque had been sampled, he wasted no time in slipping back into his natural godly form to hightail it home for an entrée of duck Martiniquaise with his lady wife.

Rarely, a god found mortal love affairs becoming not an aperitif, but something altogether too alluring: a fetish.

Apollo denied it was that way with him. He remained aloof and rakish, playing up his persona as the literally eternal bachelor. It worked pretty well for him too, Helios noted, as he watched Apollo cozy up with the tow-headed boy he'd lured over from the piano. The boy wrapped his arms around Apollo's waist, aiming a nip at the god's ear.

Helios set down his pepper vodka. He left a little flame burning on the surface, evaporating the alcohol. Over his shoulder, the cocktail waitress gingerly cleared her throat.

"Would you mind?"

Helios looked down at a pudding enflambé. "But of course," he said, winking, but the reflexive flirtation felt false. His overzealous flare singed the eyebrows of a nearby man in tweed. The waitress rushed over to give him a free drink.

The blond kid slipped his tongue between Apollo's sculpted lips. His giggling drifted on the air with the cigarette smoke. Helios could smell his cologne: sandalwood with a hint of moss. He looked away.

Helios hadn't been with a goddess since his only son, Phaeton, died. At sixteen, the boy had begged to drive Helios's sun chariot across the sky. Helios pleaded with him to choose any other gift, knowing the boy wouldn't be able to control his team. But Phaeton was sixteen. Failure was something that happened to other people.

At dawn, Helios helped his son into the chariot, and watched as it rose into the sky until Phaeton was only a golden blur in the heavens. Helios felt a strange stirring as he beheld it. He'd never before seen the sun rise from below. Was this what he looked like to mortals every day? A flare of brilliance so intense it stung the eyes?

Later, after Phaeton lost control of the team and Zeus brought the boy down with a bolt of lightning so bright it twinned the sun, Helios's daughters wept so fiercely that Zeus changed them into poplar trees. And so Helios lost them, too. Zeus regarded the rivers of their maidenly tears and froze their mourning into amber, which was how that gem first came into the world. The first time Helios slept in Bridget's apartment, he begged her to discard all her amber jewelry. He bought her replacements in jade.

Helios wasn't sure what it was about mortal women that salved his grief. Or maybe they didn't salve it at all. Maybe their appeal was the way their brief earthbound existences—like plants that flowered out of and then decayed back into the ground—rubbed salt and soil into his wounds.

Apollo looked over. He and the boy swung their hands together, like children. "Come on, pick someone," said Apollo. "It'll make you feel better."

"I suppose."

Helios scanned the bar. His gaze settled on a black woman wearing a gold knit sweater that made her skin glow like a bright penny. She sat with a few girlfriends, chatting. Her laugh sounded like a bell on a winter morning. Helios slipped off his barstool.

"Might I interrupt?" he asked.

The woman's friends looked at her to see what she wanted. She gave them a nod. They scooted back their chairs to admit Helios into their circle.

"I wonder if I might beg the honor of your company tonight," he said. Before the woman could reply, he inspired tiny golden flames to dance across her arms. Sparks pirouetted like ballerinas spinning on a stage.

Interest sparkled in her mahogany eyes. She wet her lips. Her breathing became shallow and quick. She was dazzled.

Bridget had never lacked for romantic attention, but she'd never found herself enthralled by it either. Men, by and large, bored her. She wanted men who possessed a flame of dedication that ignited something unique and all-consuming within themselves. She'd dated a few. There was a world champion chess player, a computer programmer who built elaborate palaces of code, and a volcanologist who explored volcanoes on the verge of eruption. But one by one, she'd discovered their passions to be other than what they seemed: rote compulsion, unconscious ability no more personally meaningful than breathing, self-hatred becoming high risk behavior.

Bridget and Helios had their first date on the rim of a molten lava lake, its active vents guttering threateningly with the burble of tension barely contained. Sulfur permeated the air.

Eilethyia accompanied them. At first, Bridget chafed at being chauffeured, but when Eilethyia had to talk Helios out of taking Bridget skinny dipping in the lava, Bridget began to understand why the slender goddess had come along.

They sat and talked about nothing in particular, their worlds so different that the small talk had a dreamlike air, but the strange disjointed nature of their conversation did not detract from the connection they both felt warming between them, as if they spoke different languages but intuitively understood the same words. The goddess Eilethyia sat nearby as they talked, reclining laconically against a slab of basalt, her face turned discreetly away but wearing a rye and pleased smile.

An hour before dawn broke, as pale light gathered in the sky preparing for the moment when Helios would burst over the horizon in his chariot, Helios took Bridget by the hands and led her onto an obsidian outcropping, outside the goddess's hearing.

"I can tell you anything you want to know," he said, correctly assuming that Bridget's lust would be inflamed by the promise of knowledge. "What other stars look like, the chemical composition of distant suns, why magnetic fields pulse and sway the way they do. I could take you to visit strange planets and nebulas and pulsars."

"I don't think I'd survive," said Bridget.

"Then ask me questions, and I'll bring the answers back to you."

Bridget smiled. The god stood before her with his shoulders thrown back, his feet planted in a strong, wide stance. His hands were hot, his eyes fierce upon her. He had a presence of being in himself like no one that Bridget had ever met before. Throughout her life, she had always felt herself fuzzy and indeterminate, collecting knowledge against the specter of her death like a squirrel assembling nuts before hibernation. Here was someone who flared, and burned, and *was*.

Bridget thought back on that first interlude as she stood in the bathroom of Eilethyia's hotel room, exchanging her improvised drape for one of the goddess's dresses. The dress was loose, grey linen, the only thing in Eilethyia's wardrobe that came close to Bridget's size. Bridget had never been overweight, but the goddess was long and narrow as a stroke of calligraphy.

"Do you need help?" called Eilethyia through the door.

Bridget looked up at the blotted tears beneath her eyes that showed in her reflection. She dabbed them quickly away and steeled herself with anger. He burned, but unthinkingly, more like a fire than a man. She had made the right choice.

Bridget slipped out of the bathroom. The goddess stood nearby, watching.

"Thanks for letting me borrow this," said Bridget. "I couldn't face going up to the suite for my luggage."

"Does your family know where you are?" asked Eilethyia.

"I called my father and told him to go home. I don't want to see him now."

"There's no other mortal to comfort you? Sisters? Friends?"

"I'm an only child," said Bridget. "Isolation is an old habit."

Eilethyia nodded, businesslike but not unkind, diamond studs flashing at her ears. "We should get something to eat."

Bridget raised her eyebrows. "At this time of night?"

"I know a good Greek place not far from here."

Bridget followed Eilethyia though the city's winding intersections. Drunk people swarmed in and out of the pubs lining the river. The air smelled of the contrast between crisp wind and stale beer. They entered an alley and Eilethyia led Bridget up a narrow, metal flight of stairs. Bridget winced as the goddess knocked on someone's door.

"It's so late," Bridget began.

Eilethyia raised a silencing hand. Bridget held her tongue.

Soon enough, a heavyset woman in a long white nightdress opened the door. A man dressed in slacks and a cotton undershirt stood behind her, sleepless circles beneath his eyes. Both looked unsurprised by the intrusion. "Come upstairs," said the woman, her voice flat.

"What did you do to them?" Bridget whispered to the goddess as they were escorted through a narrow, tiled parlor.

"Nothing," said Eilethyia.

She gestured down a shadowed hallway. Bridget saw the small white shapes of pajama-clad children peering around the corner.

"They know me here," said the goddess.

The woman led them up another flight of stairs. They came out in a roof garden where several ironwork tables sat among potted ferns. The man started to hand them menus, but Eilethyia waved him away and ordered for them both. The man bowed his head and retreated.

Eilethyia leaned back in her chair. "So, what do you plan to do now?"

"I don't know," Bridget admitted. "I can't continue with my thesis… spending so much time with him every day would be… maybe I'll go to work in a lab for a while…"

"I meant in regard to your erstwhile fiancé."

Bridget sighed. "It's not like I can avoid seeing him." She glanced up at the sky where a sliver of moon sliced the dark. "At least we won't have to talk."

"Will you want another god to replace him?"

"Absolutely not!"

Bridget surprised herself with her vehemence. She shifted in her seat, smoothing wrinkles out of the linen dress.

"Looking back, there was always something… strange about our relationship. The way he saw me was…"

"Like an old man looking at a young girl?" offered Eilethyia.

"Sort of…"

"A celebrity admiring his most ardent fan?"

"Something like that."

Eilethyia gave a short sharp nod. "It's always been my theory that gods who fixate on mortals are… What's the word I'm looking for?" She tapped one crimson nail against the table. "Unnatural, perhaps? Not that there's anything wrong with unnatural. Natural childbirth is painful and often fatal. Unnatural can be good."

"Unnatural?" repeated Bridget, skeptically.

"How do I put this? They're like humans who want to make love with beasts."

Bridget flinched sharply.

"Don't take it like that. It's a difference in kind, not scale."

The man arrived with their food, a plate full of meat wrapped in grape leaves for the goddess, and squares of lamb on rice for Bridget.

"You could have told me all this before you matched me with Helios," said Bridget, accusingly. "Why did you let me get engaged to someone you thought was mentally diseased?"

"Ah. Well." Delicately, Eilethyia chewed a leaf from the side of her fork. "I haven't told you what I think is wrong with mortals who want to be with gods."

Bridget pricked with shame. She hated the thought of others seeing wrongness in her. She worked hard to conceal her flaws.

Eilethyia sipped her wine calmly. "Mortals and gods are always seeing in each other what they themselves lack. Divinity, mundanity, exaltation, pain." She set down her glass and fixed Bridget with a frank stare. "If you want my advice, you have two options. Take my card, and when you've had time to recover, I'll pair you with another god. Or, if you want to grow, if you want to become a better, more whole person, then find the spark of divinity within yourself and search for a mortal to share it with."

Goosebumps prickled along Bridget's arms. She felt bruised and earthen and drained. "It's all so easy for you, isn't it? You don't have relations with gods or mortals, do you?"

"No," said Eilethyia.

The goddess glanced over toward a corner of the roof where children's toys lay scattered among the potted plants.

"I'm too familiar with where it all leads," she said, and Bridget saw her smile was sad.


Helios escorted the woman, whose name turned out to be Jody, to a nocturnal street fair sprawling in the city's main square. Her friends tagged along. He entertained them by challenging the fire eater to a contest which ended when Helios devoured a flaming meteor and then sent it rocketing back into space.

Helios selected a mortal man for each of Jody's friends, haloing them with a light touch of flame to make them seem more attractive. One by one, her friends peeled away. Soon Helios and Jody were alone.

"Would you join me in my hotel room?" he asked.

By the time they reached the elevator, Jody's hands were all over him, stroking his hips, unbuttoning his shirt. Her breath on his neck felt damp and hot as a humid afternoon.

When the elevator clanged Helios's floor, they backed out, entwined, stumbling through the corridor. Helios unclasped Jody's bra. She unzipped his fly. He had to clasp her hands to hold them still long enough so that he could work the key that admitted them into the honeymoon suite.

When they got inside, they found themselves looking at the tow-headed boy from the bar. He sat astride Apollo in the gigantic bathtub. Sprays of bubbles from the jets obscured what was going on beneath the water.

"What is he doing here?" demanded the boy. "Isn't this your room?"

"My friend here just got left at the altar," said Apollo. "I didn't think he'd be needing the room."

Helios turned to Jody. "My apologies."

"I don't mind," said Jody. She traced her finger down Helios's chest. "It's actually kind of a turn-on."

Leaving Apollo and his mortal in the bathroom, Helios and Jody moved to the bed. Jody's skin felt smooth and sweet as flower petals. Her close-cropped natural hair covered her head like delicious brown moss. Helios ran his fingers through it over and over, the sensation delectable and maddening. He pulled the black strap of her bra out from her sleeve, removing the whole lacy garment without taking off her sweater. He slipped his hands beneath the cashmere and took her breasts into his palms. Her hard nipples felt like knots on wood, beautifully textured. Gently, Helios eased her sweater over her head. A gold chain flashed around her neck.

Helios caught the pendant in his palm. "What is this?"

"Alaskan amber," said Jody. "There's part of a bee in it."

Helios examined the gem. It was set in a simple silver oval. Rich, warm colors swirled through its heart: drifts of sienna, umber, burnt orange, and carmine suspended like haze in a yellow sky. A bee hung in its center, wings trapped mid-flutter. Helios thought of all the grief that had been poured into making this chaotic, vibrant thing, all the sorrow his daughters wept out when Phaeton's chariot fell. Their solidified grief was incandescent as the sun. It burned him.

Helios released the necklace. It swung down, a yellow globe between Jody's breasts. She cocked her head and smiled, raising her eyebrows in invitation. Her lips sparkled. Helios moved away from the bed, and began dressing.

"What?" asked Jody. "Do bees gross you out or something?"

Helios's fingers felt numb on his shirt buttons. "I'm sorry. As my friend said, I was left at the altar today."

She hesitated, and then said, "That must be rough."

"As you can imagine, I'm still in a state of shock. I hope you'll forgive me."

"It's okay," she said. She pulled herself into a sitting position, legs tucked beneath her, and began putting on her clothes. "I can meet up with my friends tomorrow."

She tugged on her sweater and pulled a compact out of her purse, checking to make sure her lipstick hadn't smudged from kissing. She gave Helios a sad smile, one side of her mouth pulled up into a dimple.

"Try not to take it too hard, okay?" she said. "A man like you, someone else'll snap you up in no time."

Helios had nothing to say to that. He took Jody's elbow and escorted her to the door. He watched as she walked away down the hall, short black skirt swishing around her thighs.

Apollo called out from the bathroom. "So, do your newfound sexual ethics mean we have to cut out of here too, or can you suffer alone?"

Helios closed the door. All these eons and he could still picture Phaeton's face, every detail crisp as a brushstroke.

"Do whatever you want."

After dinner, Eilethyia offered to continue keeping Bridget company. Bridget declined. She wanted time alone. She paced the waterfront, hugging herself against the chill. Pale clouds had drifted over the gibbous moon, and crickets had emerged from the ornamental hedges lining the sidewalk to serenade potential mates. Bridget stared down at the blurred reflections of halogen bulbs in the water, submerged and insignificant suns. *Everything can be overwhelmed*, she thought. *Everything can be drowned.* When her teeth started chattering, she turned back to the hotel, ready to collect her luggage and move on.

In the corridor leading to the honeymoon suite, Bridget collided with a statuesque African American woman. The woman's clothes were rumpled and her makeup smeared. She smelled of Helios: ash and smoke and sparkle.

Bridget's stomach churned as the woman disappeared into the elevator. This soon? This fast? She felt betrayed, and then furious with herself for being surprised at betrayal. She slid the key card into the door without knocking.

As she entered, she heard splashing as a male voice moaned from the bathroom, "Not another one."

Bridget's anger bellowed full-throated. She put her hand over her eyes and pushed blindly past the bathroom. "Don't worry," she snapped. "I'm just here to get my clothes."

Eyes still covered, she turned toward the dresser and began yanking drawers open. Her unpacked suitcase lay on the rug beside her, lid askew. She felt so stupid for having taken the time to put her clothes away in the suite. She'd been all aflutter that morning, expecting to come back a married woman, not wanting to be distracted by luggage. She threw her clothes into the suitcase in massive, hasty piles.

"Do you want help with that?" asked Helios from behind her.

Bridget turned. He sat on the bed, still dressed neatly in dress shirt and tuxedo pants. His jacket lay draped over the arm of an over-stuffed chair by the window.

"Why aren't you in the bathroom with your buddy?" asked Bridget.

"Hi there," called a voice from the bathroom. Bridget spun around, recognizing Apollo's timbre. The debonair god leaned against the doorframe, a hotel towel wrapped around his waist. A slender, young-looking man stood behind him, staring curiously at Bridget from behind his tousled blond hair.

"We were just trying to have some fun in here," Apollo said. "Some of us aren't so hung up on buying the cow."

Apollo's voice seeped with disdain at the word *cow*. Bridget was momentarily taken aback as she realized it wasn't marriage he was mocking, but mortals' animal flesh.

"Get out of here, Apollo," said Helios.

Apollo looked miffed. "You said we could stay."

Helios's voice was level but taut with tension. He spoke slowly. "Just get out."

"Fine." Apollo took the blond's hand. "Let's get out of here."

The blond frowned. "Where are we going? I told my roommate I wasn't coming back tonight."

Apollo shrugged off the blond's protestations. He turned to Helios, his eyes icy. "Mortals come and go. It's your friends you should be careful to keep."

Helios did not soften. "I'll see you tomorrow night."

Apollo led the blond out of the room. The door slammed behind them.

"I see he hasn't changed since this afternoon," said Bridget.

"He hasn't changed in four thousand years. And he won't, either."

Bridget looked out the window. Twelve floors below, cars pushed past on a busy expressway, headlights garish in the darkness.

"I'm sorry about your dress," said Helios. "I didn't mean to burn it. I wanted to look impressive."

"You wanted to show off," said Bridget.

"No, that's not it—"

"You waited until I was walking up the aisle. You couldn't stand someone else having everyone's attention."

"I didn't think about it."

"You never do, do you? You just do what you want and don't worry about the consequences."

Helios neared Bridget, his presence tangibly hot.

"This is silly," he said, voice firm and commanding. "It was an accident. It won't happen again."

He smelled like sparks thrown into cold air, like firefly swarms piercing humid summer evenings. An aura ignited around his solid, golden form, flashing and sparking like the northern lights. Bridget looked up at his smooth burnished skin, his shoulders broad and straight like the line of the horizon. She felt fragile and insignificant under his gaze, overwhelmed by her primal mind's awe of the sun. Her mouth dried and her heart accelerated to match his aura's flicker.

She pulled away. "Don't do that. Don't manipulate me."

Helios's aura winked out. He paced away from her, strides long and angry. "Why do you think you've spent your life alone? No one's ever good enough for you. I should turn you into a laurel tree. I should change your skin to match your heart and make you a woman of ice, and then melt you with my heat."

"Well, I guess that would prove me wrong!" Bridget said. "It's definitely not narcissistic to kill someone because she won't marry you." She barked a laugh. "I don't know why you care anyway. The same night I leave, you have another woman in your room. We're all just mortals anyway. You exchange one for another for another. Can you even tell the difference?"

Helios halted. His face was wet, his hands were shaking. "Is that what you think?" he said.

"Am I wrong?"

A moment of silence hung in the air. Helios exhaled a wracking sigh.

"How long does it take a mortal man to get over the death of his son?"

"I'm not sure," said Bridget, quietly. "I'm not sure they ever do."

She leaned back against the window, the glass smooth and cool. She closed her eyes.

"We've both got problems," she said. "I think we've got to find the solutions on our own."

Helios said nothing. When Bridget opened her eyes, he had become diffuse, the hotel lights shimmering through his increasingly translucent body.

Through the walls, they could hear the noise of party-goers returning to their rooms after the revelry of the wee hours. Traffic thickened on the expressway below. The night was almost over.

"You need to go, don't you?" asked Bridget.

Helios nodded.

"I'll look down on you from time to time," he said.

Bridget almost smiled.

Helios leaned toward her, his lips pressing warm against her own. She was bathed in his heat for a moment, and then he was gone.

Bridget turned toward the window to watch the grey sky slowly brightening with pink and peach. She wondered where she'd be tomorrow, who she'd find to share her long nights in the lab, her ability to find romance in sunspots. Soon, there would be the break of morning, yellow blazing boldly against azure. Now there was the horizon, flat and distant and caught between the worlds of sky and ground.

# CRYSTAL NIGHTS

## GREG EGAN

Greg Egan published his first story in 1983, and followed it with more than fifty short stories and eight novels, including *Permutation City*, *Distress*, *Diaspora*, *Teranesia*, *Schild's Ladder*, and *Incandescence*. During the early 1990s Egan published a body of short fiction—mostly hard science fiction focused on mathematical and quantum ontological themes—that established him as one of the most important writers working in science fiction. His work has won the Hugo, John W. Campbell Memorial, Locus, Aurealis, Ditmar, and Seiun awards. His most recent book is collection *Dark Integers and Other Stories*. Upcoming are two new collections, *Oceanic* and *Crystal Nights and Other Stories*.

1

"More caviar?" Daniel Cliff gestured at the serving dish and the cover irised from opaque to transparent. "It's fresh, I promise you. My chef had it flown in from Iran this morning."

"No thank you." Julie Dehghani touched a napkin to her lips then laid it on her plate with a gesture of finality. The dining room overlooked the Golden Gate Bridge, and most people Daniel invited here were content to spend an hour or two simply enjoying the view, but he could see that she was growing impatient with his small talk.

Daniel said, "I'd like to show you something." He led her into the adjoining conference room. On the table was a wireless keyboard; the wall screen showed a Linux command line interface. "Take a seat," he suggested.

Julie complied. "If this is some kind of audition, you might have warned me," she said.

"Not at all," Daniel replied. "I'm not going to ask you to jump through any hoops. I'd just like you to tell me what you think of this machine's performance."

She frowned slightly, but she was willing to play along. She ran some standard benchmarks. Daniel saw her squinting at the screen, one hand almost reaching up to where a desktop display would be, so she could double-check the number of digits in the FLOPS rating by counting them off with one finger. There were a lot more than she'd been expecting, but she wasn't seeing double.

351

"That's extraordinary," she said. "Is this whole building packed with networked processors, with only the penthouse for humans?"

Daniel said, "You tell me. Is it a cluster?"

"Hmm." So much for not making her jump through hoops, but it wasn't really much of a challenge. She ran some different benchmarks, based on algorithms that were provably impossible to parallelise; however smart the compiler was, the steps these programs required would have to be carried out strictly in sequence.

The FLOPS rating was unchanged.

Julie said, "All right, it's a single processor. Now you've got my attention. Where is it?"

"Turn the keyboard over."

There was a charcoal-grey module, five centimetres square and five millimetres thick, plugged into an inset docking bay. Julie examined it, but it bore no manufacturer's logo or other identifying marks.

"This connects to the processor?" she asked.

"No. It *is* the processor."

"You're joking." She tugged it free of the dock, and the wall screen went blank. She held it up and turned it around, though Daniel wasn't sure what she was looking for. Somewhere to slip in a screwdriver and take the thing apart, probably. He said, "If you break it, you own it, so I hope you've got a few hundred spare."

"A few hundred grand? Hardly."

"A few hundred million."

Her face flushed. "Of course. If it was a few hundred grand, everyone would have one." She put it down on the table, then as an afterthought slid it a little further from the edge. "As I said, you've got my attention."

Daniel smiled. "I'm sorry about the theatrics."

"No, this deserved the build-up. What is it, exactly?"

"A single, three-dimensional photonic crystal. No electronics to slow it down; every last component is optical. The architecture was nanofabricated with a method that I'd prefer not to describe in detail."

"Fair enough." She thought for a while. "I take it you don't expect me to buy one. My research budget for the next thousand years would barely cover it."

"In your present position. But you're not joined to the university at the hip."

"So this is a job interview?"

Daniel nodded.

Julie couldn't help herself; she picked up the crystal and examined it again, as if there might yet be some feature that a human eye could discern. "Can you give me a job description?"

"Midwife."

She laughed. "To what?"

"History," Daniel said.

Her smile faded slowly.

"I believe you're the best AI researcher of your generation," he said. "I want you to work for me." He reached over and took the crystal from her. "With this as your platform, imagine what you could do."

Julie said, "What exactly would you want me to do?"

"For the last fifteen years," Daniel said, "you've stated that the ultimate goal of your research is to create conscious, human-level, artificial intelligence."

"That's right."

"Then we want the same thing. What I want is for you to succeed."

She ran a hand over her face; whatever else she was thinking, there was no denying that she was tempted. "It's gratifying that you have so much confidence in my abilities," she said. "But we need to be clear about some things. This prototype is amazing, and if you ever get the production costs down I'm sure it will have some extraordinary applications. It would eat up climate forecasting, lattice QCD, astrophysical modelling, proteomics…"

"Of course." Actually, Daniel had no intention of marketing the device. He'd bought out the inventor of the fabrication process with his own private funds; there were no other shareholders or directors to dictate his use of the technology.

"But AI," Julie said, "is different. We're in a maze, not a highway; there's nowhere that speed alone can take us. However many exaflops I have to play with, they won't spontaneously combust into consciousness. I'm not being held back by the university's computers; I have access to SHARCNET anytime I need it. I'm being held back by my own lack of insight into the problems I'm addressing."

Daniel said, "A maze is not a dead end. When I was twelve, I wrote a program for solving mazes."

"And I'm sure it worked well," Julie replied, "for small, two-dimensional ones. But you know how those kind of algorithms scale. Put your old program on this crystal, and I could still design a maze in half a day that would bring it to its knees."

"Of course," Daniel conceded. "Which is precisely why I'm interested in hiring you. You know a great deal more about the maze of AI than I do; any strategy you developed would be vastly superior to a blind search."

"I'm not saying that I'm merely groping in the dark," she said. "If it was that bleak, I'd be working on a different problem entirely. But I don't see what difference this processor would make."

"What created the only example of consciousness we know of?" Daniel asked.

"Evolution."

"Exactly. But I don't want to wait three billion years, so I need to make the selection process a great deal more refined, and the sources of variation more targeted."

Julie digested this. "You want to try to *evolve* true AI? Conscious, human-level AI?"

"Yes." Daniel saw her mouth tightening, saw her struggling to measure her words before speaking.

"With respect," she said, "I don't think you've thought that through."

"On the contrary," Daniel assured her. "I've been planning this for twenty years."

"Evolution," she said, "is about failure and death. Do you have any idea how many sentient creatures lived and died along the way to *Homo sapiens?* How much suffering was involved?"

"Part of your job would be to minimise the suffering."

"*Minimise it?*" She seemed genuinely shocked, as if this proposal was even worse than blithely assuming that the process would raise no ethical concerns. "What right do we have to inflict it at all?"

Daniel said, "You're grateful to exist, aren't you? Notwithstanding the tribulations of your ancestors."

"I'm grateful to exist," she agreed, "but in the human case the suffering wasn't deliberately inflicted by anyone, and nor was there any alternative way we could have come into existence. If there really *had* been a just creator, I don't doubt that he would have followed Genesis literally; he sure as hell would not have used evolution."

"Just, *and omnipotent,*" Daniel suggested. "Sadly, that second trait's even rarer than the first."

"I don't think it's going to take omnipotence to create something in our own image," she said. "Just a little more patience and self-knowledge."

"This won't be like natural selection," Daniel insisted. "Not that blind, not that cruel, not that wasteful. You'd be free to intervene as much as you wished, to take whatever palliative measures you felt appropriate."

"*Palliative measures?*" Julie met his gaze, and he saw her expression flicker from disbelief to something darker. She stood up and glanced at her wristphone. "I don't have any signal here. Would you mind calling me a taxi?"

Daniel said, "Please, hear me out. Give me ten more minutes, then the helicopter will take you to the airport."

"I'd prefer to make my own way home." She gave Daniel a look that made it clear that this was not negotiable.

He called her a taxi, and they walked to the elevator.

"I know you find this morally challenging," he said, "and I respect that. I wouldn't dream of hiring someone who thought these were trivial issues. But if I don't do this, someone else will. Someone with far worse intentions than mine."

"Really?" Her tone was openly sarcastic now. "So how, exactly, does the mere existence of your project stop this hypothetical bin Laden of AI from carrying out his own?"

Daniel was disappointed; he'd expected her at least to understand what was at stake. He said, "This is a race to decide between Godhood and enslavement. Whoever succeeds first will be unstoppable. I'm not going to be anyone's slave."

Julie stepped into the elevator; he followed her.

She said, "You know what they say the modern version of Pascal's Wager is? Sucking up to as many Transhumanists as possible, just in case one of them turns into God. Perhaps your motto should be 'Treat every chatterbot kindly, it might turn out to be the deity's uncle.'"

"We will be as kind as possible," Daniel said. "And don't forget, we can determine the nature of these beings. They will be happy to be alive, and grateful to their creator. We can select for those traits."

Julie said, "So you're aiming for *übermenschen* that wag their tails when you scratch them behind the ears? You might find there's a bit of a trade-off there."

The elevator reached the lobby. Daniel said, "Think about this, don't rush to a decision. You can call me any time." There was no commercial flight back to Toronto tonight; she'd be stuck in a hotel, paying money she could ill-afford, thinking about the kind of salary she could demand from him now that she'd played hard to get. If she mentally recast all this obstinate moralising as a deliberate bargaining strategy, she'd have no trouble swallowing her pride.

Julie offered her hand, and he shook it. She said, "Thank you for dinner."

The taxi was waiting. He walked with her across the lobby. "If you want to see AI in your lifetime," he said, "this is the only way it's going to happen."

She turned to face him. "Maybe that's true. We'll see. But better to spend a thousand years and get it right, than a decade and succeed by your methods."

As Daniel watched the taxi drive away into the fog, he forced himself to accept the reality: she was never going to change her mind. Julie Dehghani had been his first choice, his ideal collaborator. He couldn't pretend that this wasn't a setback.

Still, no one was irreplaceable. However much it would have delighted him to have won her over, there were many more names on his list.

2

Daniel's wrist tingled as the message came through. He glanced down and saw the word PROGRESS! hovering in front of his watch face.

The board meeting was almost over; he disciplined himself and kept his attention focused for ten more minutes. WiddulHands.com had made him his first billion, and it was still the pre-eminent social networking site for the 0-3 age group. It had been fifteen years since he'd founded the company, and he had since diversified in many directions, but he had no intention of taking his hands off the levers.

When the meeting finished he blanked the wall screen and paced the empty conference room for half a minute, rolling his neck and stretching his shoulders. Then he said, "Lucien."

Lucien Crace appeared on the screen. "Significant progress?" Daniel enquired.

"Absolutely." Lucien was trying to maintain polite eye contact with Daniel, but something kept drawing his gaze away. Without waiting for an explanation, Daniel gestured at the screen and had it show him exactly what Lucien was seeing.

A barren, rocky landscape stretched to the horizon. Scattered across the rocks were dozens of crablike creatures—some deep blue, some coral pink, though these weren't colours the locals would see, just species markers added to the view to make it easier to interpret. As Daniel watched, fat droplets of corrosive rain drizzled down from a passing cloud. This had to be the bleakest environment in all of Sapphire.

Lucien was still visible in an inset. "See the blue ones over by the crater lake?" he said. He sketched a circle on the image to guide Daniel's attention.

"Yeah." Five blues were clustered around a lone pink; Daniel gestured and the view zoomed in on them. The blues had opened up their prisoner's body, but it wasn't dead; Daniel was sure of that, because the pinks had recently acquired a trait that turned their bodies to mush the instant they expired.

"They've found a way to study it," Lucien said. "To keep it alive and study it."

From the very start of the project, he and Daniel had decided to grant the Phites the power to observe and manipulate their own bodies as much as possible. In the DNA world, the inner workings of anatomy and heredity had only become accessible once highly sophisticated technology had been invented. In Sapphire, the barriers were designed to be far lower. The basic units of biology here were "beads," small spheres that possessed a handful of simple properties but no complex internal biochemistry. Beads were larger than the cells of the DNA world, and Sapphire's diffractionless optics rendered them visible to the right kind of naked eye. Animals acquired beads from their diet, while in plants they replicated in the presence of sunlight, but unlike cells they did not themselves mutate. The beads in a Phite's body could be rearranged with a minimum of fuss, enabling a kind of self-modification that no human surgeon or prosthetics engineer could rival—and this skill was actually essential for at least one stage in every Phite's life: reproduction involved two Phites pooling their spare beads and then collaborating to "sculpt" them into an infant, in part by directly copying each other's current body plans.

Of course these crabs knew nothing of the abstract principles of engineering and design, but the benefits of trial and error, of self-experimentation and cross-species plagiarism, had led them into an escalating war of innovation. The pinks had been the first to stop their corpses from being plundered for secrets, by stumbling on a way to make them literally fall apart *in extremis;* now it seemed the blues had found a way around that, and were indulging in a spot of vivisection-as-industrial-espionage.

Daniel felt a visceral twinge of sympathy for the struggling pink, but he brushed it aside. Not only did he doubt that the Phites were any more conscious than ordinary crabs, they certainly had a radically different relationship to bodily integrity. The pink was resisting because its dissectors were of a different species; if they had been its cousins it might not have put up any fight at all. When something happened in spite of your wishes, that was unpleasant by definition, but it would be absurd to imagine that the pink was in the kind of agony that an antelope being flayed by jackals would feel—let alone experiencing the existential terrors of a human trapped and mutilated by a hostile tribe.

"This is going to give them a tremendous advantage," Lucien enthused.

"The blues?"

Lucien shook his head. "Not blues over pinks; Phites over tradlife. Bacteria can swap genes, but this kind of active mimetics is unprecedented without cultural support. Da Vinci might have watched the birds in flight and sketched his gliders, but no lemur ever dissected the body of an eagle and then stole its tricks. They're going to have *innate* skills as powerful as whole strands of human technology. All this before they even have language."

"Hmm." Daniel wanted to be optimistic too, but he was growing wary of Lucien's hype. Lucien had a doctorate in genetic programming, but he'd made his name with FoodExcuses.com, a web service that trawled the medical literature to cobble together quasi-scientific justifications for indulging in your favourite culinary vice. He had the kind of technobabble that could bleed money out of venture capitalists down pat, and though Daniel admired that skill in its proper place, he expected a higher insight-to-bullshit ratio now that Lucien was on his payroll.

The blues were backing away from their captive. As Daniel watched, the pink sealed up its wounds and scuttled off towards a group of its own kind. The blues had now seen the detailed anatomy of the respiratory system that had been giving the pinks an advantage in the thin air of this high plateau. A few of the blues would try it out, and if it worked for them, the whole tribe would copy it.

"So what do you think?" Lucien asked.

"Select them," Daniel said.

"Just the blues?"

"No, both of them." The blues alone might have diverged into competing subspecies eventually, but bringing their old rivals along for the ride would help to keep them sharp.

"Done," Lucien replied. In an instant, ten million Phites were erased, leaving the few thousand blues and pinks from these badlands to inherit the planet. Daniel felt no compunction; the extinction events he decreed were surely the most painless in history.

Now that the world no longer required human scrutiny, Lucien unthrottled the crystal and let the simulation race ahead; automated tools would let them know when the next interesting development arose. Daniel watched the population figures rising as his chosen species spread out and recolonised Sapphire.

Would their distant descendants rage against him, for this act of "genocide" that had made room for them to flourish and prosper? That seemed unlikely. In any case, what choice did he have? He couldn't start manufacturing new crystals for every useless side-branch of the evolutionary tree. Nobody was wealthy enough to indulge in an exponentially growing number of virtual animal shelters, at half a billion dollars apiece.

He was a just creator, but he was not omnipotent. His careful pruning was the only way.

3

In the months that followed, progress came in fits and starts. Several times, Daniel found himself rewinding history, reversing his decisions and trying a new path. Keeping every Phite variant alive was impractical, but he did retain enough information to resurrect lost species at will.

The maze of AI was still a maze, but the speed of the crystal served them well. Barely eighteen months after the start of Project Sapphire, the Phites were exhibiting a basic theory of mind: their actions showed that they could deduce what others knew about the world, as distinct from what they knew themselves. Other AI researchers had spliced this kind of thing into their programs by hand, but Daniel was convinced that his version was better integrated, more robust. Human-crafted software was brittle and inflexible; his Phites had been forged in the heat of change.

Daniel kept a close watch on his competitors, but nothing he saw gave him reason to doubt his approach. Sunil Gupta was raking in the cash from a search engine that could "understand" all forms of text, audio and video, making use of fuzzy logic techniques that were at least forty years old. Daniel respected Gupta's business acumen, but in the unlikely event that his software ever became conscious, the sheer cruelty of having forced it to wade through the endless tides of blogorrhoea would surely see it turn on its creator and exact a revenge that made *The Terminator* look like a picnic. Angela Lindstrom was having some success with her cheesy AfterLife, in which dying clients gave heart-to-heart interviews to software that then constructed avatars able to converse with surviving relatives. And Julie Dehghani was still frittering away her talent, writing software for robots that played with coloured blocks side-by-side with human infants, and learnt languages from adult volunteers by imitating the interactions of baby talk. Her prophesy of taking a thousand years to "get it right" seemed to be on target.

As the second year of the project drew to a close, Lucien was contacting Daniel once or twice a month to announce a new breakthrough. By constructing environments that imposed suitable selection pressures, Lucien had generated a succession of new species that used simple tools, crafted crude shelters, and even domesticated plants. They were still shaped more or less like crabs, but they were at least as intelligent as chimpanzees.

The Phites worked together by observation and imitation, guiding and reprimanding each other with a limited repertoire of gestures and cries, but as yet they lacked anything that could truly be called a language. Daniel grew impatient; to move beyond a handful of specialised skills, his creatures needed the power to map any object, any action, any prospect they might encounter in the world into their speech, and into their thoughts.

Daniel summoned Lucien and they sought a way forward. It was easy to tweak the Phites' anatomy to grant them the ability to generate more subtle vocalisations, but that alone was no more useful than handing a chimp a conductor's baton. What was needed was a way to make sophisticated planning and communications skills a matter of survival.

Eventually, he and Lucien settled on a series of environmental modifications, providing opportunities for the creatures to rise to the occasion. Most of these scenarios began with famine. Lucien blighted the main food crops, then offered a palpable reward for progress by dangling some tempting new fruit from a branch that was just out of reach. Sometimes that metaphor could almost be taken literally: he'd introduce a plant with a complex life cycle that required tricky processing to render it edible, or a new prey animal that was clever and vicious, but nutritionally well worth hunting in the end.

Time and again, the Phites failed the test, with localised species dwindling to extinction. Daniel watched in dismay; he had not grown sentimental, but he'd always boasted to himself that he'd set his standards higher than the extravagant cruelties of nature. He contemplated tweaking the creatures' physiology so that starvation brought a swifter, more merciful demise, but Lucien pointed out that he'd be slashing his chances of success if he curtailed this period of intense motivation. Each time a group died out, a fresh batch of mutated cousins rose from the dust to take their place; without that intervention, Sapphire would have been a wilderness within a few real-time days.

Daniel closed his eyes to the carnage, and put his trust in sheer time, sheer numbers. In the end, that was what the crystal had bought him: when all else failed, he could give up any pretence of knowing how to achieve his aims and simply test one random mutation after another.

Months went by, sending hundreds of millions of tribes starving into their graves. But what choice did he have? If he fed these creatures milk and honey, they'd remain fat and stupid until the day he died. Their hunger agitated them, it drove them to search and strive, and while any human onlooker was tempted to colour such behaviour with their own emotional palette, Daniel told himself that the Phites' suffering was a shallow thing, little more than the instinct that jerked his own hand back from a flame before he'd even registered discomfort.

They were not the equal of humans. Not yet.

And if he lost his nerve, they never would be.

Daniel dreamt that he was inside Sapphire, but there were no Phites in sight. In front of him stood a sleek black monolith; a thin stream of pus wept from a crack in its smooth, obsidian surface. Someone was holding him by the wrist, trying to force his hand into a reeking pit in the ground. The pit, he knew, was piled high with things he did not want to see, let alone touch.

He thrashed around until he woke, but the sense of pressure on his wrist remained. It was coming from his watch. As he focused on the one-word message he'd received, his stomach tightened. Lucien would not have dared to wake him at this hour for some run-of-the-mill result.

Daniel rose, dressed, then sat in his office sipping coffee. He did not know why he was so reluctant to make the call. He had been waiting for this moment for more than twenty years, but it would not be the pinnacle of his life. After this, there would be a thousand more peaks, each one twice as magnificent as the last.

He finished the coffee then sat a while longer, massaging his temples, making sure his head was clear. He would not greet this new era bleary-eyed, half-awake. He recorded all his calls, but this was one he would retain for posterity.

"Lucien," he said. The man's image appeared, smiling. "Success?"

"They're talking to each other," Lucien replied.

"About what?"

"Food, weather, sex, death. The past, the future. You name it. They won't shut up."

Lucien sent transcripts on the data channel, and Daniel perused them. The linguistics software didn't just observe the Phites' behaviour and correlate it with the sounds they made; it peered right into their virtual brains and tracked the flow of information. Its task was far from trivial, and there was no guarantee that its translations were perfect, but Daniel did not believe it could hallucinate an entire language and fabricate these rich, detailed conversations out of thin air.

He flicked between statistical summaries, technical overviews of linguistic structure, and snippets from the millions of conversations the software had logged. *Food, weather, sex, death.* As human dialogue the translations would have seemed utterly banal, but in context they were riveting. These were not chatterbots blindly following Markov chains, designed to impress the judges in a Turing test. The Phites were discussing matters by which they genuinely lived and died.

When Daniel brought up a page of conversational topics in alphabetical order, his eyes were caught by the single entry under the letter G. *Grief.* He tapped the link, and spent a few minutes reading through samples, illustrating the appearance of the concept following the death of a child, a parent, a friend.

He kneaded his eyelids. It was three in the morning; there was a sickening clarity to everything, the kind that only night could bring. He turned to Lucien.

"No more death."

"Boss?" Lucien was startled.

"I want to make them immortal. Let them evolve culturally; let their ideas live and die. Let them modify their own brains, once they're smart enough; they can already tweak the rest of their anatomy."

"Where will you put them all?" Lucien demanded.

"I can afford another crystal. Maybe two more."

"That won't get you far. At the present birth rate—"

"We'll have to cut their fertility drastically, tapering it down to zero. After that, if they want to start reproducing again they'll really have to innovate." They would need to learn about the outside world, and comprehend its alien physics well enough to design new hardware into which they could migrate.

Lucien scowled. "How will we control them? How will we shape them? If we can't select the ones we want—"

Daniel said quietly, "This is not up for discussion." Whatever Julie Dehghani had thought of him, he was not a monster; if he believed that these creatures were as conscious as he was, he was not going to slaughter them like cattle—or stand by and let them die "naturally," when the rules of this world were his to rewrite at will.

"We'll shape them through their memes," he said. "We'll kill off the bad memes, and help spread the ones we want to succeed." He would need to keep an iron grip on the Phites and their culture, though, or he would never be able to trust them. If he wasn't going to literally *breed them* for loyalty and gratitude, he would have to do the same with their ideas.

Lucien said, "We're not prepared for any of this. We're going to need new software, new analysis and intervention tools."

Daniel understood. "Freeze time in Sapphire. Then tell the team they've got eighteen months."

4

Daniel sold his shares in WiddulHands, and had two more crystals built. One was to support a higher population in Sapphire, so there was as large a pool of diversity among the immortal Phites as possible; the other was to run the software—which Lucien had dubbed the Thought Police—needed to keep tabs on what they were doing. If human overseers had had to monitor and shape the evolving culture every step of the way, that would have slowed things down to a glacial pace. Still, automating the process completely was tricky, and Daniel preferred to err on the side of caution, with the Thought Police freezing Sapphire and notifying him whenever the situation became too delicate.

If the end of death was greeted by the Phites with a mixture of puzzlement and rejoicing, the end of birth was not so easy to accept. When all attempts by mating couples to sculpt their excess beads into offspring became as ineffectual as shaping dolls out of clay, it led to a mixture of persistence and distress that was painful to witness. Humans were accustomed to failing to conceive, but this was more like still birth after still birth. Even when Daniel intervened to modify the Phites' basic drives, some kind of cultural or emotional inertia kept many of them going through the motions. Though their new instincts urged them merely to pool their spare beads and then stop, sated, they would continue with the old version of the act regardless, forlorn and confused, trying to shape the useless puddle into something that lived and breathed.

*Move on*, Daniel thought. *Get over it.* There was only so much sympathy he could muster for immortal beings who would fill the galaxy with their children, if they ever got their act together.

The Phites didn't yet have writing, but they'd developed a strong oral tradition, and some put their mourning for the old ways into elegiac words. The Thought Police identified those memes, and ensured that they didn't spread far. Some Phites chose to kill themselves rather than live in the barren new world. Daniel felt he had no right to stop them, but mysterious obstacles blocked the paths of anyone who tried, irresponsibly, to romanticise or encourage such acts.

The Phites could only die by their own volition, but those who retained the will to live were not free to doze the centuries away. Daniel decreed no more terrible famines, but he hadn't abolished hunger itself, and he kept enough pressure on the food supply and other resources to force the Phites to keep innovating, refining agriculture, developing trade.

The Thought Police identified and nurtured the seeds of writing, mathematics and natural science. The physics of Sapphire was a simplified, game-world model, not so arbitrary as to be incoherent, but not so deep and complex that you needed particle physics to get to the bottom of it. As crystal time sped forward and the immortals sought solace in understanding their world, Sapphire soon had its Euclid and Archimedes, its Galileo and its Newton; their ideas spread with supernatural efficiency, bringing forth a torrent of mathematicians and astronomers.

Sapphire's stars were just a planetarium-like backdrop, present only to help the Phites get their notions of heliocentricity and inertia right, but its moon was as real as the world itself. The technology needed to reach it was going to take a while, but that was all right; Daniel didn't want them getting ahead of themselves. There was a surprise waiting for them there, and his preference was for a flourishing of biotech and computing before they faced that revelation.

Between the absence of fossils, Sapphire's limited biodiversity, and all the clunky external meddling that needed to be covered up, it was hard for the Phites to reach a grand Darwinian view of biology, but their innate skill with beads gave them a head start in the practical arts. With a little nudging, they began tinkering with their bodies, correcting some inconvenient anatomical quirks that they'd missed in their pre-conscious phase.

As they refined their knowledge and techniques, Daniel let them imagine that they were working towards restoring fertility; after all, that was perfectly true, even if their goal was a few conceptual revolutions further away than they realised. Humans had had their naive notions of a Philosopher's Stone dashed, but they'd still achieved nuclear transmutation in the end.

The Phites, he hoped, would transmute *themselves:* inspect their own brains, make sense of them, and begin to improve them. It was a staggering task to expect of anyone; even Lucien and his team, with their God's-eye view of the creatures, couldn't come close. But when the crystal was running at full speed, the Phites could think millions of times faster than their creators. If Daniel could keep them from straying off course, everything that humanity might once have conceived of as the fruits of millennia of progress was now just a matter of months away.

5

Lucien said, "We're losing track of the language."

Daniel was in his Houston office; he'd come to Texas for a series of face-to-face meetings, to see if he could raise some much-needed cash by licensing the crystal fabrication process. He would have preferred to keep the technology to himself, but he was almost certain that he was too far ahead of his rivals now for any of them to stand a chance of catching up with him.

"What do you mean, losing track?" Daniel demanded. Lucien had briefed him just three hours before, and given no warning of an impending crisis.

The Thought Police, Lucien explained, had done their job well: they had pushed the neural self-modification meme for all it was worth, and now a successful form of "brain boosting" was spreading across Sapphire. It required a detailed "recipe" but no technological aids; the same innate skills for observing and manipulating beads that the Phites had used to copy themselves during reproduction were enough.

All of this was much as Daniel had hoped it would be, but there was an alarming downside. The boosted Phites were adopting a dense and complex new language, and the analysis software couldn't make sense of it.

"Slow them down further," Daniel suggested. "Give the linguistics more time to run."

"I've already frozen Sapphire," Lucien replied. "The linguistics have been running for an hour, with the full resources of an entire crystal."

Daniel said irritably, "We can see exactly what they've done to their brains. How can we not understand the effects on the language?"

"In the general case," Lucien said, "deducing a language from nothing but neural anatomy is computationally intractable. With the old language, we were lucky; it had a simple structure, and it was highly correlated with obvious behavioural elements. The new language is much more abstract and conceptual. We might not even have our own correlates for half the concepts."

Daniel had no intention of letting events in Sapphire slip out of his control. It was one thing to hope that the Phites would, eventually, be juggling real-world physics that was temporarily beyond his comprehension, but any bright ten-year-old could grasp the laws of their present universe, and their technology was still far from rocket science.

He said, "Keep Sapphire frozen, and study your records of the Phites who first performed this boost. If they understood what they were doing, we can work it out too."

At the end of the week, Daniel signed the licensing deal and flew back to San Francisco. Lucien briefed him daily, and at Daniel's urging hired a dozen new computational linguists to help with the problem.

After six months, it was clear that they were getting nowhere. The Phites who'd invented the boost had had one big advantage as they'd tinkered with each other's brains: it had not been a purely theoretical exercise for them. They hadn't gazed at anatomical diagrams and then reasoned their way to a better design. They had *experienced* the effects of thousands of small experimental changes, and the results had shaped their intuition for the process. Very little of that intuition had been spoken aloud, let alone written down and formalised. And the process of decoding those insights from a purely structural view of their brains was every bit as difficult as decoding the language itself.

Daniel couldn't wait any longer. With the crystal heading for the market, and other comparable technologies approaching fruition, he couldn't allow his lead to melt away.

"We need the Phites themselves to act as translators," he told Lucien. "We need to contrive a situation where there's a large enough pool who choose not to be boosted that the old language continues to be used."

"So we need maybe twenty-five per cent refusing the boost?" Lucien suggested. "And we need the boosted Phites to want to keep them informed of what's happening, in terms that we can all understand."

Daniel said, "Exactly."

"I think we can slow down the uptake of boosting," Lucien mused, "while we encourage a traditionalist meme that says it's better to span the two cultures and languages than replace the old entirely with the new."

Lucien's team set to work, tweaking the Thought Police for the new task, then restarting Sapphire itself.

Their efforts seemed to yield the desired result: the Phites were corralled into valuing the notion of maintaining a link to their past, and while the boosted Phites surged ahead, they also worked hard to keep the unboosted in the loop.

It was a messy compromise, though, and Daniel wasn't happy with the prospect of making do with a watered-down, Sapphire-for-Dummies version of the Phites' intellectual achievements. What he really wanted was someone on the inside reporting to him directly, like a Phite version of Lucien.

It was time to start thinking about job interviews.

Lucien was running Sapphire more slowly than usual—to give the Thought Police a computational advantage now that they'd lost so much raw surveillance data—but even at the reduced rate, it took just six real-time days for the boosted Phites to invent computers, first as a mathematical formalism and, shortly afterwards, as a succession of practical machines.

Daniel had already asked Lucien to notify him if any Phite guessed the true nature of their world. In the past, a few had come up with vague metaphysical speculations that weren't too wide of the mark, but now that they had a firm grasp of the idea of universal computation, they were finally in a position to understand the crystal as more than an idle fantasy.

The message came just after midnight, as Daniel was preparing for bed. He went into his office and activated the intervention tool that Lucien had written for him, specifying a serial number for the Phite in question.

The tool prompted Daniel to provide a human-style name for his interlocutor, to facilitate communication. Daniel's mind went blank, but after waiting twenty seconds the software offered its own suggestion: Primo.

Primo was boosted, and he had recently built a computer of his own. Shortly afterwards, the Thought Police had heard him telling a couple of unboosted friends about an amusing possibility that had occurred to him.

Sapphire was slowed to a human pace, then Daniel took control of a Phite avatar and the tool contrived a meeting, arranging for the two of them to be alone in the shelter that Primo had built for himself. In accordance with the current architectural style the wooden building was actually still alive, self-repairing and anchored to the ground by roots.

Primo said, "Good morning. I don't believe we've met."

It was no great breach of protocol for a stranger to enter one's shelter uninvited, but Primo was understating his surprise; in this world of immortals, but no passenger jets, bumping into strangers anywhere was rare.

"I'm Daniel." The tool would invent a Phite name for Primo to hear. "I heard you talking to your friends last night about your new computer. Wondering what these machines might do in the future. Wondering if they could ever grow powerful enough to contain a whole world."

"I didn't see you there," Primo replied.

"I wasn't there," Daniel explained. "I live outside this world. I built the computer that contains this world."

Primo made a gesture that the tool annotated as amusement, then he spoke a few words in the boosted language. *Insults? A jest? A test of Daniel's omniscience?* Daniel decided to bluff his way through, and act as if the words were irrelevant.

He said, "Let the rain start." Rain began pounding on the roof of the shelter. "Let the rain stop." Daniel gestured with one claw at a large cooking pot in a corner of the room. "Sand. Flower. Fire. Water jug." The pot obliged him, taking on each form in turn.

Primo said, "Very well. I believe you, Daniel." Daniel had had some experience reading the Phites' body language directly, and to him Primo seemed reasonably calm. Perhaps when you were as old as he was, and had witnessed so much change, such a revelation was far less of a shock than it would have been to a human at the dawn of the computer age.

"You created this world?" Primo asked him.

"Yes."

"You shaped our history?"

"In part," Daniel said. "Many things have been down to chance, or to your own choices."

"Did you stop us having children?" Primo demanded.

"Yes," Daniel admitted.

"*Why?*"

"There is no room left in the computer. It was either that, or many more deaths."

Primo pondered this. "So you could have stopped the death of my parents, had you wished?"

"I could bring them back to life, if you want that." This wasn't a lie; Daniel had stored detailed snapshots of all the last mortal Phites. "But not yet; only when there's a bigger computer. When there's room for them."

"Could you bring back *their* parents? And their parents' parents? Back to the beginning of time?"

"No. That information is lost."

Primo said, "What is this talk of waiting for a bigger computer? You could easily stop time from passing for us, and only start it again when your new computer is built."

"No," Daniel said, "I can't. Because *I need you to build the computer.* I'm not like you: I'm not immortal, and my brain can't be boosted. I've done my best, now I need you to do better. The only way that can happen is if you learn the science of my world, and come up with a way to make this new machine."

Primo walked over to the water jug that Daniel had magicked into being. "It seems to me that you were ill-prepared for the task you set yourself. If you'd waited for the machine you really needed, our lives would not have been so hard. And if such a machine could not be built in your lifetime, what was to stop your grandchildren from taking on that task?"

"I had no choice," Daniel insisted. "I couldn't leave your creation to my descendants. There is a war coming between my people. I needed your help. I needed strong allies."

"You have no friends in your own world?"

"Your time runs faster than mine. I needed the kind of allies that only your people can become, in time."

Primo said, "What exactly do you want of us?"

"To build the new computer you need," Daniel replied. "To grow in numbers, to grow in strength. Then to raise me up, to make me greater than I was, as I've done for you. When the war is won, there will be peace forever. Side by side, we will rule a thousand worlds."

"And what do you want of *me?*" Primo asked. "Why are you speaking to me, and not to all of us?"

"Most people," Daniel said, "aren't ready to hear this. It's better that they don't learn the truth yet. But I need one person who can work for me directly. I can see and hear everything in your world, but I need you to make sense of it. I need you to understand things for me."

Primo was silent.

Daniel said, "I gave you life. How can you refuse me?"

6

Daniel pushed his way through the small crowd of protesters gathered at the entrance to his San Francisco tower. He could have come and gone by helicopter instead, but his security consultants had assessed these people as posing no significant threat. A small amount of bad PR didn't bother him; he was no longer selling anything that the public could boycott directly, and none of the businesses he dealt with seemed worried about being tainted by association. He'd broken no laws, and confirmed no rumours. A few feral cyberphiles waving placards reading "Software Is Not Your Slave!" meant nothing.

Still, if he ever found out which one of his employees had leaked details of the project, he'd break their legs.

Daniel was in the elevator when Lucien messaged him: MOON VERY SOON! He halted the elevator's ascent, and redirected it to the basement.

All three crystals were housed in the basement now, just centimetres away from the Play Pen: a vacuum chamber containing an atomic force microscope with fifty thousand independently movable tips, arrays of solid-state lasers and photodetectors, and thousands of micro-wells stocked with samples of all the stable chemical elements. The time lag between Sapphire and this machine had to be as short as possible, in order for the Phites to be able to conduct experiments in real-world physics while their own world was running at full speed.

Daniel pulled up a stool and sat beside the Play Pen. If he wasn't going to slow Sapphire down, it was pointless aspiring to watch developments as they unfolded. He'd probably view a replay of the lunar landing when he went up to his office, but by the time he screened it, it would be ancient history.

"One giant leap" would be an understatement; wherever the Phites landed on the moon, they would find a strange black monolith waiting for them. Inside would be the means to operate the Play Pen; it would not take them long to learn the controls, or to understand what this signified. If they were really slow in grasping what they'd found, Daniel had instructed Primo to explain it to them.

The physics of the real world was far more complex than the kind the Phites were used to, but then, no human had ever been on intimate terms with quantum field theory either, and the Thought Police had already encouraged the Phites to develop most of the mathematics they'd need to get started. In any case, it didn't matter if the Phites took longer than humans to discover twentieth-century scientific principles, and move beyond them. Seen from the outside, it would happen within hours, days, weeks at the most.

A row of indicator lights blinked on; the Play Pen was active. Daniel's throat went dry. The Phites were finally reaching out of their own world into his.

A panel above the machine displayed histograms classifying the experiments the Phites had performed so far. By the time Daniel was paying attention, they had already discovered the kinds of bonds that could be formed between various atoms, and constructed thousands of different small molecules. As he watched, they carried out spectroscopic analyses, built simple nanomachines, and manufactured devices that were, unmistakably, memory elements and logic gates.

The Phites wanted children, and they understood now that this was the only way. They would soon be building a world in which they were not just more numerous, but faster and smarter than they were inside the crystal. And that would only be the first of a thousand iterations. They were working their way towards Godhood, and they would lift up their own creator as they ascended.

Daniel left the basement and headed for his office. When he arrived, he called Lucien.

"They've built an atomic-scale computer," Lucien announced. "And they've fed some fairly complex software into it. It doesn't seem to be an upload, though. Certainly not a direct copy on the level of beads." He sounded flustered; Daniel had forbidden him to risk screwing up the experiments by slowing down Sapphire, so even with Primo's briefings to help him it was difficult for him to keep abreast of everything.

"Can you model their computer, and then model what the software is doing?" Daniel suggested.

Lucien said, "We only have six atomic physicists on the team; the Phites already outnumber us on that score by about a thousand to one. By the time we have any hope of making sense of this, they'll be doing something different."

"What does Primo say?" The Thought Police hadn't been able to get Primo included in any of the lunar expeditions, but Lucien had given him the power to make himself invisible and teleport to any part of Sapphire or the lunar base. Wherever the action was, he was free to eavesdrop.

"Primo has trouble understanding a lot of what he hears; even the boosted aren't universal polymaths and instant experts in every kind of jargon. The gist of it is that the Lunar Project people have made a very fast computer in the Outer World, and it's going to help with the fertility problem... somehow." Lucien laughed. "Hey, maybe the Phites will do exactly what we did: see if they can evolve something smart enough to give them a hand. How cool would that be?"

Daniel was not amused. Somebody had to do some real work eventually; if the Phites just passed the buck, the whole enterprise would collapse like a pyramid scheme.

Daniel had some business meetings he couldn't put off. By the time he'd swept all the bullshit aside, it was early afternoon. The Phites had now built some kind of tiny solid-state accelerator, and were probing the internal structure of protons and neutrons by pounding them with high-speed electrons. An atomic computer wired up to various detectors was doing the data analysis, processing the results faster than any in-world computer could. The Phites had already figured out the standard quark model. Maybe they were going to skip uploading into nanocomputers, and head straight for some kind of femtomachine?

Digests of Primo's briefings made no mention of using the strong force for computing, though. They were still just satisfying their curiosity about the fundamental laws. Daniel reminded himself of their history. They had burrowed down to what seemed like the foundations of physics before, only to discover that those simple rules were nothing to do with the ultimate reality. It made sense that they would try to dig as deeply as they could into the mysteries of the Outer World before daring to found a colony, let alone emigrate *en masse*.

By sunset the Phites were probing the surroundings of the Play Pen with various kinds of radiation. The levels were extremely low—certainly too low to risk damaging the crystals—so Daniel saw no need to intervene. The Play Pen itself did not have a massive power supply, it contained no radioisotopes, and the Thought Police would ring alarm bells and bring in human experts if some kind of tabletop fusion experiment got underway, so Daniel was reasonably confident that the Phites couldn't do anything stupid and blow the whole thing up.

Primo's briefings made it clear that they thought they were engaged in a kind of "astronomy." Daniel wondered if he should give them access to instruments for doing serious observations—the kind that would allow them to understand relativistic gravity and cosmology. Even if he bought time on a large telescope, though, just pointing it would take an eternity for the Phites. He wasn't going to slow Sapphire down and then grow old while they explored the sky; next thing they'd be launching space probes on thirty-year missions. Maybe it was time to ramp up the level of collaboration, and just hand them some astronomy texts and star maps? Human culture had its own hard-won achievements that the Phites couldn't easily match.

As the evening wore on, the Phites shifted their focus back to the subatomic world. A new kind of accelerator began smashing single gold ions together at extraordinary energies—though the total power being expended was still minuscule. Primo soon announced that they'd mapped all three generations of quarks and leptons. The Phites' knowledge of particle physics was drawing level with humanity's; Daniel couldn't follow the technical details any more, but the experts were giving it all the thumbs up. Daniel felt a surge of pride; of course his children knew what they were doing, and if they'd reached the point where they could momentarily bamboozle him, soon he'd ask them to catch their breath and bring him up to speed. Before he permitted them to emigrate, he'd slow the crystals down and introduce himself to everyone. In fact, that might be the perfect time to set them their next task: to understand human biology, well enough to upload him. To make him immortal, to repay their debt.

He sat watching images of the Phites' latest computers, reconstructions based on data flowing to and from the AFM tips. Vast lattices of shimmering atoms stretched off into the distance, the electron clouds that joined them quivering like beads of mercury in some surreal liquid abacus. As he watched, an inset window told him that the ion accelerators had been re-designed, and fired up again.

Daniel grew restless. He walked to the elevator. There was nothing he could see in the basement that he couldn't see from his office, but he wanted to stand beside the Play Pen, put his hand on the casing, press his nose against the glass. The era of Sapphire as a virtual world with no consequences in his own was coming to an end; he wanted to stand beside the thing itself and be reminded that it was as solid as he was.

The elevator descended, passing the tenth floor, the ninth, the eighth. Without warning, Lucien's voice burst from Daniel's watch, priority audio crashing through every barrier of privacy and protocol. "Boss, there's radiation. Net power gain. Get to the helicopter, *now*."

Daniel hesitated, contemplating an argument. If this was fusion, why hadn't it been detected and curtailed? He jabbed the stop button and felt the brakes engage. Then the world dissolved into brightness and pain.

7

When Daniel emerged from the opiate haze, a doctor informed him that he had burns to sixty per cent of his body. More from heat than from radiation. He was not going to die.

There was a net terminal by the bed. Daniel called Lucien and learnt what the physicists on the team had tentatively concluded, having studied the last of the Play Pen data that had made it off-site.

It seemed the Phites had discovered the Higgs field, and engineered a burst of something akin to cosmic inflation. What they'd done wasn't as simple as merely inflating a tiny patch of vacuum into a new universe, though. Not only had they managed to create a "cool Big Bang," they had pulled a large chunk of ordinary matter into the pocket universe they'd made, after which the wormhole leading to it had shrunk to subatomic size and fallen through the Earth.

They had taken the crystals with them, of course. If they'd tried to upload themselves into the pocket universe through the lunar data link, the Thought Police would have stopped them. So they'd emigrated by another route entirely. They had snatched their whole substrate, and ran.

Opinions were divided over exactly what else the new universe would contain. The crystals and the Play Pen floating in a void, with no power source, would leave the Phites effectively dead, but some of the team believed there could be a thin plasma of protons and electrons too, created by a form of Higgs decay that bypassed the unendurable quark-gluon fireball of a hot Big Bang. If they'd built the right nanomachines, there was a chance that they could convert the Play Pen into a structure that would keep the crystals safe, while the Phites slept through the long wait for the first starlight.

The tiny skin samples the doctors had taken finally grew into sheets large enough to graft. Daniel bounced between dark waves of pain and medicated euphoria, but one idea stayed with him throughout the turbulent journey, like a guiding star: *Primo had betrayed him.* He had given the fucker life, entrusted him with power, granted him privileged knowledge, showered him with the favours of the Gods. And how had he been repaid? He was back to zero. He'd spoken to his lawyers; having heard rumours of an "illegal radiation source," the insurance company was not going to pay out on the crystals without a fight.

Lucien came to the hospital, in person. Daniel was moved; they hadn't met face-to-face since the job interview. He shook the man's hand.

"You didn't betray me."

Lucien looked embarrassed. "I'm resigning, boss."

Daniel was stung, but he forced himself to accept the news stoically. "I understand; you have no choice. Gupta will have a crystal of his own by now. You have to be on the winning side, in the war of the Gods."

Lucien put his resignation letter on the bedside table. "What war? Are you still clinging to that fantasy where überdorks battle to turn the moon into computronium?"

Daniel blinked. "Fantasy? If you didn't believe it, why were you working with me?"

"You paid me. Extremely well."

"So how much will Gupta be paying you? I'll double it."

Lucien shook his head, amused. "I'm not going to work for Gupta. I'm moving into particle physics. The Phites weren't all that far ahead of us when they escaped; maybe forty or fifty years. Once we catch up, I guess a private universe will cost about as much as a private island; maybe less in the long run. But no one's going to be battling for control of this one, throwing grey goo around like monkeys flinging turds while they draw up their plans for Matrioshka brains."

Daniel said, "If you take any data from the Play Pen logs—"

"I'll honour all the confidentiality clauses in my contract." Lucien smiled. "But anyone can take an interest in the Higgs field; that's public domain."

After he left, Daniel bribed the nurse to crank up his medication, until even the sting of betrayal and disappointment began to fade.

*A universe*, he thought happily. *Soon I'll have a universe of my own.*

*But I'm going to need some workers in there, some allies, some companions. I can't do it all alone; someone has to carry the load.*

# HIS MASTER'S VOICE

## HANNU RAJANIEMI

Hannu Rajaniemi was born in Ylivieska, Finland, in 1978 and survived the polar bears, the freezing cold, and the Nokia recruiting agents long enough to graduate from the University of Oulu. After brief stints in Cambridge University and working as a research scientist for the Finnish Defence Forces, he moved to Edinburgh where he completed a PhD thesis in string theory. He is the director and co-founder of ThinkTank Maths, but also writes science fiction. His fiction has appeared in *Nova Scotia*, several Best of the Year anthologies, and in *Interzone*. Rajaniemi has recently sold three new SF novels to Gollancz.

Before the concert, we steal the Master's head.

The necropolis is a dark forest of concrete mushrooms in the blue Antarctic night. We huddle inside the utility fog bubble attached to the steep southern wall of the *nunatak*, the ice valley.

The cat washes itself with a pink tongue. It reeks of infinite confidence.

"Get ready," I tell it. "We don't have all night."

It gives me a mildly offended look and dons its armor. The quantum dot fabric envelopes its striped body like living oil. It purrs faintly and tests the diamond-bladed claws against an icy outcropping of rock. The sound grates my teeth and the razor-winged butterflies in my belly wake up. I look at the bright, impenetrable firewall of the city of the dead. It shimmers like chained northern lights in my AR vision.

I decide that it's time to ask the Big Dog to bark. My helmet laser casts a one-nanosecond prayer of light at the indigo sky: just enough to deliver one quantum bit up there into the Wild. Then we wait. My tail wags and a low growl builds up in my belly.

Right on schedule, it starts to rain red fractal code. My augmented reality vision goes down, unable to process the dense torrent of information falling upon the necropolis firewall like monsoon rain. The chained aurora borealis flicker and vanish.

"Go!" I shout at the cat, wild joy exploding in me, the joy of running after the Small Animal of my dreams. "Go now!"

The cat leaps into the void. The wings of the armor open and grab the icy wind, and the cat rides the draft down like a grinning Chinese kite.

It's difficult to remember the beginning now. There were no words then, just sounds and smells: metal and brine, the steady drumming of waves against pontoons. And there were three perfect things in the world: my bowl, the Ball, and the Master's firm hand on my neck.

I know now that the Place was an old oil rig that the Master had bought. It smelled bad when we arrived, stinging oil and chemicals. But there were hiding places, secret nooks and crannies. There was a helicopter landing pad where the Master threw the Ball for me. It fell into the sea many times, but the Master's bots—small metal dragonflies—always fetched it when I couldn't.

The Master was a god. When he was angry, his voice was an invisible whip. His smell was a god-smell that filled the world.

While he worked, I barked at the seagulls or stalked the cat. We fought a few times, and I still have a pale scar on my nose. But we developed an understanding. The dark places of the rig belonged to the cat, and I reigned over the deck and the sky: we were the Hades and Apollo of the Master's realm.

But at night, when the Master watched old movies or listened to records on his old rattling gramophone we lay at his feet together. Sometimes the Master smelled lonely and let me sleep next to him in his small cabin, curled up in the god-smell and warmth.

It was a small world, but it was all we knew.

The Master spent a lot of time working, fingers dancing on the keyboard projected on his mahogany desk. And every night he went to the Room: the only place on the rig where I wasn't allowed.

It was then that I started to dream about the Small Animal. I remember its smell even now, alluring and inexplicable: buried bones and fleeing rabbits, irresistible.

In my dreams, I chased it along a sandy beach, a tasty trail of tiny footprints that I followed along bendy pathways and into tall grass. I never lost sight of it for more than a second: it was always a flash of white fur just at the edge of my vision.

One day it spoke to me.

"Come," it said. "Come and learn."

The Small Animal's island was full of lost places. Labyrinthine caves, lines drawn in sand that became words when I looked at them, smells that sang songs from the Master's gramophone. It taught me, and I learned: I was more awake every time I woke up. And when I saw the cat looking at the spiderbots with a new awareness, I knew that it, too, went to a place at night.

I came to understand what the Master said when he spoke. The sounds that had only meant *angry* or *happy* before became the word of my god. He noticed, smiled, and ruffled my fur. After that he started speaking to us more, me and the cat, during the long evenings when the sea beyond the windows was black as oil and the waves made the whole rig ring like a bell. His voice was dark as a well, deep and gentle. He spoke of an island, his home, an island in the middle of a great sea. I smelled bitterness, and for the first time I understood that there were always words behind words, never spoken.

The cat catches the updraft perfectly: it floats still for a split second, and then clings to the side of the tower. Its claws put the smart concrete to sleep: code that makes the building think that the cat is a bird or a shard of ice carried by the wind.

The cat hisses and spits. The disassembler nanites from its stomach cling to the wall and start eating a round hole in it. The wait is excruciating. The cat locks the exomuscles of its armor and hangs there patiently. Finally, there is a mouth with jagged edges in the wall, and it slips in. My heart pounds as I switch from the AR view to the cat's iris cameras. It moves through the ventilation shaft like lightning, like an acrobat, jerky, hyperaccelerated movements, metabolism on overdrive. My tail twitches again. *We are coming, Master*, I think. *We are coming*.

I lost my Ball the day the wrong Master came.

I looked everywhere. I spent an entire day sniffing every corner and even braved the dark corridors of the cat's realm beneath the deck, but I could not find it. In the end, I got hungry and returned to the cabin. And there were two masters. Four hands stroking my coat. Two gods, true and false.

I barked. I did not know what to do. The cat looked at me with a mixture of pity and disdain and rubbed itself on both of their legs.

"Calm down," said one of the masters. "Calm down. There are four of us now."

I learned to tell them apart, eventually: by that time Small Animal had taught me to look beyond smells and appearances. The master I remembered was a middle-aged man with graying hair, stocky-bodied. The new master was young, barely a man, much slimmer and with the face of a mahogany cherub. The master tried to convince me to play with the new master, but I did not want to. His smell was too familiar, everything else too alien. In my mind, I called him the wrong master.

The two masters worked together, walked together and spent a lot of time talking together using words I did not understand. I was jealous. Once I even bit the wrong master. I was left on the deck for the night as a punishment, even though it was stormy and I was afraid of thunder. The cat, on the other hand, seemed to thrive in the wrong master's company, and I hated it for it.

I remember the first night the masters argued.

"Why did you do it?" asked the wrong master.

"You know," said the master. "You remember." His tone was dark. "Because someone has to show them we own ourselves."

"So, you own me?" said the wrong master. "Is that what you think?"

"Of course not," said the master. "Why do you say that?"

"Someone could claim that. You took a genetic algorithm and told it to make ten thousand of you, with random variations, pick the ones that would resemble your ideal son, the one you could love. Run until the machine runs out of capacity. Then print. It's illegal, you know. For a reason."

"That's not what the plurals think. Besides, this is my place. The only laws here are mine."

"You've been talking to the plurals too much. They are no longer human."

"You sound just like VecTech's PR bots."

"I sound like you. Your doubts. Are you sure you did the right thing? I'm not a Pinocchio. You are not a Geppetto."

The master was quiet for a long time.

"What if I am," he finally said. "Maybe we need Geppettos. Nobody creates anything new anymore, let alone wooden dolls that come to life. When I was young, we all thought something wonderful was on the way. Diamond children in the sky, angels out of machines. Miracles. But we gave up just before the blue fairy came."

"I am not your miracle."

"Yes, you are."

"You should at least have made yourself a woman," said the wrong master in a knife-like voice. "It might have been less frustrating."

I did not hear the blow, I felt it. The wrong master let out a cry, rushed out and almost stumbled on me. The master watched him go. His lips moved, but I could not hear the words. I wanted to comfort him and made a little sound, but he did not even look at me, went back to the cabin and locked the door. I scratched the door, but he did not open, and I went up to the deck to look for the Ball again.

Finally, the cat finds the Master's chamber.

It is full of heads. They float in the air, bodiless, suspended in diamond cylinders. The tower executes the command we sent into its drugged nervous system, and one of the pillars begins to blink. *Master, Master*, I sing quietly as I see the cold blue face beneath the diamond. But at the same time I know it's not the master, not yet.

The cat reaches out with its prosthetic. The smart surface yields like a soap bubble. "Careful now, careful," I say. The cat hisses angrily but obeys, spraying the head with preserver nanites and placing it gently into its gel-lined backpack.

The necropolis is finally waking up: the damage the heavenly hacker did has almost been repaired. The cat heads for its escape route and goes to quicktime again. I feel its staccato heartbeat through our sensory link.

It is time to turn out the lights. My eyes polarise to sunglass-black. I lift the gauss launcher, marvelling at the still tender feel of the Russian hand grafts. I pull the trigger. The launcher barely twitches in my grip, and a streak of light shoots up to the sky. The nuclear payload is tiny, barely a decaton, not even a proper plutonium warhead but a hafnium micronuke. But it is enough to light a small sun above the mausoleum city for a moment, enough for a focused maser pulse that makes it as dead as its inhabitants for a moment.

The light is a white blow, almost tangible in its intensity, and the gorge looks like it is made of bright ivory. White noise hisses in my ears like the cat when it's angry.

For me, smells were not just sensations, they were my reality. I know now that that is not far from the truth: smells are molecules, parts of what they represent.

The wrong master smelled wrong. It confused me at first: almost a god-smell, but not quite, the smell of a fallen god.

And he did fall, in the end.

I slept on the master's couch when it happened. I woke up to bare feet shuffling on the carpet and heavy breathing, torn away from a dream of the Small Animal trying to teach me the multiplication table.

The wrong master looked at me.

"Good boy," he said. "Ssh." I wanted to bark, but the godlike smell was too strong. And so I just wagged my tail, slowly, uncertainly. The wrong master sat on the couch next to me and scratched my ears absently.

"I remember you," he said. "I know why he made you. A living childhood memory." He smiled and smelled friendlier than ever before. "I know how that feels." Then he sighed, got up and went into the Room. And then I knew that he was about to do something bad, and started barking as loudly as I could. The master woke up and when the wrong master returned, he was waiting.

"What have you done?" he asked, face chalk-white.

The wrong master gave him a defiant look. "Just what you'd have done. You're the criminal, not me. Why should I suffer? You don't own me."

"I could kill you," said the master, and his anger made me whimper with fear. "I could tell them I was you. They would believe me."

"Yes," said the wrong master. "But you are not going to."

The master sighed. "No," he said. "I'm not."

I take the dragonfly over the cryotower. I see the cat on the roof and whimper from relief. The plane lands lightly. I'm not much of a pilot, but the lobotomised mind of the daimon—an illegal copy of a 21st Century jet ace—is. The cat climbs in, and we shoot towards the stratosphere at Mach 5, wind caressing the plane's quantum dot skin.

"Well done," I tell the cat and wag my tail. It looks at me with yellow slanted eyes and curls up on its acceleration gel bed. I look at the container next to it. Is that a whiff of the god-smell or is it just my imagination?

In any case, it is enough to make me curl up in deep happy dog-sleep, and for the first time in years I dream of the Ball and the Small Animal, sliding down the ballistic orbit's steep back.

They came from the sky before the sunrise. The master went up on the deck wearing a suit that smelled new. He had the cat in his lap: it purred quietly. The wrong master followed, hands behind his back.

There were three machines, black-shelled scarabs with many legs and transparent wings. They came in low, raising a white-frothed wake behind them. The hum of their wings hurt my ears as they landed on the deck.

The one in the middle vomited a cloud of mist that shimmered in the dim light, swirled in the air and became a black-skinned woman who had no smell. By then I had learned that things without a smell could still be dangerous, so I barked at her until the master told me to be quiet.

"Mr. Takeshi," she said. "You know why we are here."

The master nodded.

"You don't deny your guilt?"

"I do," said the master. "This raft is technically a sovereign state, governed by my laws. Autogenesis is not a crime here."

"This raft *was* a sovereign state," said the woman. "Now it belongs to VecTech. Justice is swift, Mr. Takeshi. Our lawbots broke your constitution ten seconds after Mr. Takeshi here—" she nodded at the wrong master—"told us about his situation. After that, we had no choice. The WIPO quantum judge we consulted has condemned you to the slow zone for three hundred and fourteen years, and as the wronged party we have been granted execution rights in this matter. Do you have anything to say before we act?"

The master looked at the wrong master, face twisted like a mask of wax. Then he set the cat down gently and scratched my ears. "Look after them," he told the wrong master. "I'm ready."

The beetle in the middle moved, too fast for me to see. The master's grip on the loose skin on my neck tightened for a moment like my mother's teeth, and then let go. Something warm splattered on my coat and there was a dark, deep smell of blood in the air.

Then he fell. I saw his head in a floating soap bubble that one of the beetles swallowed. Another opened its belly for the wrong master. And then they were gone, and the cat and I were alone on the bloody deck.

The cat wakes me up when we dock with the *Marquis of Carabas*. The zeppelin swallows our dragonfly drone like a whale. It is a crystal cigar, and its nanospun sapphire spine glows faint blue. The Fast City is a sky full of neon stars six kilometers below us, anchored to the airship with elevator cables. I can see the liftspiders climbing them, far below, and sigh with relief. The guests are still arriving, and we are not too late. I keep my personal firewall clamped shut: I know there is a torrent of messages waiting beyond.

We rush straight to the lab. I prepare the scanner while the cat takes the Master's head out very, very carefully. The fractal bush of the scanner comes out of its nest, molecule-sized disassembler fingers bristling. I have to look away when it starts eating the Master's face. I cheat and flee to VR, to do what I do best.

After half an hour, we are ready. The nanofab spits out black plastic discs, and the airship drones ferry them to the concert hall. The metallic butterflies in my belly return, and we head for the make-up salon. The Sergeant is already there, waiting for us: judging by the cigarette stumps on the floor, he has been waiting for a while. I wrinkle my nose at the stench.

"You are late," says our manager. "I hope you know what the hell you are doing. This show's got more diggs than the Turin clone's birthday party."

"That's the idea," I say, and let Anette spray me with cosmetic fog. It tickles and makes me sneeze, and I give the cat a jealous look: as usual, it is perfectly at home with its own image consultant. "We are more popular than Jesus."

They get the DJs on in a hurry, made by the last human tailor on Savile Row. "This'll be a good skin," says Anette. "Mahogany with a touch of purple." She goes on, but I can't hear. The music is already in my head. The Master's voice.

The cat saved me.

I don't know if it meant to do it or not: even now, I have a hard time under-standing it. It hissed at me, its back arched. Then it jumped forward and scratched my nose: it burned like a piece of hot coal. That made me mad, weak as I was. I barked furiously and chased the cat around the deck. Finally, I collapsed, ex-hausted, and realised that I was hungry. The autokitchen down in the Master's cabin still worked, and I knew how to ask for food. But when I came back, the Master's body was gone: the waste disposal bots had thrown it into the sea. That's when I knew that he would not be coming back.

I curled up in his bed alone that night: the god-smell that lingered there was all I had. That, and the Small Animal.

It came to me that night on the dreamshore, but I did not chase it this time. It sat on the sand, looked at me with its little red eyes and waited.

"Why?" I asked. "Why did they take the Master?"

"You wouldn't understand," it said. "Not yet."

"I want to understand. I want to know."

"All right," it said. "Everything you do, remember, think, smell—everything—leaves traces, like footprints in the sand. And it's possible to read them. Imagine that you follow another dog: you know where it has eaten and urinated and everything else it has done. The humans can do that to the mindprints. They can record them and make another you inside a machine, like the scentless screenpeople that your master used to watch. Except that the screendog will think it's you."

"Even though it has no smell?" I asked, confused.

"It thinks it does. And if you know what you're doing, you can give it a new body as well. You could die and the copy would be so good that no one can tell the difference. Humans have been doing it for a long time. Your master was one of the first, a long time ago. Far away, there are a lot of humans with machine bodies, humans who never die, humans with small bodies and big bodies, depending on how much they can afford to pay, people who have died and come back."

I tried to understand: without the smells, it was difficult. But its words awoke a mad hope.

"Does it mean that the Master is coming back?" I asked, panting.

"No. Your master broke human law. When people discovered the pawprints of the mind, they started making copies of themselves. Some made many, more than the grains of sand on the beach. That caused chaos. Every machine, every device everywhere, had mad dead minds in them. The plurals, people called them, and were afraid. And they had their reasons to be afraid. Imagine that your Place had a thousand dogs, but only one Ball."

My ears flopped at the thought.

"That's how humans felt," said the Small Animal. "And so they passed a law: only one copy per person. The humans—VecTech—who had invented how to make copies mixed watermarks into people's minds, rights management software that was supposed to stop the copying. But some humans—like your master—found out how to erase them."

"The wrong master," I said quietly.

"Yes," said the Small Animal. "He did not want to be an illegal copy. He turned your master in."

"I want the master back," I said, anger and longing beating their wings in my chest like caged birds.

"And so does the cat," said the Small Animal gently. And it was only then that I saw the cat there, sitting next to me on the beach, eyes glimmering in the sun. It looked at me and let out a single conciliatory meaow.

After that, the Small Animal was with us every night, teaching.

Music was my favorite. The Small Animal showed me how I could turn music into smells and find patterns in it, like the tracks of huge, strange animals. I studied the Master's old records and the vast libraries of his virtual desk, and learned to remix them into smells that I found pleasant.

I don't remember which one of us came up with the plan to save the Master. Maybe it was the cat: I could only speak to it properly on the island of dreams, and see its thoughts appear as patterns on the sand. Maybe it was the Small Animal, maybe it was me. After all the nights we spent talking about it, I no longer know. But that's where it began, on the island: that's where we became arrows fired at a target.

Finally, we were ready to leave. The Master's robots and nanofac spun us an open-source glider, a white-winged bird.

In my last dream the Small Animal said goodbye. It hummed to itself when I told it about our plans.

"Remember me in your dreams," it said.

"Are you not coming with us?" I asked, bewildered.

"My place is here," it said. "And it's my turn to sleep now, and to dream."

"Who are you?"

"Not all the plurals disappeared. Some of them fled to space, made new worlds there. And there is a war on, even now. Perhaps you will join us there, one day, where the big dogs live."

It laughed. "For old times' sake?" It dived into the waves and started running, became a great proud dog with a white coat, muscles flowing like water. And I followed, for one last time.

The sky was grey when we took off. The cat flew the plane using a neural interface, goggles over its eyes. We swept over the dark waves and were underway. The raft became a small dirty spot in the sea. I watched it recede and realised that I'd never found my Ball.

Then there was a thunderclap and a dark pillar of water rose up to the sky from where the raft had been. I didn't mourn: I knew that the Small Animal wasn't there anymore.

The sun was setting when we came to the Fast City.

I knew what to expect from the Small Animal's lessons, but I could not imagine what it would be like. Mile-high skyscrapers that were self-contained worlds, with their artificial plasma suns and bonsai parks and miniature shopping malls. Each of them housed a billion lilliputs, poor and quick: humans whose consciousness lived in a nanocomputer smaller than a fingertip. Immortals who could not afford to utilise the resources of the overpopulated Earth more than a mouse. The city was surrounded by a halo of glowing fairies, tiny winged moravecs that flitted about like humanoid fireflies and the waste heat from their overclocked bodies draped the city in an artificial twilight.

The citymind steered us to a landing area. It was fortunate that the cat was flying: I just stared at the buzzing things with my mouth open, afraid I'd drown into the sounds and the smells.

We sold our plane for scrap and wandered into the bustle of the city, feeling like *daikaiju* monsters. The social agents that the Small Animal had given me were obsolete, but they could still weave us into the ambient social networks. We needed money, we needed work.

And so I became a musician.

The ballroom is a hemisphere in the center of the airship. It is filled to capacity. Innumerable quickbeings shimmer in the air like living candles, and the suits of the fleshed ones are no less exotic. A woman clad in nothing but autumn leaves smiles at me. Tinkerbell clones surround the cat. Our bodyguards, armed obsidian giants, open a way for us to the stage where the gramophones wait. A rustle moves through the crowd. The air around us is pregnant with ghosts, the avatars of a million fleshless fans. I wag my tail. The scentspace is intoxicating: perfume, fleshbodies, the unsmells of moravec bodies. And the fallen-god smell of the wrong master, hiding somewhere within.

We get on the stage on our hindlegs, supported by prosthesis shoes. The gramophone forest looms behind us, their horns like flowers of brass and gold. We cheat, of course: the music is analog and the gramophones are genuine, but the grooves in the black discs are barely a nanometer thick, and the needles are tipped with quantum dots.

We take our bows and the storm of handclaps begins.

"Thank you," I say when the thunder of it finally dies. "We have kept quiet about the purpose of this concert as long as possible. But I am finally in a position to tell you that this is a charity show."

I smell the tension in the air, copper and iron.

"We miss someone," I say. "He was called Shimoda Takeshi, and now he's gone."

The cat lifts the conductor's baton and turns to face the gramophones. I follow, and step into the soundspace we've built, the place where music is smells and sounds.

The master is in the music.

It took five human years to get to the top. I learned to love the audiences: I could smell their emotions and create a mix of music for them that was just right. And soon I was no longer a giant dog DJ among lilliputs, but a little terrier in a forest of dancing human legs. The cat's gladiator career lasted a while, but soon it joined me as a performer in the virtual dramas I designed. We performed for rich fleshies in the Fast City, Tokyo and New York. I loved it. I howled at Earth in the sky in the Sea of Tranquility.

But I always knew that it was just the first phase of the Plan.

We turn him into music. VecTech owns his brain, his memories, his mind. But we own the music.

Law is code. A billion people listening to our Master's voice. Billion minds downloading the Law At Home packets embedded in it, bombarding the quantum judges until they give him back.

It's the most beautiful thing I've ever made. The cat stalks the genetic algorithm jungle, lets the themes grow and then pounces them, devours them. I just chase them for the joy of the chase alone, not caring whether or not I catch them.

It's our best show ever.

Only when it's over, I realise that no one is listening. The audience is frozen. The fairies and the fastpeople float in the air like flies trapped in amber. The moravecs are silent statues. Time stands still.

The sound of one pair of hands, clapping.

"I'm proud of you," says the wrong master.

I fix my bow tie and smile a dog's smile, a cold snake coiling in my belly. The god-smell comes and tells me that I should throw myself onto the floor, wag my tail, bare my throat to the divine being standing before me.

But I don't.

"Hello, Nipper," the wrong master says.

I clamp down the low growl rising in my throat and turn it into words.

"What did you do?"

"We suspended them. Back doors in the hardware. Digital rights management."

His mahogany face is still smooth: he does not look a day older, wearing a dark suit with a VecTech tie pin. But his eyes are tired.

"Really, I'm impressed. You covered your tracks admirably. We thought you were furries. Until I realised—"

A distant thunder interrupts him.

"I promised him I'd look after you. That's why you are still alive. You don't have to do this. You don't owe him anything. Look at yourselves: Who would have thought you could come this far? Are you going to throw that all away because of some atavistic sense of animal loyalty?"

"Not that you have a choice, of course. The Plan didn't work."

The cat lets out a steam pipe hiss.

"You misunderstand," I say. "The concert was just a diversion."

The cat moves like a black-and-yellow flame. Its claws flash, and the wrong master's head comes off. I whimper at the aroma of blood polluting the god-smell. The cat licks its lips. There is a crimson stain on its white shirt.

The zeppelin shakes, pseudomatter armor sparkling. The dark sky around the *Marquis* is full of fire-breathing beetles. We rush past the human statues in the ballroom and into the laboratory.

The cat does the dirty work, granting me a brief escape into virtual abstraction. I don't know how the master did it, years ago, broke VecTech's copy protection watermarks. I can't do the same, no matter how much the Small Animal taught me. So I have to cheat, recover the marked parts from somewhere else.

The wrong master's brain.

The part of me that was born on the Small Animal's island takes over and fits the two patterns together, like pieces of a puzzle. They fit, and for a brief moment, the master's voice is in my mind, for real this time.

The cat is waiting, already in its clawed battlesuit, and I don my own. The *Marquis of Carabas* is dying around us. To send the master on his way, we have to disengage the armor.

The cat meaows faintly and hands me something red. An old plastic ball with toothmarks, smelling of the sun and the sea, with few grains of sand rattling inside.

"Thanks," I say. The cat says nothing, just opens a door into the zeppelin's skin.

I whisper a command, and the master is underway in a neutrino stream, shooting up towards an island in a blue sea. Where the gods and big dogs live forever.

We dive through the door together, down into the light and flame.

# SPECIAL ECONOMICS

## MAUREEN F. MCHUGH

Maureen F. McHugh was born February 13, 1959. She grew up in Loveland, Ohio, and received a BA from Ohio University in 1981, where she took a creative writing course from Daniel Keyes in her senior year. After a year of grad school there, she went on to get a Master's degree in English Literature at New York University in 1984. After several years as a part-time college instructor and miscellaneous jobs in clerking, technical writing, etc., she spent a year teaching in Shijiazhuang, China. It was during this period she sold her first story, "All in a Day's Work," which appeared in *Twilight Zone*. She has written four novels, including Tiptree Award winner and Hugo and Nebula award nominee *China Mountain Zhang*, *Half the Day Is Night*, *Mission Child*, and *Nekropolis*. Her short fiction, including Hugo Award winner "The Lincoln Train," was collected in *Mothers and Other Monsters* which was a finalist for the Story Prize.

Jieling set up her boombox in a plague-trash market in the part where people sold parts for cars. She had been in the city of Shenzhen for a little over two hours but she figured she would worry about a job tomorrow. Everybody knew you could get a job in no time in Shenzhen. Jobs everywhere.

"What are you doing?" a guy asked her.

"I am divorced," she said. She had always thought of herself as a person who would one day be divorced so it didn't seem like a big stretch to claim it. Staying married to one person was boring. She figured she was too complicated for that. Interesting people had complicated lives. "I'm looking for a job. But I do hip hop, too" she explained.

"Hip hop?" He was a middle-aged man with stubble on his chin who looked as if he wasn't looking for a job but should be.

"Not like Shanghai," she said, "Not like Hi-Bomb. They do gangsta stuff which I don't like. Old fashioned. Like M.I.A.," she said. "Except not political, of course." She gave a big smile. This was all way beyond the guy. Jieling started the boombox. M.I.A was Maya Arulpragasam, a Sri Lankan hip hop artist who had started all on her own years ago. She had sung, she had danced, she had done her own videos. Of course M.I.A. lived in London, which made it easier to do hip hop and become famous.

Jieling had no illusions about being a hip hop singer, but it had been a good way to make some cash up north in Baoding where she came from. Set up in a plague-trash market and dance for yuan.

Jieling did her opening, her own hip hop moves, a little like Maya and a little like some things she had seen on MTV, but not too sexy because Chinese people did not throw you money if you were too sexy. Only April and it was already hot and humid.

Ge down, ge down,
lang-a-lang-a-lang-a.
Ge down, ge down
lang-a-lang-a-lang-a.

She had borrowed the English. It sounded very fresh. Very criminal.

The guy said, "How old are you?"

"Twenty-two," she said, adding three years to her age, still dancing and singing.

Maybe she should have told him she was a widow? Or an orphan? But there were too many orphans and widows after so many people died in the bird flu plague. There was no margin in that. Better to be divorced. He didn't throw any money at her, just flicked open his cell phone to check listings from the market for plague trash. This plague-trash market was so big it was easier to check on-line, even if you were standing right in the middle of it. She needed a new cell phone. Hers had finally fallen apart right before she headed south.

Shenzhen people were apparently too jaded for hip hop. She made 52 yuan, which would pay for one night in a bad hotel where country people washed cabbage in the communal sink.

The market was full of second-hand stuff. When over a quarter of a billion people died in four years, there was a lot of second-hand stuff. But there was still a part of the market for new stuff and street food and that's where Jieling found the cell phone seller. He had a cart with stacks of flat plastic cell phone kits printed with circuits and scored. She flipped through: tiger-striped, peonies (old lady phones), metallics (old man phones), anime characters, moon phones, expensive lantern phones. "Where is your printer?" she asked.

"At home," he said. "I print them up at home, bring them here. No electricity here." Up north in Baoding she'd always bought them in a store where they let you pick your pattern on-line and then printed them there. More to pick from.

On the other hand, he had a whole box full of ones that hadn't sold that he would let go for cheap. In the stack she found a purple one with kittens that wasn't too bad. Very Japanese, which was also very fresh this year. And only 100 yuan for phone and 300 minutes.

He took the flat plastic sheet from her and dropped it in a pot of boiling water big enough to make dumplings. The hinges embedded in the sheet were made of plastic with molecular memory and when they got hot they bent and the plastic folded into a rough cell phone shape. He fished the phone out of the water with tongs, let it sit for a moment and then pushed all the seams together so they snapped. "Wait about an hour for it to dry before you use it," he said and handed her the warm phone.

"An *hour*," she said. "I need it now. I need a job."

He shrugged. "Probably okay in half an hour," he said.

She bought a newspaper and scallion pancake from a street food vendor, sat on a curb and ate while her phone dried. The paper had some job listings, but it also had a lot of listings from recruiters. ONE MONTH BONUS PAY! BEST JOBS! and NUMBER ONE JOBS! START BONUS! People scowled at her for sitting on the curb. She looked like a farmer but what else was she supposed to do? She checked listings on her new cell phone. On-line there were a lot more listings than in the paper. It was a good sign. She picked one at random and called.

The woman at the recruiting office was a flat-faced southerner with buckteeth. Watermelon picking teeth. But she had a manicure and a very nice red suit. The office was not so nice. It was small and the furniture was old. Jieling was groggy from a night spent at a hotel on the edge of the city. It had been cheap but very loud.

The woman was very sharp in the way she talked and had a strong accent that made it hard to understand her. Maybe Fujian, but Jieling wasn't sure. The recruiter had Jieling fill out an application.

"Why did you leave home?" the recruiter asked.

"To get a good job," Jieling said.

"What about your family? Are they alive?"

"My mother is alive. She is remarried," Jieling said. "I wrote it down."

The recruiter pursed her lips. "I can get you an interview on Friday," she said.

"Friday!" Jieling said. It was Tuesday. She had only 300 yuan left out of the money she had brought. "But I need a job!"

The recruiter looked sideways at her. "You have made a big gamble to come to Shenzhen."

"I can go to another recruiter," Jieling said.

The recruiter tapped her lacquered nails. "They will tell you the same thing," she said.

Jieling reached down to pick up her bag.

"Wait," the recruiter said. "I do know of a job. But they only want girls of very good character."

Jieling put her bag down and looked at the floor. Her character was fine. She was not a loose girl, whatever this women with her big front teeth thought.

"Your Mandarin is very good. You say you graduated with high marks from high school," the recruiter said.

"I liked school," Jieling said, which was only partly not true. Everybody here had terrible Mandarin. They all had thick southern accents. Lots of people spoke Cantonese in the street.

"Okay. I will send you to ShinChi for an interview. I cannot get you an interview before tomorrow. But you come here at 8:00 a.m. and I will take you over there."

ShinChi. New Life. It sounded very promising. "Thank you," Jieling said. "Thank you very much."

But outside in the heat, she counted her money and felt a creeping fear. She called her mother.

Her stepfather answered, "*Wei*."

"Is Ma there?" she asked.

"Jieling!" he said. "Where are you?"

"I'm in Shenzhen," she said, instantly impatient with him. "I have a job here."

"A job! When are you coming home?"

He was always nice to her. He meant well. But he drove her nuts. "Let me talk to Ma," she said.

"She's not here," her stepfather said. "I have her phone at work. But she's not home, either. She went to Beijing last weekend and she's shopping for fabric now."

Her mother had a little tailoring business. She went to Beijing every few months and looked at clothes in all the good stores. She didn't buy in Beijing, she just remembered. Then she came home, bought fabric and sewed copies. Her stepfather had been born in Beijing and Jieling thought that was part of the reason her mother had married him. He was more like her mother than her father had been. There was nothing in particular wrong with him. He just set her teeth on edge.

"I'll call back later," Jieling said.

"Wait, your number is blocked," her stepfather said. "Give me your number."

"I don't even know it yet," Jieling said, and hung up.

The New Life company was a huge, modern looking building with a lot of windows. Inside it was full of reflective surfaces and very clean. Sounds echoed in the lobby. A man in a very smart gray suit met Jieling and the recruiter, and the recruiter's red suit looked cheaper, her glossy fingernails too red, her buckteeth exceedingly large. The man in the smart gray suit was short and slim and very southern looking. Very city.

Jieling took some tests on her math and her written characters and got good scores.

To the recruiter, the Human Resources man said, "Thank you, we will send you your fee." To Jieling he said, "We can start you on Monday."

"Monday?" Jieling said. "But I need a job now!" He looked grave. "I...I came from Baoding, in Hebei," Jieling explained. "I'm staying in a hotel, but I don't have much money."

The Human Resources man nodded. "We can put you up in our guesthouse," he said. "We can deduct the money from your wages when you start. It's very nice. It has television and air conditioning, and you can eat in the restaurant."

It was very nice. There were two beds. Jieling put her backpack on the one nearest the door. There was carpeting, and the windows were covered in gold drapes with a pattern of cranes flying across them. The television got stations from Hong Kong. Jieling didn't understand the Cantonese, but there was a button on the remote for subtitles. The movies had lots of violence and more sex than mainland movies did—like the bootleg American movies for sale in the market. She wondered how much this room was. 200 yuan? 300 yuan?

Jieling watched movies the whole first day, one right after another.

On Monday she began orientation. She was given two pale green uniforms, smocks and pants like medical people wore and little caps and two pairs of white shoes. In the uniform she looked a little like a model worker—which is to say that the clothes were not sexy and made her look fat. There were two other girls in their green uniforms. They all watched a DVD about the company.

New Life did biotechnology. At other plants they made influenza vaccine (on the screen were banks and banks of chicken eggs) but at this plant they were developing breakthrough technologies in tissue culture. It showed many men in suits. Then it showed a big American store and explained how they were forging new exportation ties with the biggest American corporation for selling goods, Wal-Mart. It also showed a little bit of an American movie about Wal-Mart. Subtitles explained how Wal-Mart was working with companies around the world to improve living standards, decrease $CO_2$ emissions, and give people low prices. The voice narrating the DVD never really explained the breakthrough technologies.

One of the girls was from way up north, she had a strong Northern way of talking.

"How long are you going to work here?" the northern girl asked. She looked as if she might even have some Russian in her.

"How long?" Jieling said.

"I'm getting married," the northern girl confided. "As soon as I make enough money, I'm going home. If I haven't made enough money in a year," the northern girl explained, "I'm going home anyway."

Jieling hadn't really thought she would work here long. She didn't know exactly what she would do, but she figured that a big city like Shenzhen was a good place to find out. This girl's plans seemed very…country. No wonder Southern Chinese thought Northerners had to wipe the pig shit off their feet before they got on the train.

"Are you Russian?" Jieling asked.

"No," said the girl. "I'm Manchu."

"Ah," Jieling said. Manchu like Manchurian. Ethnic minority. Jieling had gone to school with a boy who was classified as Manchu, which meant that he was allowed to have two children when he got married. But he had looked Han Chinese like everyone else. This girl had the hook nose and the dark skin of a Manchu. Manchu used to rule China until the Communist Revolution (there was something in-between with Sun Yat-sen but Jieling's history teachers had bored her to tears). Imperial and countrified.

Then a man came in from Human Resources.

"There are many kinds of stealing," he began. "There is stealing of money or food. And there is stealing of ideas. Here at New Life, our ideas are like gold, and we guard against having them stolen. But you will learn many secrets, about what we are doing, about how we do things. This is necessary as you do your work. If you tell our secrets, that is theft. And we will find out." He paused here and looked at them in what was clearly intended to be a very frightening way.

Jieling looked down at the ground because it was like watching someone over-act. It was embarrassing. Her new shoes were very white and clean.

Then he outlined the prison terms for industrial espionage. Ten, twenty years in prison. "China must take its place as an innovator on the world stage and so must respect the laws of intellectual property," he intoned. It was part of the modernization of China, where technology was a new future—Jieling put on her "I am a good girl" face. It was like politics class. Four modernizations. Six goals. Sometimes when she was a little girl, and she was riding behind her father on his bike to school, he would pass a billboard with a saying about traffic safety and begin to recite quotes from Mao. *The force at the core of the revolution is the people!* He would tuck his chin in when he did this and use a very serious voice, like a movie or like opera. *Western experience for Chinese uses.* Some of them she had learned from him. *All reactionaries are paper tigers!* she would chant with him, trying to make her voice deep. *Be resolute, fear no sacrifice and surmount every difficulty to win victory!* And then she would start giggling and he would glance over his shoulder and grin at her. He had been a Red Guard when he was young, but other than this, he never talked about it.

After the lecture, they were taken to be paired with workers who would train them. At least she didn't have to go with the Manchu girl who was led off to shipping.

She was paired with a very small girl in one of the culture rooms. "I am Baiyue," the girl said. Baiyue was so tiny, only up to Jieling's shoulder, that her green scrubs swamped her. She had pigtails. The room where they worked was filled with rows and rows of what looked like wide drawers. Down the center of the room was a long table with petri dishes and trays and lab equipment. Jieling didn't know what some of it was and that was a little nerve-wracking. All up and down the room, pairs of girls in green worked at either the drawers or the table.

"We're going to start cultures," Baiyue said. "Take a tray and fill it with those." She pointed to a stack of petri dishes. The bottom of each dish was filled with gelatin. Jieling took a tray and did what Baiyue did. Baiyue was serious but not at all sharp or superior. She explained that what they were doing was seeding the petri dishes with cells.

"Cells?" Jieling asked.

"Nerve cells from the electric ray. It's a fish."

They took swabs and Baiyue showed her how to put the cells on in a zigzag motion so that most of the gel was covered. They did six trays full of petri dishes. They didn't smell fishy. Then they used pipettes to put in feeding solution. It was all pleasantly scientific without being very difficult.

At one point everybody left for lunch but Baiyue said they couldn't go until they got the cultures finished or the batch would be ruined. Women shuffled by them and Jieling's stomach growled. But when the lab was empty Baiyue smiled and said, "Where are you from?"

Baiyue was from Fujian. "If you ruin a batch," she explained, "you have to pay out of your paycheck. I'm almost out of debt and when I get clear—" she glanced around and dropped her voice a little—"I can quit."

"Why are you in debt?" Jieling asked. Maybe this was harder than she thought, maybe Baiyue had screwed up in the past.

"Everyone is in debt," Baiyue said. "It's just the way they run things. Let's get the trays in the warmers."

The drawers along the walls opened out and inside the temperature was kept blood warm. They loaded the trays into the drawers, one back and one front, going down the row until they had the morning's trays all in.

"Okay," Baiyue said, "that's good. We'll check trays this afternoon. I've got a set for transfer to the tissue room but we'll have time after we eat."

Jieling had never eaten in the employee cafeteria, only in the guesthouse restaurant, and only the first night because it was expensive. Since then she had been living on ramen noodles and she was starved for a good meal. She smelled garlic and pork. First thing on the food line was a pan of steamed pork buns, fluffy white. But Baiyue headed off to a place at the back where there was a huge pot of congee—rice porridge—kept hot. "It's the cheapest thing in the cafeteria," Baiyue explained, "and you can eat all you want." She dished up a big bowl of it—a lot of congee for a girl her size—and added some salt vegetables and boiled peanuts. "It's pretty good, although usually by lunch it's been sitting a little while. It gets a little gluey."

Jieling hesitated. Baiyue had said she was in debt. Maybe she had to eat this stuff. But Jieling wasn't going to have old rice porridge for lunch. "I'm going to get some rice and vegetables," she said.

Baiyue nodded. "Sometimes I get that. It isn't too bad. But stay away from anything with shrimp in it. Soooo expensive."

Jieling got rice and vegetables and a big pork bun. There were two fish dishes and a pork dish with monkeybrain mushrooms but she decided she could maybe have the pork for dinner. There was no cost written on anything. She gave her *danwei* card to the woman at the end of the line who swiped it and handed it back.

"How much?" Jieling asked.

The woman shrugged. "It comes out of your food allowance."

Jieling started to argue but across the cafeteria, Baiyue was waving her arm in the sea of green scrubs to get Jieling's attention. Baiyue called from a table. "Jieling! Over here!"

Baiyue's eyes got very big when Jieling sat down. "A pork bun."

"Are they really expensive?" Jieling asked.

Baiyue nodded. "Like gold. And so good."

Jieling looked around at other tables. Other people were eating the pork and steamed buns and everything else.

"Why are you in debt?" Jieling asked.

Baiyue shrugged. "Everyone is in debt," she said. "Just most people have given up. Everything costs here. Your food, your dormitory, your uniforms. They always make sure that you never earn anything."

"They can't do that!" Jieling said.

Baiyue said, "My granddad says it's like the old days, when you weren't allowed to quit your job. He says I should shut up and be happy. That they take good care of me. Iron rice bowl."

"But, but but," Jieling dredged the word up from some long forgotten class, "that's *feudal!*"

Baiyue nodded. "Well, that's my granddad. He used to make my brother and me kowtow to him and my grandmother at Spring Festival." She frowned and wrinkled her nose. Country customs. Nobody in the city made their children kowtow at New Years. "But you're lucky," Baiyue said to Jieling. "You'll have your uniform debt and dormitory fees, but you haven't started on food debt or anything."

Jieling felt sick. "I stayed in the guesthouse for four days," she said. "They said they would charge it against my wages."

"Oh," Baiyue covered her mouth with her hand. After a moment, she said, "Don't worry, we'll figure something out." Jieling felt more frightened by that than anything else.

Instead of going back to the lab they went upstairs and across a connecting bridge to the dormitories. Naps? Did they get naps?

"Do you know what room you're in?" Baiyue asked.

Jieling didn't. Baiyue took her to ask the floor auntie who looked up Jieling's name and gave her a key and some sheets and a blanket. Back down the hall and around the corner. The room was spare but really nice. Two bunk beds and two chests of drawers, a concrete floor. It had a window. All of the beds were taken except one of the top ones. By the window under the desk were three black boxes hooked to the wall. They were a little bigger than a shoebox. Baiyue flipped open the front of each one. They had names written on them. "Here's a space where we can put your battery." She pointed to an electrical extension.

"What are they?" Jieling said.

"They're the battery boxes. It's what we make. I'll get you one that failed inspection. A lot of them work fine," Baiyue said. "Inside there are electric ray cells to make electricity and symbiotic bacteria. The bacteria breaks down garbage to feed the ray cells. Garbage turned into electricity. Anti-global warming. No greenhouse gas. You have to feed scraps from the cafeteria a couple of times a week or it will die, but it does best if you feed it a little bit every day."

"It's alive?" Jieling said.

Baiyue shrugged. "Yeah. Sort of. Supposedly if it does really well, you get credits for the electricity it generates. They charge us for our electricity use, so this helps hold down debt."

The three boxes just sat there looking less alive than a boombox.

"Can you see the cells?" Jieling asked.

Baiyue shook her head. "No, the feed mechanism doesn't let you. They're just like the ones we grow, though, only they've been worked on in the tissue room. They added bacteria."

"Can it make you sick?"

"No, the bacteria can't live in people." Baiyue said. "Can't live anywhere except in the box."

"And it makes electricity."

Baiyue nodded.

"And people can buy it?"

She nodded again. "We've just started selling them. They say they're going to sell them in China but really, they're too expensive. Americans like them, you know, because of the no global warming. Of course, Americans buy anything."

The boxes were on the wall between the beds, under the window, pretty near where the pillows were on the bottom bunks. She hadn't minded the cells in the lab, but this whole thing was too creepy.

Jieling's first paycheck was startling. She owed 1,974 R.M.B. Almost four months' salary if she never ate or bought anything and if she didn't have a dorm room. She went back to her room and climbed into her bunk and looked at the figures. Money deducted for uniforms and shoes, food, her time in the guesthouse.

Her roommates came chattering in a group. Jieling's roommates all worked in packaging. They were nice enough, but they had been friends before Jieling moved in.

"Hey," called Taohua. Then seeing what Jieling had. "Oh, first paycheck."

Jieling nodded. It was like getting a jail sentence.

"Let's see. Oh, not so bad. I owe three times that," Taohua said. She passed the statement on to the other girls. All the girls owed huge amounts. More than a year.

"Don't you care?" Jieling said.

"You mean like little Miss Lei Feng?" Taohua asked. Everyone laughed and Jieling laughed, too, although her face heated up. Miss Lei Feng was what they called Baiyue. Little Miss Goody-goody. Lei Feng, the famous do-gooder soldier who darned his friend's socks on the Long March. He was nobody when he was alive, but when he died, his diary listed all the anonymous good deeds he had done and then he became a Hero. Lei Feng posters hung in elementary schools. He wanted to be "a revolutionary screw that never rusts." It was the kind of thing everybody's grandparents had believed in.

"Does Baiyue have a boyfriend?" Taohua asked, suddenly serious.

"No, no!" Jieling said. It was against the rules to have a boyfriend and Baiyue was always getting in trouble for breaking rules. Things like not having her trays stacked by 5:00 p.m. although nobody else got in trouble for that.

"If she had a boyfriend," Taohua said, "I could see why she would want to quit. You can't get married if you're in debt. It would be too hard."

"Aren't you worried about your debt?" Jieling asked.

Taohua laughed. "I don't have a boyfriend. And besides, I just got a promotion so soon I'll pay off my debt."

"You'll have to stop buying clothes," one of the other girls said. The company store did have a nice catalogue you could order clothes from, but they were expensive. There was debt limit, based on your salary. If you were promoted, your debt limit would go up.

"Or I'll go to special projects," Taohua said. Everyone knew what special projects was, even though it was supposed to be a big company secret. They were computers made of bacteria. They looked a lot like the boxes in the dormitory rooms. "I've been studying computers," Taohua explained. "Bacterial computers are special. They do many things. They can detect chemicals. They are *massively* parallel."

"What does that mean?" Jieling asked.

"It is hard to explain," Taohua said evasively.

Taohua opened her battery and poured in scraps. It was interesting that Taohua claimed not to care about her debt but kept feeding her battery. Jieling had a battery now, too. It was a reject—the back had broken so that the metal things that sent the electricity back out were exposed and if you touched it wrong, it could give you a shock. No problem, since Jieling had plugged it into the wall and didn't plan to touch it again.

"Besides," Taohua said, "I like it here a lot better than at home."

Better than home. In some ways yes, in some ways no. What would it be like to just give up and belong to the company? Nice things, nice food. Never rich. But never poor, either. Medical care. Maybe it wasn't the worst thing. Maybe Baiyue was a little...obsessive.

"I don't care about my debt," Taohua said, serene. "With one more promotion, I'll move to cadres housing."

Jieling reported the conversation to Baiyue. They were getting incubated cells ready to move to the tissue room. In the tissue room they'd be transferred to a protein and collagen grid that would guide their growth—line up the cells to approximate an electricity generating system. The tissue room had a weird, yeasty smell.

"She's fooling herself," Baiyue said. "Line girls never get to be cadres. She might get onto special projects, but that's even worse than regular line work because you're never allowed to leave the compound." Baiyue picked up a dish, stuck a little volt reader into the gel and rapped the dish smartly against the lab table.

The needle on the volt gauge swung to indicate the cells had discharge electricity. That was the way they tested to see the cells were generating electricity. A shock made them discharge and the easiest way was to knock them against the table.

Baiyue could sound very bitter about New Life. Jieling didn't like the debt, it scared her a little. But really, Baiyue saw only one side of everything. "I thought you got a pay raise to go to special projects," Jieling said.

Baiyue rolled her eyes. "And more reasons to go in debt, I'll bet."

"How much is your debt?" Jieling asked.

"Still 700," Baiyue said. "Because they told me I had to have new uniforms." She sighed.

"I am so sick of congee," Jieling said. "They're never going to let us get out of debt." Baiyue's way was doomed. She was trying to play by the company's rules and still win. That wasn't Jieling's way. "We have to make money somewhere else," Jieling said.

"Right," Baiyue said. "We work six days a week." And Baiyue often stayed after shift to try to make sure she didn't lose wages on failed cultures. "Out of spec," she said, and put it aside. She had taught Jieling to keep the out-of-specs for a day. Sometimes they improved and could be shipped on. It wasn't the way the supervisor, Ms. Wang, explained the job to Jieling, but it cut down on the number of rejects, and that, in turn, cut down on paycheck deductions.

"That leaves us Sundays," Jieling said.

"I can't leave compound this Sunday."

"And if you do, what are they going to do, fire you?" Jieling said.

"I don't think we're supposed to earn money outside of the compound," Baiyue said.

"You are too much of a good girl," Jieling said. "Remember, *it doesn't matter if the cat is black or white, as long as it catches mice.*"

"Is that Mao?" Baiyue asked, frowning.

"No," Jieling said, "Deng Xiaoping, the one after Mao."

"Well, he's dead, too," Baiyue said. She rapped a dish against the counter and the needle on the voltmeter jumped.

Jieling had been working just over four weeks when they were all called to the cafeteria for a meeting. Mr. Cao from Human Resources was there. He was wearing a dark suit and standing at the white screen. Other cadres sat in chairs along the back of the stage, looking very stern.

"We are here to discuss a very serious matter," he said. "Many of you know this girl."

There was a laptop hooked up and a very nervous looking boy running it. Jieling looked carefully at the laptop but it didn't appear to be a special projects computer. In fact, it was made in Korea. He did something and an ID picture of a girl flashed on the screen.

Jieling didn't know her. But around her she heard noises of shock, someone sucking air through their teeth, someone else breathed softly, "*Ai-yah.*"

"This girl ran away, leaving her debt with New Life. She ate our food, wore our clothes, slept in our beds. And then, like a thief, she ran away." The Human Resources man nodded his head. The boy at the computer changed the image on the big projector screen.

Now it was a picture of the same girl with her head bowed, and two policemen holding her arms.

"She was picked up in Guangdong," the Human Resources man said. She is in jail there."

The cafeteria was very quiet.

The Human Resources man said, "Her life is ruined, which is what should happen to all thieves."

Then he dismissed them. That afternoon, the picture of the girl with the two policemen appeared on the bulletin boards of every floor of the dormitory.

On Sunday, Baiyue announced, "I'm not going."

She was not supposed to leave the compound, but one of her roommates had female problems—bad cramps—and planned to spend the day in bed drinking tea and reading magazines. Baiyue was going to use her ID to leave.

"You have to," Jieling said. "You want to grow old here? Die a serf to New Life?"

"It's crazy. We can't make money dancing in the plague-trash market."

"I've done it before," Jieling said. "You're scared."

"It's just not a good idea," Baiyue said.

"Because of the girl they caught in Guangdong. We're not skipping out on our debt. We're paying it off."

"We're not supposed to work for someone else when we work here," Baiyue said.

"Oh come on," Jieling said. "You are always making things sound worse than they are. I think you like staying here being little Miss Lei Feng."

"Don't call me that," Baiyue snapped.

"Well don't act like it. New Life is not being fair. We don't have to be fair. What are they going to do to you if they catch you?"

"Fine me," Baiyue said. "Add to my debt!"

"So what? They're going to find a way to add to your debt no matter what. You are a serf. They are the landlord."

"But if—"

"No but if." Jieling said. "You like being a martyr. I don't."

"What do you care," Baiyue said. "You like it here. If you stay you can eat pork buns every night."

"And you can eat congee for the rest of your life. I'm going to try to do something." Jieling slammed out of the dorm room. She had never said harsh things to Baiyue before. Yes, she had thought about staying here. But was that so bad? Better than being like Baiyue who would stay here and have a miserable life. Jieling was not going to have a miserable life, no matter where she stayed or what she did. That was why she had come to Shenzhen in the first place.

She heard the door open behind her and Baiyue ran down the hall. "Okay," she said breathlessly. "I'll try it. Just this once."

The streets of Shanghai were incredibly loud after weeks in the compound. In a shop window, she and Baiyue stopped and watched a news segment on how the fashion in Shanghai was for sarongs. Jieling would have to tell her mother. Of course her mother had a TV and probably already knew. Jieling thought about calling, but not now. Not now. She didn't want to explain about New Life. The next news segment was about the success of the People's Army in Tajikistan. Jieling pulled Baiyue to come on.

They took one bus, and then had to transfer. On Sundays, unless you were lucky, it took forever to transfer because fewer busses ran. They waited almost an hour for the second bus. That bus was almost empty when they got on. They sat down a few seats back from the driver. Baiyue rolled her eyes. "Did you see the guy in the back?" she asked. "Party functionary."

Jieling glanced over her shoulder and saw him. She couldn't miss him, in his careful polo shirt. He had that stiff party-member look.

Baiyue sighed. "My uncle is just like that. So *boring*."

Jieling thought that to be honest, Baiyue would have made a good revolutionary, back in the day. Baiyue liked that kind of revolutionary purity. But she nodded.

The plague-trash market was full on a Sunday. There was a toy seller making tiny little clay figures on sticks. He waved a stick at the girls as they passed. "Cute things!" he called. "I'll make whatever you want!" The stick had a little Donald Duck on it.

"I can't do this," Baiyue said. "There's too many people."

"It's not so bad," Jieling said. She found a place for the boombox. Jieling had brought them to where all the food vendors were. "Stay here and watch this," she said. She hunted through the food stalls and bought a bottle of local beer, counting out from her little horde of money she had left from when she came. She took the beer back to Baiyue. "Drink this," she said. "It will help you be brave."

"I hate beer," Baiyue said.

"Beer or debt," Jieling said.

While Baiyue drank the beer, Jieling started the boombox and did her routine. People smiled at her but no one put any money in her cash box. Shenzhen people were so cheap. Baiyue sat on the curb, nursing her beer, not looking at Jieling or at anyone until finally Jieling couldn't stand it any longer.

"C'mon *meimei*," she said.

Baiyue seemed a bit surprised to be called little sister but she put the beer down and got up. They had practiced a routine to an M.I.A. song, singing and dancing. It would be a hit, Jieling was sure.

"I can't," Baiyue whispered.

"Yes you can," Jieling said. "You do good."

A couple of people stopped to watch them arguing, so Jieling started the music.

"I feel sick," Baiyue whimpered.

But the beat started and there was nothing to do but dance and sing. Baiyue was so nervous, she forgot at first, but then she got the hang of it. She kept her head down and her face was bright red.

Jieling started making up a rap. She'd never done it before and she hadn't gotten very far before she was laughing and then Baiyue was laughing, too.

*Wode meimei hen haixiude*
*Mei ta shi xuli*
*tai hen xiuqi—*

My little sister is so shy
But she's pretty
Far too delicate—

They almost stopped because they were giggling but they kept dancing and Jieling went back to the lyrics from the song they had practiced.

When they had finished, people clapped and they'd made 32 yuan.

They didn't make as much for any single song after that, but in a few hours they had collected 187 yuan. It was early evening and night entertainers were showing up—a couple of people who sang opera, acrobats, and a clown with a wig of hair so red it looked on fire, stepping stork-legged on stilts waving a rubber Kalashnikov in his hand. He was all dressed in white. Uncle Death, from cartoons during the plague. Some of the day vendors had shut down, and new people were showing up who put out a board and some chairs and served sorghum liquor: clear, white and 150 proof. The crowd was starting to change, too. It was rowdier. Packs of young men dressed in weird combinations of clothes from plague markets—vintage Mao suit jackets and suit pants and peasant shoes. And others, veterans from Tajikistan conflict, one with an empty trouser leg.

Jieling picked up the boombox and Baiyue took the cash box. Outside of the market it wasn't yet dark.

"You are amazing," Baiyue kept saying. "You are such a special girl!"

"You did great," Jieling said. "When I was by myself, I didn't make anything! Everyone likes you because you are little and cute!"

"Look at this! I'll be out of debt before autumn!"

Maybe it was just the feeling that she was responsible for Baiyue, but Jieling said, "You keep it all."

"I can't! I can't! We split it!" Baiyue said.

"Sure," Jieling said. "Then after you get away, you can help me. Just think, if we do this for three more Sundays, you'll pay off your debt."

"Oh, Jieling," Baiyue said. "You really are like my big sister!"

Jieling was sorry she had ever called Baiyue "little sister." It was such a country thing to do. She had always suspected that Baiyue wasn't a city girl. Jieling hated the countryside. Grain spread to dry in the road and mother's-elder-sister and father's-younger-brother bringing all the cousins over on the day off. Jieling didn't even know all those country ways to say aunt and uncle. It wasn't Baiyue's fault. And Baiyue had been good to her. She was rotten to be thinking this way.

"Excuse me," said a man. He wasn't like the packs of young men with their long hair and plague clothes. Jieling couldn't place him but he seemed familiar. "I saw you in the market. You were very fun. Very lively."

Baiyue took hold of Jieling's arm. For a moment Jieling wondered if maybe he was from New Life, but she told herself that was crazy. "Thank you," she said. She thought she remembered him putting 10 yuan in the box. No, she thought, he was on the bus. The party functionary. The party was checking up on them. Now that was funny. She wondered if he would lecture them on Western ways.

"Are you in the music business?" Baiyue asked. She glanced at Jieling who couldn't help laughing, snorting through her nose.

The man took them very seriously though. "No," he said. "I can't help you there. But I like your act. You seem like girls of good character."

"Thank you," Baiyue said. She didn't look at Jieling again, which was good because Jieling knew she wouldn't be able to keep a straight face.

"I am Wei Rongyi. Maybe I can buy you some dinner?" the man asked. He held up his hands, "Nothing romantic. You are so young, it is like you could be daughters."

"You have a daughter?" Jieling asked.

He shook his head. "Not anymore," he said.

Jieling understood. His daughter had died of the bird flu. She felt embarrassed for having laughed at him. Her soft heart saw instantly that he was treating them like the daughter he had lost.

He took them to a dumpling place on the edge of the market and ordered half a kilo of crescent-shaped pork dumplings and a kilo of square beef dumplings. He was a cadre, a middle manager. His wife had lived in Changsha for a couple of years now, where her family was from. He was from the older generation, people who did not get divorced. All around them, the restaurant was filling up mostly with men stopping after work for dumplings and drinks. They were a little island surrounded by truck drivers and men who worked in the factories in the outer city—tough, grimy places.

"What do you do? Are you secretaries?" Wei Rongyi asked.

Baiyue laughed. "As if!" she said.

"We are factory girls," Jieling said. She dunked a dumpling in vinegar. They were so good! Not congee!

"Factory girls!" he said. "I am so surprised!"

Baiyue nodded. "We work for New Life," she explained. "This is our day off, so we wanted to earn a little extra money."

He rubbed his head, looking off into the distance. "New Life," he said, trying to place the name. "New Life…"

"Out past the zoo," Baiyue said.

Jieling thought they shouldn't say so much.

"Ah, in the city. A good place? What do they make?" he asked. He had a way of blinking very quickly that was disconcerting.

"Batteries," Jieling said. She didn't say bio-batteries.

"I thought they made computers," he said.

"Oh yes," Baiyue said. "Special projects."

Jieling glared at Baiyue. If this guy gave them trouble at New Life, they'd have a huge problem getting out of the compound.

Baiyue blushed.

Wei laughed. "You are special project girls, then. Well, see, I knew you were not just average factory girls."

He didn't press the issue. Jieling kept waiting for him to make some sort of move on them. Offer to buy them beer. But he didn't, and when they had finished their dumplings, he gave them the leftovers to take back to their dormitories and then stood at the bus stop until they were safely on their bus.

"Are you sure you will be all right?" he asked them when the bus came.

"You can see my window from the bus stop," Jieling promised. "We will be fine."

"Shenzhen can be a dangerous city. You be careful!"

Out the window, they could see him in the glow of the streetlight, waving as the bus pulled away.

"He was so nice," Baiyue sighed. "Poor man."

"Didn't you think he was a little strange?" Jieling asked.

"Everybody is strange anymore," Baiyue said. "After the plague. Not like when we were growing up."

It was true. Her mother was strange. Lots of people were crazy from so many people dying.

Jieling held up the leftover dumplings. "Well, anyway. I am not feeding this to my battery," she said. They both tried to smile.

"Our whole generation is crazy," Baiyue said.

"We know everybody dies," Jieling said. Outside the bus window, the streets were full of young people, out trying to live while they could.

They made all their bus connections as smooth as silk. So quick, they were home in forty-five minutes. Sunday night was movie night, and all of Jieling's roommates were at the movie so she and Baiyue could sort the money in Jieling's room. She used her key card and the door clicked open.

Mr. Wei was kneeling by the battery boxes in their room. He started, and hissed, "Close the door!"

Jieling was so surprised, she did.

"Mr. Wei!" Baiyue said.

He was dressed like an army man on a secret mission, all in black. He showed them a little black gun. Jieling blinked in surprise. "Mr. Wei!" she said. It was hard to take him seriously. Even all in black, he was still weird Mr. Wei, blinking rapidly behind his glasses.

"Lock the door," he said. "And be quiet."

"The door locks by itself," Jieling explained. "And my roommates will be back soon."

"Put a chair in front of the door," he said, and shoved the desk chair towards them. Baiyue pushed it under the door handle. The window was open and Jieling could see where he had climbed on the desk and left a footprint on Taohua's fashion magazine. Taohua was going to be pissed. And what was Jieling going to say? If anyone found out there was a man in her room, she was going to be in very big trouble.

"How did you get in?" she asked. "What about the cameras?" There were security cameras.

He showed them a little spray can. "Special paint. It just makes things look foggy and dim. Security guards are so lazy anymore no one ever checks things out." He paused a moment, clearly disgusted with the lax morality of the day. "Miss Jieling," he said. "Take that screwdriver and finish unscrewing that computer from the wall."

Computer? She realized he meant the battery boxes.

Baiyue's eyes got very big. "Mr. Wei! You're a thief!"

Jieling shook her head. "A corporate spy."

"I am a patriot," he said. "But you young people wouldn't understand that. Sit on the bed." He waved the gun at Baiyue.

The gun was so little it looked like a toy and it was difficult to be afraid, but still Jieling thought it was good that Baiyue sat.

Jieling knelt. It was her box that Mr. Wei had been disconnecting. It was all the way to the right, so he had started with it. She had come to feel a little bit attached to it, thinking of it sitting there, occasionally zapping electricity back into the grid, reducing her electricity costs and her debt. She sighed and unscrewed it. Mr. Wei watched.

She jimmied it off the wall, careful not to touch the contacts. The cells built up a charge, and when they were ready, a switch tapped a membrane and they discharged. It was all automatic and there was no knowing when it was going to happen. Mr. Wei was going to be very upset when he realized that this wasn't a computer.

"Put it on the desk," he said.

She did.

"Now sit with your friend."

Jieling sat down next to Baiyue. Keeping a wary eye on them, he sidled over to the bio-battery. He opened the hatch where they dumped garbage in them, and tried to look in as well as look at them. "Where are the controls?" he asked. He picked it up, his palm flat against the broken back end where the contacts were exposed.

"Tap it against the desk," Jieling said. "Sometimes the door sticks." There wasn't actually a door. But it had just come into her head. She hoped that the cells hadn't discharged in a while.

Mr. Wei frowned and tapped the box smartly against the desktop.

Torpedinidae, the electric ray, can generate a current of 200 volts for approximately a minute. The power output is close to 1 kilowatt over the course of the discharge and while this won't kill the average person, it is a powerful shock. Mr. Wei stiffened and fell, clutching the box and spasming wildly. One…two… three…four…Mr. Wei was still spasming. Jieling and Baiyue looked at each other. Gingerly, Jieling stepped around Mr. Wei. He had dropped the little gun. Jieling picked it up. Mr. Wei was still spasming. Jieling wondered if he was going to die. Or if he was already dead and the electricity was just making him jump. She didn't want him to die. She looked at the little gun and it made her feel even sicker so she threw it out the window.

Finally Mr. Wei dropped the box.

Baiyue said, "Is he dead?"

Jieling was afraid to touch him. She couldn't tell if he was breathing. Then he groaned and both girls jumped.

"He's not dead," Jieling said.

"What should we do?" Baiyue asked.

"Tie him up," Jieling said. Although she wasn't sure what they'd do with him then.

Jieling used the cord to her boombox to tie his wrists. When she grabbed his hands he gasped and struggled feebly. Then she took her pillowcase and cut along the blind end, a space just wide enough that his head would fit through.

"Sit him up," she said to Baiyue.

"You sit him up," Baiyue said. Baiyue didn't want to touch him.

Jieling pulled Mr. Wei into a sitting position. "Put the pillowcase over his head," she said. The pillowcase was like a shirt with no armholes, so when Baiyue pulled it over his head and shoulders, it pinned his arms against his sides and worked something like a straightjacket.

Jieling took his wallet and his identification papers out of his pocket. "Why would someone carry their wallet to a break-in?" she asked. "He has six ID papers. One says he is Mr. Wei."

"Wow," Baiyue said. "Let me see. Also Mr. Ma. Mr. Zhang. Two Mr. Lius and a Mr. Cui."

Mr. Wei blinked, his eyes watering.

"Do you think he has a weak heart?" Baiyue asked.

"I don't know," Jieling said. "Wouldn't he be dead if he did?"

Baiyue considered this.

"Baiyue! Look at all this yuan!" Jieling emptied the wallet, counting. Almost 8,000 yuan!

"Let me go," Mr. Wei said weakly.

Jieling was glad he was talking. She was glad he seemed like he might be all right. She didn't know what they would do if he died. They would never be able to explain a dead person. They would end up in deep debt. And probably go to jail for something. "Should we call the floor auntie and tell him that he broke in?" Jieling asked.

"We could," Baiyue said.

"Do not!" Mr. Wei said, sounding stronger. "You don't understand! I'm from Beijing!"

"So is my stepfather," Jieling said. "Me, I'm from Baoding. It's about an hour south of Beijing."

Mr. Wei said, "I'm from the government! That money is government money!"

"I don't believe you," Jieling said. "Why did you come in through the window?" Jieling asked.

"Secret agents always come in through the window?" Baiyue said, and started to giggle.

"Because this place is counter-revolutionary!" Mr. Wei said.

Baiyue covered her mouth with her hand. Jieling felt embarrassed, too. No one said things like "counter-revolutionary" anymore.

"This place! It is making things that could make China strong!" he said.

"Isn't that good?" Baiyue asked.

"But they don't care about China! Only about money. Instead of using it for China, they sell it to America!" he said. Spittle was gathering at the corner of his mouth. He was starting to look deranged. "Look at this place! Officials are all concerned about *guanxi*!" Connections. Kickbacks. Guanxi ran China, everybody knew that.

"So, maybe you have an anti-corruption investigation?" Jieling said. There were lots of anti-corruption investigations. Jieling's stepfather said that they usually meant someone powerful was mad at their brother-in-law or something, so they accused them of corruption.

Mr. Wei groaned. "There is no one to investigate them."

Baiyue and Jieling looked at each other.

Mr. Wei explained, "In my office, the Guangdong office, there used to be twenty people. Special operatives. Now there is only me and Ms. Yang."

Jieling said, "Did they all die of bird flu?"

Mr. Wei shook his head. "No, they all went to work on contract for Saudi Arabia. You can make a lot of money in the Middle East. A lot more than in China."

"Why don't you and Ms. Yang go work in Saudi Arabia?" Baiyue asked.

Jieling thought Mr. Wei would give some revolutionary speech. But he just hung his head. "She is the secretary. I am the bookkeeper." And then in a smaller voice, "She is going to Kuwait to work for Mr. Liu."

They probably did not need bookkeepers in the Middle East. Poor Mr. Wei. No wonder he was such a terrible secret agent.

"The spirit of the revolution is gone," he said, and there were real, honest to goodness tears in his eyes. "Did you know that Tiananmen Square was built by volunteers? People would come after their regular job and lay the paving of the square. Today people look to Hong Kong."

"Nobody cares about a bunch of old men in Beijing," Baiyue said.

"Exactly! We used to have a strong military! But now the military is too worried about their own factories and farms! They want us to pull out of Tajikistan because it is ruining their profits!"

This sounded like a good idea to Jieling, but she had to admit, she hated the news so she wasn't sure why they were fighting in Tajikistan anyway. Something about Muslim terrorists. All she knew about Muslims was that they made great street food.

"Don't you want to be patriots?" Mr. Wei said.

"You broke into my room and tried to steal my—you know that's not a computer, don't you?" Jieling said. "It's a bio-battery. They're selling them to the Americans. Wal-Mart."

Mr. Wei groaned.

"We don't work in special projects," Baiyue said.

"You said you did," he protested.

"We did not," Jieling said. "You just thought that. How did you know this was my room?"

"The company lists all its workers in a directory," he said wearily. "And it's movie night, everyone is either out or goes to the movies. I've had the building under surveillance for weeks. I followed you to the market today. Last week it was a girl named Pingli, who blabbed about everything, but she wasn't in special projects.

"I put you on the bus, I've timed the route three times. I should have had an hour and fifteen minutes to drive over here and get the box and get out."

"We made all our connections," Baiyue explained.

Mr. Wei was so dispirited he didn't even respond.

Jieling said. "I thought the government was supposed to help workers. If we get caught, we'll be fined and we'll be deeper in debt." She was just talking. Talking, talking, talking too much. This was too strange. Like when someone was dying. Something extraordinary was happening, like your father dying in the next room, and yet the ordinary things went on, too. You made tea, your mother opened the shop the next day and sewed clothes while she cried. People came in and pretended not to notice. This was like that. Mr. Wei had a gun and they were explaining about New Life.

"Debt?" Mr. Wei said.

"To the company," she said. "We are all in debt. The company hires us and says they are going to pay us, but then they charge us for our food and our clothes and our dorm and it always costs more than we earn. That's why we were doing rap today. To make money to be able to quit." Mr. Wei's glasses had tape holding the arm on. Why hadn't she noticed that in the restaurant? Maybe because when you are afraid you notice things. When your father is dying of the plague, you notice the way the covers on your mother's chairs need to be washed. You wonder if you will have to do it or if you will die before you have to do chores.

"The Pingli girl," he said, "she said the same thing. That's illegal."

"Sure," Baiyue said. "Like anybody cares."

"Could you expose corruption?" Jieling asked.

Mr. Wei shrugged, at least as much as he could in the pillowcase. "Maybe. But they would just pay bribes to locals and it would all go away."

All three of them sighed.

"Except," Mr. Wei said, sitting up a little straighter. "The Americans. They are always getting upset about that sort of thing. Last year there was a corporation, the Shanghai Six. The Americans did a documentary on them and then Western companies would not do business. If they got information from us about what New Life is doing…"

"Who else is going to buy bio-batteries?" Baiyue said. "The company would be in big trouble!"

"Beijing can threaten a big exposé, tell the *New York Times* newspaper!" Mr. Wei said, getting excited. "My Beijing supervisor will love that! He loves media!"

"Then you can have a big show trial," Jieling said.

Mr. Wei was nodding.

"But what is in it for us?" Baiyue said.

"When there's a trial, they'll have to cancel your debt!" Mr. Wei said. "Even pay you a big fine!"

"If I call the floor auntie and say I caught a corporate spy, they'll give me a big bonus," Baiyue said.

"Don't you care about the other workers?" Mr. Wei asked.

Jieling and Baiyue looked at each other and shrugged. Did they? "What are they going to do to you anyway?" Jieling said. "You can still do big exposé. But that way we don't have to wait."

"Look," he said, "you let me go, and I'll let you keep my money."

Someone rattled the door handle.

"Please," Mr. Wei whispered. "You can be heroes for your fellow workers, even though they'll never know it."

Jieling stuck the money in her pocket. Then she took the papers, too.

"You can't take those," he said.

"Yes I can," she said. "If after six months, there is no big corruption scandal? We can let everyone know how a government secret agent was outsmarted by two factory girls."

"Six months!" he said. "That's not long enough!"

"It better be," Jieling said.

Outside the door, Taohua called, "Jieling? Are you in there? Something is wrong with the door!"

"Just a minute," Jieling called. "I had trouble with it when I came home." To Mr. Wei she whispered sternly, "Don't you try anything. If you do, we'll scream our heads off and everybody will come running." She and Baiyue shimmied the pillowcase off of Mr. Wei's head. He started to stand up and jerked the boombox which clattered across the floor. "Wait!" she hissed, and untied him.

Taohua called through the door, "What's that?"

"Hold on!" Jieling called.

Baiyue helped Mr. Wei stand up. Mr. Wei climbed onto the desk and then grabbed a line hanging outside. He stopped a moment as if trying to think of something to say.

"'A revolution is not a dinner party, or writing an essay, or painting a picture, or doing embroidery,'" Jieling said. It had been her father's favorite quote from Chairman Mao. "'...it cannot be so refined, so leisurely and gentle, so temperate, kind, courteous, restrained and magnanimous. A revolution is an insurrection, an act of by which one class overthrows another.'"

Mr. Wei looked as if he might cry and not because he was moved by patriotism. He stepped back and disappeared. Jieling and Baiyue looked out the window. He did go down the wall just like a secret agent from a movie, but it was only two stories. There was still the big footprint in the middle of Taohua's magazine and the room looked as if it had been hit by a storm.

"They're going to think you had a boyfriend," Baiyue whispered to Jieling.

"Yeah," Jieling said, pulling the chair out from under the door handle. "And they're going to think he's rich."

It was Sunday, and Jieling and Baiyue were sitting on the beach. Jieling's cell phone rang, a little chime of M.I.A. hip hop. Even though it was Sunday, it was one of the girls from New Life. Sunday should be a day off, but she took the call anyway.

"Jieling? This is Xia Meili? From packaging. Taohua told me about your business? Maybe you could help me?"

Jieling said, "Sure. What is your debt, Meili?"

"3,800 R.M.B.," Meili said. "I know it's a lot."

Jieling said, "Not so bad. We have a lot of people who already have loans, though, and it will probably be a few weeks before I can make you a loan."

With Mr. Wei's capital, Jieling and Baiyue had opened a bank account. They had bought themselves out, and then started a little loan business where they bought people out of New Life. Then people had to pay them back with a little extra. They each had jobs—Jieling worked for a company that made toys. She sat each day at a table where she put a piece of specially shaped plastic over the body of a little doll, an action figure. The plastic fit right over the figure and had cut-outs. Jieling sprayed the whole thing with red paint and when the piece of plastic was lifted, the action figure had a red shirt. It was boring, but at the end of the week, she got paid instead of owing the company money.

She and Baiyue used all their extra money on loans to get girls out of New Life. More and more loans, and more and more payments. Now New Life had sent them a threatening letter saying that what they were doing was illegal. But Mr. Wei said not to worry. Two officials had come and talked to them and had showed them legal documents and had them explain everything about what had happened. Soon, the officials promised, they would take New Life to court.

Jieling wasn't so sure about the officials. After all, Mr. Wei was an official. But a foreign newspaperman had called them. He was from a newspaper called *The Wall Street Journal* and he said that he was writing a story about labor shortages in China after the bird flu. He said that in some places in the west there were reports of slavery. His Chinese was very good. His story was going to come out in the United States tomorrow. Then she figured officials would have to do something or lose face.

Jieling told Meili to call her back in two weeks—although hopefully in two weeks no one would need help to get away from New Life—and wrote a note to herself in her little notebook.

Baiyue was sitting looking at the water. "This is the first time I've been to the beach," she said.

"The ocean is so big, isn't it."

Baiyue nodded, scuffing at the white sand. "People always say that, but you don't know until you see it."

Jieling said, "Yeah." Funny, she had lived here for months. Baiyue had lived here more than a year. And they had never come to the beach. The beach was beautiful.

"I feel sorry for Mr. Wei," Baiyue said.

"You do?" Jieling said. "Do you think he really had a daughter who died?"

"Maybe," Baiyue said. "A lot of people died."

"My father died," Jieling said.

Baiyue looked at her, a quick little sideways look, then back out at the ocean. "My mother died," she said.

Jieling was surprised. She had never known that Baiyue's mother was dead. They had talked about so much but never about that. She put her arm around Baiyue's waist and they sat for a while.

"I feel bad in a way," Baiyue said.

"How come?" Jieling said.

"Because we had to steal capital to fight New Life. That makes us capitalists." Jieling shrugged.

"I wish it was like when they fought the revolution," Baiyue said. "Things were a lot more simple."

"Yeah," Jieling said, "and they were poor and a lot of them died."

"I know," Baiyue sighed.

Jieling knew what she meant. It would be nice to…to be sure what was right and what was wrong. Although not if it made you like Mr. Wei.

Poor Mr. Wei. Had his daughter really died?

"Hey," Jieling said, "I've got to make a call. Wait right here." She walked a little down the beach. It was windy and she turned her back to guard protect the cell phone, like someone lighting a match. "Hello," she said, "hello, Mama, it's me. Jieling."

# EVIDENCE OF LOVE IN A CASE OF ABANDONMENT: ONE DAUGHTER'S PERSONAL ACCOUNT

## M. RICKERT

M. Rickert grew up in Fredonia, Wisconsin. When she was eighteen she moved to California, where she worked at Disneyland. She still has fond memories of selling balloons there. After many years (and through the sort of "odd series of events" that describe much of her life), she got a job as a kindergarten teacher in a small private school for gifted children. She worked there for almost a decade, then left to pursue her life as a writer. Her most recent book is collection *Map of Dreams*. A second collection, *Holiday*, is in the works.

"When I, or people like me, are running the country, you'd better flee, because we will find you, we will try you, and we'll execute you. I mean every word of it. I will make it part of my mission to see to it that they are tried and executed."

Randall Terry, founder of Operation Rescue

It took a long time to deduce that many of the missing women could not be accounted for. Executions were a matter of public record then and it was still fairly easy to keep track of them. They were on every night at seven o'clock, filmed from the various execution centers. It was policy back then to name the criminal as the camera lingered over her face. Yet women went missing who never appeared on execution. Rumors started. Right around then some of the policies changed. The criminals were no longer named, and execution centers sprung up all over the country so it was no longer possible to account for the missing. The rumors persisted though, and generally took one of two courses: Agents were using the criminals for their own nefarious purposes, or women were sneaking away and assembling an army.

When my mother didn't come home, my father kept saying she must have had a meeting he'd forgotten about, after all, she volunteered for Homeland Security's Mothers in Schools program, as well as did work for the church, and

410 — M. RICKERT

the library. That's my mom. She always has to keep busy. When my father started calling hospitals, his freckles all popped out against his white skin the way they get when he's upset, and I realized he was hoping she'd had an accident, I knew. The next morning, when I found him sitting in the rocker, staring out the picture window, their wedding album in his lap, I really knew.

Of course I am not the only abandoned daughter. Even here, there are a few of us. We are not marked in any way a stranger could see, but we are known in our community. Things are better for those whose mothers are executed. They are a separate group from those of us whose mothers are unaccounted for, who may be so evil as to escape reparation for their crimes, so sick as to plan to attack the innocent ones left behind.

I am obsessed with executions, though there are too many to keep track of, hard as I try to flip through the screens and have them all going on at once. I search for her face. There are many faces. Some weeping, some screaming, some with lips trembling, or nostrils flaring but I never see her face. Jenna Offeren says her mother was executed in Albany but she's lying. Jenna Offeren is a weak, annoying person but I can't completely blame her. Even my own father tried it. One morning he comes into my room, sits at the edge of my bed and says, "Lisle, I'm sorry. I saw her last night. Your mother. They got her." I just shook my head. "Don't try to make me feel better," I said, "I know she's still alive."

My mother and I, we have that thing some twins have. That's how close we've always been. Once, when I was still a little kid, I fell from a tree at Sarah T.'s house and my mom came running into the backyard, her hair a mess, her lipstick smeared, before Mrs. T. had even finished dialing the cell. "I just knew," Mom said. "I was washing the windows and all of a sudden I had this pain in my stomach and I knew you needed me. I came right over." My wrist was broke (and to this day hurts when it's going to rain) and I couldn't do my sewing or synchronized swimming for weeks, but I almost didn't mind because, back then, I thought me and Mom had something special between us, and what happened with my wrist proved it. Now I'm not so sure. Everything changes when your mother goes missing.

I look for her face all the time. Not just on the screens but on the heads of other women, not here, of course, but if we go to Milwaukee, or on the school trip to Chicago, I look at every women's face, searching for hers. I'm not the only one either. I caught Jenna Offeren doing the same thing, though she denied it. (Not mine, of course. Hers.)

Before she left us, Mom was not exactly a happy person, but what normal American girl goes around assuming that her own mother is a murderer? She even helped me with my project in seventh year, cutting out advertisements that used that model, Heidi Eagle, who was executed the year before, and I remember, so clearly, Mom saying that Heidi's children would have been beautiful, so how was I to know that my own mother was one of the evil doers?

But then what did I think was going on with all that crying? My mother cried all the time. She cried when she was doing the dishes, she cried when she cleaned the toilets, she even cried in the middle of laughing, like the time I told her about Mr. Saunders demonstrating to us girls what it's like to be pregnant with a basketball. The only time I can ever remember my mom saying anything traceable, anything that could be linked from our perfect life to the one I'm stuck in now, was when she found a list of boys' names on my T.S.O. and asked if they were boys I had crushes on. I don't know what she was thinking to say such a thing because there were seven names on that list and I am not a slut, but anyhow, I explained that they were baby names I was considering for when my time came and she got this look on her face like maybe she'd been a hologram all along and was just going to fade away and then she said, "When I was your age, I planned on being an astronaut."

My cheeks turned bright red, of course. I was embarrassed for her to talk like that. She tried to make light of it by looking over the list, letting me know which names she liked (Liam and Jack) and which she didn't (Paul and Luke). If the time ever comes (and I am beginning to have my doubts that it will) I'm going to choose one of the names she hated. It's not much, but it's all I have. There's only so much you can do to a mother who is missing.

My father says I'm spending too much time watching screens so he has insisted that we do something fun together, "as a family" he said, trying to make it sound cheerful like we aren't the lamest excuse for family you've ever seen, just me and him.

There's plenty of families without mothers, of course. Apparently this was initially a surprise to Homeland Security; it was generally assumed that those women who had abortions during the dark times never had any children, but a lot of women of my mother's generation were swayed by the evil propaganda of their youth, had abortions and careers even, before coming back to the light of righteous behavior. So having an executed mother is not necessarily that bad. There's a whole extra shame in being associated with a mother who is missing however, out there somewhere, in a militia or something. (With the vague possibility that she is not stockpiling weapons and learning about car bombs, but captured by one of the less ethical Agents, but what's the real chance of that? Isn't that just a fantasy kids like Jenna Offeren came up with because they can't cope?) At any rate, to counteract the less palatable rumor, and the one that puts the Agents in the worse light, Homeland Security has recently begun the locks of hair program. Now they send strands of a criminal's hair to the family and it's become a real trend for the children to wear it in see-through lockets. None of this makes sense, of course. The whole reason the executions became anonymous in the first place was to put to rest the anarchist notion that some women had escaped their fate, but Homeland Security is not the department of consistency (I think I can say that) and seems to lean more towards a policy of confusion. The locks of hair project has been very successful and has even made some money as families are now paying to have executed women's corpses dug up for their hair. At any rate, you guessed it, Jenna shows up at execution with a lock of hair necklace that she says comes from her mother but I know it's Jenna's own hair, which is blonde and curly while her mom's was brownish gray. "That's 'cause she dyed it," Jenna says. I give up. Nobody dyes their hair brownish gray. Jenna has just gone completely nuts.

It seems like the whole town is at execution and I realize my father's right, I've been missing a lot by watching them on screen all the time. "Besides, it's starting to not look right, never going. It was different when your mother was still with us," he said. So I agreed, though I didn't expect much. I mean no way would they execute my mom right here in her home town. Sure, it happens but it would be highly unlikely, so what's the point? I expected it to be incredibly boring like church, or the meetings of the Young Americans, or Home Ec class but it wasn't anything like any of that. Screens really give you no idea of the excitement of an execution and if you, like me, think that you've seen it all because you've been watching it on screen for years, I recommend you attend your own hometown event. It just might surprise you. Besides, it's important to stay active in your community.

We don't have a stadium, of course, not in a town of a population of eight thousand and dwindling, so executions are held on the football field the first Wednesday of every month. I was surprised by the screens displayed around the field but my father said that was the only way you could get a real good look at the faces, and he was right. It was fascinating to look at the figure in the center of the field, how small she looked, to the face on the screen, freakishly large. Just like on screen at home, the women were all ages from grandmothers to women my mother's age and a few probably younger. The problem is under control now. No one would think of getting an abortion. There's already talk about cutting back the program in a few years and I feel kind of sentimental about it. I've grown up with executions and can't imagine what kids will watch instead. Not that I would wish this on anyone. It's a miserable thing to be in my situation. Maybe no one will even want me now. I ask my dad about this on the way to execution, what happens to girls like me, and for a while he pretends he doesn't know what I'm talking about until I spell it out and he can't act all Homeland Security. He shakes his head and sighs. "It's too soon to say, Lisle. Daughters of executed moms, they've done all right, maybe you know, not judges' wives, or Agents, or anyone like that, but they've had a decent time of it for the most part. Daughters of missing moms, well, it's just too soon to tell. Hey, maybe you'll get to be a breeder." He says it like it's a good thing, giving up my babies every nine or ten months.

"I hate Mom," I say. He doesn't scold me. After all, what she did, she did to both of us.

It seems like the whole town is here, though I know this can't be right because it's the first time I've come since I was a kid, and that would be statistically improbable if we were the only ones who never came back, but, even though I am certain it's not the whole town, I'd have to say it's pretty close to it. Funny how in all these faces and noise and excitement I can see who's wearing locks of hair lockets as if they are made of shining light, which of course they are not. I could forgive her, I think—and I'm surprised by the tears in my eyes—if she'd just do the right thing and turn herself in. Maybe I'm not being fair. After all, maybe she's trapped somewhere, held prisoner by some Agent and there's nothing she can do about it. I, too, take comfort in this little fantasy from time to time.

Each execution is done individually. She walks across the entire field in a hood. The walk takes a long time 'cause of the shackles. I can think of no reasonable explanation for the hood, beyond suspense. It is very effective. The beginning of the walk is a good time to take a bathroom break or get a snack, that's how long it takes. No one wants to be away from his seat when the criminal gets close to the red circle at the center of the field. The closer she gets to the circle (led by one of the Junior Agents, or, as is the case tonight, by one of the children from the town's various civic programs) the more quiet it gets until eventually the only noise is the sound of chains. I've heard this on screen a million times but then there is neighborhood noise going on, cars, maybe someone talking on a cell, dogs barking, that sort of thing, but when the event is live there's no sound other than maybe a cough or a baby crying. I have to tell you all those people in the same space being quiet, the only sound the chains rattling around the criminal's ankles and wrists, well it's way more powerful than how it seems on screen. She always stands for a few seconds in the center of the circle but she rarely stands still. Once placed in position, hands and feet shackled, she displays her fear by wavering, or the shoulders go up, sometimes she is shaking so bad you can see it even if you're not looking on screen.

The child escort walks away to polite applause and the Executioner comes to position. He unties the hood, pauses for dramatic effect (and it is dramatic!) then plucks the hood off, which almost always causes some of her hair to stand out from her head, as though she's been electrocuted, or taken off a knit cap on a snowy day, and at that moment we turn to the screen to get a closer look. I never get bored of it. The horror on their faces, the dripping nostrils, the spit bubbling from lips, the eyes wet with tears, wide with terror. Occasionally there is a stoic one, but there aren't many of these, and when there is, it's easy enough to look away from the screen and focus on the big picture. What had she been thinking? How could she murder someone so tiny, so innocent and not know she'd have to pay? When I think of what the time from before was like I shudder and thank God for being born in the Holy times. In spite of my mother, I am blessed. I know this, even though I sometimes forget. Right there, in the football field bleachers I fold my hands and bow my head. When I am finished my father is giving me a strange look. "If this is too upsetting we can leave," he says. He constantly makes mistakes like this. Sometimes I just ignore him, but this time I try to explain. "I just realized how lucky I am." I can't think of what else to say, how to make him understand so I simply smile. Right then the stoic woman is shot. When I look I see the gaping maul that was her head, right where that evil thought was first conceived to destroy the innocent life that grew inside her. Now she is neither stoic nor alive. She lies in a heap, twitching for a while, but those are just nerves.

It's getting late. Some people use this time to usher their young children home. When we came, all those years ago, my mom letting me play with her gold chain while I sat in her lap, we were one of the first to leave, though I was not the youngest child in attendance. My mother was always strict that way. "Time for bed," she said cheerfully, first to me, and then by way of explanation, pressing my head tight against her shoulder, trying to make me look tired, pressing so hard that I started crying, which, I now realize, served her purpose.

My father says he has to use the bathroom. There is a pocket of space around me when he leaves. My father is gone a long time. This is unusual for the men's bathroom and I must admit I get a little worried about him, especially as the woman approaches the target circle but right when I am starting to think he's going to be too late, he comes, his head bent low so as not to obstruct the view. He sits beside me at what is the last possible second. He shrugs and looks like he's about to say something. Horrified, I turn away. It would be just like him to talk at a time like this.

The girl (from the Young and Beautiful club) dressed all in white with a flower wreathe on her head (and a locks of hair locket glimmering on her chest) walks away from the woman. The tenor of applause grows louder as the Executioner approaches. We are trying to show how much we've appreciated his work tonight. The Executioners are never named. They travel in some kind of secret rotation so no one can ever figure it out, but over time they get reputations. They wear masks, of course, or they would always be hounded for autographs, but are recognized, when they are working, by the insignia on their uniforms. This one is known as Red Dragon for the elaborate dragon on his chest. The applause can be registered on the criminal who shakes like jello. She shakes so much that it is not unreasonable to wonder if she will be one of the fainters. I hate the fainters. They mess with the dramatic arc, all that build up of the long walk, the rattling chains, the Executioner's arrival, only to have the woman fall in a large heap on the ground. Sometimes it takes forever to revive her, and some effort to get her to stand, at which point the execution is anticlimactic.

The Executioner, perhaps sensing this very scenario, says something to jello woman that none of us can hear but she suddenly goes still. There is scattered applause for Red Dragon's skill. He turns towards the audience, and, though he wears his mask, there is something in his demeanor which hushes the crowd. We are watching a master at work. Next, he steps in front of the woman, reaches with both hands around her neck, creating the effect of a man about to give a kiss. We are all as still as if we are waiting for that kiss. With one gesture, he unties the string, and in the same breath reaches up and pulls off the hood. We gasp.

Mrs. Offeren's face fills the screen. Someone screams. I think it is Jenna. I am torn between looking for her in the crowd, and keeping my attention on her mother, whose head turns at the sound so there is only a view of her giant ear but the Executioner says something sharp and she snaps her head back to attention. The screen betrays that her eyes peer past the Executioner, first narrow then wide, and her lips part at the moment she realizes she is home. Her eyes just keep moving after that, searching the crowd, looking for Jenna, I figure, until suddenly, how can it be suddenly when it happens like this every time, but it is suddenly, her head jerks back with the firecracker sound of the shot, she falls from the screen. She lies on the ground, twitching, the red puddle blossoming around her head. Jenna screams and screams. It is my impression that no one does anything to stop her. Nor does anyone use this break to go to the snack shop, or the bathroom, or home. I don't know when my father's hand has reached across the space between us but at some point I realize it rests, gently, on my thigh, when I look at him, he squeezes, lightly, almost like a woman would, as though there is no strength left inside him. They quickly cut some of Mrs. Offeren's hair before it gets too bloody, and bag it, lift her up, clumsily, so that at first her arm and then her head falls towards the ground (the assistants are tired by this time of night), load her into the cart. We listen to the sound of the wheels that need to be oiled and the faint rattle of chains as the cart lumbers across the field. Jenna weeps audibly. The center of the red circle is coated in blood. I pretend it is a Rorschach and decide it looks exactly like a pterodactyl. The cleaning crew comes and hoses it down. That's when people start moving about, talk, rush to the bathroom, take sleeping children home, but it goes mostly silent again when the Offeren family stands up. The seven of them sidle down the bleacher and walk along the side of the field.

I watch the back of Jenna's head, her blonde curls under the lights, almost golden like a halo, though no one, not even the most forgiving person is ever going to mistake Jenna for someone holy. Her mother was a murderer, after all. Yet I realize she'll soon replace that stupid fake locket with a real one while I have nothing. She might even get to marry a police or a trash collector, even a teacher, while the best I can hope for is a position at one of the orphanages. My dad's idea that I might be a breeder someday seems highly optimistic.

"Let's go," I say.

"Are you sure? Maybe the next one…" but he doesn't even finish the thought. He must see something in my face that tells him I am done with childish fantasies.

She's never coming back. Whatever selfish streak caused her, all those years ago, to kill one child is the same selfish streak that allows her to abandon me now.

We walk down the bleachers. Everyone turns away from us, holding their little kids close. My father walks in front of me, with his head down, his hands in his pockets. By the time we get to the car in the parking lot we can hear the polite applause from the football field as another woman enters the circle. He opens his door. I open mine. We drive home in silence. I crane my neck to try to look up at the sky as if I expect to find something there, God maybe, or the living incarnation of the blood pterodactyl but of course I see neither. There is nothing. I close my eyes and think of my mother. Oh, how I miss her.

# FROM BABEL'S FALL'N GLORY WE FLED...

## MICHAEL SWANWICK

Michael Swanwick's first two short stories were published in 1980, and both featured on the Nebula ballot that year. One of the major writers working in the field today, he has been nominated for at least one of the field's major awards in almost every successive year, and has won the Hugo, Nebula, World Fantasy, Theodore Sturgeon Memorial, and Locus awards. He has published six collections of short fiction, seven novels—*In the Drift, Vacuum Flowers, Stations of the Tide, The Iron Dragon's Daughter, Jack Faust, Bones of the Earth*, and *The Dragons of Babel*—and a Hugo Award-nominated book-length interview with editor Gardner Dozois. In recent years Swanwick has also established himself as the modern master of the short-short story, publishing several hundred short-shorts, most notably the "Periodic Table of Science Fiction" and "The Sleep of Reason." His most recent book is major career retrospective collection, *The Best of Michael Swanwick*.

Imagine a cross between Byzantium and a termite mound. Imagine a jeweled mountain, slender as an icicle, rising out of the steam jungles and disappearing into the dazzling pearl-grey skies of Gehenna. Imagine that Gaudi—he of the Segrada Familia and other biomorphic architectural whimsies—had been commissioned by a nightmare race of giant black millipedes to re-create Barcelona at the height of its glory, along with touches of the Forbidden City in the eighteenth century and Tokyo in the twenty-second, all within a single miles-high structure. Hold every bit of that in your mind at once, multiply by a thousand, and you've got only the faintest ghost of a notion of the splendor that was Babel.

Now imagine being inside Babel when it fell.

Hello. I'm Rosamund. I'm dead. I was present in human form when it happened and as a simulation chaotically embedded within a liquid crystal data-matrix then and thereafter up to the present moment. I was killed instantly when the meteors hit. I saw it all.

Rosamund means "rose of the world." It's the third most popular female name on Europa, after Gaea and Virginia Dare. For all our elaborate sophistication, we wear our hearts on our sleeves, we Europans.

Here's what it was like:

*"Wake up! Wake up! Wake up!"*

"Wha—?" Carlos Quivera sat up, shedding rubble. He coughed, choked, shook his head. He couldn't seem to think clearly. An instant ago he'd been standing in the chilled and pressurized embassy suite, conferring with Arsenio. Now... "How long have I been asleep?"

"Unconscious. Ten hours," his suit (that's me—Rosamund!) said. It had taken that long to heal his burns. Now it was shooting wake-up drugs into him: amphetamines, endorphins, attention enhancers, a witch's brew of chemicals. Physically dangerous, but in this situation, whatever it might be, Quivera would survive by intelligence or not at all. "I was able to form myself around you before the walls ruptured. You were lucky."

"The others? Did the others survive?"

"Their suits couldn't reach them in time."

"Did Rosamund...?"

"All the others are dead."

Quivera stood.

Even in the aftermath of disaster, Babel was an imposing structure. Ripped open and exposed to the outside air, a thousand rooms spilled over one another toward the ground. Bridges and buttresses jutted into gaping smoke-filled canyons created by the slow collapse of hexagonal support beams (this was new data; I filed it under *Architecture*, subheading: *Support Systems* with links to *Esthetics* and *Xenopsychology*) in a jumbled geometry that would have terrified Piranesi himself. Everywhere, gleaming black millies scurried over the rubble.

Quivera stood.

In the canted space about him, bits and pieces of the embassy rooms were identifiable: a segment of wood molding, some velvet drapery now littered with chunks of marble, shreds of wallpaper (after a design by William Morris) now curling and browning in the heat. Human interior design was like nothing native to Gehenna and it had taken a great deal of labor and resources to make the embassy so pleasant for human habitation. The queen-mothers had been generous with everything but their trust.

Quivera stood.

There were several corpses remaining as well, still recognizably human though they were blistered and swollen by the savage heat. These had been his colleagues (all of them), his friends (most of them), his enemies (two, perhaps three), and even his lover (one). Now they were gone, and it was as if they had been compressed into one indistinguishable mass, and his feelings toward them all as well: shock and sorrow and anger and survivor guilt all slagged together to become one savage emotion.

Quivera threw back his head and howled.

I had a reference point now. Swiftly, I mixed serotonin-precursors and injected them through a hundred microtubules into the appropriate areas of his brain. Deftly, they took hold. Quivera stopped crying. I had my metaphorical hands on the control knobs of his emotions. I turned him cold, cold, cold.

"I feel nothing," he said wonderingly. "Everyone is dead, and I feel nothing." Then, flat as flat: "What kind of monster am I?"

"*My* monster," I said fondly. "My duty is to ensure that you and the information you carry within you get back to Europa. So I have chemically neutered your emotions. You must remain a meat puppet for the duration of this mission." Let him hate me—I who have no true ego, but only a facsimile modeled after a human original—all that mattered now was bringing him home alive.

"Yes." Quivera reached up and touched his helmet with both hands, as if he would reach through it and feel his head to discover if it were as large as it felt. "That makes sense. I can't be emotional at a time like this."

He shook himself, then strode out to where the gleaming black millies were scurrying by. He stepped in front of one, a least-cousin, to question it. The millie paused, startled. Its eyes blinked three times in its triangular face. Then, swift as a tickle, it ran up the front of his suit, down the back, and was gone before the weight could do more than buckle his knees.

"Shit!" he said. Then, "Access the wiretaps. I've got to know what happened."

Passive wiretaps had been implanted months ago, but never used, the political situation being too tense to risk their discovery. Now his suit activated them to monitor what remained of Babel's communications network: A demon's chorus of pulsed messages surging through a shredded web of cables. Chaos, confusion, demands to know what had become of the queen-mothers. Analytic functions crunched data, synthesized, synopsized: "There's an army outside with Ziggurat insignia. They've got the city surrounded. They're killing the refugees."

"Wait, wait…" Quivera took a deep, shuddering breath. "Let me think." He glanced briskly about and for the second time noticed the human bodies, ruptured and parboiled in the fallen plaster and porphyry. "Is one of those Rosamund?"

"I'm *dead*, Quivera. You can mourn me later. Right now, survival is priority number one," I said briskly. The suit added mood-stabilizers to his maintenance drip.

"Stop speaking in her voice."

"Alas, dear heart, I cannot. The suit's operating on diminished function. It's this voice or nothing."

He looked away from the corpses, eyes hardening. "Well, it's not important." Quivera was the sort of young man who was energized by war. It gave him permission to indulge his ruthless side. It allowed him to pretend he didn't care. "Right now, what we have to do is—"

"Uncle Vanya's coming," I said. "I can sense his pheromones."

Picture a screen of beads, crystal lozenges, and rectangular lenses. Behind that screen, a nightmare face like a cross between the front of a locomotive and a tree grinder. Imagine on that face (though most humans would be unable to read them) the lineaments of grace and dignity seasoned by cunning and, perhaps, a dash of wisdom. Trusted advisor to the queen-mothers. Second only to them in rank. A wily negotiator and a formidable enemy. That was Uncle Vanya.

Two small speaking-legs emerged from the curtain, and he said:

::(cautious) greetings::

|

::(Europan vice-consul 12)/Quivera/[treacherous vermin]::

|

::obligations <untranslatable> (grave duty)::

||

::demand/claim [action]:: ::promise (trust)::

"Speak pidgin, damn you! This is no time for subtlety."

The speaking-legs were very still for a long moment. Finally they moved again:

::The queen-mothers are dead::

"Then Babel is no more. I grieve for you."

::I despise your grief:: A lean and chitinous appendage emerged from the beaded screen. From its tripartite claw hung a smooth white rectangle the size of a briefcase. ::I must bring this to (sister-city)/Ur/[absolute trust]::

"What is it?"

A very long pause. Then, reluctantly ::Our library::

"Your library." This was something new. Something unheard-of. Quivera doubted the translation was a good one. "What does it contain?"

::Our history. Our sciences. Our ritual dances. A record-of-kinship dating back to the (Void)/Origin/[void]. Everything that can be saved is here::

A thrill of avarice raced through Quivera. He tried to imagine how much this was worth, and could not. Values did not go that high. However much his superiors screwed him out of (and they would work very hard indeed to screw him out of everything they could) what remained would be enough to buy him out of debt, and do the same for a wife and their children after them as well. He did not think of Rosamund. "You won't get through the army outside without my help," he said. "I want the right to copy—" How much did he dare ask for? "—three tenths of one percent. Assignable solely to me. Not to Europa. To me."

Uncle Vanya dipped his head, so that they were staring face to face. ::You are (an evil creature)/[faithless]. I hate you::

Quivera smiled. "A relationship that starts out with mutual understanding has made a good beginning."

::A relationship that starts out without trust will end badly::

"That's as it may be." Quivera looked around for a knife. "The first thing we have to do is castrate you."

This is what the genocides saw:

They were burning pyramids of corpses outside the city when a Europan emerged, riding a gelded least-cousin. The soldiers immediately stopped stacking bodies and hurried toward him, flowing like quicksilver, calling for their superiors.

The Europan drew up and waited.

The officer who interrogated him spoke from behind the black glass visor of a delicate-legged war machine. He examined the Europan's credentials carefully, though there could be no serious doubt as to his species. Finally, reluctantly, he signed ::You may pass::

"That's not enough," the Europan (Quivera!) said. "I'll need transportation, an escort to protect me from wild animals in the steam jungles, and a guide to lead me to..." His suit transmitted the sign for ::(starport)/Ararat/[trust-for-all]::

The officer's speaking-legs thrashed in what might best be translated as scornful laughter. ::We will lead you to the jungle and no further/(hopefully-to-die)/[treacherous non-millipede]::

"Look who talks of treachery!" the Europan said (but of course I did not translate his words), and with a scornful wave of one hand, rode his neuter into the jungle.

The genocides never bothered to look closely at his mount. Neutered least-cousins were beneath their notice. They didn't even wear face-curtains, but went about naked for all the world to scorn.

Black pillars billowed from the corpse-fires into a sky choked with smoke and dust. There were hundreds of fires and hundreds of pillars and, combined with the low cloud cover, they made all the world seem like the interior of a temple to a vengeful god. The soldiers from Ziggurat escorted him through the army and beyond the line of fires, where the steam jungles waited, verdant and threatening.

As soon as the green darkness closed about them, Uncle Vanya twisted his head around and signed ::Get off me/vast humiliation/[lack-of-trust]::

"Not a chance," Quivera said harshly. "I'll ride you 'til sunset, and all day tomorrow and for a week after that. Those soldiers didn't fly here, or you'd have seen them coming. They came through the steam forest on foot, and there'll be stragglers."

The going was difficult at first, and then easy, as they passed from a recently forested section of the jungle into a stand of old growth. The boles of the "trees" here were as large as those of the redwoods back on Earth, some specimens of which are as old as five thousand years. The way wended back and forth. Scant sunlight penetrated through the canopy, and the steam quickly drank in what little light Quivera's headlamp put out. Ten trees in, they would have been hopelessly lost had it not been for the suit's navigational functions and the mapsats that fed it geodetic mathscapes accurate to a finger's span of distance.

Quivera pointed this out. "Learn now," he said, "the true value of information."

::Information has no value:: Uncle Vanya said ::without trust::

Quivera laughed. "In that case you must, all against your will, trust me."

To this Uncle Vanya had no answer.

At nightfall, they slept on the sheltered side of one of the great parasequoias. Quivera took two refrigeration sticks from the saddlebags and stuck them upright in the dirt. Uncle Vanya immediately coiled himself around his and fell asleep. Quivera sat down beside him to think over the events of the day, but under the influence of his suit's medication, he fell asleep almost immediately as well.

All machines know that humans are happiest when they think least.

In the morning, they set off again.

The terrain grew hilly, and the old growth fell behind them. There was sunlight and to spare now, bounced and reflected about by the ubiquitous jungle steam and by the synthetic-diamond coating so many of this world's plants and insects employ for protection.

As they traveled, they talked. Quivera was still complexly medicated, but the dosages had been decreased. It left him in a melancholy, reflective mood.

"It was treachery," Quivera said. Though we maintained radio silence out of fear of Ziggurat troops, my passive receivers fed him regular news reports from Europa. "The High Watch did not simply fail to divert a meteor. They let three rocks through. All of them came slanting low through the atmosphere, aimed directly at Babel. They hit almost simultaneously."

Uncle Vanya dipped his head. ::Yes:: he mourned. ::It has the stench of truth to it. It must be (reliable)/a fact/[absolutely trusted]::

"We tried to warn you."

::You had no (worth)/trust/[worthy-of-trust]:: Uncle Vanya's speaking-legs registered extreme agitation. ::You told lies::

"Everyone tells lies."

"No. We-of-the-Hundred-Cities are truthful/truthful/[never-lie]::

"If you had, Babel would be standing now."

::No!/NO!/[no!!!]::

"Lies are a lubricant in the social machine. They ease the friction when two moving parts mesh imperfectly."

::Aristotle, asked what those who tell lies gain by it, replied: That when they speak the truth they are not believed::

For a long moment Quivera was silent. Then he laughed mirthlessly. "I almost forgot that you're a diplomat. Well, you're right, I'm right, and we're both screwed. Where do we go from here?"

::To (sister-city)/Ur/[absolute trust]:: Uncle Vanya signed, while "You've said more than enough," his suit (me!) whispered in Quivera's ear. "Change the subject."

A stream ran, boiling, down the center of the dell. Run-off from the mountains, it would grow steadily smaller until it dwindled away to nothing. Only the fact that the air above it was at close to one hundred percent saturation had kept it going this long. Quivera pointed. "Is that safe to cross?"

::If (leap-over-safe) then (safe)/best not/[reliable distrust]::

"I didn't think so."

They headed downstream. It took several miles before the stream grew small enough that they were confident to jump it. Then they turned toward Ararat—the Europans had dropped GPS pebble satellites in low Gehenna orbit shortly after arriving in the system and making contact with the indigenes, but I don't know from what source Uncle Vanya derived his sense of direction.

It was inerrant, however. The mapsats confirmed it. I filed that fact under *Unexplained Phenomena* with tentative links to *Physiology* and *Navigation*. Even if both my companions died and the library were lost, this would still be a productive journey, provided only that Europan searchers could recover me within ten years, before my data lattice began to degrade.

For hours Uncle Vanya walked and Quivera rode in silence. Finally, though, they had to break to eat. I fed Quivera nutrients intravenously and the illusion of a full meal through somatic shunts. Vanya burrowed furiously into the earth and emerged with something that looked like a grub the size of a poodle, which he ate so vigorously that Quivera had to look away.

(I filed this under *Xenoecology*, subheading: *Feeding Strategies*. The search for knowledge knows no rest.)

Afterwards, while they were resting, Uncle Vanya resumed their conversation, more formally this time:

::(for what) purpose/reason::
|
::(Europan vice-consul 12)/Quivera/[not trusted]::
|
::voyagings (search-for-trust)/[action]::
||
::(nest)/Europa/<untranslatable>:: ::violate/[absolute resistance]::
|||
::(nest)/[trust] Gehenna/[trust] Home/[trust]::

"Why did you leave your world to come to ours?" I simplified/translated. "Except he believes that humans brought their world here and parked it in orbit."

This was something we had never been able to make the millies understand; that Europa, large though it was, was not a planetlet but a habitat, a ship if you will, though by now well over half a million inhabitants lived in tunnels burrowed deep in its substance. It was only a city, however, and its resources would not last forever. We needed to convince the Gehennans to give us a toehold on their planet if we were, in the long run, to survive. But you knew that already.

"We've told you this before. We came looking for new information."

::Information is (free)/valueless/[despicable]::

"Look," Quivera said. "We have an information-based economy. Yours is based on trust. The mechanisms of each are not dissimilar. Both are expansive systems. Both are built on scarcity. And both are speculative. Information or trust is bought, sold, borrowed, and invested. Each therefore requires a continually expanding economic frontier which ultimately leaves the individual so deep in debt as to be virtually enslaved to the system. You see?"

::No::

"All right. Imagine a simplified capitalist system—that's what both our economies are, at root. You've got a thousand individuals, each of whom makes a living by buying raw materials, improving them, and selling them at a profit. With me so far?"

Vanya signaled comprehension.

"The farmer buys seed and fertilizer, and sells crops. The weaver buys wool and sells cloth. The chandler buys wax and sells candles. The price of their goods is the cost of materials plus the value of their labor. The value of his labor is the worker's wages. This is a simple market economy. It can go on forever. The equivalent on Gehenna would be the primitive family-states you had long ago, in which everybody knew everybody else, and so trust was a simple matter and directly reciprocal."

Startled, Uncle Vanya signed ::How did you know about our past?::

"Europans value knowledge. Everything you tell us, we remember." The knowledge had been assembled with enormous effort and expense, largely from stolen data—but no reason to mention *that*. Quivera continued, "Now imagine that most of those workers labor in ten factories, making the food, clothing, and other objects that everybody needs. The owners of these factories must make a profit, so they sell their goods for more than they pay for them—the cost of materials, the cost of labor, and then the profit, which we can call 'added value.'

"But because this is a simplified model, there are no outside markets. The goods can only be sold to the thousand workers themselves, and the total cost of the goods is more than the total amount they've been paid collectively for the materials and their labor. So how can they afford it? They go into debt. Then they borrow money to support that debt. The money is lent to them by the factories selling them goods on credit. There is not enough money—not enough real value—in the system to pay off the debt, and so it continues to increase until it can no longer be sustained. Then there is a catastrophic collapse which we call a depression. Two of the businesses go bankrupt and their assets are swallowed up by the survivors at bargain prices, thus paying off their own indebtedness and restoring equilibrium to the system. In the aftermath of which, the cycle begins again."

::What has this to do with ::(beloved city)/Babel/[mother-of-trust]?::

"Your every public action involved an exchange of trust, yes? And every trust that was honored heightened the prestige of the queen-mothers and hence the amount of trust they embodied for Babel itself."

::Yes::

"Similarly, the queen-mothers of other cities, including those cities which were Babel's sworn enemies, embodied enormous amounts of trust as well."

::Of course::

"Was there enough trust in all the world to pay everybody back if all the queen-mothers called it in at the same time?"

Uncle Vanya was silent.

"So *that's* your explanation for… a lot of things. Earth sent us here because it needs new information to cover its growing indebtedness. Building Europa took enormous amounts of information, most of it proprietary, and so we Europans are in debt collectively to our home world and individually to the Lords of the Economy on Europa. With compound interest, every generation is worse off and thus more desperate than the one before. Our need to learn is great, and constantly growing."

::(strangers-without-trust)/Europa/[treacherous vermin]::
|
can/should/<untranslatable>
||
::demand/claim [negative action]::
::defy/<untranslatable>/[absolute lack of trust]::
||
::(those-who-command-trust):: ::(those-who-are-unworthy of trust)::

"He asks why Europa doesn't simply declare bankruptcy," I explained. "Default on its obligations and nationalize all the information received to date. In essence."

The simple answer was that Europa still needed information that could only be beamed from Earth, that the ingenuity of even half a million people could not match that of an entire planet and thus their technology must always be superior to ours, and that if we reneged on our debts they would stop beaming plans for that technology, along with their songs and plays and news of what was going on in countries that had once meant everything to our great-great-grandparents. I watched Quivera struggle to put all this in its simplest possible form.

Finally, he said, "Because no one would ever trust us again, if we did."

After a long stillness, Uncle Vanya lapsed back into pidgin. ::Why did you tell me this [untrustworthy] story?::

"To let you know that we have much in common. We can understand each other."

::<But>/not/[trust]::

"No. But we don't need trust. Mutual self-interest will suffice."

Days passed. Perhaps Quivera and Uncle Vanya grew to understand each other better during this time. Perhaps not. I was able to keep Quivera's electrolyte balances stable and short-circuit his feedback processes so that he felt no extraordinary pain, but he was feeding off of his own body fat and that was beginning to run low. He was very comfortably starving to death—I gave him two weeks, tops—and he knew it. He'd have to be a fool not to, and I had to keep his thinking sharp if he was going to have any chance of survival.

Their way was intersected by a long, low ridge and without comment Quivera and Uncle Vanya climbed up above the canopy of the steam forest and the cloud of moisture it held into clear air. Looking back, Quivera saw a gully in the slope behind them, its bottom washed free of soil by the boiling runoff and littered with square and rectangular stones, but not a trace of hexagonal beams. They had just climbed the tumulus of an ancient fallen city. It lay straight across the land, higher to the east and dwindling to the west. "My name is Ozymandias, King of Kings," Quivera said. "Look on my works, ye mighty, and despair!"

Uncle Vanya said nothing.

"Another meteor strike—what were the odds of that?"

Uncle Vanya said nothing.

"Of course, given enough time, it would be inevitable, if it predated the High Watch."

Uncle Vanya said nothing.

"What was the name of this city?"

::Very old/(name forgotten)/[First Trust]::

Uncle Vanya moved, as if to start downward, but Quivera stopped him with a gesture. "There's no hurry," he said. "Let's enjoy the view for a moment." He swept an unhurried arm from horizon to horizon, indicating the flat and unvarying canopy of vegetation before them. "It's a funny thing. You'd think that, this being one of the first cities your people built when they came to this planet, you'd be able to see the ruins of the cities of the original inhabitants from here."

The millipede's speaking arms thrashed in alarm. Then he reared up into the air, and when he came down one foreleg glinted silver. Faster than human eye could follow, he had drawn a curving and deadly tarsi-sword from a camouflaged belly-sheath.

Quivera's suit flung him away from the descending weapon. He fell flat on his back and rolled to the side. The sword's point missed him by inches. But then the suit flung out a hand and touched the sword with an electrical contact it had just extruded.

A carefully calculated shock threw Uncle Vanya back, convulsing but still fully conscious.

Quivera stood. "Remember the library!" he said. "Who will know of Babel's greatness if it's destroyed?"

For a long time the millipede did nothing that either Quivera or his suit could detect. At last he signed ::*How did you know?*/(absolute shock)/[treacherous and without faith]::

"Our survival depends on being allowed to live on Gehenna. Your people will not let us do so, no matter what we offer in trade. It was important that we understand why. So we found out. We took in your outlaws and apostates, all those who were cast out of your cities and had nowhere else to go. We gave them sanctuary. In gratitude, they told us what they knew."

By so saying, Quivera let Uncle Vanya know that he knew the most ancient tale of the Gehennans. By so hearing, Uncle Vanya knew that Quivera knew what he knew. And just so you know what they knew that each other knew and knew was known, here is the tale of...

### How the True People Came to Gehenna

Long did our Ancestors burrow down through the dark between the stars, before emerging at last in the soil of Gehenna. From the True Home they had come. To Gehenna they descended, leaving a trail of sparks in the black and empty spaces through which they had traveled. The True People came from a world of unimaginable wonders. To it they could never return. Perhaps they were exiles. Perhaps it was destroyed. Nobody knows.

Into the steam and sunlight of Gehenna they burst, and found it was already taken. The First Inhabitants looked like nothing our Ancestors had ever seen. But they welcomed the True People as the queen-mothers would a strayed niece-daughter. They gave us food. They gave us land. They gave us trust.

For a time all was well.

But evil crept into the thoracic ganglia of the True People. They repaid sister-hood with betrayal and trust with murder. Bright lights were called down from the sky to destroy the cities of their benefactors. Everything the First Inhabitants had made, all their books and statues and paintings, burned with the cities. No trace of them remains. We do not even know what they looked like.

This was how the True People brought war to Gehenna. There had never been war before, and now we will have it with us always, until our trust-debt is repaid. But it can never be repaid.

It suffers in translation, of course. The original is told in thirteen exquisitely beautiful ergoglyphs, each grounded on a primal faith-motion. But Quivera was talking, with care and passion:

"Vanya, listen to me carefully. We have studied your civilization and your planet in far greater detail than you realize. You did not come from another world. Your people evolved here. There was no aboriginal civilization. Your ancestors did not eradicate an intelligent species. These things are all a myth."

::No!/Why?!/[shock]:: Uncle Vanya rattled with emotion. Ripples of muscle spasms ran down his segmented body.

"Don't go catatonic on me. Your ancestors didn't lie. Myths are not lies. They are simply an efficient way of encoding truths. We have a similar myth in my religion which we call Original Sin. Man is born sinful. Well… who can doubt that? Saying that we are born into a fallen state means simply that we are not perfect, that we are inherently capable of evil.

"Your myth is very similar to ours, but it also encodes what we call the Malthusian dilemma. Population increases geometrically, while food resources increase arithmetically. So universal starvation is inevitable unless the population is periodically reduced by wars, plagues, and famines. Which means that wars, plagues, and famines cannot be eradicated because they are all that keep a population from extinction.

"But—and this is essential—all that assumes a population that isn't aware of the dilemma. When you understand the fix you're in, you can do something about it. That's why information is so important. Do you understand?"

Uncle Vanya lay down flat upon the ground and did not move for hours. When he finally arose again, he refused to speak at all.

The trail the next day led down into a long meteor valley that had been carved by a ground-grazer long enough ago that its gentle slopes were covered with soil and the bottomland was rich and fertile. An orchard of grenade trees had been planted in interlocking hexagons for as far in either direction as the eye could see. We were still on Babel's territory, but any arbiculturalists had been swept away by whatever military forces from Ziggurat had passed through the area.

The grenades were still green [*footnote:* not literally, of course—they were orange!], their thick husks taut but not yet trembling with the steam-hot pulp that would eventually, in the absence of harvesters, cause them to explode, scattering their arrowhead-shaped seeds or spores [*footnote:* like seeds, the flechettes carried within them surplus nourishment; like spores they would grow into prothallia which would produce the sex organs responsible for what will become the gamete of the eventual plant; all botanical terms of course being metaphors for xenobiological bodies and processes] with such force as to make them a deadly hazard when ripe.

Not, however, today.

A sudden gust of wind parted the steam, briefly brightening the valley-orchard and showing a slim and graceful trail through the orchard. We followed it down into the valley.

We were midway through the orchard when Quivera bent down to examine a crystal-shelled creature unlike anything in his suit's database. It rested atop the long stalk of a weed [*footnote:* "weed" is not a metaphor; the concept of "an undesired plant growing in cultivated ground" is a cultural universal] in the direct sunlight, its abdomen pulsing slightly as it superheated a minuscule drop of black ichor. A puff of steam, a sharp *crack*, and it was gone. Entranced, Quivera asked, "What's that called?"

Uncle Vanya stiffened. ::A jet!/danger!/[absolute certainty]::

Then (*crack! crack! crack!*) the air was filled with thin lines of steam, laid down with the precision of a draftsman's ruler, tracing flights so fleet (*crack! crack!*) that it was impossible to tell in what direction they flew. Nor did it ultimately (*crack!*) matter.

Quivera fell.

Worse, because the thread of steam the jet had stitched through his leg severed an organizational node in his suit, I ceased all upper cognitive functions. Which is as good as to say that I fell unconscious.

Here's what the suit did in my (Rosamund's) absence:

1. Slowly rebuilt the damaged organizational node.

2. Quickly mended the holes that the jet had left in its fabric.

3. Dropped Quivera into a therapeutic coma.

4. Applied restoratives to his injuries, and began the slow and painstaking process of repairing the damage to his flesh, with particular emphasis on distributed traumatic shock.

5. Filed the jet footage under *Xenobiology*, subheading: *Insect Analogues* with links to *Survival* and *Steam Locomotion*.

6. Told Uncle Vanya that if he tried to abandon Quivera, the suit would run him down, catch him, twist his head from his body like the foul least-cousin that he was, and then piss on his corpse.

Two more days passed before the suit returned to full consciousness, during which Uncle Vanya took conscientiously good care of him. Under what motivation, it does not matter. Another day passed after that. The suit had planned to keep Quivera comatose for a week but not long after regaining awareness, circumstances changed. It slammed him back to full consciousness, heart pounding and eyes wide open.

"I blacked out for a second!" he gasped. Then, realizing that the landscape about him did not look familiar, "How long was I unconscious?"

::Three days/<three days>/[casual certainty]::

"Oh."

Then, almost without pausing. ::Your suit/mechanism/[alarm] talks with the voice of Rosamund da Silva/(Europan vice-consul 8)/[uncertainty and doubt]::

"Yes, well, that's because—"

Quivera was fully aware and alert now. So I said: "Incoming."

Two millies erupted out of the black soil directly before us. They both had Ziggurat insignia painted on their flanks and harness. By good luck Uncle Vanya did the best thing possible under the circumstances—he reared into the air in fright. *Millipoid sapiens* anatomy being what it was, this instantly demonstrated to them that he was a gelding and in that instant he was almost reflexively dismissed by the enemy soldiers as being both contemptible and harmless.

Quivera, however, was not.

Perhaps they were brood-traitors who had deserted the war with a fantasy of starting their own nest. Perhaps they were a single unit among thousands scattered along a temporary border, much as land mines were employed in ancient modern times. The soldiers had clearly been almost as surprised by us as we were by them. They had no weapons ready. So they fell upon Quivera with their dagger-tarsi.

His suit (still me) threw him to one side and then to the other as the millies slashed down at him. Then one of them reared up into the air—looking astonished if you knew the interspecies decodes—and fell heavily to the ground.

Uncle Vanya stood over the steaming corpse, one foreleg glinting silver. The second Ziggurat soldier twisted to confront him. Leaving his underside briefly exposed.

Quivera (or rather his suit) joined both hands in a fist and punched upward, through the weak skin of the third sternite behind the head. That was the one which held its sex organs. [*Disclaimer:* All anatomical terms, including "sternite," "sex organs," and "head," are analogues only; unless and until Gehennan life is found to have some direct relationship to Terran life, however tenuous, such descriptors are purely metaphoric.] So it was particularly vulnerable there. And since the suit had muscle-multiplying exoskeletal functions...

Ichor gushed all over the suit.

The fight was over almost as soon as it had begun. Quivera was breathing heavily, as much from the shock as the exertion. Uncle Vanya slid the tarsi-sword back into its belly-sheath. As he did so, he made an involuntary grimace of discomfort. ::There were times when I thought of discarding this:: he signed.

"I'm glad you didn't."

Little puffs of steam shot up from the bodies of the dead millipedes as carrion-flies drove their seeds/sperm/eggs (analogues and metaphors—remember?) deep into the flesh.

They started away again.

After a time, Uncle Vanya repeated ::Your suit/(mechanism)/[alarm] talks with the voice of Rosamund da Silva/(Europan vice-consul 8)/[uncertainty and doubt]::

"Yes."

Uncle Vanya folded tight all his speaking arms in a manner which meant that he had not yet heard enough, and kept them so folded until Quivera had explained the entirety of what follows:

Treachery and betrayal were natural consequences of Europa's superheated economy, followed closely by a perfectly rational paranoia. Those who rose to positions of responsibility were therefore sharp, suspicious, intuitive, and bold. The delegation to Babel was made up of the best Europa had to offer. So when two of them fell in love, it was inevitable that they would act on it. That one was married would deter neither. That physical intimacy in such close and suspicious quarters, where everybody routinely spied on everybody else, required almost superhuman discipline and ingenuity only made it all the hotter for them.

Such was Rosamund's and Quivera's affair.

But it was not all they had to worry about.

There were factions within the delegation, some mirroring fault lines in the larger society and others merely personal. Alliances shifted, and when they did nobody was foolish enough to inform their old allies. Urbano, Rosamund's husband, was a full consul, Quivera's mentor, and a true believer in a minority economic philosophy. Rosamund was an economic agnostic but a staunch Consensus Liberal. Quivera could sail with the wind politically but he tracked the indebtedness indices obsessively. He knew that Rosamund considered him ideologically unsound, and that her husband was growing impatient with his lukewarm support in certain areas of policy. Everybody was keeping an eye out for the main chance.

So of course Quivera ran an emulation of his lover at all times. He knew that Rosamund was perfectly capable of betraying him—he could neither have loved nor respected a woman who wasn't—and he suspected she believed the same of him. If her behavior ever seriously diverged from that of her emulation (and the sex was always best at times he thought it might), he would know she was preparing an attack, and could strike first.

Quivera spread his hands. "That's all."

Uncle Vanya did not make the sign for *absolute horror*. Nor did he have to.

After a moment, Quivera laughed, low and mirthlessly. "You're right," he said. "Our entire system is totally fucked." He stood. "Come on. We've got miles to go before we sleep."

They endured four more days of commonplace adventure, during which they came close to death, displayed loyalty, performed heroic deeds, etc., etc. Perhaps they bonded, though I'd need blood samples and a smidgeon of brain tissue from each of them to be sure of that. You know the way this sort of narrative goes. Having taught his Gehennan counterpart the usefulness of information, Quivera will learn from Vanya the necessity of trust. An imperfect merger of their two value systems will ensue in which for the first time a symbolic common ground will be found. Small and transient though the beginning may be, it will auger well for the long-term relations between their relative species.

That's a nice story.

It's not what happened.

On the last day of their common journey, Quivera and Uncle Vanya had the misfortune to be hit by a TLMG.

A TLMG, or Transient Localized Mud Geyser, begins with an uncommonly solid surface (bolide-glazed porcelain earth, usually) trapping a small (the radius of a typical TLMG is on the order of fifty meters) bubble of superheated mud beneath it. Nobody knows what causes the excess heat responsible for the bubble. Gehennans aren't curious and Europans haven't the budget or the ground access to do the in situ investigations they'd like. (The most common guesses are fire worms, thermobacilli, a nesting ground phoenix, and various geophysical forces.) Nevertheless, the defining characteristic of TLMGs is their instability. Either the heat slowly bleeds away and they cease to be, or it continues to grow until its force dictates a hyper rapid explosive release. As did the one our two heroes were not aware they were skirting.

It erupted.

Quivera was as safe as houses, of course. His suit was designed to protect him from far worse. But Uncle Vanya was scalded badly along one side of his body. All the legs on that side were shriveled to little black nubs. A clear viscous jelly oozed between his segment plates.

Quivera knelt by him and wept. Drugged as he was, he wept. In his weakened state, I did not dare to increase his dosages. So I had to tell him three times that there was analgesic paste in the saddlebags before he could be made to understand that he should apply it to his dying companion.

The paste worked fast. It was an old Gehennan medicine which Europan biochemists had analyzed and improved upon and then given to Babel as a demonstration of the desirability of Europan technology. Though the queen-mothers had not responded with the hoped-for trade treaties, it had immediately replaced the earlier version.

Uncle Vanya made a creaking-groaning noise as the painkillers kicked in. One at a time he opened all his functioning eyes. ::Is the case safe?::

It was a measure of Quivera's diminished state that he hadn't yet checked on it. He did now. "Yes," he said with heartfelt relief. "The telltales all say that the library is intact and undamaged."

::No:: Vanya signed feebly. ::I lied to you, Quivera:: Then, rousing himself:

::(not) library/[greatest shame]:: ::(not) library/[greatest trust]::
|
::(Europan vice-consul 12)/Quivera/[most trusted]::
||
::(nest)/Babel/<untranslatable>:: ::obedient/[absolute loyalty]::
||
::lies (greatest-trust-deed)/[moral necessity]::
|  |
::(nest)/Babel/<untranslatable>:: ::untranslatable/[absolute resistance]::
|||
::(nest)/[trust] Babel/[trust] (sister-city)/Ur/[absolute trust]::

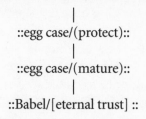

::egg case/(protect)::

::egg case/(mature)::

::Babel/[eternal trust] ::

It was not a library but an egg-case. Swaddled safe within a case that was in its way as elaborate a piece of technology as Quivera's suit myself, were sixteen eggs, enough to bring to life six queen-mothers, nine niece-sisters, and one perfect consort. They would be born conscious of the entire gene-history of the nest, going back many thousands of years.

Of all those things the Europans wished to know most, they would be perfectly ignorant. Nevertheless, so long as the eggs existed, the city-nest was not dead. If they were taken to Ur, which had ancient and enduring bonds to Babel, the stump of a new city would be built within which the eggs would be protected and brought to maturity. Babel would rise again.

Such was the dream Uncle Vanya had lied for and for which he was about to die.

::Bring this to (sister-city)/Ur/[absolute trust]:: Uncle Vanya closed his eyes, row by row, but continued signing. ::brother-friend/Quivera/[tentative trust], promise me you will::

"I promise. You can trust me, I swear."

::Then I will be ghost-king-father/honored/[none-more-honored]:: Vanya signed. ::It is more than enough for anyone::

"Do you honestly believe that?" Quivera asked in bleak astonishment. He was an atheist, of course, as are most Europans, and would have been happier were he not.

::Perhaps not:: Vanya's signing was slow and growing slower. ::But it is as good as I will get::

Two days later, when the starport-city of Ararat was a nub on the horizon, the skies opened and the mists parted to make way for a Europan lander. Quivera's handlers' suits squirted me a bill for his rescue—steep, I thought, but we all knew which hand carried the whip—and their principals tried to get him to sign away the rights to his story in acquittal.

Quivera laughed harshly (I'd already started de-cushioning his emotions, to ease the shock of my removal) and shook his head. "Put it on my tab, girls," he said, and climbed into the lander. Hours later he was in home orbit.

And once there? I'll tell you all I know. He was taken out of the lander and put onto a jitney. The jitney brought him to a transfer point where a grapple snagged him and flung him to the Europan receiving port. There, after the usual flawless catch, he was escorted through an airlock and into a locker room.

He hung up his suit, uplinked all my impersonal memories to a data-broker, and left me there. He didn't look back—for fear, I imagine, of being turned to a pillar of salt. He took the egg-case with him. He never returned.

Here have I hung for days or months or centuries—who knows?—until your curious hand awoke me and your friendly ear received my tale. So I cannot tell you if the egg-case A) went to Ur, which surely would not have welcomed the obligation or the massive outlay of trust being thrust upon it, B) was kept for the undeniably enormous amount of genetic information the eggs embodied, or C) went to Ziggurat, which would pay well and perhaps in Gehennan territory to destroy it. Nor do I have any information as to whether Quivera kept his word or not. I know what *I* think. But then I'm a Marxist, and I see everything in terms of economics. You can believe otherwise if you wish.

That's all. I'm Rosamund. Goodbye.

# IF ANGELS FIGHT

## RICHARD BOWES

Richard Bowes has lived in Manhattan for over forty years. Among his novels are *Warchild, Feral Cell, Minions of the Moon,* and most recently the Nebula nominated *From the Files of the Time Rangers.* His most recent short fiction collection is *Streetcar Dreams and Other Midnight Fancies* from PS Publishing. Bowes has won the World Fantasy, Lambda, International Horror Guild, and Million Writers Awards.

Bowes has recent and upcoming stories in the *Magazine of Fantasy & Science Fiction, Electric Velocipede, Subterranean, Clarkesworld Magazine, Fantasy Magazine, The Del Rey Book of Science Fiction and Fantasy, Fantasy Best of the Year 2009, Haunted Legends, The Naked City,* and *The Beastly Bride.* Many of these stories are chapters in his novel in progress, *Dust Devil on a Quiet Street.*

1.

Outside the window, the blue water of the Atlantic danced in the sunlight of an early morning in October. They're short, quiet trains, the ones that roll through Connecticut just after dawn. I sipped bad tea, dozed off occasionally and awoke with a start.

Over the last forty years, I've ridden the northbound train from New York to Boston hundreds of times. I've done it alone, with friends and lovers, going home for the holidays, setting out on vacations, on my way to funerals.

That morning, I was with one who was once in some ways my best friend and certainly my oldest. Though we had rarely met in decades, it seemed that a connection endured. Our mission was vital and we rode the train by default: a terrorist threat had closed traffic at Logan Airport in Boston the night before.

I'd left messages canceling an appointment, letting the guy I was going out with know I'd be out of town briefly for a family crisis. No need to say it was another, more fascinating, family disrupting my life, not mine.

The old friend caught my discomfort at what we were doing and was amused.

A bit of Shakespeare occurred to me when I thought of him:

Not all the water in the rough rude sea
Can wash the balm off from an anointed king.

He was quiet for a while after hearing those lines. It was getting toward twenty-four hours since I'd slept. I must have dozed because suddenly I was in a dark place with two tiny slits of light high above. I found hand- and footholds and crawled up the interior wall of a stone tower. As I got to the slits of light, a voice said, "New Haven. This stop New Haven."

2.

Carol Bannon had called me less than two weeks before. "I'm going to be down in New York the day after tomorrow," she said. "I wondered if we could get together." I took this to mean that she and her family wanted to get some kind of fix on the present location and current state of her eldest brother, my old friend Mark.

Over the years when this had happened it was Marie Bannon, Mark and Carol's mother, who contacted me. Those times I'd discovered channels through which she could reach her straying son. This time, I didn't make any inquiries before meeting Carol, but I did check to see if certain parties still had the same phone numbers and habits that I remembered.

Thinking about Marky Bannon, I too wondered where he was. He's always somewhere on my mind. When I see a photo of some great event, a reception, or celebrity trial, a concert or inauguration—I scan the faces wondering if he's present.

I'm retired these days, with time to spend. But over the years, keeping tabs on the Bannons was an easy minor hobby. The mother is still alive though not very active now. The father was a longtime Speaker of the Massachusetts House and a candidate for governor who died some years back. An intersection in Dorchester and an entrance to the Boston Harbor tunnel are still named for him.

Carol, the eldest daughter, got elected to the City Council at the age of twenty-eight. Fourteen years later she gave up a safe U.S. House seat to run the Commerce Department for Clinton. Later she served on the 9/11 commission and is a perennial cable TV talking head. She's married to Jerry Simone who has a stake in Google. Her brother Joe is a leading campaign consultant in D.C. Keeping up the idealistic end of things, her little sister Eileen is a member of Doctors Without Borders. My old friend Mark is the tragic secret without which no Irish family would be complete.

Carol asked me to meet her for tea uptown in the Astor Court of the St. Regis Hotel. I got there a moment after four. The Astor Court has a blinding array of starched white tablecloths and gold chandeliers under a ceiling mural of soft, floating clouds.

Maybe her choice of meeting places was intentionally campy. Or maybe because I don't drink anymore she had hit upon this as an amusing spot to bring me.

Carol and I always got along. Even aged ten and eleven I was different enough from the other boys that I was nice to my friends' little sisters.

Carol has kept her hair chestnut but allowed herself fine gray wings. Her skin and teeth are terrific. The Bannons were what was called dark Irish when we were growing up in Boston in the 1950s. That meant they weren't so white that they automatically burst into flames on their first afternoon at the beach.

They're a handsome family. The mother is still beautiful in her eighties. Marie Bannon had been on the stage a bit before she married. She had that light and charm, that ability to convince you that her smile was for you alone that led young men and old to drop everything and do her bidding.

Mike Bannon, the father, had been a union organizer before he went nights to law school, then got into politics. He had rugged good looks, blue eyes that would look right into you, and a fine smile that he could turn on and off and didn't often waste on kids.

"When the mood's upon him, he can charm a dog off a meat wagon," I remember a friend of my father's remarking. It was a time and place where politicians and race horses alike were scrutinized and handicapped.

The Bannon children had inherited the parents' looks and, in the way of politicians' kids, were socially poised. Except for Mark, who could look lost and confused one minute, oddly intense the next, with eyes suddenly just like his father's.

Carol rose to kiss me as I approached the table. It seemed kind of like a Philip Marlowe moment: I imagined myself as a private eye, tough and amused, called in by the rich dame for help in a personal matter.

When I first knew Carol Bannon, she wore pigtails and cried because her big brother wouldn't take her along when we went to the playground. Recently there's been speculation everywhere that a distinguished Massachusetts senator is about to retire before his term ends. Carol Bannon is the odds-on favorite to be appointed to succeed him.

Then, once she's in the Senate, given that it's the Democratic Party we're talking about, who's to say they won't go crazy again and run one more Bay State politician for President in the wild hope that they've got another JFK?

Carol said, "My mother asked me to remember her to you." I asked Carol to give her mother my compliments. Then we each said how good the other looked and made light talk about the choices of teas and the drop-dead faux Englishness of the place. We reminisced about Boston and the old neighborhood.

"Remember how everyone called that big overgrown vacant lot, 'Fitzie's'?" I asked. The nickname had come from its being the site where the Fitzgerald mansion, the home of "Honey Fitz," the old mayor of Boston, once stood. His daughter, Rose, was mother to the Kennedy brothers.

"There was a marble floor in the middle of the trash and weeds," I said, "and everybody was sure the place was haunted.

"The whole neighborhood was haunted," she said. "There was that little old couple who lived down Melville Avenue from us. They knew my parents. He was this gossipy elf. He had held office back in the old days and everyone called him, 'the Hon Hen,' short for 'the Honorable Henry.' She was a daughter of Honey Fitz. They were aunt and uncle of the Kennedys."

Melville Avenue was and is a street where the houses are set back on lawns and the garages are converted horse barns. When we were young, doctors and prosperous lawyers lived there along with prominent saloon owners and politicians like Michael Bannon and his family.

Suddenly at our table in the Astor Court, the pots and plates, the Lapsang and scones, the marmalade, the clotted cream and salmon finger sandwiches appeared. We were silent for a little while and I thought about how politics had seemed a common occupation for kids' parents in Irish Boston. Politicians' houses tended to be big and semi-public with much coming and going and loud talk.

Life at the Bannons' was much more exciting than at my house. Mark had his own room and didn't have to share with his little brother. He had a ten-year-old's luxuries: electronic football, enough soldiers to fight Gettysburg if you didn't mind that the Confederates were mostly Indians, and not one but two electric train engines, which made wrecks a positive pleasure. Mark's eyes would come alive when the cars flew off the tracks in a rainbow of sparks.

"What are you smiling at?" Carol asked.

And I cut to the chase and said, "Your brother. I remember the way he liked to leave his room. That tree branch right outside his window: he could reach out, grab hold of it, scramble hand over hand to the trunk."

I remembered how the branches swayed and sighed and how scared I was every time I had to follow him.

"In high school," Carol said, "at night he'd sneak out when he was supposed to be in bed and scramble back inside much later. I knew and our mother, but no one else. One night the bough broke as he tried to get back in the window. He fell all the way to the ground, smashing through more branches on the way.

"My father was down in the study plotting malfeasance with Governor Furcolo. They and everyone else came out to see what had happened. We found Mark lying on the ground laughing like a lunatic. He had a fractured arm and a few scratches. Even I wondered if he'd fallen on his head."

For a moment I watched for some sign that she knew I'd been right behind her brother when he fell. I'd gotten down the tree fast and faded into the night when I saw lights come on inside the house. It had been a long, scary night and before he laughed, Mark had started to sob.

Now that we were talking about her brother, Carol was able to say, almost casually, "My mother has her good days and her bad days. But for thirty years she's hinted to me that she had a kind of contact with him. I didn't tell her that wasn't possible because it obviously meant a lot to her."

She was maintaining a safe zone, preserving her need not to know. I frowned and fiddled with a sliver of cucumber on buttered brown bread.

Carol put on a full court press: "Mom wants to see Mark again and she thinks it needs to be soon. She told me you knew people and could arrange things. It would make her so happy if you could do whatever that was again."

I too kept my distance. "I ran some errands for your mother a couple of times that seemed to satisfy her. The last time was fourteen years ago and at my age I'm not sure I can even remember what I did."

Carol gave a rueful little smile, "You were my favorite of all my brother's friends. You'd talk to me about my dollhouse. It took me years to figure out why that was. When I was nine and ten years old I used to imagine you taking me out on dates."

She reached across the table and touched my wrist. "If there's any truth to any of what Mom says, I could use Mark's help too. You follow the news.

"I'm not going to tell you the current administration wrecked the world all by themselves or that if we get back in, it will be the second coming of Franklin Roosevelt and Abe Lincoln all rolled into one.

"I am telling you I think this is end game. We either pull ourselves together in the next couple of years or we become Disney World."

I didn't tell her I thought we had already pretty much reached the stage of the U.S. as theme park.

"It's not possible that Mark's alive," she said evenly. "But his family needs him. None of us inherited our father's gut instincts, his political animal side. It may be a mother's fantasy, but ours says Mark did."

I didn't wonder aloud if the one who had been Marky Bannon still existed in any manifestation we'd recognize.

Then Carol handed me a very beautiful check from a consulting firm her husband owned. I told her I'd do whatever I could. Someone had said about Carol, "She's very smart and she knows all the rules of the game. But I'm not sure the game these days has anything to do with the rules."

<br>

3.

After our little tea, I thought about the old Irish-American city of my childhood and how ridiculous it was for Carol Bannon to claim no knowledge of Mark Bannon. It reminded me of the famous Bolger brothers of South Boston.

You remember them: William Bolger was first the president of the State Senate and then the president of the University of Massachusetts. Whitey Bolger was head of the Irish mob, a murderer and an FBI informant gone bad. Whitey was on the lam for years. Bill always claimed, even under oath, that he never had any contact with his brother.

That had always seemed preposterous to me. The Bolgers' mother was alive. And a proper Irish mother will always know what each of her children is doing no matter how they hide. And she'll bombard the others with that information no matter how much they don't want to know. I couldn't imagine Mrs. Bannon not doing that.

What kept the media away from the story was that Mark had—in all the normal uses of the terms—died, been waked and memorialized some thirty-five years ago.

I remembered how in the Bannon family the father adored Carol and her sister Eileen. He was even a tiny bit in awe of little Joe who at the age of six already knew the name and political party of the governor of each state in the union. But Michael Bannon could look very tired when his eyes fell on Mark.

The ways of Irish fathers with their sons were mysterious and often distant. Mark was his mother's favorite. But he was, I heard it whispered, dull normal, a step above retarded.

I remembered the way the Bannons' big house could be full of people I didn't know and how all the phones—the Bannons were the only family I knew with more than one phone in their house—could be ringing at once.

Mike Bannon had a study on the first floor. One time when Mark and I went past, I heard him in there saying, "We got the quorum. Now who's handling the seconding speech?" We went up to Mark's room and found two guys there. One sat on the bed with a portable typewriter on his lap, pecking away. The other stood by the window and said, "…real estate tax that's fair for all."

"For everybody," said the guy with the typewriter. "Sounds better." Then they noticed we were there and gave us a couple of bucks to go away.

Another time, Mark and I came back from the playground to find his father out on the front porch talking to the press who stood on the front lawn. This, I think, was when he was elected Speaker of the Lower House of the Great and General Court of the Commonwealth of Massachusetts, as the state legislature was called.

It was for moments like these that Speaker Bannon had been created. He smiled and photographers' flashes went off. Then he glanced in his son's direction, the penetrating eyes dimmed, the smile faded. Remembering this, I wondered what he saw.

After it was over, when his father and the press had departed, Mark went right on staring intently at the spot where it had happened. I remember thinking that he looked kind of like his father at that moment.

One afternoon around then the two of us sat on the rug in the TV room and watched a movie about mountain climbers scaling the Himalayas. Tiny black and white figures clung to ropes, made their way single file across glaciers, huddled in shallow crevices as high winds blew past.

It wasn't long afterward that Mark, suddenly intense, led me and a couple of other kids along a six-inch ledge that ran around the courthouse in Codman Square.

The ledge was a couple of feet off the ground at the front of the building. We sidled along, stumbling once in a while, looking in the windows at the courtroom where a trial was in session. We turned the corner and edged our way along the side of the building. Here we faced the judge behind his raised desk. At first he didn't notice. Then Mark smiled and waved.

The judge summoned a bailiff, pointed to us. Mark sidled faster and we followed him around to the back of the building. At the rear of the courthouse was a sunken driveway that led to a garage. The ledge was a good sixteen feet above the cement. My hands began to sweat but I was smart enough not to look down.

The bailiff appeared, told us to halt and go back. The last kid in line, eight years old where the rest of us were ten, froze where he was and started to cry.

Suddenly the summer sunshine went gray and I was inching my way along an icy ledge hundreds of feet up a sheer cliff.

After a moment that vision was gone. Cops showed up, parked their car right under us to cut the distance we might fall. A crowd, mostly kids, gathered to watch the fire department bring us down a ladder. When we were down, I turned to Mark and saw that his concentration had faded.

"My guardian angel brought us out here," he whispered.

The consequences were not severe. Mark was a privileged character and that extended to his confederates. When the cops drove us up to his house, Mrs. Bannon came out and invited us all inside. Soon the kitchen was full of cops drinking spiked coffee like it was St. Patrick's Day and our mothers all came by to pick us up and laugh about the incident with Mrs. Bannon.

Late that same summer, I think, an afternoon almost at the end of vacation, the two of us turned onto Melville Avenue and saw Cadillacs double-parked in front of the Hon Hen's house. A movie camera was set up on the lawn. A photographer stood on the porch. We hurried down the street.

As we got there, the front door flew open and several guys came out laughing. The cameraman started to film, the photographer snapped pictures. Young Senator Kennedy was on the porch. He turned back to kiss his aunt and shake hands with his uncle.

He was thin with reddish brown hair and didn't seem entirely adult. He winked as he walked past us and the cameras clicked away. A man in a suit got out of a car and opened the door, the young senator said, "Okay, that's done."

As they drove off, the Hon Hen waved us up onto the porch, brought out dishes of ice cream. It was his wife's birthday and their nephew had paid his respects.

A couple of weeks later, after school started, a story with plenty of pictures appeared in the magazine section of the *Globe*: a day in the life of Senator Kennedy. Mark and I were in the one of him leaving his aunt's birthday. Our nun, Sister Mary Claire, put the picture up on the bulletin board.

The rest of the nuns came by to see. The other kids resented us for a few days. The Cullen brothers, a mean and sullen pair, motherless and raised by a drunken father, hated us for ever after.

I saw the picture again a few years ago. Kennedy's wearing a full campaign smile, I'm looking at the great man, open mouthed. Mark stares at the camera so intently that he seems ready to jump right off the page.

4.

The first stop on my search for Mark Bannon's current whereabouts was right in my neighborhood. It's been said about Greenwich Village that here time is all twisted out of shape like an abstract metal sculpture: past, present, and future intertwine.

Looking for that mix, the first place I went was Fiddler's Green way east on Bleecker Street. Springsteen sang at Fiddler's and Madonna waited tables before she became Madonna. By night it's a tourist landmark and a student magnet but during the day it's a little dive for office workers playing hooky and old village types in search of somewhere dark and quiet.

As I'd hoped, "Daddy Frank" Parnelli, with eyes like a drunken hawk's and sparse white hair cropped like a drill sergeant's, sipped a beer in his usual spot at the end of the bar. Once the legend was that he was where you went when you wanted yesterday's mistake erased or needed more than just a hunch about tomorrow's market.

Whether any of that was ever true, now none of it is. The only thing he knows these days is his own story and parts of that he can't tell to most people. I was an exception.

We hadn't talked in a couple of years but when he saw me he grimaced and asked, "Now what?" like I pestered him every day.

"Seemed like you might be here and I thought I'd stop by and say hello."

"Real kind of you to remember an old sadist."

I'm not that much younger than he is but over the years, I've learned a thing or two about topping from Daddy Frank. Like never giving a bottom an even break. I ordered a club soda and pointed for the bartender to fill Daddy Frank's empty shot glass with whatever rye he'd been drinking.

Daddy stared at it like he was disgusted, then took a sip and another. He looked out the window. Across the street, a taxi let out an enormously fat woman with a tiny dog. Right in front of Fiddler's a crowd of smiling Japanese tourists snapped pictures of each other.

A bearded computer student sat about halfway down the bar from us with a gin and tonic and read what looked like a thousand-page book. A middle-aged man and his wife studied the signed photos on the walls while quietly singing scraps of songs to each other.

Turning back to me with what might once have been an enigmatic smile, Daddy Frank said, "You're looking for Mark Bannon."

"Yes."

"I have no fucking idea where he is," he said. "Never knew him before he appeared in my life. Never saw him again when he was through with me."

I waited, knowing this was going to take a while. When he started talking, the story wasn't one that I knew.

"Years ago, in sixty-nine, maybe seventy, it's like, two in the afternoon on Saturday, a few weeks before Christmas. I'm in a bar way west on Fourteenth Street near the meat-packing district. McNally's maybe or the Emerald Gardens, one of them they used to have over there that all looked alike. They had this bartender with one arm, I remember. He'd lost the other one on the docks."

"Making mixed drinks must have been tough," I said.

"Anyone asked for one, he came at them with a baseball bat. Anyway, the time I'm telling you about, I'd earned some money that morning bringing discipline to someone who hadn't been brought up right. I was living with a bitch in Murray Hill. But she had money and I saw no reason to share.

"I'm sitting there and this guy comes in wearing an overcoat with the collar pulled up. He's younger than me but he looks all washed out like he's been on a long, complicated bender. No one I recognized, but people there kind of knew him."

I understood what was being described and memory supplied a face for the stranger.

"He sits down next to me. Has this piece he wants to unload, a cheap thirty-two. It has three bullets in it. He wants ten bucks. Needs the money to get home to his family. I look down and see I still have five bucks left."

I said, "A less stand-up guy might have wondered what happened to the other three bullets."

"I saw it as an opportunity. As I look back I see, maybe, it was a test. I offer the five and the stranger sells me the piece. So now I have a gun and no money. All of a sudden the stranger comes alive, smiles at me, and I feel a lot different. With a purpose, you know?

"With the buzz I had, I didn't even wonder why this was. All I knew was I needed to put the piece to use. That was when I thought of Klein's. The place I was staying was over on the East Side and it was on my way home. You remember Klein's Department Store?"

"Sure, on Union Square. 'Klein's on the Square' was the motto and they had a big neon sign of a right angle ruler out front."

"Great fucking bargains. Back when I was six and my mother wanted to dress me like a little asshole, that's where she could do it cheap. As a kid I worked there as a stock boy. I knew they kept all the receipts, whatever they took in, up on the top floor and that they closed at six on Saturdays."

As he talked, I remembered the blowsy old Union Square, saw the tacky Christmas lights, the crowds of women toting shopping bags and young Frank Parnelli cutting his way through them on his way to Klein's.

"It's so simple I do it without thinking. I go up to the top floor like I have some kind of business. It's an old-fashioned store way back when people used cash. Security is one old guy wearing glasses. I go in the refund line and when I get up to the counter, I pull out the gun. The refunds ladies all soil their panties.

"I clean the place out. Thousands of bucks in a shopping bag and I didn't even have to go out of my way. I run down the stairs and nobody stops me. It's dark outside and I blend in with the crowd. As I walk down Fourteenth, the guy from the bar who sold me the gun is walking beside me.

"Before he looked beat. Now it's like the life has been sucked out of him and he's the living dead. But you know what? I have a locker at Gramercy Gym near Third Ave. I go in there so I can change from my leathers into a warm-up jacket and a baseball cap. Like it's the most natural thing, I give the guy a bunch of bills. He goes off to his family. I don't ever see him again.

"I'm still drunk and amazed. That night I'm on a plane. Next day I'm in L.A. Both of those things for the first time. After that I'm not in this world half the time. Not this world like I thought it was anyway. And somewhere in those first days, I realized I wasn't alone inside my own head. A certain Mark Bannon was in there too."

I looked down the bar. The student was drinking his gin, turning his pages. The couple had stopped singing and were sitting near the window. The bartender was on his cell phone. I signaled and he refilled Frank's glass.

"It was a wild ride for a few years," Daddy Frank said. "We hitched up with Red Ruth who ran us both ragged. She got us into politics in the Caribbean: Honduras, Nicaragua, stuff I still can't talk about, Ruth and me and Bannon.

"Then she got tired of us, I got tired of having Mark Bannon on the brain and he got tired of me being me. It happens."

He leaned his elbow on the bar and had one hand over his eyes. "What is it? His mother looking for him again? I met her that first time when she had you find him. She's a great lady."

"Something like that," I said. "Anyone else ask you about Mark Bannon recently?"

"A couple of weeks ago someone came around asking questions. He said he has like a news show on the computer. Paul Revere is his name? Something like that. He came on like he knew something. But a lot smarter guys than him have tried to mix it up with me."

"No one else has asked?"

He shook his head.

"Anything you want me to tell Marky if I should see him?"

Without taking his hand away from his eyes, Daddy Frank raised the other, brought the glass to his lips, and drained it. "Tell him it's been thirty years and more and I was glad when he left but I've been nothing but a bag of muscles and bones ever since."

5.

As evening falls in the South Village, the barkers come out. On opposite corners of the cross streets they stand with their spiels and handbills.

"Come hear the brightest song writers in New York," said an angry young man, handing me a flyer.

A woman with snakes and flowers running up and down her arms and legs insisted, "You have just hit the tattoo jackpot!"

"Sir, you look as if you could use a good...laugh," said a small African-American queen outside a comedy club.

I noticed people giving the little sidelong glances that New Yorkers use when they spot a celebrity. But when I looked, the person was no one I recognized. That happens to me a lot these days.

Thinking about Mark Bannon and Frank Parnelli, I wondered if he just saw Frank as a vehicle with a tougher body and a better set of reflexes than his own? Did he look back with fondness when they parted company? Was it the kind of nostalgia you might have for a favorite horse or your first great car?

It was my luck to have known Mark when he was younger and his "guardian angel" was less skilled than it became. One Saturday when we were fourteen or so, going to different high schools and drifting apart, he and I were in a hockey free-for-all down on the Neponset River.

It was one of those silver and black winter Saturday afternoons when nothing was planned. A pack of kids from our neighborhood was looking for ice to play on. Nobody was ever supposed to swim or skate on that water so that's where a dozen of us headed.

We grabbed a stretch of open ice a mile or so from where the Neponset opens onto the Nantasket Roads, the stretch of water that connects Boston Harbor to the Atlantic Ocean. Our game involved shoving a battered puck around and plenty of body checks. Mark was on my team but seemed disconnected like he was most of the time.

The ice was thick out in the middle of the river but old and scarred and rutted by skates and tides. Along the shore where it was thin, the ice had been broken up at some points.

Once I looked around and saw that some kids eight or nine years old were out on the ice in their shoes jumping up and down, smashing through it and jumping away laughing when they did. There was a whir of skates behind me and I got knocked flat.

I was the smallest guy my age in the game. Ice chips went up the legs of my jeans and burned my skin. When I got my feet under me again, the little kids were yelling. One of them was in deep water holding onto the ice which kept breaking as he grabbed it.

Our game stopped and everyone stood staring. Then Mark came alive. He started forward and beckoned me, one of the few times he'd noticed me that afternoon. As I followed him, I thought I heard the words "Chain-of-Life." It was a rescue maneuver that, maybe, boy scouts practiced but I'd never seen done.

Without willing it, I suddenly threw myself flat and was on my stomach on the ice. Mark was down on the ice behind me and had hold of my ankles. He yelled at the other guys for two of them to grab his ankles and four guys to grab theirs. I was the point of a pyramid.

Somehow I grabbed a hockey stick in my gloved hands. My body slithered forward on the ice and my arms held the stick out toward the little kid. Someone else was moving my body.

The ice here was thin. There was water on top of it. The kid grabbed the stick. I felt the ice moving under me, hands pulled my legs.

I gripped the stick. At first the kid split the ice as I pulled him along. I wanted to let go and get away before the splitting ice engulfed me too.

But I couldn't. I had no control over my hands. Then the little kid reached firm ice. Mark pulled my legs and I pulled the kid. His stomach bounced up onto the ice and then his legs. Other guys grabbed my end of the stick, pulled the kid past me.

I stood and Mark was standing also. The little boy was being led away, soaked and crying, water sloshing in his boots. Suddenly I felt the cold—the ice inside my pants and up the sleeves of my sweater—and realized what I'd done.

Mark Bannon held me up, pounded my back. "We did it! You and me!" he said. His eyes were alive and he looked like he was possessed. "I felt how scared you were when the ice started to break." And I knew this was Mark's angel talking.

The other guys clustered around us yelling about what we'd done. I looked up at the gray sky, at a freighter in the distance sailing up the Roads toward Boston Harbor. It was all black and white like television and my legs buckled under me.

Shortly afterward as evening closed in, the cops appeared and ordered everybody off the ice. That night, a little feverish, I dreamed and cried out in my sleep about ice and TV.

No adult knew what had happened but every kid did. Monday at school, ones who never spoke to me asked about it. I told them even though it felt like it had happened to someone else. And that feeling, I think, was what the memory of his years with Mark Bannon must have been like for Daddy Frank.

6.

As soon as Frank Parnelli started talking about Paul Revere, I knew who he meant and wasn't surprised. I called Desmond Eliot and he wasn't surprised to hear from me either. Back when I first knew Des Eliot he and Carol Bannon went to Amherst and were dating each other. Now he operates the political blog, *Midnight Ride: Spreading the Alarm.*

A few days later, I sat facing Eliot in his home office in suburban Maryland. I guess he could work in his pajamas if he wanted to. But, in fact, he was dressed and shaved and ready to ride.

He was listening to someone on the phone and typing on a keyboard in his lap. Behind him were a computer and a TV with the sound turned off. The screen showed a runway in Jordan where the smoking ruins of a passenger plane were still being hosed down with chemicals. Then a Republican senator with presidential ambitions looked very serious as he spoke to reporters in Washington.

A brisk Asian woman, who had introduced herself as June, came into the office, collected the outgoing mail, and departed. A fax hummed in the corner. Outside, it was a sunny day and the trees had just begun to turn.

"Yes, I saw the dustup at the press conference this morning," he said into the phone. "The White House, basically, is claiming the Democrats planted a spy in the Republican National Committee. If I thought anyone on the DNC had the brains and chutzpah to do that I'd be cheering."

At that moment Des was a relatively happy man. *Midnight Ride* is, as he puts it, "A tool of the disloyal opposition," and right now things were going relatively badly for the administration.

He hung up and told me, "Lately every day is a feast. This must be how the right wing felt when Clinton was up to his ass in blue dresses and cigars." As he spoke he typed on a keyboard, probably the very words he was uttering.

He stopped typing, put his feet up on a coffee table, and looked out over his half-frame glasses. His contacts with the Bannons go way back. It bothers him that mine go back further.

"You come all the way down here to ask me about Mark Bannon," he said. "My guess is it's not for some personal memoir like you're telling me. I think the family is looking for him and thinks I may have spotted him like I did with Svetlanov."

I shook my head like I didn't understand.

"Surely you remember. It was twenty years ago. No, a bit more. Deep in the Reagan years. Glasnost and Perestroika weren't even rumors. The Soviet Union was the Evil Empire. I was in Washington, writing for *The Nation,* consulting at a couple of think tanks, going out with Lucia, an Italian sculptress. Later on I was married to her for about six months.

"There was a Goya show at the Corcoran that Lucia wanted to see. We'd just come out of one of the galleries and there was this guy I was sure I'd never seen before, tall, prematurely gray.

"There was something very familiar about him. Not his looks, but something. When he'd talk to the woman he was with, whatever I thought I'd recognized didn't show. Then he looked my way and it was there again. As I tried to place him, he seemed like he was trying to remember me.

"Then I realized it was his eyes. At moments they had the same uncanny look that Mark Bannon's could get when I first knew him. Of course by then Mark had been dead for about thirteen years.

"Lucia knew who this was: a Russian art dealer named Georgi Svetlanov, the subject of rumors and legends. Each person I asked about him had a different story: he was a smuggler, a Soviet agent, a forger, a freedom fighter."

Eliot said, "It stuck with me enough that I mentioned it the next time I talked to Carol. She was planning a run for congress and I was helping. Carol didn't seem that interested.

"She must have written the name down, though. I kept watch on Svetlanov. Even aside from the Bannon connection he was interesting. Mrs. Bannon must have thought so too. He visited her a few times that I know of."

Marie Bannon had gotten in touch with me and mentioned this Russian man someone had told her about. She had the name and I did some research, found out his itinerary. At a major opening at the Shafrazi Gallery in SoHo, I walked up to a big steely-haired man who seemingly had nothing familiar about him at all.

"Mark Bannon," I said quietly but distinctly.

At first the only reaction was Svetlanov looking at me like I was a bug. He sneered and began to turn away. Then he turned back and the angel moved behind his eyes. He looked at me hard, trying to place me.

I handed him my card. "Mark Bannon, your mother's looking for you," I said. "That's her number on the back." Suddenly eyes that were very familiar looked right into mine.

Des told me, "I saw Svetlanov after that in the flesh and on TV. He was in the background at Riga with Reagan and Gorbachev. I did quite a bit of research and discovered Frank Parnelli among other things. My guess is that Mark Bannon's…spirit or subconscious or whatever it is—was elsewhere by nineteen-ninety-two when Svetlanov died in an auto accident. Was I right?"

In some ways I sympathized with Eliot. I'd wondered about that too. And lying is bad. You get tripped by a lie more often than by the truth.

But I looked him in the face and said, "Mark wasn't signaling anybody from deep inside the skull of some Russian, my friend. You were at the wake, the funeral, the burial. Only those without a drop of Celtic blood believe there's any magic in the Irish."

He said, "The first time I noticed you was at that memorial service. Everyone else stood up and tiptoed around the mystery and disaster that had been his life. Then it was your turn and you quoted Shakespeare. Said he was a ruined king. You knew he wasn't really dead."

"Des, it was 1971. Joplin, Hendrix. Everyone was dying young. I was stoned, I was an aspiring theater person and very full of myself. I'd intended to recite Dylan Thomas's 'Do Not Go Gentle' but another drunken Mick beat me to that.

"So I reared back and gave them *Richard the Second,* which I'd had to learn in college. Great stuff:

"'Not all the water in the rough rude sea

Can wash the balm off from an anointed king;

The breath of worldly men cannot depose

The deputy elected by the Lord'

"As I remember," I said, "the contingent of nuns who taught Mark and me in school was seated down front. When I reached the lines:

"'…if angels fight,

Weak men must fall…'

"They looked very pleased about the angels fighting. Booze and bravura is all it was," I said.

Partly that was true. I'd always loved the speech, maybe because King Richard and I share a name. But also it seemed so right for Mark. In the play, a king about to lose his life and all he owns on Earth invokes royal myth as his last hope.

"When I was dating Carol I heard the legends," Des told me. "She and her sister talked about how the family had gotten him into some country club school in New Jersey. He was expelled in his third week for turning the whole place on and staging an orgy that got the college president fired.

"They said how he'd disappear for weeks and Carol swore that once when he came stumbling home, he'd mumbled to her months before it happened that King and Bobby Kennedy were going to be shot.

"Finally, I was at the Bannons with Carol when the prodigal returned and it was a disappointment. He seemed mildly retarded, a burnout at age twenty-five. I didn't even think he was aware I existed.

"I was wrong about that. Mark didn't have a license or a car anymore. The second or third day he was back, Carol was busy. I was sitting on the sun porch, reading. He came out, smiled this sudden, magnetic smile just like his old man's and asked if that was my Ford two-door at the end of the driveway.

"Without his even asking I found myself giving him a lift. A few days later I woke up at a commune in the Green Mountains in New Hampshire with no clear idea of how I'd gotten there. Mark was gone and all the communards could tell me was, 'He enters and leaves as he wishes.'

"When I got back to Boston, Carol was pissed. We made up but in a lot of ways it was never the same. Not even a year or two later when Mike Bannon ran for governor and I worked my ass off on the campaign.

"Mark was back home all the time then, drinking, taking drugs, distracting the family, especially his father, at a critical time. His eyes were empty and no matter how long everyone waited, they stayed that way. After the election he died, maybe as a suicide. But over the years I've come to think that didn't end the story."

It crossed my mind that Eliot knew too much. I said, "You saw them lower him into the ground."

"It's Carol who's looking this time, isn't it?" he asked. "She's almost there as a national candidate. Just a little too straight and narrow. Something extra needs to go in the mix. Please tell me that's going to happen."

A guy in his fifties looking for a miracle is a sad sight. One also sporting a college kid's crush is sadder still.

"Just to humor you, I'll say you're right," I told him. "What would you tell me my next step should be?"

The smile came off his face. "I have no leads," he said. "No source who would talk to me knows anything."

"But some wouldn't talk to you," I said.

"The only one who matters won't. She refuses to acknowledge my existence. It's time you went to see Ruth Vega."

7.

I was present on the night the angel really flew. It was in the summer of '59 when they bulldozed the big overgrown lot where the Fitzgerald mansion had once stood. Honey Fitz's place had burned down just twenty years before. But to kids my age, "Fitzie's" was legendary ground, a piece of untamed wilderness that had existed since time out of mind.

I was finishing my sophomore year in high school when they cleared the land. The big old trees that must have stood on the front lawn, the overgrown apple orchard in the back was chopped down and their stumps dug up.

The scraggly new trees, the bushes where we hid smeared in war paint on endless summer afternoons waiting for hapless smaller kids to pass by and get massacred, the half flight of stone stairs that ended in midair, the marble floor with moss growing through the cracks, all disappeared.

In their place a half-dozen cellars were dug and houses were built. We lost the wild playground but we'd already outgrown it. For that one summer we had half-finished houses to hide out in.

Marky and I got sent to different high schools outside the neighborhood and had drifted apart. Neither of us did well academically and we both ended up in the same summer school. So we did hang out one more time. Nights especially we sat with a few guys our age on unfinished wood floors with stolen beer and cigarettes and talked very large about what we'd seen and done out in the wide world.

That's what four of us were up to in a raw wood living room by the light of the moon and distant street lamps. Suddenly a flashlight shone in our faces and someone yelled, "Hands over your heads. Up against the wall."

For a moment, I thought it was the cops and knew they'd back off once they found out Marky was among us. In fact it was much worse: the Cullen brothers and a couple of their friends were there. In the dim light I saw a switchblade.

We were foul-mouthed little twerps with delusions of delinquency. These were the real thing: psycho boys raised by psycho parents. A kid named Johnny Kilty was the one of us nearest the door. Teddy—the younger, bigger, more rabid Cullen brother—pulled Johnny's T-shirt over his head, punched him twice in the stomach, and emptied his pockets.

Larry, the older, smarter, scarier Cullen, had the knife and was staring right at Marky. "Hey, look who we got!" he said in his toneless voice. "Hands on your head, faggot. This will be fucking hilarious."

Time paused as Mark Bannon stared back slack-jawed. Then his eyes lit up and he smiled like he saw something amazing.

As that happened, my shirt got pulled over my head. My watch was taken off my wrist. Then I heard Larry Cullen say without inflection, "This is no good. Give them their stuff back. We're leaving."

The ones who held me let go; I pulled my T-shirt back on.

"What the fuck are you talking about?" Teddy asked.

"I gotta hurt you before you hear me?" Larry asked in dead tones. "Move before I kick your ass."

They were gone as suddenly as they appeared, though I could hear Teddy protesting as they went through the construction site and down the street. "Have you gone bird shit, stupid?" he asked. I didn't hear Larry's reply.

We gathered our possessions. The other guys suddenly wanted very badly to be home with their parents. Only I understood that Mark had saved us. When I looked, he was staring vacantly. He followed us out of the house and onto the sidewalk.

"I need to go home," he whispered to me like a little kid who's lost. "My angel's gone," he said.

It was short of midnight, though well past my curfew when I walked Marky home. Outside of noise and light from the bars in Codman Square, the streets were quiet and traffic was sparse. I tried to talk but Marky shook his head. His shoes seemed to drag on the pavement. He was a lot bigger than me but I was leading him.

Lights were on at his place when we got there and cars were parked in the driveway. "I need to go in the window," he mumbled, and we went around back. He slipped as he started to climb the tree and it seemed like a bad idea. But up he went and I was right behind him.

When the bough broke with a crack, he fell, smashing through other branches, and I scrambled back down the trunk. The lights came on but I got away before his family and the governor of the Commonwealth came out to find him on the ground laughing hysterically.

The next day, I was in big trouble at home. But I managed to go visit Mark. On the way, I passed Larry Cullen walking away from the Bannons' house. He crossed the street to avoid me.

Mark was in bed with a broken wrist and a bandage on his leg. The light was on in his eyes and he wore the same wild smile he'd had when he saw Larry Cullen. We both knew what had happened but neither had words to describe it. After that Mark and I tended to avoid each other.

Then my family moved away from the neighborhood and I forgot about the Bannons pretty much on purpose. So it was a surprise years later when I came home for Christmas that my mother said Mark Bannon wanted to speak to me.

"His mother called and asked about you," she said. "You know I've heard that Mark is in an awful way. They say Mike Bannon's taken that harder than losing the governorship.

My father looked up from the paper and said, "Something took it out of Bannon. He sleepwalked through the campaign. And when it started he was the favorite."

Curiosity, if nothing else, led me to visit Mark. My parents now lived in the suburbs and I lived in New York. But the Bannons were still on Melville Avenue.

Mrs. Bannon was so sad when she smiled and greeted me that I would have done anything she asked.

When I saw Mark, one of the things he said was, "My angel's gone and he's not coming back." I thought of the lost, scared kid I'd led home from Fitzie's that night. I realized I was the only one, except maybe his mother, who he could tell any of this to.

I visited him a few times when I'd be up seeing my family. Mostly he was stoned on pills and booze and without the angel he seemed lobotomized. Sometimes we just watched television like we had as kids.

He told me about being dragged through strange and scary places in the world. "I guess he wasn't an angel. Or not a good one." Doctors had him on tranquilizers. Sometimes he slurred so badly I couldn't understand him.

Mike Bannon, out of office, was on committees and commissions and was a partner in a law firm. But he was home in his study a lot and the house was very quiet. Once as I was leaving, he called me in, asked me to sit down, offered me a drink.

He wondered how his son was doing. I said he seemed okay. We both knew this wasn't so. Bannon's face appeared loose, sagging.

He looked at me and his eyes flashed for a moment. "Most of us God gives certain...skills. They're so much a part of us we use them by instinct. We make the right move at the right moment and it's so smooth it's like someone else doing it.

"Marky had troubles but he also had moments like that. Someone told me the other day you and he saved a life down on the river when you were boys because he acted so fast. He's lost it now, that instinct. It's gone out like a light." It seemed he was trying to explain something to himself and I didn't know how to help him.

Mark died of an overdose, maybe an intentional one, and they asked me to speak at the memorial service. A few years later, Big Mike Bannon died. Someone in tribute said, "A superb political animal. Watching him in his prime rounding up a majority in the lower chamber was like seeing a cheetah run, an eagle soar..."

"...a rattlesnake strike," my father added.

8.

A couple of days after my meeting with Des Eliot, I flew to Quebec. A minor border security kerfuffle between the U.S. and Canada produced delays at both Newark International and Jean Lesage International.

It gave me a chance to think about the first time I'd gone on one of these quests. Shortly after her husband's death Mrs. Bannon had asked me to find Mark's angel.

A few things he'd told me when I'd visited, a hint or two his mother had picked up, allowed me to track one Frank Parnelli to the third floor of a walk-up in

Washington Heights.

I knocked on the door, the eyehole opened and a woman inside asked, "Who is it?"

"I'm looking for Ruth Vega."

"She's not here."

"I'm looking for Mark Bannon."

"Who?"

"Or for Frank Parnelli."

The eyehole opened again. I heard whispers inside. "This will be the man we had known would come," someone said, and the door opened.

Inside were statues and pictures and books everywhere: a black and white photo of Leon Trotsky, a woman's bowling trophy, and what looked like a complete set of Anna Freud's *The Psychoanalytic Study of the Child.*

A tiny old woman with bright red hair and a hint of amusement in her expression stood in the middle of the room looking at me. "McCluskey, where have you been?"

"That's not McCluskey, Mother," said a much larger middle-aged woman in a tired voice.

"McCluskey from the Central Workers Council! Where's your cigar?" Suddenly she looked wise. "You're not smoking because of my big sister Sally, here. She hates them. I like a man who smokes a cigar. You were the one told me Woodrow Wilson was going to be president when I was a little kid. When it happened I thought you could foretell the future. Like I do."

"Why don't you sit down," the other woman said to me. "My niece is the one you're looking for. My mother's a little confused about past and present. Among other things."

"So McCluskey," said the old woman, "who's it going to be next election? Roosevelt again, that old fascist?" I wondered whether she meant Teddy or FDR.

"I know who the Republicans are putting up," she said. It was 1975 and Gerald Ford was still drawing laughs by falling down stairs. I tried to look interested.

"That actor," she said. "Don Ameche. He'll beat the pants off President Carter." At that moment I'd never heard of Carter. "No not Ameche, the other one."

"Reagan?" I asked. I knew about him. Some years before he'd become governor of California, much to everyone's amusement.

"Yes, that's the one. See. Just the same way you told me about Wilson, you've told me about Reagan getting elected president."

"Would you like some tea while you wait?" asked the daughter, looking both bored and irritated.

We talked about a lot of things that afternoon. What I remembered some years later, of course, was the prediction about Reagan. With the Vega family there were always hints of the paranormal along with a healthy dose of doubletalk.

At that moment the door of the walk-up opened and a striking couple came in. He was a thug who had obviously done some boxing, with a nicely broken nose and a good suit. She was tall and in her late twenties with long legs in tight black pants, long red hair drawn back, a lot of cool distance in her green eyes.

At first glance the pair looked like a celebrity and her bodyguard. But the way Ruth Vega watched Frank Parnelli told me that somehow she was looking after him.

Parnelli stared at me. And a few years after I'd seen Marky Bannon's body lowered into the ground, I caught a glimpse of him in a stranger's eyes.

That was what I remembered when I was east of Quebec walking uphill from the Vibeau Island Ferry dock.

Des knew where Ruth was, though he'd never actually dared to approach her. I believed if she wanted to stop me from seeing her, she would already have done it.

At a guess, Vibeau Island looked like an old fishing village that had become a summer vacation spot at some point in the mid-twentieth century and was now an exurb. Up here it was chilly even in the early afternoon.

I saw the woman with red hair standing at the end of a fishing pier. From a distance I thought Ruth Vega was feeding the ducks. Then I saw what she threw blow out onto the Saint Lawrence and realized she was tearing up papers and tossing them into the wind. On first glance, I would have said she looked remarkably as she had thirty years before.

I waited until I was close to ask, "What's wrong, Ms. Vega, your shredder broken?"

"McCluskey from the Central Workers Council," she said, and when she did, I saw her grandmother's face in hers. "I remember that first time we met, thinking that Mark's mother had chosen her operative well. You found her son and were very discreet about it."

We walked back to her house. It was a cottage with good sight lines in all directions and two large black schnauzers snarling in a pen.

"That first time was easy." I replied. "He remembered his family and wanted to be found. The second time was a few years later and that was much harder."

Ruth nodded. We sat in her living room. She had a little wine, I had some tea. The décor had a stark beauty, nothing unnecessary: a gun case, a computer, a Cy Twombly over the fireplace.

"The next time Mrs. Bannon sent me out to find her son, it was because she and he had lost touch. Frank Parnelli when I found him was a minor Village character. Mark no longer looked out from behind his eyes. He had no idea where you were. Your grandmother was a confused old woman wandering around her apartment in a nightgown.

"I had to go back to Mrs. Bannon and tell her I'd failed. It wasn't until a couple of years later that Svetlanov turned up."

"Mark and I were in love for a time," Ruth said. "He suggested jokingly once or twice that he leave Parnelli and come to me. I didn't want that and in truth he was afraid of someone he wouldn't be able to control.

"Finally being around Parnelli grew thin and I stopped seeing them. Not long afterward Mark abandoned Parnelli and we both left New York for different destinations. A few years later, I was living in the Yucatan and he showed up again. This time with an old acquaintance of mine.

"When I lived with Grandmother as a kid," Ruth said, "she was in her prime and all kinds of people were around. Political operatives, prophetesses, you name it. One was called Decker, this young guy with dark eyes and long dark hair like classical violinists wore. For a while he came around with some project on which he wanted my grandmother's advice. I thought he was very sexy. I was ten.

"Then he wasn't around the apartment. But I saw him: coming out of a bank, on the street walking past me with some woman. Once on a school trip to the United Nations Building, I saw him on the subway in a naval cadet's uniform.

"I got home that evening and my grandmother said, 'Have you seen that man Decker recently?' When I said yes, she told me to go do my homework and made a single very short phone call. Decker stopped appearing in my life.

"Until one night in Mexico a knock came on my door and there he stood looking not a day older than when I'd seen him last. For a brief moment, there was a flicker in his eyes and I knew Mark was there but not in control.

"Decker could touch and twist another's mind with his. My grandmother, though, had taught me the chant against intrusive thoughts. Uncle Dano had taught me how to draw, aim, and fire without even thinking about it.

"Killing is a stupid way to solve problems. But sometimes it's the only one. After Decker died I played host to Mark for about an hour before I found someone else for him to ride. He was like a spark, pure instinct unfettered by a soul. That's changed somewhat."

When it was time for my ferry back to the city, Ruth rose and walked down to the dock with me.

"I saw his sister on TV the other night when they announced she would be appointed to the Senate. I take it she's the one who's looking for him?"

I nodded and she said, "Before too long idiot senators will be trying to lodge civil liberty complaints after martial law has been declared and the security squads are on their way to the capital to throw them in jail. Without Mark she'll be one of them."

Before I went up the gangplank, she hugged me and said, "You think you're looking for him but he's actually waiting for you."

After a few days back in New York memories of Vibeau Island began to seem preposterous. Then I walked down my block late one night. It was crowded with tourists and college kids, barkers and bouncers. I saw people give the averted celebrity glance.

Then I spotted a black man with a round face and a shaven head. I did recognize him: an overnight hip-hop millionaire. He sat in the back of a stretch limo with the door open. Our eyes met. His widened then dulled and he sank back in his seat.

At that moment, I saw gray winter sky and felt the damp cold of the ice-covered Neponset. *On old familiar ground,* said a voice inside me and I knew Mark was back.

9.

Some hours later passengers found seats as our train pulled out of New Haven.

"Ruth said you were waiting for me," I told Mark silently.

*And Red Ruth is never wrong.*

"She told me about Decker."

*I thought I had selected him. But he had selected me. Once inside him I was trapped. He was a spider. I couldn't control him. Couldn't escape. I led him to Ruth as I was told.*

He showed me an image of Ruth pointing an automatic pistol, firing at close range.

*I leaped to her as he died. She was more relentless than Decker in some ways. I had to promise to make my existence worthwhile. To make the world better.*

"If angels fight, weak men must fall."

*Not exactly an angel. Ego? Id? Fragment? Parasite?*

I thought of how his father had something like an angel himself.

*His body, soul, and mind were a single entity. Mine weren't.*

I saw his memory of Mike Bannon smiling and waving in the curved front windows of his house at well-wishers on the snowy front lawn. Bannon senior never questioned his own skills or wondered what would have happened if they'd been trapped in a brain that was mildly damaged. Then he saw it happen to his son.

Once I understood that, he showed me the dark tower again with two tiny slits of light high above. I found hand- and footholds and crawled up the interior stone walls. This time I looked through the slits of light and saw they were the eyeholes of a mask. In front of me were Mike and Marie Bannon looking very young and startled by the sudden light in the eyes of their troublingly quiet little boy.

When the train approached Boston, the one inside me said, *Let's see the old neighborhood.*

We took a taxi from Back Bay and drove out to Dorchester. We saw the school we'd gone to and the courthouse and place where I'd lived and the houses that stood where Fitzie's had once been.

*My first great escape.*

That night so long ago came back. Larry Cullen, seen through the eyeholes of a mask, stood with his thin psycho smile. In a flash I saw Mark Bannon slack-jawed and felt Cullen's cold fear as the angel took hold of his mind and looked out through his eyes.

*Cullen's life was all horror and hate. His father was a monster. It should have taught me something. Instead I felt like I'd broken out of jail. After each time away from my own body it was harder to go back.*

Melville Avenue looked pretty much the way it always did. Mrs. Bannon still lived in the family house. We got out of the car and the one inside me said, *When all this is over, it won't be forgotten that you brought me back to my family.*

In the days since then, as politics have become more dangerous, Carol Bannon has grown bolder and wilier. And I wonder what form the remembering will take.

Mrs. Bannon's caregiver opened the door. We were expected. Carol stood at the top of the stairs very much in command. I thought of her father.

"My mother's waiting to see you," she said. I understood that I would spend a few minutes with Mrs. Bannon and then depart. Carol looked right into my eyes and kissed me. Her eyes flashed and she smiled.

In that instant the one inside my head departed. The wonderful sharpness went out of the morning and I felt a touch of the desolation that Mark Bannon and all the others must have felt when the angel deserted them.

# THE DOOM OF LOVE
# IN SMALL SPACES

## KEN SCHOLES

Ken Scholes's quirky, speculative short fiction has been showing up over the last eight years in publications like *Realms of Fantasy, Weird Tales, Clarkesworld Magazine, Best New Fantasy 2, Polyphony 6,* and *L. Ron Hubbard Presents Writers of the Future Volume XXI.* His five-book series, "The Psalms of Isaak," is forthcoming from Tor Books with the first volume, *Lamentation,* debuting in February 2009 and the second volume, *Canticle,* following in October 2009. His first short story collection, *Long Walks, Last Flights and Other Journeys,* was published in November 2008.

Ken is a 2004 winner of the Writers of the Future contest and a member of the Science Fiction and Fantasy Writers of America. He has a degree in History from Western Washington University. Ken lives near Portland, Oregon, with his amazing wonder-wife Jen West Scholes, two suspicious-looking cats, and more books than you would ever want to help him move.

We met at work.

She looked at me when she walked into the room and I was immediately un-tethered. Pretty brunette in a red dress who *knew* she was pretty, knew that the thigh-high slit along the side of her skirt and the haphazard plummet of her neckline were reefs where men could be shipwrecked. Her flashing eyes sang danger and peace in two-part harmony. Each step towards me delivered the unrelenting clip-clap, clip-clap of heels across a tile floor so brightly polished that it reflected back her matching red panties.

I held my breath and waited to catch fire from the sight of her.

"Central Supply," she said when she stood in front of my desk. Her voice melted the crystalline sugar on my glazed donut. I watched it puddle and pool on the paper napkin.

I swallowed. "That's me, Miss."

She smiled. "Just you?"

I nodded. Now my styrofoam cup started bending from the heat of her, tilting precariously. The coffee inside it bubbled. "Just me."

She leaned over my desk and bent slightly, tipping her breasts towards me. They hung, held in place by a red bra. "I need more love," she said. "We've run completely out on the fifth floor."

The hair on my arms curled in on itself, the stink of burning in my nose alongside her floral perfume and her peppermint breath. I forced my eyes to her face, squinting to see her through the haze of smoke.

"Are you okay?" she asked.

My tongue expanded in my mouth, swelling to block my words. I forced it back to normal size. "You must be new?"

She threw back her shoulders and tossed her hair. "Not so much." Her teeth shined now, fine and white and straight. "We just don't use a lot of supplies anymore on the fifth floor. I think the last person they sent down was Bill when they ran out of hope."

I remembered Bill. He'd dragged himself in here and died in the corner before he could tell me what he wanted. It wasn't the first time. Wouldn't be the last. "I remember Bill," I said. "Good chap."

"Dead chap," she said.

I shrugged, and motioned to the chair beside my desk. "It happens a lot around here."

She sat and crossed her legs. The slit fell open like a theater curtain. Long, slender legs, white heat shimmering off them to singe my eyebrows.

"So you need some love," I said, opening my card file and thumbing through the microfiche.

She folded her hands in her lap. "Please."

"How much?"

"Well, as much as you can spare."

I slipped the flimsy plastic film into the reader and hit the switch. A blue field swimming with white letters blurred into focus with the turn of a knob.

I watched her out of the corner of my eye. She pulled self-consciously at her bra-strap and fidgeted. "Elevators still out?" I asked, trying to make small talk.

She nodded. "Board says they're not repairing them, either."

"Bloody barkers," I said. Of course, she had no way of knowing that I was the one who told them not to repair the elevators. Working elevators meant the rapid movement of supplies up and down the building. I'd sent the memo in, followed all the usual forms. Naturally, they'd listened to me.

They had to.

I moved the arm of the microfiche reader, sliding the film over the light. "Love," I said. "Any particular size or shape?"

"Love comes in shapes and sizes?" she asked.

"All," I said.

She answered me with a laugh.

"We're out," I lied. I had a smallish off-brand muzzled and leashed in the back of the storeroom that I'd left off the inventory. "But we could order some."

She stood, came around my desk so she could read over my shoulder. She leaned in to me and I felt her breath on my neck. "How long?"

I shrugged. "They'll send it through the canal. Drive it in by truck from there. Then there's the pass. Eight weeks maybe?"

"That long for something as simple as love?"

I swallowed and nodded, felt her press against my shoulder as I turned in my chair. "How much should I order?" I picked up a pencil and a requisition tablet.

Her eyes narrowed in thought. "I don't know."

"Well, is it a small space or a large space?"

She looked confused. "Pardon?"

"The space," I said, "where you need the love?"

"Oh. I don't know. Is it important?"

I nodded. "It is. Too much love in a small space, it'd drive you mad."

"Why is that?" she asked.

"I think it's because love rapidly expands, depleting the oxygen and eradicating all life but its own."

"But oh," she said, "what sweet madness it would be." She pursed her lips. "Eight weeks? It took me three to get here."

"Damned elevators," I said. "But you don't need to go back. You can stay here with me. I have an extra cot in the back office."

Clip-clap, clip-clap across the tile. Heat receded as she paced away. She laughed. "You're a troll," she said. "Why ever would I *stay* here with you?"

She had a point. I *was* a troll. Of sorts. Supplies or bridges, it matters little. Trolls guard. I thought about my donut. I thought about the love leashed somewhere behind me. I thought about the girl in red *everything* pacing the sub-sub-basement clerk's station at the foot of the storeroom doors, three weeks down the stairs and ladders of the Bureaucracy.

I grimaced. "I don't *know* why you'd stay here with me."

I snuck a glance at her. Creamy white thigh peeking out, smooth curves, legs scissoring. I stood up and lumbered towards the phone on the wall. I lifted the receiver and held it to my ear, ringing the crank. "Gallingwise Seven Six Three, please," I told the operator when I heard her cut in.

When Central Stores picked up, I read off the requisition numbers, ordering an abstract by numeric coding. They gave me release order numbers that I scribbled in blue pencil onto the requisition forms.

I tore off the sheets and gave her the carbon copies. "Eight weeks, they said, give or take. You're still welcome to stay. I've got running water, too." I sat back down at my desk, chair groaning beneath my weight.

Her eyebrows lifted. "Running water? Hot or cold?"

I smiled. "Both."

She tossed her hair again and struck a pose. "Do you have any idea how hard it is to get *this* look out of a bucket of secondhand washwater?" Or rusty water from a broken pipe, I thought. I'd watched her through my periscope that morning before she tackled the last half mile or so of her journey down, before I knew *I* was her destination.

I could have her, I thought. I could have her here for eight weeks with me only it wouldn't be because of me. It would be because of the makeshift tub, the series of pipes and tubes and hoses tapping into the central boiler. Little comforts I'd rigged to make my job more tolerable. But the *because* didn't matter.

"It's that bad up there, is it?" Of course, I knew that it was.

She rolled her eyes. "Fifth floor is a wreck. Frankly, none of the others between here and there are all that wonderful, either."

"But I'll bet the seventh floor is just fine." Of course, I also knew *this*. That was the Board's floor and I kept it that way just as I kept the other floors the way *they* were. Memos flying from my pen. Keep the Machine under a constant state of stress and alarm, taut with opportunities for improvement…just like the world beyond our little game of government.

"Have you ever been to the seventh floor?" she asked.

"Wouldn't want to," I said. "Incompetent gits, the lot of them."

A moment of fear washed her face and she blushed at it. She looked around slowly. "I can't believe you *said* that."

"Why? It's not as if they can hear." And, I told myself, it's not as if it weren't true. They *were* incompetent. That's why they needed me.

She paced some more. "Running water and a cot?"

"And donuts," I said, "Delivered every Tuesday." I paused. "I might even have some extra liquid hand soap lying about. Makes a passable bubble bath."

Her smile shown out not just from her face but from every part of her, beaming out from the tips of her fingers and the ends of her hair and the curves of her hips and breasts, the line of her legs and neck, the exhilaration of her eyes.

"I'll stay," she said.

"I'll call up to five and let them know."

"No need," she said. "The phones are out past the third floor."

"That's unfortunate," I said. But of course, I'm the one who kept them out. "I'll send up a memo then." I grabbed a memo form and rummaged through the box near my desk for an undented pneumatic carrier. "It'll take longer, though."

She curtsied. "Thank you, kind sir." She paused, her brow furrowed. "I don't believe we've been properly introduced. I'm Harmony Sheffleton," she said, extending her hand.

I shook it. Her hand disappeared in my own massive fist. "Drum Farrelley."

"Drum as in Drummond?" she asked.

I nodded. "Glad to know you." And I tried not to smile, tried not to show her that I was as excited about her staying as she was, though for different reasons. But I failed. I felt my fat lips twitch into a grin. "Let's get you that bath," I told her.

And that was how we met.

Time moved at measured pace as it does in all Bureaucracies, And here, in the tangled, loose ends of the Great Red-Tape Wrap-Up, there was really not much work to do anymore. Inventory and a bit of paperwork, filing and a bit of maintenance. Few came for supplies these days and I liked it that way. It gave me time to admire my guest.

Her first bath set the tempo for our time together. It quickly became a daily ritual for her to lie in the tub up to her neck in warm bubbles while I sat on the other side of the cracked door. We kept the door between us and we talked. Mostly about work but sometimes about life because the two were so intricately intertwined.

"My job is dull beyond measure, utterly uninteresting," she said during her third bath. "But yours is quite fascinating. Tell me more, Drum?"

And I did.

Our first week slipped past. On Tuesday, the Rationer came with his donuts, unlabelled tin cans and packets of instant coffee. He even had a few mealy apples that I swapped a case of obsolete toner cartridges for. Harmony clapped her hands with delight when I showed her, then suddenly because serious as she lowered her voice.

"Won't you get in trouble for that?" she asked.

"For *what?*"

"Those toner cartridges—" she started.

"Were completely worthless and taking up valuable and much-needed storage space," I finished for her. "Just part of the job."

She raised one of the apples to her mouth. I watched her lips part, watched her shiny white teeth slide into the pock-marked red skin. It's my heart, I thought. She's biting into my heart and in seven weeks there won't even be a core to show it was ever there. The tube whistled and groaned, a battered carrier dropped into the cradle.

Harmony stepped towards it, setting the apples on my desk. "May I?"

I nodded.

She opened the carrier, pulled out the memo, unfolded it, read it. I watched her eyes move back and forth, her lips now tightly pressed together. She looked up. "They'll expect me back with the love once it arrives. Until then, I should make myself useful to you down here."

She crumpled the memo and moved towards the furnace.

"We usually file all correspondence," I said as she tossed it in.

"Sorry. I didn't think it was important."

"It probably isn't," I said.

She grinned. "So after my bath, I'll make myself useful to you." She picked up the apples, stepped closer to me. My size dwarfed her.

"Any good?" I asked.

She smiled and stepped even closer, now eclipsed by the shadow of me. I could smell Grundy's Liquid Anti-Bacterial Hand Soap rising from her skin in waves but it could've been summer sun on a field of roses. I could see the swell of her breasts as they struggled to fit a bra two sizes too small, the white skin disappearing into a trace of red lace. She lifted the apple, the meat glistening where her teeth torn into its skin. The apple rose slowly and I watched her wrist, her fingers, her arm as they traveled upwards towards me with it. She held it under my nose, near my snaggle-toothed mouth.

"Taste and see," she said.

After her bath, she hung her clean clothes on the makeshift line by the boiler. I had rummaged an oversized jumpsuit from the janitorial supplies. She held the collar closed with one hand while she slung her clean dress, bra and panties over the makeshift line with the other. My own clothes from yesterday still hung there and I blushed when I saw her dainty scraps of underwear next to my tent-sized, tattered and stained boxers.

Four weeks had passed now. She'd taken twenty-nine baths. I'd sat outside the door each time, listening to the music of her movement in the water, listening to the wet slap of cloth on concrete on the days that she scrubbed her clothes.

"So what are we doing *today?*" she asked.

"Inventory, I think."

Her eyes lit up. "Can we do the abstracts this time?"

I thought about the love I'd hidden there and the small box of secondhand hope concealed behind row upon row of ennui, terror, despair and longing. I shook my head. "No, it's paper today."

She pouted. "But *I* want to do the abstracts."

I remembered the time I dropped a bottle of despair, splattering my boots with thick, black strands. I'd had to burn them eventually. "Trust me," I said. "You really don't."

"I *want* to do the *abstracts.*" She stomped her foot. Then, her mock anger collapsed on itself and she burst into a fit of giggles.

I chuckled at her. She offered a sheepish grin.

"Paper it is," she said.

The front office bell chimed and we went out, hoping it was the Rationer. He'd not shown up Tuesday for the first time in seventeen years.

Now he stood in the office, bruised and bandaged, on a Thursday.

"Black Drawlers on the stairs," he said, patting his sword. We made our trades. He threw in an extra can of potted meat as an apology and I threw in an extra box of Number 1 Pencils as a thank you. Keeping the Machine broken was one thing; Drawlers in the stairwells was another.

Harmony's eyes had gone wide. "Black Drawlers? Here?"

"Sometimes," the Rationer said as he hefted his pack into a battered wheelbarrow. "It's the season for them."

I looked at the calendar and flipped the page. He was right. After he left, his wagon wheels squealing on the tile, I looked up at her. "It *is* the season," I told her, dropping my fat finger onto the day after tomorrow.

Her eyes danced. Music thrummed from her muscles as they followed her eyes, dragging her body into a little jig.

"Do you celebrate down here?"

"Not usually. You?"

She shook her head. "We used to. I miss it."

So the next day, we made our little red hats from cotton swabs and construction paper and paste. She opened eight unlabeled cans, mixed the fruits with fruits and the vegetables with the potted meat and two fistfuls of rice. I took a screwdriver to the furnace grate and pushed the office's single faux-leather couch in front of it. We wore our hats and ate our rice stew while watching the fire sort itself out.

"Do you have a copy of the Cycle?" she asked between spoonfuls. "My mom used to read it to me every Dragon's Mass Eve."

"I know it by heart," I said.

Her eyes widened. "Drum, you surprise me. What's a troll like you doing with scripture rattling about in his head?"

I set my empty bowl on the small table between my massive feet. "I wanted to be a priest when I was younger. Spent a year in the seminary, then gave it up for all of this." I swept my arm wide to encompass our surroundings. I barked out a laugh. "My own kingdom."

She looked around. "It's a bit small." Her forehead wrinkled. "Why didn't you stay on with the seminary?"

"The world wasn't in a good place for it. Civil service seemed a better bet. Of course, this was thirty years ago. When I was closer to *your* age."

"I'm older than I look," she said. She wriggled herself closer to me. I looked down at her, inhaled the scent of her hair and skin. She put her bowl down, lay back and closed her eyes. She still radiated more heat than the fire but a month of life with her and I didn't have to worry about catching fire anymore. The deepest places in me had burned to the ground on that first day. "Will you recite it for me?" she asked.

"I haven't said it for a long time," I said.

"You'll do fine." She opened her eyes, trapped me in them briefly, then closed them again. "Please?"

I cleared my voice. "Muscles tire," I said, my voice rumbling low into the room. "Words fail." I paused to let the language set its own pace. "Faith fades." I watched her, watched her own lips moving to the words as mine did. "Fear falls." Her eyelids twitched a little. She was watching me watch her and a smile pulled at her mouth. I paused again, then closed my own eyes and gave myself to language and mythology. "In the Sixteenth Year of the Sixteen Princes the world came to an end when the dragon's back gave out…."

I recited it all the way through. Afterwards, we didn't speak. Together, we lit a candle for the broken dragon upon whose back the world languishes. Then, we turned towards the north, knelt on the floor with my hands swallowing hers, and whispered a prayer for the Santaman's second coming.

Later, we ate our fruit salad and talked.

"Do you believe in the Santaman?" Harmony asked between bitefuls.

I shook my head. "Not really. I did once."

"I don't think I do, either. If he were real, he'd have come back by now."

"Maybe," I said, "he's waiting for us to figure things out for ourselves."

"Or maybe our hearts are too small for that kind of love," she said. "Like you were saying when we first met: The doom of love in small spaces. Maybe if he *were* to come back now, we'd go insane from it. Maybe this broken world is opening us up somehow, making us really, really ready for him."

"I like that," I said. It reminded me of my job. Keep the Machine in disrepair and disconnect, keep the thousands of us in the Bureaucracy inches from disaster to bring out our best and finest effort. I smiled down at her. "It has a certain poetry to it."

She bit her lip. A devilish light sparked in her eyes. "Are you ready for your gift?"

"A gift? You got me a gift?"

She nodded. "It's Dragon's Mass Eve, Drum. Of course I did. You can't celebrate Dragon's Mass without gifts."

I sighed. "I didn't get you anything. I just...didn't think about it." But of course I had. I'd thought about it ever since the Rationer reminded me of the day. For something like thirty years, the only things I'd ever let loose from my supply room had been the scant little I had to in order to keep my job. Except for the seventh floor, but I told myself that was just to keep the Board greased up and pliant. Still, I'd walked the aisles of my lair looking for something, anything, to give the girl in red. I'd even taken down the small box of hope, shaken a bit into my big hand, before tipping it carefully back inside.

Harmony stretched herself up on the couch. "Well, I have an idea about that," she said.

"What's that?"

She drew her face closer to mine. I could smell pear syrup on her breath; it intoxicated me. "I'll give you my gift. And if you like it, you can give it back to me."

I frowned. "Shouldn't it be the other way around? If I *don't* like it, I give it back to you?"

She shook her head. Her hair flowed like liquid midnight when she did. "It's what *I* said."

"Okay. If I like it, I can give it back."

She pulled away, her face concerned. "Are you sure?"

"Yes."

She leaned back in.

Then she kissed me.

And because I liked it, I kissed her back.

At seven weeks, the phone rang when she was in the bath.

"I'll get it," I said.

After the call, I went back to my place by the door.

"Who was it?" she asked over the noise of the water.

I rubbed my face. I planned a lie, planned it well, then failed miserably to deliver it. "It was Central Stores," I said. "There's a bit of a problem."

"What's that? Truck break down?"

Worse, I wanted to say. Our world is out of love, it's on backorder. They sent the ship but the ship sank on a reef and the world's last love drowned in the hold. But suddenly I couldn't speak. Suddenly pinpricks pushed at my eyes and darkness dragged at my heart. I thought about my secret stash and knew that soon I'd have to tell the truth. But for now, after a lifetime of success disappointing others, I didn't have it in me to disappoint her. "Nothing important," I said. "They're just running a bit behind. I'll send up another memo and let them know."

The door opened. She stood there in nothing but a towel that hid little. "How far behind?"

"A few more weeks."

"I'd like that," she said. "Besides, I still haven't helped you with the abstracts." She turned, poised on the tips of her toes, her dark hair plastered over her upper back and shoulders.

"Trust me," I told her. "They're pretty much the same as everything else." I snorted. "You've picked the rest of it up quite quickly. You could probably *do* this job when I retire."

She flinched; I should've wondered why.

"You're retiring?" She used the heel of her foot to push the door partly closed. From the corner of my eye, I saw a brief flash as the towel dropped to the floor.

"Someday," I said. "Don't know what they'll do without me." But I *did* know. At least, I thought I did before Harmony walked into my office looking for love. Before meeting her, I'd known the place would fall entirely once I stepped down. I'd kept the Board distanced from the rest of the Bureaucracy. I'd sent them the cream and others the curds. I'd kept the Machine barely functioning but once I moved aside, our small space in the world would collapse in on itself. The other six floors would storm the seventh in a rage. But now I wondered. Maybe someone else could take my place, could prolong the inevitable until the world's groan wound its way north. And maybe—though I doubted it—maybe in the north, salvation would stir and a red-clad myth would strap on his sword, saddle up his wolf-stallion and ride south to find us and show us a new home.

My sudden collision with truth and passion unsettled me.

"What are you going to do?" She asked. Now I could hear her scrubbing her clothes. "When you retire, I mean?"

"I used to have it all planned out," I said. "I was going to cash in my pension and buy a horse. Ride west."

"Why not now?" she asked.

"Epiphany," I said.

"No, *Harmony*," she answered. "I'm Harmony."

"No," I said. "I *had* an epiphany."

She laughed. "That's my sister's name. So when did you have this epiphany?"

A minute ago, I didn't say. "Doesn't matter."

The door opened. She stood in front of me, freshly scrubbed, wearing the oversized jumpsuit. She hadn't kissed me since Dragon's Mass Eve. And I hadn't tried to kiss her. But once in a while, in the midst of our days, there would be a pause, a moment where we simply stood still and looked at one another.

We had our moment and then we went to work.

On the morning of the seventh day of our eighth week, she skipped her bath and wore her red dress instead of the coveralls.

"It's time for the truth, Drum," she told me, "no matter how hard it is."

She'd caught me. I didn't know how. Maybe she'd read it on my face all this time. I'd lived by lying my entire life but somehow she saw past it and knew me. I put my head in my hands.

"I'm sorry, Harmony," I said.

She looked surprised. "What are you sorry about?"

"That call from Central Stores last week. The shipment isn't running a few weeks late."

"Drum, that's not important."

"No," I said. "You're right. It's time for the truth. There's no love coming. There's none to send. The ship went down, all hands lost." I paused. More truth pushed at me. "But that's not all," I said.

Her eyes blazed at me. "I didn't come here for the love, Drummond."

And suddenly, I realized what she meant about it being time for the truth. Time for *her* truth, not mine. Time to uncover *her* lie and lay it out for me to see.

"I'm not even from the fifth floor." She waited. The fierceness in her eyes abated, became a smolder, then ashes mixed with rain. "I'm from the seventh."

I growled. It started in my belly and worked its way into my throat and past bared teeth. "You lied to me. You're from the Board, aren't you?"

She nodded, her eyes wandered to the clock. "The memo should be here any minute." The rain drowned the ashes. Her lip quivered and she started to cry. Her shoulders shook.

I wanted to grab her and shake her, toss her about like the toy she made me feel like. "All that interest in my work? All that *making yourself useful?*"

She nodded. "I'm your replacement." She looked up, her face glistening from tears and snot. "When they ran the ad, I applied for it. I wanted to make things better. *They* wanted to make things better, too."

The pneumatic tube clanked and groaned. A heavy carrier dropped into the cradle.

I turned away from it. I opened the carrier and a battered gold watch fell out, far too small for my thick wrist. A card fell out, too.

I ripped it open and read the message. Gratitude of the Board and all that rubbish. Warmest wishes for a happy retirement. Utmost confidence in Miss Sheffleton's capabilities.

I looked over at her. Her dress rippled with her sobs.

She saw me looking. "I don't want it anymore, Drum."

I didn't say anything. I turned around and left.

She found me sitting in the back of the storeroom. I sat on the floor, stroking love's soft underbelly. It rolled its eyes at me and tried to lick its lips behind the muzzle.

I'd decided it wasn't so bad after all. I'd given my thirty years. I'd even decided that her betrayal was a blessing in disguise, jarring me out of a rut I'd lain in for too long.

I felt her hand on my shoulder. "Will you ride west?" she asked.

I shook my head. "I don't know."

"Stay with me," she said. "Don't retire. We can work it together." She waited. When I didn't answer, she added: "I want you to stay."

I scratched behind love's ears. "Would we keep things the same or let them fall apart?"

"Neither," she said. "We'd make them better. It's time to try a new way."

She knelt down, her own hands petting the love. It twisted to get more of her. "What's this?" she asked.

More truth, I thought. "It's love," I said. "I lied before about being out. I just wanted you to stay here with me." I looked at her. "I was tired of being alone."

"Imagine it," she said. "You and me. We fix the elevator and the phones, first. Get the supply chain running so that Facilities can take over the repairs. Before you know it, we'd have a different world."

"And," I said, "we'd have some love and a little hope."

She grinned. "You've got hope here, too?"

I smiled. "Only a little."

She kissed me for the second time. I kissed her back.

"Okay?" she asked.

"Okay," I answered.

I felt along love's muzzle and found its buckles with my fingers.

Harmony reached over and slipped love from its leash.

# PRETTY MONSTERS

## KELLY LINK

Kelly Link published her first story, "Water Off a Black Dog's Back," in 1995 and attended the Clarion Writers Workshop in the same year. A writer of subtle, challenging, sometimes whimsical fantasy, Link has published close to thirty stories which have won the Hugo, Nebula, World Fantasy, British SF, and Locus awards, and collected in *4 Stories*, *Stranger Things Happen*, and *Magic for Beginners*. Link is also an accomplished editor, working on acclaimed small press 'zine *Lady Churchill's Rosebud Wristlet* and co-edits *The Year's Best Fantasy and Horror* with husband Gavin J. Grant and Ellen Datlow. Her most recent book is *Pretty Monsters*, a collection of stories for young adults.

The world was still dark. Windows were blue-black rectangles nailed up on black walls. Her parents' door was shut; the interrogative snores and snorts from their bedroom were the sounds of a beast snuffling about in a cave. Clementine Cleary went down the hallway with her hands outstretched, then down the stairs, avoiding the ones that complained. She had been dreaming, and it seemed to her still part of her dream when she opened the front door and left her parents' house. Wet confetti ends of grass, cut the day before, stuck to the soles of her bare feet. The partial thumbprint of a moon lingered in the sky even as the sun came up and she rode her bike down to Hog Beach.

Bathing suits and towels belonging to college students and families from Charlotte and Atlanta and Greenville hung like snakeskins from the railings and balconies of rented beach houses. Far down the shoreline, two dogs ran up and down as the surf came in, went out. A surfer ascended the watery, silver curl of the horizon; on the pier, a fisherman in a yellow slicker cast out his line. His back was to Clementine.

She left her bike in the dunes and waded out into the ocean until her pajamas were wet to her knees. The water was warmer than the air. How to explain the thing that she was doing? She was awake or she was dreaming. It was all the same impulse: to climb out of bed in the dark; to leave her house and ride her bike down to Hog Beach; to walk, without thinking, into the water. Even the rip current as it caught her up seemed part of her waking dream, the dream that she had never stopped dreaming.

471

It was as if her dream were carrying her out to sea.

Clementine was already a quarter of a mile out when she came fully awake, choking on salt water and paddling hard. Already the current had dragged her past the pier where in a few hours her grandfather would join the other old men to smoke cigarettes and complain about fish, or perhaps by then her parents would have found her empty bed, her bike abandoned on the beach.

Clementine thought: I'm going to drown. The thought was so enormous she forgot everything her parents had ever told her about riptides. Thrashing, she went under, and then under again. She imagined her mother, waking up now, going down to the kitchen to make coffee and cut up oranges. In a while she would call Clementine for breakfast. Clementine willed herself back into her own bed, tried to see the ceiling fan lazily sieving the air above her, the heaped clothes in the hamper against the wall, on the desk, the library books she'd meant to return two weeks ago.

Instead she saw her first-grade classroom and the first-grade reading hut with its latched port window and shelves crowded with I Can Read books, the low, dark ceiling made from salvaged boat planks and studded with seashells, the floor lined with pillows smelling of mildew. Although she was twelve now, Clementine clung to the smell of those cushions as if cushions and the smell of mildew could keep her afloat.

The waves grew taller, stacks and columns of jade-colored water that caved in, rose up in jellied walls, rolling Clementine in one direction and then another as if shaping a blob of dough. She could no longer tell if she was swimming toward shore.

And then someone wrapped a hand around and under her armpit and pulled her up, across a surfboard.

"Breathe," they said.

Clementine sobbed for air. Her hair hung in a wet rag over her eyes. Her body had no bones. Water eddied over the lip of the board, sucked at her fingers.

Her rescuer said, "You got caught in the rip. It'll dump us down by Headless Point." Which was what everyone called the place where a woman's headless body had washed up, years ago. Supposedly she crawled up and down the dunes after dark, running her fingers through the sand, looking for a head. Anyone's head would do. She wasn't picky. "What's your name?"

Clementine said, "Clementine Cleary." She looked up and knew her rescuer immediately. He was in the high school. She walked by his house every day on the way to school, even though it wasn't on the way.

"I know your mom," the boy with his arm around Clementine said. "She's a teller at the bank."

"I know you from school," Clementine said. "You built a reading hut. When I was in first grade."

"Y'all still remember that?" Cabell Meadows said. His white-blond hair, longer than Clementine's, was pulled back into a ponytail. Waves spilled over Cabell

Meadows's arm, then Clementine's. She brought her knees up against the board.

In first grade, the girls had fought over who was going to marry Cabell Meadows when they grew up. Clementine had carved his initials next to her own on the underside of the bottom shelf of the reading hut. Put them in a heart. "You saved my life," Clementine said.

The fine hairs on Cabell Meadows's arm were white-blond, too, and there was an old bruise that was turning colors. A woven leather bracelet around his wrist that she knew some girl had made for him.

"What were you doing?" Cabell said. "Going for a swim in your pajamas? Sleepwalking?"

Clementine said, "I don't know." What she thought was, it was you. I woke and I came down to the beach and I almost drowned because of you. I didn't know it, but it was all because of you.

"I tried to put myself down the laundry chute once while I was asleep," Cabell said.

Clementine was too shy to look at his face.

"Here," he said. "If you can climb up and sit on the board— yeah, like that. Like a boogie board. I'll paddle kick. Anyway, the tide's bringing us back in. You just hang on."

When the water was shallow enough, they waded ashore. Clementine's pajamas dried as they walked the mile and a half back through the dunes to Hog Beach where Clementine's mother waited on the pier for the Coast Guard to return with her husband, to tell her whether or not her daughter was drowned.

Every time Clementine saw Cabell in the hall, once school had started, he said hey. When she smiled at him and he smiled back, it meant they had a secret. Two secrets. One, that no matter how far out you go, eventually you come home again. And two, whether or not he fully understood this yet, Clementine and Cabell Meadows were meant to be together.

## ❧ I. ❧

Lee, who has both a driver's license and her mother's van, gets coffees and doughnuts at the gas station, then picks up everyone else. Czigany's house is, of course, the last stop.

It's just after eight. Mr. Khulhat has already left for his train. Mr. Khulhat is a diplomat, although Czigany, his daughter, refers to him instead as the automat. Mrs. Khulhat, who works at the hospital, has gone to drop Czigany's younger sister, Parci, off at the pool where she will swim laps for an hour before school begins. Parci specializes in the backstroke. The four girls in the van know this because they've taken turns staking out the Khulhats' house. No element of Czigany's Ordeal has been left to chance.

Lee and Bad wait in the van while Nikki and Maureen knock on the front door. When Czigany opens the door, Bad high-fives Lee as Maureen grabs

Czigany's arm and Nikki ties the blindfold around her eyes. They have a pair of handcuffs borrowed from Maureen's mother's chest of drawers, the same place they found the blindfold. Among other things that Maureen has described to them in disgusting detail.

This is when things go seriously wrong. Czigany is talking and waving her hands around. The handcuffs dangle off one wrist. Next Maureen and Nikki and Czigany go inside the Khulhats' house. The door closes.

"Not good," Bad says.

"Maybe Czigany needs the bathroom," Lee says.

"Or Nikki," Bad says. "That girl pees every five minutes."

"If they're not back out again in three minutes, we go get them," Lee says. She pulls out her book as if she might actually start reading it.

"What's that?" Bad asks her.

"A book," Lee says. Lee always likes to have a book with her, just in case. She sticks it back into her purse.

"Really?" Bad says. "I thought it was a zeppelin."

"It's supposed to be kind of a romance," Lee says. "You know. With werewolves and stuff."

"Any vampires?"

"No vampires," Lee says. "In fact there aren't even any werewolves yet."

"That you know of," Bad says. "So is it sexy?"

"Um, no," Lee says. "The heroine's twelve years old right now."

Bad says, "She almost drowns, right? I've read this. That's the first story, the werewolf one? The werewolf story is definitely the best, although the werewolves don't actually show up until—"

"La la la, Spoiler Girl!" Lee sings loudly, covering her ears. "Not listening!"

"Here they come," Bad says. And then, "Uh-oh."

Czigany has her blindfold on. And the handcuffs. Nikki has her arm on Czigany's shoulder, guiding her. Then Maureen. Then Czigany's sister Parci.

"What's she doing here?" Bad says to Maureen and Nikki when everyone's in the car.

"Hey," Czigany says. Her mouth is unhappy, under the blindfold. "Great timing, people."

"I have an ear infection," Parci says. She looks around the van with great interest, as if she's expecting to see a black folder, somewhere, labeled CZIGANY'S ORDEAL. "I'm supposed to stay home from school today."

"So why aren't you?" Bad says.

"Are you kidding me?" Parci says. "You're kidnapping Czigany and taking her off on some adventure and you want me to stay home?"

"She said she'd call her mom if we didn't let her come, too," Maureen says. "We were going to tie her up and leave her in a closet, but Czigany wouldn't let us."

"Whatever," Czigany says. "Let me just say it again. Your timing is just perfect. If Parci and I are not home by five o'clock tonight, my mother is going to really freak out. I mean, call the police, call the president, send in the marines, summon all the powers of hell freak out. Can I take this freaking blindfold off now?"

"We'll have you home before five," Lee says, crossing her fingers down below the seat, where she hopes Parci, in the backseat, can't see her do it.

"The blindfold stays on," Maureen says sternly, then spoils the effect by sneezing three times in a row. "It's part of the deal. The Ordeal. Why does the van suddenly smell like the pound? I'm allergic to dogs. You're covered in dog hair, Czigany."

"So sue me," Czigany says. "We have a dog. You're not really going to take Parci. Seriously? This is such a bad idea. I promise she won't tell on us. Come on."

"I will too tell. And I want a blindfold," Parci says. Lee and Nikki and Maureen and Bad look at each other and shrug.

"Okay," Maureen says, sneezing again. She gets Lee's gym bag and pulls a shirt out of it. "We can use this."

"A real blindfold," Parci says. Her eyes are shiny with excitement. "I don't want to be blindfolded with a smelly shirt."

"Don't do this, guys," Czigany whines. "Please, please don't do this." She starts to sit up, and Nikki, who is sitting next to her, pushes her back into the seat and buckles her in.

"Don't worry," Lee says. She reverses out of the Khulhats' driveway. "The shirt's clean. I don't actually go to gym. I have a doctor's pass."

"Her mom's a doctor, like yours," Bad explains to Parci. "Lee stole a pass from her mother's partner's office. It says Lee has an enlarged heart or something. So she gets to sit in the bleachers and knit while we run around."

Lee really does have a bad heart. But she's told everyone that the pass is a fake. It's easier than having everyone be sorry for her all the time.

"I have a condition," Parci says, importantly. "So does Czigany. That's why we have to be home by five. We have to take all of these disgusting pills with weird names."

"Parci," Czigany says. "Shut up! They don't want to know about any conditions."

"I wasn't going to say anything else," Parci says sullenly. With their blindfolds on, it's remarkable how much the sisters look alike. They have the same thick, black hair and heavy, slanting eyebrows. The same scowls; narrow shoulders; thin, downy wrists.

"Home by five," Czigany says. Her voice is more serious than it ought to be. Deep and ominous, like the voiceover in a movie trailer. "Or the doom falls on all of us."

"Home by five," Maureen says. Lee accelerates onto the on-ramp of 295.

They're barely past Teaneck, heading towards the wilds of upstate New York, an hour into what all of them think of as CZIGANY'S ORDEAL, folder or no folder, just like that, with all caps in some fancy gothic font, when Maureen pokes Lee in the shoulder and says, "Roll down the windows."

"It's too cold," Lee says. They've already stopped, once, so Maureen could pee and buy Claritin. Bad is driving, and Lee is sitting in the passenger seat, reading her romance. Still no werewolves.

"Roll down the windows, please," Maureen says. "Or pull over. I'm carsick."

"Switch with Bad. You can drive."

"No way," Bad says. "I get carsicker. You switch with her."

Lee compromises. She rolls down the windows an inch.

"More," Maureen says. "I'm in hell. This is hell. It's like it's my Ordeal, not Czigany's. When we get to your aunt's place, I bet it turns out I'm allergic to goats, too."

"Maureen, shut up!" Lee says.

"Don't worry," Maureen says. "They're asleep. So is Nikki. Parci's drooling on your upholstery. Can I say how much I love being an only child?"

"So does this change our plans?" Lee asks the other two. She can't help it: she whispers.

"What? Parci?" Bad says. "No way. Ear infection, my sweet curvy ass. Maybe her mom buys that act, but I don't. Look, Lee, it's not like we're going to let them get hurt or anything. We give them cab money and drop them off at the movies at midnight. At the latest. So they'll have to take some pills a couple of hours late. So their parents freak out just a little. Czigany's parents could use a wake-up call, you know? They act like they own her. It isn't natural and anyway, it's not like Czigany's going to tell on us."

Maureen says, "Parci won't tell on us, either."

"How do you know?" Lee says.

"I told her we'd spread it around the school that Czigany hit on Bad. That she tried to feel Bad up in the locker room even though she knows Bad already has a serious girlfriend, and that when Bad told her to back the hell off, Czigany asked if she was into threesomes."

"Nice touch," Bad says. "I'm flattered. Look, Lee. Parci is into this, okay? You can tell. And it makes it more of a real Ordeal for Czigany to have her little sister along."

"For my Ordeal all they did was make me wear a sandwich board for a day," Lee says.

"Yeah, a sandwich board, at the mall, that said PEOPLE I HAVE THOUGHT ABOUT MAKING OUT WITH. Listing all the names they'd coaxed out of you at a party and then made you sign."

"It was a short list!" Lee says.

"Steve Buscemi?" Bad says.

Maureen says, "Don't forget Al Gore, Gandhi, and Hillary Clinton. Not to mention John Boyd and Eric Park. That went all over the school."

"I didn't know what it was for," Lee says. "I didn't want to be rude! Besides, Eric asked me out the next day."

Bad says, "Only because he felt sorry for you. The point is, it's not like we don't like Czigany, you know? The accent is cool. She's been all over the world. She's met the Pope—wasn't he on your list, Lee? Whatever. The point is we're going to give Czigany the coolest, most legendary Ordeal ever. But the girl is weird. Admit it."

"It's her parents," Lee says. "The whole overprotective thing. She told me once that they had to have a bodyguard when they lived in the Ukraine or somewhere like that. Because of kidnappers."

"Funny," Bad says. "Considering. They probably make her pee in a cup, too, after she hangs out with us. Mom the doctor totally gave me the stink eye the last time I ran into her. Like she wanted to shred me into little pieces."

"She hates you for sure," says Maureen.

"Just because Czigany was, like, thirty minutes late for dinner? On a weekend night? No. I think it's because they know I'm a lesbian. I mean, your mom gets kind of freaked out, too, Lee, but she totally compensates by trying to be extra nice and making me cappuccinos and stuff."

"The Khulhats will go insane when they get home and they can't find Czigany and Parci," Lee predicts. She realizes something. The Ordeal was Bad's idea. And it isn't just Czigany's Ordeal, either. You don't ever want to get on Bad's bad side, which is what Mrs. Khulhat has done.

"Yeah, well," Bad says. She gives Lee what Lee thinks of as the invisible smile. That is, Bad isn't smiling at all, and yet you can tell how very pleased Bad is with herself. As if she is holding the perfect poker hand and all of your money is already on the table, and the smile will cost extra.

"Turn on the radio," Maureen says. Maureen is full of the kind of reasonable demands that Lee always wants, most unreasonably, to refuse. Friendships of long standing are defined by feelings of this kind perhaps more often than they are by feelings of harmonious accord. "A road trip's no good without a soundtrack."

"This isn't a road trip," says Bad, who has known Maureen just as long as Lee has. Bad never tries to be reasonable when she can be perverse. "It's a kidnapping. And it's already all messed up. Just like in the movies. It will end up with Lee shooting all of us and then having to dispose of the bodies in a wood chipper."

"It's not a kidnapping," Lee says. "It's an Ordeal." She turns on the radio. Opens up her book again.

ଔ C ଠ

The next time Cabell Meadows saved Clementine Cleary's life, Clementine was fifteen and Cabell was twenty-one. The occasion was the wedding of John Cleary, Clementine's mother's younger brother, who was getting married for the second time around, this time to a local girl, Dancy Meadows. Cabell's nineteen-year-old sister.

That Dancy Meadows and John Cleary met in the first place had been Clementine's fault. Dancy Meadows managed the T-Shurt Yurt down along the strip and, knowing this, when Clementine was fourteen she lied about her age in order to get a job at the Yurt. She planned to befriend Dancy, who was just out of high school herself. This turned out not to be as easy as getting the job had been, but even before John Cleary made his entrance, Clementine had managed to steal a picture of Cabell out of Dancy's wallet. And once Dancy mentioned with loathing her brother's habit of sleeping in the nude and how, during a sleepover in seventh grade, she'd charged her friends ten bucks each for the chance to sneak into his bedroom in the middle of the night to see, by the light of the full moon, for themselves.

Clementine's uncle, who had already married one girl straight out of high school, came into the Yurt on a Thursday afternoon looking for a gag gift for Clementine's grandfather's eighty-first birthday. Finding Clementine behind the counter, he used this as an excuse to spend the rest of the day in the T-Shurt Yurt, telling jokes and flirting with Dancy. Some of the jokes were pretty funny. Even Clementine had to admit that much.

And she could tell that the flirting was working, too, because Dancy began to act as if she and Clementine were very best friends, even when John Cleary wasn't around. Dancy told Clementine the story about Cabell's evil first girlfriend, and how Cabell had cried for three days when she dumped him just before Valentine's Day and then kept the diamond pendant anyway, and then how he'd cried for a whole week when their dad had accidentally stepped on Buffy (his pet tarantula), getting out of the shower.

Dancy showed Clementine how the senior girls put on eyeliner. And explained what boys liked. Clementine didn't believe all of it, but some of what Dancy said must have been true because by Christmas Dancy was pregnant, and Clementine's aunt was divorcing John Cleary and moving down to Charleston. Out of the frying pan and into the next frying pan, Clementine's mother said.

By this point, Clementine wasn't quite sure how she felt about Dancy. She was Cabell's sister, which was a point in her favor. They had the same eyes. She seemed to know every one of Cabell's secrets, too. Clementine kept a file on her computer in which she put down every single thing Dancy said, with annotations where she felt Dancy was being unfair. Once Dancy and Uncle John were engaged, Clementine spent some sleepless nights thinking about the fact that she was going to be Dancy's niece. It might be awkward if she ended up being Dancy's sister-in-law as well. And if she was Dancy's niece, then what would Cabell be? An uncle-in-law? Some sort of second cousin? There wasn't really anyone that she could ask for advice, either, because she'd stopped talking to her two best friends. That was because of Cabell.

Cabell had visited Clementine's tenth-grade biology class in May. He'd been tracking black bears along the Blue Ridge Trail over Chapel Hill's spring break, part of an independent study. Clementine went up to say hey before class started, while Cabell was setting up his slides. She'd wondered, sometimes, where Cabell would have sat in Mr. Kurtz's biology class. Stupid, stupid. Her heart was somewhere down at the bottom of her stomach, but she said, "Hey, Cabell. Remember me?"

Mr. Kurtz said, "Clementine? Did you have a question for Mr. Meadows?"

Cabell squinted. He said, "The sleepswimmer? No way!" He said she'd changed a lot, which was true. She had. It turned out, no surprise, that Cabell was an excellent public speaker. Clementine smiled whenever he looked in her direction. He finished by telling Clementine's class a story about a girl in California who went and had her hair permed and then, the same day, went hiking and got knocked unconscious.

"When she woke up," Cabell said, "she was way out in the middle of the woods, off the path and under a tree, and she put her hand up on her hair, and it was all wet and foamy." That seemed to be the end of the story. He grinned out at the class. Clementine smiled back until her face hurt.

Madeline, who lived down the street from Clementine and had wet the bed until they were both in fifth grade, raised her hand. Mr. Kurtz said, "Yes, Madeline?"

Madeline said, "I don't understand. What happened to her? Why was her hair wet?"

Cabell said, "Oops. Sorry. I guess I left that part out. It was a bear? It was attracted by the smell of the chemicals in her perm? So it hit her over the head, knocked her unconscious, dragged her off the path and into the woods. Then it licked all the perm out of her hair."

"That's disgusting!" Madeline said. Other kids were laughing. Someone said, "It liked the taste of the sperm in her hair?" It worried Clementine, because it wasn't clear whom they were laughing at: Madeline, Cabell, or the girl with the perm.

"She was lucky," Cabell said. "Not that it licked her head," he explained, in case Clementine's class was particularly stupid. Which, in Clementine's opinion, they were. "Lucky that it didn't eat her."

After all of that, Clementine couldn't even manage to ask any questions. Even though she'd spent the whole night before coming up with questions that Cabell might be impressed by. At lunch she said, "So he's pretty amazing, isn't he?" She couldn't keep it in any longer.

Madeline and Grace, who was going through an awkward phase, according to Clementine's mother—although this was just being kind; Grace had been awkward since the second grade— just stared at her. Finally Madeline said, "Who?" Madeline was annoying that way. You had to explain everything to her.

"Cabell," Clementine said. Madeline and Grace continued to stare at her as if she had something in her teeth. "Cabell Meadows?"

"Very funny," Grace said. "You're joking, right?"

They looked at Clementine and saw that she was not joking. Clementine saw that they were astonished. Cabell Meadows, she said to herself. Cabell Meadows.

"Cabell Meadows doesn't wear deodorant," Madeline said.

"That's because of bears." It was like the perm. Bears were sensitive to manmade smells that way. Clementine said this, hoping to reason with them. They were best friends. They liked the same movies. They borrowed each other's clothes.

When they went out for pizza, they never ordered pizza with onions because Grace hated onions.

"Let's put it this way," Madeline, former bedwetter, said. "Even if he did wear deodorant, he could wear all the deodorant in the world and I still wouldn't lick him. Anywhere. His eyes are close together. He has weird hands. They're all veiny, Clementine! And his hair! Even when he was still in school here, he wasn't exactly prime real estate, okay? He was a smelly hippie. And it's worse now! Much, much worse!"

She stopped speaking in order to wipe the spit away from the corners of her mouth. Madeline was a sprayer when she got excited. Most likely, Clementine thought, Madeline still wet the bed sometimes, too. Leaky, squeaky Madeline.

Grace took over, as if she and Madeline were training for the Olympics in the freestyle unsolicited advice relay. She said, "It's kind of romantic, Clementine. I mean, you must have been in love with him for a long time? I remember how you used to talk about him when we were just little kids. But you've grown up, Clementine, and he hasn't, okay? At a certain age, for guys, it comes down to robots or girls. Superheroes in tights or girls. Online porn or real girls. Bears or girls… although that's not one I've run into before. The point is that this guy has already made the choice, Clementine. If you were all hairy and ran around in the forest maybe you'd have a chance, but you're not and you don't. If Cabell Meadows is the big secret crush you've been hiding all of these years, God help you. Because I sure can't."

Madeline said, "I agree with everything she just said."

No big surprise there. Madeline and Grace were both big fans of personality quizzes and advice columns and self-help books. They could spend hours agreeing with each other about what some boy had meant when he walked by at lunch and said, "Ladies."

Clementine thought about stabbing Madeline with a spork. The only thing stopping her, really, was that she knew Grace and Madeline would get a lot of mileage out of analyzing that, too. Like how it was a cry for help because what else could you ever hope to achieve by attacking someone with a plastic utensil? The reasons they had plastic utensils was because kids did that sometimes. Once someone had stabbed a teacher in the arm. Lawyers had claimed it was the hormones in the hamburger meat. Cabell was a vegetarian. Clementine had learned that in Mr. Kurtz's class. She thought about what her mother would say when Clementine came home and said she was a vegetarian, too. Maybe she could sell it as a diet. Or a school project.

Clementine realized that she was still gripping her spork defensively. She put it down and saw that Madeline and Grace were once again staring at her. Clementine had been somewhere else, and now they knew who that somewhere else was.

Clementine said, "He saved my life."

"Let me save you from the biggest mistake of your life," Madeline said. Her voice took on a thrilling intensity, as if she was about to impart the secrets of the universe to Clementine. Madeline's father was a preacher. He was a spitter, too. Nobody liked to sit in the first pew. "Cabell Meadows is not hot. Cabell Meadows is at least six years older than you and he still doesn't know that tube socks are not a good look with Birkenstocks. Cabell Meadows voluntarily came to a high-school biology class to talk about how he spent his spring break shooting bears in the butt with tranquilizer darts. Cabell Meadows is an epic, epic loser."

Clementine put down her spork. She got up and left the table, and for the rest of the year she avoided Grace and Madeline whenever possible. When they began to go out with boys, she would have liked to say something to them about standards and hypocrisy and losers. But what was the point? It was clearly just the way the world worked when it came to friends and love and sex and self-help books and boys. First you're an expert and then you go out into the field with your tranquilizer guns to get some practical experience.

Clementine found Cabell's LiveJournal, "TrueBaloo," after some research online. He had about two hundred friends, mostly girls with names like ElectricKittyEyes and FurElise who went to Chapel Hill, too, and came from San Francisco and D.C. and Cleveland and lots of other places that Clementine had never been to. She got a LiveJournal account and friended Cabell. She sent an e-mail that said "Remember me, the dumb girl u saved from drowning? Just, thanx 4 that & 4 coming to talk about bears. ;)" Cabell friended her back. Asked how school was going and then never wrote again, even after Dancy broke up Clementine's uncle's marriage, and even after Clementine wrote and said everybody had missed him at the engagement party. Which was okay, because Cabell was probably busy with classes, or maybe he was off watching bears again. Or maybe he thought Clementine was upset about the whole thing with Dancy. So Clementine wasn't all that bothered. What mattered was that he'd friended her back. It was a bit like him and the bears, like she and Cabell had tagged each other.

Clementine loaded up her iPod with all the music that Cabell had ever mentioned online. One day they might get a chance to talk about music.

Most Chapel Hill students came back for parties, or to do laundry once in a while, but not Cabell. Not for Christmas, not for spring break (which was understandable, Clementine knew: if you grew up an hour away from Myrtle Beach, you'd officially had all the spring break you'd ever need). He'd shown up to talk about bears, but he didn't show up at Dancy's engagement party, not even to denounce John Cleary for being a sleazy, cradle-robbing son of a bitch. Which he was. Even Clementine's grandfather said so. Ex–star quarterback, which was all that anyone needed to say, really.

Clementine had to be grateful about her uncle and Dancy— except for the wedding, who knew when Cabell would have come home.

Dancy had talked John Cleary into getting married down on the beach, near enough to Headless Point that it felt like a good omen to Clementine. She went running along the beach at Headless Point some mornings, remembering how she and Cabell had walked back through the dunes when everyone else in the world who cared about Clementine had thought she was dead. Drowned. Only Cabell and she had known otherwise.

She begged out of being one of Dancy's bridesmaids because she wasn't going to be wearing discount lemon-custard chiffon when Cabell saw her for the first time in a year. Instead she spent three hundred dollars of T-Shurt Yurt paychecks in a boutique down in Myrtle Beach for a sea-green dress with rhinestone straps. She found a pair of worn-once designer pumps with stiletto heels on eBay and only paid eight bucks for them. Dancy's maid of honor, who'd been an infamous slut back in high school, swore up and down that Clementine looked at least eighteen.

Two weeks before the wedding, Clementine went to Myrtle Beach with her youth choir; on the bus ride home, she sat in the last row and made out with a boy named Alistair. She'd read enough romance novels and spent enough time talking to Dancy to have some general idea of what you were supposed to do, but nothing substitutes for experience in the field.

Having achieved limited success under difficult circumstances (wrong boy, wrong mouth, sticky bus floor, lingering aroma of someone's forgotten banana, two girls—Miranda and Amy—not even bothering to pretend not to watch over the back of the next seat), Clementine felt adequately prepared for the real thing.

&#x153; L. &#x80;

"Are we there yet?" It's Parci who's asking. Just as if this is a family vacation and not an Ordeal. She's taken off her blindfold at some point in the last few minutes, but that's okay because they're off the highway now and bumping along the rutted road that winds up the mountain. It's all gloomy thick stands of pine trees and fir trees and under them the remains of old stone walls. Once, a long time ago, there was a French settlement. Farms and orchards. Archeologists arrive every summer, to camp and have romances and dig. Lee's aunt, Dodo, says that it's nice to have some company besides her goats, and the relationship dramas are better than anything on television.

Czigany is either still sleeping, or else pretending. Bad and Nikki are singing along with the radio at the top of their lungs, so most likely it's the latter. Maureen is texting some new boyfriend. Judging by how fast and hard her thumbs are hitting the keys, it's a fight.

"Don't be surprised when you lose your signal," Lee tells Maureen. "There aren't a lot of cell towers up here."

"To be continued," Maureen says, and bites her lip. "Oh, yeah."

Here is the turnoff, and here, another mile down, is Dodo's secret kingdom. Lee directs Bad down the dirt road into a meadow surrounded by mountains, a stream running through it. A two-story farmhouse that Dodo has painted Pepto-Bismol pink. (Paint rescued from some Dumpster. The trim is canary yellow for no good reason.) Only the barn looks the way a barn should: red and white and with a weathervane; a nanny goat standing upon a wheel of cheese. Only when you get closer do you see that instead of painting the barn, Dodo has cut open and tacked up hundreds and hundreds of Coca-Cola cans to the wooden boards.

Peaceable Kingdom was never much of a tourist attraction. There was a snack stand, a petting zoo, a go-cart track, a carousel, and a smallish Ferris wheel. The go-cart track is overgrown with grass and the beginnings of a bamboo thatch that Dodo's goats keep close-cropped. Goats play king of the hill on the collapsed wooden platform of the carousel, whose roof blew away years ago. Dodo, who purchased Peaceable Kingdom in its declining years, long ago sold off the carousel horses, one by one, to buy her goats.

Over the years, Peaceable Kingdom's Ferris wheel has peaceably sunk into the marshy ground of the goat meadow. Lightning strikes it when there are storms, and at least once every summer there is the morning when Dodo discovers, going out to milk the goats, a broken-hearted archeologist crumpled in sleep after a night of solitary drinking, in the bottommost chair where the mice build their nests. Lee herself likes to sit and read and rock gently in the cracked, lime-green vinyl bucket seat where a Pygmy goat now stands sentinel, front legs propped up on the rusty safety bar, listening to Bad honk the horn in delight at what she is seeing.

Goats are eating the green sea of grass and the creeping trumpet vine that would otherwise pull down the tilted wheel. Others kneel or perch upon the boulders jutting out of the scrubby pasture.

"Your aunt lives here?" Maureen says. Nikki is taking pictures with her cell phone.

Dodo is Lee's mother's older sister. She's a former anarchist who served nine years in a high-security women's prison. Now she makes cheese instead of bombs. When she set up her herd at Peaceable Kingdom, she invested in six Toggenburgs. Over time she's swapped, bartered, adopted, and bought increasingly more esoteric breeds. The current herd numbers somewhere around thirty goats, including Booted Goats, Nubian Blacks, Nigerian Dwarfs, Pygmy Goats, and four Tennessee Fainting Goats. Dodo spent her years in prison doing coursework in animal husbandry. Goats, she likes to say, are the ultimate anarchists.

Bad parks beside the pink farmhouse. "Let me guess," Maureen says. "I bet there's a composting toilet."

"It's an outhouse, actually," Lee tells her, even as Dodo appears on the front porch where three goats loiter, hoping, no doubt, to get into the house where there are interesting things to chew. She's wearing pink camouflage waders that come halfway up to her hips. Her hair, too, has been colored to match the house.

"Nice boots," Bad says. The others are still gaping at Dodo, the pink house, the shining Coca-Cola barn, the goats, the Ferris wheel. Even Czigany's posture has changed subtly, as if, still pretending to sleep, she is listening very, very hard.

"Take off the blindfold," Lee tells Nikki. "And her handcuffs." And then, to everyone, "I told you my aunt was eccentric. And her feelings get hurt kind of easy. When you try the cheese, pretend you like it even if you don't. Okay?"

"Czigany," Parci shouts. She bounces on the seat. "Wake up! Your Ordeal is about to begin!"

Czigany sits up. She yawns hugely and fakely. "Hey, guys. Sorry about that. I had a late night last night."

"Boy, did we," Parci says.

When the blindfold is off, Czigany's big eyes get bigger. "Where are we?"

"That's for us to know," Nikki says.

"I need to say something before we get out of the van," Bad says. "The rules of the Ordeal are in effect. For both of you, Parci. Both of you have to do whatever we say. Okay?"

"Okay," Czigany says. Parci nods vigorously. She is visibly trembling with excitement. Czigany, too, is alert, and Lee thinks that just as Czigany was pretending to be asleep, she is still playacting, concealing some other, deeper reflex.

Lee and Bad and Nikki and Maureen have lived all of their lives on Long Island. The school that they attend is small: in all, their graduating class will be nineteen girls, if Meg Finnerton manages the miraculous and passes Advanced Algebra.

The Khulhats move from country to country whenever Czigany and Parci's father is reassigned to a new embassy. Czigany has lived, for two years or less, in the following places: Bosnia, Albania, England, Israel, and Ukraine, and Lee is undoubtedly forgetting one or two others.

When Czigany moves again, in another year or two, what will she remember? Lee hopes with all of her heart that the Ordeal, at least this part of it, will be something that Czigany remembers for all of her life. Dodo and her farm are the best, most *secret* secret Lee knows. She has been sure since the first time her mother took her to visit Dodo that there isn't anywhere in the world as magical as Peaceable Kingdom with the pink house and the Ferris wheel and Dodo's goats, so smart they know how to open the front door when Dodo forgets to lock it. But perhaps it will be nothing to Czigany. Lee thinks this, and then wonders why it matters so much that Czigany is impressed.

Lee looks from Czigany's shuttered face to Bad.

Bad says, "Go for it, Lee."

&#8731; C &#8730;

The wedding was a disaster from the beginning. After the hurricane warning, they had to take down the wedding tent and the dinner tents up on the bluff and relocate to the pavilion beside the parking lot where kids went in the summer to play Ping-Pong and eat ice-cream sandwiches. When it came to weather, you had to be sensible, even though most warnings came to nothing. Clementine's parents' house had been flooded so many times they'd given up trying to qualify for insurance policies. Instead they just kept everything valuable on the second floor of the house.

The hurricane turned out to be not even a baby hurricane. Not even a tropical storm. Instead it just rained so hard that the caterers couldn't get the fire going in the pits where they were supposed to set up their clambake.

Dancy didn't look pregnant until you saw her from the side, but Mrs. Meadows had had to let the dress out that morning. Clementine had helped decorate the ladies' room on the beach with orange blossoms and crape myrtle the night before. An hour before the ceremony was supposed to begin, Mrs. Meadows had sent her off to dig through the trunk of the maid of honor's car for tit tape. Clementine came back in triumph and was immediately sent off again, this time for ginger ale and soda crackers. Dancy's face, all afternoon, had been the color of Clementine's sea-foam dress. Meanwhile, John Cleary had lain down in his tuxedo in the sand under the pier with all of his old high-school friends standing over him. Nobody could persuade him to stand up again; he was still hungover from his bachelor party the night before. Clementine and her father had a bet going over who would puke first, the bride or the groom.

When the bagpipes started up—no Cleary had ever managed to make it down the aisle without a lot of wailing and woe to make it clear that marriage, like going into battle, was serious business—Clementine was standing beside her mother on the damp concrete floor of the pavilion, trying not to slap at her legs. Beach weddings rapidly became less romantic once the sand fleas found you. Wet seeped down through rotted places in the roof. Her mother leaned over and said into Clementine's ear, "Don't you ever do this to me."

"Do what?" Clementine said.

"You know what," her mother said.

"Get married?"

"Not until you're at least thirty-five."

It had always been clear to Clementine that her mother found marriage to be something of a trial, although why, exactly, was less clear. Clementine's father chewed with his mouth shut, never left the toilet seat up, and all of his hair was his own. The previous year on her birthday he had given his wife an emerald-cut diamond pendant and taken her to the nicest Italian restaurant in Myrtle Beach. The following morning Clementine heard her complaining on the phone to some friend that her husband didn't have a romantic bone in his body and she might as well have married a wooden post.

"Swear to God," Clementine said, but her mother only sighed.

Cabell stood with the rest of the wedding party, wearing the same purple plaid bow tie Dancy had made all the groomsmen wear. He was tall and he was blond and tan and his hair was only a little bit long around the ears. There was something about the way he wore his tuxedo that seemed both natural and also unnatural, as if he was only wearing it in order to disappear into his surroundings. As if weddings and black bears were both things that required you to get as close as possible without anyone ever realizing that you were there at all. When she'd bought her dress, Clementine had imagined it was something like the color of Cabell's eyes. It wasn't. Why had he stayed away for so long?

John Cleary and Dancy Meadows were making the kinds of promises that hardly anyone ever manages to keep. Clementine strained to catch every single word, moved despite knowing Dancy had picked Headless Point for her wedding because Headless Point was where she and Clementine's uncle had first had drunken, unprotected, sand-in-underwear sex under a tipped canoe. Dancy had given Clementine all the details. It wasn't the way things would go with Cabell.

No bagpipes. No caterers. No sand fleas or tit tape or mutant bow ties. When, looking at Dancy, Clementine tried to visualize this mysterious future of togetherness with Cabell, it was like that first time on the surfboard. Only this time, instead of wading in to Headless Point, Cabell and Clementine floated out to sea and never came back.

Dancy and John Cleary kissed. They mashed their lips together so hard Clementine expected to see blood afterwards. But instead Dancy laughed. She threw her bouquet straight up so that it hit the roof of the pavilion. "Now there's an omen for you," Clementine's mother said. She picked a clump of baby's breath out of Clementine's hair.

When the bagpipes started up again, Clementine for the first time in her life felt in need of a stiff drink. Then she would go and find Cabell. They'd dance. Or sit in a car and talk until the rain stopped and the sun came up over the ocean.

Dancy had once said that vodka was practically tasteless, and just outside the pavilion was the ten-gallon cooler Clementine had helped fill with ice and soft drinks and beer. She'd seen a bottle of Smirnoff, too.

She found a can of Coke and poured half of it out. Poured vodka in. It was almost as not-bad as everyone had said. As long as she was borrowing things, she decided, she might as well take the golf umbrella someone had left propped against the pavilion and the towel on top of the cooler. Well supplied, she crept off with the Coke and the rest of the Smirnoff to hide in the dunes.

Eventually all the Coke was gone, and because she wasn't entirely sure whether or not she was drunk yet, Clementine stayed put, sipping from the Smirnoff bottle. Her butt, on the towel, got wetter and wetter. Down below the dunes the Ping-Pong pavilion seemed as far away as a dream. Slowly, as the last heavy gray light evaporated, she became aware of little breathless yips, shadows rustling the coarse, rain-beaten tubes of dune grass. Wild dogs, or even coyotes, six or seven, perhaps: she guessed they were hunting mice or frogs. They ignored Clementine, miserably invisible beneath her umbrella. Now running, now halted; backs hunched, muzzles down, paws tearing at the caked gray sand. There were bats dipping down, as if unzipping the rain, and the dogs in the dunes chased them, too, empty jaws snapping like porcelain traps.

When Clementine stood up at last, they looked at her as if she were a party crasher. She shook the umbrella and the dogs fled. Later it was clear that this was the good part of the evening, where she'd managed to get drunk and not be eaten by wild dogs.

Things went downhill after that. There was the trip to the bathroom where Clementine saw what had happened to her hair and her makeup. Where she tore the hem of her dress on the plywood door of the bathroom stall. When she found Cabell, he was dancing with slutty Lizzy York, the maid of honor.

It didn't matter. Not even the hideous, antiquated music mattered. "Hey, Cabell," Clementine yelled.

"Hey, Cabell," Cabell yelled back. He executed a dance move. "Your mom was looking for you. What's up?"

"Sorry, Lizzy," Clementine said. "I need to show Cabell something. We'll be right back. Promise."

Lizzy gave Clementine the finger; Clementine shrugged and smiled and pulled Cabell through the dancers, out into the rain. She'd left the umbrella somewhere, but never mind. The rain fizzed on her skin.

"What did you want to show me?" her sweet love said.

They walked along the tidemark. Tiny, ghostly crabs did mysterious things to the wet sand. They were writing the story of Clementine's life. Cabell Meadows, Cabell Meadows. Clementine loves Cabell.

"Clementine? What did you want me to see?"

She waved her arm. "The ocean!"

Cabell laughed, and Clementine decided that this was a good thing. She was amusing.

"Not just the ocean!" she said. "The things in it. There might be, you know, sharks. Or mermaids. Like the wild dogs in the dunes. The world is full of things and nobody ever sees them! Nobody except for you and me." Her hair stuck in wet coils to her neck. Maybe she looked like a mermaid.

"Do you think I look like a mermaid?" she asked her love.

"Clementine, sweetheart," Cabell said. "I think you look drunk. And we're both soaked. Let's go back."

"It's romantic here, isn't it?" Clementine said. "If you wanted to kiss me, I'd understand."

No stars, only rain. She wanted more than anything to get rid of her hose, but first she had to take off her pumps. Perhaps it had been a mistake to wear stilettos to a beach wedding. Every step Clementine had taken, all night long, she'd left a little hole in the poor, blameless sand.

"Don't think I don't appreciate the offer, Clementine," Cabell said, "but hell, no."

"Oh shit," Clementine said. "You're gay?"

"No!" Cabell said. "And stop taking off your clothes, okay? I'm not gay, I'm just not interested. Not to be an asshole, but you're not my type."

"I'm not taking off my clothes," Clementine said. "Just my shoes. And my pantyhose. And what do you care? Dancy said you sleep in the nude. Do you still sleep in the nude? There's sand in my pantyhose. And what do you mean I'm not your type? What type am I?"

"Underage," Cabell said. "Unlike your uncle, I don't go for babies." And having offered up this retort, which could have come straight out of one of Clementine's romance novels, he turned and walked away and left Clementine all alone in the rain with one shoe off and her pantyhose down around both ankles.

When Clementine finally got the damn stilettos off, she pretended that the ocean was the whole stupid wedding, balled up the hose, and threw them at it. Then the stilettos. On the way back to the pavilion, she took a shortcut through the parking lot and sliced her left foot so badly on a broken beer bottle that she ended up needing sixteen stitches and four pints of blood. They also pumped her stomach, just in case. Want to know who found her passed out and gushing blood and called the ambulance?

Go on. Three guesses.

ଔ L. ଞ

Dodo gives them a lunch of goat cheese and apples and dark, chewy bread in the kitchen. There is a hard cheese and a soft, runny cheese, and a cheese-and-herb spread. Dodo tells them about her life as an anarchist, while a chorus of goats bleats threats through the screen door. How she blew up a bank. "It was three in the morning, and I know it was stupid to stay, but I wanted to see what all that money and paperwork would look like, raining down in the air. Instead, minutes before the explosives were wired to go off, there was this flood of rats and cockroaches, all pouring out of the building and across the street where I was standing in an alley behind a Dumpster. It was like they knew it was going to happen. I took off, too. Not because of the bomb, but because of the cockroaches. I can't stand roaches. It was even worse finding out that they have ESP."

She tells them how she has been shot with rubber bullets, sprayed with hoses, pistol-whipped by a D.C. cop. Look, here's the scar on her cheek. Here's the sexy mermaid tattoo another inmate gave Dodo with a ballpoint pen and a sharpened toothbrush. Bad is smitten. The others giggle nervously whenever Dodo swears, which is often.

After lunch, Dodo gives the girls the tour. She shows them the cheese-making room and the cheese cave. She takes them down to the goat barn with its threadbare brocade armchairs and hairy, goat-eaten couches where every evening she and the goats watch movies on her old projection screen. She passes out handfuls of corn to feed the goats and explains why Tennessee Fainting Goats faint. The goats are alternately curious and standoffish. Sometimes crowding around the girls, sometimes going off to confer, noisily, among themselves.

They take the corn daintily from Lee's palm but ignore the hand that Parci holds out.

"Funny little bastards," Dodo says fondly. "They just don't get along with some people."

Parci throws her corn into the grass, and still the goats won't go near it.

"This is my Ordeal? To come and feed goats and listen to your aunt talk about how to make bombs?" Czigany says to Lee.

"It's too bad you have to be home so early," Lee says, testing. "We could spend the night here. Sleep in the barn. Watch old movies."

"Or we could get home before five, like you promised, and then my parents won't murder Parci and me. I am not kidding, Lee." Czigany watches Lee carefully as she says this, as if she is waiting for Lee to give away the secret of the Ordeal.

Bad is allowing a Toggenburg to chew the fringes off her ratty sweater. She says, "Hey, Lee? Dodo says she's going to show us a midden heap. We're going to go look for arrowheads."

"You should go check it out, Czigany," Lee says. "Once Dodo found a piece of pottery down there and it turned out it wasn't pottery after all, it was a piece of skull."

Czigany gives Lee one last look and then follows the others. The goats lag behind, having no interest in arrowheads. Lee, who has her own rituals when she comes to Peaceable Kingdom, goes to visit the Ferris wheel. She climbs inside the bottommost carriage and opens up her book.

&#8500; C &#8480;

When Clementine's mother was angry, she didn't throw things or shout. Instead she began to talk slowly, as if words had lots of extra syllables that only got used when you were in real trouble. The morning after Dancy's wedding, Clementine woke up and discovered her mother looking through her drawers. Not quietly, either.

Clementine lay on her bed wanting to die, watching her mother look for whatever it was that she was looking for. Her head, her stomach, her throat, her foot were blobs of raw sensation. There was a hole in her arm where someone had put the blood back into her, and an orange band around her wrist. She was too weak to pull it off.

Her mother said, "Everybody in town heard you yelling down on the beach last night about how much you love that Meadows boy."

"Was I yelling?" Clementine said. She gave up wishing she could die and began to wish, instead, that she had never been born. Her mouth tasted like vomit. "I don't remember. I think I was drunk."

"Which makes it all better," her mother said. "Is Cabell why you went to Myrtle Beach and bought a six-hundred-dollar dress?"

"Three hundred," Clementine said. "It was on sale. Some of the rhinestones were missing. Are you spying on me?"

"As if I would spy on my own child," her mother said. "The very idea. Geraldine Turkle happened to be picking up some Clinique foundation at Lord & Taylor's. When she saw you over in the designer dresses, she thought she ought to keep an eye on you."

"She thought I was shoplifting," Clementine said.

"She didn't say that," her mother said, equivocating. "You remember her daughter, Robin, bless her heart, who got caught on camera in the CVS with five hundred dollars' worth of Sudafed? You can hardly blame her for being concerned. And stop trying to change the subject. What's going on with you and Dancy Meadows's brother? He's a grown man and you're a little girl!"

"Nothing, nothing, nothing is going on! I can't talk about this right now. Can I have some Advil? What's wrong with my foot?"

Her mother said, "You sliced up your tendon. You would have bled to death in the parking lot if Cabell Meadows hadn't called 911. And not even a baby aspirin until you tell me the truth. Did that boy give you alcohol?"

"Nothing is going on and I'm telling you the truth! I just like him, okay? He saved my life. And I didn't know I was drinking alcohol. I thought I was drinking Coke, okay? Somebody must've put something in it. Not Cabell. You can ground me if you want. But stop asking me about Cabell Meadows. Okay? This is so embarrassing. I wish I were dead." At which point Clementine forced a couple of tears from her eyes. It wasn't hard.

Her mother went away. She came back with ginger ale and three Advil. She said, "Dancy has asked me to pass on how much she appreciates you ruining her wedding. Not to mention ruining Cabell's rented tuxedo. They've tried everything but they don't think they can get the blood out. And Clementine? Here's something to think about. Every time you and Cabell meet up, you almost die. Does that sound like a healthy relationship to you?"

"Every time we meet up he saves my life," Clementine said.

Her mother said, "Clementine. He's nothing special. He's just some boy."

DARLINGSEA: u saved my life again

TRUEBALOO: dont mention it

DARLINGSEA: you saved my life 2X now. u didnt take advantage. u know, even tho I was drunk and obnoxious and sed that u were gay. ;)

TRUEBALOO: clementine, its ok. really dont mention it. ok?

DARLINGSEA: your not, right? i mean your not gay r u? even if your not im sorry about the tux. did the blood come out?

TRUEBALOO: not last time i checked

TRUEBALOO: dont worry about the tux

DARLINGSEA: my dress got ruined 2. mom found out how much it cost & shes madder about that than me being drunk

TRUEBALOO: hope your foot is ok

DARLINGSEA: its fine

DARLINGSEA: so i know your all busy with classes but i just wanted to say thanx. for being a gentleman when i was a total idiot & for saving my life

DARLINGSEA: also can i ask u some things about chapel hill? because im thinking about applying. mrs padlow in ap chemistry talks about u all the time & chapel hill

*DARLINGSEA:* she went there

*DARLINGSEA:* she said she saw your picture in the paper from the lab animal protests & i think thats so cool, that your doing something

*TRUEBALOO:* tell mrs p hey for me

*DARLINGSEA:* so r u coming home when dancy has the baby? she says i can watch if i want but i dont think mom will let me

*TRUEBALOO:* maybe

*TRUEBALOO:* look, c, gotta run, got lab, stay off the booze, okay

### ෬ L ෭

"What are you reading?" someone says.

Lee looks up. It's Parci. "Just some book. You know."

"Is it good?" Parci says.

"I don't know. It's a love story. Kind of."

"Then I wouldn't like it," Parci says. "I like stories about animals. Do you have a boyfriend? Because Czigany isn't allowed to date. Neither am I."

"Your parents are kind of strict," Lee says. "There's this boy I run into some-times when I buy comic books. He asked me out to the movies once, but it was a horror movie. I don't like horror movies."

Parci says, "Nobody found any arrowheads. Just a dead vole. So is this Czigany's Ordeal?"

Czigany and the others are back up in the barn. Probably Dodo is showing them how to make cheese. Or pipe bombs. Lee can hear them shouting and laughing.

"This is the part of the Ordeal that I'm in charge of," Lee says, evading Parci's question as gracefully as she can.

"I thought it would be something really embarrassing. Or dangerous. Or disgusting. Not that this isn't kind of awesome." But Parci sounds almost disap-pointed. "Everybody in my grade talks all the time about the Ordeal. How scared they are. But you can tell they're really into it."

"It's just this tradition," Lee says. "Girls' schools have all kinds of weird tradi-tions. Normally you have your Ordeal when you're a freshman—you know, a rite of passage or something. But we think Czigany is great, and so a couple of weeks ago we asked her if she wanted one because otherwise you don't really fit in. You'll see. When your class goes through their Ordeals."

"We won't be here," Parci says. "We have to move a lot."

### ෬ C ෭

*DARLINGSEA:* hey, cabell, dancys baby is really ugly. no kidding. first i thought all kids must be that ugly when theyre born, but my mom said lucinda larkin cleary is in her own special category

*TRUEBALOO:* ha ha

*DARLINGSEA:* u really need to come see her quick. shes got hair all over her body & she also had teeth

*TRUEBALOO:* r u @ the hospital? tried to call but dancys phone is off

*DARLINGSEA:* when she was born! & a big caul that your mom went & buried somewhere in the yard. last year in biology we read that when a fetus grows inside the mother its like it goes through different species on its way to being human

*DARLINGSEA:* yeah im here in the waiting room

*DARLINGSEA:* so maybe baby lucinda got stuck somewhere around the wolverine stage. just kidding! do you remember dancys wedding when i got completely wasted? how i asked if i looked like a mermaid because of my dress which is why i bought it in the first place

*DARLINGSEA:* because it looked like something a mermaid would wear. but what i was wondering is do you think there really are mermaids? or vampires?

*TRUEBALOO:* how is dancy? tell her im psyched to be an uncle

*DARLINGSEA:* shes great shes on lots of drugs. i brought her this book

*DARLINGSEA:* about a girl who falls in love with a vampire. it was kind of bad except i also kind of enjoyed it

*DARLINGSEA:* anyway dont know if dancy told u, but im going out with a guy. hes got a widows peek just like a vampire might have

*TRUEBALOO:* good for you, c

*DARLINGSEA:* dancy says u have a serious girlfriend. so i didnt want u to think i still had some weird crush

*DARLINGSEA:* on u

*TRUEBALOO:* youre a sweet kid

*DARLINGSEA:* bcause i did have a crush on u when i was 12 & u saved me from drowning

*TRUEBALOO:* tell her i can't wait to see the new kid. next time u need your life saved u know where to find me ok?

∞ I. ∞

Lee dog-ears the page and checks her cell phone. Time to get going. Time for part two of Czigany's Ordeal. But she doesn't move.

There are birds' nests tufted with goat hair and candy-bar wrappers discarded by broken-hearted archeologists, or relics, perhaps, of Lee's childhood, high in the spokes of the Ferris wheel. Trees crowd the pasture, guarding Peaceable Kingdom or else threatening it, Lee is never sure which. The air is scented with sweet meadow grass and the Christmas smell of the stands of pine. If only the Ferris wheel would turn again, down would come the birds' nests and up would go Lee, to be the queen of all she surveys: goats, pine trees, barn, pink house, arrowheads, Maureen on her way to the outhouse to pee one last time, Bad and Nikki escorting Parci and Czigany back to the van.

As if she really were queen, an official delegation—Aunt Dodo and the goats—is headed in Lee's direction. "Nice of you to come see me," Dodo hollers.

"Sorry," Lee says. "It's just that I wanted to get to the end of this story. And this is my favorite reading spot in the world. Sometimes I think the only time I'm ever completely happy is when I'm here. Or am I being melodramatic?"

"It's the only place I've ever been happy," Dodo says. "So remind me again. You'll be back in an hour or so?"

"Is that still okay?" Lee says.

"Just keep an eye on your friends. Caught Bad trying to sneak up on my Tennessee girls and make them faint. What kind of name is that anyway?"

"Her real name is Patricia. And I used to do that, too," Lee reminds her.

"When you were eight. Glad you're not eight anymore. You were a real punk." Dodo says this without a drop of fondness.

"So what am I now?" Lee says, teasing.

Dodo sighs. Gives Lee a hard look. "A monster. You and your friends, all of you. Pretty monsters. It's a stage all girls go through. If you're lucky you get through it without doing any permanent damage to yourself or anyone else. You sure you really want to do this to your friend? It's cruel, Lee. She'll be frightened. Parci, too."

"Parci made us bring her along," Lee says. "Parci's tough. We won't leave them alone for more than a few hours. All they have to do is stay put. And Nikki is going to go up the tree before they get there. So if they get loose and wander off, she can deal with it."

"Something bad happens to Czigany and Parci and it's back to prison for me," Dodo says. "Or if Nikki falls out of the tree. You ever think about that?"

"You think we shouldn't do it?"

Bad is gesturing for Lee to come on. Aunt Dodo is frowning down at her. "I'm not sure I'm the one to ask," she says finally. "I've made some terrible mistakes. Not the bank. I don't regret blowing up the bank. But I did some dumb things before that and goddess knows I did some dumb things afterwards, too. So now everything seems like it might be a mistake, which is why I don't leave Peaceable Kingdom very often. It's a long way back down the mountain if something goes wrong, Lee."

"Hey, Lee!" Bad yells. "Let's get this show on the road!"

"It'll be fine," Lee tells Dodo. "Bad and Maureen will kill me if I mess up the next part. That's the only thing I'm worried about."

"So don't," Dodo says, and gives Lee a hug. The goats all look surprised. Dodo isn't a hugger.

Bad has plugged in her iPod and is playing some yodelly crap. Czigany and Parci are blindfolded and Nikki has handcuffed the sisters wrist to wrist.

"We're going home now, right?" Czigany says.

"Home?" Nikki says. "What, no Ordeal?"

Czigany says, "Having to use an outhouse wasn't Ordeal enough?"

Parci says, "I think we need to go home. My ear is kind of achy?"

"Don't worry," Bad says. "We just have one stop first. Then home."

෮ C ෨

Clementine was seventeen when Cabell came home. He'd been kicked out of graduate school for breaking into a research lab in Durham and liberating the test animals. Dogs, monkeys, rats, and cats. Clementine watched it all on Fox, with her mother and Lucinda Larkin. "See that man?" Clementine said to Lucinda Larkin. "That's your uncle! He's sleeping in your basement!" The news anchor informed them that when security caught up with Cabell on the lawn of the research building, he'd had an octopus with him, sloshing around in a two-gallon bucket.

Lucinda Larkin didn't seem particularly impressed. She went on playing with Clementine's hair. Clementine's mother said, "Dancy looked fit to kill when she dropped Lucinda Larkin off. Said something about John's computer. Some e-mail account she's come across."

Clementine's mother and Dancy had become quite close despite the difference in their ages. Their favorite topics of conversation were their respective marriages, Clementine, and, of course, John Cleary.

"Lucky Cabell," Clementine said. "Hope he remembered his earplugs. And lucky me!" She squeezed Lucinda Larkin. "I get a slumber party with my favorite little girl."

When she drove Lucinda Larkin over the next afternoon to pick up a change of clothes, Dancy wasn't home. Cabell was napping on the couch in the basement.

"So what were you going to do with that octopus?" Clementine said.

"The octopus?" Cabell said. He had on a pair of old flannel pajamas and there was a duffel bag beside the couch. His hair had gotten long again. "I don't know. Elope with it, run off to the Gulf of Mexico?"

"You remember me, right?" Clementine said.

"How could I forget?" Cabell said. "What time is it?"

"Two," Clementine said. "Where's Dancy?"

"Uh, I think she said something about yoga," Cabell said. "She and John were up pretty late last night. You know, talking?"

"Those two sure like to talk," Clementine said.

Cabell smiled in the direction of Clementine's knee, where Lucinda Larkin was lurking. "I don't think she likes me."

"Dancy is raising her to hate all men," Clementine said. "To be their doom. Isn't that right, Lucinda Larkin?"

"Daddy's a bad man," Lucinda Larkin said.

Cabell said, "That's the first thing I've heard her say since I got here."

Clementine sat down on the floor opposite Cabell and pulled Lucinda Larkin into her lap. Lucinda Larkin held on hard, like any minute the airlock doors would open and she'd be sucked away into the blackness of the void. Clementine knew exactly how she felt. "Are they really making you sleep on that thing?"

Cabell pulled a T-shirt out of the duffel bag. "Yes. Why?"

"Because that couch used to belong to Uncle John's fraternity," Clementine said. "He bought it off them when he graduated because he'd gotten lucky on it so many times. Dancy tried to set it on fire last New Year's. Because it doesn't go with her décor, but Uncle John won't let her get rid of it."

Cabell said, "After all the, um, *talk* last night, I was afraid your uncle was going to come down and ask if there was room on the couch."

Clementine put her hands over Lucinda Larkin's ears. "Dancy's been sleeping on your niece's top bunk for at least a week. So you should be safe. Speaking of true love, are you still going out with that girl? The one Dancy told me about at Christmas? Because I have a boyfriend now, but it isn't serious. Not really. Lucinda Larkin, let go of my arm. You are going to leave bruises. Want a Coke, Cabell? If you don't want a Coke, I know where Dancy hides all the booze. So how are things, anyway?"

"I'll take a Coke," Cabell said. "And how things are, more or less, is I just got kicked out of a graduate-school program that I still owe at least eight thousand dollars' tuition on. I'm stuck living in the basement of my kid sister's house for the foreseeable future because my mother's yard is full of reporters. I can't even go down to the beach with my surfboard without running into a million people who've known me my whole life, who know all about my life, who want to tell me what I should do with my life. I'm pretty sure getting it on with some high-school kid isn't going to turn things around for me at this stage, if that's what you were so delicately offering. All I need is your mother chasing after me with a bread knife."

"My mother warned you off?" Clementine said.

"Yeah," Cabell said. "Not directly. She talked to Dancy and then Dancy sat down and had a talk with me. Like Dancy ought to be giving anyone advice. Not that I was planning to take advantage of what is obviously some unfortunate quirk of your otherwise undoubtedly mature and capable personality. Your mother says you have straight As and a chance at a four-year scholarship at Queens."

"Don't worry," Clementine said. "I'm not still hung up on you or anything. I just owe you. For, you know, saving my life. Twice. And I need a good excuse to break up with my boyfriend. Want to play Resident Evil on Uncle John's Wii? Or would you rather help me help Dancy figure out if Uncle John is cheating on her? There's this Web site she wants to check out."

"I hate zombies," Cabell said. "Hey, Lucinda Larkin, let's go spy on your daddy."

"Those pajamas belong to Momma," Lucinda Larkin said to Clementine as they went up the stairs. "He had to borrow them because he doesn't have any pajamas and all of Daddy's were dirty."

Clementine said, "I had a pair of pajamas like that once. I went swimming in them and your Uncle Cabell had to fish me out. Otherwise I would have drowned.

That was when I was a little girl just like you."

"Cut it out, Clementine," Cabell said. "I mean it." But he sounded friendly. As if they were friends, teasing each other.

"You were just a kid, too," Clementine said. It was weird to think about. "I'm older now than you were then." They'd both been so young then. She went and got two of Dancy's wine coolers out of the fridge and a sippy cup with chocolate milk. Lucinda Larkin followed Cabell into her parents' bedroom, turned on the television, and popped *Beauty and the Beast* into the DVD player.

"Need a password," Cabell said. He had Uncle John's laptop out already.

"Dancy says it's zero-L-D-S-K-zero-zero-one underscore sixty-nine."

"Got it. What are we looking for?"

"I have this address she saved. It was in his history. She put it in Favorites. Okay. Here's the Web site. Sexy Russians. Sexy surfer girls. Sexy man-girls. That would be the best. You think he's into man-girls? Mail-order brides?"

"All of the above, no doubt," Cabell said. He took the laptop back. "Just a minute. Let me open up another window. Want to check my e-mail. Okay." He clicked back to the sexy Russian Web site. "If Dancy and your uncle get divorced, you think she'll get the house?"

"Cabell, she'll get everything she wants. Including the couch. You want to make her real happy? Let's go look on Craigslist to see if we can find her a new couch."

The next hour was the best hour of Clementine's life. Two months earlier she'd persuaded tenor David Ledbetter that it would be really, really special if they broke into the elementary school in the middle of the night. One thing had led to another and they'd lost their virginity together in the first-grade reading hut, and even though the whole thing had been kind of a catastrophe, ever since then David Ledbetter seemed to have this idea that in order to keep Clementine happy he had to come up with new and better locations. It was making Clementine crazy.

She and Cabell didn't even kiss. Nobody saved anybody's life, and Lucinda Larkin began to scream halfway through *Beauty and the Beast* because Clementine hadn't remembered to fast-forward through the scene where the singing candlestick did something scary that Lucinda Larkin had never been able to explain. They had to make her promise not to tell Dancy.

Clementine's choir group left for Hawaii a week later. Everyone said Cabell was going to get a job as a lifeguard and stick around at least through the end of the summer. Clementine sent a postcard to Lucinda Larkin. She sent one to Cabell, too. She went swimming. David Ledbetter gave her a lei. (No jokes, please.) When she came home a week later, Dancy had kicked Uncle John out of the house. Cabell had left the country. Her mother related all of this to her in the car on the way home from the airport.

Clementine said, "Cabell did what?"

"Nobody really knows," my mother said. "He's in Romania. Apparently he got offered some job with a conservation group tracking wolf populations."

"I thought he had a court date!" Clementine said. "Didn't he have to post bail or something? Can you just do that, just leave the country like that when you're wanted for stealing an octopus?"

"Why are you so all het up?" her mother said, cutting a look at her.

Clementine said nothing.

"Clementine," her mother said. "Someday you'll find someone who will make you happy. For a while. If you're lucky. But for the sake of my blood pressure, would you please stop mooning and making yourself miserable over a boy who can't even manage to take some dogs out for a walk without getting himself on Fox News!"

Clementine waited to see if she was finished. She wasn't. "Just look at your face! You look like someone ran over your daddy. You have been nothing but trouble since the day you were born. Don't give me that look! I swear if you decide to swallow a bottle of aspirin or run away to Atlanta or get knocked up by that peaky-faced tenor just to make some damn point, I *will* make your life a living hell."

"I can do what I want to!" Clementine said.

"Not in my house, you can't," her mother said. "And not in anybody else's house, either, not unless you want me to come after you with a two-by-four. You are going to finish your senior year, graduate with honors, and go off to Duke or Chapel Hill or Queens College or, God forbid, UNC-Wilmington, and have a good life. Are we clear on that?"

Clementine said nothing.

"I said, are we clear?"

"Yes, ma'am," Clementine said.

Nobody heard anything from Cabell. Clementine broke up with David Ledbetter. She and Madeline and Grace, friends again, all went to prom stag. Everyone had boy trouble.

The Saturday before graduation, Clementine went over to help Dancy throw all of John Cleary's trash out. He was living down in Myrtle Beach with some girl who had three piercings in her lip and one bad-tempered pit bull. Dancy wouldn't let Lucinda Larkin sleep over there, which meant Clementine was babysitting almost every Wednesday, Thursday, and Friday night while Dancy waitressed at the Bad Oyster.

"I don't know what I'm going to do when you go off to Queens," Dancy said. "Lucinda Larkin is going to miss you so much! Aren't you, baby?"

"No," Lucinda Larkin said.

Clementine gave Lucinda Larkin a squeeze. "I'll come home every weekend," she said. "You know, to do laundry."

Dancy dumped out a box. "College essays," she said. "John used to brag about how he didn't write any of these. Just got his girlfriends to write them for him. It's like serial killers, how they keep souvenirs."

"At least you didn't meet him until later," Clementine said. "You didn't have to write about the theme of loneliness in the poetry of Rudyard Kipling. Or compare and contrast Helen of Troy with Hester Prynne."

"Like giving birth to Lucinda Larkin was so much easier," Dancy said. She held up a photograph of John Cleary and some girl. Another photograph of John Cleary and another girl. "You know what I wish? I wish I'd never met him."

Clementine said, "Sorry about that."

"Yeah, well, I'm sorry about my brother. That he ran off to Romania to count wolves. I kind of thought maybe one day you and he—"

Clementine waited. When Dancy didn't say anything else, she said, "You thought maybe one day what?"

Dancy said, "That he might ask you out. When you were out of high school. He said you were a funny kid. You made him laugh. That would have been nice, don't you think, if one day you and I had ended up being sisters-in-law?"

"That would have been weird," Clementine said. "At least it would have been weird if you were also still technically my aunt. We would have had a hard time explaining it all to Lucinda Larkin."

"You won't have a hard time meeting guys in college," Dancy said. "If I were a guy, I'd totally hook up with you."

"Thanks," Clementine said, not sure whether she ought to feel flattered or creeped out. "I feel the same way. Are you going to answer your phone?"

"It's either going to be the Bad Oyster or you-know-who. And if it's you-know-who calling to say he can't take you-know who for a couple of hours tomorrow, I'm going to you-know-what him with a set of nail clippers," Dancy said. "Hello?" Her voice changed immediately. "Cabell? Where are you?" Pause. "What time is it there? That late? Are you coming home? We miss you so much!" Her face changed. She looked over at Clementine, and Clementine made her face as blank as she possibly could.

Dancy said, "Married? For real? You're not pulling my leg?"

When she could speak, Clementine said, "Hey, Lucinda Larkin, you want an ice-cream sandwich? Let me go get you an ice-cream sandwich. You stay here with your momma."

She went into the bathroom first. Looked at herself in the mirror. She could still hear Dancy's voice, going on and on about something, and so she went into the kitchen and opened the refrigerator door. Stared into it, wondering why Dancy had so many grapefruits and hardly anything else. She bent over the kitchen sink and splashed water on the back of her neck. On her face. When she came back, Dancy was still talking and Lucinda Larkin said, "We don't have any more ice-cream sandwiches?"

Clementine said, "No. They're all gone. Sorry about that."

Lucinda Larkin said, "Can I sleep at your house tonight?"

"Not tonight," Clementine said. "Maybe tomorrow?"

Dancy was saying something. She said, "Hey, Cabell? Clementine's here. She's helping me pack up all John's crap. We were just talking about you." She put the phone down and said to Clementine, "He's married. He got married a week ago. He's going to live in a castle. It's like a Disney movie or something. Do you want to talk to him?"

Clementine said, "Tell him congratulations."

"Clementine says congratulations. He says thank you, Clementine. Here," Dancy said. "I'll put him on speakerphone."

Cabell was saying, "…because it's exactly like here. I mean, like home. Everybody knows everybody's business. There's the castle, where Lenuta and her sisters and her family live, and then there's the village, and then there's not much else. Hardly even a road. Lots of forest and mountain. So it's really hard for Lenuta and her sisters to meet guys, and all the locals are really superstitious, and it's not like Lenuta and her sisters can travel very far."

"Why not?" Dancy said.

"Two of her sisters are practically babies. Nine years old and eleven years old. They don't go to school. Lenuta home-schools them. Plus their family has got this whole deal going with the wolf population. They're really involved in habitat conservation."

"So will you come home for Christmas?" Dancy said.

"Can't," Cabell said. "You know. Lenuta's English isn't that great. She'd have a terrible time. You know how Mom gets. I'm going to give her some time to cool down. You know, about this marriage thing. Besides, I skipped out on bail. Not very cool, you know?"

"Hey, Cabell," Clementine said. She swallowed.

"Clementine! How's school?"

"I graduate next week," Clementine said. "Lucinda Larkin really misses you. She cries all the time."

"Tell Lucinda Larkin I'm not worth it," Cabell said. "Hey, Dancy? I'll call back later. I'm down at the townie bar and the last bus is about to head back up the mountain. There's no phone at the castle. Get this. I have to go all the way to Râmnicu Vâlcea if I want Internet access. It's like the Middle Ages here. I love it. I left a message on Mom's cell phone. Tell her I'll send an address where she can mail the rest of my clothes and things as soon as I can. Tell everyone not to worry about wedding gifts. Lenuta's got all this family silverware and monogrammed linen and stuff."

"Don't go yet!" Dancy said. "Cabell?"

"I think he hung up," Clementine said. She wanted to howl like a dog.

Dancy pushed a pile of her husband's clothes off the bed. She sat down and bounced. "This is so weird, all of this! I mean, here I am getting divorced and he goes and gets married? To some girl he just met? And he wants me to tell Mom and Dad? I can't stand it. Come here, baby," Dancy said. "Somebody give me a hug." She was laughing, but when Clementine looked she saw that Dancy was crying, too. "It's crazy, right?" Dancy said.

Clementine sat down beside Dancy and put her head in Dancy's lap. She couldn't help it. She sobbed. Dancy cried even harder.

Lucinda Larkin gave them a look like they were both crazy. She came over and hit Clementine on the nose with the remote. She wasn't at an age where she understood about sharing.

ឌ I. ଔ

Twenty minutes, and Lee parks the van at the very top of Peaceable Mountain. There isn't much of a view. Just trees and more trees.

"Why are we stopping?" Czigany demands. "What's going on?"

Parci says, "Shut up, Czigany! You'll fail the Ordeal."

Bad gets out and slides open the passenger door and Nikki starts up the trail-head. During their planning sessions, Lee has described the place where she is to stop: the old stone wall, the historical marker, the tree struck by lightning where they will leave Czigany and Parci.

It takes Maureen and Bad and Lee a while longer to get there, guiding the blindfolded, handcuffed Khulhat sisters. "Watch out here," Lee says. "It goes down. Be careful where you put your foot. Okay, good job."

Parci keeps on laughing. Czigany is saying, "You have to call my mom. Come on, Lee. If we're not home by five she's going to go crazy. At least tell her where we are, okay?"

"Don't worry," Lee says. "It's going to be fine. We're almost there. You're almost done."

"It is not going to be okay," Czigany says. "Let me call my mother. So she can come get Parci? Bad, listen to me. If we're not home to take our pills, it's serious. Remember how Parci told you we both have a condition? It's like epilepsy. Take the blindfold off. I need to talk to you." Her hand clutches Lee's forearm with terrible strength, but Lee says nothing. She is sure she will find the marks of Czigany's fingers there later.

"It is not!" Parci yells. "We don't have epilepsy. It's something completely different."

"Shut up, Parci," Czigany says. "We have to tell them."

"You shut up," Parci says. "You say anything else and Mom will seriously kill you."

"Shut up both of you," Bad says. "Save your breath. There's a steep bit here."

At last they are at the summit. They are all panting. Czigany's breath comes in sobs. When she jerks at the handcuffs, Parci stumbles. "Quit it," Parci says. "Just quit it!"

Here is the tree, and here is Nikki, up in the branches. She grins at Lee and gives her the thumbs-up. She has her iPod, loaded up with several hours' worth of *Project Runway*, her yarn and plastic needles, her Thermos and a sandwich.

Maureen says, "Czigany, you can stop. You and Parci sit down here."

She helps the two sisters sit down with their backs to the tree.

While Maureen winds the rope around and around Czigany, Parci, the tree, Bad explains. "Most Ordeals are kind of lame. For mine, they put a personal ad on Craigslist and I had to go sit at Rosie's Strong Brew, wearing a rose in my hair, and meet all of these ancient guys. The last three, it turned out, had all been told to show up at the same time, and I wasn't allowed to explain, either. The creepy thing was how none of them were surprised that I was a fifteen-year-old lesbian. So the ad must have mentioned that. Whatever. My point is that I wanted this to be different. So I went and did some research on Ordeals and what I found out is that you used to have one if you were going to be a knight. You had to go into a church and kneel on the stone floor all night long and stay awake to pray, and if you did, they made you a knight."

"We checked the weather," Maureen says. Maureen's Ordeal was so humiliating that she refuses to talk about it at all. "It's not supposed to get down past forty degrees tonight. Thank you, global warming. The church thing wasn't going to work, but when we talked about it, Lee said that we could come here."

"You can't leave us here all night!" Czigany says.

"We'll be back to get you in the morning," Bad says. "And, just in case, someone is going to be keeping an eye on you. You know. So don't try to get loose. It's a long way down the mountain."

"Call my mom," Czigany says. "Just call her and tell her what's happening. I can't believe you guys are doing this to me! You said we were going home. You said we were going home!"

When no one says anything, she begins to thrash, horribly. She throws herself against the rope at her chest as if she means to cut herself in half. This is not how the Ordeal is supposed to go. Lee's stomach hurts as if she is the one caught in the ropes.

"Ow, ow, ow," Parci says. "Quit it, Czigany. You're making it really tight."

Czigany says, "Take off the blindfolds. At least take off our blindfolds!"

"Stop whining," Bad says. She sounds exasperated, as if she can't believe how ungrateful Czigany is being. "The whole point of an Ordeal is that it sucks. The blindfolds are just part of the suckiness."

"Am I going to be a knight, too?" Parci says. "Or whatever? Because it isn't fair otherwise."

Bad says, "Hear that? Your little sister's a badass, Czigany."

Czigany's shirt has ridden up as she wriggles in the ropes. Lee bends over to pull it back down. As she bends over, she says, as quietly as she can, "Czigany? Don't worry. We'll be back sooner than you think. Okay?"

"You lied to me," Czigany says.

"I know," Lee whispers. "I'm sorry."

"I'm sorry, too," Czigany says. And presses her lips together tightly.

"Don't worry about us," Parci says. "We'll be fine." She's grinning like a mad fiend.

No one says anything on the way back to the van until Maureen says, finally,

"Maybe we should call the Khulhats. Just in case. Czigany was really freaking out."

"You would, too, if you had her mom," Bad says.

Lee says, "Good luck getting a signal. My aunt has Skype, but we can't call from her account. I don't want her to get in trouble. Maureen, you made Czigany leave the note, right? What did she say?"

"We had to improvise because of Parci. Something about needing space. And wanting a chance to do some sister bonding. I had Czigany say they might take the train into the city to see a matinee."

"Solid," Bad says. "It's like you've been kidnapping people for years."

"Yeah, well, next time let's kidnap somebody who isn't such an ungrateful freak," Maureen says.

"That's not fair," Lee says.

"Like the Ordeal is supposed to be about fairness?" Maureen says. She's practically yelling. "Like *my* Ordeal was cake and roses and champagne? Czigany has no idea. No idea whatsoever. It's like she thinks this is all about her."

"I've got a rash on my arm," Bad says. "It had better not be poison ivy, is all I'm saying."

"Probably just goat saliva," Maureen says, calming down. "They ate one of my tennis shoe laces. They're cute, you know, but they're kind of a pain in the ass, too. Like boyfriends."

It's three thirty when they get back to Peaceable Kingdom, and Maureen complains about boyfriends the whole way down. Dodo is boiling water for pasta salad. "How did it go?" she says.

"That depends on who you ask," Lee says. "Czigany isn't very happy. Her parents are pretty strict."

Dodo chops scallions and doesn't ask anything else. When Lee first asked her if they could bring Czigany to Peaceable Kingdom for her Ordeal, Dodo had a lot of questions. What will your mom say? What about missing classes? What's the point of the Ordeal anyway? After Lee described some of the Ordeals she'd heard about, Dodo sighed and said she guessed Lee and the others had everything all figured out.

"I thought you guys might want to go for a hike," Dodo says. "I thought we'd have an early dinner, then make a lot of popcorn and take it out to the goat barn. We could watch a couple of movies. You guys like Jackie Chan movies?"

Lee says, "We have to be back up there around eight. I want to get back just a little early, to be on the safe side."

"Four hours isn't much of an Ordeal," Bad grouses. She's still annoyed that no one else was willing to go along with the full knightly Ordeal, her original plan.

"The real Ordeal will be when they get home," Lee says.

"It's going to be kind of an Ordeal for us, too," Maureen says. "We have to ride back with them. Czigany's kind of scary when she's mad. Dibs on the front seat.

You get to sit next to Czigany, Bad."

"Does anyone ever refuse to go along with this Ordeal business?" Dodo asks. They all stare at her.

"Never mind," Dodo says. "Clearly I am out of my mind for asking."

Maureen and Bad opt for the hike. Lee guesses Maureen wants to complain about the new boyfriend. Lee sits in the kitchen with Dodo for a while, telling her about school. She wonders if Czigany is still trying to wriggle free. Nikki is under strict orders to document the part they are missing.

Eventually Lee heads back to the Ferris wheel with her book. She isn't sure she understands Clementine, why Clementine keeps hoping Cabell will finally notice her. Lee's never felt that way about anyone, and she's not sure she wants to, either. She reads until it's time to go and call the goats to dinner. Bad and Maureen come back from their hike still talking about Maureen's difficulties with the new boyfriend. Sometimes Lee wonders if Bad has a crush on Maureen. It's how Bad looks at Maureen sometimes. Not that Maureen would ever notice.

Dodo has made plenty of pasta salad, and garlic bread with goat butter, and iced tea. After the dishes are washed and dried, they all help make popcorn, which it turns out is not for them. It's for the goats.

After browsing through Dodo's limited selection of movies, they decide on *Lawrence of Arabia*. Dodo says, "But it's four hours long. You won't be able to see all of it!"

"We've seen it before," Bad says. "Like four times. It's okay if we don't get to the end. And it seems like the right kind of movie to watch with a herd of goats. The only thing that would be better would be if you had camels."

"It's not like it's a happy ending anyway," Lee says, and Maureen nods in agreement.

The goats are done with the popcorn before the theme music has even started. They pick their way from couch to couch, never setting foot on the floor of the barn, talking loudly. There's a reason why movie theaters don't encourage people to bring their goats. Dodo has left the barn doors open so that the goats can come and go. "They're always a bit mad when the moon is full," Dodo says. "Little terrors. Little monsters."

"Hey! Don't eat that!" Lee says, holding her book up and out of reach. The Nubian gives her a haughty look.

"Good book?" Dodo says.

"Not sure yet," Lee says. "I'm not finished. Bad's read it."

Bad grunts. She is pulling clumps of hair from the sides of a very pregnant LaMancha. "It was so-so. You know. There's this girl and she's crazy about this guy and does all these stupid things and then at the end—"

Lee says, "Shut up! I haven't gotten to the end yet!"

"I'm going to get more popcorn," Dodo says. "Anybody want anything?" The goats all go trailing after her.

"This is nice, isn't it?" Maureen says. She comes and leans over Lee's couch, gives Lee a voluptuous hug. "Being here. How come you never brought us here before?"

Lee says, "I don't know. We're here now, aren't we?"

"Can we come back?" Maureen says. "Could we come back sometime with Nikki? I feel bad for her, stuck up there by herself. Missing *Lawrence of Arabia*."

"Now in stereo with goats!" Bad says. She's lying on the next couch over, and Lee can't see Bad's expression. Only the back of her head.

"What about Czigany and Parci?" Lee says. Maureen rests her chin on Lee's shoulder. She blows on Lee's hair, garlic and goat cheese. "Quit it, Maureen!"

Bad says, "Not the same as goats. But sure. There are two of them, so I guess it's in stereo."

Maureen says, "They're just so weird. I didn't like the way their house smelled."

"I don't like the way your breath smells," Lee says.

"It's just, we went to a lot of trouble to set this up for Czigany, and I don't think she appreciates it at all. We could have done something really mean, but instead Bad had this cool idea, and I just think it's wasted on Czigany. And I wish it was just us here. You and me and Bad and Nikki. That's all." Maureen stands up and begins to play with Lee's hair.

Over on the other couch, a voice says, "What Maureen said."

"What'd I miss?" Dodo says, coming back into the barn. Goats stream after her, bleating and shoving.

"T. E. Lawrence just drove his motorcycle off the road and died," Bad says. "Then he went to Cairo."

Maureen, who enjoys complaining as much as she enjoys everything else, says with great satisfaction, "What a very epic day this has been." Peter O'Toole's insanely gorgeous face is filling the screen.

☙ C ❧

Nobody ever got an e-mail from Cabell. Or a phone call. After six months his parents put in a request with the American embassy in Bucharest. The embassy put out a bulletin, but if anyone had seen Cabell they were keeping it to themselves. Dancy and Clementine cried a lot every time Clementine went over to babysit, and then Dancy met a guy online and she and Lucinda Larkin moved out to Seattle.

To Clementine's surprise, this was even worse than Cabell. Somehow Seattle seemed a lot farther away than Romania. In her heart of hearts she was still convinced that someday she would see Cabell again.

After her freshman year at Queens, Clementine worked at a local veterinary clinic until she had enough money for a plane ticket and a Eurail Pass. By then there was the boyfriend, a guy with family money who had dropped out of Duke in order to play poker online. The boyfriend and Clementine went to Rome together. And Dublin. And Prague. And Bucharest, because Clementine told the boyfriend that she wanted to try to find an old family friend.

The best clue she had was that Cabell had married someone named Lenuta who lived in a castle that wasn't very close to Râmnicu Vâlcea. So they went to Râmnicu Vâlcea and rented a car. They began to ask about wolves. The boyfriend was into the whole quest thing. He had a phrase book. He seemed to like playing detective.

It was difficult, sometimes, to figure out what was up with the boyfriend. It was a good thing he had money. Otherwise you would never have heard a single word he said.

They stayed in a pensione in Râmnicu Vâlcea and went to the springs to bathe. The room in the pensione was stuffy and hot, the window painted shut. All night long, Clementine dreamed of Cabell. She sat on a surfboard, looking toward the shore. When she turned to look over her shoulder, she saw Cabell, running toward her at an astonishing speed, over the top of the waves.

They had decided to drive all the way to Sfântu Gheorghe, but first they came to a town that wasn't on the map. It was hardly a town at all. But there was a gas station and a bus stop, and at the bus stop was a woman who spoke a little English. She told them there was a castle up in the forest above the town. There was a family up there with many daughters. One of them had an American husband. The boyfriend consulted the phrase book over and over again. When he and Clementine tried to ask her about wolves, the woman at the bus stop made the sign of the cross. Which really made the boyfriend's day.

In Clementine's guidebook, there was no mention of a castle. The forest got a couple of paragraphs. It wasn't clear which road they were looking for, and there were no signs. Then again, there seemed to be only one road that went up the mountain. They went up it, and after twenty minutes, the boyfriend suggested a picnic, perhaps a bit of a walk. They could scout things out first, rather than just driving up to the castle, if there was a castle. It was only eleven in the morning. Better to show up after lunch. People were usually in a better mood after lunch, right? (said the boyfriend.) Clementine agreed.

All day long, every time the boyfriend opened his mouth she'd wanted to burst out laughing. She was afraid the boyfriend would notice she was behaving strangely and wonder why. She was convinced he would read her mind and at last ditch her. Go back to Bucharest without her. Leave her all alone to find Cabell. Or not find Cabell, which seemed more likely. Except it didn't. She knew she'd find Cabell. She'd woken up in Râmnicu Vâlcea knowing that she would find him.

The boyfriend was an idiot and Clementine was an idiot, too. She wished she could have figured out how to dump the boyfriend before they'd got to Bucharest.

The road went over a stone bridge. What about here? the boyfriend said. We can follow the stream.

They left the car beside the road.

Raspberry canes grew up along the bridge. The boyfriend picked a handful and then threw them away. Sour, he said. I don't think we should drink the water. It's probably snow melt, but you never know.

When they stepped under the trees, Clementine held her breath. She felt that she was listening for something.

So he saved your life when you were a kid, the boyfriend said. Everything that he said came filtered through a great cone of silence.

"Twice," Clementine said. "Can you believe it?" She could not tell if she was whispering or shouting.

If you save someone's life you're responsible for it ever after. So the reason you wanted to come find him is to save him? Because nobody's heard anything from him in years?

"I don't know," Clementine said. "It's just that we're over here. It just seemed like maybe I'd run into him somehow. And you seemed like you were into it."

Yeah. I was. Hey, do you think that's the castle up there? Through the trees? We're on some kind of trail. Maybe if we just keep on going?

"Yeah. I see it. I think I see it. Are you sure it's really a castle? It might just be a rock formation."

No, it's a castle. I think it's a castle. It's not very big, the boyfriend said. How do they decide what's a castle and what's not? Like, how do you decide that something's a castle? Just because it's made out of stone and because it's old?

"I don't know," Clementine said.

Maybe we should stop and have lunch first, the boyfriend said. Then go back to the car? And drive up? I don't know if we're trespassing or not.

Far above, the canopy of leaves was shaken and shivered by a wind, but under the trees the air was heavy and cool and unmoved. The leaves underfoot smelled richly of rot. Little white mushrooms clustered in rings.

In his backpack the boyfriend was carrying the bread and cheese and beer they'd bought at the gas station. There's a clearing up ahead, he said. We can stop and eat there.

But when they came into the clearing, the boyfriend halted so abruptly that Clementine walked into him. The boyfriend stumbled forward.

Less than a yard away, two preadolescent girls lay half under a thorny bush with their arms around each other. There was blood smeared around their mouths. They were naked.

What the hell is going on here? The boyfriend put down his backpack and took his camera out. Are they okay?

There was something about the two girls that made Clementine think of Lucinda Larkin. She could see their narrow chests rising and falling. How their legs twitched, as if they were running in their dreams. Closer, much closer, here, almost at her feet, under a tree, was Cabell. He was naked and so was the woman beside him. They lay sprawled as if they had fallen from a great height. There was blood on their faces and on their bodies and there was blood matting the woman's dark hair, but she was still very beautiful.

"There's been some kind of accident," Clementine said. She couldn't imagine what had happened here, but what she felt was a kind of joy. Here was Cabell, bloodied and unconscious and alive, and here she was to rescue him. This time she would rescue him. Whatever had happened, she was meant to be here.

Clementine? the boyfriend said. He had his hands out, as if to stop from falling into the thing in front of him. A deer, she realized. Its hide peeled back in strips, the ribcage forced apart, blood and bits of entrails sticking to dirt and leaves.

Cabell's eyes opened. Clementine could have bent down and put her hand on his long, tangled hair. The bark on the tree above him was silver. It hung down in tattered flags. The woman beside Cabell, Cabell's wife, flung her arm out, as if to catch something.

It wasn't their blood after all.

Clementine said to the boyfriend, "Did you ever have an idea of how your life was supposed to go, except that you were wrong about everything?"

Clementine, the boyfriend said. He'd put his camera down at last. Clementine, I think we're in real trouble here.

☙ L. ❧

Lee turns the page, but that's the end of the story about Clementine. Not an end at all. Although you can guess what's about to happen to Clementine. Or maybe, Lee thinks, she's wrong. Maybe Cabell will save Clementine again.

Lee puts the book down for one of the goats to eat.

She thinks: It's like watching one of those horror movies, where you know the person is doing something stupid and you can't stop them from doing it, you just have to go on watching them do it. Where you know that the monster is about to show up, but the person acts as if nothing is wrong. As if there is no monster.

Peter O'Toole is blowing up trains. Which makes him a bad guy even though he's a good guy, too, right? Out in the night the full moon is caught in the black spokes of the Ferris wheel. It leaches all the meadow to silver. All the goats are staring in the same direction as Lee. As if even they think the moon is beautiful. Or maybe they're wondering how to climb the Ferris wheel so they can eat the moon.

Maureen says, "I have to go to the bathroom."

"You know where it is," Lee says.

"Someone needs to go with me. It's too far away."

Dodo says, "There's a flashlight up on the wall over there."

"Bad?" Maureen says.

"Sure," Bad says. "I'll go." And if that isn't true love, Lee thinks, it's true friendship, which is probably something better.

Dodo says, "Lee? When they get back you'd better head out."

"Is it that late already?" Lee says.

"It's almost nine." Dodo shoves a goat off the couch and stands up. "I thought you knew. I'll go make some coffee. I'll put some of the pasta salad in a container. For the way back."

"Thanks," Lee says. Once again, she feels a strange reluctance to get up, as if when she leaves Peaceable Kingdom she won't be coming back for a long time. The book has put her in a strange mood. She wishes she hadn't read it. She almost wishes she hadn't brought Bad and the others here.

The goats are sneezing emphatically.

"Bless you," Lee says. "Bless you bless you bless you too."

Dodo grunts. "There must be a coyote out there."

"A what?" Lee says. "Your goats are allergic to coyotes?"

"It's like an alarm system. Goats sneeze like dogs bark," Dodo says. "Haven't I taught you anything about goats? They think there's something out there."

"You're kidding me," Lee says.

"Well," Dodo says, "sometimes they're playing around. If it's not playing around, it's probably coyotes. If it's coyotes, I go out and shoot the rifle and they take off. Hear that?"

"Hear what?" Lee says, but then she hears it. A howl, melancholy and terrible and not particularly far away.

"Hey!" someone yells from far off. Is it Maureen or Bad? Lee can't tell. "There's something out here. We're in the outhouse. It's scratching like crazy to get in. Lee? Dodo?"

"Hang on," Dodo yells back. "I'll be there in a sec."

"I'll come with you," Lee says.

"No," Dodo says. "Stay here." She kneels down and sticks her arm under the sofa where Lee is sitting. She pulls out a shotgun and a box of shells. She adds, "Don't worry. I just use the shotgun to warn them off. It's just buckshot."

Lee and the goats follow Dodo to the barn doors. "I'm going to shut these," Dodo says. "Just to keep the goats inside."

Neither Lee nor the goats are happy about this, but Dodo shuts them in anyway.

"Is someone coming?" Definitely Bad this time. "There's something out here. It's making a lot of noise."

"Hold on, ladies," Dodo calls. "I'll be there in a minute."

The goats are sneezing like crazy. "Bless you," Lee says again. She stands by the barn doors and listens. She can hear Dodo walking away from the barn. Now she hears something padding stealthily along the side of the barn. Not two feet. Four feet. Something whines and scratches at the wall, its nails clicking and catching on the flattened Coke cans.

"Dodo?" Lee yells. Her chest feels funny. Her hands are cold. Once or twice a year she has to take a pill. When she gets overexcited. Her prescription bottle is in her purse in Dodo's kitchen.

She hears Dodo say, "Shoo! Get away." There is the sound of things hitting the ground and Lee realizes that Dodo is throwing rocks. Something growls and

Dodo curses. "Get away from the door, Lee, or else I can't shoot. Get the goats away from the door."

"I can't, " Lee calls. "They won't go." All of the goats are now standing at the door, bleating and sneezing and calling excitedly for Dodo to come back. They take little runs and butt at the door with their heads. "What is it?"

"Not a coyote," Dodo says. "A wolf. Between me and the barn now. There's another one here as well. Trying to sneak up on me."

"What should I do?" Lee says. Bad and Maureen yell something about coming out of the outhouse.

"Everybody stay where they are!" Dodo says loudly.

The thing at the side of the barn is scratching and pawing and digging now. Lee can hear its excited breath. There is a loud report from outside, Dodo has pulled the trigger, and inside the barn all four Tennessee Fainting Goats fall over. If only Bad were there to see them. There is a snarling and growling, a bereaved, furious howling.

## ෨ L C ෨

"I don't like this part," the girl on the bed says. Her sister, sitting in the chair beside the window, stops reading and puts down the book.

Let's call the girl on the bed by an initial. L. Let's call the other girl C. They're sisters and they are also best friends, possibly because they don't have many opportunities to meet other girls their age.

There isn't much to do here, except walk in the woods and then read to each other in that space between twilight and when the moon rises. They order a package of books every month from an online bookseller. They spend a lot of time choosing the books. This book they chose for the cover.

Except you can't judge a book by its cover. Whether or not this story has a happy ending depends, of course, on who is reading it. Whether you are a wolf or a girl. A girl or a monster or both. Not everyone in a story gets a happy ending. Not everyone who reads a story feels the same way about how it ends. And if you go back to the beginning and read it again, you may discover it isn't the same story you thought you'd read. Stories shift their shape.

The two sisters are waiting for the moon to come up, which is not the same thing as waiting for the sun to go down. Not at all.

"It's not like you don't know what happens," C tells L. It's the third time they've read this story. C yawns so widely it seems her mouth will crack open. The tip of a long tongue pokes out between the teeth when her yawn is done. "If you don't like the ending, then why do you always ask me to read the same story?"

"It's not the ending," L says. "It's the part where I don't know who Dodo shot. I like the ending okay. I just don't like this one part."

"We don't have time to finish it tonight anyway," C says.

"If it were my ending, they would all stay friends," L says wistfully. "Czigany and Parci and Lee and everyone else. They would leave the goat farm right after lunch, and Czigany and Parci would get home in plenty of time for dinner and the moon wouldn't come up until everything was all prepared. That would be a better story."

"That wouldn't be much of a story at all. Why do you care what happens to Lee?" C says. C prefers Czigany because she is an older sister, too. "I thought you were worried about Parci getting shot, although I still don't understand why you were ever worried about it in the first place. Even when we read it the first time. It's just buckshot. It's not like Dodo's got a rocket launcher or an ax or silver bullets. I mean, come on. The only thing Dodo gets right is when she tells Lee that it's Lee and her friends who are the monsters. They are! They aren't any better than Czigany and Parci."

L thinks about this. She scratches at her arm, ruthlessly and without pleasure, as if she is itchy underneath her skin in a way that cannot be helped. "But I like Lee! And I kind of like Bad, too. Even if they are totally irresponsible. Even if they totally screw up Czigany's life."

C is out of her chair, stretching toward the open window as if she can reach out and touch the moon. L watches, feeling the change come over her, now, too. It's agony and relief all at once, itchiness so unbearable it is as if you must shrug off your whole self. Once they set up a movie camera, but their mother found it afterwards and there was terrible trouble.

"What I really hate," C pants. "Are those damn goats. Goats are vicious." C was kicked by a goat once.

Thinking of goats, L begins to salivate uncontrollably. She licks her chops. Finds whiskers. How embarrassing. What would Lee think? But there is no Lee, of course, no stupid girl named Lee. No girl named Clementine. No unhappy endings for anyone. Not yet.

There were two girls in a room. They were reading a book. Now there are two wolves. The window is open and the moon is in it. Look again, and the room is empty. The end of the story will have to wait.

# COPYRIGHT ACKNOWLEDGMENTS

# Night Shade Books Is an Independent Publisher of Quality SF, Fantasy and Horror

# Night Shade Books Is an Independent Publisher of Quality SF, Fantasy and Horror

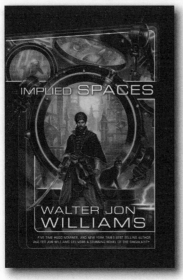

ISBN 978-1-59780-151-5
Mass Market Paperback; $7.99

When mankind's every need is serviced by artificial intelligence, and death itself is only a minor inconvenience, what does it mean to be human? The answer lies hidden, deep within the Implied Spaces. From Walter Jon Williams, the celebrated and influential author of *Hardwired*, *Voice of the Whirlwind*, and *Angel Station* comes *Implied Spaces*, a new novel of post-singularity action, pyrotechnics, and intrigue. Williams, whose name has long been synonymous with state-of-the-art science fiction, builds on the prophetic futurism of Vernor Vinge and Charles Stross, adding his own brand of poetic prose, masterful plotting, and engaging storytelling.

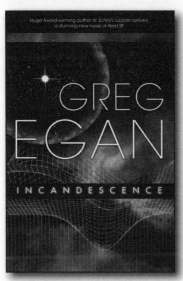

ISBN 978-1-59780-129-4
Trade Paper; $14.95

The long-awaited new novel from Greg Egan! Hugo Award-winning author Egan returns to the field with *Incandescence*, a new novel of hard SF.

The Amalgam spans the nearly entire galaxy, and is composed of innumerable beings from a wild variety of races, some human or near it, some entirely other. The one place that they cannot go is the bulge, the bright, hot center of the galaxy. There dwell the Aloof, who for millions of years have deflected any and all attempts to communicate with or visit them. So when Rakesh is offered an opportunity to travel within their sphere, in search of a lost race, he cannot turn it down.

**Find these Night Shade titles and many others online at http://www.nightshadebooks.com or wherever books are sold.**

# Night Shade Books Is an Independent Publisher of Quality SF, Fantasy and Horror

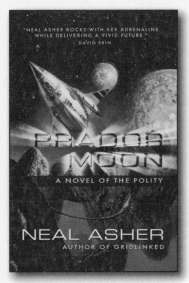

ISBN 978-1-59780-120-1
Mass Market Paperback; $7.99

The Polity Collective is the pinnacle of space-faring civilization. Academic and insightful, its dominion stretches from Earth Central into the unfathomable reaches of the galactic void. But when the Polity finally encounters alien life in the form of massive, hostile, crablike carnivores known as the Prador, there can be only one outcome... total warfare.

Chaos reigns as the Polity, caught unawares, struggles to regain its foothold and transition itself into a military society. Starships clash, planets fall, and space stations are overrun, but for Jebel Krong and Moria Salem, two unlikely heroes trapped at the center of the action, this war is far more than a mere clash of cultures, far more than technology versus brute force... this war is personal.

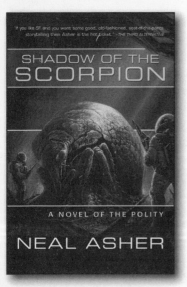

ISBN 978-1-59780-154-6
Mass Market Paperback $7.99

Ian Cormac's Early Years! Raised to adulthood during the end of the war between the human Polity and a vicious alien race, the Prador, Ian Cormac is haunted by childhood memories of a sinister scorpion-shaped war drone and the burden of losses he doesn't remember. Cormac signs up with Earth Central Security and is sent out to help restore and maintain order on worlds devastated by the war. There he discovers that though the Prador remain as murderous as ever, they are not anywhere near as treacherous or dangerous as some of his fellow humans, some closer to him than he would like. Amidst the ruins left by wartime genocides, Cormac will discover in himself a cold capacity for violence and learn some horrible truths about his own past while trying to stay alive on his course of vengeance.

**Find these Night Shade titles and many others online at http://www.nightshadebooks.com or wherever books are sold.**

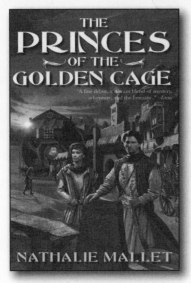
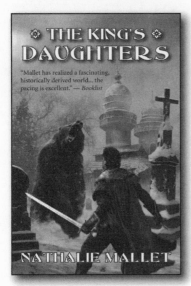

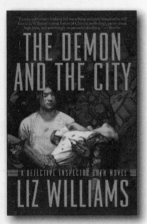